Pride and Pleasure

ALSO BY SYLVIA DAY

Bad Boys Ahoy!

Ask for It

Passion for the Game

A Passion for Him

Don't Tempt Me

The Stranger I Married

Seven Years to Sin

SYLVIA DAY, WRITING AS LIVIA DARE

In the Flesh

ANTHOLOGIES

Perfect Kisses

Published by Kensington Publishing Corp.

Pride and Pleasure

SYLVIA DAY

KENSINGTON PUBLISHING CORP.
www.kensingtonbooks.com

This one is for Kate Duffy, friend and mentor, for her countless contributions to my writing, career, and general well-being. She was incomparable. I miss her fiercely.

ACKNOWLEDGMENTS

Huge thanks to my editor, Alicia Condon. Her edits to this book were invaluable, and her willingness to learn/work with my process is deeply appreciated.

There aren't words to describe my appreciation for my agent extraordinaire, Robin Rue. If I listed all the ways she facilitated the writing of this book, it would fill as many pages as the story. Suffice it to say—she rocks!

I owe a huge debt of gratitude to cover goddess Kristine Mills-Noble, who knocked it out of the park with the cover for this book. She's been giving me great covers for years, but this one is definitely my favorite so far.

Hugs to my BFFs Karin Tabke and Shayla Black, who know how close this book came to killing me. Their support kept me going when I didn't think I could take another step.

And major love to all the readers who waited a few years for me to release another historical. I hope you love Jasper and Eliza's story.

Chapter 1

London, England, 1818

As a thief-taker, Jasper Bond had been consulted in a number of unusual locations, but today was the first in a church. Some of his clients were at home in the rookeries his crew haunted. Others were most comfortable in the palace. This particular prospective client appeared to be one of strong faith since he'd designated St. George's as the location of their assignation. Jasper suspected it was considered a "safe" place, which told him this person was ill at ease with retaining an individual of dubious morality. That suited him fine. He would probably be paid well and kept at a distance: his favorite sort of commission.

Alighting from his carriage, Jasper paused to better appreciate the impressive portico and Corinthian columns of the church's façade. Muted singing flowed outward from the building, a lovely contrast to the frustrated shouts of coachmen and the clatter of horses' hooves behind him. His cane hit the street with a thud, his gloved palm wrapped loosely around the eagle's-head top. With hat in hand, he waved his driver away.

Today's appointment had been arranged by Mr. Thomas

Lynd, a man who shared Jasper's trade and confidence for many reasons, not the least of which was his mentorship of Jasper in the profession. Jasper would never presume to call himself a moral man, but he did function under the code of ethics Lynd had taught him—help those in actual need of it. He did not extort protection money as other thief-takers did. He did not steal goods with one hand in order to charge for their return with the other. He simply found what was lost and protected those who wanted security, which begged the question of why Lynd was passing on this post. With such similar principles, either of them should have been as good as the other.

Because Jasper had an inordinate fondness for puzzles and mysteries, he was too intrigued by Lynd's motives to do anything besides follow through. This, despite the location being one that necessitated his handling the inquiry personally, which was something he rarely did. He preferred to work through trusted employees to retain the anonymity necessary to his greater personal plans.

Mounting the steps, he entered St. George's and paused to absorb the wave of music that rolled over him. Near the front on the right side was the raised canopied pulpit; on the left, the bi-level reading desk. The many box pews were empty of the faithful. Only the choir occupied the space, their voices raised in musical praise.

Jasper withdrew his pocket watch and checked the time. It was directly on the hour. In his profession, he found it highly useful to be a slave to punctuality. He moved to the stairs that would take him up to the right-side gallery for his appointment.

When he reached the landing, he paused. His gaze was drawn to and held by wild tufts of white hair defying gravity. One hopelessly overworked black ribbon failed to tame the mass into anything but a messy, lopsided queue. As he watched, the unfortunate owner of the horrendous coiffure reached up and scratched it into further disarray.

So fascinated was Jasper with the monstrosity of that hair, it took him a moment to register the petite form beside its owner. Once he did, however, his interest was snared. In complete opposition to her companion, the woman was blessed with glossy tresses of a reddish-blond hue so rare it was arresting. They were the only two people in the gallery, yet neither had the tense expectation inherent in those who were awaiting an individual or event. Instead they were singularly focused on the choir below.

Where was the individual he was scheduled to meet?

Sensing she was the object of perusal, the woman turned her head and met Jasper's weighted gaze. She was attractive. Not in the exceptionally remarkable way of her hair but pleasing all the same. Deep blue eyes stared at him from beneath thick lashes. She had an assertive nose and high cheekbones. When she bit her lower lip, she displayed neat white teeth, and when her lips pursed, she revealed a tiny dimple. It was a charming face rather than beautiful, and notable for her seeming displeasure at the sight of him.

"Mr. Bond," she said, after a slight delay. "I did not hear you approach."

One could blame the choir's singing for that. However, the truth of it was that he walked silently. He'd learned the skill long ago. It had saved his life then and continued to do so in recent years.

Standing, she moved toward him with a determined stride and thrust out her hand. As if cued, the singers below ended their hymn, leaving a sudden silence into which she said, "I am Eliza Martin."

Her voice surprised him. Soft as a summer breeze, but threaded with steel. The sound of it lingered, stirring his imagination to travel in directions it shouldn't.

He shifted his cane to his other hand and accepted her greeting. "Miss Martin."

"I appreciate your courtesy in meeting with me. However, you are exactly what I feared you would be."

"Oh?" Taken aback by her direct approach, he found himself becoming more intrigued. "In what way?"

"In every way, sir. I contacted Mr. Lynd because we require a certain type of individual. I regret the need to say you are not he."

"Would you object to my request for elaboration?"

"The points are too numerous," she pronounced.

"Nevertheless, a man in my position seeks predictability in others but fears it in himself. Since you state I am the epitome of what you did *not* want, I feel I must request an accounting of the criteria upon which you based your judgment."

Miss Martin seemed to ponder his response for a moment. In the brief time of introspection, Jasper collected what his instincts had recognized upon first sight: Eliza Martin was intensely aware of him. Without her cognizance, her baser senses were reacting to him much the way his were to her: her delicate nostrils flared, her breathing quickened, her body swayed with the undercurrent of agitation . . . a doe sensing the hunter nearby.

"Yes," she said, with a catch in her voice. "I can see why that would be true."

"Of course it's true. I never lie to clients." He never bedded them either, but that was about to change.

"You have not been engaged," she reminded, "so I am not a client."

The man with the frightening hair intruded. "Eliza, marry Montague and be done with this farce."

With the voicing of that one name, Jasper knew why he'd received the referral and how little chance Eliza Martin had of dismissing him.

"I will not be bullied, my lord," she said firmly.

"Invite Mr. Bond to sit, then."

"That won't be necessary."

Skirting her, Jasper settled into the pew behind the one they occupied.

"Mr. Bond . . ." Miss Martin gave a resigned exhalation. "My lord, may I present Mr. Jasper Bond? Mr. Bond, this is my uncle, the Earl of Melville."

"Lord Melville." Jasper greeted the earl with a slight bow of his head. He knew of Melville as the head of the Tremaine family, a lot renowned for their eccentricities. "I believe you will find me to be highly suitable for any task in want of a thief-taker to manage it."

Miss Martin's blue eyes narrowed on him in silent reproach for attempting to circumvent her. "Sir, I am certain you are capable in most circumstances. However—"

"About the many points . . . ?" he interjected, circling back. He disliked proceeding when there were still matters left unaddressed.

"You are overly tenacious." She remained standing, as if prepared to show him out.

"An excellent trait to have in my profession."

"Yes, but that doesn't mitigate the rest."

"What rest?"

The earl's gaze darted back and forth between them.

She shook her head. "Can we not simply leave it at that, Mr. Bond?"

"I would rather we didn't." He set his hat on the seat beside him. "I have always taken pride in my ability to manage any situation put before me. How will I provide exemplary service if I can no longer make that claim?"

"Really, sir," Miss Martin protested. "I did not say you are unsuitable for your trade as a whole, only in regards to our situation—"

"Which is . . . ?"

"A matter of some delicacy."

"I cannot assist you if I am ignorant of the details," he pointed out.

"I do not want your assistance, Mr. Bond. You fail to collect that."

"Because you refuse to explain yourself. Mr. Lynd thought I was suitable and you trusted his judgment enough to arrange this meeting." Jasper would pay Lynd handsomely for the referral. It had been far too long since he'd felt this level of interest in anything beyond his need for vengeance.

"Mr. Lynd does not have the same considerations I do."

"Which are . . . ?"

"Sir, you are exasperating."

And she was fascinating. Her eyes sparkled with irritation, her right foot tapped against the floor, and her fisted hands moved often as if to rest on her hips. But she resisted the urge. He found her resistance most appealing. What would it take to break it and see her unrestrained? He couldn't wait to find out.

"I will compensate you for your time today," she said, "so all is not a complete loss to you. There is no need to continue this discussion."

"You overlook the possibility that I might have intended to assign a member of my crew to you, Miss Martin. I would, however, need to know what your situation is so I can determine whose skills would best suit your requirements." He intended to service her himself, but he wasn't above a little subterfuge when the prize was this delicious.

"Oh." She bit her lower lip again. "I hadn't considered that."

"So I noted."

Miss Martin finally sank back onto the pew in a movement of eminent grace. "Just so we are clear you won't do."

"It isn't clear." He set his cane between his legs and

placed his hands atop it, one over the other. "At least, not to me."

She glanced at his lordship, then—reluctantly—back to Jasper. "You force me to say what I would rather not, Mr. Bond. Frankly, you are too handsome for the task."

He was stunned into momentary silence. Then, he relished an inner smile. How delightful she was, even when cross.

"Mr. Lynd was less conspicuous than you," she continued. "You are quite large and, as I said, far too comely."

Lynd was a score of years older and average in height, features, and build. Jasper looked to the earl and found the man staring at his niece with confusion. "I fail to see what bearing my face has on my investigative skills."

"In addition—" her voice grew stronger as she warmed to the topic of his faults, "—it would be impossible to disguise the air about you which distinguishes you."

"Pray tell me what that is." He was beginning to find it difficult to hide his growing enjoyment of the conversation.

"You are a predator, Mr. Bond. You have the appearance of one, and you carry yourself like one. To be blunt, you are clearly capable of being a dangerous man."

"I see." Fascination deepened into captivation. Perhaps she wasn't so innocent, after all. He spent obscene amounts of coin on his attire, deliberately crafting an appearance so polished very few saw past it to the rough edges underneath.

"I doubt you would be effective at your profession if you were not possessed of both predatory and dangerous qualities," she qualified in a conciliatory tone.

"And many others," he offered.

Miss Martin nodded. "Yes, I suspect the trade requires you to be well versed in a multitude of skills."

"It certainly helps."

"However, your masculine beauty negates all of that."

Jasper was ready to move forward. "Would you get to the

point, Miss Martin? What—exactly—did you intend to hire me to accomplish?"

"Quite a bit, actually. Protection, investigation, and . . . to act as my suitor."

"I beg your pardon?" Bond's voice rumbled through the air between them.

Eliza was flustered and out of sorts, and her state was entirely his fault. She had not anticipated that he would be so persistent or so curious. And she had certainly not expected a man of his appearance. Not only was he the handsomest man she had ever seen, but he was dressed in garments fit for a peer and he carried his large frame with a sleek, predaceous grace.

He also regarded her in a manner that would only lead to trouble.

To receive such an examination from a man who looked like Jasper Bond was highly disconcerting. Men such as he usually dismissed women of average appearance the moment they saw them. That was why she took such pains to be as unobtrusive in her attire selections as possible. Why encourage responses she was ill-equipped to deal with?

Perhaps his interest was engaged by the color of her hair? Her mother had posited that some men had a peculiar preference for specific parts of the female body and for tresses of a certain hue.

"Repeat yourself, please, Miss Martin," Bond said, watching her with those dark and intense eyes.

It was her curse to feel compelled to gaze directly at the person with whom she was speaking. She found it difficult to think quickly when awed by Jasper Bond's perfection. Stunning as he was from the shoulders down, he was more so from the shoulders up. His hair was as thick and dark as her favorite ink, and blessed with a similar sheen. The length—

slightly overlong—was perfect for framing his features: the distinguished nose, the deep-set eyes, the stern yet sensual mouth. It was a testament to the way he carried himself that he could be so formidable with such a pretty face. He was very clearly not a man one wished to cross.

"I need protection—" she said again.

"Yes."

"Investigation—"

"I heard that part."

"And—" her chin went up, "—a suitor."

He nodded as if that were a mundane request, but the glitter in his eyes was anticipatory. "That's what I thought you said."

"Eliza . . ." The earl stared at his clasped hands and shook his head.

"My lord," Bond began in a casual tone. "Were you aware of the nature of Miss Martin's inquiry?"

"Trying times these are," Lord Melville muttered. "Trying times."

Bond's precise gaze moved back to Eliza. Her brow lifted.

"Is he daft?" Bond queried.

"His brain is so advanced, it stumbles over mediocrity."

"Or perhaps it's tangled by your reasoning in this endeavor?"

Her shoulders went back. "My reasoning is sound. And sarcasm is unproductive, Mr. Bond. Please refrain from it."

"Oh?" His tone took on a dangerous quality. "And what is it you hope to produce by procuring a suitor?"

"I am not in want of stud service, sir. Only a depraved mind would leap to that conclusion."

"Stud service . . ."

"Is that not what you are thinking?"

A wicked smile came to his lips. Eliza was certain her heart skipped a beat at the sight of it. "It wasn't, no."

Wanting to conclude this meeting as swiftly as possible, she rushed forward. "Do you have someone who can assist me or not?"

Bond snorted softly, but the derisive sound seemed to be directed inward and not at her. "From the beginning, if you would please, Miss Martin. Why do you need protection?"

"I have recently found myself to be a repeated victim of various unfortunate—and suspicious—events."

Eliza expected him to laugh or perhaps give her a doubtful look. He did neither. Instead, she watched a transformation sweep over him. As fiercely focused as he'd been since his arrival, he became more so when presented with the problem. She found herself appreciating him for more than his good looks.

He leaned slightly forward. "What manner of events?"

"I was pushed into the Serpentine. My saddle was tampered with. A snake was loosed in my bedroom—"

"I understand it was a Runner who referred you to Mr. Lynd, who in turn referred you to me."

"Yes. I hired a Runner for a month, but Mr. Bell discovered nothing. No attacks occurred while he was engaged."

"Who would want to injure you, and why?"

She offered him a slight smile, a small show of gratitude for the gravity he was displaying. Anthony Bell had come highly recommended, but he'd never taken her seriously. In fact, he had been amused by her tales and she'd never felt he was dedicated to the task of discovery. "Truthfully, I am not certain whether they intend bodily harm, or if they simply want to goad me into marriage as a way to establish some permanent security. I see no reason to any of it."

"Are you wealthy, Miss Martin? Or certain to be?"

"Yes. Which is why I doubt they sincerely aim to cause me grievous injury—I am worth more alive. But there are some who believe it isn't safe for me in my uncle's household. They claim he is an insufficient guardian, that he is touched and ready for Bedlam. As if any individual capable of compassion would put a stray dog in such a place, let alone a beloved relative."

"Poppycock," the earl scoffed. "I am fit as a fiddle, in mind and body."

"You are, my lord," Eliza agreed, smiling fondly at him. "I have made it clear to all and sundry that Lord Melville will likely live to be one hundred years of age."

"And you hope that adding me to your stable of suitors will accomplish what, precisely?" Bond asked. "Deter the culprit?"

"I hope that by adding *one of your associates,*" she corrected, "I can avoid further incidents over the next six weeks of the Season. In addition, if my new suitor is perceived to be a threat, perhaps the scoundrel will turn his malicious attentions toward him. Then, perhaps, we can catch the fiend. Truly, I should like to know by what methods of deduction he formulated this plan and what he hoped to gain by it."

Bond settled back into his seat and appeared deep in thought.

"I would never suggest such a hazardous role for someone untrained," she said quickly. "But a thief-taker, a man accustomed to associating with criminals and other unfortunates . . . I should think those who engage in your profession would be more than a match for a nefarious fortune hunter."

"I see."

Beside her, her uncle murmured to himself, working out puzzles and equations in his mind. Like herself, he was most comfortable with events and reactions that could be quantified or predicted with some surety. Dealing with issues defying reason was too taxing.

"What type of individual would you consider ideal to play this role of suitor, protector, and investigator?" Bond asked finally.

"He should be quiet, even-tempered, and a proficient dancer."

Scowling, he queried, "How do dullness and the ability to dance signify in catching a possible murderer?"

"I did not say 'dull,' Mr. Bond. Kindly do not attribute words to me that I have not spoken. In order to be acknowledged as a true rival for my attentions, he should be someone whom everyone will believe I would be attracted to."

"You are not attracted to handsome men?"

"Mr. Bond, I dislike being rude. However, you leave me no recourse. The fact is, you clearly are not the sort of man whose temperament is compatible with matrimony."

"I am quite relieved to hear a female recognize that," he drawled.

"How could anyone doubt it?" She made a sweeping gesture with her hand. "I can more easily picture you in a swordfight or fisticuffs than I can see you enjoying an afternoon of croquet, after-dinner chess, or a quiet evening at home with family and friends. I am an intellectual, sir. And while I don't mean to imply a lack of mental acuity, you are obviously built for more physically strenuous pursuits."

"I see."

"Why, one has only to look at you to ascertain you aren't like the others at all! It would be evident straightaway that I would never consider a man such as you with even remote seriousness. It is quite obvious you and I do not suit in the most fundamental of ways, and everyone knows I am too observant to fail to see that. Quite frankly, sir, you are not my type of male."

The look he gave her was wry but without the smugness that would have made it irritating. He conveyed solid self-confidence free of conceit. She was dismayed to find herself strongly attracted to the quality.

He would be troublesome. Eliza did not like trouble overmuch.

He glanced at the earl. "Please forgive me, my lord, but I must speak bluntly in regard to this subject. Most especially because this is a matter concerning Miss Martin's physical well-being."

"Quite right," Melville agreed. "Straight to the point, I always say. Time is too precious to waste on inanities."

"Agreed." Bond's gaze returned to Eliza and he smiled. "Miss Martin, forgive me, but I must point out that your inexperience is limiting your understanding of the situation."

"Inexperience with what?"

"Men. More precisely, fortune-hunting men."

"I would have you know," she retorted, "that over the course of six Seasons I have had more than enough experience with gentlemen in want of funds."

"Then why," he drawled, "are you unaware that they are successful for reasons far removed from social suitability?"

Eliza blinked. "I beg your pardon?"

"Women do not marry fortune hunters because they can dance and sit quietly. They marry them for their appearance and physical prowess—two attributes you have already established I have."

"I do not see—"

"Evidently, you do not, so I shall explain." His smile continued to grow. "Fortune hunters who flourish do not strive to satisfy a woman's intellectual needs. Those can be met through friends and acquaintances. They do not seek to provide the type of companionship one enjoys in social settings or with a game table between them. Again, there are others who can do so."

"Mr. Bond—"

"No, they strive to satisfy in the only position that is theirs alone, a position some men make no effort to excel in. So rare is this particular skill that many a woman will disregard other considerations in favor of it."

"Please, say no—"

"Fornication," his lordship muttered, before returning to his conversation with himself.

Eliza shot to her feet. "My lord!"

As courtesy dictated, both her uncle and Mr. Bond rose along with her.

"I prefer to call it 'seduction,' " Bond said, his eyes laughing.

"I call it ridiculous," she rejoined, hands on her hips. "In the grand scheme of life, do you collect how little time a person spends abed when compared to other activities?"

His gaze dropped to her hips. The smile became a full-blown grin. "That truly depends on who else is occupying said bed."

"Dear heavens." Eliza shivered at the look Jasper Bond was giving her. It was . . . expectant. By some unknown, godforsaken means she had managed to prod the man's damnable masculine pride into action.

"Give me a sennight," he suggested. "One week to prove both my point and my competency. If, at the end, you are not swayed by one or the other, I will accept no payment for services rendered."

"Excellent proposition," his lordship said. "No possibility of loss."

"Not true," Eliza contended. "How will I explain Mr. Bond's speedy departure?"

"Let us make it a fortnight, then," Bond amended.

"You fail to understand the problem. I am not an actor, sir. It will be evident to one and all that I am far from 'seduced.' "

The tone of his grin changed, aided by a hot flicker in his dark eyes. "Leave that aspect of the plan to me. After all, that's what I am being paid for."

"And if you fail? Once you resign, not only will I be forced to make excuses for you, I will have to bring in another thief-taker to act in your stead. The whole affair will be entirely too suspicious."

"Have you had the same pool of suitors for six years, Miss Martin?"

"That isn't—"

"Did you not just state the many reasons why you feel I am not an appropriate suitor for you? Can you not simply reiterate those points in response to any inquiries regarding my departure?"

"You are overly persistent, Mr. Bond."

"Quite," he nodded, "which is why I will discover who is responsible for the unfortunate events besetting you and what they'd hoped to gain."

She crossed her arms. "I am not convinced."

"Trust me. It is fortuitous, indeed, that Mr. Lynd brought us together. If I do not apprehend the culprit, I daresay he cannot be caught." His hand fisted around the top of his cane. "Client satisfaction is a point of pride, Miss Martin. By the time I am done, I guarantee you will be eminently gratified by my performance."

Chapter 2

"There are times when I impress myself with my own brilliance," Thomas Lynd crowed when entering Jasper's study with hat in hand.

One could always trust Lynd to eschew the services of a formal butler. He preferred lackeys over servants whose training in deportment exceeded his own.

Jasper settled back in his chair with a smile of welcome. "You've outdone yourself this time."

As usual, Lynd's garments were overdone in style and underwhelming in fit. The result of a poor tailor provided with expensive material yet lacking the knowledge of how best to utilize it. Regardless, Lynd presented a decidedly more refined appearance than others of their profession. He walked a fine line, one that enabled him to remain respected and welcomed by the lower classes, while presenting himself in a way the peerage found nonthreatening.

Lynd dropped into one of the two seats set in front of the desk. "The moment she mentioned Montague, I had no doubt."

Although he visited Jasper's home with regularity, he surveyed the room as if seeing it for the first time. His gaze lingered on the mahogany bookshelves lining the far wall and the sapphire-hued velvet drapes framing the windows opposite. "Besides, she wanted a bloody lapdog, and none of our acquaintances can boast your pedigree."

"Bastardy is no advantage in any situation." Jasper straddled the line Lynd traversed so well, which worked—surprisingly—to Jasper's benefit. He was often hired by those who wanted his services to go unnoticed and were capable of paying the added expense such stealth required. That proclivity enabled him to work with Eliza Martin, because his face was not well known.

"It is in this one." Lynd ran a hand through brown hair as yet unaffected by the graying of age. "It takes breeding to tolerate the sorts of pompous asses Melville's niece expects you to rub along with, and you will be far less noticeable in the venues she will expect you to attend than anyone else I could think of."

Standing, Jasper moved to the console table by the window where decanters of liquors and crystal tumblers waited. Lynd was one of very few individuals who were aware of Jasper's lineage. He had Jasper's confidence because he'd once shown Jasper's mother a kindness when she desperately needed it.

As Jasper poured two rations of Armagnac, his gaze took in the two disreputable-looking lackeys who waited out on the street. Lynd's men.

It had taken Jasper some time to locate a respectable neighborhood that would accommodate his activities without undue strain. His neighbors tolerated the endless comings and goings of his crew because they found his presence useful in minimizing footpad crimes in the immediate vicinity. He considered his services to the community a small price to pay to avoid residing in the areas surrounding Fleet Street and the Strand, where Lynd and many other thief-takers lived. It was nigh impossible to abide the stench from the sewer ditch, which was an inescapable odor embedded into the very walls of the surrounding buildings.

Returning to his seat, Jasper set Lynd's glass at the edge of the desk. "I have an appointment with Miss Martin this afternoon. I'll learn then how serious Montague is about winning her hand. Perhaps he has grown desperate enough to become foolish."

"Preposterous," Lynd scoffed. "The whole affair. If someone is so determined to marry the chit, he should ask her outright. But then, I suppose the entire lot of hopefuls is daft or desperate beyond reason to mix their lineage with the Tremaines'. She should be grateful her late father's fortune has attracted suitors to her. She would have a devil of a time enticing a man without it."

Jasper's brow went up. He'd been enticed the moment she first opened her mouth.

"Truly," Lynd went on, "she should just pick a poor fellow and be done with it. Any other woman would. Been allowed to run amok, that one. She took it upon herself to engage a thief-taker to intercede and his lordship is too preoccupied with the maze of his mind to rein her in. Melville's participation in my interview was only with himself."

"Do you have a point to this disparagement of my client?"

"Six weeks will seem a lifetime, I vow. No compensation can restitute the loss of your sanity. She is contrary in the extreme. Unnatural in a female. She had the gall to look down her nose at me—a feat, I must say, since I'm taller—and tell me I would do well to hire a decent tailor. No polish to her at all. I could barely tolerate her for the length of the interview. Made my teeth grind."

"Good of you to decline the post, then," Jasper drawled. "Clearly you would not have made a convincing suitor."

"If you manage to be, I'd say you missed your true calling as a man of the stage."

"So long as Montague fails to acquire the funds he needs to regain his marker from me, I can do whatever is required." It was a delectable twist that the best way to foil Montague's suit was to woo Eliza Martin himself.

"Revenge has a way of eating at you, my boy, like a cancer. Best to keep that in mind."

Jasper smiled grimly.

Shrugging, Lynd said, "But you'll do as you like, you always have."

The marker Jasper held was for a deed to a parcel of land in Essex that boasted only a modest home and was by far the smallest property Jasper laid claim to. Regardless, its value was priceless. It represented years of meticulous planning and the retribution due him. And in a mere six weeks it would be irrevocably his to destroy or flaunt at his whim.

Jasper withdrew a waiting coin purse from his desk drawer and pushed it to the edge of the desk.

Lynd hesitated before collecting the silken bag. "I wish I could afford not to accept this."

"Nonsense. I owe you more than I could ever repay."

Rounding his desk, Jasper escorted Lynd to the foyer and saw him off. Once his visitor was gone, he shot a quick glance at the clock above the mantel in his office.

He was only a few hours away from paying a call on Miss Eliza Martin. He was anticipating it far more than was seemly. He should not be thinking of her at all, a woman who inferred he was more brawn than intellect. His goals were met by dealing with each challenge at the proper time and with the whole of his attention. Eliza's appointed time was later; there were other items needing to be addressed now. Yet he stood on the threshold of his office where pressing matters awaited him, thinking instead of how he should attire himself to call on her, contemplating whether he should dress to impress or whether mimicking her somber style would better achieve his aim.

Jasper found himself wanting to meet with her approval. It would be hard won, which made it worth the effort.

"The *trone d'amour*," he murmured to himself, touching his cravat. Decided on a style, Jasper headed to his desk and determined he wouldn't think of his newest employer for at least an hour.

Jasper's foot crossed the threshold of the Melville front door at precisely eleven o'clock. Snapping his pocket watch shut, he waited only a moment while the butler dealt with his hat and cane. But it was a moment he relished for the expectation weighting it. He'd considered the possible reasons why he should be so confoundedly eager to reach this portion of his schedule and come to the conclusion it was Eliza Martin's ability to surprise him that he enjoyed.

The realization came with the sudden understanding that nothing surprised him anymore. He knew precisely what others would say before they said it and how they would respond before they did so. It was the way of the world, the rules of decorum, and his own acute appreciation of human nature. Socializing was like a scripted play, with all the actors aware of what their lines were and when they should be spoken.

Eliza had yet to say anything he expected her to say.

"This way, sir."

Jasper followed the butler to a study and paused on the threshold while he was announced. With his hands clasped at the small of his back, he took in the room, noting how the heavy masculine furniture was offset by flowery pastel drapes and artwork featuring picturesque country landscapes. As if the space had once been a man's domain and was no longer.

"Ah, good morning, Mr. Bond."

The butler bowed and stepped aside, exposing the slender woman who'd been hidden by his tall frame. Eliza sat at a walnut desk so large she appeared dwarfed behind it. Her gaze was downcast, her hair piled high in soft curls, and her shoulders partially hidden by the fine lace decorating a modest bodice.

Jasper entered fully and moved to one of the two carved wooden chairs facing the desk. Before he sat, he glanced down at what occupied her. Ledgers. She worked over them studiously, filling the columns with impressive speed and painfully neat numerals.

"Once again," she murmured, "you are precisely on time."

"Another of my faults?" he asked.

She glanced up at him, studying him beneath the veil of thick auburn lashes. "Would you care for tea?"

"No, thank you."

She set her quill aside and waved the butler away. "The trait of punctuality simply tells me that you value time. It suggests you will value mine as well, which I appreciate."

"What else do you value, Miss Martin?"

"I fail to see how that signifies."

Jasper smiled. "If I am to be a lovelorn swain or even simply a fortune hunter who has set his cap for you, I am expected to know things about you."

"I see." A slight wrinkle marred the space between her brows, then she said, "I value my privacy, solitude, the books in my library, my horse, and my money."

He watched the way her fingertips tapped lightly atop the ledger in front of her. "You keep your own accounts?"

"As my father did before me."

"Why have you not wed?"

Eliza sat back and crossed her arms. "Are you married, Mr. Bond?"

"Jasper," he corrected, wanting to hear his given name spoken in her soft, yet steely voice. "And no, I'm not married."

"Then I ask the same question of you. Why have *you* not wed?"

"The manner in which I live my life doesn't lend itself to matrimony. I keep odd hours and odder company."

"Hmm . . . Well, I have not wed because I've yet to find an individual whose company is worth the expense." She lifted one shoulder in an offhand shrug. "Frankly, marriage for me is an extremely expensive proposition. In addition to the loss of control over my own funds, I'd be agreeing to spend an inordinate amount of time with another person. It makes me odd, I know—or perhaps it just makes me a Tremaine—but I find socializing with others is more exhausting than refreshing. I have to consider everything I want to say, and then filter it through my mind before I speak so what emerges from my mouth doesn't offend with its bluntness."

And there it was, the key to wooing her into bed: encourage her to be herself. Not a problem for him at all, since he enjoyed her unpolished pronouncements and reasoned judgments. He looked forward to the challenge of unveiling the woman beneath the brain.

"Eliza," he purred, watching her reaction to his uninvited familiarity—the slight dilation of her irises, the unaffected flutter of her lashes, and the quickening tempo of the pulse visible at her throat. "I must confess, I was very much looking forward to our meeting this morning precisely because of what emerges from your mouth."

Which led to thoughts of what else he liked about that particular feature. Such as the full curve of her bottom lip, and the way it pursed lightly when he goaded her. Even the way it moved when she spoke. The things he wanted to do to that mouth shocked even him. He wanted to feel it move over his skin, whispering lewd taunts and pressing soft kisses. Teasing. Suckling. . . .

He inhaled sharply, displeased for the first time in his life with the finely honed instincts he'd long relied on to survive. It was one thing to be sexually aware of a woman—something he found quite stimulating and enjoyable. It was quite another to be physically affected by that awareness.

"It's rare," he continued, forcing his thoughts back to the business at hand, "for a client to be so forthcoming. It makes my efforts far more effective when they are."

Her head tilted to the side, causing two curls to sway beside a delicately shaped ear. She seemed prepared to speak, but then she didn't. Instead, she withdrew a piece of paper from beneath her leather-bound ledger and offered it to him.

He leaned forward and accepted it, turning it around so he could read what was written. As with her bookkeeping, the columns were neat and tidy, yet the way in which she formed her letters was different. Highly slanted as opposed to straight, elongated at the highs and lows, bleeding at the point of ink refill as if she was too hurried to shake off the excess properly. He mulled this over as he read—the care over numerals versus the carelessness over proper names was telling. The list catalogued her suitors by peerage rank—if applicable—as well as length of suit, age, brief but concise physical descriptions, and anomalous traits such as throat clearing and nose twitching. He would easily be able to put a name to a face with the information she provided.

"I'm impressed with the thoroughness of your observation skills," he praised, looking up at her.

A ghost of a smile curved her lips, making him realize he had yet to see her smile in truth. "Thank you. I came to the conclusion last evening that this would be my final Season. I secured an agreement from my uncle long ago that six Seasons would be all he'd ask of me . . . but I was undecided about holding him to the promise. He asks so little of me, after all."

"I see." He should feel no guilt in enjoying her, then. He would not be ruining her if she was seated firmly on the shelf.

"And so I've also decided to utilize your services for the

entirety of the six weeks remaining in this Season, Mr. Bond. If you will advise me of the cost of securing your services for that length of time, I'll see you are paid by the end of the day tomorrow."

Jasper leaned back in his chair, considering. There was something about the way she eyed him that set off a quiet alarm. He appreciated being paid for services rendered—as anyone did—but he wondered if more than the balance of her accounts and a wish to absolve a debt was motivating her. He'd dealt with members of the peerage who felt the act of paying him put him in his place. Once he'd accepted money, he was no longer a businessman but a commodity they had rights and power over. In most instances, he cared not at all what clients told themselves to assuage their pride. In this case, he would not allow Eliza to think she could control him with her money.

"We have an agreement," he said, smiling slightly to soften the rigidity of his position on the matter. "A fortnight without pay. If I have satisfied you at that time, you may make restitution then."

There was a flash of wariness in her blue eyes. Barely there and then gone. "But I do not intend to replace you."

"Excellent. I do not intend to be replaced." He held the list aloft. "Did you, perchance, put these in order of most suspicious to least likely?"

"Yes, of course." She stood and rounded the desk.

He rose quickly, watching in surprise as she settled into the seat beside him. She leaned over the armrest and gestured for him to sit. "If you have any questions, I'm most willing to answer them to the best of my ability."

As Jasper lowered himself back into the chair, he inhaled the rather exotic scent of her perfume, appreciating how different it was from her modest mode of dress. She was a study in contradictions, from her appearance to her voice to her handwriting. "Why is the Earl of Montague so near the bottom?"

Eliza's head tilted so she could better see where he pointed. It was the closest proximity they'd shared yet, affording him the opportunity to note the smattering of light freckles over the bridge of her nose. "Why shouldn't he be within the 'least likely' section? His lordship is handsome and charming and—"

"Desperately in debt." It was by dint of will alone that he managed not to crush the foolscap in his hand. What natural attraction he felt for her was increased by a sense of possessiveness. Damned if Montague would get his hands on Eliza or her money.

"Yes. I know. But so are many of the men on the list. Those who are not in debt are of limited means." She saw his raised brows and another slight smile curved her lips. "I've looked into the circumstances of every gentleman who calls upon me, even the ones whose motives are clear straightaway."

"And how did you manage that?"

"I may not have a bookkeeper, Mr. Bond—"

"Jasper," he corrected, yet again.

Her shoulders went back. "Such familiarity is inappropriate in business dealings."

"Not so." It appeared he was correct about her wish for distance. "And especially not in this instance. You should be more than a little fond of me. I collect that you find it difficult to contemplate, since I am not your type of male, but the use of given names and time spent in my company will help to alleviate any awkwardness you might feel, creating a more believable presentation."

"You said to leave that aspect of the plan to you."

"Quite right. I will lead, you will follow." He used the tone of voice that never failed to pull others into line. He knew if he gave Eliza the slightest opportunity, she would run roughshod over him. "Now, about how you acquired your information . . . ?"

Her lips pursed. Clearly she was not a woman used to being managed. *Been allowed to run amok, that one,* Lynd had said. Jasper wouldn't change that about her, even if afforded the opportunity, but he also wouldn't be led around by the nose.

"I have a man of affairs," she said, "who makes discreet inquiries for me as necessary. One cannot be too careful."

Jasper leaned back, settling into a comfortable position to better enjoy the conversation. "And what sort of information did you glean from these inquiries? Were you made aware of the full extent of Lord Montague's debts?"

"I know enough to be wary."

"Then why put him in such an elevated position on your list?"

"As I said, he is charming and could certainly secure a better match than me. I think he uses me to make other women jealous. My mother used to say, 'there's nothing so attractive as a man who belongs to another woman.' Montague may be financially troubled, but few know that. He's managed to hide it well. And he is handsome enough to cover many faults in some women's eyes." Her gaze narrowed, and she raked him from head to toe. "In fact, you two are similar in height and coloring. Build, too, although he is not nearly as . . . broad."

It took great effort not to tense and betray his unease at her perceptiveness. "And yet you claimed others would see me and know straightaway I was not like your other suitors at all."

"You have an astonishingly good memory, Mr. Bond."

"Jasper."

She took a deep breath. "Your sharp recollection is laudable . . . Jasper."

"Thank you, Eliza." He held back a satisfied smile at the tiny bit of progress. "I've found the skill quite useful. But I confess, I'm perplexed by your contradictory statements."

"I said there were similarities, but they are not overly evident." She didn't intend for her perusal to be invigorating, but it most definitely was. "He is handsome, yes. As are you. But you are flamboyantly so. It's astonishing really, the way the first sight of you arrests the brain. Whenever I initially catch sight of you, it takes a moment to pull my thoughts together."

"I am gratified you find me appealing." And relieved that the fraternal similarities she'd noted were so quickly dismissed.

"Fustian. I'm certain you must be accustomed to all the attention by now. What is it like, by the way? Having people admire you when you enter a room or pass them by?"

"I don't notice such things."

"Truly?"

"I am usually intent on whatever purpose I have for being in any given location or situation."

"Oh, I see." Eliza nodded. "Yes, you are quite focused. Intensely so. It's another trait distinguishing you."

He swiftly utilized the avenue provided by her curiosity. "Tomorrow, I intend to take you to the Royal Academy of Art. You can see for yourself how others perceive me."

"An outing?" She frowned. Oddly, he liked that as much as her hint of a smile. Her face was so expressive, it took much of the guesswork out of wondering what was on her mind. "I suppose that's the best way to expose me and lure the culprit out."

"I would never use you as bait. It's my intention to become the target instead." He took care to fold the list neatly. "Over the next several weeks, you and I will be spending a great deal of time together. The more you are seen with me, the bigger a threat I will become."

She watched him tuck the folded paper into a pocket of his waistcoat.

"In addition," he went on, "I will need to meet with your man of affairs."

"Why?"

"Some men do not appreciate having their private matters examined, discreetly or not. And I must ask about your investments and Lord Melville's activities."

Her face took on an appearance of great interest. "You suspect another motivation."

"It's a possibility. Malicious intent can be incited by many things: love, money, and vengeance are at the top of the list. You are wealthy, others are not. If any of your investments or ventures has caused an individual to feel wronged, there is motive there. If anyone holds ill-will toward Melville, hurting someone close to him could be motive as well." Jasper held her gaze. "Personally, I can understand why someone would go to great lengths to win you. But to take it to the point of injury against you . . . I cannot wait to learn the identity of our mystery assailant. I anticipate that introduction with great relish."

Eliza did not appear to be alarmed by his fervent hope for violence. "I'm grateful for your attention to the task."

"You would not accept anything less."

She stood, and he stood with her. Her head tilted back to maintain eye contact. "Mr. Lynd and the Runner I hired both seemed to think I was daft. It isn't a pleasant feeling to be treated as mentally inferior. It was a brief glimpse, I suppose, of what Melville bears with terrible frequency."

"Is that one of the reasons why you resist marriage? For your uncle's benefit?"

"No. He's quite capable of caring for himself, at least to the extent that he employs a trustworthy and efficient staff to manage the minutiae he has no patience for." Her gaze moved to the clock on the mantel. "Today I am at home to callers. Will you be one of them?"

"Will it settle your mind if I am?"

Her head gave a slight shake. "Here at home, I feel safe enough."

"Then I shall refrain. I think it will be more effective if I'm not one of the many. Tomorrow will be our first public appearance together, and you will be granting me your undivided attention. That will establish my connection with you in a more prominent way. We'll require a chaperone who gossips. Do you know of someone who will suffice?"

"I'll see to it. What do I say to those who ask about you? What reply can I give to inquiries about your people and situation?"

He breathed in her scent with a deep inhalation, one last delay before revealing a truth no one else knew. "You may tell them I am the nephew of the late Lord Gresham of County Wexford, and our families are old friends from long ago."

"Oh . . ."

Jasper knew little of his mother's relations. Diana Gresham had been disowned after her pregnancy became evident, a circumstance affording her no way out of the hell she'd died in. When Jasper tracked Gresham down years later, the only regret he felt at learning of his lordship's recent passing was that he'd lost the opportunity to repay his uncle in kind.

"You are a conundrum, aren't you?" Eliza said softly. "I should like to figure you out."

"If you have a question, ask me."

"Will you answer?"

That made him smile. When he heard her breath catch, his inner predator licked its lips and purred. For all her protests regarding the suitability of his appearance, it was undeniable that it pleased her. "My past and my future are irrelevant. You have my present. In that, yes, ask away. I will answer."

"I knew you would be troublesome, Mr. Bond."

"Jasper."

"But I believe you will resolve my dilemma, and I find a measure of relief in that." Rounding the desk, she resumed her seat. Her manner changed, became distant. She opened a drawer and withdrew a small book. "Here is a copy of my social calendar for the remainder of the Season as it stands so far. I will keep a list of future invitations I accept."

"Your thoroughness is admirable."

"I think you and I shall work well together. Is there anything else? Or are we finished for today?"

He found himself wanting to linger, knowing it was still early in the day and the most interesting part of it would now be behind him. "These lists are sufficient at present. I'll need to be apprised of the other matters we discussed—your investments, your man of affairs, and anything in Lord Melville's past that might put a loved one at risk."

"An investment pool managed by Lord Collingsworth and rental properties," she answered, with her head already bent and quill in hand. "Both residential and commercial. I can take you to them, if you like."

"I would."

"Will the day after tomorrow be soon enough for a tour and meeting with my man of affairs, Mr. Reynolds?"

"Quite. I will also need a list of your tenants."

She glanced up at him. "Your attention to detail is very impressive."

He bowed. "I do try. I will call on you tomorrow at one."

"I'll be ready."

Turning about, Jasper moved to leave the room. On the threshold, he looked back, finding a small bit of pleasure in catching Eliza staring after him, despite the frown marring her brow. She looked down quickly.

When he reached the foyer, he pulled out his pocket watch and was startled by the time. He'd overstayed his visit by nearly ten minutes, making him late for his next appointment.

Bloody hell. He had completely forgotten the time.

Chapter 3

Eliza was compiling the list of property holdings Jasper had requested when her man of affairs was announced. She looked up at the somberly dressed but friendly-faced man in her study doorway, and gestured for him to take a seat before her desk. "Good morning, Mr. Reynolds."

"An excellent morning, Miss Martin." Terrance Reynolds sat and placed his satchel at his feet.

She shook her head at the butler, who'd been waiting to relay a tea service request to the housekeeper. While she knew she should offer the courtesy, she truly didn't have much to say, and she dreaded the awkwardness that would arise when she couldn't fill the additional time with conversation. Some women possessed a talent for charming but meaningless discourse. Sadly, she was not one of them.

"You will be happy to hear," Reynolds began, "that I've found a shopkeeper for the vacant space on Peony Way. A purveyor of soaps, candles, and such."

"Excellent. You are most efficient, Mr. Reynolds."

"Thank you."

She set her quill aside, noting how much more comfortable she was talking to Reynolds than she was to Mr. Bond . . . *Jasper*. Yet that wasn't to say she preferred the comfort of one over the excitement of the other, which made no sense, considering she'd never been one to enjoy excitation overmuch. Her mother's life had forever been a series of crises and bursts of happiness interspersed with heated arguments and the depths of despair. Eliza had grown so weary of Georgina Tremaine Martin Chilcott's incessant drama that she'd taken great pains to moderate her own life. She preferred private dinners to lavish balls, and the comfort of laying on her boudoir chaise with a book over literary luncheons. There was nothing at all soothing about Jasper Bond, and she was intrigued by the fact that she missed the heightened awareness she felt in his presence.

Eliza returned her attention to the man sitting across from her. "You mentioned last week that your brother's employer had passed on. Is he still in search of employment?"

The males in the Reynolds family were all in trade as men of affairs and bookkeepers. She'd been briefly introduced to another of the siblings, Tobias Reynolds, who was possessed of the same golden locks and green-as-glass eyes as Terrance. She had henceforth inquired about Tobias on occasion—part of a well-meant but surprisingly arduous attempt to be more personable—and she'd learned of his misfortune in the course of those inquiries.

"He's been assisting our father and other brother," Reynolds replied, "but yes, Tobias is without a permanent post at the moment."

"I should like to engage him, if he's so inclined. He will have to travel and leave quickly, but the recompense should be sufficient to mitigate such inconveniences."

Reynolds frowned. "Where would you like him to go?"

"County Wexford. There is a person of interest there I would like to know better. Family, circumstances, community stature. Things of that nature." Eliza ignored the hint of unease that briefly plagued her. Yes, Jasper asserted that his past was irrelevant, and he was not a man one wished to cross. However, she had a right to know if she would be lying on his behalf, or if there was indeed more to her thief-taker than met the eye. "As always, discretion is the rule, but more so in this instance. I don't want Lord Gresham to be aware of my interest. And timeliness will be rewarded.

"Would you prefer me to see to it personally?" he offered.

"No. I need you here. We'll be advancing the monthly tour of my properties to the day after tomorrow."

"As you wish, Miss Martin. I will speak with my brother as soon as I depart."

"If you could also ascertain the extent of the allowance he feels will be sufficient to support the endeavor, I will ensure I have the amount available before he departs."

"Certainly." He didn't query her about the nature of her interest, which was why they worked well together. She did not like to justify her expenses to anyone.

"Thank you." She managed a smile. "That will be all for now, Mr. Reynolds. I appreciate you, as always."

After he left, Eliza glanced at the clock on her desk. Her nose wrinkled. The morning was gone, and the afternoon was rushing by as swiftly. Soon, she would be welcoming guests into her parlor and engaging in conversation so inane she wouldn't remember later what she discussed.

She was disappointed Jasper wouldn't be there. The time would be much more engrossing if he were. When she considered all the amusements used to enliven events that never engaged her—the pianoforte, singing, card games, and chess—she was taken by the realization it was a man best used as a blunt-force instrument who interested her most.

There were some days when Eliza actually enjoyed riding through Hyde Park, despite the torturously slow pace of the congestion and the need for endless smiling that pained her cheeks. Today was one of those good days. The soft breeze and gentle warmth of the sun were refreshing, and the need to prepare quick and appropriate responses to greetings kept her thoughts free of Jasper.

"You seem to be enjoying yourself today, Miss Martin," the Earl of Montague said from his seat beside her. He'd arrived for their agreed-upon outing in a new and clearly expensive curricle. When he first began pursuing her in earnest, she'd wondered why a peer of seemingly substantial wealth would show such dogged interest in her of all people. Then she learned he maintained the appearance of solvency through prudence—and luck—at the gaming tables. It was a clever ruse and one few bothered to delve into.

She looked at him with a frown, slightly chagrined by her inability to navigate the social waters without bumping into things. "Is it so obvious that I usually do not?"

"Not so obvious, no," he said, while deftly handling the ribbons. He maneuvered through the multitude of conveyances on South Carriage Drive with admirable skill. "But I've taken to paying close attention to you, Miss Martin. And I collect that you have little interest in Society as a whole."

"To put it bluntly, my lord."

Montague grinned, his teeth white despite the shadow cast by the brim of his hat. Of all her suitors, she would say he was the most attractive. His dark hair was so thick and glossy she thought it might feel like silk if she touched it, and his eyes were extremely expressive. Similar in color to Jasper's, but nowise near as shuttered.

"I understand," he went on, "that a woman loses a measure of freedom when she takes a husband."

"Most vexing, to be sure."

"And I appreciate your reticence. You see, I've come to the delayed understanding that people in general perplex you."

Eliza's brows rose. "You have?"

"I realize now I was going about this business of courting you all wrong. Most women want wooing—flowers and tokens of affection, focused attention, and the like."

"The flowers you send weekly are lovely," she said automatically, although she thought it a shame for such beautiful living things to be cut away from their source of nourishment.

"I'm gratified you think so. But I believe you wouldn't miss them if I ceased making the gesture. You would not experience hurt feelings or attribute emotional reasons to my actions based on conjecture."

He offered a genuine smile, and she stared, seeing a charm in it she'd missed previously. It was an aftereffect of Jasper that she was now overly attentive to other males. She wanted to discern why the thief-taker affected her so strongly.

"I am sorely inept at interpreting such things," she agreed, adjusting the angle of her parasol to better shield her face. The slightest touch of sun on her nose would result in more freckles.

"No, you are perfectly reasoned," his lordship argued. "And that's where I erred. I was pandering to your softer nature, when I should have been appealing to your intellect. Therefore, I will not insult your intelligence any further. I'm in need of your fortune, Miss Martin."

Intrigued, she shifted on the seat to better study him. "A novel approach, I must say. Quite bold."

His grin held shades of triumph. "And you like it. For the first time in our acquaintance, I feel as if I have your attention in its entirety."

Montague paused to tip his hat to Lord and Lady Grayson as they passed. When he looked back at Eliza, there was a new gleam in his eye, reminiscent of the way Jasper looked at her. It lacked the ability to make her breath catch, but she recognized it for what it was—the earl was suddenly more intrigued by her as well.

"The best approach to you is so obvious," the earl continued, "that I'm quite put out by my failure to see it before. Whether or not I have elevated feelings for you isn't of enough value to you to equal what you believe you will lose. In the simplest of terms, I haven't shown you that I am a good investment."

Captured by the uniqueness of the conversation, Eliza wished they were not in public so she could fully enjoy the surprise without interruption. "Please, go on."

"First and foremost, the Montague lands are vast and with proper care would yield a tidy return."

"Why isn't the estate supporting you now?"

"My father suffered from a loose hand with coin, an untrustworthy steward, and a greedy mistress. I assure you, however, I am not my father."

"Perhaps not, but you *are* a gamester, my lord. You have managed to do well enough with your winnings." She gestured at his fashionable equipage. "But luck at the tables is a fickle thing, and certainly you would eventually contract mistresses of your own. Perhaps you will become smitten by a paramour who is also afflicted with avarice. I would not take kindly to destitution due to gambling or the waste of *my* funds on another woman who was enjoying the companionship of *my* husband. I expect to own the things I pay for, and I rarely lend them out."

"Ah, so," he said softly, with another warm glance in her direction. "You know, Miss Martin, the more I know of you, the more taken I am."

"Today, I find myself enjoying your company as well. But forgive me, my lord, I have no desire to marry you."

"There are other benefits." Outwardly, nothing changed, but Eliza sensed a new weight of expectation, as if he were debating whether or not to continue with his thought. "Aside from financial considerations, there are other ways in which a man and his wife reach an accord. I want to assure you, you would not find married life to be distasteful. I've no wish for disharmony in my home. I would make every effort to see that you were satisfied in sharing your life with me."

For a moment, she was perplexed by his statement. Did they not have an accord now? Then she recalled the conversation she'd had with Melville and Jasper about the things women wanted from men. Which led her to thinking about the things a peer would want from a woman. . . .

"Are you referring to procreation, my lord?"

Montague visibly jolted. Staring straight ahead, he seemed unable to respond. And then he laughed. It was a full, open-throated sound that drew stares from every quarter. "No wonder you find the usual discourse less than interesting. Speaking one's mind is much more stimulating."

Eliza opened her mouth to reply, then shut it again as her attention was snared by a familiar shade of blue velvet. Montague's carriage continued to move forward, but Eliza's eyes remained riveted to Jasper, who sat astride a black steed just off the Row, watching her with the fiercely intense stare that set butterflies to flight in her stomach. Her response was so strong, it was unnerving. Her palms grew damp, conveying a heat that had nothing to do with the weather. It was rather like spotting a crouched panther in the brush, its rapacious gaze following the prey it intended to pounce upon at any moment.

Without conscious prompting, she straightened in her seat and her hand lifted to the brim of her simple straw hat.

Jasper was such a compelling figure, even the dappled light afforded by an overhanging tree could not diminish his vibrancy. A thrill of awareness moved through her, as did a strong appreciation for the sight of him. How long had he been there? She could have sworn he hadn't been under that tree mere seconds before.

The earl spoke, drawing her thoughts back to him.

She tore her gaze from Jasper. "I beg your pardon, my lord?"

"Wed me," he repeated. "I will give you things you don't yet know you want. I understand you, Miss Martin. We are different in all the best ways. A collaboration between us would be to the advantage of us both."

"I have a better idea. I will find you a more suitable candidate."

Montague's mouth curved. "You intend to play matchmaker?"

"In a fashion." Eliza was keenly aware of Jasper's gaze following her.

"Miss Martin, I want to be clear about my intentions. I've decided you will suit me best of all. I will not be easily dissuaded from my aim of proving I can complement you as well."

"As you wish." She sighed. "Please do not make a nuisance of yourself in the effort, Lord Montague. You've always been one of the more agreeable of my suitors. I should like you to stay that way, if possible."

Montague laughed again and looked at her with sparkling eyes. "You are a delightful surprise. I wish I'd been wiser earlier in the Season."

Eliza looked behind her to where Jasper had been.

He was gone, leaving behind a marked absence.

As Jasper urged his mount away from South Carriage Drive toward the adjacent Rotten Row, the member of his crew assigned to watching Eliza also turned with him.

"She has an eye for you," Aaron White said, gesturing at another crew member further up the Drive who would continue surveillance.

Jasper nodded. He had come without thought. It wasn't until he'd caught sight of Eliza that he realized why. A vague notion had played in his mind—a budding desire to see her glorious hair in sunlight—and somehow it led him here. Ridiculously sentimental. Completely out of character. Her time in his schedule had passed, and he had other matters to attend to.

"Of course," Aaron continued, "you made certain she saw you."

Jasper could shine in a crowd or hide among it in the space of a breath merely by making miniscule changes in his deportment and posture. He'd been an unnoticed observer until Montague said something to Eliza that snared her attention completely. Jasper had wanted to steal her regard, and he'd done so. "It's best that she not seem too taken with any of her other suitors. Defeats the effectiveness of my plan to secure her safety."

"And your pronounced interest in her has nothing to do with it," Aaron teased, holding his reins loosely in one hand while the other rested atop his thigh. He was a young lad, short and stocky, a hard worker with three small mouths to feed. For that reason, Jasper kept him away from the more hazardous assignments. Watching out for Eliza was perfect.

"Her attractiveness makes the job more agreeable." That was all Jasper intended to say on the matter.

Aaron's gaze followed Montague. "The earl appears to agree. He seems genuinely taken with her."

The sound of Montague's recent laughter lingered in Jasper's mind, and his gloved grip tightened on his reins. "She would be miserable with him. He cares for nothing so much as his own self-interest. I'm doing her a favor."

"That's one way of looking at the ruination of a proper society miss." There was amusement in Aaron's tone, which was understandable considering Jasper's rule against dallying with ladies of quality. It was a rule he was clearly intent on breaking.

"I am not ruining her. She decided long ago she would

never wed, and she reiterated that intention to me only hours ago."

"And you'll show her the joys of shagging, so she doesn't die ignorant? Another favor? By God, Bond, you're damn near saintly in your generosity."

Jasper shot the younger man a fulminating glare.

Aaron raised both hands in a gesture of surrender. "You're a shrewd businessman above all. Makes me right curious as to why you plan to stop short of the big prize. Since you're taking her to bed, why not also take her to wife? Add her fortune to the other benefits of the association."

"Wanting and wedding are two very different things. She would be equally miserable with me. I've no notion of how to keep a woman happy outside of the bedroom."

"Don't let her out of bed. Problem solved."

"I am not amused."

"Merely a suggestion." Aaron grinned. "Not sure why I mentioned it, considering I benefit from your remaining just as you are now. If you became obscenely wealthy, you wouldn't work so hard, and I would have fewer opportunities to earn my wages."

Jasper's gaze followed Eliza until Montague's equipage was lost in the crowd. Out of sight, out of mind. He hoped. He withdrew his pocket watch and checked the time. Eliza would return home shortly and begin preparations for the evening.

How would she appear when dressed formally? Not that she would put any effort into it, which he found refreshing. Some women spent excessive amounts of time on their exteriors. Eliza's most attractive qualities weren't the most obvious ones. The hints of stronger passions were so subtle, even she was not aware of them. She was of the introspective sort, quietly curious and sharply intelligent.

Jasper, by contrast, preferred a more hectic pace of living. He kept his hours filled from the time he awoke until he couldn't fight sleep a moment longer. Such preoccupation afforded less time to ruminate on the thorn wedged in his side. Eliza both helped and hindered in that regard. When he was with her, he was so mindful of her there was no room for awareness of anything else. And that was a problem. He could not afford to lose his focus now. Not when he was so close to achieving his aims.

He growled and tugged his hat lower on his brow, hating to be in public while so disconcerted. Over a spinster who thought he was too handsome and too dangerous.

"I shall leave Miss Martin in your capable hands," he said.

"You might consider occupying *your* hands with a visit to the upper floor of Remington's," Aaron suggested. "To take the edge off."

The prod to partake in the more carnal offerings at his favorite gentlemen's club came from keen observation. Although Aaron's observant nature was one of the reasons why Jasper had employed him, it was damned inconvenient when aimed in his direction. "Watch her. Not me."

He turned about in search of another familiar figure. As luck would have it, he didn't have far to look.

The gentleman Jasper sought was en route to him, weaving through the many riders with one hand lifted to his hat brim in perpetual greeting. Gabriel Ashford, ninth Earl of Westfield, was a gazetted rake of prominent family and fortune, which ensured that an inordinate number of female stares were directed his way. Although his exploits were known to include nearly every vice, there were no signs of dissipation marring the features that incited some women to swoon. He looked fit and lean, and his easy smile was on full display.

As Westfield drew near, his countenance changed subtly. The façade he wore so well slipped a little, revealing the true man beneath. A good and kind man whom Jasper had taken into his confidence. A gentleman he considered a friend.

"Good afternoon, Bond."

Jasper tipped his hat. "My lord."

"I saw you eyeing Montague." Westfield drew abreast of Jasper's mount. "Are you worried he'll get his hands on Miss Martin's fortune and settle his debt?"

"Actually, it was Miss Martin who held my interest."

"Ah . . . I failed to collect that elusive bluestockings were to your taste."

"Paying clients are always to my taste."

"Interesting." Westfield's brows rose. "Why does Miss Martin require your services?"

Jasper spurred his horse into motion. The earl followed suit.

"What do you know of her and her kin?" Jasper asked.

"The Tremaine brood is unquestionably an odd lot, which makes them fiendishly easy to gossip about. The males are known to be brilliant to the point of madness, and the females are blessed with that stunningly beautiful shade of hair. Miss Martin seems to have inherited a bit of both traits in addition to her sizeable fortune. As for her parents, Mr. Martin was a man of trade and Lady Georgina was known to be charming and vivacious. Although Miss Martin seems as indifferent to men as her mother was appreciative, I've wondered if a deeper resemblance between them is simply untapped. Intriguing to contemplate."

"Are you saying her mother was indiscriminate?"

"Lady Georgina was known to have a fondness for the social company of men. Does that mean she took many to her bed?" Westfield shrugged. "I cannot say. However, she married Martin immediately following her presentation. She would have had her pick of peers, but instead jumped into matrimony with a commoner. Why, unless it was a love match? And if it was a love match, I doubt she would stray."

"What do you know of Mr. Martin?"

"I know his death was shocking to many. He was said to have a vigorous constitution. He was built like a laborer and often pitched in as one when the opportunity presented itself. A servant found him dead in his office when he failed to appear for supper. A weak heart was blamed."

Jasper decided he would have to dig further back, before Eliza's present-day suitors, to see if the trouble plaguing her had begun long before now.

Westfield inclined his head at a passing acquaintance. "Many have speculated that the vagaries of the family he married into might have hastened him to his grave. His due, so to speak, for his lofty marital aspirations. After his passing, Lady Georgina married again, to another commoner."

A woman of high passions and a lack of prejudice. Did Eliza carry those inclinations? How delicious if she did . . .

Jasper shook off the tangential thought. "Miss Martin has a stepfather?"

"Had. Lady Georgina and Mr. Chilcott were killed together in a carriage accident before Miss Martin's first Season. The poor girl has been sorely afflicted with tragedy."

Did she grieve? Jasper wondered. Had she always been so detached from others or was that a recently acquired safety mechanism?

"Now tell me," the earl said, "what has Miss Martin engaged you to do?"

"She has cause to fear for her safety."

Westfield's brows rose. "Truly? Who would want to injure her? She's worth more alive than dead."

"She believes someone—perhaps an overzealous suitor— is trying to goad her into marriage as a means of protecting herself. I haven't yet decided if she's correct, but hearing about her parents' untimely demise only incites further concern."

"How diverting," the earl said. "Can I assist you in any way?"

"I was hoping you would ask." Jasper reached into his pocket and withdrew the small book containing Eliza's social calendar. It was an unavoidable fact that there were some doors he needed a peer to open. "I must attend as many of these functions as possible."

The earl flipped through the small bound pages with one hand. "I see I will have to refrain from arranging a liaison tomorrow evening, so I can squire you about."

"I appreciate your sacrifice," Jasper drawled.

"I should hope so." Westfield's tone was droll. In truth, he enjoyed participating in Jasper's work when the circumstances allowed. He was even known to become somewhat of a pest, if Jasper went too long without enlisting him for some task or another. "See you at ten?"

"Perfect."

Eliza had just pulled on a dressing gown and settled in front of her vanity mirror when a knock came to her boudoir door. When bade to enter, a white-capped maid stepped in and curtsied. "His lordship asks for you, miss."

"Thank you."

Frowning, Eliza watched the servant back out of the room. She'd enjoyed tea with her uncle just an hour before, listening fondly as he spoke at length and with great animation about his latest botanical experiments. Once, their solarium had been filled with comfortable chaises and short bookcases. Now, it housed rows of long tables supporting various potted plants. Eliza didn't mind the loss of her former favorite reading spot, appreciating how the experiments in the glass space exposed his lordship to sunlight and fresh air.

What would cause him to ask for her now, at an hour when she was beginning preparations for the evening's social events? Perhaps he had an epiphany of some sort or something of a celebratory nature to share? He once woke her before sunrise because a splicing experiment yielded unexpectedly delightful results.

She stood and pulled a comfortable house gown out of the wardrobe. Then she called for her abigail, Mary, who entered the room from the bathing chamber and assisted Eliza in securing the row of buttons following the length of her spine. Despite skipping her chemise and stays, it took long moments to become presentable. Eliza tied a quick ribbon around her unbound hair and considered herself ready enough.

"What will you wear tonight?" Mary asked.

"Lay out three of your favorites." Eliza opened the door to the gallery. "I'll pick one when I return."

She often left the selection of clothing to her abigail. It didn't matter what Mary chose—Eliza always picked the gown on the farthest right. Her dresses were all impeccable, if unremarkable, having been created by a seamstress who was in high demand for her skill. The *modiste* had originally protested Eliza's selection of colors that, while fashionable, did little to emphasize the hue of her hair. But eventually the hopelessness of the objections became patently clear, and Eliza was spared from hearing them. She felt it was only fair to avoid giving anyone the notion she was attempting to entice or set a lure. Since the most popular shades were pastels and she looked best in darker colors, there was no excuse for her to dress with self-flattery in mind.

She left the room and headed directly to the family parlor on the same floor. The door was ajar. A fire crackled merrily in the grate, and his lordship paced before it in his usual state of dishabille—mussed hair, lopsided cravat, and unevenly buttoned waistcoat sans coat.

Eliza entered with a brisk stride. "My lord?"

He faced her with a distracted smile. "I'm sorry to disturb you, my dear, but you have a visitor."

She glanced down at her hastily composed presentation. "A visitor? Downstairs?"

"Good evening, Miss Martin."

Jasper's voice. A shiver coursed down her spine at the sound. Pivoting, she found him standing behind the door. His gaze was narrowed, his face austere. He was dressed in the same riding garments he had been wearing when she'd seen him in the park, but his cravat was less crisp and the outside of his boots bore traces of scuffing.

As they did every time she saw him, her thoughts skidded to a halt. It took her the length of several heartbeats to remember to speak.

There was no hiding the way her breath hitched when she greeted him. "Mr. Bond."

Chapter 4

"Behave yourself as promised, young man," Melville said, before hurrying from the room. Clearly, he was eager to return to whatever he'd been doing before being interrupted. The door was left open, but Eliza doubted such measures would impede a man like Jasper if he was of a mind to act scandalously.

"You have my word, my lord," Jasper said softly.

There was a pregnant pause after the earl departed. Jasper raked her with a heated gaze, from top to toe and back again. Then he averted his head, exposing a clenched jaw and rapid pulse. Eliza realized he was aware she'd skipped undergarments in her haste. He knew she was unbound and unfettered.

And it was adversely affecting him.

His reaction to her was creating a corresponding reaction to him. The tempo of her heartbeat increased.

Eliza covered her discomposure by moving to the settee and sitting. Smoothing her floral skirts with restless hands, she looked at Jasper's savagely masculine profile and said the first thing that came to mind. "I apologize for not being more presentable."

"How can I accept an apology"—his gaze slowly returned to her face—"for something that brings me such pleasure?"

She swallowed hard, hating that her mouth was so dry. His eyes followed the working of her throat. A thick, hot current of awareness flowed through her. It was difficult to see him there in the private room where only family and close friends gathered. An intimacy was established by his presence. She felt exposed without the stricture of her stays. Vulnerable in a way she'd never known before.

Forcing her hands to be still, she said, "I saw you this afternoon."

She didn't confess that she'd been smitten by the sight of him in his rakishly angled hat.

He nodded. "You should be cautious around Montague."

"I sincerely doubt he is the culprit."

"Why?"

"He is an intelligent man. He must be aware of more productive ways to win my hand. In fact, he said as much to me today. He believes he understands me now and presented himself as a sound investment. He's come to the conclusion that appealing to my reason is far more likely to yield the results he hopes for than attempting to engage my emotions."

Jasper's chest lifted and fell deeply. "The man gambles obsessively."

"Those who lose to him do so by their own choice. His skill is widely lauded. They know what they risk by playing against him."

"Up to this point," he murmured, "I considered you remarkably reasoned."

Eliza's chin lifted. "You are provoking me."

"I'm being frank." He approached, but his gait lacked the seductiveness she'd come to anticipate. Instead, it was determined. "Is Montague your favorite of your suitors?"

"I enjoy his lordship's company," she answered carefully.

"However, I enjoy most every gentleman who comes calling. I would avoid anyone whose companionship I didn't find agreeable. In fact, I warned Lord Montague this afternoon to be careful not to become troublesome."

He paused on the opposite side of the low table. "What would prompt you to make such a statement?"

"He has become impatient to wed and claims he is determined to have me. His approach—while unique—did not sway me, but I seem to have become something of a curiosity to him."

"The Quality is ever in pursuit of relief from boredom. After all, it's so tedious to be blessed with the wherewithal to do anything one desires."

There was an undertone to his words that set Eliza on alert. Jasper wasn't simply voicing an offhand observation.

Exhaling harshly, he altered direction toward the grate, his boots thudding softly across the well-worn rug. Resting a forearm on the mantel, he stared into the glowing coals. His dark hair gleamed with vitality. The strands sweeping forward to frame his temples and brow were uniquely appealing despite the popularity of the style. Burnished by firelight, Eliza found the lines of his large body to be magnificent. He was exceedingly male, like a glass filled overfull. She wondered how women managed a sip without spilling all over themselves.

Not a poetic thought and definitely an unseemly one, but she chose not to delude herself. She was attracted to him. His mere presence made her highly conscious of her own femininity.

"Why are you here?" she asked, twisting to face his back.

There was a long hesitation, then he said, "Your father's death. Did it come as a surprise to you?"

"Yes." Eliza's fingers linked together in her lap.

Jasper looked at her over his shoulder. "You answered

too swiftly. I need you to be honest with me, if I'm to succeed."

The way he stared at her gave her pause.

"Very well," she amended. "I was surprised and not. I knew he was unwell, but I believed he had an affliction of the mind. Not the body."

"Affliction of the mind, you say? Was he lacking reason?"

"He wasn't mad. Although I sometimes thought my mother was determined to drive him to it."

He focused more intently on her. "Explain."

"He was unhappy, which contributed to an excessive fondness for strong spirits, but I did not collect how sick he'd become until it was too late. Why do you ask?"

"You lost both of your parents too early. I must be certain their fate isn't linked to your present situation in some way. Are you quite confident your father's death was natural in cause?"

"It was expected," she qualified. "I wouldn't call it natural. As you said, he died before his time."

"And your mother's death? Are you confident it was an accident?"

"The only surprise about her demise was how long it took to happen," she said sharply.

"Eliza . . ." Jasper came to sit beside her.

The air around her became charged with his energy.

I never feel so alive as I do when I am the object of a man's desire, her mother had said, while spinning like a giddy girl with her skirts held in each hand. *The blood sings, Eliza. The heart races. It is the most glorious feeling in the world.*

Why did Jasper have to be the man to awaken such reactions in her? Why did he have to prove, just by breathing, that she wasn't immune to needing someone after all? She was so disappointed to realize there were indeed some shades of pleasure that could be colored only by another hand.

His dark eyes were warm with concern. "Please understand, I only wish to be thorough. Your safety is of the utmost importance to me."

She nodded, believing the sincerity in his tone. A lock of her hair was dislodged by the movement, slipping free of her hastily tied ribbon to slide over her shoulder.

He stood. Holding out a hand, he assisted her to her feet. "Turn around."

As Eliza pivoted, she disturbed the air, allowing the primitive scent that clung to him—horses and leather, tobacco and bergamot—to tease her senses. She jumped slightly at the feel of his fingers against her nape. Awareness of him swept outward, flowing across her skin like warm water. He lifted the curl from her shoulder and rubbed it between his fingers.

"Like fine silk," he murmured. He loosened the ribbon securing her hair, returned the errant lock to its former place, and retied the whole more securely.

Her gaze darted around the room, hyperaware of her surroundings. Everything was rendered in brilliant clarity, from the crystals hanging from the many ornate candlesticks to the inlaid mother-of-pearl glimmering from the tops of the end tables.

In the swirling confusion, she grasped the first thought that came to her. "Are you one of those gentlemen who has an unusually strong interest in red hair?"

"I have an unusually strong interest in you." He pressed his lips to the bare skin between her shoulder and throat.

"Jasper," she whispered, shocked by the violent quiver that moved through her. "What are you doing? Why did you come now . . . tonight . . . when I'll be seeing you tomorrow?"

His hands fell to his sides. "I saw the way you looked at Montague. What he said made you see him in a way you haven't before."

Eliza faced him. He was more than a head taller, but his frame curved toward her in a way that made their proximity searingly intimate. As if he was about to twirl her into a waltz.

Her heart beat a little faster. Her breathing quickened. "I don't understand."

He cupped her chin and tilted her face upward. "You looked at him the way you look at me."

"That's impossible." Montague incited none of this turmoil.

"I need you to regard me in the same manner with which I regard you."

She was arrested by the way he looked her over. So intent. With a gaze that was fierce. Fervent. His fingertips followed the path of his perusal. Touching her forehead. Tracing her brows. Following the bridge of her nose.

Eliza, in turn, studied him unabashedly. His features were so perfectly formed, beautiful in their symmetry but masculine in their lines. It was such a pleasure to look upon him; he made her want to stare.

"How do I regard you now?" she queried breathlessly.

"Too aware. Trying to reason your way out of this attraction. Stop thinking," he murmured. Tilting his head, he lowered his mouth toward hers. The approach was slow and deliberate. His grip was loose and without force. "Let yourself feel it."

She stumbled back, panting because she couldn't breathe when he was so close.

Jasper watched her retreat with hooded eyes. She was nearly beyond arm's reach when he growled and caught her back. His lips sealed over hers with a boldness that stole what was left of her air. With one hand at her nape and an arm around her waist, Jasper took her mouth as if he owned it. Undeniably skilled and . . . hungry. A slanting, suckling, ferocious possession that stunned her completely.

Eliza sagged into him, unable to comprehend the ardor with which he kissed her. His body was astonishingly hard, like warm marble. From shoulder to thigh, he pressed un-yieldingly against her. Without the barrier of her stays the sensation was . . . Dear God, she couldn't describe the need she had to touch more of him. Her hands clenched and re-leased at her sides, reaching for him, then falling away.

Where should—could—she touch him?

As if he understood, Jasper's hand at her nape followed the length of her arm down to her wrist. His fingers circled it, then lifted her hand to his chest. Between his coat and waistcoat he urged her palm to splay over his heart. His skin burned through the layers of clothing between them. His heartbeat raced with the same recklessness as hers.

Her other hand clenched the hem of his coat. She whim-pered, overwhelmed.

Her capitulation gentled him. The press of his lips soft-ened and his grip slackened enough to allow her lungs to ex-pand. Teasing rather than taking, Jasper licked the lower curve of her lip, goading her to taste him back. She did, trembling, uncertain.

At the first flick of her tongue, he captured it with soft suction. Startled, Eliza jerked in his arms, her breasts flat-tening against his chest. His groan vibrated against her, tum-bling across sensitized nerve endings.

"Eliza."

The clock on the mantel began to chime on the half hour, but Eliza was lost to time, focused instead on the luxuriant licks stroking deep into her mouth. Her hand moved across Jasper's torso, feeling the muscles tense beneath her touch. A sound escaped her, a soft plea.

Jasper lifted his head, breathing hard. With heavy-lidded eyes, he studied her face.

"This," he said gruffly, "is how you should look at me, the way you look at no one else. As if you long for me to finish what I've started. As if you ache to feel my mouth on you, my hands on you."

She did ache. And felt unappeased, as if she had an unquenched thirst. Her skin was too sensitive. Her fingers trembled. She was far too hot.

He stepped back and turned away in a motion as elegant as it was powerful. She couldn't help but follow him with her gaze. He was such a large and finely built man, yet he moved with such grace.

"Jasper." Her pulse leaped at the look he shot her. "Tomorrow night . . . I will save the first waltz for you."

She hadn't meant to say that. In retrospect, she wasn't certain she'd had anything to say at all. She simply felt the unaccountable urge to stay him and keep him just a little while longer. And she wanted to dance with him, to stand within the circle of his arms in a place where there was safety in numbers.

He returned. Reaching for her hand, he lifted it and pressed a kiss to the back, giving her fingers a squeeze that only added to the tingling his lips had evoked. "I'm not well versed in dancing. Let me rephrase: I do not know how."

"You don't?" Eliza was astonished by the pronouncement and the lack of education it implied. But he comported himself without fault and was well-spoken.

It would be weeks before Tobias Reynolds returned. How would she bear the wondering about his origins until then?

Jasper's smile chased her ruminations away and curled her toes. "I shall endeavor to please you in other ways. Be assured, I will not rest until you're completely satisfied. Until tomorrow."

He departed the room. It was several minutes later before Eliza felt steady enough to do the same.

It was a beautiful afternoon. A brief spate of rain before the sun rose had cleared the worst of the soot from the air, leaving behind a pale blue sky. It was the kind of day that lightened moods and increased the proliferation of smiles.

But Eliza was nervous.

It was a rarity for her to feel out of sorts. There were very few things that affected her mood in a negative way, because reason so often provided the answers required to accept any given situation. But physical attraction had no reason. It was instinctual and separate from the mind. And she wasn't immune to it, as she'd hoped she would be.

What was she to say to Jasper, who was waiting in the parlor to escort her about town for the day? She sighed and turned away from the cheval mirror. Perhaps it would be best to leave the opening of discussion to him. A man such as Jasper Bond must be familiar with such circumstances.

She descended to the ground-level floor with studiously controlled speed, her hand coasting along the top of the wooden handrail to support less than steady steps. She was still chastising herself for deliberately selecting a pale yellow gown, one of the few pastel colors that suited her. It hadn't been laid out on the far right. What did she hope to gain by encouraging Jasper's interest?

On the other hand, what did she have to lose?

"Mr. Bond," she said as she entered the parlor, steeling herself for the sight of him and finding the effort ineffective. When her brain stopped, her feet followed suit by abruptly halting their forward movement. She stumbled.

In the process of standing, Jasper was agile enough to lunge forward and catch her by the elbows. He steadied her with a frown. "Eliza."

"Thank you." She pulled free and stepped back, needing some distance to catch her breath.

How dangerously handsome he was. The fine cut and quality of his dark green velvet coat and the beautiful silver-threaded embroidery in his pale green waistcoat enticed the eye to linger and admire. His fawn-colored breeches hugged powerful horseman's thighs, a sight that made her feel things she oughtn't. But that was merely the packaging. It was the man inside the trappings who so appealed to her. The magnetism he exuded. The sense that at any moment something extraordinary would happen. The phantom tingling of her lips that brought heated reminiscences of his kiss to mind.

She looked away, seeking the clock to distract herself.

"You're early." She startled herself by feeling . . . *pleased* by that.

"You wreak havoc on a man's schedule," he said with a slight smile to soften the sting.

The tiny warmth in her chest blossomed.

"You look lovely, Eliza." His voice lowered. "I wanted a few moments of your time before I'm restrained by decorum."

"*You will be restrained by* me, *young man.*"

Eliza turned as Regina, Lady Collingsworth, entered the room like a whirlwind. She was a guinea-blond matron with piercing blue eyes and cherry-red cheeks. A sweet and pleasant woman for the most part, she was capable of a great force of will, and she took in Jasper's appearance with a steely glance.

Wagging a closed fan at him, she said, "You are a pretty fellow, Mr. Bond. Accustomed to testing your boundaries and finding little resistance, I bet. But I will not tolerate such nonsense. You'll behave yourself. If you want the right to be naughty, you will have to provide more than charm and a smile."

The top of her ladyship's head barely reached Jasper's shoulder, but there was no doubt she could manage him.

Eliza quickly introduced them. "Her ladyship and her son, Lord Collingsworth, will be escorting us today."

Jasper sketched a faultlessly elegant bow. "A pleasure, Lady Collingsworth."

"Let us see if you feel the same by the end of the afternoon."

In short order they were on their way, comfortably seated in Lord Collingsworth's barouche with the men on one side, and Eliza and Regina on the other. Eliza studied the two gentlemen from beneath the shade of her wide-brimmed hat, attempting to resolve in her mind why she should be so attracted to one man above all others. Was it because Jasper seemed to be equally attracted to her? If so, perhaps the simplest solution was to discuss it with him and see if he wouldn't be willing to be less overt. He'd given no serious indication that he was doing anything more than being very, very thorough about his work. And she knew she wasn't the sort of female who incited raging passions in men.

The thought had a depressive effect on her sprits.

Determined to be less maudlin, she moved her attention to Lord Collingsworth. The epitome of aristocratic excellence, his lordship was tall and slender with stern lips and an aquiline nose. His hair was as light as his mother's, but he lacked her liveliness. Collingsworth had lost both wife and unborn child a year ago, and the light of joy that once filled him had died along with them. His grief was reflected in the somberness of his clothing and the rarity of his smiles. Eliza was still trying to comprehend why the things that brought him happiness before his marriage were no longer capable of doing so now. Yes, he'd lost what Lady Collingsworth had brought to him, but surely he retained the interests he'd had as a bachelor?

Clearly, she was missing something required to reason out

the answer. She was becoming resigned to the notion that she would never be capable of understanding romantic natures.

Jasper's boot tapped against the side of her foot. She met his gaze with raised brows.

Look at me, he mouthed with darkened eyes.

Did he not understand how difficult that was? Of course he didn't. He did not feel overheated and confused when he looked at her. He didn't struggle to understand why the act of pressing their lips together had created overwhelming feelings in other parts of the anatomy.

Frustrated, she crossed her arms and looked at the passing carriages.

The toe of his boot touched her ankle, then slid up along the back of her lower calf.

Eliza froze. Her lungs seized, holding her breath. A shiver moved up her leg to unmentionable places. Wide-eyed, she glanced at him.

Jasper winked. As indignation welled up within her, his tongue traced the curve of his lower lip in a slow, sensual glide. Her breath left her in a rush. Instantly and viscerally she recalled the feel of that talented tongue against her lips and in her mouth, thrusting deep and sure in imitation of a far more intimate act.

Her breasts grew heavy and tender. The beat of her heart quickened and her skin tingled from her head to the place where his boot stroked her. It suddenly struck her that Jasper was deliberately arousing her. In the middle of the day. In the center of town. Seated inches away from two other people.

His hand lifted to an unsecured button on his coat. Strong fingers grasped it, the pad of his thumb rubbing leisurely against the outer curve. She watched, mesmerized, imagining him touching her skin that way. On the curve of her shoulder, perhaps. Or somewhere else.

He would know the best place to focus that caress.

The thought of his skill thrilled her.

Her face heated. She shifted restlessly on the squab, hoping to find a more comfortable position and worsening her predicament instead. She clutched her throat, rubbing it to facilitate her breathing. She felt as if she might pant, as if her stays were too tight and she might soon become dizzy.

Jasper's gaze settled on her gently heaving breasts. She knew she should look away and collect herself, but she could not. Her brain writhed in dismay, horrified that her body would so completely fail to function properly for no other reason than that Jasper Bond was undressing her in his mind. She knew he was remembering her as she'd been last night. Partially dressed. Easily bared.

The barouche slowed to a stop.

"Here we are," Lady Collingsworth said with customary cheerfulness.

Jasper broke the connection first, his head turning toward Somerset House. Eliza looked down, watching as his foot withdrew from beneath her skirts.

How she made the journey from the carriage to the interior of the edifice was a mystery to her. By the time she recovered the full use of her mental and physical faculties, they were entering the Exhibition Hall. Light poured into the large room from the arched windows high above the hall floor. The walls were covered in paintings, the gilded frames butting against each other, occupying every tiny bit of space.

As they neared the center of the room, Jasper slowed their progress to a standstill. Eliza looked at him, surprised to find him staring raptly at the images before him. His head was tilted back to the point that the rear of his hat brim nearly touched his back.

Eliza took stock of the room's other occupants, noting that the nearest individual was a few feet away. She leaned nearer to Jasper and whispered his name.

"Hmm . . . ?"

"Do you remember saying you would answer any question I asked, so long as it pertained to the present?"

"Yes." He did not cease his enthralled perusal of the art. "Ask me anything."

She cleared her throat. "Do you . . . want to . . . mate with me?"

He jolted so violently, the reaction shook her, too. His wide-eyed gaze darted to hers. "Eliza."

"I do not see why you should look so astonished," she said, "after kissing me last night, and considering your actions during the ride here."

His gaze warmed. A smile curved his lips. He relaxed, focusing completely on her. "Forgive me. Your choice of wording combined with our location took me aback."

"I didn't expect to have to discuss such things with you," she muttered. "I apologize if I say things incorrectly. But I must know if you can refrain from provoking me. Does the thoroughness of our presentation have to be established with the tactics you've utilized thus far or—"

"—or do I indeed want to *mate* with you?" Jasper's smile widened. "Is that what you want to know?"

Eliza nodded briskly, feeling anxious even though her question was perfectly sound considering their circumstances.

He squeezed her hand where it rested on his forearm. "You are wondering if I'm manipulating the performance I want out of you, or if my blood is so hot for you I cannot bear for you not to feel similarly?"

She averted her gaze. Described in that way, her query sounded ridiculous. Jasper was a dazzlingly handsome man. Even now, as she looked around the room to avoid his stare, she found a number of women ogling him or casting surreptitious glances in his direction at regular intervals. He could have any woman he wanted. One who was charming and flirtatious. Knowledgeable.

"Miss Martin."

Eliza turned her attention to the man who intruded on their conversation. "Sir Richard," she managed. "How lovely to see you here."

Sir Richard Tolliver was an average man, neither young nor old, neither tall nor short, neither portly nor lean. His hair was a soft brown and his eyes a gentle green. He was quiet and unassuming, one of the least aggressive of her suitors.

"You remember my sister, Miss Amanda Tolliver," he said, with a sidelong glance at Jasper.

"Yes, of course. Good to see you, Miss Tolliver." Eliza made the appropriate introductions offhandedly. But when Jasper bowed over Miss Tolliver's hand and the young lady blushed to the roots of her lovely dark hair, Eliza found her mood altering drastically.

Sir Richard offered a tight smile. "I see now why you declined my invitation to escort you to the exhibition, Miss Martin. I did not understand you had a prior engagement."

Eliza realized with some surprise that he was upset. He felt slighted, although that hadn't been her intent. She'd simply been aware that accepting his offer of escort would lead to spending hours in the company of someone with whom she had nothing in common. She thought it best to spare them both the awkwardness.

That was not, however, the explanation she could give. Conversing in society had little to do with truth. It was more about keeping everyone's feelings as neutral as possible. For many, the truth was not a neutral topic.

She was considering how she could reply in an acceptable manner when Miss Tolliver batted her thick lashes at Jasper. Eliza froze with her mouth partially formed around a word.

Suddenly she knew precisely how Tolliver felt, and how little sound reasoning had to do with it.

What a morass the art of courting was.

"Will I see you tonight at the Lansing rout, Sir Richard?" she asked.

"If you will be there, Miss Martin, I will certainly attend."

"If you are obliged, I should like to save the first waltz for you."

Tolliver's sudden grin lit up the room. Eliza was slightly frightened by its fervency.

"What about you, Mr. Bond?" Miss Tolliver asked. "Will you be at the Lansing rout? Shall I save a place on my dance card for you?"

Eliza felt Jasper's forearm tense beneath her fingers. When he said nothing, she realized he didn't know how to reply. The truth he'd shared so readily with her was not one he wished to share with others.

"Mr. Bond was injured yesterday," she lied. "His horse was ill-mannered and stepped quite harshly on his foot. While he can walk, dancing is out of the question for now."

"Oh. I'm so sorry to hear that." Miss Tolliver did indeed look crestfallen. "I hope you recover quickly, Mr. Bond."

Jasper nodded and bid the siblings farewell. He led Eliza away with a briskness that belied the injury she'd invented for him. He drew to a halt when they reached a corner and glared at the painting in front of him.

His foot tapped against the floor. "The dance you gave to Tolliver was mine."

Eliza was confused. "But you do not dance."

"Moments ago," he said in a low, biting tone, "you were asking if I wanted to be inside you and the next, you're encouraging another man's obvious interest in you."

Astonished by the physical response she had to his choice

of phrasing, she stared at the painting he was directing his ire at and tried to piece an explanation together.

"I was not encouraging him," she said carefully. "I was commiserating with him. I collected that he was perturbed and perhaps felt . . . marginalized."

Jasper glanced at her with a sardonically raised brow. "You know how he feels, but not how I feel. Care to explain why?"

"Miss Tolliver is clearly taken with you, and she's lovely and charming. As many times as we've met before, today was the first time I resented those qualities in her."

He grew very still.

Unsure if that was a positive or negative sign, she pressed on. "Sir Richard must feel similarly in regards to you. How can he compete with a man such as yourself? I vow there isn't another male in the world who is as stunning. In the face of what must have been a crushing feeling of inferiority, offering a dance seemed the least I could do."

Jasper's face gave away none of his thoughts. After a torturously long delay, he said, "You have no notion that the room just tilted on its axis, do you?"

Chapter 5

Jasper watched as Eliza's gaze darted around the Exhibition Hall in search of proof to support his claim. A rush of tenderness tightened his chest and prevented him from explaining.

Eliza returned her attention to him. "Lady Collingsworth doesn't look as if something so phenomenal has happened."

"Ah, Eliza," he murmured, warmly amused. "Lynd said you would drive me mad, and he was correct, as usual."

Her pretty mouth pursed into a tight line. "I begin to feel as if I am lacking wits," she groused. "I have been at a loss to understand anything since I woke this morning."

He found her confusion poignantly endearing. He wished he could reply to her in a gentler manner, but he was not a gentle man. As surprising as her use of "mate" had been earlier, he found it brilliantly apt now. His desire for her was at a fever pitch, his blood hot and his patience far too thin. If they'd been alone, he would be fucking her now. *Mating* with her. Pumping his cock so deep into her she would have no doubt that her public performance was the furthest thing from his mind.

Rolling his shoulders back, he tried to ward off the tension building there. He could not talk about sex right now, even to say that he wanted it with her. The words would be too coarse, his vehemence too frightening. And he wasn't yet sure that she wanted it with him. Her body did, yes. Watching her melt for him in the barouche had been singularly the most arousing experience of his life. But she had been overwhelmed and not thinking properly at the time. Eliza needed to be cognizant of her decision to take him to her bed if he was to have her as he wanted.

She watched him now, wary and unsure.

He urged her to walk with him, needing to be in motion. It didn't escape his notice that she had him in this state by speech alone. Not with a look or a touch, but with innocently spoken, artlessly truthful words.

"I want you to teach me how to dance," he said.

"Truly?" The excitement in her voice was its own reward.

"It's the only way to make restitution for giving my dance to someone else." And another way to add a block of time with her to his schedule.

Her smile was a sight to behold. "I must warn you, I am not a very good instructor of anything. I lack patience and become easily frustrated."

"I am a speedy learner," he assured, intending to make the lessons worth her while in many ways.

"Very well, then. I would be happy to try."

Returning his attention to the portraits on the wall, Jasper acknowledged that he enjoyed the exhibition. He had not expected to, as he wasn't fond of crowds. The room was almost full and the hum of conversation was a steady but not-unpleasant drone. He should not have felt comfortable there. He was a mongrel among purebreds, yet Eliza made him feel as if he was right where he should be. At the very least, right where he wanted to be.

"Which is your favorite so far?" she asked.

"I think that one." He pointed to an image of a galloping horse. "I can almost feel the wind when I look at it."

"Mine is this one." She pulled him forward and singled out a portrait of a dancing nymph with flowing hair and ribbons. "The skill involved in turning mere paints into an image that looks as if it can walk right off the canvas . . . I am awed by it."

"I'm glad you came with me and not with Tolliver," he said.

She squeezed his arm. "I am, too."

They continued around the room at a leisurely pace, pausing every few feet to take in the many paintings occupying the soaring walls.

After an hour, Eliza begged to be excused. "Will you be comfortable if I leave you alone for a moment?"

Jasper wanted to say no. "Only a moment."

She moved away. He expected her to speak to someone she knew or visit with Lady Collingsworth for a time. Instead, she left the room. He moved to follow, wanting to ensure her safety by keeping her in sight.

Lady Collingsworth deftly intercepted him.

"My lady," he said, with a slight inclination of his head.

She wrapped her hand around his forearm and waved him forward with her fan. "I would like to become better acquainted with you, Mr. Bond."

"Oh?" He looked toward the exit in time to see Sir Richard Tolliver and his sister make their egress.

"Eliza's mother and I were dear friends. After Lady Georgina's passing, I took Eliza under my wing. I couldn't love her more if she was my own child."

"She is an exceptional young woman."

"Not so young," she said, eyeing him. "She has had six failed Seasons."

"By her choice. And she is young in more than her years. She has an almost childlike comprehension of emotions."

"You sound as if you know her well, yet I have never heard of you prior to yesterday. Why are you here, Mr. Bond? And when will you return to the place whence you came?"

They rounded a corner of the room and Jasper considered his reply. A hastily spoken falsehood could breach Eliza's privacy. "I am here on business."

"You are in trade?" Her ladyship pulled away enough to facilitate studying his attire. "Successfully, it would appear."

Jasper smiled. "Is it a mark in my favor that I am not in pursuit of Miss Martin's fortune?"

"Depends on what else you are in pursuit of. I am not blind. I see the way you look at her."

"I am not blind either."

"Cheeky fellow," she admonished, but there was a twinkle in her eye. "What are your intentions?"

He stared at a painting nigh the size of his curricle and mulled over his reply. In the end, he circumvented the question. "I want her to be safe and happy."

And yet his "intentions," such as they were, might very well put her safety and happiness at risk. For her, there must be some comfort in her ignorance of softer emotions. Already their association had caused her to feel bewildered and to act against sound reasoning.

"Excellent sentiments," Lady Collingsworth said. "I could not agree more. Might I suggest you pay your addresses sooner, rather than later? It would be lovely for her to enjoy a few weeks of the Season as an affianced woman."

The tension in Jasper's shoulders returned, but for a different reason. Speaking carefully, he answered, "I am not certain she would be best served with me."

"I see." There was a long moment wherein her ladyship drummed her gloved fingertips into his forearm. "Do you know, Mr. Bond, I can count on my fingers the number of times I have seen Eliza smile in public?"

"She does not smile often," he agreed, feeling more than a little triumph that she'd smiled so brilliantly at him today.

"I would suggest you leave the determination of what makes Eliza feel safe and happy to her. Speculation is necessary in business, but in affairs of the heart, it often leads to poor judgments."

"I will take that under advisement."

Her mouth curved on one side. "I can see what she likes about you, Mr. Bond. You listen. I suspect you don't always act on what you've heard, but you listen in any case."

They returned to the entrance and she released him. Jasper bowed, then ducked out of the room with unseemly haste. But he was stopped once again by Lord Westfield, who was a few feet away from reaching the Exhibition Hall with a delicate-looking blonde on his arm.

"Why, Bond," Westfield called out. "Where are you running off to?"

His lordship leaned down and whispered something to his companion. When his head lifted, she was smiling in a way that promised all sorts of delicious things. She moved into the room without him, leaving him to speak to Jasper.

"Miss Martin left the room some minutes ago," Jasper said.

"And you are following her with notable eagerness."

"I have been waylaid twice now." His glare made it clear who the second delay was.

"Well, then," his lordship said, "the least I can do is show you where the ladies' retiring rooms are, as I would imagine that's where she went. Unless you frightened her into fleeing. I say, your scowl is fearsome even to me."

Jasper growled softly.

Westfield laughed and gave concise directions. Jasper was grateful for the assistance, but was less appreciative of the note of amusement that colored its delivery.

With a quick salute of fingertips to his hat brim, he set off in search of Eliza. Several minutes had passed since she parted from him, an inconsiderable amount of time for many women but slightly too long for a lady who didn't fret about her appearance. He turned the corner and heard Eliza's voice float toward him, but he could not see her. There was a statue of a man between them, in the center of the hallway on a platform of rollers. She was speaking with calm efficiency to the men laboring to move the obstruction, explaining that one of the wheels seemed to be caught by the runner protecting the floor.

Shaking his head, Jasper started forward. How like her to linger and offer engineering advice, even of such a small nature. A fond smile curved his lips. She said he was a man clearly suited to more strenuous pursuits and he would not argue the point. However, it appeared a quick mind was as arousing to him as a naked woman.

"Miss Martin," he called out.

"Mr. Bond." She peeked around the thigh of the statue. "I have been eye level with the backside of this artwork for long moments now. It seems one of the wheels is indisposed to motion."

"Perhaps you should just squeeze around the platform?" he suggested, gauging the space on either side. There wasn't much room, despite the generous size of the hallway. In fact, the piece was so large it towered above them.

He slowed as he neared. "Is there another way around?" he asked, directing his question at the two red-faced men straining to push the piece down a tributary hallway.

"Aye," the larger of the two gasped. Straightening, he pulled a handkerchief from his pocket and mopped his brow.

The smaller man, seemingly unwilling to be delayed by courtesy toward a lady, charged into the base with his shoulder. The jolt dislodged the stuck wheel, causing the platform and statue to lurch forward. The wood creaked in protest.

One of the thick lines of rope securing the heavy piece snapped. The resulting noise was like the crack of a whip. Jasper watched in horror as the statue listed away from him.

"Eliza!" he shouted, lunging forward but having no way to reach her.

The platform cracked and the troublesome wheel broke away, tumbling a short ways down the hall.

The rest was over far too quickly. The crash was deafening in the enclosed space. Debris from the shattered art piece billowed into the air in a hazy cloud.

Jasper could not see Eliza among the ruins.

Scrambling over the destruction, he reached the spot where he last saw her standing. The torso of the figure lay there in a solid piece. He was so stunned, he couldn't think. His chest was so tight, he swayed on his feet.

Shouts from other parts of the building grew in volume, competing with the thunderous sound of the blood rushing through his ears.

"Heavens," Eliza said. "What a mess."

Jasper's gaze followed the voice. She stood in a nearby doorway, staring at the disorder.

Dear God . . .

He clambered over wobbling chunks of decimated statue and crushed her to his chest.

"It looked as if the rope might have been cut at least partway through." Jasper held his third glass of brandy and continued to pace before the unlit fireplace in his study. His coat and waistcoat had been tossed over the arm of a wingback chair, yet still he felt too constricted. "But there's no way to be certain. I was only granted a brief look at it."

"You don't believe it was an accident," Westfield queried from his position on the settee, "despite the prominence of the location and the randomness of the event?"

"Miss Martin says the statue was waiting in a secondary

hall when she went into the retiring room. Upon her emergence, she found it had been moved into her path."

"Two men were having a devil of a time pushing it," the earl reminded. "A lone individual would have found the task impossible."

"But one wheel was troublesome. Perhaps, not by chance." Jasper downed the contents of his tumbler in one swallow, seeking to warm the spot inside him chilled by the near miss. "Is it possible for one person to be the victim of so much misfortune?"

Setting the glass down on his desktop with a harsh thud, he glanced at the clock. It would be hours before he saw Eliza again at the Lansings' rout. He was certain to be in a state of high agitation until then. Assigning more men to watch the Melville household was small comfort.

Westfield made a noise suspiciously like a snort. "You are positively high-strung about the business, while Miss Martin seemed to take the happenings in stride."

"Because she trusts me to manage everything and keep her safe," Jasper said tightly.

"I trust you will, as well. But you appear less confident in your own abilities."

"The gravity of this 'accident' is also responsible for her lack of anxiety. The irony of that . . . Because this was by far the most dangerous event, she believes it's unrelated to the rest."

"Are you saying she's less concerned because she was almost killed?"

Jasper glanced at the earl and noted the amused interest on his lordship's face. For a brief moment, he was enraged by the entertainment Westfield appeared to be taking from the events of the afternoon. In the earl's privileged, pampered, ennui-afflicted life even the misfortune of others could enliven spirits.

Reining in his temper, Jasper turned away. He kneaded

the back of his neck with a firm grip. "I am doing all I can. There is nothing to be done about my concern that I'm not doing enough."

He was meeting with Eliza's man of affairs tomorrow, and together they would be visiting her rental properties. His men were looking into the circumstances of her present tenants and recent ones. He intended to speak with Lord Collingsworth this evening about joining the investment pool Eliza mentioned, and he was waiting on word from Lord Melville regarding a time when they could meet. There were still her two fathers—Mr. Martin and Mr. Chilcott—to delve into, but he would see to those inquiries himself. Eliza's family secrets were not ones he wished anyone else to know about, despite the trust he placed in his crew.

"If it's any consolation," Westfield said, pushing to his feet, "you are engaged in a singularly unique investigation, while playing a role far outside your experience. Feeling as if you might be missing something is to be expected. But I'm here for you, if you need. I have the experience you lack. In fact, if you would like me to assume the courting of Miss Martin while you focus on the investigation, I would be happy to do so."

Jasper bared his teeth in a semblance of a smile. "That's quite all right."

The earl laughed. "The offer stands, if you should change your mind. In the meantime, I must eat and prepare for the evening's festivities. You should have a meal as well, and attempt some moderation in your drinking. Otherwise, you won't be much good to anyone."

Waving Westfield away with an impatient flick of his wrist, Jasper sank heavily into the chair behind his desk and mentally took apart every bit of information he'd gleaned so far, looking for any clue he might have missed.

He could not fail in this. Client satisfaction and point of pride be damned. He was acting on his own behalf, stricken by the memory of those brief moments when he'd feared Eliza had been gravely wounded . . . or worse.

It was not a feeling he intended to experience ever again.

"Bloody hell," Westfield grumbled, snatching two glasses of champagne from a passing servant's tray. He shoved one toward Jasper, causing the wine to slosh precariously up to the lip. "I'd forgotten how unintelligible Lady Lansing becomes when excited. I could not comprehend a word she said. How long were we held captive? Twenty minutes? Half an hour?"

"Ten, my lord. At most." Jasper's gaze searched the ballroom from one end to the other. It was a long and narrow space, with inlaid marble floors and three large chandeliers. Fluted columns surrounded the perimeter, as did the occasional potted fern. The far wall consisted entirely of French doors, most of which were thrown wide to allow the night air to circulate.

"Interminable." Westfield tossed back the contents of his glass. "The things I do for you, Bond."

"You should be flattered. Your illustrious presence singlehandedly made Lady Lansing's ball a resounding success."

"I am not appeased."

"I owe you a debt, as well, of course," Jasper murmured, distracted by his inability to find Eliza. "Does that soothe your ire?"

The Lansing's ballroom was neither overly large nor overly filled. There was a respectable showing of guests, but it wasn't yet a crush. Why, then, couldn't he locate her glorious red hair?

Are you one of those gentlemen who have an unusually strong interest in red hair?

He hadn't been. He had considered all women equally endowed. Now, here he was, completely oblivious to every other hue but that novel fiery one.

The earl caught his arm. "Walk this way," Westfield urged, attempting to tug him along. "Someone is approaching whom I'd rather not speak to."

With a rueful smile, Jasper followed. They rounded the perimeter at a torturously slow pace due to the number of attendees who wished to greet the earl. Jasper was about to leave Westfield behind when he finally spotted her.

His step faltered. Westfield bumped into him.

"Damnation, Bond, what the devil are you—" The earl fell silent.

Jasper gave a low, appreciative whistle. Uncouth, to be sure, and an undeniable betrayal of his commonness, but it was sincere. He could find no words.

"Why," Westfield said in a contemplative tone, "I have clearly been remiss in not paying proper attention to Miss Martin."

Eliza stood amid a circle of acquaintances, most of whom were gentlemen. Her glorious hair had been arranged in abundant curls that framed her face and caressed her nape. Her body was clad in sapphire satin, the bold color incongruous amid the paler hues worn by the other women in attendance. There would have been no way to miss her, had she not been shorter than the crowd of salivating males around her.

What in God's name was she wearing?

Unable to help himself, Jasper stared with clenched fists. Riveted. The deep color of her gown showcased the creamy hue of her skin and the richness of her tresses to supreme advantage. The cut of the garment was painfully simple, with minimal detail. The gown's true beauty lay in how it clung to its wearer. How the low bodice hugged full, firm breasts and bared more than a glimpse of cleavage. How the long skirts emphasized the length of her legs. The short puffed sleeves failed to meet the uppermost end of Eliza's long white gloves, revealing a sprinkling of freckles on her upper arms that he found enchanting.

He was struck with fierce longing, like a man gone too long without a meal who doesn't realize he's starving until presented with the sight and smell of food.

An amused masculine voice intruded. "Glad to see I'm not the only man to lose all sense of social grace."

Jasper tore his gaze away from Eliza to see who spoke to him.

"Lord Brimley," Westfield said. "Good to see you again."

As the earl made the appropriate introductions, Jasper studied Baron Brimley with his usual thoroughness. The baron was a head shorter than both himself and Westfield, and far more slender. Although Brimley's hairline was receding with regretful swiftness, Jasper guessed he was younger than he appeared.

"Surprised to see you, Westfield," Brimley said after greeting Jasper. "Did word of Miss Martin's transformation spread so quickly?"

"Actually," the earl drawled, "I simply dropped all of this evening's invitations into a hat and withdrew a few. The 'transformation,' as you call it, is an unexpected boon."

"Mr. Tomlinson is of the mind that Miss Martin finally seeks to throw off the mantle of spinsterhood," Brimley relayed.

"Perhaps," Jasper suggested, feeling proprietary, "she's taken a fancy to someone and hopes to encourage him."

"You don't say?" Brimley's eyes were wide. "Care to guess who it is?"

"I am at a disadvantage, I'm afraid. I have yet to become acquainted with every moth circling her flame."

"Moth to flame, eh? Poetic and apt. Well, I shall take it upon myself to discover his identity."

Westfield clapped him on the shoulder. "You will, of course, be sporting and share your findings."

Brimley's chest puffed up. "Certainly, Westfield."

Jasper gave in to his impatience. With a slight bow, he sidestepped away. "If you will excuse me, my lords."

"Not so fast, Bond," Westfield said quickly. "I shall accompany you in your journey to pay court to the lovely Miss Martin. Excuse us, Brimley. Do keep us apprised of your discoveries."

The tension in Jasper's shoulders increased. Bringing Eliza to Westfield's attention—and the reverse—was not something he should view as threatening, but the feeling was there. He remembered what Eliza had said about her unexpected feelings of animosity toward Miss Tolliver and he admired her candor even more.

She caught sight of him when he was several feet away. Courtesy of her décolletage, he saw her breath catch and a gentle flush spread across her luminous skin. She stared, unblinking, and masculine triumph surged through him. She was clearly smitten by the sight of him, yet he had not provoked that response from her with any effort on his part.

He drew to a halt on the fringes of her circle. A pathway was made for him with obvious reluctance.

"Miss Martin."

She lowered her gaze and curtsied. "Good evening, Mr. Bond."

Jasper obliged Westfield with the necessary introductions, then backed away. For a while, he simply observed her in this new environment, smiling inwardly when she spoke so bluntly those around her momentarily lost their way in the conversation. As dramatic as her change of appearance was, she was still Eliza. While others spoke with great animation about the tale of her mishap at the Royal Academy, she frowned and bit her lower lip, clearly not reconciling the expanded tales with the actual reality. She looked at him often, seeming to take comfort in his proximity. He recalled his earlier thoughts about how at ease she made him feel in situations where he was feeling his way blind.

They were not so different. More than anything, he was drawn to the affinity they shared in unexpected and deeply seated ways.

In order to see him schooled properly, Jasper's mother had paid for his education with her pride and her life. He'd protested the expense, knowing what it would cost her, but she would not be swayed. In the end, he conceded only because he intended to support her, not for the reason she espoused—to impress his sire, a man well-versed in ignoring his many bastard issue.

Jasper blamed opium for his mother's failure to see the hopelessness of her quest. Certainly no one possessed of full mental faculty would hold the dream that a handsome son with a decent education and proper speech would engender fondness and paternal pride in a dissolute reprobate like the late Earl of Montague. Yes, Jasper was well-spoken and possessed of a refined sense of style. He could read and write. He was capable with numbers, although he lacked the fondness for them Eliza had. In short, he should fit in, but he did not. And he knew Eliza felt the same way.

A violin played a few opening notes, signaling an end to the orchestra's short break. Guests began to line up along the center of the parquet floor. Eliza shot him a long, meaningful glance and he knew she was going to be dancing *his* dance.

She took to the floor with Sir Richard Tolliver. Riveted by the elegant grace with which she glided across the room, Jasper could not take his eyes from her. The sapphire gown's skirts were noticeably fuller than those worn by the other females in attendance; he thought the style suited Eliza perfectly. There were more layers to her than most women.

The musicians began the opening notes of a waltz. Eliza

stepped nearer to Tolliver and clasped his hand. With an accomplished flourish, he began the requisite series of steps.

Jasper frowned, thinking. There had been two Tollivers at the Exhibition Hall. They'd left the room shortly after Eliza and followed in her direction. On Eliza's list of suitors, Tolliver's name had been placed above Montague's, in part because he had a sister who could use a dowry to secure a more advantageous match.

Turning away, Jasper expected the other sibling would be nearby. He had only to find her.

Chapter 6

"You are a vision this evening, Miss Martin," Sir Richard said, as they circled the dance floor along with the other couples.

"Thank you." Eliza wondered if she should say more than that. What did one say that wouldn't sound awkward? She always considered such praise to be a platitude. She was well aware she was no classic beauty. However, since she'd put effort into looking attractive this evening, it would be disingenuous to assume none of the compliments were sincere. Especially considering she was wearing one of her mother's gowns.

Eliza was still stunned at her decision. Her mother was someone she never wanted to emulate. Lady Georgina had been irrepressible and impetuous. She'd paid little heed to the consequences of her actions and how they might affect others. For years, Eliza had asked herself the question "What would Mother do?" so she could choose the reverse option. But after this afternoon, she wanted to do something nice for Jasper. He'd been so distraught after the unfortunate event at Somerset House. It meant a great deal to her that he cared so much for her well-being. If she were completely honest, she would also say she hoped her attire might goad an answer from him in regards to her earlier question about mating.

Of course, there was also the reasonable explanation for her choice: it signaled to one and all that a drastic change had occurred in her life. She'd known the very day her mother had taken a fancy to Mr. Chilcott. Lady Georgina's blue eyes had been bright, her lips red, and her cheeks flushed. She had hummed to herself and burst out in song at odd moments. Over the following week, she'd smiled incessantly. But most telling of all was the way she altered her mode of dress. She'd begun choosing gowns with conservative adornments and richer colors, as if she knew her smitten glow was accessory enough. Eliza understood that she could not continue to go about looking as ordinary as possible and expect others to believe she was extraordinarily attached to a particular man.

Sir Richard cleared his throat. "I pray you'll forgive me, Miss Martin, but I am concerned for you."

"Concerned?"

"I detest stepping into affairs that are removed from me," he said, sounding anything but reluctant. "However, I fear your laudable discrimination in selecting a spouse has become lax."

Her brows rose. "Lax?"

"I speak of Mr. Bond, of course."

"I see." Although Tolliver had been paying court to her for two Seasons now, this was the first display of condescension she'd witnessed. She did not like his tone at all. It was one a parent or tutor would use with a recalcitrant child.

"There is something about Mr. Bond that doesn't sit well with me. I cannot put my finger on it, but something is not right with him."

She turned her head and located Jasper standing by a fluted column with crossed arms and hooded eyes. Not for the first time, she noted how he didn't look at her as he had on the day they'd met. His stare now was hotter, more aware, and it awakened an answering awareness in her. Warmth blossomed in the pit of her stomach and expanded. They had known each other only a few days, but she was irrevocably changed by his acquaintance, newly cognizant of a baser sensibility previously veiled from her.

As for Tolliver's assertions, although she didn't appreciate the manner of their delivery, she could not fault him for making them. Jasper's attire was the only thing polished about him. Although he appeared innocuous on the surface, those with keen perception would recognize how incongruous he was among the crowd. There was a razor's edge of menace to him and a sleek grace to his movements that was inherently predaceous.

"I see no evidence of unsuitability," she lied. "In truth, I find him quite acceptable."

"Miss Martin, I must say, I am alarmed by your estimation. Who are his people?"

"His father is known to Lord Melville." Eliza followed Sir Richard's lead through an unusually vigorous turn. He was such an accomplished dancer; his uncustomary carelessness was telling.

"I suspect he is in want of funds, and you have them."

"That applies to many gentlemen of my acquaintance, wouldn't you agree? But I'm curious. What led you to the assumption that Mr. Bond is a fortune hunter and more of a hazard than my other suitors? Certainly his appearance refutes such a conclusion."

Jasper looked beyond reproach this evening. Dressed in a dark gray velvet coat and a pale blue waistcoat, he looked accomplished and elegant. The expert tailoring of the whole ensemble displayed the power of his body to advantage. She fully appreciated how strong and capable he was. She felt safe knowing he was nearby. The only person capable of harming her when Jasper was near was Jasper himself.

"Miss Martin." Tolliver looked pained. "I must advise you that it's most disconcerting to dance with a female who spends the duration of the waltz admiring another gentleman."

"I am not admiring him, sir." At least, not verbally. "I am merely requesting that you expound upon the methods of deduction you used to reach your conclusion. You say he is in want of funds, I see no evidence of such. I should like to know what you see that I don't."

"A lady of your refined reasoning is at a disadvantage in this situation." His brown eyes were somber. "I shall explain. He's regarding you in an inappropriate fashion, Miss Martin."

"Are you saying," she asked carefully, "Mr. Bond must be in want of money because he cannot take his eyes off me? I don't understand the logic. Isn't it possible Mr. Bond might find something visually appealing about me? Perhaps my trim figure has garnered his admiration?"

"Your form is attractive," he conceded gruffly.

"Or my hair? Some men are excessively fascinated by certain hues, I'm told."

A flush rose from beneath his cravat to color his cheekbones. "You have lovely hair."

"But my attractive form and lovely tresses are not enough to explain why Mr. Bond regards me so intently? I suppose that's due to his exceedingly comely face and its ability to captivate anyone with unhindered vision. Correct me if I'm wrong, but I understand you to mean that my limited physical charms are no match for his. He can certainly find a far more beautiful female." Eliza wrinkled her nose, as if in deep thought. "Well, then, perhaps it's my brain he finds so interesting."

"I agree you are extremely clever, Miss Martin," he said in a fervent rush, swiftly grasping at the change of topic. "It's why I like you so well, and why I'm certain we will enjoy each other's companionship for an indefinite period of time. However, Mr. Bond obviously lends more attention to cultivating his exterior than his interior. One does not attain that physical size through intellectual exertions. I doubt he's capable of grasping the worth of your brain. In fact, in your position, I would wonder if it was even possible to have meaningful discourse with him."

Eliza nodded. "I understand now. Ruling out my mental and physical attributes would leave only my fortune as an enticement for handsome men. I'm quite enlightened, Sir Richard."

The waltz ended. She retreated the moment the last strains faded away. "Thank you. This discussion has been most informative. However, I seek clarification on one point: If attractive men find only my fortune alluring and you find my brain alluring, does that make you unattractive?"

Tolliver's mouth opened, then closed. Then opened again. Nothing came out.

After an abbreviated curtsy, Eliza spun about and left the dance floor. She intended to go to Jasper, but he was no longer where she last saw him.

Jasper found Miss Tolliver on the dance floor. Shortly afterward, he was himself found by Lord Westfield.

"I'm almost inclined to wed posthaste," his lordship said, "to spare myself further pre-matrimonial torment."

"Because post-matrimonial torment is eminently more bearable," Jasper said dryly.

"I don't have unreasonable qualifications for a spouse," Westfield said with some defensiveness. "So long as she doesn't aggravate me unduly, and I'm not averse to bedding her, I am open to anyone of suitable breeding."

"How progressive of you."

The earl arched a brow. "Your tone leaves something to

be desired. Now, tell me there's something to be done here. I'm bored."

"When Miss Tolliver exits the dance floor, I should like her to know my theory regarding today's events."

"Ah, you want to see how she reacts. Personally, I don't see how a woman could have moved that statue. And you cannot tell me Sir Richard helped her. I'm not even certain he could lift his sibling."

"Leave no stone unturned."

When the waltz ended, they made certain to place themselves in Miss Tolliver's path. She greeted Westfield with a charming and studied curtsy.

"Miss Tolliver." Westfield gave an elegant bow. "A pleasure to see you."

"Thank you, my lord." She offered a sympathetic smile to Jasper. "How is your foot this evening, Mr. Bond?"

"Improving, Miss Tolliver. Thank you."

The pretty brunette offered a flirtatious smile. The pale yellow gown she wore was more heavily adorned than the similarly shaded gown Eliza had worn earlier in the day. Such details were not something Jasper was accustomed to noting. What a woman wore or how she styled her hair was inconsequential to him.

But Eliza's appearance tonight was such a contrast to her usual mode of dress he suspected she purposely minimized her beauty before. It made him consider the attire of others with a more discerning eye, part of his careful reflection on the desire he had for her. Only days into their acquaintance and he knew he would not be ready to part from her in the foreseeable future. He also knew he was willing to go to great lengths to have her.

"I heard about the unfortunate incident at the Royal Academy." Miss Tolliver shook her head. "How terrifying for Miss Martin! I am certain I would be bedridden for a sennight after such a shock."

"She is managing extraordinarily well," he agreed.

"Especially considering the circumstances," Westfield said, in a confidential tone.

She frowned. "Circumstances?"

The earl leaned closer. "There is some speculation that the rope securing the statue might have been deliberately cut."

"No!" Her hand went to her throat. "Why would anyone do something so heinous? Especially to Miss Martin."

"I didn't say she was the intended target," he qualified, straightening. "She might simply have been in the wrong place at the wrong time."

"Well, there is some small comfort in that." She exhaled audibly. "Deliberately cut, you say. I wonder why?"

She looked away and worried her lower lip with her teeth.

"I wouldn't dare speculate," Westfield said. "It's rarely good to have one's name associated with such sensational tales."

"True of us all," she said gravely, dipping into another curtsy. Miss Tolliver excused herself, and Jasper followed her with his gaze. She headed directly to a group of women.

"She spreads the tale," Westfield murmured, turning his back to her.

"That's no proof of innocence. In fact, a clever person might assume that bearing the news to others would lighten suspicion. After all, what reasonable person would air their misdeeds to all and sundry?" Jasper intended to have both Tollivers followed for a time. He would not take any chances.

"Excellent point."

"What do you know of the investment pool managed by Lord Collingsworth?"

"I participated for a time, but Collingsworth is too conservative for my taste. You might feel similarly."

How like Eliza to be cautious. Money was vitally important to her, not for what it could buy, but for the measure of freedom and control its possession granted her. "Do you know who the other investors are?"

"A few. Not all. Why?"

"Miss Martin is one of them."

"Truly?" Westfield's brows rose. "Wasn't aware of that. Does that make me a suspect?"

Smiling, Jasper said, "Possibly."

The earl grabbed a glass of champagne from a passing servant. "How delicious."

"Not if you're at fault." Jasper moved forward.

"Was that a threat, Bond?"

"Not if you are at fault," he said again. "In that case, it would be a promise."

"Where are you going?"

"To the card room. Perhaps the scent of desperation will lead me in a new direction."

"You never answered my question about what you'll do once you own Montague's property." Although Westfield was the public face of the wager that secured the property, Jasper hadn't revealed why he wanted it.

However, he had no hesitation in revealing what he would do with it. "I will raze the house, then leave England."

"For parts unknown?"

"Didn't I tell you?" Jasper looked at him. "I've purchased a plantation in the South Seas."

"Good God." The earl choked on his champagne. "Only you would find peace living among savages."

"I think similarly about your life."

A brilliant shade of sapphire blue in the periphery of Jasper's vision caught his interest. He turned his head to catch Eliza moving toward one of three sets of French doors leading outside to a wide veranda.

She shot him a look over her shoulder. It was not the calculated look of a practiced flirt. It was simpler and more sincere, betraying pleasure at seeing him and the hope he might follow.

He smiled and inclined his head in acknowledgment.

"I will go ahead without you," Westfield murmured.

"I'll only be a moment."

"You disappoint me, Bond. When a beautiful woman looks at you in that manner, you should need far more time than that."

Eliza moved toward the nearest exterior exit with the hope that her dark gown would blend somewhat with the darkness of night and provide her a brief spell of anonymity. She felt Jasper's stare following her and fought the urge to quicken her pace. Not because she wished to avoid him, but because it was instinctive to run when caught in the sights of a hunter.

The anticipation of capture was its own pleasure. The hair on her nape stood on end and gooseflesh covered the parts of her arms exposed above her long gloves. When the warmth of a large hand surrounded her elbow, she couldn't fight the shiver that moved through her.

"Miss Martin." Jasper's deep voice caused a tingling in her stomach. With an easy grip, he led her outdoors to where several guests were paired in quietly voiced conversations. "You might have warned me that you would steal my breath upon sight."

"Thank you." Unlike Tolliver's compliment, Jasper's praise did not make her feel awkward. Instead, she felt warm and slightly giddy.

"Altering your appearance to goad speculation was an excellent plan." He looked down at her with warm appreciation. "In case I've failed to mention it, I love the way you think."

Eliza flushed. "Would you admire my intellect less to know I hoped my presentation would impress you as much as my reasoning?"

"No. I would be deeply flattered."

"I feel silly," she confessed. "Simply knowing you goads me into acting in ways I normally wouldn't."

Jasper smiled, and she found him so handsome it made her chest tighten. "Would it ease your nervousness to know I have second-guessed every aspect of my attire from the knot of my cravat to the shoes on my feet before every meeting I've had with you since the first? I believe it's part of the mating ritual."

He slowed as they stepped outside the circle of light cast by the ballroom chandeliers. There were torches set around the veranda, but they were spaced at wide intervals to provide just enough illumination to delineate where stone gave way to lawn.

"Part of the charade?" she asked.

"I've yet to feign anything with you, Eliza."

Unsure of how to banter flirtatiously, she moved on to safer topics. "How do you know Lord Westfield?"

"Lucian Remington introduced us one evening."

She was momentarily surprised Jasper would boast membership in such an exclusive establishment as Remington's Gentlemen's Club. Then, she recalled that Lucian Remington was the bastard son of the Duke of Glasser. He was known to allow gentlemen of any background to join his club . . . so long as they could afford it. The practice was tolerated by those born of higher station because Remington's was grand on the grandest scale. They were loath to deny themselves such luxury.

"Have you known one another long?"

"Not excessively long, no."

Although he didn't move, she sensed the change in him. The sudden alertness. It was similar to being doused by chilled water. She sometimes forgot she and Jasper Bond hardly knew one another, because her overwhelming physical attraction to him fostered an illusion of intimacy.

Eliza deliberately kept her tone light when she said, "Forgive me for prying into your personal matters. They are none of my concern."

She would do well to follow his example and keep to safer topics in their relations. He worked for her, and an employee was all he would ever be to her. Perhaps it would slow her fascination with him to keep that in mind.

How deeply could one fall when the pool was shallow?

While there was no outward sign of it, Jasper knew Eliza had withdrawn and he'd lost ground with her. Relationships were complications for just that reason—at some point, women expected full disclosure. He found the need mystifying.

But he wasn't willing to cede any of the progress he had made with Eliza, regardless of the points on which he would have to bend.

"I met him two years ago," he elaborated. "He finds the work I do interesting and from that interest, we became . . . friends."

"You say the word 'friends' so strangely."

"It's not one I am accustomed to using."

She nodded and softened toward him, both physically and otherwise. "I understand."

Jasper looked at the stone beneath his feet. Of course she would understand. There was an unusual affinity between them. On the surface, they could not be more wrong for one another. In private moments, however, nothing had ever felt more right.

"Ah, there you are, Miss Martin," a confident and familiar voice called out.

Turning his head, Jasper watched Lord Montague exit the ballroom. Wearing dark emerald velvet and an artful amount of diamond accoutrements, the earl looked solvent and unflappable. It was a feat made more impressive by Jasper's knowledge of the truth. Montague's circumstances could not be shakier. Still, the earl's wide smile and bright eyes made it clear he was genuinely pleased to see Eliza. Or at the very least, the fortune she represented.

Jasper straightened. He'd never resented his younger brother for bearing the title and privileges that came with it—until the present. In the case of Eliza, Montague's advantages now posed the first real threat to Jasper's aims. Jasper could provide only intangibles, such as passion, acceptance, adventure, which were things Eliza had only recently shown an interest in. If she came to the conclusion that she needed matrimony to have sex . . .

There was the possibility that in seducing her, he was pushing her into marriage.

Extending his hand, Jasper waited for Eliza to set hers atop his palm. He kissed the back, hating the white satin barring his lips from her soft, pale skin. "I shall leave you to your admirer," he murmured, giving her fingers a reassuring squeeze.

As much as he disliked it, the best way to establish the distinction between himself and Montague was to let her experience it firsthand.

He passed the earl with no more than a slight tilt of his head as acknowledgment, feeling more than a little satisfaction that he held the marker to the peer's beloved property and the earl didn't know it.

Jasper moved directly toward the card room. Now was as good a time as any to see which of Eliza's swains was dependent upon the whims of chance. In that enterprise, at least, he had no competition.

* * *

"Mr. Bond is an exceptionally fine-looking young man," Lady Collingsworth said from her seat on the opposite squab. The Collingsworth carriage inched its way through the congested streets. While most of the other conveyances squired their passengers from one society event to another, Eliza and her ladyship were retiring to their respective homes.

"You mentioned that earlier." Eliza draped her long gloves over her lap. She'd found the sight of Jasper in finery so pleasant, she would have liked to see him again before the evening ended. Their brief discussion on the veranda had been long enough only to make her wish for more time.

"There are certain types of handsomeness that are so compelling you tell yourself later you must have exaggerated the appeal in your mind. When you see the man again and he exceeds your embroidery, it's impossible not to remark upon it." Although the lamps were turned down low, there was enough light to see her ladyship's smile.

"He does render one speechless," Eliza agreed. "Sir Richard Tolliver felt the need to warn me that a man as comely as Mr. Bond would set his cap for me only because of my purse."

"Good heavens." Regina's ramrod-straight spine stiffened further. "Tolliver is blind and desperate. I paid a great deal of attention to Mr. Bond over the course of the day. He most definitely has tender feelings for you. Enough so he fears being unable to make you happy."

"How did you reach that conclusion?"

"Mr. Bond said as much to me."

Eliza's brows rose. "Did he?"

"He did indeed. Are you considering his suit?"

"To answer that conclusively, I would need to know him better."

Lady Collingsworth linked her hands together in her lap. "The responsibility I was given for you is a deep honor. As you know, your mother meant a great deal to me. I loved Georgina as I would a sibling. I wish most sincerely to do well by you."

"You have been wonderful." She wanted to say that Regina had done far better than her own mother would have, but she bit her tongue. She would never understand what the sweet, generous Lady Collingsworth had seen in the self-centered, mercurial Georgina. Whatever it was, it had inspired an abiding loyalty that persisted beyond the grave. Eliza learned long ago to voice no disparagement of her mother to Regina. To do so was to invite extensive reprimand and extolments of her mother's worth.

"You are kind to say so." Her ladyship smiled. "You look so like Georgina in that gown. I was taken aback upon first sight of you. For a moment, it felt almost as if time had moved backward."

Eliza didn't see the resemblance beyond the hue of her hair and eyes, but again, she said nothing. Then, she realized she should offer thanks for the voiced observation. Her ladyship would perceive it to be a compliment. "Thank you."

"You are a remarkably sensible young woman," Regina continued. "You are cautious and prefer not to leave anything to chance. But matrimony is all about taking chances. Do you know how much time Collingsworth and I spent together before he paid his addresses? If you consider only the moments we actually spoke to one another, it was no more than a handful of hours. There were parties and dinners and picnics and such, but always with others nearby impeding any chance for quiet, meaningful discourse. You speak of knowing someone well, but in truth there is very little you need to know. Does an attraction exist between you? Do you both wish to see the other happy or, at the very least, reasonably content? If you have those things, you have all you need to enjoy a comfortable marriage."

"And what if there are things he refuses to share with

me? How can there be trust, if there are aspects of one another we don't know?"

"Are there not parts of yourself that you would rather keep private?" Regina challenged. "Things you would choose not to discuss? Of course there are. Women are entitled to their mysteries, and men are entitled to their secrets. Frankly, some secrets are painful and best left alone."

Eliza considered this information carefully. There were indeed things she would prefer never to discuss again. It stood to reason that Jasper, too, would have memories he would like to forget. The person he was today might have been shaped by past events, but they didn't rule him now. Why should they rule her?

"You can manage a man," her ladyship coached, "if you pander to his pride and innate sense of self-importance. Convince him that your idea is his and he'll follow it through. When handled correctly, marriage can be a useful enterprise."

"The effort you describe is altogether too much work, in my opinion." But perhaps worth the effort for a man such as Jasper Bond. Shockingly, Eliza was contemplating all the things she might have to concede if she wanted to have Jasper in her life for longer than the length of the Season.

"My dear child. You extract from life what you put into it." Regina leaned forward. "Your coin will be of little comfort to you during chilly nights and solitary meals. I want a happier future for you. Someone to look after you. Children to love. This is a man's world, Eliza. Whether we like it or not, there is no help for it. You think you have freedom and independence now, but marriage would grant you even greater license. And Mr. Bond appears to have means of his own, so you might have everything to gain and nothing to lose."

The carriage rolled to a halt outside the Melville town house.

Eliza caught her ladyship's hand and gave it an affectionate squeeze. "Thank you, Regina. You've given me a great deal to think about."

"I'm available to you, if you need me."

As Eliza climbed the steps to the front door, she recognized that a decisive shift had taken place in her world. It was as if she'd been sleeping in a moving carriage, content to move in any general direction. Now she was awakened and feeling the need to change course. Unfortunately, she had no notion of where she wanted to go. She was, however, beginning to think that wherever the destination, having Jasper with her would make the journey far more interesting.

Chapter 7

"This is the last one." Mr. Terrance Reynolds consulted the sheaf of notes in his lap. "As I mentioned during our last meeting, Miss Martin, your newest tenant creates perfumed soaps, bath oils, and candles to order. Business is slow at present, but having purchased some of Mrs. Pennington's products for my wife, I think that will soon change."

Jasper kept his gaze on Eliza, who sat on the opposite squab. It was nearing two o'clock in the afternoon. They'd been visiting her various properties for nearly three hours now, solidifying in his mind just how wealthy Eliza was. He could easily see how someone would find the lure of her fortune overwhelming, but a suitor would have to be capable of looking beneath the surface to discover it. In her business dealings, Eliza went to great efforts to hide her gender and, therefore, her identity.

"I'll pay a visit to this store," she said, looking out the window of Jasper's unmarked, enclosed town carriage. "It will be interesting to see the scent the proprietress chooses to create for me."

Jasper wanted to tell Eliza that he liked the way she smelled already, but could not with Mr. Reynolds present. In addition to the safety considerations that prompted today's excursion, the exercise also brought to light how much he enjoyed talking with Eliza and listening to her view of situations. He missed being able to speak with her freely, but felt it best to keep the arrangement between himself and Eliza private. To Mr. Reynolds' knowledge, Jasper was a friend of Melville's and a possible investor in Eliza's proposed plan to modernize the amenities in a few of her older properties.

"How close are we to the store?" Jasper asked.

"A few blocks," Reynolds replied. "We're almost there."

Rapping on the roof, Jasper signaled for his driver to stop. "I'll walk from here. That will give us a sufficient length of time between Miss Martin's arrival and mine so it doesn't appear as if we came together."

An odd look crossed Eliza's features before she nodded. He made a note to ask her later what prompted it. Alighting from the carriage, he accepted the cane she passed to him through the open door.

"Pink and white striped awning," Reynolds advised.

"Thank you." Jasper saluted Eliza with a quick touch to the brim of his hat, then he set off.

Today, he'd learned more than just how wealthy she was. Though neither Eliza nor Mr. Reynolds said so outright, Jasper noted that she leased her properties predominantly to women. He expected his investigation would prove her tenants to be mostly spinsters and widows. It was an honorable endeavor, and he admired her for undertaking it. However, the practice made it less likely that one of her tenants was to blame for her recent troubles. She would engender gratitude before malice. He would need to cast his net wider to include those whose rental applications had been denied. Meanwhile, every day that passed without a stronger lead aggravated him more. The work itself was not an issue. It was the threat to Eliza's safety that made Jasper dread every moment she was out of his sight.

In short order, he spotted the cheery awning and his waiting carriage nearby. This time, it was Reynolds who remained out of view while Eliza entered the store. One of the most important lessons Lynd had taught Jasper was to surround himself with trustworthy staff and to pay them well enough to keep them happy. *Better to have two people you trust with your life, than a dozen you can't vouch for.* Eliza appeared to have the same sensibility. Terrance Reynolds was paid handsomely. That fact was made obvious by the quality of his attire and his accessories, from his gold pocket watch to his leather satchel. In return, the man seemed genuinely fond of Eliza and intent on serving her interests well.

As Jasper entered the store, the bell above the door jingled to herald his arrival. The interior of the shop was perfectly sized for an establishment catering to the sense of smell. The air was fragrant without being overpowering. A variety of cloth-covered round tables were placed at set intervals around the room, displaying wares in colorful groupings.

He removed his hat.

"Good afternoon, sir."

Jasper found the speaker to his left, arranging items on a tabletop in front of Eliza. The shopkeeper was young and beautiful, blond and blue-eyed. As shapely as a prized courtesan, but with the face of an angel. He bowed in greeting, then shifted his attention to Eliza. The hue of her hair made her initially more arresting to the eye than the paler tresses of the proprietress, but she lacked the fullness of curves and classic beauty of the other. That didn't alter the fact that he found Eliza to be far more pleasing to look upon. From the first, she'd called to him on a physical level. There was raw magnetism between them, unique in its form. Bedding her would not be about the appeasement of his hunger, but a celebration of it. He'd never felt that for anyone else. With her it was the journey to be savored, not the destination.

"Miss Martin," he drawled. "Fancy meeting you here. It's a lovely day, wouldn't you agree?"

"I would indeed, Mr. Bond." Her eyes sparkled with genuine pleasure. The manner in which she looked at him always stirred him. She lacked the artifice to hide how much she enjoyed his appearance.

Jasper couldn't look away.

Eliza blushed when he continued to stare. She caught her lower lip between her teeth and a wash of heat swept over him.

He could arouse her with a glance. Did she know what that did to him?

"Is there something in particular I can help you find?" the blonde asked, excusing herself from Eliza. She wiped her hands on the apron tied around her waist, then gestured at the goods around them. "Floral or fruity? Musky or spicy? If you tell me the age and gender of the person you're shopping for, I can help you find just the thing. Or I can create something unique."

"What would you suggest for a young woman of discriminating taste, high intelligence, and deep passions? Nothing ordinary or expected, please. She is neither."

"Is she a wife or a lover?"

He considered the inquiry a moment, both the boldness of the question and his possible answer.

"It's best if I ask," she explained, glancing back at Eliza. "Providing you with the best possible product will ensure both your future business and your referral, and I need one as much as the other."

"How can I argue with that, Miss . . . ?"

"*Mrs.* Pennington." In close proximity, she appeared to be no older than Eliza.

"Why don't I look around," he suggested, "while you assist Miss Martin?"

Once again, Mrs. Pennington looked over her shoulder. "She's selecting a half dozen of her favorite scented oils, which is what I would like you to do."

"I will start with the same offerings, then."

Mrs. Pennington gestured toward the back of the store. Jasper followed her prompting. As she opened up free space on a table, she continued to cast furtive glances at Eliza. Perhaps she feared thievery?

He held back and remained silent, not wanting to distract her from finishing her task as soon as possible. When she straightened, he listened to her instructions and assured her that he could whittle down the choices without further help.

When she left him, he watched her return to the front of the store and waited to see if she would eye him as often as she had Eliza. She did not. But Eliza did.

He'd never known it could be so arousing to be ogled. He supposed it was because he had never been ogled by the right person.

Once Eliza was home again, she stripped off her gloves in the foyer, then looked at the post lying on a silver salver atop the console table. She set aside the few letters for Melville that appeared to be of a personal nature and collected the rest, intent on taking them up to her room. She wanted nothing so much as something to eat and a cup of tea.

She was halfway up the stairs when Melville called her name from below. Turning on the step, she smiled at him. "Yes, my lord?"

"Could I have a moment of your time?" he queried, frowning while trying to straighten his crooked waistcoat.

"Of course." As she descended, her gaze met the butler's. "Could you ask Mrs. Potts to bring tea to his lordship's laboratory?"

The servant's tall and lean frame moved quickly out of range of her sight.

Eliza followed Melville around the base of the staircase and collected his mail at the console. They passed her study door, then turned to the right at the end of the parquet-lined hallway. The room where his lordship spent much of his time was there. She made a chastising clicking noise with her tongue when she found the drapes drawn tight. A copious number of candles were scattered around the room, offering plenty of light . . . and smoke.

"It's a glorious day outside," she chastised, dropping the day's post onto one of the long, slender laboratory tables before moving briskly over to the windows. She drew the drapes aside, then systematically unlocked each of the windows lining the length of the wall and pushed up the sashes.

"Too bright," his lordship groused, blinking like an owl.

"You need sunlight. We humans don't thrive in dark places as mushrooms are wont to do."

"Mushrooms!" He snapped his fingers. "Brilliant, Eliza."

Melville quickly rounded his desk and began writing.

She pulled out one of the wooden stools that butted against a table bearing various-sized glass tubes and bottles. Waiting patiently, she blew out nearby candles that were unnecessary now that sunlight illuminated the large, disorganized space. The multitude of colorful liquids in jars cast jeweled beams of light onto the floor. In that moment, it was possible to see how Melville could become entranced by the mysteries he researched.

When Mrs. Potts bustled in with tea service on a tray, the intrusion seemed to snap his lordship into a renewed awareness of his location and his visitor.

"Oh, Eliza!" his lordship cried, scratching his head. "I apologize."

Eliza laughed softly. "It's quite all right."

She enjoyed these quiet moments with her uncle. In addition to being the only family she had remaining, he did not seek to fill perfectly good moments of silence with inane chatter. She did not have to consider—and reconsider—everything she said, or phrase her words in ways that made them more understandable while also diluting their meaning.

Sliding off the stool, she stood in front of the tea service and began to prepare the tea.

"Montague paid a call on me today," Melville said.

"Oh?" Her brows went up. "Why does that make me apprehensive?"

"Because you know why he came. He asked for permission to pay his addresses."

Eliza's breath left her in a rush. "Did he give you cause to believe I would welcome his offer?"

"On the contrary, he made it quite clear that while you find him to be one of the more agreeable of your suitors, you are not inclined to wed him."

That made her smile. "Yet he made his request, regardless."

"He was concerned by speculation regarding events at Somerset House yesterday. Some talk of your accident not truly being an accident at all." His lordship accepted the cup and saucer she passed to him. "Why didn't you tell me about what happened?"

"There was no need to bother you with the tale," she protested. "It was unfortunate, but no harm was done."

Melville gave her a calculated look. "You hired a thief-taker to protect you because of threats to your person, yet you dismiss this egregious event out of hand?"

"Because the flagrant nature of the event makes it unlikely to be unrelated to the rest," she argued. "I could have been killed. What purpose would that serve anyone? And the location was so prominent, increasing the possibility of exposure. It doesn't align with the other attacks at all."

"Regardless, I granted Montague's request."

Eliza knew that tone; Melville's mind was set. "I suspected you had."

"My years are advancing. I would like you to have someone in your life to look after your well-being, someone whose loyalty is not bought with coin."

"I can look after myself." Wielding a pair of silver tongs, she prepared a plate for him, artfully arranging a freshly baked scone alongside slices of shaved ham.

"By hiring someone."

"Marrying Montague would be nigh on the same thing," she pointed out.

"With the addition of children and a permanent companion. Not to mention a title and the many responsibilities you would gain with it. You would be busy, fulfilled, and rarely alone."

"I enjoy being alone."

"I cannot bear the thought of it." Melville set his cup down. "I haven't forgotten our agreement. I know this is your sixth and final Season. You think you'll be happier rusticating in the country, but I disagree."

"Rusticating is not quite what I had in mind."

"I told Montague he had my permission to make the attempt to change your mind, and I wished him well. No harm in that, is there?"

"Would you be happy if I married anyone at all?" she queried, adding milk to her tea. "Or only Montague? You seem to like him quite well."

"I met his father once or twice." Melville shrugged. "He seemed to be a pleasant enough fellow. And Montague is determined to have you. There is something to be said for that. But if there's someone else you prefer, I would champion him over Montague."

"Thank you, my lord. I will keep that in mind."

"You're humoring me," he said dryly.

Eliza's lips curved against the rim of her cup. "I am not. In fact, this discussion has me seeing Lord Montague in an entirely new light. You are correct: there's something to be said for his determination. And yours. Which I think was his point. He wanted me to know he's serious, and he wanted to ascertain whether or not he would have your support. He said he understands me better now, and perhaps that's true. Flowers will not win me, but cunning and unorthodox methods . . . At the very least, I admire his approach."

Not enough to wed him, but she didn't see any benefit to reiterating that point. She was enjoying tea with her uncle far too much to ruin it by being unnecessarily contrary. She gestured at his plate in a silent urging to eat.

"Good girl," he praised. "How is Mr. Bond's investigation progressing? Is he equally unconcerned by large statues nearly crushing you?"

Just the sound of Jasper's name caused the tempo of her heartbeat to alter. "No. He was upset enough for both of us. If there's anything nefarious to be uncovered, he will find it. He would also like to meet with you."

"Yes, yes. Tell him to come by whenever is convenient for him. If he waits for me to remember to make an appointment, we shall never meet. I doubt I'll be of much help, however. I have never been with you when you've been accosted."

"He is investigating beyond the present," she explained. "He wishes to exclude anyone who might hold resentment toward you, Mother, or Mr. Chilcott."

"Ah, so . . . well, that's a reasonable avenue of inquiry."

They ate in companionable silence for a time, during which Eliza considered his comment about having a permanent companion. Up until now, she thought repasts such as she shared with Melville were all she needed. They rarely spoke while eating, and she enjoyed that. She hadn't considered how the silence might be deafening if she was the only one to fill it. There was a large difference between sitting quietly with someone else and sitting alone. She realized there was a certain comfort in knowing one could speak if one wanted to and chose not to, rather than being unable to speak because no one was there to listen.

"What troubles you, my dear?"

"Nothing, my lord."

"I am aware denial is a common female response. But you are too direct for such evasions."

Eliza shook her head. "I've found it best to hold my tongue, if choosing to do otherwise is guaranteed to lead to fruitless argument."

"Ah . . . Your mother. You will have to speak of her sometime."

"I don't see why."

"Perhaps then," he mumbled around a bite, "you will stop thinking of her before making decisions."

"I do not—" she started to protest, then fell silent when he shot her a look. He was right, as always.

Eventually, Melville drifted back to his notes and Eliza slipped off the stool with the intent of moving upstairs. The day's post caught her eye and she scooped it up, carrying it over to the small, shallow basket where Melville kept his mail. It was nearly overflowing. She shook her head. She'd long ago learned to separate Melville's personal correspondence from the rest—so that outstanding accounts were paid in a timely manner—but clearly he was also neglecting to keep in touch with those who reached out to him.

"What will it take," she asked, as she added to the pile, "to motivate you to whittle this down?"

"What?" He looked up at her, then down at the basket. "Good God."

"My thoughts exactly." She pulled five off the top and brought them to him. "Can we start with these?"

He sighed. "If you insist."

Eliza kissed his cheek. "Thank you."

"Ha." He snorted. "You are exacting your pound of flesh for Montague."

She was laughing as she left the room.

Jasper leaned back in his chair and drummed his fingertips on the desktop. "How long was he there?"

"About an hour," Aaron said, holding his hat to his chest with both hands. He stood just inside the doorway of Jasper's study, rocking back on the heels of his boots. "Perhaps a little longer."

"You know why Montague paid that call," Westfield prompted from his usual spot on the settee.

"No, I do not. She refused him," Jasper bit out.

"All the more reason to gain Melville's support. Don't be obtuse, Bond. Women bow to familial pressure to marry men they don't want. It happens all the time."

Jasper's fingers curled into his palm.

"Do you believe Montague is responsible for Miss Martin's troubles?" the earl asked.

"I cannot be certain one way or the other."

"What will you do now?"

"Speak to her." How had she taken the news? How far would she go to make Melville happy?

The thought of Eliza with Montague did horrible things to him.

It was a new sort of torment to be unable to see her now, to be barred from her company by rules and dictates he'd ignored for years.

Straightening, he uncovered his inkwell and stabbed a quill into it. He dashed off a quick note, powdering the ink with fine-grained sand before folding. Then he sealed the whole and waved it at Aaron. "Take this to the Melville residence."

Aaron approached and collected the missive.

"Miss Martin may need you after she reads it. Linger to be sure and if so, assist her. When you've finished with that," Jasper went on, "I want you to look into a Mrs. Pennington, who runs a newly opened shop on Peony Way. Pink-striped awning out front, lovely blonde inside. There is something not right with her. Find out what it is."

"Will do, Bond."

After the young man left, Westfield stood and walked to the console to avail himself of Jasper's brandy. "It's unfortunate Montague made so bold a move. Had it been anyone else paying addresses, you could have killed two birds with one stone by encouraging her to marry the gentleman— Montague would be barred from Miss Martin's fortune, and you could wipe your hands clean of the business by entrusting her safety to her future husband. Assuming you would be able to ascertain that her betrothed was not our culprit, of course."

"Of course." The thought didn't improve Jasper's mood at all. In fact, it worsened with the understanding that foiling Montague and successfully completing his assignment had fallen behind his desire to possess Eliza.

"It might also explain why he sent along the missive today," Westfield continued. "The assurance that he would be buying back the marker to his mother's property was prompted by something."

"Like his father, he is arrogant to the point of idiocy." Unless Montague had something else shoring up his confidence . . . Jasper would research the possibility posthaste.

"What do you expect you can accomplish by talking to Miss Martin?" Westfield asked, turning to face him. "Does she trust you to play matchmaker as well as suitor?"

Jasper snorted.

"You are so touchy lately, Bond," the earl complained. "Perhaps you should take the evening off and indulge yourself at Remington's for a few hours."

"Montague can have any heiress he wants. Why is he so determined to have this one? Someone clearly on the shelf and possessed of a rare temperament? Someone who's told him she does not want him?"

"Perhaps that's the lure." Westfield sank into a chair in front of Jasper's desk. The earl looked both comfortable and bored, two states of being that were unknown to Jasper. "A woman can be a bloody nuisance when she is overly fond of a man. If Miss Martin is inclined to spend much of her time in the country, Montague could have all of the benefits of marrying an attractive yet mature heiress, with none of the detriments. I know you find it hard to believe, Bond, but sometimes there are sound reasons for doing something. Not everything in this world is motivated by some evil plan."

"It is with Montague."

"Are you quite certain the son is so like the father? Or does that matter to you?"

Jasper stood. "Quite certain."

"Look on the bright side. Perhaps Montague's move will speed things up a bit with your investigation. Now there's a more immediate timeline for the culprit to work against."

"It's a sorry thing indeed when the reason for celebrating is that a madman could now be feeling desperate enough to act rashly."

Westfield sipped his libation and watched Jasper carefully. "You are like a caged beast. There is such an air of disquiet about you. I have never seen you this way before. Is ruining Montague so important to you?"

It took Jasper a long moment to answer. He didn't want to share his state of mind; it was too personal and intemperate. "Have you ever wanted something so badly you couldn't imagine not having it?"

"Like what?"

"Anything at all."

"There was a gelding once." Westfield held his glass between both palms, warming the liquor with his body heat. "At Tattersall's. I underbid. I stewed for weeks afterward. If I had the chance again, I would not be so cautious."

"Had you ridden it?"

"No. But I watched him be put through his paces. I examined him myself. Beautiful animal. I knew the moment I saw him that we would suit beautifully together."

"Do you still regret the loss?"

The earl shrugged. "On occasion. Not often. It was some time ago. I tell myself surely there was something wrong with the beast and I'm fortunate to have avoided being saddled with it. Otherwise, fate would have seen fit to give him to me."

"I don't believe in fate. I believe we make our own destiny." Jasper rubbed his jaw, absently noting that he should shave again. It was early evening and his skin was no longer smooth. It might burn Eliza when he kissed her.

If she came . . .

"Certainly my situation is nothing like yours," Westfield said. "Your need is rather like a thirst, is it not?"

"Thirst . . . yes." It was clear the earl was mistaking Jasper's lust for Eliza for a lust for vengeance. Jasper chose not to correct the assumption. "That's apt."

Unfolding from the chair, the earl polished off the last of his brandy. "I will continue to assist you in your quest for revenge, Bond. You are not alone in this endeavor, whether you appreciate that or not."

How well the earl knew him to comprehend that he disliked being dependent upon anyone. "You've done more than enough. The marker for Montague's property is my greatest wish realized."

"I'm merely your mask." Westfield's smile was grim.

"You are the one who has interceded in every investment that might have saved him. You are the one who funded the seasoned gamblers capable of winning against him. You are the one who has worked tirelessly for years to earn enough to squander a fortune to ruin him. Remind me never to anger you, Bond. You aren't a very nice fellow to those you dislike."

"You are too honorable a man to do anything that would completely alienate me." With a smile, Jasper tossed the earl's words back at him, "Whether you appreciate hearing that or not."

"Good God, don't make that statement within earshot of others, please." The earl looked at the clock. "Should I return at ten o'clock to begin our shadowing of Miss Martin?"

Jasper considered the time. It was shortly after five. "Let's make it eleven, shall we?"

"You will hear no complaints from me," Westfield said as he made his egress. "I've spent more time with you over the last few days than I have with a woman. No offense, but you aren't nearly as charming."

"I should hope not," Jasper muttered, following the earl out to the hall en route to his rooms upstairs.

"I beg you to follow my lead and consider indulging in some female companionship yourself. It would be a relief to find you less surly this evening."

Jasper paused with his foot on the bottom step, absorbing the now familiar thrum of anticipation he felt whenever time with Eliza approached. "Don't feel the need to be excessively timely," he said over his shoulder, before ascending the staircase two steps at a time.

"This coming from a man who is a stickler for punctuality?" Westfield called after him. "I believe you have caught the Melville madness."

Jasper thought that was apt, too.

* * *

Eliza wondered what the house looked like from the front. Alighting from the carriage in the mews afforded her only a backside glimpse of Jasper's home.

The young man who couriered Jasper's note to her urged her expeditiously through an iron gate and along a cobblestone pathway bisecting a garden that was immaculate, if uninspired. She was still absorbing the severity of the rear lawn when Jasper appeared. A shiver of delight moved through her.

He filled the doorway leading into the house, his broad shoulders and tall frame backlit by the interior candlelight. His stance was wide, allowing light to shine between his legs, detailing the length and power of his thighs. He was fully dressed, but the expert fit of his breeches left nothing to the imagination. For the first time, she found the sight of a man's body inflaming. From the moment she first laid eyes on him, she'd felt a disturbing and significant physical response to his proximity. It intensified daily, encouraged by every heated look and every casual touch.

"Eliza." There was something intimate about the way he said her name.

She gained the first stair leading up from the garden and he held his hand out to her. It was gloveless and looked so strong and capable. She decided she loved his hands.

She tugged off her glove before she accepted his assistance, wanting to feel the warmth of his skin. A frisson of heated awareness moved up her arm. His grip tightened for a moment, as if he felt it, too. Looking up at him from beneath the hood of her cloak, she noted the stark austerity of his handsome features. He seemed so somber. So grave.

"Is something wrong?" she asked, having been concerned from the moment his summons arrived.

"Come inside."

Glancing behind her, she saw that the young man who'd

accompanied her had departed. There had been others with him, but they hadn't entered the gardens with her. Jasper's note advised her to ask his man to accompany her back, *if* she chose to visit him as he requested. Once she relayed her acquiescence, everything was arranged with amazing swiftness. She'd been squired from Melville's house through the delivery alley and seen into a hired hackney. The winding and repetitive route they'd taken ensured she wasn't followed.

Jasper led her inside and took her to a study. Her senses were engaged by the feel of the room the moment she entered it. The mixture of blue hues and mahogany wood was surprising; although she couldn't say what else she might have chosen for him. Large wingback chairs and overly stuffed settees spoke of comfort as well as functionality. She knew instantly that he spent a great deal of time in this room, which made her want to explore every corner of it.

He came up behind her and set his hands on her shoulders. She stiffened, not with fear or apprehension, but expectantly. She heard him inhale slowly and deeply, as if savoring her scent. The action suited him. He was a man firmly attuned to his baser nature, reliant on his senses and instincts as all predatory and dominant creatures were. She was attracted to that side of him, deriving a potent thrill from being capable of stirring it.

"May I?" he asked, referring to her cloak.

Eliza nodded.

Her hood was lifted and pulled back, exposing her face to light from all around. He paused, his frame emanating an unmistakable tension. The act of removing her cloak suddenly became far more revealing. She understood then that he hadn't summoned her to discuss urgent business or anything else. The divestment of her exterior garments was the first step in the removal of all her clothing.

Her breath caught audibly and a fine tremor rippled through her.

Jasper's chin came to rest atop the crown of her head. His hands gripped her upper arms in a gentle yet unshakeable hold. "Will you stay?" he asked gruffly.

She hesitated only a moment. "Yes."

Chapter 8

Eliza felt Jasper relax. She did not. How could she, having just agreed to give herself to a man she barely knew? For the first time in her life, she had ignored all reason and acted purely on feeling.

Just like her mother would have done . . .

She pushed the thought aside. She'd made her decision and she would not regret it. "What would you have done if I said no?"

"Changed your mind." His fingers deftly released the frog at her throat. Her cloak began to slip and he caught it with a flourish.

Turning to face him, she watched as he draped the black velvet garment over the back of one of the pale blue settees. "I'm agreeing to something I have no knowledge of," she pointed out. "Perhaps I will change my own mind."

Jasper stepped closer and cupped her face in his hands. "If so, I will desist. But I fully intend for you to beg me not to stop."

The physical response she had to his words was so violent it took her by surprise. He took advantage, his mouth sealing over hers and taking it, his tongue thrusting fast and deep. Eliza caught his wrists to keep her balance, her body otherwise frozen by the onslaught. A whimper escaped her and was swallowed by his answering groan.

He released her as quickly as he'd caught her, stepping back and leaving her to stumble from the loss of his support. His chest lifted and fell rapidly. His gaze was heavy-lidded and hot.

"This is my study," he said in a hoarse voice. "When I'm home, this is the most likely place to find me."

Stunned by the sudden change in conversation and the distance between them, Eliza took a moment to register what he'd said. "It suits you," she managed.

"Come along." Jasper held his hand out to her.

He pulled her gently from the room and back out to the visitor's foyer. There was a longcase clock against the wall, a large console with a lone silver salver atop it, and a rack for Jasper's cane. It was a purely functional space, lacking any adornments.

"The parlor is here," he said, steering her across a round Aubusson rug covering the marble floor.

From the threshold, she saw a fire in the grate and playing cards scattered across two separate tables. It looked as if a gathering had recently been there and would be returning shortly. The room was decorated in shades of yellow and cream. There was a large quantity of furniture, all of which was oversized and sturdily built. Still, the space felt sterile and uncluttered.

"At any given hour," he said, "many of my employees can be found in here. The downstairs is often noisy, filled with bawdy conversations and raucous laughter. This is the first time this room has been empty in many years."

"Oh . . ." Eliza understood that he'd sent the men away because of her. "When will they be back?"

"Not for many hours."

Her palms grew damp, a reaction he couldn't fail to note with her hand in his. "Were you so certain of my capitulation?"

"Far from it, but I couldn't proceed as if failure was inevitable." He tugged her from the room. "There is also a dining room and ballroom on this floor, but I use neither, so they're unfurnished."

They moved toward the staircase and started to climb. With every step they took, her excitement mounted. Her breathing quickened and her face felt hot. There was an unmistakable finality to their upward progression, as if her fate had been set and she couldn't turn back now. Far from feeling trapped, she felt liberated. All afternoon, she'd thought of Melville and Regina and Montague. She had weighed their admonishments and advice. And she'd felt the mounting pressure to conform, to cede to the expected behavior and cast aside any lingering hope for independence.

"The third floor," he said, "has three bedrooms and a nursery, which has been converted into a room for guests. Sometimes my men stay here, for various reasons. No one is here now. If you would like to see the rooms, I'll show them to you."

If he was trying to give her time to change her mind, it wasn't working. She was growing more agitated by the moment. Impatient. Restless. "Why?"

Jasper glanced at her. "Does anything about my home strike you in an unusual way?"

"It's lovely," she said. "Beautifully furnished. However, it is also oddly barren. Nothing adorns the walls or table surfaces. You've hung no portraits of loved ones or pleasing landscapes. I had hoped to learn more about you by visiting, but I've seen very little that tells a story."

"One has to *want* things in order to purchase them. There's nothing I want. There has been nothing I've seen in a shop window or in someone else's home that I have coveted." He paused with one foot on the next step. "I think you might understand that lack of wanting. You attire yourself for purpose, not for vanity. You did not refurnish Melville's study when you commandeered it. You replaced what needed to be replaced and made do with the rest."

"Many people find that art and sentimental objects provide comfort and enjoyment. I, too, own a few items that are impractical but give me pleasure."

"Am I such to you?" he asked, his dark eyes shadowed with some emotion she couldn't name. "An impractical pleasure?"

"Yes."

He started forward again. They reached the second floor landing and Eliza looked down the lone hallway, searching for and finding a lack of wall adornment. Aside from sconces to light the way, there was nothing to relieve the long expanse of soft green damask covering the walls.

His pace slowed from brisk to a near stroll. "I have only ever wanted intangible things—health and happiness for my mother, justice for wrongdoings, satisfaction in a job well done—things of that nature. I have never understood why others become focused on particular objects. I've never comprehended obsession or overwhelming need."

He spoke without inflection. There was nothing in what he said that betrayed any emotion, yet she felt a deeper undercurrent to his words.

"Why are you telling me this?" she asked softly, clutching his hand with both of her own.

"I'm the only one who uses this floor." He started forward. "Aside from my own rooms, the rest are vacant."

His repeated evasion of her questions was growing tiresome. She could not understand his mood. With her own emotions a confusing jumble, she didn't have the wherewithal to translate his feelings, too.

They reached a set of open double doors. Jasper gestured her in ahead of him.

Taking a deep breath, Eliza crossed the threshold. Like her room in Melville's house, Jasper's sitting room was predominantly burgundy in tone with occasional splashes of cream to alleviate the dark hue. But unlike her space, his was thoroughly masculine. There were no tassels or patterns to any of the materials, and no carvings in the wooden arms and legs of the chairs and tables.

The air smelled of him. She breathed the scent into her nostrils, finding it calming to her jangled nerves. Then, she looked at the open doorway to her left, the portal to Jasper's bedchamber, and her stomach knotted all over again.

"There are games women play," he murmured, his gaze hot enough to heat her skin. "Tests they devise to gauge a man's interest."

"What sorts of tests?"

"They make certain a man learns of their favorite flower or color or important dates, then wait to see if he will remember and gift them accordingly."

Her hands linked together nervously. Should she sit? Or remain standing as he did? She escaped into the conversation, not knowing what else to do. "The objects of feminine and masculine sentimentality are often widely different. To expect a man to assume what might be an unnatural form of sentiment to prove devotion is an unreasonable experiment with a high probability of failure. Why not accept his instinctual gestures of affection in whatever manner they are manifested? They likely mean more to him and reveal more about his character."

Jasper's smile curled her toes. "Do you have any notion of how sexually arousing I find your intellect? One day I should like you to expound upon this topic while I'm inside you. I suspect I would find it highly erotic."

A flush swept over her face.

He shut the door to the hallway and locked it. The soft click of the latch rippled through her.

"I tested you today," he said, with his back to her. "Considering how irritating I find such ploys, it astonishes me that I did so."

"Did I pass?"

Facing her, he shrugged out of his coat. "You are in my home, so I would say so."

He swiftly unfastened the buttons of his waistcoat. Eliza found she could not look away, despite the voice in her head that lectured about privacy and proper maidenly modesty.

She cleared her throat so she could speak. "You sent for me without telling me why."

"If Montague had sent for you, would you have gone?"

"Of course not. He does not work for me."

Jasper stiffened. When he returned to the act of shaking off his waistcoat, it was with notable impatience. "If Reynolds had sent for you, would you have gone?"

"No."

"But he works for you."

Clearly the expected responses were not the ones he wanted to hear. He wanted the truth.

"I would not have expended the effort for anyone else," she admitted, her mouth drying as he untied and unwound his cravat, baring his throat. The sight was intensely provocative to her. His skin was darker than her own, firmer. She wanted desperately to touch it, to feel him swallow beneath her fingertips.

He toed off his buckled shoes. "That was the test. I needed to know if you would place me in a different category from other men you know. I was also curious to see how deep your adventuresome proclivities were buried."

"I am far from adventuresome," she protested.

"You would like to believe that." Jasper tossed his cravat on the floor, then yanked his shirtsleeves over his head.

Eliza's knees weakened and she staggered over to the nearest chair, half-sinking and half-falling into it.

Dear God, he was beautiful. Astonishingly, breathtakingly so. She remembered how he'd urged her to touch him the first time he kissed her. He had been so hard beneath her questing fingers, like stone. She could see why. Her hand lifted to her throat. As dry as her mouth had been, it was now flooded with moisture.

She had never seen a rendering of a male body that could compare. The washboard-like cording of muscles across his abdomen and the light dusting of dark hair that thinned into a fine line were new to her. And delightful. Her gaze followed the trail to where it disappeared beneath the placket of his breeches.

Then lower . . .

He was hard there, too. Cupped by the expertly tailored doeskin, the outline of his erection was thick and prominent. The knot in her stomach tightened. He was such a blatantly masculine creature. Primitive in the most vital of ways. A male whose appetites were undoubtedly fierce and expansive. How could she, a woman who knew nothing about exploiting her own femininity, sate such a man?

When he didn't move, she jerked her gaze upward to find him staring back at her. A tight smile preceded him taking a seat on the opposite settee. He had allowed her to look her fill, she realized. Unashamed of the visible proof of his lust. Unabashed.

Jasper rolled down his hose, one leg at a time. "I *need* you to be adventuresome, Eliza. You wouldn't tolerate me and my profession for long if you were not."

"I do more than tolerate you," she rejoined softly, having lost the strength to speak louder.

He stood, and her eyes stung. She was enamored with the sight of him. Smitten as she'd thought she could never be. There was nothing she would alter about him, nothing she found fault with. In that moment, she was certain she would pay any price for the pleasure of looking upon him indefinitely. The sensations moving through her were drugging and addictive. She wondered helplessly if there was any way she could feel like this every day.

Approaching her with hand outstretched, he said, "From the moment I first saw you, I desired you and knew I had to have you. Since then, I have come to realize it isn't mere craving that drives me. It is wanting, Eliza. I *want* you. I've never wanted anything in my life, until you. Nothing. Do you understand what I'm saying? Gaining and losing a possession means nothing to me. There is always a replacement."

"I understand." She allowed him to pull her to her feet. "But I don't know what conclusion to draw from that understanding."

He gestured for her to face away from him. "I ceased trying to find reason in it. I cannot waste any more time trying to puzzle out what I don't know. I must act on what I do know—you are the one thing in the world I want, and I can have you. I'm also lacking the scruples that would prevent me from doing whatever is necessary to keep you. The details can be dealt with later, when I can once again think about something other than bedding you."

His fingers went to the buttons that secured the back of her gown and released them with laudable dexterity.

"Have I no say in the matter?" she asked.

He pressed his lips to the top of her bared shoulder. "If you intend to say you have no objections, speak away. Otherwise, I ask that you give me the next few hours before voicing anything that might make my task more difficult for me."

Eliza looked straight ahead, which was a straight-line view into Jasper's bedroom. The bed was directly in front of her, custom-made from the size of it. The back of her gown gaped open and he pushed it free of her shoulders, then down to the floor. "Step out," he ordered.

She obeyed, too overwhelmed to do otherwise. "You are giving me too much time to think," she groused, averting her gaze from the bed.

Jasper laughed softly, the moment of levity sufficient to lighten some of the incertitude preying on her. "Would you prefer to be ravished?"

"I would prefer not to have these fits of nerves."

"I should like to ravish you." He loosened her stays. "Not tonight, when I need both of us to have no doubt that you came to my bed willingly, but soon."

Crossing her arms over her chest, she held her loosened corset to her breasts. Jasper rounded her and backed up, putting distance between them.

"I'm almost naked," she bit out, wanting him to do *something*. Why was he standing so far away? Even if he extended his arms their full length, he wouldn't be able to reach her.

"I am highly aware of that fact." Reaching down, he stroked himself through his breeches, his long fingers rubbing along the length of the pronounced bulge.

"Have you no shame?" Her tone was curt, her emotions high. She was a virgin, for God's sake, and he was giving her too much breathing room. She was achingly aware of everything around her, when what she wanted was to be lost to the barrage of sensations he could so easily overwhelm her with.

"None at all. And I would like for you to have none either. Eliza . . ." His tone softened. "Did I not explain myself clearly? Don't you understand that you are uniquely appealing to me? You worry that exposing your body will make you vulnerable, but I'm the one who will be left raw by the experience."

She stood there for a long moment, lip quivering. He was

forcing her to reason everything out during the one occasion when she didn't want to think at all.

Jasper watched her with those intense dark eyes, his body made golden by the flickering candlelight. How many times had he experienced this sequence of events to be so nonchalant? Dozens? More . . . ?

She would not be surprised. What woman could resist him?

She was resisting him. . . .

Her jaw clenched. He was right to avoid responsibility for her choice to be here. It was her decision, and she needed to claim it. Why should she tell herself that she was acting on instinct when that was a lie?

She was not like her mother. She was not driven to rashness by passion. She knew damn well what she was doing.

Eliza launched herself at him. Two running steps and a wild leap, and she was upon him. He caught her, laughing. Lifting her feet from the floor, he spun and strode into the bedroom.

"Not adventuresome?" he teased, setting her down at the foot of the bed. He looked at her with such an expression of proprietary pride that her throat tightened.

Pivoting on his bare feet, Jasper locked the bedroom door.

"I thought we were the only ones here?" she queried, her heart still racing from her leap off the proverbial cliff.

"You are assuming I'm locking others out, instead of locking you in . . ."

The thought of capture excited her. She had run willingly into the lion's den, and now there was no turning back.

He leaned back against the door, his palms pressed flat to the panels and one ankle crossed over the other. The perfect appearance of insouciant leisure. But he'd never been able to hide his predaceous nature from her. She had seen it from the first and she saw it now: the high color on his throat and cheekbones, the fine sheen of sweat on his chest, the flaring of his nostrils, and the narrowed, concentrated gaze.

One wrong move and he would pounce . . .

Reaching up, she began to pull the pins from her hair. She dropped them on the floor, one by one, as he'd done with his cravat. There was something oddly freeing in that carelessness. The act of tossing aside the trappings that restrained. Here in this room with Jasper, she could finally cast off the confusing strictures of society and be what she had always wanted to be—liberated and independent.

After the last pin dropped, she shook out her hair, relishing the tingling of her scalp. She was clad in only her loosened stays and pantalettes, but she was not embarrassed or cold. There was no way she could be, when warmed by a stare as heated as Jasper's.

He didn't move, barely blinked. As the silence lengthened, she lost courage and clasped her hands in front of her.

"You are so beautiful, Eliza." His hand lifted to his chest and rubbed, as if to soothe a pain there. "I adore your freckles. Do you have them everywhere?"

She bit her lower lip and nodded. "It is the bane of red hair, I'm afraid."

"I will kiss every one of them," he vowed. "They are delightful."

"Fustian," she scoffed. "No one likes freckles."

Jasper's eyes twinkled in the light of the bedside tapers. "Isn't there anything about me you adore? Any part of me you want to kiss?"

"I am mad for every inch of you," she pronounced with heartfelt fervency. "The way you smell. The cut of your hair. The line of your jaw. I'm especially taken with your hands. I can feel the strength in them when you touch me. You could crush my bones in your grip, but instead you are so gentle."

He held both hands out, offering them to her. She rushed

forward, knowing his touch would calm and distract her. "Sometimes I fear crushing you," he confessed with a hitch in his voice.

Catching his hands with hers, Eliza pressed a kiss into each palm. "Is that why you stand so still?"

"Yes."

"What would you do, if you had no need for restraint?"

As before, he brought her hand to rest over his heart, allowing her to feel its racing. "I would pin you to this door behind me and take you, swift and hard. Then I would lay you on the floor, spread you wide, and have you again. Slowly. Deeply. Eventually, we might make it to the bed, but I couldn't guarantee it."

"It sounds . . . savage."

"You make me feel that way. If I could curb the need I have for you, I would. Perhaps, after tonight, it will be more manageable. I pray that's the case."

The roughness in his voice was a caress of its own. Freed from the pressure of her stays, the tips of her breasts throbbed and puckered tight. She was eye level with his chest, which made her wonder if his nipples were as sensitive as hers. The flat disks were surrounded by gooseflesh. Giving in to the urge, Eliza leaned forward and warmed one with a lick of her tongue.

"Bloody hell," he bit out, jerking violently.

Jasper spun her away from him in a dizzying pivot. The ripping of her stays was like a crack of thunder in the room, followed by the rush of cool air across her back and the soft tickle of her hair beneath her shoulder blades. Her pantalettes were next, the tie at her waist digging briefly into her flesh before breaking in half. The flesh-colored stockinette was rent into two halves that clung to her ankles by the fastenings there.

She'd barely registered that she was excited by his loss of

control when a hand at her lower back steered her forward, straight up the short steps at the foot of the bed and onto the mattress.

On her hands and knees, she crawled across the burgundy counterpane, highly conscious of everything she was exposing to him in the process. His hand caught her ankle when she reached the middle of the massive bed, halting her. She dropped to her stomach in a bid for modesty. The remnants of her pantaloons were stripped from her legs and discarded.

Eliza didn't move, barely breathed.

"Are you frightened?" he asked gruffly.

She had to force herself to think about her feelings. "I d-don't know."

Jasper stretched out beside her, his arm extended above their heads. With his other hand, he urged her to roll to her side, so that her back was against his sweat-dampened chest. He leaned forward and rested his cheek against her shoulder, his silky hair brushing softly against her skin. His arm came around her waist and held her tightly to him. He didn't move. Eventually, she relaxed into his warmth, inhaling the scent of him, which was made stronger by the tremendous heat of his body. He felt fevered against her flesh.

It took long moments, but over time his temperature cooled and his breathing slowed.

"Jasper . . . ?"

His hand at her waist moved higher, cupping a breast. She tensed again at the unfamiliar touch.

"Shh," he murmured, gentling her.

The feel of his breath gusting across her ear made her nipple harden into his palm. A rough sound escaped him and his hand flexed convulsively around her.

"Let me show you what you did to me," he whispered, withdrawing enough to coax her onto her back.

Eliza stared up at him, awed anew by how handsome he

was. How was it possible that such a man would find her so desirable?

She didn't care. She was just grateful for her good fortune.

With no further warning, he lowered his head and surrounded her nipple with the humid heat of his mouth. She arched upward with a gasp, startled by the violence of her response. His tongue curled around the aching tip, and his cheeks hollowed on a deep suckle. She cried out, her nails scratching into the velvet coverlet. His callused fingertips rolled her other nipple, then tugged. She began to pant.

"Jasper."

He growled and sucked harder, his tongue stroking the underside of the straining point with wicked skill. The flesh between her thighs pulsed in time to the rhythm of his mouth, clenching deep and feeling empty. Her hips lifted, seeking. The hand at her breast slid lower, across the flat of her belly and into the dark red curls at the apex of her thighs.

The shock of the caress froze her. She was too sensitive there, too wet and swollen.

"Touch me." His voice was so gruff, she barely recognized it.

He withdrew and caught her wrist, urging her hand to mold around the outline of his erection. He showed her how to move, rubbing her palm up and down his thick length. Heat rushed up her arm and spread throughout her body, easing her stiffened muscles. Exploiting her distraction, he resumed his quest, his fingers slipping through the lax barrier of her thighs. His palm cupped her, the breadth of his hand easily laying claim to the part of her that had always been intensely private.

His dark head lifted. He watched her reaction as his fingers moved, gliding through the slickness clinging to the entrance of her body.

"Open," he breathed. "Let me feel how wet you are."

When she hesitated, he took her mouth, his lips slanting across hers in a brazen seduction. His tongue followed the outer curve of her lower lip, tracing the shape before teasing the seam with flirtatious licks. She opened with rapacious hunger, her head lifting in an attempt to deepen the kiss. He pulled back, maintaining the provocative distance between them, denying her the full possession she sought.

Eliza made a frustrated sound and his fingers tapped lightly against her sex.

Challenged by his silent bargain, she spread her legs, draping one thigh over his so nothing was barred from him.

"Yes." His lips lowered to hers. "Be wanton . . ."

His tongue and fingertip breached her simultaneously, above and below. She writhed into the unexpected intrusion, moaning as sweat misted her skin. She gripped his erection with desperately clenching fingers. Bolder than she'd ever imagined she could be.

"So snug." His finger pushed inexorably deeper, then pulled back. When he stroked back into her, her legs fell open, and her hips arched. "Snug and very hot."

Her fingertips found the plush head of his penis straining above the waistband of his breeches. She hungrily explored the satiny curve, fascinated with the heat and silky smooth texture. Moisture beaded on the crown. She wished she could clench the length of him, caress him fervently from root to tip.

"No more," he said harshly, pulling back from her.

She grasped for him to no avail. He slipped further down the bed, away from her greedy lips and tormented breasts.

"Jasper!" she protested, trying to sit up but losing the leverage to do so when he pushed his shoulders under her legs.

There was a blazing moment when she realized what he wanted, then her thoughts scattered beneath the lash of his tongue. An unvoiced protest died on her lips. She couldn't muster the will to stop him, even to appease her scandalized sense of modesty. Instead she moaned and rocked into his mouth, trying to find his rhythm so she could ease the terrible yearning within her.

"That's the way," he coaxed darkly, lifting her hips.

His tongue lapped through the tender folds of her sex, parting her, licking her with velvet roughness. He toyed with her, flickering over the knot of nerves with the pointed tip of his tongue. She bucked upward, knowing there had to be more. Wanting more. Needing it. She mewled in torment.

His finger returned, sliding easily through greedily clenching tissues.

"Oh . . ." she moaned, her eyes squeezing shut against the unbearable intimacy. "Oh, God!"

In and out. Pushing and withdrawing. Pumping. She writhed, and he pinned her hips with a heavy arm.

Two fingers. Her body shuddered violently at the unfamiliar stretching. His mouth surrounded her, tongued her, sucked her . . .

Eliza climaxed with a serrated cry, her fingers digging into the counterpane, her thighs quivering.

At the height of her pleasure, Jasper thrust his fingers deep and scissored them, rending the barrier of her virginity. She scarcely felt the pain, so lost was she to the wonder of his talented tongue.

He didn't stop, groaning as if he felt the same surfeit of feeling, prolonging the waves of sensation until she pushed his head away, unable to bear any more.

Chapter 9

Jasper pressed a kiss to a freckle on Eliza's thigh before sliding off the end of the bed. She curled onto her side, flushed and trembling, her slim, pale limbs drawn tight to her body. Her blue eyes followed his movements, looking dazed and sated at once.

His blood was raging, his cock throbbing. He yanked open the placket of his breeches and pushed them down. Kicking them aside, he took his penis in his hand and stroked the pulsing length. Crimson skeins of moisture—her virginal blood—clung to his fingers. The sight aroused him, luring his seed to leak from the tip of his cock.

He'd pushed her far and fast, needing to take her past the twin hurdles of inexperience and virginity so he could have her as he needed to. He had tried to warn her, attempted to explain, forced himself to give voice to a craving he didn't understand. Small comfort to a woman overwhelmed by her first physical attraction.

Jasper had taken advantage of that fact, remembering how riotous the flush of first lust was, how ill-considered and desperate it felt. He remembered it well, because Eliza made him feel that way again. Hot-blooded. Randy. Impatient.

With harsh strides, he went to the washstand and grabbed a handful of freshly laundered towels. On the way back to the bed, he caught up the bottle of oil he'd purchased at Mrs. Pennington's shop. He tossed the towels on the counterpane, then poured a small pool of the fragrant golden liquid into his palm. The bottle was set aside on the nightstand by Eliza's head.

Deliberately, he rubbed his hands together, releasing the scent of bergamot and spice into the air. He'd chosen a masculine scent on purpose, wanting it to linger in her mind after the night was over, goading her to remember the things he had done to her body. Thus far she hadn't been subject to the sorts of lewd imaginings he suffered through, but he intended that to change. Whether she was balancing her ledgers or dancing with blasted suitors, Jasper wanted her to be thinking of sex with him.

Eliza watched, riveted, as he gripped his cock at the root and stroked upward, pulling and stretching, swelling further until he was certain he'd never been this hard and thick. Ropey veins coursed the length of him, making him look as brutal as he felt. His bollocks were drawn up tight and hard, his seed churning with the need for release.

She made a soft, anxious noise.

"Are you frightened?" he asked for the second time that evening. Knowing she had to be. Aware that he would have been kinder to shield her from his size until she knew enough to appreciate it. But he was willing to cast aside what little gentlemanly considerations he had to gain what he wanted from her, using every advantage he possessed to distinguish himself from the others who hoped to win her and take her from him. She liked to look at him. And she was attuned to him on the most basic level. Her mind might shy away from his primitive display, but her body understood . . . and would react accordingly.

"Yes," she answered softly, her knees drawing closer to her abdomen. "I have always known you were too much for me."

"But you want me regardless. Face the other way."

Rolling, she gave him her back. She curled in a manner that drew her feet up to the lush curve of her buttocks. The discovery of her voluptuous derriere had been a delightful surprise when she'd crawled across his bed earlier. On the surface, Eliza appeared as moderate in form as she was in temperament, but even in this, her private landscape was the most picturesque. He was certain her backside was the most perfect he'd ever seen.

"Who knew you hid such a curvaceous bottom beneath your clothes?" he murmured, joining her and pressing a kiss to a cluster of freckles on her shoulder.

"You tease me," she accused without heat.

"You spoke of men who appreciate certain hues of hair." Jasper wrapped his body around her, pulling her against his chest with an arm around her slender waist. "Is it so hard to believe I might have my own preferences?"

"For freckles and buttocks?"

"You, Eliza. All of you." He inhaled sharply when she leaned into him, and he became further inflamed by the smell of her. "My patience is thinner than I would wish," he confessed hoarsely. "I must beg you in advance for greater license. You trust me with your life; will you trust me in this? Trust me to give you pleasure, even if I am rough or hurried?"

She looked at him over her shoulder. Her lower lip was caught between her teeth and her eyes were shadowed, but she nodded.

With no further preliminaries, he took his cock in his hand and arched his hips forward. Her breath hissed out when he tucked the thick head against her and slid upward, parting the slick folds of her sex and gliding across her clitoris. Up, then down. On the downstroke, the furled under-side of his cockhead caught the swollen knot of nerves. On the upstroke, the swollen crest rubbed over it. He notched the tiny protrusion into the weeping hole at the tip of his cock and stroked himself from root to crown with his fist. A hot pulse of pre-ejaculate flowed over her sensitive flesh. She moaned, arching backward.

Jasper restrained her with a hand at her breast, fighting his turbulent need to pound into her and spew violently, ex-pending his lust in a violent taking that would slake his crav-ing. The sense of desperation was nigh intolerable. He couldn't shake the apprehension that she might be removed from his grasp before he was ready. It was too soon. His need for her too sharp . . .

Eliza's hand covered his.

Her nipple pebbled into his palm, tightening deliciously. He felt its sensitivity when he kneaded the whole of her breast. Her entire body trembled, and her hips pushed back. Her legs parted, one foot hooking behind his calf, giving her leverage to undulate against him.

She was finally unrestrained, and it was better than he'd imagined. She whispered his name. He pulled back, finding the clutching entrance to her body. There was a moment of hesitation; a brief second when reason reminded him that she was above him in station. Too good for him.

His jaw clenched. He pushed his cockhead deliberately into her tight, resisting flesh. She was scorching hot and drenched.

"Christ," he hissed, seared by the silken heat of her. The delicate muscles inside her bore down on the exquisitely sensitive head of his cock. A violent shudder wracked his frame.

Eliza's head thrashed against his chest. Her nails dug into the forearm he pinned her with. Her movements altered, writhing away instead of into him. She tried to close her legs, but he blocked her, moving his hand from her breast to her cunt in a lightning-quick lunge.

"Trust me," he said gruffly, pushing deeper. "Breathe."

Registering the tremendous strain in Jasper's voice, Eliza tried to obey, gasping air into seized lungs. He slid deeper, despite the panicked clench of untried tissues. She understood the use of the oil now. It gave her body no traction to deny him, no means of resistance.

Her eyes closed on a shuddering exhale. Her mind filled with the vision of Jasper standing beside the bed fully naked, skin gleaming, abdominal and chest muscles rippling from the rough movement of his hands on his magnificent erection. She knew how to judge proportions. She'd known she could never accommodate him, but she wanted to. Needed to.

He withdrew a scant inch. She sucked air into her burning lungs, and his hips lunged forward, tunneling his rigid penis into her. She made a broken sound, unprepared for the feeling of being so utterly possessed.

"God." He stilled, panting, his chest working like a great bellows against her back. His cheek nuzzled against her temple. "Am I hurting you?"

"No . . . Too full." Stretched to the point of aching, but she was not pained.

"You can take me." His fingers rubbed between her legs, starting a hot, sweet trickle of sensation in her core. "Let me in, Eliza. Don't fight it."

Eyes stinging, she gave a tentative, tiny swivel of her hips. He slid a fraction deeper.

"Yes," he purred, nudging forward then withdrawing. "Like that."

She forced her taut frame to relax, sagging back against his supportive chest and deliberately modifying her breathing. Slow deep breath in. Steady breath out. She concentrated on his touch, the way he expertly circled her clitoris with callused fingertips, urging pleasure outward across devastated nerve endings.

On her next inhale, he thrust, sinking into her until his thighs were pressed tight to hers. Her held fell forward on a low moan.

"Eliza."

Dear God, he was so deep in her . . .

He pulled out with painstaking slowness, then filled her again. With every withdrawal and return, his movements became more fluid. Practiced. His expertise became apparent. He knew just how far to pull out, how leisurely to push in, how deep to penetrate to drive her mad for the feel of him inside her. Her enjoyment grew, until she sought the pleasure purposefully, writhing into his thrusts to feel the sweet fullness she craved.

A low rumble of approval vibrated against her back. "You like this."

She gasped at a particularly masterful stroke. The intimidating size of his erection was now something she relished. He was so long and thick. The largeness of him ensured that he rubbed and stretched every sensitive spot, awakening a voracious hunger. She struggled against him, resisting the position he kept her in that prevented her from increasing his depth and pace.

"Tell me you like this," he coaxed darkly, rolling his hips and fingers simultaneously, arousing her with consummate skill so she clenched greedily around him. "Say it."

"Yes." She whimpered in torment, aching every time he pulled out and left her empty. "But . . ."

"I can give it to you." His tone was rough and deeply sexual. "Tell me what you want, Eliza, and you can have it."

"More," she begged, shameless in her yearning. "Give me more . . ."

Jasper's hand cupped her swollen sex and pulled her back into a powerful lunge of his hips. Heat washed over her. His pace increased, the flat of his palm applying just enough pressure to stimulate her on the outside as well as within. Sweat coated her skin and his, making them slide along each other, releasing the fragrance of the oil and Jasper's scent into the air. The room became hot and the counterpane damp, creating a lush humidity that intensified the experience. He whispered lewd praise, his words slurring with pleasure, his abdomen and thighs flexing powerfully as he drove into her. Tears filled her eyes, the tension so fine she felt as if she might break at any moment.

"Please," she sobbed. *"Please!"*

"Right there," he groaned, holding still at the deepest point and grinding against her, screwing into her another fractional bit. "Right there."

She arched violently. The climax hit, her vision narrowing until it blackened completely. Her mouth opened in a silent cry of pleasure. Inside, she convulsed, tightening on him in the most intimate of embraces. Blood roared in her ears, drowning out all sound.

A thick wash of heat flooded the depths of her. Jasper cursed and jerked against her, shuddering in unison with every wrenching spurt.

Eliza felt her name on his lips as he emptied himself inside her, his mouth moving against her shoulder in a sweetly broken litany.

There was no place in Jasper's life for Eliza Martin.

He lay on his side with his head propped in his hand, watching her as she napped. Strands of her beautiful hair clung to her damp forehead and cheeks. Her lips were parted, her chest lifting and falling in the measured tempo of slumber. She lay on her stomach, baring twin dimples in each curve of her extremely enticing buttocks.

Spread out as she was, naked and rosy-skinned and debauched, it was easy to imagine keeping her there in his bed. But it was only an illusion. His gaze lifted and swept around the nearly empty room. Aside from the bed and washstand, there was only a wardrobe and chair for furnishings. This evening with Eliza was the longest stretch of time he'd spent awake in his bedchamber since he took up residence in the house. In the normal course of his life, there would be laughter and loud voices filtering up from the lower floor. He would be adhering to a tight schedule, working as many hours as possible to keep income flowing. After all, there was nothing he wanted done that didn't require coin to see to it.

Try as he might, Jasper couldn't picture Eliza in any part of his home beyond this private space. The men who worked for him were coarse and sometimes ill-mannered. They would have no notion of what to do with a lady like Eliza. He had no dining table at which to feed her, no formal parlor in which she could entertain what few guests would deign to call on her here. His home was less than half the size of Melville's and located in a part of town that, while acceptable, had never been fashionable.

Things would have to change drastically . . .

Eliza made a soft noise. He looked at her and found her rousing. She blinked, then rubbed at her eyes. He watched her vision focus on him. Awareness swept over her face along with a heated blush. She grew unnaturally still.

"Ah," he murmured, smiling. "You look scandalized."

"You look smug," she accused, but with warmth in her eyes.

"Do I?" He stroked his hand down the curve of her back. How could he resist, when she looked at him as she was doing now? "If I do, so should you."

He knew some of her feelings were inspired by the aftermath of orgasmic bliss and gratitude for it, but some of them were more deeply rooted. God knew he had never expected nor wanted anyone to love him, but he'd have a better chance of keeping Eliza if her attachment deepened.

She looked at her fingers, which toyed with a wrinkle in the counterpane. "I did nothing."

Jasper tapped the end of her nose with his finger. "You'll have to take my word for it. There are many ways to have sex, ranging from horribly disappointing to quite nicely done. What you and I just experienced is another sort of matter altogether. It takes two people with singular chemistry to achieve such a delectable end."

Eliza remained strangely quiet.

"Sixpence for your thoughts," he said, aware of tension eating into his contentment. "Is regret setting in?"

"No. No regrets," she replied carefully, glancing at him. "The first day we met, you spoke of rare skills in sexual congress, and clearly you have them. What woman could regret ending up in your bed?"

"Your thoughts on the matter are the only ones that concern me."

"I fail to see how that can be true. I didn't even touch you. You were required to do all of the work—"

Laughing, he leaned over and pressed a kiss to her shoulder. "Sweetheart, that was far from 'work.' "

"I should have done something!" she protested, looking less shy and more animated. She set her chin in her hand, which elevated her torso just enough to bare the upper curve of her breasts. "I feel sorely inadequate."

Jasper was somewhat startled by the ferocity with which he was stirring again, simply from the sight of her and the thought of her deliberately arousing him. "Rubbish. If you had been any more adequate, the business would have been done before I was inside you. That's why I made a point of facing you away from me."

"You made certain I could not participate?" Eliza frowned. "I find that very unsporting."

"Unsporting?" He grinned, enjoying her immensely as always. In all of his days, he'd yet to bed a woman who wanted to put more effort into pleasing him. Leastwise, not any he hadn't paid for their services.

He gestured at his cock, which was half-hard. The semierection should not have been possible, not after the galvanic orgasm he'd been devastated by only a short time ago. "Men are easily enticed into the necessary physical state for sexual congress. It takes considerably more effort to arouse a woman. That's why so many are left disappointed—in the race to climax, men always run the distance faster."

"Disappointed? How can—"

"You asked me for more," he reminded. "Imagine if I had given you less, or worse, said I was finished and it was a shame you couldn't keep pace."

"Oh . . . But you would never do that."

"I would never do that," he agreed. Even if it meant nearly killing himself every time he had her.

She pushed up, stealing his wits with the unexpected view of her perfect breasts. They were neither large—as he'd erroneously thought he preferred—nor small. When she sat back on her heels with her hands on her knees, he found himself speechless.

Then, her eyes widened and she bit her lower lip. Redfaced, she made a move as if to leave the bed.

He caught her wrist. "What is it?"

"I need a towel," she whispered.

Sitting up, he grabbed one he'd thrown on the bed earlier. With his other hand, he gestured for her to widen her kneeling stance.

"Jasper . . ." Eliza was clearly mortified.

"It's mine," he said, tapping his shoulder in a silent order for her to put her hand there for balance. "Let me."

His cock hardened at the visible evidence of how explosively he'd climaxed. She was soaked with his semen. Thick trickles of it coursed down either thigh. He could hardly believe he was ready for her again. By all rights, he should be drained dry.

He cleaned her as gently as possible.

"You knew to have towels ready," she noted breathlessly, as he parted her delicately and dried the dark red curls between her legs. "I should have suggested sheep-gut condoms. I . . . I wasn't thinking clearly."

"It was my responsibility to do that."

"It's *my* body."

"Only in public and when you are dressed. When you're naked, your body belongs to me."

Her chin lifted. "Does your body belong to me when it's bared?"

"Clothed and unclothed, for as long as you'll have me." If he had his way, even longer than that . . .

Jasper looked her in the eye. "I always use French letters, Eliza. I haven't gone without one since I was young and too ignorant to know better. I assure you, that was many years ago."

"Did you forget tonight? Or find you lacked—"

"I never forget." He paused in his ministrations. "Tomorrow, when you're repaired and rested and feeling entirely in control of your mental faculties, we'll discuss everything that transpired tonight."

Her fingertips dug into his shoulder. "You deliberately spilled your seed inside me? Did you not think of the consequences I might face? Have you no care for me?"

Dropping the towel, Jasper caught her around the waist and tugged her against him. "I would do anything for you. Break any law, violate every rule, circumvent any competition—"

"Montague," she interjected, comprehension leaving her jaw slack. "You know he visited with Melville, and why."

"To hell with Montague," he said fiercely. "I want you. That's all there is to it."

"I gave myself to you freely." Eliza tried to wriggle away. "You didn't have to . . . *mark* me, as if you were marking your territory."

"I did." He gripped her with as much tenderness as her resistance allowed. "The moment you saw me, you knew what I was. My nature is no surprise to you."

"I hired you to protect me!"

Jasper inhaled sharply, cut to the quick by the truth of what she said. "Christ, Eliza."

He released her, but she didn't pull away. Instead she stared at him, breathing roughly. With her face and pale shoulders framed by gloriously hued tousled locks, she was the loveliest creature he'd ever seen.

"I'm sorry," he muttered, running a hand through his hair.

"Not for what you did," she surmised. "But because I'm unhappy about it."

There was nothing he could say to that. Lying to her was not an option.

The silence stretched out. They were only inches apart, both kneeling. He sat on his heels; she was upright, bringing them nearly eye to eye. He waited on tenterhooks, wondering if she would want to leave and what he could do to convince her to stay. Seducing a woman in a temper often led to hot sex, but the fury afterward was hotter still. He couldn't risk pushing her any further away.

Damnation, he would give anything to know what she was thinking . . .

"I can almost hear your brain working," Eliza said, studying him. "Care to tell me what thoughts occupy you so completely?"

"My brain isn't as refined as yours, so I am at a loss for what to do. Tell me how to sweeten you toward me again."

"I'm mystified by the ferocity of your possessiveness. You could have anyone." She swallowed hard. "The only thing distinguishing me is my fortune. Is that what you covet so strongly?"

"You don't believe that," he scoffed. "And I will point out that you, too, could have anyone."

She gave his shoulder a little push. "Lie down."

Jasper fell to his back without reservation, willing to do whatever she required to redeem himself. However, there was nothing repentant about his cockstand, which eagerly extended almost to his navel. He'd progressed from nearly erect to flagrantly so the moment she became aggressive.

"Since your body is now mine, by your own admission," she murmured, "I should like to examine it."

He lay unmoving, submitting . . . for now.

Eliza gestured at his penis. "I should like to see it at rest sometime."

"Little chance of that happening. Merely thinking of you makes me hard." He should, perhaps, couch his sentiments more delicately, but since his lust for Eliza was raw, it was more honest to word it thusly.

She reached out and caressed his biceps. When the muscle twitched beneath her touch, she pulled back with a squeak.

Jasper caught her hand and put it back. "Don't be frightened or shy. Whatever you do, I promise to enjoy it."

"I do not want you to simply *enjoy* it," she argued, meeting his gaze. "I want to be exceptionally good at pleasing you. I want to be memorable."

Jasper exhaled in a rush, the allusion to temporariness goading every proprietary instinct he possessed.

Eliza's fingers moved featherlight over the flesh of his upper arm. Then, she grew bolder and squeezed.

"You are so hard," she whispered. Her gaze moved over

his chest and abdomen, followed by her hands. She lingered over his stomach, tracing every ridge of muscle. "And large. You are like a great, sleek beast. A virile animal."

A visible shiver moved through her, which set off an answering response in him. "You like that about me."

"I shouldn't. You are too wild and undisciplined. I'm not woman enough to tame you."

"You wouldn't want me tamed." He caught her hand again and urged it to his cock, prodding her fingers to wrap around him. Her tentative touch was like lightning, causing the hair on his legs to prickle. "Part of you may be appalled at my primitive approach to certain matters, but part of you wouldn't have me any other way."

"You are very arrogant."

"I take no credit for your attraction. My parents are responsible for my appearance, and my ruthlessness is equally inherent. I am, however, grateful they win your regard. Contrary to your opinion, you are the perfect female for me."

Her other hand joined the first, cupping him. Her hands were so slender; she could not circle him in her grip.

"What wins your regard?" she asked, tracing a thick vein with her fingertip.

"Your honesty and good s-sense," he hissed, shuddering as she clasped the head of his cock in her palm. "Your agile mind and independent thought. And the way you respond to me physically. By God, I cannot get enough of that. You melt for me, softening all those hard edges you use to keep others at bay."

Eliza's tongue followed the curve of her lower lip. Her eyes had grown heavy-lidded, betraying how well she enjoyed touching him so intimately. Or perhaps it was what he'd said. Jasper reached up and cupped her breast, his thumb and forefinger surrounding the delicate peak and tugging. She made a soft noise of pleasure.

"Lie atop me," he said hoarsely.

She hesitated, looking unsure. He showed her the way, steadying her with his hands on her waist as she draped her slim body over him. Cupping her nape, he pulled her lips down to his. He kissed her with open-mouthed hunger, drinking her in with deep draws on her tongue. She kissed him back with equal fervency, her lips slanting across his, her hands clutching the counterpane on either side of him.

He groaned, feeling ravenous but wanting no more than this for now. It wasn't enough and yet it was too much, the act of kissing both erotic and sweet. The feel of her slight weight stretched across him was one he adored, and the sudden smattering of tiny kisses she pressed all over his lips made him laugh with delight.

"I'm sorry," he said again, knowing he could never give up this intimacy. He was willing to grovel to keep it. "I will make mistakes. I don't know how to do this, how to be what you deserve."

Eliza kissed him quiet. "We'll show one another how to be what the other needs," she breathed. "I want to be the one who gets inside you. The one you cannot forget . . ."

Jasper thrust his fingers into her hair and took her mouth in a long, deep kiss. He had no notion of what time it was, and he didn't care. He just knew he didn't want it to end.

Chapter 10

Eliza had never fully appreciated the restorative properties of salt baths. However, Jasper insisted she take one before leaving his home the evening before and suggested she might avail herself of one in the morning as well. Having taken his advice, she felt much better, although there was still lingering soreness in unmentionable places.

She was also starving, as she often was after strenuous activity. She ate far more at breakfast than was usual and remained at the table for some time after Melville excused himself. With the late morning sunshine slanting through the window at her back, Eliza read the paper and chose not to think about all the many things she should be thinking about. Instead she chose to dissect the waltz in her mind, remembering the way it was taught to her and improving upon that teaching method.

Jasper would be calling later for his first dance lesson. She was eager for him to become proficient so she could share a dance with him in public. A thrill moved through her at the thought of being in his arms in full view of everyone. It would be a delicious challenge to be decorous at a time when she would be so physically stimulated.

Eliza turned the page and tapped her foot to a tune playing in her head. After returning home at ten o'clock the night before, she'd stayed in. She was perfectly content to read the various renditions of last night's events in the gazettes, having previously come to the conclusion that the printed tales were often more entertaining than the reality.

"Eliza."

Glancing up, she smiled as her uncle reentered the room. "Yes, my lord?"

He rounded the long wooden table with a frown. Today was one of the few days when every piece of his attire was the way it should be, signaling a hard-won victory for his lordship's valet.

"The Earl of Westfield is here," he said, pausing beside her.

"Oh?"

"He has expressed an interest in paying his addresses to you."

Eliza blinked up at him. "Beg your pardon?"

"He wants to wed you. And speak with you. He awaits you in the parlor."

She folded the paper carefully, her thoughts rushing forward and stumbling all over themselves. With her brain arrested by confusion, her attention moved to the delicate lace runner that bisected the table. Her gaze slowly shifted to the brass candelabra that stood in the center. The antique piece was surrounded by a ring of pink roses, just as she was surrounded by sudden marriage proposals.

Melville cleared his throat and pulled her chair back from the table. "I was not aware you and Westfield were well acquainted."

Eliza stood. "I hardly know him."

"It would be an excellent match, much more advantageous than marrying Montague."

"Absolutely," she agreed, linking her arm with his and following his lead toward the door. Westfield was handsome, wealthy, and widely respected. He was also a friend of Jasper's, which made his offer decidedly more curious.

"How do you feel about this?" his lordship asked as they left the room.

"I wish I knew. Perhaps I'll have a better idea after I speak with him. How did you respond?"

"I wished him luck."

"What about me? Do you wish me luck, too?"

"I wish you happy, dear. In whatever form suits you best." He kissed her cheek. "Now, go on. Don't keep Westfield waiting."

Eliza set off on her own toward the front of the house. It was late enough in the day that the sun no longer shined directly through the glass around the front door. The familiar stillness of her home was usually comforting, but today it emphasized the disturbance created by the earl's visit. A second offer of marriage in as many days. She could hardly credit it.

As she entered the formal parlor, Eliza collected that Westfield's reason for visiting wasn't the sole cause of her unease. His physical presence was palpable. His person fairly crackled with a vibrant energy very much at odds with Jasper's quiet, intensely watchful air.

"Good morning, my lord," she said.

"Miss Martin." Westfield stood. He was as tall as Jasper, though not as broad or muscular. If pressed for a description, she would call him "elegant" and very dashing. "You look radiant."

"Thank you. I should return the compliment and say you look quite nice."

He grinned. "How are you faring this fine day? I hope you're well. You were missed about town last night."

Eliza chose to sit in the pale yellow velvet wingback facing the doorway. She lowered herself into the seat and smoothed her floral-patterned muslin skirts. The earl settled opposite her with practiced grace, a man of understated power and privilege. She decided that "polished" was a more apt descriptor than "elegant." Jasper had a sharper edge to him.

"I'm well," she answered. "I stayed in by choice, not due to any malaise. I don't enjoy the events of the Season as much as others do, I suspect."

She mentioned her sentiments deliberately, knowing Westfield would need an accomplished hostess for a wife if he hoped to achieve his political and social aims.

"Not surprising," he said, "considering what a danger they have become to you."

"Beg your pardon?"

"I'm aware of the nature of your association with Mr. Bond."

Eliza was too startled to blink. "Oh."

"Please don't hold his disclosures against him. He confided in me because he knows I am trustworthy."

"He may trust you with his own personal matters, but trusting you with mine is an avenue I wish he'd discussed with me." She wondered how much information the earl was privy to. Considering he was offering marriage, she expected he was aware of more than she was comfortable with.

"I appreciate your concern, I assure you." He paused as the tea service was brought in and placed before Eliza on the low table between them. He eyed Mrs. Potts with what appeared to be astonishment, a reaction Eliza was quite used to. The housekeeper was tall and slender as a reed, her arms seemingly too frail to support the weight of the heavy service. But she was far stronger than she looked, capable of lifting items even Melville struggled with.

After Mrs. Potts left, Westfield continued. "My intention is to help you and Bond. And myself, of course."

"By offering to resolve a temporary problem by binding

me to a permanent one?" Eliza turned her attention to the preparation of tea.

"You just called me a permanent problem," he pointed out dryly.

"Not *you*," she corrected, measuring the tea leaves. "Marriage to you. We know very little about each other, and if we were to consider what we do know, I doubt we'd find ourselves to be aligned."

"I know I'm appreciative of the way you responded to a statue nearly braining you," he argued, leaning forward. "I thought you displayed considerable fortitude and courage. You proved yourself capable of addressing any situation presented to you, Miss Martin, and that is a trait I've not previously been wise enough to consider."

Taking more time and care than necessary, Eliza balanced a strainer atop the lip of a cup. Her mind was focused on identifying how she felt about Jasper's betrayal of her confidence. She knew she shouldn't take the matter lightly—not after the examples of foolish choices her mother had made in the throes of an infatuation—but she found herself making excuses for Jasper. Attempting to find a mitigating circumstance she could accept. Surely he had good reason for sharing what happened between them the night before, if only she could think of it. It was difficult for her to decide whether she was showing good faith or poor judgment.

"I understand my desire to remain unencumbered by marriage is incomprehensible to most," she said finally. "All young women are expected to select a husband as they would a new bonnet or pelisse, because a spouse is as necessary a female accessory as outerwear. But I need no support, financial or otherwise. I have most of what I need, and I can afford to buy the rest. Frankly, my lord, while your solvency is most refreshing, I don't see what use I would have for you personally."

"No?" His mouth lifted on one side in a manner she

knew many women would find appealing. "You would be free of the suitors plaguing you, including Montague, who is becoming impatient. Bond has only your best interests at heart, but he's blinded by his own personal motivations, and now they are contributing to your dilemma. Seeing you safely wed to someone he can trust is the most responsible way to address your situation."

"I dislike talking in half-measure, my lord. I lack the talent required to translate and decipher. Since I don't believe you would offer marriage in the name of friendship, regardless of the circumstances, I should like for you to speak bluntly and honestly."

Eliza chose not to elaborate on what those circumstances might be, because she still wasn't certain how much the earl knew. If he was aware of her indiscretion and the possible ramifications, it would explain his address. But what would motivate a man in his position to step into such a situation?

Westfield waved off her offer of sugar. "I'm not being completely altruistic. You are sensible, attractive, and willing to take extraordinary measures to accomplish necessary tasks."

"I'm certainly not the only female to meet those qualifications."

"You are wealthy, intelligent, and determined," he enumerated. "You have sufficient breeding, but come unencumbered by tiresome, troublesome, or expensive siblings. You speak your mind and force me to speak mine. What more could I ask for?"

"Desire? Elevated feelings? Youth?" She could tell by the momentarily blank expression on his face that her first suggestion took him aback. However, she felt the question was warranted by his offer.

"Four and twenty is a perfectly acceptable age. As to the rest, a lifetime is a long time to commit to another individual. I'd rather not enter into such an extended association based on higher sentiments."

"That isn't why you make this offer. You see an opportunity in me, yes. But finding a suitable wife is not all you want."

Westfield straightened. Although his gaze didn't narrow, his focus did. "What else would it be?" he drawled.

It was the drawl that proved her point. "Perhaps you seek a shield or a barrier. Someone to deflect attention from you. Or an innocuous person to fill a hole you find painful."

"Can I add 'imaginative' to the list of your attributes?"

The sound of masculine voices in the foyer drew Eliza's attention to the open parlor door. A moment later, the butler appeared with a calling card borne atop a salver. A quick glance at the clock on the mantel told her it was Jasper. He was timely as usual, arriving just a few minutes early.

She nodded at the butler in a silent acknowledgment that he should show Jasper in. "Mr. Bond is here, my lord."

When Jasper appeared in the doorway, her fingers linked tightly within her lap. For such a large man, he moved with an effortless silence. His attire was notably understated, comprised of shades of gray. His Hessians were polished to a shine rivaling the luster of his gleaming hair, and he stood with a widened stance, a position that emphasized how solid he was. How well-anchored and stable.

Jasper drew to a halt just inside the threshold, looking at Westfield in a way that said he wasn't surprised to see the earl visiting. Either his men watching the house had informed him, or he'd known from Westfield. Eliza didn't know how she felt about the latter possibility.

What she did know was that their relationship was irrevocably changed. Although he was dressed from his neck to his toes, in her mind's eye she saw him as he'd been last night—flushed and disheveled, naked and vulnerable. He had been so open then, so willing to bare his thoughts and feelings, even when he didn't understand them. The knowledge of that hidden side to him created a nearly unbearable yearning. A part of her believed she "knew" him. It was not reasonable for her to feel thusly, considering how little about his life and past was known to her, but it wasn't her mind making the determination.

From the way he was looking at her, he was remembering the night before, too. But if he felt the same deep connection, why had Westfield come to call on her?

"Miss Martin." Jasper bowed, his voice lingering in the air for a delicious moment. He straightened and pivoted to face the earl. "My lord."

Westfield stood. "Bond. How fortuitous your arrival is."

"Is that so?" Jasper looked at her. "Why?"

Eliza understood from Jasper's low tone that he was in a volatile mood. She hesitated a moment before answering, unsure how to relay the events of her morning. "Lord Westfield has come to offer his assistance."

Visually, there was no change in Jasper's countenance, but his clipped response spoke volumes. "With what?"

She looked at Westfield, turning the conversation over to him.

Jasper's arms crossed.

The earl smiled. "I'm simply following through with what we discussed last night. Seeing Miss Martin wed might resolve the problems of everyone involved."

"Wed to whom?"

"To me, of course."

"Of course." Jasper shifted slightly, in the manner of a stirring beast.

Eliza, who was uncertain of what was transpiring, thought it best to keep her own counsel.

Westfield's smile began to fade as the silence stretched out.

Jasper glanced at Eliza. "Have you answered him?"

"Not yet, sir."

"Why the delay? Westfield is suitable in every way."

Stiffening against a sharp pain in her chest, Eliza lifted her chin and replied, "Perhaps I was waiting for your endorsement, Mr. Bond."

"Damned if I'll give it to you," he snapped.

She blinked.

The earl looked equally stunned. "Now, see here, Bond—"

"What is your answer, Eliza?" Jasper stared hard at her.

She looked at his hands, noting the whiteness of his knuckles as he gripped his biceps. She forced herself to look away and give Lord Westfield her full attention. Her fingers were linked so tightly, they hurt. Even lacking refinement in social graces, she knew what she was about to do was wrong in many ways, but she also knew Jasper needed to hear she wanted him as well. He required it said aloud, with a witness. As confident and aggressive as he could be when in his element, he was as lost as she was when it came to intimacy.

After a deep inhalation, she said, "As honored as I am by your address, my lord, I must decline. My feelings are engaged elsewhere."

Westfield's brows rose.

"Right, then," Jasper said, breaking his stillness. "Out you go, Westfield. I'll see you this evening. Come early. You and I have matters to discuss."

Frowning, the earl stood. "My offer will stand through the end of the Season, Miss Martin. As for you, Bond—" Westfield's face took on a hardened cast—"we do, indeed, have matters to discuss."

Eliza was vaguely aware of holding out her hand to Westfield, who lifted it to firm lips and kissed the back. She might have said something inane, he might have as well, but she was so taken aback by the intensity with which he stared at her that she missed the rest. It was a searching look, one she couldn't answer.

He left shortly after, with Jasper following him to the front door. Eliza took the brief moment of solitude to take a fortifying drink of her now tepid cup of tea.

Equanimity. She missed it. Feeling so unsettled and confused was anathema to her. This was exactly the sort of situation her mother had so often wallowed in, the sort of situation Eliza long promised herself to avoid.

"Eliza."

"What did you tell him?" Her head lifted so she could see Jasper's face, then lowered again as he sank to one knee in front of her. Her heart thudded violently. Her free hand fisted in her lap.

He urged her grip to relax by gently prying open her fingers. "The only thing Westfield knows is the reason why you hired me. I needed someone who had invitations to the events you attend, so I could gain entry."

"Of course." As he massaged her palm, the tingles that coursed up her arm weren't entirely due to a returning flow of blood. "You didn't know he intended to—"

"No."

"I thought, perhaps, it was your way of protecting me from the consequences of last night."

He took the cup from her other hand. "I'm not that selfless. Regardless, the memory belongs only to us, and I would never share it."

She swallowed hard. "Why are you kneeling in that way?"

A slow, self-deprecating smile curved his mouth. "If I'm able to secure Melville's blessing, would you have me?"

"*Jasper.*"

"Westfield is correct. It would solve many problems. I would have greater access to you, the person who wishes to harm you would have less access, we would have more time to—"

"We hardly know one another!" she protested, while a rush of warm and sweet feelings tightened her chest.

"We have honesty and desire." He brought her hands to his lips and kissed the knuckles. His eyes were dark, his words delivered with heartrending earnestness. "You have money and breeding; I work in trade, and my blood is worthless. But I would spill it for you."

Eliza sucked in a shaky breath. "What are you saying?"

"Marry me."

"I don't want to marry."

"But you want me." Jasper reached up and cupped her nape, his thumb stroking across her throbbing pulse.

"Why can't I have you without a ring?"

He snorted. "Only you would prefer to be a man's mistress instead of his wife."

"You should prefer me that way, too!"

"While other men line up to ask for your hand and claim rights to you that are mine? I think not."

"In a month, the Season will be over—"

"But our relationship will not be. You don't yet see it, but you are visibly changed by what transpired between us last night. The more I have you, the more obvious it will become, and other men will be drawn to that new awareness in you."

She absorbed his words, startled to think that the lush languidness she felt might be obvious to others. Studying Jasper, she searched for signs of change in *his* appearance.

His mouth curved. "I am down on one knee, Eliza. If that isn't a reflection of change, I have no notion what would be."

"Please do not make light of this. You don't want to marry either. You said you have no place in your life for a wife."

"I can make a place for *you*. We've both thought of matrimony in terms of how it would limit our lives, but marriage can be useful in some regards. A married woman has far more freedom than a spinster."

"How would it be useful to you?"

"It would settle me." His touch moved downward to cup her cheek. "In the last few days, I've been pulled in two directions—between work that must be done and thoughts of you. If you were mine, you would be close and protected. I could focus on the tasks at hand in the thorough manner I'm accustomed to."

She gripped his other hand tightly in her lap. "Perhaps it would be best for both of us if we went our separate ways and resumed our lives as we knew them."

"Eliza." He made a frustrated noise. "Don't ask me to come to you as Montague and Westfield did, with practical reasons and sound arguments. If pressed, I would have to say we have no business in one another's lives and we would be mad to marry."

"I know."

"But I can make you happy. We are alike in many ways, yet different enough to complement one another. You can show me how to be more circumspect; I can afford you the opportunity to be as adventuresome as you like."

An odd sort of delight bubbled within her. Like champagne, it made her slightly giddy. "I'm not nearly as confident in my ability to make you happy. Most people find me to be aloof and too quiet. I am proficient with the pianoforte, but I'm a terrible singer. I—"

He laughed and leaned forward to kiss the end of her nose. "I don't want to be entertained. I want you. Just the way you are."

"You worry about the possibility I might be with child," she argued.

"I take that very seriously, yes. But why ask for marriage now, instead of waiting to be certain?" Jasper leaned back.

"Tell me truthfully, Eliza. Is your fortune an obstacle between us? Do you think it matters to me?"

She shook her head without hesitation. When he continued to seem expectant, she spoke the negation aloud, "No."

"Good." He released her, and set both his hands on his upraised knee. "Let us make a bargain, shall we? I will secure Lord Melville's blessing, and you'll say 'yes' to me—"

"Jasper, I would swiftly bore you."

"Then," he pressed on, "the banns will be read. That will give us the time we need to find the source of your trouble, discern whether or not you are increasing, and spend some time together. If, after all of that, you still believe we don't suit and cannot be happy together, we'll break the engagement at the end of the Season. Is that reasonable enough for you?"

"It isn't easy to break an engagement."

"But it can be done."

"You claim not to be reasoned about this, yet you present me with a practical plan that affords me the opportunity to reach solid conclusions." She sighed. "I'm faced with two difficult choices: Make a decision now with too little information, or progress further than I ever intended in order to gather the information I believe we both need."

"If only you were impulsive," he teased. "I might have been able to convince you to elope with me and spare you all the rumination."

"How can you be so confident about this?" she complained. "Why can I not have some of that surety?"

"I make my decisions here"—he tapped his abdomen—"and they are usually instantaneous. You make your decisions here"—he tapped her temple with his index finger—"and that takes more time. I'm trying to give you that time, Eliza, while staving off my own impatience. An engagement is the compromise we reach."

Worrying her lower lip, Eliza struggled to find the courage to say what she shouldn't.

"Talk to me," he urged.

"I cannot decide if it's desire goading me to agree against my better sense, and I'm also concerned that as the novelty of bedding me becomes less engaging you will want me less and less, until eventually you no longer want me at all. After we are bound to one another, it will be too late to realize we had only lust, which was quickly sated."

His nostrils flared. "If the possibility of waning interest concerns you, I can prove I desire you for more than sex. I won't ask you to give yourself to me again until we are wed, but I'm available to you whenever and wherever you want me. Chivalry and mores are no restraints to me. I learned long ago never to spite myself; the only person who loses is me. You should know of that aspect of my character, I suppose, before you wed me."

To be wanted so keenly . . . Eliza finally understood why her mother had been addicted to the feeling. It was so very tempting. And Jasper was irresistible.

To have him whenever she wanted. The thought of commanding sex from him, at any time and in any place, was impossibly arousing.

"Eliza," he murmured, drawing her focus back to him. "Give yourself permission to take what you want, for once. You might enjoy it more than you think."

That was partially what she was afraid of. But her fear wasn't a strong enough deterrent to mitigate her memories of the night before and the lingering happiness she'd felt upon waking.

"Speak to Melville," she said. "Then, ask me again."

Chapter 11

"I would never have expected this of you," Westfield said, rocking back on his heels.

"That makes two of us," Jasper said dryly.

The Valmont ballroom was larger than many, but the broad expanse and thirty-foot ceilings did little to ease the crush of guests. Worse than the crowd was Jasper's realization that he was an object of curiosity. Having spent the entirety of his life avoiding notice whenever possible, he found it decidedly uncomfortable to be the center of attention. But the news of the notoriously reticent Miss Eliza Martin's betrothal to a man few people had ever heard of was apparently the most interesting item of discussion. His appearance was being examined by nearly everyone, as if the reason he'd won her could be determined visually.

Mindful of Eliza's pride, he had dressed with care. While he'd elected to wear black to minimize his size, his coat and breeches were flawlessly tailored. The materials used were exceptional, as were the diamond in his cravat pin and the sapphire in the ring on his right hand. The result was understated yet expensive elegance, which he hoped mitigated any speculation that he wanted Eliza for her fortune.

"You are completely inappropriate for her," the earl went on.

"Agreed."

Jasper looked for Eliza and found her. She appeared composed, if slightly irritated. The frown marring her brow betrayed both her peevishness and bemusement. He smiled, appreciating her artless honesty.

"She would be better served with me," Westfield said. "How can any woman live the life you do, Bond?"

"I expect Miss Martin and I will discover the answer as time progresses."

Westfield stepped forward, then turned to face him, effectively taking up the entirety of his view. "Is there anything you will *not* do in your quest to ruin Montague?"

"This has nothing to do with Montague."

"Of course it does."

"On the periphery," Jasper conceded, sidestepping to resume his viewing of Eliza.

"Wait." The earl moved in front of him again. "Were you talking about her last night? That nonsense about wanting something badly?"

"Yes." He wanted her now. Eliza had worn another of her mother's gowns, this one in a lovely rose hue. It was as simple in cut as the sapphire gown she'd worn days ago, but the bodice was provocatively low and the waist perfectly snug. The slender beauty of her figure was a joy to behold.

"Bloody hell." Westfield looked over his shoulder at Eliza. "Do you love her?"

"I enjoy her, and I can make her happy."

"I doubt you can. Not for the long term. And how does enjoyment signify? I enjoy half a dozen women any given fortnight, yet you don't see me proposing to any of them."

"Therein lies the difference between us," Jasper drawled. "There are very few things I've enjoyed in my life, and none to the degree with which I enjoy Miss Martin's company."

"Now, you have me intrigued," Westfield complained. "I'll forever be wondering what I missed about Miss Martin."

"No, you will not. You'll forget about her in any other capacity than as my wife, and that will be the end of it."

"Hmm . . ." Westfield turned around, searching. "I have yet to see Montague. I should like to know how he's taking the news of your engagement."

Jasper didn't care what Montague thought.

The moment the realization hit, his spine straightened and his breath hissed out between his teeth. Shifting his position, he canted his body away from Eliza, his hands flexing at his sides. Soon, he would be able to put Montague behind him, but not now. Not yet. The earl had still to pay for his sins and the sins of his father.

Eliza. She made him forget himself, which was one of the reasons why he needed her. But she couldn't serve that purpose now. Not yet. His plan was in the final stages after years of frustrated waiting and endless hours of work.

"Mr. Bond."

Turning his head, Jasper watched as Sir Richard Tolliver approached. Although Jasper had believed Tolliver couldn't be any thinner, it appeared he was tonight. His dark coat hung loosely on his shoulders and his modestly embroidered waistcoat gaped a little just above the top button. "Good evening, Sir Richard."

"I hear congratulations are in order," Tolliver said, looking far from congratulatory.

"They are. Thank you."

"How fortuitous that Miss Martin should decide to marry so soon after you returned to her life. Almost as if she were waiting for you these last few years."

"Poetic," Westfield drawled. "Perhaps if you'd shared your talent for romantic thought and turns of phrase with Miss Martin, you might have had more luck with her."

"What talent did *you* share?" Tolliver shot back, glaring at Jasper.

"Be very careful when maligning me," Jasper warned softly. "Should you inadvertently cast aspersions on Miss Martin's character, I assure you, I won't take it well."

Tolliver's foot tapped against the floor. "Your long familial friendship with the Tremaines makes it decidedly odd that Miss Martin can share little about you."

"Cannot? Or will not?" Jasper challenged. "She understands the value of privacy. It's one of the many qualities she and I have in common. Now, cease being a nuisance. Go find a new heiress to woo."

Tolliver remained in place for a long moment. Finally, he spoke between clenched teeth, "Good evening, Mr. Bond. And to you as well, my lord." He turned about and stalked away.

"You're making friends already," Westfield said, staring after Tolliver. "I have to say, I never guessed he had such forcefulness in him. Perhaps his feelings for Miss Martin were true after all."

"Nothing so sublime." Jasper rolled his shoulders back. This was what he'd wanted—to attract the attention of whoever was endangering Eliza. But he hadn't anticipated the feeling of jealousy. Tolliver had roused his proprietary instincts and his discomfort was certain to worsen as time progressed.

The sound of Montague's name being bandied around them drew Jasper's attention toward the farthest entrance. "He came," he murmured. "I'd begun to doubt he would."

"Look at this place." Westfield gestured with a jerk of his chin. "Lady Valmont hasn't enjoyed a gathering of this size in many years. The curious come en masse to see Miss Martin's transformation and the man responsible for it. She changed her appearance for you, did she not?"

"She did it for the investigation. At first." Jasper gave himself permission to look at her again. He was torn between his two goals—winning Eliza's hand and staying focused on his vengeance. "Tonight, I think she did it for me."

"So she was being truthful when she said she had feelings for you?" Westfield snorted. "What in God's name does she see in you?"

"I wish I knew. I would show her more of it."

Montague's progress through the room was marked by a noticeable ripple in the throng. He was heading toward Eliza, who stood on the opposite side of the room.

Jasper started in that direction. Westfield fell in line. They worked their way through the crowd, their path repeatedly blocked by one inquisitive well-wisher after another.

"Is your marriage a sign that Montague's destruction is now assured?" the earl asked.

"Not yet. I have learned he's forming a pool of investors for a coal mine speculation." Jasper grabbed a glass of lemonade from the tray of a passing footman.

"Is that what shored up his confidence about his finances and prompted him to contact me about retrieving his marker?"

"I hope to know the answer tomorrow. Either he's falling deeper into ruin or digging himself out of it."

Westfield grabbed his elbow and pulled him to a halt. "Bond."

Jasper's brows rose in silent inquiry.

"Have you considered embracing your new life with Miss Martin and leaving Montague's future to fate? In my experience, deserving fellows have a way of finding their own sorry end."

"*I* am Montague's end," Jasper said, before tossing back the contents of his glass. He started forward again, lamenting the beverage's inability to make the scrutiny directed his way more tolerable.

* * *

"I am so happy for you." Lady Collingsworth beamed like a proud parent. Dripping in sapphires and adorned with white plumes in her hair, she carried herself with the sort of regal confidence that supported such accessories instead of depended upon them.

"Thank you." Eliza ran a hand over her unsettled stomach.

"I admire you for following your heart," Regina went on. "I know how difficult the decision to marry was for you."

"I've tried to understand why it is so hard for me and not for so many others. Certainly I am not privy to information other women do not have."

"Of course you are. Only you lived with your mother."

Eliza's eyes widened. It was the closest the countess had ever come to speaking harshly about Georgina.

"Why do you look so surprised, dear? I'm aware of how you feel about your mother and her choices. She wed two different men because she cared for them, and neither marriage ended well. The fact that her second husband was a fortune hunter sealed your opinion of matrimony. I understand the preconceptions you had to overcome before accepting Mr. Bond's proposal." Regina looked past Eliza, focusing on something or someone behind her. "I can only hope that the indecent way he looks at you had a hand in your capitulation. I do believe his regard elevates the temperature in the room."

"Regina!" Eliza resisted the urge to glance at Jasper, knowing if she did, she would become flushed and distracted. All evening long, he'd been staring at her as if she was naked.

"Stuff," the countess retorted. "What happens in the privacy of the marital bed is of equal importance to what happens outside of it. A marriage cannot thrive if there is disharmony in the bedroom."

"Can it survive if pleasure is all there is?"

"My dear girl, pleasure is what is lacking in most marriages. Don't take it for granted."

"It seems so frivolous a reason," Eliza muttered.

"You are too smart to make frivolous decisions. I'm certain if you made a list of Mr. Bond's good and bad points, you would find the good far outweighs the bad."

No longer able to resist looking at Jasper, Eliza turned her head to find him. En route, her attention was caught by a familiar tall figure. The Earl of Montague was cutting through the crowd, his handsome face lit with a charming grin. Although he was frequently held back by those who wished to greet him, it was obvious he was on a direct path to her.

"Montague seems to be in good spirits," Regina noted. "It was good of you to tell him directly about your engagement to Mr. Bond."

"Leaving the matter to Melville would have been too distant and insincere." Eliza offered a smile to Regina that was filled with heartfelt gratitude. "I wouldn't have had the courage to meet with him without you. Thank you for accompanying me."

"Accompanying you where?"

Eliza was warmed by the sound of Jasper's voice behind her. The occupants of the room receded, her awareness of the noise fading into insignificance. She faced him. "To the park this afternoon."

"For a meeting with Montague?"

"Yes. To tell him about our engagement."

A shadow passed over Jasper's features. "You should not have done that."

She stiffened at his tone, unaccustomed to being gainsaid. "It was the least he deserved."

"You have no notion of what he deserves."

"Bond." Westfield's low, warning tone stole Eliza's attention. She looked at the earl, who stood just beyond Jasper's left shoulder. Like Montague, Westfield cut a dashing figure, and when he looked at her, his eyes were kind.

Two peers. Both were attractive, solicitous, and willing to marry her. Yet she had chosen the wild commoner of indeterminate origins. A man she could never hope to tame. She felt a frisson of disquiet over her decision.

Jasper's jaw tensed, as if he sensed her sudden confusion. The affection that had been in his eyes when they'd first reunited this evening was far less evident now. To her, the distance between them seemed almost tangible.

Regina cleared her throat. "Perhaps you might accompany me to the drinks table, Lord Westfield. My throat is dry."

"Of course." The earl shot a meaningful glance at Jasper, before leading Lady Collingsworth away.

Jasper stepped closer to Eliza. "How can I protect you when you deliberately put yourself in danger?"

"What danger? I met with Lord Montague in public, with Lady Collingsworth in attendance. Your men were certainly somewhere nearby. Or were they not? Is that why your mood is so foul?"

"You hired me to investigate your suitors. Then you meet with one privately to tell him he's losing any chance of laying claim to your money, putting him in a desperate position!"

"What could he have done?"

"Abscond with you. Hold you for ransom. Anything."

"Montague?" she scoffed. "A man of his station would not—"

"You don't know him, Eliza, or what he is capable of."

"And you do?"

"Stay away from him."

Her brow rose. "Is that an order?"

Jasper's jaw clenched. "Don't turn this into a battle of wills."

"You are attempting to limit my freedom. It's unreasonable to expect me not to fight for it."

He caught her by the elbows and tugged her scandalously close, as if they were alone and not surrounded on all sides by prying eyes. "I am attempting to keep you safe."

"Your advice is duly noted." Eliza knew she was goading his temper, but his clipped responses made her wonder if she wasn't giving him precisely what he wanted. He seemed to be spoiling for a fight.

"You must heed me." His eyes were so dark, they were nearly black.

"Your concern is unfounded. I foresee no occasion where Lord Montague and I would have cause to meet again outside of social settings."

"Cause or not, I want you to keep your distance." He released her. "From Tolliver, as well."

Irritation swelled within her. "Tell me why."

"Tolliver is not taking the news of our engagement well."

"And Montague? He smiled when I told him and wished me happy."

"He cares for no one's happiness but his own."

"And I'm just to take your word for this, with no explanation provided?"

"Yes."

"Already exerting your husbandly right to control me in whatever manner you see fit?" Her grip on her fan tightened to the point that the wood creaked in protest.

"I will not allow you to turn a discussion about your safety into an argument about independence and the drawbacks of matrimony."

"Won't allow. I see. Is this acceptance and rejection of acquaintances reciprocal? Can I forbid you to meet with Lord Westfield?"

"You are deliberately baiting me."

"I am simply attempting to discern where the boundaries are, and if they apply equally to both of us."

"Westfield is no danger to anyone."

"Maybe I know something you do not," she challenged. "Of course, if I follow your example, I don't have to share what I know with you."

She looked away to hide the prickling of tears and saw Lord Montague approaching. Her shoulders went back.

"Miss Martin." Montague kissed the back of the hand she extended to him, then released her with a stately dip of his head. He looked at Jasper. "Mr. Bond. May I extend felicitations to you?"

Jasper's lips curved in a teeth-baring smile. "You may, my lord. I accept them with pleasure."

Eliza knew the rigidness of her posture betrayed the oppositional nature of her conversation with Jasper, but she was too frustrated to care overmuch.

"Is it too much to hope, Miss Martin," the earl said, "that you might still have room on your dance card for me?"

"The next waltz is yours."

A tic in Jasper's jaw filled her with acrimonious satisfaction.

She'd deliberately withheld the evening's two waltzes. Not for Montague, but as a token gesture for Jasper. She had intended for her next waltz to be with him, even though it would take weeks for him to learn the steps and absorb them into memory.

"It appears I, too, am fortunate," Montague said. "Although not to the same degree as you, Mr. Bond."

"So it seems." Jasper's features were set in hard lines.

The orchestra played a few brief notes to alert the guests that the next dance would soon begin. Eliza gratefully excused herself and searched for her partner, Baron Brimley. As she moved away from the terrible tension emanating from

Jasper, her breathing became easier. Reason returned to her, swiftly followed by regret. She disliked that they'd quarreled. Worse, she disliked herself.

Jasper watched Eliza walk away with undue haste and berated himself for sparking their first argument. He *knew* he had to tread lightly with her or risk her thrusting issues of money and independence between them, but he'd been discomfited into acting rashly. The surprise of learning that she'd met with Montague drove him to be harsh and unyielding, yet his ignorance was his own fault. Lynd had called upon him unexpectedly, and Jasper made the mistake of delaying the daily reports in order to accommodate his old mentor.

How could he have been so careless? He lived by rigid schedules and timetables for a reason—they kept things running smoothly and without startling incidents. Compounding his error by expelling the anger that should rightly have been self-directed only made the situation worse. He'd now caused a rift between him and Eliza that he could ill-afford.

"You have Byron's brooding countenance mimicked to perfection," Montague said. "I didn't try that tactic when attempting to woo Miss Martin."

Jasper's head turned slowly, his expression altering to reveal no emotion whatsoever. He and his half-brother were nearly of a height. The similarities between them were numerous enough that Jasper shifted slightly to put more distance between them. "I cannot say I'm sorry you lost her to me."

Montague smiled and rocked back on his heels, blissfully oblivious to the resemblance between them and the reason for it. "You are somewhat of a mystery, Mr. Bond."

"Ask me what you want to know. Perhaps I'll answer you."

"How do you feel about coal?"

A ripple of satisfaction moved through Jasper. Could acquiring the information he needed be so easy? "It's a necessity. Life would be miserable without it."

"My thoughts exactly." The earl's smile turned into a grin. "I have a speculation you might find interesting."

Jasper pushed Eliza from his mind and managed a smile. "You have the entirety of my attention, my lord."

By the time the Earl of Montague collected Eliza for their waltz, her ire had vanished. Still, she was completely out of sorts. For the first time, she understood that she'd lived her life without conflict after her mother passed on. No one disagreed with her because there were no points of contention; she was not obliged to explain herself nor meld her viewpoint with anyone else's. The result of her unchallenged independence was that she was sorely unprepared for arguments. Her entire body responded negatively to discord. She had a headache, and her stomach was upset, even though she was no longer angry.

"I've never seen you look lovelier, Miss Martin," Montague murmured, as he set his hand at her waist.

"Thank you." She stared at his cravat, noting its elaborate style and thick starching.

Montague had dressed flamboyantly in peacock blue velvet and a multi-colored waistcoat. His attire was far removed from Jasper's more somber style, and yet the earl's height and physical coloring were uncannily accurate substitutes for Jasper. The similarity caused Eliza to focus on how the earl made allowances for her shorter stature when an upraised arm position dictated it. He was a highly accomplished dancer, leading her expertly through the steps. She took mental notes for use in Jasper's dancing lessons, grateful the preoccupation afforded her some respite from her emotional turmoil.

"You have aroused my curiosity," he said.

"In what regard?"

"Your matchmaking skills."

Eliza frowned. "I didn't say I possessed any. Only that I could find someone more suitable for you than I."

"Suggestions?" His dark eyes were laughing.

"I believe any unmarried woman in attendance tonight would fit that criterion."

"For shame," he cried, laughing, and thereby turning heads toward them. "To foster hope, only to dash it with a cruel jest."

"Fustian. You could have anyone."

"Except for you."

It took her a moment to realize he was teasing her. "How about Audora Winfield?" she offered.

"Her laugh drives me to madness."

"Jane Rothschild?"

"I frighten her. She stammers and turns red. The best we've managed were short stretches of time at a house party where I spoke incessantly to fill the void and she nodded vigorously to everything I said."

"Poor thing. Perhaps more time spent with her will alleviate her nervousness?"

"Too torturous for both of us, I think. Certainly too much work."

"Lady Sarah Tanner?"

He shook his head.

"What fault does she have?" Eliza asked.

Montague hesitated a moment, then said, "She is . . . overbold."

"Oh. I see." She found herself at a loss. There were others, she was sure, but she couldn't name them offhand. "Perhaps you would be best served by waiting for a new Season and new debutantes?"

"As recently as yesterday, I would have said I could not afford to wait that long."

"And today?"

"Today, I have renewed hope that I can buy the time necessary to find a suitable replacement for you. I believe I have found a solid investment with a high probability of return. Mr. Bond might join me in the pool. We have plans to discuss it further tomorrow."

"Do you?"

Why would Jasper consider investing with Montague when he claimed not to trust the earl and knew him to be insolvent? It was unreasonable. And that wasn't her only concern. What was Jasper's experience with investments? Did he know what he was involving himself in?

In the morning, she would ask Reynolds to look into Montague's speculation and assess its potential. Then, she'd approach Jasper directly and ask him to explain. If he refused to answer, she would give him an ultimatum—share with her or lose her.

They could progress no further as a couple with so much unsaid between them.

Chapter 12

"I'm sorry."

Eliza turned away from the French doors leading to the rear garden and faced Jasper. He entered the Melville ballroom with a determined, forceful stride. There were over one hundred feet of marble floor between them, but she felt his presence keenly.

"Close the door," she said.

He drew to a halt. The massive room was dimly lit, with only the indirect morning sunlight at her back offering any illumination. She heard him take a deep breath before turning around and returning to the door.

As the click of the latch echoed through the room, she asked, "Did you sleep well?"

"No." Jasper resumed the long walk to where she stood, passing the many mural vignettes without looking. "But then, I've never slept well. There is too much to be done and not enough time in the day."

"I didn't sleep well either." She absorbed the rush of sensation she always felt upon first sight of him. Interspersed between the Georgian-era vignettes of a picnic party were long, slender mirrors framed by cream-colored molding.

The result was many Jaspers filling the room. Her reaction was equally magnified.

"I apologize for last night," he said again, reaching for her and pulling her into his arms. Lowering his head, he sealed his mouth over hers.

There was nothing remorseful about his kiss. It was hot, fierce, and lustful. Jasper's tongue teased her lips open, then licked inside. The taste of him exploded across her senses, awakening a powerful need to possess him.

Eliza caught him to her with fevered desperation. Her arms encircled his shoulders, her fingers pushed into his silky hair and cupped his nape. Her breasts swelled against his chest, the lingering soreness between her legs forgotten in a rush of slick moisture. She wanted to bare his skin, rub her open mouth across it, caress him with her hands and un-inhibited undulations of her body.

He groaned and twisted his mouth away.

"Jasper . . . ?"

"I handled myself poorly." He rested his temple against hers. "I know you won't tolerate being dictated to."

She no longer wanted to talk, but knew they must. Sexual passion could not be all they had. "H-how do you know that?"

"Because I pay attention to you." He set her away from him. "And I'm a good judge of character."

"You have me at a disadvantage. I know nothing about you beyond your livelihood and your wish to marry me."

"You know how I look without my clothes on. And how I feel inside you."

She wanted him inside her now. Ached for the feeling of fullness and delicious friction. The incendiary rush of climax and the repletion that followed.

Eliza linked her hands behind her back and circled him, her green skirts swaying around her legs. "That isn't enough for me in quiet, contemplative moments. I think of you and how I act when I'm around you, and I do not recognize myself. You are the catalyst for the changes in me, yet you're an enigma. Can you understand how difficult it is for me to experience such upheaval with no foundation upon which to lay it?"

He turned his head to keep their gazes connected. "I know it appears as if I haven't altered as much or sacrificed as much as you have."

"You aren't the only one sorry about their behavior last night. I said and did things I regretted almost the moment they happened. I was irritated with you and reacted unthinkingly."

"Relationships are fraught with such behavior. It's perfectly normal."

"It will not be normal for us, or I want nothing to do with it."

His stance widened. "What are you saying?"

Slowing in front of him, she eyed him from head to toe. He was dressed for riding in snug doeskin breeches and polished Hessians. The powerful muscles of his thighs and calves were clearly delineated. He crossed his arms, as if in preparation for a confrontation, and his flexing biceps strained the seams of his dark gray coat.

He was the most attractive, sexually alluring man she'd ever crossed paths with.

"I cannot hide how I want you," she said huskily. "I want to be in your bed even now, despite the fact that it's the middle of the morning. I want you so badly I burn with it."

"Eliza."

"See how you've changed me, that I can say such things aloud? But desire alone won't be enough impetus to wed you. I could insist on an affair instead." She rounded him again. "I agreed to your proposal because you've been honest with me. Although you haven't revealed much of your-self, what you have shared up to this point has been truth-ful."

Jasper caught her arm as she came around. "I'm different with you, as well. I am learning to adjust. You will, too."

"Not unless you become more than a stranger to me. You once said your past and future are irrelevant. But since then, you've asked me to blend your future with mine. To create a joint future. *Our* future. In order for that to happen, you have to show me the road upon which you travel. I cannot be led along blindly. If you won't commit to sharing, then we are finished before we begin."

"The future is shaped by the past." His throat worked on a hard swallow. "My past will alter your view of me. The risk of you turning away from what I am is too great."

Eliza cupped his cheek. With every inhale, she smelled the beloved scent of his skin. "What kind of life would we have together, if we continue to do and say things to each other we lament? It's the worst sort of dishonesty. I've seen it be-fore, and I know it ends in sorrow and misery. I don't want that for you, or for me. I do not want that for *us*."

He caught her hand and kissed her palm. "You speak of your parents."

"There was so much left unsaid between them. Their in-fatuation brought them together, but it wasn't strong enough to bear the weight of their façades. They quarreled often and said unkind things. Eventually, apologies were no longer enough to mend the rift between them. How could they be, when they continued to repeat the mistakes they apologized for?" Her fingertips drifted across his firm lips. "If only they'd been honest about themselves and what they needed. Per-haps they could have made each other happy."

"The moment you walked away from me last night, I re-gretted my brusqueness. I considered climbing through your bedroom window just to reassure myself that you would still receive me."

"Would you have revealed the truth to me then?"

Jasper offered a rueful smile. "I doubt it. Surely, the convenience of finding you in bed would have distracted me."

"How swiftly you tell the truth when it's not tied to your past."

He urged her closer and pressed a kiss to her forehead. Then, he walked away and spoke over his shoulder. "Pull the pins from your hair. I'll speak for as long as it takes you to let it down completely."

"What game is this?"

"I intend to learn how to dance with you. We cannot have every lesson delayed by interruptions, despite how pressing they might be. We need a way to measure the time spent."

"Your pocket watch will not suffice?"

"That isn't nearly as fun."

Reaching up with both hands, she obliged. Slowly. Pulling out one pin and carefully lowering her arm to drop it on the floor.

He gave an approving nod, then began to follow the length of the wall. "There are some individuals who lack empathy for others. They are unable to create or sustain emotional connections, and their vision of the world is limited to their own viewpoints."

"My stepfather was such a person. Chilcott was entirely self-absorbed."

Jasper's voice rose to compensate for the growing distance between them. "In addition to that defect of character, Montague is also cursed with aberrant sexual appetites."

Eliza paused in the act of withdrawing another pin. "How do you know this?"

"I have crossed paths with women who've had the misfortune of catching his eye. He prefers unwilling partners and the infliction of pain. My understanding is he cannot perform otherwise."

"Unwilling . . ." Her stomach turned at the thought of being forced to share the intimacies of sexual congress with someone who was cruel and malicious. "How does one acquire such deviant tastes?"

"Through the blood, perhaps? Or a defect of the soul." He shrugged. "Who knows?"

Her hands fell to her sides. She walked toward him with her hair loosened and threatening to fall around her shoulders. "Why didn't you tell me this earlier? How could you keep such things from me?"

"When could I have told you?"

"Don't be coy!"

He altered direction to meet her halfway, his booted steps more silent than her slippered ones. "I would give up a great many things to spare you such sordidness. I knew you were decided against marriage, which made the possibility of your ever learning of Lord Montague's activities very slim indeed."

"I would not have met with him yesterday if I'd known!" As she reached him, her hands went to her hips. "And you and I would not have quarreled."

"I also feared what would happen if he discovered you knew of his darker nature. Your face is so expressive. You will not be able to hide your condemnation, and he's a desperate man. His good name is all he has left. He cannot afford to have it sullied by gossip."

Although she didn't approve of his methods, she hadn't the heart to argue about his reasoning. He wanted to protect her in every respect. "Do you think he's the one who has been plaguing me?"

"I wouldn't put it past him." Jasper beckoned her closer with a crook of his finger. "He is teetering on the verge of utter ruination. He's gambled away or sold every non-entailed property, and he does not have the means to support the holdings he has left. His debts are such that he's being denied credit. Soon, he will have nowhere to turn."

"And yet you're considering investing with him?" Eliza stepped into his open arms. "What are you thinking?"

He set his chin atop her head. "I want him ruined. I cannot allow him to find a means of salvation. If feigning interest is required to glean the information I need to thwart him, it's a small price to pay."

His tone was so vitriolic, it didn't sound like Jasper at all. Eliza leaned back to study his features. "Why?"

"Retribution for a . . . friend."

Jealousy stung her. "A lover?"

"No." His hands stroked the length of her spine. "Before you there was sex. You have been my only lover."

Her fingers straightened his already immaculate cravat. "Will I always be?"

"Are you asking if I'll be steadfast? Of course."

"You answer so easily."

His beautiful mouth curved with amusement. "As if I practiced my response for just such a question? And here I thought we'd established I have yet to tell you a falsehood."

Eliza looked up at him from beneath her lashes. "I find the thought of another woman enjoying you as I have to be extremely vexing."

"Vexing," he repeated, grinning.

"Intolerable," she amended.

"We certainly cannot have you vexed. Therefore, I must be faithful."

Unsatisfied by his response, she goaded him. "I shall follow your lead in this aspect of our association, as I have in everything else."

"Why, Miss Martin," he drawled. "I do believe that was a threat."

Her gaze dropped to where her fingers lay against white linen. "Only if you stray."

He laughed. Picking her up, he spun her around.

"Jasper!" Wide-eyed, she looked into his face. Something in his expression flushed her skin.

"You delight me." His voice was slightly husky.

"You confound me. And charm me."

"And arouse you."

"Too easily." She ran her hands through his hair, unable to resist its thick silky texture.

"I want you even when we're not together. Can you say the same?"

"Yes, in the moments when I'm not questioning myself for jumping into a situation with my eyes closed."

Jasper set her down and touched her falling hair with reverent fingers. "Your mind wants to make sense of what you feel. I've forsaken any effort to understand it, but you will not. It's one of the many things I admire about you. Just promise me that when you have doubts or concerns, you'll come to me as you did today. Tell me what you need, and I will find a way to give it to you."

Eliza believed him. He made her feel as if she was important to him. Necessary. She'd never been necessary to anyone before. It was a novel feeling, one she was still attempting to assimilate.

"What I need," she began, catching his hand in hers and setting her left hand on his shoulder, "is for you to learn how to waltz. I want to dance with you."

He positioned his hand at her waist. "From the very first, you listed dancing as a requirement in your suitors."

"I'll enjoy dancing with you best of all." Eliza smiled. "You have that air of danger about you, and a very seductive way of moving. The inherent sensuality of the waltz was made for a man such as you."

His smile made her pulse race. "I want to commission a

new gown for you to wear during our first public waltz. Will you wear it?"

Pleased by the thought of a gift, she nodded. It had been a long time since someone who cared for her bought her a present. Melville rarely knew what day of the week it was; special occasions were beyond him.

"I cannot wait," he purred, his spine straightening beautifully. "Teach me quickly."

"It will be my pleasure." Her tone changed, became more clipped and direct. "There are nine positions in the German waltz. However, we must start with a rule: this precise distance between us should always be maintained."

"You're too far away," he complained, shooting a pointed glance down at the floor between them.

"Stuff. The waltz is the only dance in which pairs are set apart from the assemblage and focused on each other. There is no way to be more intimate."

"Without a bed."

Eliza bit back an indulgent smile. Certainly she shouldn't encourage his roguish tendencies, but she adored them. He was unlike any man she knew—wicked in all the best ways.

"Pay attention," she said sternly. "Your feet should be turned outward when stepping"—she demonstrated—"and the lift of your leg should be pronounced."

Although he continued to make provocative statements, Eliza remained focused. She walked him carefully through the steps. At first, he seemed almost afraid to move. When she pointed it out, he groused, "Damned if I'll trample you."

But he soon learned to appreciate her responsiveness. He became more confident and sure-footed. The steps became more natural, his arm movements accomplished with more flourish. She praised him when his form was perfect, and teased him when it wasn't.

As time passed and they continued their exertions, his scent of spice and bergamot filled the air between them. The advance and retreat of the steps became foreplay to her. The twisting movements limbered her, while the too-brief moments of proximity began to titillate her senses. His powerful shoulder flexed beneath her hand, reminding her of how delicious he was when naked and passionate and aroused. Her breathing quickened.

Jasper watched her with an enigmatic smile. "I like this."

"The dance?"

"The way you follow my lead. The feel of your body moving in just the way I want, with only the slightest urging."

"You like being in control."

Jasper paused mid cross step. Their faces were turned toward one another, their lips only inches apart. "And you like me in control."

"Perhaps"—she lowered her gaze to his lips—"being out of control is my aim."

His hand tightened on her waist. "Are you propositioning me, Miss Martin?"

"What would you do if I did?"

"Anything you want."

He sidestepped, so that their bodies were aligned. Face-to-face. Jasper was such a large, strong man. She felt so delicate when she was with him, yet never overpowered.

"You know what I want," she whispered, blushing.

"A kiss?" He gently pulled another pin from her hair. "An embrace?"

"More."

"How much more?"

She bit her lower lip.

Jasper caught her chin. "Shyness has no place between us."

"I don't want to be . . . overbold."

"Sweetheart." His tone was soft and warm. "Can you still be unaware of how I relish your esteem and desire?

Haven't I told you how deeply they please me and how much satisfaction I derive from them?"

"As if I'm the only woman to admire you," Eliza said wryly.

"You're the only woman whose admiration has value to me."

"Why? There's nothing special about me. Whatever pleasing traits I possess are better represented in other females."

"Not in the combination with which you are blessed." His hand drifted from her jawline and closed around her breast. He studied her reaction as his thumb circled a highly sensitive nipple. "I love that you are beautiful and clever and carry a constant desire for me. You could not be more perfect."

Her body responded instantly to his expert touch—her nipples tightened into aching points and the flesh between her legs throbbed with need.

"Tell me what you want," he coaxed, anchoring her with a hand at her hip. With two fingers, he rolled and tugged the erect point of her breast, the pressure too light to offer any relief.

She felt pliable and wanton. Intoxicated. They'd been alone for an hour, only inches apart; his body had been in motion the entire time. Watching him move was a seduction in and of itself. She couldn't keep herself from wanting him. Her infatuation was far too great to be moderated.

"I want you naked," she breathed.

A soft rumbling came from his chest, sounding suspiciously like a purr. "Why?"

Her hands moved of their own volition, catching the lapels of his coat. "Take this off."

His wicked smile made her toes curl. He shrugged out of the expensive garment and let it fall to the floor. "Better?"

"Not nearly." She caressed his arms through his shirtsleeves. Looking behind him at the mirror on the opposite wall, she drank in the view of his buttocks and thighs. The sight, smell, and feel of him were all aphrodisiacs to her.

He glanced over his shoulder. "You surprise me in all the best ways. Should I hang a mirror above our bed?"

"Jasper . . ." A shiver of mortified delight moved through her. "I would never be able to look."

"I think you won't be able to look away. Shall we prove it?"

Eliza stilled. "Here?"

"Would Melville disturb us?"

She shook her head. "How . . . ?"

Her mind rushed forward, planning how they could manage a coupling without a bed.

"Your nipples are so pretty," he murmured, drawing her attention to her bodice. She was shamelessly, visibly aroused. "So tiny and petite."

He stayed her when she moved to cover herself. "Unfair for you to hide when I cannot."

She followed the gesturing sweep of his hand and found the bold outline of his erection straining the placket of his breeches. A soft sound of yearning escaped her. She wished for nothing more than to be naked with him, his powerful body flexing and working atop hers, his long thick penis pushing deep into her. Despite her lingering soreness, the lure of orgasm was too potent to be denied.

He stroked himself brazenly through the doeskin. "You cannot have this again so soon."

"Why not?" she demanded, her gnawing desire making her audacious.

"You're sore, and I'm not in possession of a condom."

Knowing he was vulnerable to her, she closed the distance between them. With one hand at his nape and the other gripping his buttock possessively, she rubbed against him like a cat.

Jasper's chest vibrated with a chuckle, stimulating her already tender nipples. "Vixen," he murmured, bending his knees and notching his erection against her swollen sex. He worked her against him, stroking where she ached with the stone-hard length of him.

"Yes," she panted, her nails digging into his skin. "I want this."

His lips moved against the shell of her ear. "You can't have it, I told you. But I can make you come. Would you like that, Eliza?"

"Please." She felt feverish.

"Are you wet for me?"

"Jasper!"

"Show me." He backed away. "Lift your skirts and bare yourself."

Despite the extremity of her desire, Eliza was still mortified by the request. It was one thing to be in his arms and lost to his skill. It was quite another to stand alone and lewdly display herself. "I cannot."

His eyes were so very dark. "I promise to reward your courage."

She fought against years of training and memories of her mother's promiscuity to blossom as he wished her to do. She'd always believed intimacy was built through time and familiarity. Now she knew it could also be based simply on trust.

She clutched her skirts in her hands. "I suppose you've seen countless pantalettes before."

The corner of Jasper's mouth twitched. "Countless? How debauched do you think I am?"

"Enough to ask me to do this."

"True enough," he conceded with a regal bow of his dark head. "But I did not *ask*."

She might have taken him to task for his arrogance, if her brain hadn't leaped in another direction. *So rare is this par-*

ticular skill that many a woman will disregard other consid-erations in favor of it, he'd said the day they had first met. And she'd laid claim to a man who possessed such expertise and wanted to practice it on her. How foolish was she to deny herself?

Before she altered her mind, Eliza yanked up her narrow skirts.

The way he looked at her caused the hairs on her nape to stand on end. "How brave you are," he praised.

Emboldened by his admiration, she untied the ribbon that secured her pantalettes around her waist. The lace-hemmed linen fell to the floor and pooled around her ankles.

"Sweet Eliza," he murmured, his foot deliberately catching on his discarded coat and sliding it across the floor to a spot directly in front of her. "You are more generous than I deserve."

He sank to his knees.

As he stared at the dark red curls between her legs, Eliza became so aroused she could no longer stand still. She swayed slightly, and he caught her hip with one hand. With the other, he caught the waistband of her pantalettes and silently urged her to step out of them.

He kept her legs wide by gripping her ankle and keeping it in place. The hand at her hip moved between her legs, parting her and stroking gently through the slickness of her desire.

"I believe you were made for me," he said huskily, rubbing her flesh with a callused finger. "Look how wet you are."

Her hips rolled into his teasing caresses. "Jasper . . ."

Leaning forward, his breath ruffled her damp curls. She tensed in anticipation.

He licked his lips and purred, "Let's see how wet you can get."

Chapter 13

Eliza watched as Jasper leaned forward and licked lightly across the quivering flesh exposed by the spread of his fingers. The sensation was exquisite torment. Her thighs shook with the strain of yearning for orgasm. The sight of him on his knees, servicing her with such tenderness, was too stimulating to bear. He was so beautiful. So big and strong. So confident and self-possessed. To see him subjugating himself to her desire filled her with a sense of feminine power she'd never known.

And Jasper had introduced her to that power. Shown her it existed. Reveled in her wielding of it. She cherished him for that gift and his confidence in giving it to her.

Cupping the back of his head, she held her breath in anticipation.

"Open to me," he said softly, tapping the top of his shoulder.

It took the space of a heartbeat to comprehend what he wanted. He held out his hand to help her balance and she carefully, hesitantly lifted one leg. As the back of her knee settled over his shoulder, the thrill of dominance increased. Heat raced across her skin. The lush weight of her breasts strained her bodice. The illicitness of what they were doing only added to her excitement. Her entire body felt ripe with erotic promise, fluid and languid, restless and alluring.

Jasper tilted his head back to look up at her. His expression—lust laced with fondness and admiration—tightened her chest. "You've discovered your ability to enslave a man. And you like it."

She ran her fingers through his hair, grateful she had the right to do so. "With you, I seem to like everything."

He caressed her thigh with a firm, yet gentle grip. With a turn of his head, he pressed a kiss to the skin above the tie of her stocking. His tongue flickered, so swift and fleeting she wondered if she imagined it.

"Don't tease me," she pleaded. "I am already overwrought."

"Patience is a virtue."

"Do I look virtuous to you?" she cried, so frustrated by desire she had to look away.

It was then that the mirror behind him snared her attention. Her breath caught sharply at the reflected view—her leg slung dominantly over Jasper's broad shoulder, her toes pointed from the delicious expectation, her hands cupping his head and urging him toward the eager flesh between her thighs.

"Are you watching?" he asked with a dark note of devilish provocation.

"Yes . . ." Eliza stared, unblinking, as his head canted to the side and he leaned into her. A second later, his mouth was on her, his firm lips surrounding her clitoris in a heated embrace. The flat of his tongue rubbed across the distended knot of nerves, and she cried out as tiny spasms rippled through her.

Jasper pulled back, licking his lips. "One day soon, I will spread you across my bed and feast on you for hours, just to hear the sounds you make when I pleasure you."

His words created a vision in her mind that inspired a heated rush of moisture. He hummed with approval and leaned forward, his hands cupping her buttocks and holding her still. The restraint he'd shown so far disappeared in a voracious assault of lips and tongue that destroyed any remaining rational thought.

Driven to wildness by his ardor, Eliza held his head and rocked into his working mouth. In the mirror, her reflection was both aggressive and wanton, her calf flexing against his back, urging him on. She was red-faced and gasping, her eyes glassy and her hair in disarray. She looked ravished and debased and more sensual than she ever thought she could be.

She looked like a woman who might enslave a man like Jasper Bond.

He hefted her higher with effortless strength, forcing her to balance on the tips of her toes. His tongue pushed into her and she moaned, pleasure sizzling across oversensitive nerve endings. Stabbing fierce and fast, Jasper breached the clenching tissues and drank the flow of silky liquid that welcomed a deeper, thicker penetration.

All the while the mirror starkly displayed her frantic writhing. She ground her throbbing flesh against Jasper's mouth, riding his thrusts in a mindless quest for orgasm. His tongue withdrew, and he caught her clitoris in a hot, wet kiss. With suction and the pointed tip of his tongue, he set off a climax so intense her vision blackened. Sobbing in the grip of violent shudders, Eliza hunched over him, attempting to pull away from his fervent suckling but unable to escape him. As the gripping ecstasy eased, the circle of his lips tightened, hurtling her headlong into another furious release.

Her nails dug into his shoulders. Tears burned her eyes and sweat bloomed from her skin in a humid mist. As she listed and began to fall, Jasper shrugged out from under her leg and caught her to him, tumbling backward so she sprawled across him.

She clung to him weakly, breathing his name.

"Shh," he soothed, his hands stroking her trembling back. "I have you."

He did. Completely.

Jasper stared up at the murals of circling olive branches surrounding each of the three massive chandeliers in the Melville ballroom. He knew time was rushing by while he lay on hard marble with Eliza draped bonelessly atop him. However, he didn't care about the time or the discomfort of his position. There was nowhere else he would rather be. Aside from a bed, perhaps . . .

"Jasper?" Eliza's normally clipped voice was passion-hoarse. He enjoyed the sound so much, he was prompted to press a quick hard kiss to her forehead.

"Um?" His fingers played with the disheveled strands of her tumbling hair.

Her head lifted and she looked at him. "How can you imbue so much smugness into one little sound?"

"Should I not be smug? You just melted in my mouth."

Gaze narrowed, she rose to a kneeling position beside him and set her hands on her knees. Her expressive face took on a look of examination and calculation. When her focus settled on his groin, his subsiding cockstand swelled to renewed life. He almost held his breath, wondering how far she would go.

"I cannot allow you to leave with that," she pronounced.

He grinned, adoring her. "Oh? But it is attached, I'm afraid. Fortunately, we are to be married, and you'll soon have more frequent access to it."

She gave his shoulder a push. "Not the penis itself. The erection, you vexing man."

"Ah . . . I always have one when I part ways with you."

Her blue eyes widened. "You do not!"

"I do. Not to this extent, but to some degree."

Eliza appeared to consider this information carefully. "Have you always been so randy?"

"Not prior to meeting you. My natural appetite for sex was previously sated by twice-weekly visits to Remington's." He rubbed a strand of her hair between his thumb and fore-finger, remembering the flaming tresses spilling across his pillows.

"Courtesans?" One of her hands lifted to rest on his abdomen. "Have you never had a woman who was special to you? One to whom you were attached enough to see more than once?"

"There are some who are . . . easier to pass the time with. They eschew conversation and work diligently. If they're available, I will choose one of them over the others. But attachment? No."

"Sex without affection? That sounds very lonely to me."

"I don't know what loneliness is." It was not in his nature to discuss feelings and such. Jasper shifted uncomfortably, but answered directly. The more he revealed, the less hesitant Eliza became. That result was worth any discomfort. "There are goals to be met and work to be done. There is no time in my day to wish for things I don't have. Except for you."

"I will never understand why you like me so well." The tiny dimple he'd first noted on the day they'd met winked at him. "But I won't complain about my good fortune."

Enamored with that dimple, he grabbed her hand and tugged her toward him. "Kiss me."

"You like kissing. Not that I'm complaining. You are very accomplished."

"I never liked the act prior to meeting you. Now, I cannot

get enough. Sometimes the urge to kiss you is so fierce I have a damnable time resisting it."

Her eyes widened. "Truly? I cannot fathom your disregard. I love your lips. And your kisses."

"I never considered my mouth a particularly erotic part of my anatomy. There are other places on my body I preferred directing attention to."

"Can I kiss you somewhere else?" A blush swept upward, over her chest to her cheeks. "Here, perhaps."

Her hand moved lower and stroked him through his breeches.

"Bloody hell," he hissed, unprepared for his impossibly swift reaction to her boldness.

"Too much?" she whispered, withdrawing.

"No." He caught her retreating hand and put it back, mentally kicking himself for startling her away from an act he wanted as much as his next breath. The level of trust she was displaying—from speaking freely to indulging his lustful whims—humbled him. He'd done nothing in his life to deserve her.

"Have your wicked way with me," he urged. "I beg you."

Eliza raked him with a heated glance, from head to toe. He felt that gaze like a tangible caress. "Teach me how to please you. Show me the way to be the only woman you will ever need or want."

Jasper yanked the placket of his breeches open and pushed his smalls out of the way. His cock sprang free of its confinement, straining toward his navel in a display of brute male arrogance.

"My God," she breathed. "Every part of you is magnificent."

The awed note in her voice sent relief rushing through him, swiftly followed by rampant desire. He watched as she reached for him, her slim white hands enclosing his scorching length in cool satin skin. His neck arched, his teeth gritting together in a bid for control. A few pumps of his hand and he could finish this. He was primed to blow after Eliza's earlier display of total abandon. Her scent clung to his lips, filling his nostrils with every drawn breath, spurring his lust to previously unattained heights.

Her fingertips slid delicately up and down his cock, exploring. Jasper exhaled in a rush. His bollocks were drawn up tight, his seed churning and pushing its way up his shaft to leak out the tip.

Eliza touched the first drop, then lifted her finger toward her mouth.

"You might not like it," he warned. "Some women do not."

Her brow arched defiantly. Her mouth formed an O, and she pushed the glistening fingertip inside. She hummed softly, and that was his undoing.

"Put your mouth on me," he said gruffly. "Wrap your lips around the head."

She bent over him without hesitation. Her hair—still partially pinned—drifted over her shoulders, with some freed pieces falling to pool on his stomach. He reached up with one hand and pushed her hair out of the way of his view.

He watched her lips part, her head lower, his cock disappear inside her . . . Her mouth fastened on the plush head, and he groaned raggedly. The drenching heat and gentle suction were torturous.

"That's good," he gasped. "Take more."

Her lips slid farther down, pushing his cockhead deeper into the narrowing channel of her mouth.

"Suck. Ah . . . yes, like that." Sweat dotted his brow and upper lip. "God . . . your tongue . . ."

A moan vibrated along the length of his shaft.

Any worry he'd had that she would find the act distasteful vanished with that sound. Her hand pushed into his breeches and cupped his testicles. Her avid tongue rubbed the underside of his cock. Her head bobbed up and down his length, her mouth sucking so forcefully it was audible. The wet smacking echoed through the massive room, then rippled through him in a wracking shudder.

As frenzied as she'd been in her own extremis, she was similarly ravenous for his. Eliza worked his cock as if starved for the taste of him. The sight of her fervor, the feel of her hands and mouth, the sounds she made . . . it was all so erotic he lost himself to her.

"You make me so hard," he growled. "Desist. Let me finish this."

In response, she took him as deep as she could, her tongue pinning him to the curved roof of her mouth. She sucked him so vigorously his thighs shook with the pleasure.

"Christ." His hips lunged upward. The first furious spurt of semen felt as if it was wrenched from his spine.

Eliza swallowed deeply and worked her hand on him, pumping his seed up the length of his shaft and into her eager mouth. Groaning and sweating, Jasper clenched his jaw shut and fucked his cock through her swollen lips, spewing his lust in an orgasm so intense it was painful. The rush of climax was endless, his cum spilling over her stroking tongue in thick, creamy washes. She took every wrenching pulse with unmitigated greed, urging him on with muffled moans.

Jasper collapsed to the floor with arms outstretched, muscles twitching from his calves to his shoulders, his lungs fighting for every serrated breath. His cock began to soften, as exhausted as he was, but she didn't cease her ministrations. The tip of her tongue dipped into the tiny hole at the crown, drinking the last bit of semen he had left. He closed his eyes, drunk on the repletion sinking into the very marrow of his bones.

"Come here," he murmured, needing to hold her.

As she curled against his side on the marble and entwined

her legs with his, Jasper didn't recognize the feeling gripping his chest in a vise.

It was hours later when he realized the sensation might have been joy.

"Good morning, Miss Martin."

Eliza welcomed the distraction provided by the arrival of her man of affairs shortly after eleven o'clock two days later. Jasper had sent a note, excusing himself from their scheduled morning meeting, and while it expressed regret, the missive gave no explanation for why he'd canceled. The last time they spoke at length was during yesterday's dance lesson in the ballroom—a space she would never think of in the same way again.

"Good morning, Mr. Reynolds," she replied briskly, closing her ledger and smiling.

He stared at her, blinking, as if taken aback, which brought to her attention how readily she smiled of late.

Clearing his throat, he took a seat in front of her desk. She was pleased to see he'd procured a new satchel. Unlike his previous one, this one was made of butter-soft burgundy leather ornamented with gold hardware. He was a wonderful employee, one who worked hard and performed well, and she paid him accordingly. It was good to see him indulging himself.

"I understand congratulations are in order," he said.

"Yes. Thank you." Eliza linked her fingers on the desktop. "How is Mrs. Reynolds?"

"Very well."

He told a story about his wife's social pursuits that Eliza made every effort to appear interested in. She was grateful when he moved on and said, "I've also received word from my brother."

"Oh?" A quiver moved through her tummy. Jasper's agreement to be more forthcoming about his situation put her in an awkward position. She'd grown more and more apprehensive about sending Tobias Reynolds to Ireland. Although she had engaged Tobias before beginning an intimate relationship with Jasper, she was nevertheless circumventing the man she intended to marry by researching his past without his knowledge or consent.

Reynolds settled more comfortably into the chair. "He arrived safely and has begun the initial inquiries."

She reminded herself to trust her instincts. "I would like to recall him. I have the information I need."

"If you're certain . . ."

"I am. He'll still be paid the agreed-upon fee for his time, of course."

"I never doubted it." His fingers curled and uncurled around the wooden arms of his chair. "May I speak freely, Miss Martin?"

"Always," she assured. "I value honesty above all else. I'd expect you would know that by now."

"I do. However . . ." He inhaled deeply, then exhaled in a rush of words. "Have I been remiss in my duties or disappointing in some way? Have I given you cause to distrust me?"

"No." Her spine straightened with alarm. "Why would you have such concerns?"

"You've always asked me to investigate your suitors. Therefore, I was startled to learn of your engagement to a gentleman whose circumstances I was not asked to explore. I know he is a friend of Lord Melville, but he's also a possible investor and even in that capacity, you did not ask me to verify his solvency."

Eliza was impressed. "Your thoroughness is laudable, sir."

"I'm relieved to hear you say so." He leaned forward. "I had only yesterday and this morning to inquire, but I must confess, what little I've gleaned has made me uneasy."

"Uneasy?" Certainly Terrance Reynolds wasn't the only enterprising and curious individual in town. What could be learned about Jasper through cursory inquiry?

"His residence is in a less-than-fashionable area of town. He has all manner of disreputable-looking individuals coming and going as they please. I'm not yet certain, but I believe he engages in trade. I suspect he makes a comfortable living, but it's doubtful he has your means."

"Few do. Regardless, Mr. Bond counts the Earl of Westfield as a close acquaintance."

"There is that," Reynolds conceded. "Frankly, your betrothed is a bit of an enigma."

Much obliged by his loyalty, Eliza felt it best to offer a truthful explanation for Jasper, so Reynolds would no longer be troubled. "Mr. Bond is a thief-taker."

"A thief-taker!" There was a pause, during which he blinked rapidly. Finally, he said, "Not one of the better-known ones."

"No, of course not. It would have been impossible for Mr. Bond to assume the guise of a viable suitor if he was a familiar personage. I found him through a referral."

"Found . . . ? You *sought* a thief-taker? I don't understand."

"Do you recall when Mrs. Peachtree experienced monetary troubles earlier this year?" she asked, referring to a tenant who'd suspected one of her employees of pilfering from the till. "You reported that she hired a Runner. When my situation arose, I approached her for his name and engaged the same man. However, Mr. Bell was unable to assist me. He referred me to Thomas Lynd, who suggested Mr. Bond would be more suitable."

"Dear God." Reynolds flushed. "You've done so much without my assistance . . . I cannot help feeling superfluous."

"Quite the opposite. You're an excellent man of affairs,

sir, and valuable to me. Therefore, I was unwilling to endanger you. You see, I have recently found myself to be prone to accidents of a disturbing and suspicious nature."

"Accidents!" He paled. "What . . . ? Why . . . ? Damnation! *Who* would have reason to harm you?"

"That's what I hired Mr. Bond to discover."

"I wish you'd seen fit to include me. Tobias and I could have overseen a thief-taker or Runner on your behalf. You could have avoided the ruse of an engagement to Mr. Bond."

"It isn't a ruse." She lamented the shadow of confusion that swept over his features. "My relationship with Mr. Bond is twofold."

Reynolds began to shift uncomfortably in his seat. He looked pained.

"If you have something to say, sir," she prompted. "Please feel free. I respect your opinions and viewpoints as they relate to my business matters."

He cleared his throat again. "I find the novelty of the series of events leading to the hiring of Mr. Bond to be . . . dubious. The circle begins when you're subjected to incidences causing you to fear for your safety. Then, you hire a thief-taker. The result of which leads to the thief-taker successfully wooing you into accepting his proposal of marriage, despite his lack of suitability. I cannot help wondering if the end ties back to the beginning in a manner more closely related than surface appearances indicate."

"You're wondering whether it's possible Mr. Bond is the source of my problem, as well as the solution to it? No, do not look chagrined! It is a fascinating hypothesis. I'm embarrassed I didn't think of it myself." She leaned back in her chair and allowed her mind to toy with the idea. "Mr. Bond would indeed be quite clever if he arranged to create circumstances necessitating his hiring, then used his employment to gain access to wooing me. However, considering my former aversion to marriage, I cannot see how anyone would imagine such machinations would be successful."

"Your financial means and familial circumstances would certainly make the effort worthwhile. What would Mr. Bond have to lose? At the very least, he would be paid to solve a mystery of his own making, ensuring a satisfying conclusion for you and a financial reward for him."

Eliza smiled. "I'm congratulating myself for hiring such a creative thinker for my man of affairs."

Reynolds looked embarrassed. "You have always been so circumspect, especially about your suitors. Please allow me to continue investigating Mr. Bond. I'll accept no fee for my services. Putting your mind at ease is the very least I can do."

"I am not uneasy, Mr. Reynolds. Trust is of equal value to me as honesty. I've extended mine to Mr. Bond without reservation, and I have no wish to erode that foundation with needless doubts."

He nodded. "As you wish."

"Thank you, Mr. Reynolds. However, I do have something for you to look into. The Earl of Montague is creating an investment pool. I should like to know what speculation has garnered his interest and how you assess its viability."

"Are you interested in joining the pool?"

"Not at this time. Lord Montague approached Mr. Bond about it, and I'm concerned as to whether or not the investment is sound."

Reynolds withdrew his weekly report from his satchel and stood. "I'll begin my inquiries straightaway."

Eliza accepted the papers with a brisk nod. "Godspeed, sir."

He gave a slight bow. "To you as well, Miss Martin."

For the hour following Terrance Reynolds's departure, Eliza worked diligently on a list of garments and items she would need for her trousseau. Her desire to replace her entire wardrobe with gowns of brighter hues and more provocative lines was just another sign of how much she'd changed since meeting Jasper. It was not an alteration of character she took lightly.

After contemplating the matter thoroughly, she understood that Jasper wasn't the entirety of the reason why she was able to abandon long-held attitudes and beliefs. Her own ability to trust him enabled her transformation. She'd watched her mother falter through one relationship after another, spiraling deeper into melancholia with every failed romance. Whatever it was Georgina had been seeking in a partner, she'd been unable to find it. Eliza now suspected a lack of trust and honesty was to blame. All this time, she'd thought avoidance of romantic entanglements was the solution. In truth, the answer was simply to find a partner whom she could trust. Now she had only to cultivate her bond with Jasper through transparency and forthrightness.

A soft rapping on her open study door drew Eliza's attention from the papers on her desk. Robbins stood on the threshold with the post in hand.

"Excuse me, miss."

The butler entered and set the salver on the edge of her desk. "Will you be taking tea here, or with his lordship?"

"With Melville, thank you."

Eliza stared at the unusually large pile of letters in front of her. She shifted through them, separating Melville's correspondence from her own. The majority of her post was invitations, far more than she was accustomed to receiving. Confused by the sudden influx, she collected Melville's missives and stood. She went to her uncle's study and discovered him absent, then moved on to the conservatory. There she found him watering the plants he experimented with. The afternoon sunlight poured in through the many windows, warming the enclosed space and creating a noticeable humidity.

"Good afternoon, my lord," she said upon entering.

Melville presented his cheek to her, and she pressed a kiss to it. "Eliza," he said breathlessly. "Remember the splicing I shared with you? Look how it's thriving!"

Eliza examined the two disparate plants, now connected at the stem. It made her think of her relationship with Jasper. "Beautiful. I can see why you're so pleased."

"Normally these plants grow best in a tropical climate, so I am doubly pleased by the success." He beamed with pride, then noted the letters she carried. His smile faded, and he held out his hand with a sigh.

She handed the post to him. "Are you making any progress with responding to those who write to you?"

His wince was answer enough.

She shook her head. "Do you never miss the company of others, my lord?"

"I have all I need right here." He set the mail atop potting soil scattered on the table.

"Perhaps others need *you*. Clearly they continue to extend their friendship to you, even though you don't reply."

Melville's well-being was a growing concern to her. What would happen to him when they no longer shared a roof? She was his sole human connection to the world at large. Would he soon become completely estranged from Society, reliant upon the gazettes for news? It broke her heart to think of it.

He returned his attention to watering his plants. "Were you not determined to live a solitary life until a short time ago? Content with quiet walks, good books, and uninterrupted time with your ledgers?"

"I have you."

"For how long? Eventually, I will move on to my reward."

Eliza drew swirls in the soil with her fingertip. "The time you speak of is still far away."

Melville glanced at her, but blessedly did not continue to speak of his demise. Instead he said, "Regardless, I am relieved to see you out of your mother's shadow. It does my old heart good to know you've found someone with whom to share your life."

"My mother's shadow," she repeated softly. "Have I moved out of it? I resemble her, and I've chosen a man similar to my father. Perhaps I have assumed her shadow and made it my own?"

"You have her beauty," Melville agreed. "But also a steadfastness she lacked. Your footing is solid. Georgina's was often unsteady."

"You mean to say she was irresponsible."

"I mean to say she was unstable. She could not maintain an even keel. She listed from one side to the other." He flicked a small bug off a plant leaf. "Georgina is the reason I acquired an interest in horticulture. My hope was to find some combination of herbal elements to tame the mercurial quality of her moods."

Eliza remembered those fluctuations all too well. Georgina would be giddy with happiness one week, then unable to rise from bed the next. "You think her ailment was physical? I have always believed she simply had poor judgment."

"I was willing to consider any possibility. I would've searched the world for the key to her happiness, just as I would do for you."

"Mr. Bond makes me happy. The only worry I have now is for you."

He reached over and patted the back of her hand. "I'll be well, so long as you are."

Turning her hand over, she squeezed his. "Shall we retire to your study for tea?"

"Is it time already?" As if cued, Melville's stomach grumbled with hunger. He set the watering pot down and dusted off his hands. Then, he proffered his forearm to her.

"Don't forget the mail I brought you."

He groaned, but gathered up the post. "You are certainly stubborn like your mother."

They exited the conservatory and strolled the distance to his study in companionable silence. When they stepped into his private domain, Eliza took in the space where her uncle spent the majority of his day and knew she would miss these moments with him. For all his idiosyncrasies and foibles, she loved him dearly. She wondered how much time she might have to visit with him once she lived with Jasper. When Melville retreated to the country, would he be alone for months at a time? Now that she thought of it, she suspected Jasper spent all of the year in London due to his trade.

Melville set the latest post atop the leaning pile of mail in the basket by the door. Unable to bear the additional weight, the mass shifted to the side and dozens of letters tumbled to the floor. "Bloody nuisance," he muttered, squatting to pick up the wayward missives.

Eliza joined him, raking letters toward her with widespread fingers.

"How odd," he said to himself.

"What's odd?" she queried.

"This seal."

She focused on the black wax seal gracing the letter he held out to her. "It looks to be a sword crossing over . . . something."

"An hourglass."

"Interesting. To whom does that seal belong?"

"I've no notion. But there is another one . . ." He dug

into the pile at his feet and withdrew a second letter bearing the same image in black wax. "See here."

He opened the letter, dropping the others to the floor in the process. As he read, he frowned. Then, he grew very pale.

"What is it?" she asked, alarmed.

"It appears to be a threat of violence"—Melville held the letter out to her—"against you."

Chapter 14

Standing, Jasper set both palms flat on Eliza's desk and surveyed the five open letters spread out before him. They were obviously all penned by the same female hand. The delicate swirls and flowing script were clearly the handiwork of a woman.

He glanced up at Melville and Eliza, both of whom sat in chairs facing him. "Are there more?"

"Those were all we could find," Eliza said, looking remarkably composed.

"Do you have any notion of when the first of these arrived? Or the last?"

She shook her head.

Jasper's fingertips drummed on the desktop. "This changes everything."

"Yes," she murmured. "It certainly does."

Each missive warned Melville to retire with Eliza to the country or she would pay the consequences, completely contradicting Eliza's original assumption that she was being pushed toward matrimony.

He looked at the earl. "Would you, perchance, be able to assist with the procurement of a Special License?"

Eliza jolted visibly. "Beg your pardon?"

"Special License?" the earl asked, frowning and scratching his head. "Who's getting married?"

"I will take that as a 'no.' " Jasper was certain Melville's hair was even more of a fright today than it had been the previous times he'd seen it. "Perhaps Westfield can be useful in that regard."

"Jasper." Eliza no longer looked placid. "What are you about?"

Straightening, he set his hands on his hips. "It appears there's a woman out there who perceives you to be a threat. It's likely she has an interest in one of your suitors."

"An unhealthy interest."

"One can only hope that it's Montague who has enamored her to the point of violence."

She shot him an arch look.

His smile was unapologetic. "Regardless, taking you out of competition could likely remove you from danger straightaway."

"Perhaps the news of my engagement will suffice, if we give it a chance to spread?"

"I would rest easier if you and I resided under the same roof." In truth, he doubted he would rest at all if they shared a bed, but that was a topic for another discussion.

Melville nodded. "Quite right. I've proven to be unsuitable for the task of protecting you."

Eliza's gaze dropped to her lap.

"Eliza." Jasper made every effort to keep his voice modulated. "I should like to hear your thoughts on the matter."

She took a deep breath. "I'm not prepared to leave Melville at this time."

"Is he your only concern?"

Her head lifted. "Am I overlooking something else?"

"No." He relaxed. "I could take up residence here with you until the end of the Season. As your husband."

The softness that stole into her eyes when she looked at

him was worth far more than the concession deserved, but he wouldn't complain about that.

"Would you?"

"I will do whatever you need."

"Thank you." Her smile lit up the room.

A surge of adrenaline pushed through him. Eliza would be his within the week. "Make whatever arrangements you need, but please avoid leaving the house whenever possible."

She nodded.

"I will see to my end of things." He cast one last glance at the letters laid out before him. Fury resurfaced with biting swiftness. He would find the author of the threats and ensure that the culprit never posed a hazard to Eliza again.

Marriage would not be the end of his hunt.

Jasper urged his horse away from Lambeth Palace. He cast a final look at the brick gatehouse and Lollard's Tower, then set his hand lightly over the Special License tucked into his coat's inner pocket.

Drawing abreast of him, Westfield said, "You have yet to tell me precisely what the letters said. Since their contents incited our mad rush to the archbishop, you have to know I'm overset with curiosity."

"The missives were brief. A few lines each, almost in rhyme, with the same admonishment to retire from the city. Two made indirect references to sidesaddles and the Serpentine, both of which relate to accidents Miss Martin experienced."

"Nothing about the falling statue at the Royal Academy? Perhaps it *was* an accident."

"Perhaps. I'm at a disadvantage in many respects. I don't know if the letters arrived before the events, which might suggest violence was not the culprit's first choice. Or if the letters arrived after the fact and served as taunts."

"Written by a woman, you say?" Westfield whistled. "There is some sense in that. A man who wished to prevent her from marrying could simply compromise Miss Martin."

"I doubt she would have conceded, despite the damage to her reputation. She has an aversion to being managed and a limited appreciation for Society's mores."

"Truly?" The earl tugged the brim of his hat down as a shield against the late afternoon sun. "The more I learn of her, the more I like. Who would have thought a spinster's sixth Season would cultivate such drama and intrigue?"

"Which begs the question: why now? Melville's correspondence has been accumulating for years. His housekeeper was able to present a small trunk of past letters, and there were no threats prior to this Season."

"I assume you won't be abandoning your work in favor of a honeymoon?"

The mention of a honeymoon was all it took to fill Jasper's mind with lascivious thoughts. "If only I were so fortunate."

"You are extremely fortunate."

Jasper's brows rose. "Oh?"

"You knew precisely what you wanted, and made certain you attained it."

Directing his gaze forward, Jasper pondered the somber note in the earl's normally droll tone. "Is all well with you, my lord?"

"Of course. Nothing is ever wrong in my world, Bond. There are no surprises. No challenges. Equanimity rules the day."

"There is something to be said for that."

"Yes, it's boring."

Laughing, Jasper urged his mount into a canter, leaving the Thames behind. There was a great deal to be done before he could end the day. "You are welcome to stay in my world for a while longer, if you prefer. Never a dull moment."

"Wait until you're married," Westfield drawled.

Jasper entered his house to the sound of raucous laughter floating out of the downstairs parlor. Behind him, Westfield barely stepped onto the marble floor of the visitor's foyer when Herbert Crouch caught sight of them.

Herbert, who'd been leaning against the parlor doorjamb as if awaiting them, pulled his hands out of his pants' pockets and straightened. He was one of Jasper's most seasoned employees; old enough that his two grown sons also worked for Jasper. He lumbered over with a broad grin that peeked out from the frame of a bushy, unkempt beard.

The Crouches were an odd-looking lot as a whole. Herbert was of a height with Jasper, but considerably broader. Many of his progeny were near giants; the top of their sire's head barely reached their shoulders.

Herbert mussed his wheat-colored hair with a meaty hand, disrupting the perfectly molded shape of his hat's interior. "I 'ave news that might be interesting."

Gesturing toward his study, Jasper passed his hat and gloves to his butler, but kept his coat on. The Special License in his pocket wasn't something he was willing to allow out of his immediate reach.

He settled behind his desk. Westfield moved over to the console to help himself to the Armagnac. Herbert sank heavily onto one of the settees.

With libation in hand, Westfield faced the center of the room and leaned back against the console with his hip. He crossed his legs at the ankle and enjoyed a deep swallow of brandy. "How fare you, Crouch?"

Jasper studied him. The earl seemed to be imbibing more of late. If he continued along the same vein, Jasper intended to bring the matter up for discussion. It was not a subject he looked forward to broaching, but the health of his friend warranted his concern.

"As well as can be expected, mi'lord." Herbert didn't smile, which was unusual for him. Jasper knew the commoner was ill-at-ease conversing socially with an earl.

"How are Mrs. Crouch and your brood?"

"All are well. The missus is increasin' again."

"Again? Dear God." Westfield took another drink. "How many children do you have now?"

"Eighteen. Until the birthin'."

"You are a stronger man than I, Crouch."

Herbert gave an awkward pull on his beard and looked at Jasper almost pleadingly.

Jasper took pity on the man and said, "Before you begin, it is important to know we're now looking for a woman."

"I knew it!" Herbert slapped his knee.

"Of course you did." Jasper was more than satisfied with the strengths of his crew. Herbert in particular had an instinct for hunting, becoming quite dogged when he sensed something was amiss. "What did you uncover?"

"I still 'ave a few more questions of my own to answer 'bout some o' the renters, but there's one I'm fair certain isn't what she says she is."

"Who?"

"Vanessa Pennington. Aaron and I 'ave asked around, but we can't find any proof of a Mr. Pennington. No ring on 'er finger, no papers or letters, no portraits—"

"Perhaps she keeps such sentimental items in a private place," Westfield suggested.

"I checked," Herbert said.

"How—?" Westfield paused. "Forget I asked."

Jasper's mouth curved. "Her residence is above the store, yes?"

Herbert nodded. "Aside from the agreement to rent the

space from Miss Martin, I couldn't find anything with the name 'Pennington' on it. But I did find several receipts and such addressed to 'Vanessa Chilcott.' "

"Chilcott." Jasper leaned back heavily into his chair. "Bloody hell."

"A ne'er-do-well clan of thieves and miscreants." Westfield straightened and took the seat opposite Herbert. "Perhaps their past success with Lady Georgina has made them bold in regards to the Tremaine family."

"How is Vanessa Chilcott related to Miss Martin's stepfather?" Jasper asked.

Herbert lifted one sturdy shoulder in a shrug. "Aside from praising her face and figure, the other shopkeepers in the area 'ad little to say 'bout her. She keeps to 'erself."

Westfield snorted. "I've been told the Chilcotts are all remarkably good looking. Which is not enough to make *me* foolish, but clearly the same cannot be said of everyone, or the family wouldn't be so successful in their subterfuges."

Jasper averted his gaze. Eliza was too intelligent to miss seeing the parallels between her relationship with him and her mother's with Chilcott. She had to overlook prejudicial experiences in order to extend her trust to him, which made her credence all the more valuable. He would have to tread carefully or risk losing something priceless.

"I want Miss Chilcott watched at all hours until further notice," he told Herbert. "I want to know whom she speaks to, where she goes, and what hours she keeps. And I need to know how she's related to Miss Martin."

"I'll see to it." Herbert pushed heavily to his feet.

Jasper watched the man depart, then looked at Westfield. "I visited the Pennington store with Miss Martin, and she had no notion the proprietress was anything more than a stranger. Miss Chilcott, however, appeared to be greatly interested in Miss Martin."

"That's to be expected." The earl made a careless gesture

with his hand. "She is residing and conducting business in space owned by Miss Martin."

"Miss Chilcott should not be aware of that fact. Miss Martin takes great pains to remain anonymous, conducting most transactions through her man of affairs. She believes it eases the way for everyone involved if her gender remains unknown." Jasper rapped his knuckles against the desk in frustration. "Damnation. If I'd retained the sales receipt from my purchase, I could have compared Vanessa Chilcott's penmanship to that of the letters Melville received."

"I still don't understand why Miss Chilcott would want to prevent Miss Martin from marrying. Pettiness?"

"There is an obligation created with their business relationship that doesn't exist otherwise," Jasper reasoned, "a legal agreement between two parties with responsibilities and ramifications on both sides. As a former step-relation, whatever grievance Miss Chilcott may have against Miss Martin clearly has no weight or she would have pursued it legally. Without legal basis, there's no possibility of restitution. But as a tenant, if she was to create a circumstance in which Miss Martin was seen as liable for damages or loss of income, Miss Chilcott could possibly negotiate a financial settlement."

"I see. Miss Martin is accountable as a landlord in ways she isn't as a relation-by-marriage. Exploiting their business association for monetary gain wouldn't be too far outside the realm of possibility, considering the Chilcott family's larcenous reputation."

"My thoughts exactly. It would also explain why Miss Chilcott hid her true identity."

"But would an assumed guise withstand further scrutiny in a court of law?" Westfield queried.

"Assuming I'm correct, I doubt she intends her plan to go that far. If she was able to gain leverage of some sort against

Miss Martin, I believe the result would be a quiet exchange of funds in order to maintain the business anonymity Miss Martin prizes. However, if Miss Martin had a spouse, *he* would have greater license to mount a public defense, because he would have no reason to hide."

"Extortion is a nasty business. Best not to have anything requiring concealment."

Jasper's foot tapped restlessly. "I'm due to retrieve the balance of my purchases from Miss Chilcott's store—customized items requiring preparation time."

Westfield set his glass on the low table with a dull thud and rose gracefully to his feet. "I'm coming with you, of course. I should like to see what happens next."

"Let us hope you see the end of Miss Martin's troubles." Jasper pulled out his pocket watch and checked the time. He cursed.

"Running behind again, are you?" There was laughter in the earl's voice. "Tardiness is becoming a habit with you. Here I thought you would corrupt Miss Martin's finer points, but perhaps the opposite is true."

Jasper might have been chagrined if not for the fact that the swifter time passed, the sooner Eliza would be his wife. "Step lively, Westfield."

But haste didn't help him achieve his aim. Although they arrived at Miss Chilcott's shop within posted business hours, the proprietress was not in evidence.

"Shoddy way to run a new business," Westfield muttered, tilting his head back to eye the pink-striped awning.

"Only if you mean to make a success of it. By your accounts, the Chilcotts aren't ones to work for their keep."

Jasper waited for Peter Crouch to return from checking the rear exterior staircase leading to the domicile on the second floor. When the young man appeared, he was shaking his head.

"Damn and blast," Jasper muttered. "I cannot wait for Miss Chilcott to return. I'm to meet Montague at Remington's in an hour to discuss his idiotic mining speculation."

Westfield looked at him. "Despite an imminent wedding and the nefarious Miss Chilcott, you still won't allow Montague to meet his own fate? You know as well as I he's destined to destroy himself."

"He and his family owe me far better than that. I want his destruction to come by *my* hand, and I will not rest until I've seen the deed through to the last."

The earl sighed and turned away from the building. "I'll accompany you to Remington's, then part ways with you for the evening. With the announcement of Miss Martin's engagement to you, you won't be needing me to gain entry to anyplace you choose to go. I, however, am in dire need of a strong drink and a soft woman. Or two."

"Easy on the drink," Jasper said, walking back to his horse.

"And ride hard on the woman? Excellent idea."

Neither man could see the eavesdropper in the room above them. She sat on the floor beneath the barely raised sash and listened to the masculine voices drifting up to her. A smile curved her lovely lips. With a rapacious gleam in her blue eyes, she began to plan . . .

It was difficult for Eliza to refrain from fidgeting when she knew she was to be married the next day. However, the Cranmores' ballroom was not the place to appear anxious.

A few years had passed since she'd last been invited to a Cranmore event. Lady Cranmore was a consummate hostess whose entertainment innovations were often copied, and her expertise was widely evident tonight. Tulle and ivy wrapped Ionic columns. Harp players filled every corner with music when the orchestra was quiet. Outside, the rear lawn was dotted with dramatically blazing torches. The result was one of Grecian decadence, and everyone in attendance appeared to be in high spirits.

Eliza, however, was feeling high-strung. She was filled with a mixture of exhilaration and apprehension such as she'd never known. Tomorrow, she would be wed. After so many years of making certain she did nothing as her mother would have, she was no longer allowing Georgina to rule her actions from the grave. Which made every aspect of the coming day momentous.

"I am so pleased," Lady Collingsworth said, looking at Eliza with bright eyes. "I must confess, when you told me you would be married tomorrow, I doubted I could do justice to the occasion with such short notice."

Personally, Eliza thought nothing more than family and close friends were necessary, but she guessed that saying so would only disappoint and hurt Regina. "Thank you," she said instead. "You're too kind to me."

"Stuff." Regina waved one gloved hand carelessly. "I had given up on your ever marrying. I'm so very happy you found someone precious to you after all."

"Precious," Eliza repeated, her head turning to find Jasper. He stood on the edge of the ballroom speaking with Montague. She'd previously taken note of Westfield's absence.

"You are full of surprises lately," Regina murmured. "To think . . . Secret proposals from *two* of the most eligible bachelors of the ton. Absolutely delicious. Does Mr. Bond know who his competition was?"

"Yes."

"Lord Montague is being laudably gracious. Look at him speaking so civilly with your betrothed. And what a pair they make. From this distance, one could almost imagine them as brothers."

"My understanding is that the similarities between the two exist only on the exterior."

Regina leaned closer. "Your tone is intriguing."

Eliza lowered her voice to a whisper. "Have you ever heard anything of a worrisome nature about Lord Montague?"

"Such as?"

"Never mind. There are some things it's best not to know."

"You cannot initiate such a topic, only to abandon it!"

When it became apparent Eliza would say no more, Regina snapped open her fan with a flourish. "Hmph . . . With your engagement, I'd hoped that poor Rothschild girl would finally capture Montague's attention, but you have me wondering if he's not such a prize after all."

"Jane Rothschild?" Eliza frowned.

"Over there." Regina gestured to where Miss Rothschild was hovering behind a column near Montague and Jasper. "See how she stares at him, looking so forlorn? I've noticed her lingering in his general vicinity, as if she hopes he'll notice her. Her behavior is sadly untoward, but exception must be made for her common origins."

Jane was a pretty girl with soft brown hair and eyes, and a rather curvaceous figure. An air of melancholy clung to her. Perhaps it was the way her mouth turned down at the corners, or how she shifted so restlessly, as if the disquiet inside her was so great it manifested itself physically.

"Montague told me he attempted to court Miss Rothschild," Eliza said, "but she was unreceptive."

"I cannot believe that," Regina scoffed. "Her parents would pay a fortune for an earldom, and her actions speak for her."

Eliza could argue with neither point. Curious, she excused herself and moved toward the other woman. Why would Montague say Miss Rothschild was averse to his suit, when it appeared she was in fact openly seeking his regard? It was a puzzle, especially considering how dire Montague's financial situation was reported to be and how wealthy the Rothschilds were.

As she drew closer, Montague parted from Jasper and moved toward the open doors leading to the moonlit garden. Jane prepared to follow the earl outside, but Eliza spoke out.

"Miss Rothschild. How are you this evening?"

Jane cast an almost frantic glance at Montague's back, then faced Eliza with a weak smile. "I'm well, Miss Martin. Thank you for inquiring. Congratulations on your betrothal."

With proximity, Eliza noted Jane's wan complexion and the dark circles under her eyes. "Thank you. Would you care for something to drink? A lemonade, perhaps?"

"No." Jane looked out the door again. "I'm not thirsty."

"Miss Martin."

Jasper's voice drew Eliza's attention. His gaze was blatantly inquisitive.

Jane bolted. "Excuse me, Miss Martin. I wish you a good evening."

Eliza gaped as the woman hurried out to the garden.

Drawing abreast of her, Jasper queried, "Is everything all right?"

"I doubt it."

He leaned over her, his proximity far too close to be seemly, but she couldn't complain. The thrill she felt at his nearness was worth any censure.

"What do you know of your stepfather's relations?" he asked.

"Extremely little. I avoided speaking with him whenever possible."

Jasper's gaze moved over her face, searching. "What was it about him you disliked so intensely?"

"You would have had to know my mother to understand.

She was . . . erratic. Impulsive. What she needed was a firm hand, such as my father's, but Mr. Chilcott was overly indulgent. He encouraged her wild notions and sudden changes of agenda. His enabling of her behavior led to their deaths. She decided they absolutely had to travel north to celebrate the passing of six months of marriage. She ignored warnings of muddy roads due to torrential downpours, and he didn't have the sense or will to stay her."

"I see."

Eliza looked out to the rear lawn, but could no longer see Jane Rothschild or Lord Montague. The Cranmores had a heterogeneous garden featuring a hedgerow maze, a pagoda, various-sized obelisks, a recreation of a Grecian temple ruin, and a gazebo covered in climbing roses. It was an expansive outdoor space that could not be seen fully while standing in the ballroom.

"What are you looking for?" Jasper asked.

"Escort me outside."

With one brow arched in a silent show of curiosity, he offered his arm and led her to the garden.

They reached the gravel-lined path beyond the terrace and began to stroll. There were several groups of guests enjoying the many sights, but the distance between parties was sufficient to keep the conversations private.

"What, precisely, are we doing?" he inquired.

Although she was focused on finding Jane Rothschild, Eliza was taken by Jasper's warm tone. She glanced at him. "We're searching for a quiet corner."

"Are you attempting to compromise me, Miss Martin?"

"I confess, the notion is tempting. If you were of a mind to steal a few moments of my time away from prying eyes and ears, where in this garden would you go?"

He raked their surroundings with a considering glance. "Not the maze. Nor the gazebo. The temple might have promise, if you could restrain those sweet whimpers of yours that drive me to distraction."

"You are not quiet in your pleasures either."

"Because of you, love. Only with you."

Her breath hitched at his endearment. Embarrassed by the depth of her reaction, she looked away . . . and noted footprints moving off the pathway onto the adjacent lawn. She tugged Jasper's arm to stay him, then pointed at the ground.

His lips pursed, contemplatively.

Only two prints were visible before the rest became hidden by low-lying ferns. A large Italian alder spread its branches above them, providing a slightly shadowy cover from the moonlight.

Releasing him, Eliza looked around to be sure no one was watching, then she followed the trail by stepping deliberately into the preceding footprints. She knew Jasper was with her even though she didn't hear him behind her. As she approached the tree, she picked out the sound of voices. One was feminine and pleading, the other masculine and biting.

Jasper caught her elbow and pulled her to the side, then urged her to crouch behind a boxwood shrub. Eliza bunched up her pale green skirts to keep the hem from becoming damp and dirty. They were on the far side of the tree from where they'd left the path. She couldn't see the other couple from their vantage, but the sound was much improved.

"You cannot leave me in this state!" Jane cried.

"I can do anything I desire. Haven't we already determined that?"

The identity of the speakers was clear to Eliza. When she looked at Jasper, she knew he recognized Montague's voice, if not Jane Rothschild's.

"You leave me no choice," Jane said, with steel in her

tone. "I shall tell my parents what you did to me at the Hammonds' house party. They will know I carry your child."

"Is it mine?" Montague rejoined smoothly. "I think not. You are a promiscuous piece of baggage. I'm certain I can locate others who would attest to sampling your dubious charms."

Jasper jolted physically, eliciting Eliza's concern. Reaching out, she set her hand atop his forearm and found it to be hard as marble. He looked stone-faced and furious, his jaw clenched so tightly the tautness of the muscles was visible. He did not, however, look the least bit as surprised as she knew she did.

"I was untouched," Jane said with more dignity than Eliza thought she would manage under similar circumstances. "You forced this child on me. You must make this right. Your misdeed can no longer remain hidden."

"Rape is a serious allegation, Miss Rothschild. In fact, I find it so egregious I'm considering leveling an allegation against you in response: *scandalum magnatum*. While antiquated, it would still serve to protect my good name. You would go to prison, Jane, for libel against a peer of the realm. Not the most hospitable accommodations for a woman who is *enceinte*."

"You're a monster. Vile and debased. Filled with the devil's own taste for depravity and lust."

"And you want to wed me." Montague laughed. "What does that make you?"

"Desperate," Jane hissed.

Eliza swayed with a rush of nausea. Jasper grabbed her elbow and stood, dragging her up with him. He propelled her away from their hiding spot and back out to the pathway, nearly running into Sir Richard Tolliver and his sister, who were strolling away from the manse.

"I say," Tolliver muttered. "What were you doing back there, Mr. Bond?"

Jasper moved to step around the siblings. "We were momentarily lost."

"Lost?" Tolliver snorted. "Ridiculous. Have you no care for Miss Martin's reputation? Certainly my sister and I will be discreet, but you should—"

"Your discretion is appreciated. Excuse us." Jasper gave a quick bow and set off toward the house, forcing Eliza into an indecorous pace to keep up.

As they fled, she glanced behind her. Tolliver was engaged in spirited debate with his sister. Chagrined to have been caught stumbling out of the bushes with Jasper, Eliza was turning her gaze forward again when a shifting shadow beneath the alder caught her eye. A chill moved through her.

Had Jane Rothschild noted their departure? Or worse, had Montague?

Chapter 15

"Forgive the delay, Mr. Reynolds." Eliza hurried into her study. "I wasn't expecting you this morning."

Reynolds rose swiftly to his feet. "My apologies, Miss Martin. I have some information I feel you must know, and I thought it best to bring it to you directly."

"Oh?" Rounding the desk, she sat for the first time since breakfast. She shot a quick look at the window, noting the persistence of the early morning drizzle. In her opinion, the gray and overcast sky was ill-fitting for her wedding day, but she thought it matched Jasper's mood of the evening before. He'd seen her safely back to Lady Collingsworth, admonished her to stay far away from Montague, and departed in a rush. She was anxious to see him again and ascertain how he was feeling on the day of their wedding. "My curiosity is duly aroused."

Her man of affairs remained standing for a few moments longer; his attention caught by the parade of footmen and hired staff flowing past the open doorway. "I don't recall ever seeing such a flurry of activity on the premises."

"Mr. Bond and I are to be married late this afternoon," she explained, somewhat startled to realize she would rather return to the interrupted fitting for her wedding gown than participate in a discussion of business matters.

"Married?" Mr. Reynolds lowered himself into his chair. "So soon?"

"Why wait?"

"I wish you happy, Miss Martin. But I'm also exceedingly grateful I called on you this morning."

"Thank you, sir. I appreciate your sentiments."

He nodded. "As for why I'm here . . . By some stroke of good fortune, my father's employer, Lord Needham, recently learned of a business associate who was approached by Lord Montague to join the investment pool you asked me to look into. My father began an investigation into the viability of the speculation at that time, which was a few days ago. Sadly, it would appear it *isn't* sound, and we recommend against participation."

"I see." Eliza couldn't muster even a modicum of concern for Montague. She was still horrified to realize how consummate his façade was, how perfectly it shielded him, and how ugly he was behind it.

"Considering Lord Montague's financial state, I wondered why he would risk his few remaining funds on such a risky prospect. Once again, my father was of great assistance. It seems Lord Needham was a player in a card game that also boasted Lord Westfield and Lord Montague as participants. Lord Westfield was the victor, and the winnings included the deed to a property in Essex that has been in the late Lady Montague's family for generations. Montague is said to have been overwrought at the loss, which was instigated in large part by Westfield. I assume the property has sentimental value. It's Montague's last remaining unentailed holding. He sold everything else long ago."

"Instigated?" She frowned. "In what way?"

"Montague was prepared to withdraw from the game

when Westfield put a deed into the pot. He then went to great lengths to goad Montague into doing the same by making thinly veiled references to Montague's poor financial situation. It escalated to the point where Montague was faced with the choice of folding under the cloud of insolvency or continuing in an effort to maintain the guise of affluence."

"Dear God," she muttered, somewhat disgusted by the carelessness inherent in gambling. She valued her financial security too deeply to leave its fate up to chance. "I still don't see how Westfield can be held in any way responsible for Montague's stupidity."

"The property Westfield wagered is actually deeded to Mr. Bond."

Eliza went very still for a moment, then she exhaled in a rush. "Well . . . that alters the situation a bit, does it not?"

The Earl of Westfield was an extremely wealthy man who owned both entailed and unentailed properties. If he wished to gamble with such high stakes, he didn't require Jasper's means to do it. Jasper, however, held a deep dislike for Montague, and he'd apparently been aware of the earl's dissolute and immoral private life. He would insist against Westfield risking anything in the process of providing assistance, and so would supply the property to be wagered to mitigate any possibility of loss.

What had Montague done to garner Jasper's wrath? And how far was Jasper willing to go to gain whatever recompense he sought?

Reynolds continued. "Westfield also ensured Montague's bet by offering unusual terms: if Montague lost, he would have until the end of the Season to buy the marker back. Albeit at considerable expense, far more than the property is worth."

"Montague thought he had little chance of losing the deed permanently." Her hand lifted to her knotting stomach. Would Jasper go so far as to marry her to prevent Montague from gaining access to her funds, which the earl could then use to recover his marker?

"I believe the investment pool Lord Montague is forming is actually a means to gather the funds necessary to regain his mother's property before time runs out. He can tell the investors later that the speculation was unsuccessful, resulting in a loss, or perhaps he intends to marry or gamble successfully to repay the investors without the pressure of an end-of-Season deadline."

"It is tremendously hazardous to play such games." In truth, she couldn't care less whether or not Montague was ostracized. It was the very least he deserved. She spoke only to fill the silence, absentmindedly attempting to hide how unsettled she felt.

"Montague seems to have little choice." Reynolds looked grim. "I cannot help wondering how involved Mr. Bond is in this affair. Is he assisting Lord Westfield? Or is Westfield assisting him? And why?"

She kept her face impassive. "The Rothschilds would gladly take Montague as a son-in-law, but he resists. If he was of a mind to recover his deed, he could do so through Jane Rothschild's dowry."

"Montague would never marry Miss Rothschild," he scoffed. "Both of her parents are of common stock. Montague has approached only tradesmen to invest in his pool, and he refuses to gamble at tables where commoners are seated."

"I am astonished at how little I knew about someone I saw with fair regularity."

"Is the same not true of the man you intend to marry today?"

"No." She said no more. There was no need to explain her or Jasper's personal affairs.

"With his participation in Westfield's wager, Bond, too, is

playing a hazardous game against a peer of the realm. And his profession . . . will he continue it? If so, doesn't that present a separate set of challenges? The danger he faces daily will be brought home to you. Those he angers will seek you out—"

"Is that all, Mr. Reynolds?" she said sharply. She could hardly tolerate hearing him speak so reasonably about a matter she was too emotionally invested in to view impartially. Where was her good sense? Her reason? Her desire for self-preservation?

"I've angered you. That was not my intent." His stiff posture deflated. "Providing you information with which to make decisions has been my position for so long, it's now second nature to me. But I should know better than to step into your personal and private affairs."

Eliza immediately regretted her harsh tone. "This is as uncharted for me as it is for you. I will never hold your concern for me against you. Your loyalty is why I retain you, after all."

"I promise to speak no more on the matter. Not ever."

"Please, rest easy, Mr. Reynolds," she said softly, because her throat was too tight to allow for greater volume. "I didn't make my decision regarding Mr. Bond lightly."

"I understand. Your feelings are engaged. I should be celebrating your good fortune, not questioning it. Lord knows having my wife, Anne, in my life has made my world a richer place." He managed a smile. "There is risk in love, but it can be worth taking."

Eliza searched her own heart, something she was not accustomed to doing. She'd always questioned what purpose feelings served when the reasonable course of action was best decided with the mind. But it seemed her heart refused to be denied. Even now, it raced with something akin to panic at the thought of losing Jasper. Despite everything she'd learned from her mother, and everything she knew from observation, and everything years of dealing with her own business affairs had taught her, she couldn't imagine turning away from him now. Despite whatever his goals or motivations might be. Despite the heartache she invited by proceeding with marriage to a man who hid so many things from her.

She—a reasonable woman who prized her equanimity to the point of excessive caution—was faced with the realization that the only avenue she could bear taking was the most hazardous and unreasonable one.

She'd given Jasper her trust, and she would not take it back. She couldn't. She loved him too much.

"I brought this for you."

Jasper turned away from his bed, where several garments were laid out for his selection. He smiled at Lynd, who entered through the sitting room door. His mentor held a folded square of white cloth in his hand. When Jasper accepted it, he saw the letter *L* embroidered in the corner.

"It was my grandfather's," Lynd explained, shoving his hands into the pockets of his overly elaborate coat of fine wool. He rocked back on his heels in an uncustomary nervous gesture. "It was passed to my father, then to me. I want you to have it on your wedding day."

The monogram distorted as Jasper's eyes stung. Lynd was the closest thing to a father he'd ever had. It meant a great deal to him that Lynd regarded him as a son. "Thank you."

Lynd waved the gratitude away with a shaky hand.

That telltale sign of deep emotion goaded Jasper to step forward and embrace his old friend. There was a moment of crushing, then back slapping.

"Who would have thought you would marry an heiress?" Lynd said in a gruff voice. "And an earl's niece in the bargain!"

Jasper set the kerchief carefully on his bed. "I'm not certain *I* will believe it until the vows are said and the deed done."

"The chit is fortunate to have you. If she has a brain in her head, she knows it."

"She's the most intelligent person I know. Oddly humorous. Lacking all guile." Glancing around the room, Jasper remembered Eliza in the space. "And passionate in ways one would not expect."

"I certainly would not expect it," Lynd muttered. To which Jasper laughed.

Lynd studied him with an odd half-smile. "She has changed you. I didn't realize until this moment that this is a love match."

Jasper breathed deeply. He hadn't named his feelings for Eliza. Perhaps he'd been afraid to. He wanted and needed her, and he could have her. He'd been content with that.

Turning away, he gestured at an ensemble of light gray breeches, a silver-threaded waistcoat, and a charcoal gray coat. "What do you think of this?"

Lynd drew abreast of him and set his hands on his hips. "Have you nothing less plain?"

Remembering Eliza's commentary on Lynd's need for a proper tailor, Jasper hid a smile and shook his head. "I'm afraid not. This is for you, you see. I cannot have you better dressed than me at my own wedding, can I?"

Wide-eyed, Lynd looked at him. "You would have me at your wedding?"

"I would not have the wedding without you. Who will stand beside me, if not for you, my old friend?"

Lynd's nose reddened, swiftly followed by his eyes.

A knock came from the open doorway. Jasper looked over his shoulder. Patrick Crouch stood on the threshold with the top of his head nearly touching the lintel. "There is a woman 'ere to see you. I told 'er you weren't seeing anyone today, but she mentioned Lord Montague and I thought I should tell you."

"Is she still here?"

"Aye."

Jasper moved to the chair by the door where he'd tossed his coat earlier.

Lynd cleared his throat. "I'll come down with you."

They descended to the ground floor and took up positions in Jasper's study—Jasper leaned into the front of his desk, while Lynd settled into a wingback with one ankle set atop the opposite knee. In short order, a petite brunette entered the room. She was lovely, with sable-dark hair and cornflower blue eyes. Her back was ramrod straight and her head held high. She declined to pass her fur-lined cape and muff to the butler, and spent a long moment sweeping the room from one end to the other with an examining glance.

Finally, she returned her attention to Jasper and said, "Mr. Bond, I presume."

"Yes."

"Mrs. Francesca Maybourne." She brushed off the immaculate damask of his settee with a gloved hand before perching delicately on the edge. She fluffed her rain-dampened skirts with little regard for Jasper's rug.

Lynd rolled his eyes.

Jasper crossed his arms. "This is my associate, Mr. Lynd. How can we help you, Mrs. Maybourne?"

"I trust I have your discretion," she said in a clipped tone.

"I would not be successful in my profession if I weren't discreet."

She weighed his assurance for a second, then nodded. "My sister is in trouble, Mr. Bond. I'm at my wits' end trying to help her."

"Can you elaborate?"

She met his gaze directly. "Eloisa is young and impetuous. She has yet to learn how to deny herself anything. Recently, she began a flirtation with the Earl of Montague. I thought it was ridiculous, but relatively harmless. After all, my sister is a married woman."

Jasper's brows rose.

"However, it has come to my attention that Lord Montague is a scoundrel of the worst sort." Mrs. Maybourne's nose wrinkled, which softened her sharpness somewhat. "My sister came to me this morning in tears. It seems Lord Montague asked her for a token of her affection. I was horrified when she told me this! To give irrefutable evidence of an indiscretion . . . I cannot imagine what she was thinking."

"What was this trinket?"

"A sapphire and diamond necklace, sir. One of great value. And if that were not bad enough, it's a family heirloom on her husband's side. There is no doubt he will notice its loss."

"Has she asked for the necklace back?"

"Many times. Prior to today, Lord Montague said he would return it. Then, this morning, he said he intended to sell it. He gave her the name of the jeweler and said she could contact the proprietor any time after three o'clock this afternoon to repurchase it." Mrs. Maybourne sighed and wrung her hands. "The necklace is worth a small fortune, sir. There is no way for her to obtain the funds necessary to reclaim it without her husband becoming aware."

Jasper's lips pursed. He glanced at Lynd. Montague had devised a way to obtain the funds needed to buy back his marker. Yet by some twist of fate, the knowledge had been brought to Jasper. It seemed he was destined to destroy Montague.

He looked back at Mrs. Maybourne. "You want me to retrieve the necklace before he pawns it."

"Yes."

"Perhaps he already has."

She shook her head, causing thick glossy curls to sway around her piquant face and long, slender neck. "I pray that's not the case. I approached a Runner, but because a peer is involved, he refused the commission. Mr. Bell recommended you, sir. In the interim, he ascertained that the necklace had not yet been brought into the store as of an hour ago. He agreed to watch the premises until you make an appearance. Perhaps you will arrive too late. I won't hold anyone but my sister responsible for such a lamentable end. But if God is kind, you will precede Montague and find a way to bring this debacle to a successful resolution."

"This is no easy task you set," Jasper warned.

"My sister cannot afford to buy the necklace, Mr. Bond. But she and I are capable of affording you."

"Bond." Lynd uncrossed his legs and leaned forward. "May I have a word with you?"

"Time is of the essence!" she cried.

Lynd managed a ghost of a smile. "It won't take but a moment."

Jasper followed Lynd out to the foyer. "What are the odds that this should fall in my lap?"

"Tony Bell is a good man. Certainly an excellent source of new business." Lynd stopped in the center of the circular rug and turned around. "Let me manage this task for you. You cannot take this on today, yet the opportunity isn't one you can allow to slip through your fingers."

Growling, Jasper ran a hand through his hair and damned the timing of this unexpected boon. "I cannot send you out to accost a peer. If things go awry, the penalty could be your life."

"That's what masks are for, my boy." Lynd grinned. "I'll put on that suit you have for me, and add a wig. If Montague attempts to identify me later, he'll describe a very different fellow. With any luck, I will even arrive at the wedding on time."

"Montague is my cross to bear."

"Bloody hell." Lynd shook his head. "You know how I feel about this vendetta you wage—it cannot help your mother now. That said, you are so close to achieving your final aim, and I would rest easier knowing you've put the past behind you. But I'm not certain you can do so until you see this matter of Montague's property through to the end."

Jasper's head fell forward. For all of his life, the one thing he'd needed was justice for his mother. And now, with the end in sight after years of planning, he could no longer deny he wanted Eliza more. He wanted her so badly that when faced with the choice of foiling Montague or getting married, the latter was the event he couldn't bear to miss. Even while the thought of Montague slipping through his fingers caused his gut to knot and sweat to mist his skin, the response was only a shadow of what he felt when contemplating the loss of Eliza.

Torn, he spoke gruffly. "I'm certain I will not rest easy until I've seen my plan through to the end. Montague's ruination is all I have lived for, for so long. How can I abandon the cause in the final hour? How could I face my reflection in the mirror every morning, knowing I deserted my life's goal only days before fruition?"

"By having something else in your life more fulfilling," Lynd posited. "You are young yet. There is a world out there to be explored. I know that's what your mother would have wished for you."

A thought that had eluded Jasper previously came to him in that moment. Was it possible that the tutoring she'd secured for him had not been for his father's benefit at all? Perhaps a secure and brighter future for her son had been the true aim.

Regardless, it wasn't his mother's wishes—whatever they may have been—that decided him. He made his choice based on the instincts that had saved his life so many times before.

"I cannot lose Eliza," Jasper said with total, unequivocal conviction. With her, he had no sordid past. There was only the future, one he looked forward to and . . . needed. "If you can see to Montague, I'd be eternally grateful. As for myself, I have a wedding to attend."

"Right, then." Gesturing toward the study, Lynd said, "You deal with the matter of the retainer and collect the necessary information. I'll change my garments."

"Thank you." Jasper clasped him on the shoulder.

Lynd flushed. "Consider it a wedding gift. Now off with you. There is work to be done and vows to be spoken."

Jasper arrived at the Melville house precisely at three o'clock. Eliza delayed the donning of her wedding gown for his arrival and rushed to the lower floor to meet him. She came to a halt partway down the last flight of stairs, arrested by the sight of him. He'd dressed in the same garments he wore on the day they'd met, and the sentimentality of the gesture touched her so deeply her chest ached with it. His dark hair was slightly windblown and his cheekbones burnished by the cold. He was beautiful in every way. Flawless to her eyes.

Smitten, she sighed. Jasper heard. His gaze lifted to find her, and she watched his expression change, becoming fiercely focused.

"Eliza."

She barely heard her name, but she felt it. She rushed down the remaining steps and stopped a few feet away from him. "How are you?"

"Better, now that I'm with you."

Eliza gestured toward the parlor, then led the way. As always, she knew he followed even though he moved silently. She sat, and he took a seat beside her on the settee.

They were to be married in an hour. She felt more joy than apprehension about that.

"I am so glad you came early." She fought the urge to reach for his hand. "I've been worried about you since we parted last night."

He nodded. "Montague is very much like his father. The manner in which he spoke was difficult to tolerate."

"His father . . . ?"

"I've come to you now because we have something to discuss before the wedding, something you must know before we say our vows to one another. I can only pray you'll still have me, once the truth is out."

Eliza was made wary by his tone and her own lingering anxiety from Reynolds' visit. "You can tell me anything. I want to support you, Jasper. You no longer have to carry your burdens alone."

His dark eyes were contemplative and somber. "It's my goal to commit myself to you unencumbered. I am working diligently in that regard."

She was waiting patiently for him to continue when a violent pounding came to the front door. The sound echoed through the lower floor and brought them both to their feet.

Somehow, without appearing to run, Robbins reached the entrance before they did. The butler opened the door and revealed one of Jasper's crew, the handsome young man who'd escorted her to Jasper's home the night she shared his bed. Aaron yanked off his hat when he saw Eliza. His wild eyes caused her alarm.

Jasper quickly outdistanced her with his longer stride. "What is it?"

"The store. It's ablaze."

"Pennington's?"

Eliza's heart lodged in her throat. "What is ablaze? What's happening?"

"Stay with her," Jasper ordered, running down the front steps to where a footman held the reins to Aaron's mount. Catching the pommel with both hands, he vaulted into the saddle and galloped away.

As he disappeared from view, Eliza stared out the open doorway, confused and frightened. Aaron stepped into the house, panting. She caught him by a thick biceps before he moved past her. Their gazes met directly. "Where has he gone?"

"To your property on Peony Way."

One meaningful glance at Robbins was all it took to set things in motion. Within twenty minutes a carriage was hitched and brought around front. During that time, Eliza spoke with Regina and Melville, explaining the delay and assuring them all would be well. She ignored admonishments to await Jasper's return.

"We're to be married in half an hour," she argued. "Regardless of the circumstances or location, I intend to be with him at that time."

Aaron followed her down the front steps to the street. "He wouldn't want you there. For your own safety."

"While he risks his own for me?"

"Bond is not unprepared for this event. I'm certain the situation will be well in hand before we arrive."

"Then he should have no cause for objection." She pulled together the sides of her hastily donned pelisse and secured the buttons.

Eliza was tying the ribbon to her bonnet when a familiar figure rode up to the house and drew to a halt.

"Don't tell me I missed the nuptials," Westfield called out, pushing up the brim of his rakishly angled hat.

"Mr. Bond and I will return shortly, my lord." She accepted the footman's assistance up the carriage steps. "Please see yourself inside. Lady Collingsworth will receive you."

The earl dismounted and approached, catching either side of her carriage's doorframe with both hands and leaning in. All levity was gone from his features. "What has you so anxious?"

"One of my properties has caught fire. Mr. Bond has gone on ahead."

"To Peony Way," Westfield said.

Eliza blinked, understanding that everyone had a piece of the puzzle she was missing. "Perhaps you should ride with me."

He nodded and climbed in. Aaron joined them, sharing the opposite squab with the earl.

With a crack of the coachman's whip, the carriage jolted forward.

Her foot rapped an impatient staccato against the floorboards. "Why is the incident at the Peony property of surprise only to me?"

Westfield explained. "The tenant you know as Mrs. Vanessa Pennington is, in truth, Miss Vanessa Chilcott. Bond suspected Miss Chilcott of intending to use her business relationship with you to create a financial liability on your part."

Eliza felt oddly still inside, her thoughts strangely quiet. She wondered if it was shock she felt or simply resignation. The nature of the Chilcott brood was well-known to her, but she'd thought herself beyond their avarice since her mother's passing.

"Such as a fire on the property," she said without inflection. "If I was neglectful as a landlord or deliberately failed to address a safety issue in the building, she might have a claim then."

"Precisely. Bond believed you might pay a handsome

settlement to keep your gender and evidence of your holdings out of the courts."

A cold fury moved through her. "But such a quiet transaction would no longer be likely to occur once I marry. Hence the need for her to act before the vows are spoken."

As they neared Peony Way, they found the street blocked off by wagons set perpendicular to the flow of traffic. Thick, black smoke mushroomed into the air and burned her airways. Eliza withdrew a kerchief from her reticule and held it against the lower half of her face.

They alighted from the carriage at the makeshift barrier and traversed the rest of the distance on foot, pushing their way through crowds of onlookers who fought tenaciously to retain their vantages. Westfield led the way while Aaron brought up the rear, both men attempting to cushion her from the crush but being only moderately successful.

When they neared the charred storefront, they found their way impeded by members of the fire brigade working on behalf of Eliza's insurance company to minimize the damage. She explained who she was, her eyes on the building's façade. Allowed to pass through, she searched the sea of people clogging the immediate area and spotted Jasper's tall frame.

"There." She pointed.

Westfield caught her elbow and shepherded her closer. When they were only a few feet away, the crowd parted and a cleared path appeared, revealing Jasper standing by Mrs. Penning—*Miss Chilcott*. The woman's gown and apron were both singed and covered in ash. Her blond hair was darkened by soot, as was her face, which had a swelling bruise around her left eye. The resemblance to Eliza's stepfather was so obvious, it would be impossible to miss if one was paying attention, which Eliza hadn't been when they'd met. A morning spent with Jasper in the close confines of his carriage, followed by his entrance into the Pennington shop so swiftly on the heels of her own had kept her too preoccupied to pay any mind to the other woman.

It was a testament to Vanessa Chilcott's beauty that she was still riveting in her disheveled condition. Westfield faltered slightly when she turned toward them, his breath leaving his lungs in an audible rush.

"Eliza." Jasper did not appear to be overly surprised to see her. "Why did I know you wouldn't heed caution and stay home?"

"I go where you go." She examined him for signs of injury. He was dirty with ash and soot, as if he'd been in the building as well, but he didn't appear to be hurt.

She turned her attention to the woman standing beside him. "Miss Chilcott."

Vanessa Chilcott's blue eyes were red-rimmed and somewhat vacant. She replied in a painfully hoarse voice. "Miss Martin."

"What happened here?"

Jasper had begun to reply when a fireman approached.

"The fire is contained," the man said. "We found the body and a can of paraffin oil, just as Mrs. Pennington described."

"Body?" Eliza felt ill. "Dear God ... Someone was caught in the fire?"

Jasper nodded. "Miss Chilcott went up to her flat to retrieve a special order and caught Terrance Reynolds in the act of setting the place ablaze. They fought, and she brained him with a poker. She barely made it out before the fire engulfed the space. I attempted to retrieve him ... but it was too late."

"Mr. Reynolds?" Eliza repeated.

Her man of affairs had been excruciatingly thorough in his vetting of prospective tenants. By God, he'd discovered Jasper's ownership of the property Westfield wagered against Montague, despite the intricate nature of the inquiry and formidable time constraints. He would not have missed discovering that Mrs. Pennington was actually Vanessa Chilcott. Why had he withheld the information? What reason would he have to allow a Chilcott to rent space from her?

She looked at Vanessa. "You were his insurance. He hid your identity from me to use at his convenience. What role do you play in this subterfuge?"

"None." Vanessa's chin lifted. "I am more ignorant of this matter than you are."

"What relation are you to my stepfather?"

"I am your stepsister."

Staggered by the day's revelations and the understanding that the employee she'd trusted so keenly had betrayed her, Eliza swayed on her feet. Jasper caught her close.

She clung to him. "I saw him only hours ago. He came with information about you. Information intended to make me doubt the wisdom of marrying you."

He stiffened. "What information?"

"Your participation in the wager between Westfield and Montague over land in Essex. He suggested you offered for me as a way to prevent Montague from laying claim to my money, which would afford him the opportunity to reclaim his marker."

"And you were not swayed by this?"

"No. Which left him no option, I suppose, aside from this last-minute attempt to delay the ceremony." She looked up, finding Jasper watching her with a dark, fierce gaze. "But it would only delay the inevitable. Surely, he knew that. What was his aim? I had no intention of releasing him from his position. His circumstances would not have altered."

"We'll uncover his secrets, love." He sheltered her in his embrace, anchoring her as no one else in her life ever had. "I promise you that. Every last one of them."

Chapter 16

With Westfield at his side, Jasper escorted Eliza and Vanessa Chilcott into the Melville residence. Disheveled and reeking of smoke, the four of them were incongruous in a household prepared for the celebration of a wedding. They stood shoulder to shoulder in the foyer, hard-faced and bemused.

Lady Collingsworth hurried from the ballroom where the ceremony was to take place and came to an abrupt halt a few feet away. "Dear God," she muttered. "The parson awaits you, but it's clear I should reschedule."

"No," Eliza said, astonishing Jasper. "If he can wait an hour, I can be ready."

Recovering, Jasper said, "I can be repaired within an hour as well."

Blinking rapidly, Lady Collingsworth took in Miss Chilcott's appearance.

"Regina," Eliza said briskly, "this is Miss Vanessa Chilcott, my stepsister. Vanessa, this is the dowager Countess of Collingsworth."

"My lady," Vanessa whispered, curtseying.

Admiration and pride filled Jasper. He could think of no other woman who would wade through the morass of the

day's events with such aplomb. Eliza could have left Miss
Chilcott to her own devices after learning the truth of her
identity. Instead, she had asked one question of the woman—
"Why?"—to which Miss Chilcott replied, "I want to be self-
sufficient and independent. Who better to learn from than
you? And how else to manage it, but to shed the Chilcott
name that has defined my life thus far?"

Eliza had offered to take the woman in for now, since
Miss Chilcott's residence and all her possessions had been
lost in the fire. At the very least, it kept the woman close
while they delved into her circumstances. They would address other considerations tomorrow.

"Miss Chilcott will need a bath and a room," Eliza said.
"If you could see to that, Regina, I would be deeply grateful."

"Of course." Lady Collingsworth looked at Jasper. "You
have visitors, Mr. Bond. In the parlor."

Jasper met Eliza's querying gaze by extending his arm. *I
go where you go,* she'd said, and despite everything, she
wished to be married to him with as much haste as he felt.
He treasured her for that and countless other things.

Westfield set off to join the handful of other guests in the
ballroom. Jasper and Eliza moved into the formal parlor.
There were five people in the room. The Crouch twins,
Lynd, Anthony Bell, and Mrs. Francesca Maybourne.

Surveying the group with raised brows, Jasper wondered
why the lot of them was in attendance. He was about to ask
that very question, when Eliza spoke.

"Good afternoon, Mrs. Reynolds," she said softly. "After
today's events, I was not expecting to see you again."

"I went to the jeweler," Lynd explained, "but Bell was
nowhere to be found, which raised my suspicions."

Eliza continued listening to the recounting of the second
half of the Reynolds's plot with a heavy heart. While she

was deeply grateful for the plan's failure, she was painfully conscious that the hazard would not have existed if Jasper wasn't determined to destroy Montague. How much of his energy was focused on that endeavor? Would she ever have all of him? Or was the largest piece of his heart given to the woman from his past whom Montague had destroyed?

And yet she had to take heart. He'd come to marry her and sent Lynd after Montague in his stead.

"Sometimes," Jasper said quietly, "what looks too good to be true is precisely that."

Lynd nodded. "It was wise of you to send the Crouches with me. Together we watched the street for close to an hour and we noted one hackney that was a fixture the entire time. Patrick walked by it and—aided by his tremendous height—was able to see Mrs. Reynolds waiting inside with a pistol in her lap. I sent Peter to fetch Bell so he could confirm the story she gave us. Bell didn't know her, but apparently she knew enough about him, you, and Montague to create the perfect lure to draw you out. We brought her here to see what you thought of it all, having no notion her identity was false or that Miss Martin would know who she truly was."

Eliza eyed Anne Reynolds with something akin to hatred, an emotion she'd never truly felt before. "Were you going to shoot Mr. Bond? Was it your intention to kill him?"

The brunette lowered the sodden kerchief she'd been sobbing into since learning of her husband's demise and glared daggers at Jasper. "That isn't his name. I have no notion what his given name truly is, but I can tell you his surname is Gresham. He is the son of Diana Gresham, who was a whore for Lord Montague until her death from a wasting disease."

Jasper became so still it frightened Eliza. "Moderation would be wise," he warned with dangerous softness.

"I know everything about you, Mr. Gresham," Anne spat. "I told Mr. Reynolds to share what he knew with Miss

Martin. After all, she's the one who hired my brother-in-law to investigate your connection to Lord Gresham in County Wexford. 'Tell her he isn't what he says he is,' I told him, but he insisted Miss Martin had only to believe you wanted her money to set you aside. He also feared rousing her concern if she was to learn he never recalled Tobias from Ireland. 'She might wonder what other orders I've disobeyed,' he said. He should have listened to me."

The explosive tension in the room was palpable. Eliza rushed to fill the void before Anne could ignite the situation further. "You wrote the threatening letters Lord Melville received." It was not a question. "Why? What purpose did this all serve?"

Anne's chin lifted and she looked away. "As if I would say anything further. I have done nothing wrong."

"What of the incident at the Royal Academy?" Jasper asked with ice in his tone.

"Dear God. You cannot think we had anything to do with that! We are not murderers. I've had enough of this." She stood. "You have no right to detain me."

"I'll be taking you in to Bow Street," Bell said, rocking back on his heels. He was a short and slender man, almost delicate looking. "We'll see if the magistrate agrees with you. 'Til then, sit down."

"That's an expensive cape you wear," Jasper noted. "And sizable emeralds at your ears and throat. Either you came into your marriage with money, or Miss Martin paid your husband exceedingly well."

Unaccustomed to noting such things, Eliza reevaluated the woman's attire. Anne Reynolds's ensemble did indeed seem far finer than Eliza's own accoutrements. She looked at Jasper. "How? I manage my own funds . . . keep my own ledgers . . ."

"You do not deal directly with your tenants. Who collects the rents?"

"Mr. Reynolds."

"Right," Lynd said. "Is it possible what you believe you are charging and collecting isn't what the tenants are actually paying to Reynolds?"

Eliza paled. "I suppose it's possible, if he was clever enough about it." Which she knew he could have been. She looked at Anne, who was also wan, if defiant. "If he raised the rents over time without my knowledge, or charged for miscellaneous items of which I wasn't aware. We should ask Miss Chilcott and my other tenants. Dear God . . . they are all as much victims as I am."

"That's likely why Reynolds wanted Bond dead," Bell said. "Once you had a husband to assist you, the embezzlement might've been discovered or Reynolds' duties reduced. I'm sorry I didn't believe you when you hired me, Miss Martin. Let that be a lesson to me in the future."

Jasper remained deadly quiet and expressionless.

"This was to be my last Season," Eliza said softly. "I intended to retire to the country with Melville, at which point a greater portion of my affairs would have been left in Mr. Reynolds's hands. He and his wife were so close to achieving their aims that my sudden decision to marry Mr. Bond must have made them desperate."

"If you marry him," Anne said coldly, "you deserve what comes to you. At least Mr. Reynolds was concerned about building your wealth. Gresham, I am certain, intends to squander it."

Eliza pushed to her feet, unable to bear any more. "I shall leave this matter to you, Mr. Bell. I'm confident you will apprise me of the necessary information."

The Runner gave a curt nod. "Of course."

"Mr. Bond," Eliza murmured, which caused Anne to laugh. "Would you accompany me, please?"

"In a moment," he said without inflection. "I'll find you."

Eliza made her egress on wooden legs, wondering if she would, indeed, be found, or if Jasper would now be lost to her. Perhaps he'd never truly been hers to begin with. For all their promises to be truthful to one another, it seemed they'd kept more secrets than they'd shared.

Jasper reached the top of the staircase and turned to the right, following the directions to Eliza's room that Lady Collingsworth had given him. If the dowager countess thought it was inappropriate for him to ask for them, she gave no outward indication. Instead, she told him the parson was having a fine time with both the champagne and Lord Westfield's witty discourse, and he'd agreed to stay as long as they wanted him to.

Inhaling deeply, Jasper lifted his hand to knock on Eliza's boudoir door. As he waited for her to answer, he struggled against the feeling of being made of glass; he felt as if he might break at any moment. Perhaps it was the endless string of unexpected revelations that had him so unsettled. Or perhaps he was simply experiencing a bridegroom's expected nervousness. He thought it might be terror over the prospect of losing something irreplaceable, but he didn't have any frame of reference to be certain.

The door opened, and Eliza stood there. She was in a dressing gown, and her eyes and nose were red. He remembered when they'd first met, he'd thought her pretty enough but no raving beauty. He couldn't comprehend that determination now. He was certain she was the loveliest woman he'd ever seen.

Stepping back, she made room for him to enter, then she shut the door quietly behind him.

Her rooms were decorated in the same hues of cream and burgundy as his own. He noticed that immediately, and took an odd sort of comfort in the similarity. He shouldn't forget how alike they were in the most fundamental of ways. If only they could strip away their exteriors and bare that affinity . . .

"I should have told you—"

They spoke and ended in unison. Startled to have said the same thing at once, they stared at one another. He waited for her to speak first. After the day's revelations, she deserved the opportunity to give him a tongue-lashing.

Her hands tightened the belt at her waist. "I hired Tobias Reynolds in the beginning, when I knew nothing about you. You said the connection between you and Lord Gresham would withstand greater scrutiny, and I told myself I was only confirming the claim before someone else had a mind to. But I recalled Mr. Reynolds from the task before he reported anything. I wanted you to be the one to tell me whatever you felt I should know, in your own good time."

Jasper nodded and linked his fingers behind his back. "I should have told you about my mother. I knew I would have to, but I thought we had time—"

"We do." She stepped closer. "All the time you need."

"The time is now, Eliza. You should know me before you wed me. I couldn't bear for you to turn away from me after you're mine."

"I cannot turn away. I love you."

His eyes closed on a shuddering breath. "Eliza—"

"I don't want you to say anything," she interrupted quickly, "until after we are man and wife. I need to marry you with my heart, not my mind. I need to trust in my own instincts, over my reason, so I can make the changes necessary to be what you require, to be whole. I need you to know I accept you just the way you are, without reservation or doubt, so you can—God willing—someday grow to love me, too."

Eliza was defying all of her routines, setting aside habits of a lifetime, deliberately making one concession after another . . . *for him.* She was determined to leave herself open to trusting him, even when everything suggested she shouldn't.

"I love you," she said again.

He looked at her. She'd taken a seat upon one of the settees with her hands clasped demurely in her lap. Insanely, that aroused him—the vision of her so controlled, when he knew how wild she could be in his arms. It was the way she revealed her deeper self when they were intimate, even more than the physical pleasure, that drove his sexual craving for her.

"I am undone," he said hoarsely. "You rule me completely. I would do anything to possess you."

Eliza's hand lifted to her throat, her fingers wrapping around the graceful column. He crossed the room to her and caught that alabaster hand. Jasper pressed a kiss to the back of it, then moved to the tips of her fingers. He licked the end of the one that would bear his ring by the close of the day, and she shivered. Her lashes lowered and her lips parted on soft panting breaths.

Opening his mouth, he sucked the slender digit inside, swirling his tongue around it until a whimper escaped her.

The sound of surrender freed him from any restraint.

He reached down and opened the placket of his breeches with his free hand. His cock fell heavily into his palm, so thick and hard he fisted himself to stave off his hunger.

"Jasper."

His mouth slid free of her trembling fingers. "I need you."

Eliza fumbled with the belt at her waist. Jasper sank to the floor on his knees and pushed up her chemise, his hands rough with impatience. He caught her hips and tugged her down to his lap, her legs straddling his. The cleft of her sex pressed against the silky length of him.

He caught her nape in his hand, forcing her to look straight into his eyes. "I need to be in you."

"Yes." She grew slick with welcome due to the heat of his rut. She loved him like this, uncontrolled and lustful.

He shifted her, urging her up and then over him, the thick crest of his penis gliding along her slit and nudging her clitoris. She moaned and caught his shoulders, tense with impatience and greedy for pleasure.

When he notched himself at her clenching opening, she trembled. With a groan, he thrust, pushing his thickly veined cock deep into her.

"*Eliza.*" His arms tightened around her, crushing the air from her lungs and immobilizing her against him.

She clawed at his back, writhing. The heat of his skin burned through the linen and velvet of his garments.

"Please," she begged, quivering around him. "*Please.*"

Jasper gripped her hips, lifting and dropping her. Working her onto his rigid length. Pumping her up and down. Grinding and screwing deep.

Eliza sobbed with the pleasure. "Yes!"

"I will addict you to this," he promised in a dark, dangerously rough voice. "Addict you to me. Soon, you'll seek me out in public, unable to wait another moment. You will lift your skirts and beg for my mouth on you, my tongue in you. In the extremity of your lust, you won't care where we are. You will crave the taste of me. You will sink to your knees and service me with your mouth, sucking my cock until I spill into you, thick and hot and mad with hunger."

She wrapped her arms around his shoulders, eyes closing as he surged repeatedly inside her. The feeling was incredible. She would never have enough of it. The stroking of the furled underside of his crown rubbed deliciously, finding her most sensitive nerve endings and setting them afire.

He slid inside her, deeply, filling her with the heat and hardness of him. Filling her with pleasure that made her arch wildly. His possession was indescribably erotic. As addicting as he threatened.

He withdrew, and she felt empty. He returned, and she bit her lip to hold back cries that would betray their actions to a multitude of guests.

But Jasper would abide no restraint. "Let me hear you," he coaxed. "Let me hear how much you want this."

His free hand cupped her thigh, opening her wider so that he could thrust deeper. Swiveling his hips, he worked her into a frenzy with ruthless skill, making her insensate with lust and hungry for more. Always more. As much as he gave her, it wasn't enough.

Eliza gasped and dug her nails into the flexing muscles of his back. The horrors of the day created a sharp urgency. "Finish me."

"Too soon," he ground out, sweat dripping down his temple.

"We have forever to go slower. Don't make me wait now."

He crushed her to him. "I love you. Eliza . . . love you."

She climaxed with a force that left her shaking. Jasper followed swiftly, his hips ramming upward with ferocious speed. She felt his climax building, felt the tensing of his muscles and the frantic heaving of his powerful chest. When he came, it was violent, his thick penis jerking inside her with every molten spurt of his seed. Her name fell brokenly from his lips until she kissed him, swallowing the sounds of his pleasure with unconditional love in her heart.

They were married an hour later. Aside from the parson, who was flushed and happy with drink, it was a somber wedding. If the stamp of Jasper's passion was evident in Eliza's appearance, no one said anything to her, and she was certain Regina would have.

Jasper's hair was still damp when he said his vows. He'd

sent the Crouches back to his home to retrieve fresh clothes, then bathed in a guest bedroom to save time.

Fewer than a dozen people witnessed the short ceremony. The celebration afterward was equally abridged, since everyone had been present for hours by the time the vows were said.

Eliza wore a new cream-hued satin gown with fine lace sleeves and bodice. It was cut and fashioned in the latest style, the first of many that would assist her transformation. She intended to enhance what beauty God had given her, using every weapon in her feminine arsenal to please her husband and deepen his love for her.

When the time came to retire, Jasper was relieved. Eliza led him to her suite of rooms with his hand in hers.

"I have something for you," he said, when they were alone.

"Oh." She bit her lower lip. "I did not think of a wedding gift for you."

"You're all the gift I need." He reached into the inner pocket of his coat and withdrew a lady's signet ring.

He held his hand out for hers, slipping the golden circlet onto the ring finger of her right hand. "It was my mother's."

Eliza looked up at him with luminous eyes. "Thank you."

He nodded and shrugged out of his coat. "Would you care for a drink?" he asked solicitously. Having taken her body so peremptorily earlier, he intended to savor her now.

"No. I want you."

Satisfaction surged through him. His chest expanded on a deep inhale. His blood thickened and flowed hotly. "Have you no reservations? No questions?"

"Why are you still talking?" She presented her back to him.

"Will you always surprise me?" He approached her and reached for the first button of her gown.

"Haven't we had enough unpleasantness for one day? Tomorrow is soon enough to address the rest."

He pressed his lips to her shoulder, grateful for her.

Her head turned, and her gaze met his. "If you'd gone to the jeweler's today instead of Lynd . . ."

"Eliza . . ."

She pivoted into his arms, catching his mouth with her own in a fervent, awkward kiss. He caught her close, lifting her feet from the floor. Her slender arms wrapped around his neck, her fingers pushed into his hair in the way that never failed to inflame him.

"I want you naked," she breathed, making his cock hard. "I want to touch you everywhere, and your clothing makes that impractical."

"We cannot have impracticality in our bedroom," he said, biting back a smile. Setting her down on the edge of the mattress, Jasper stepped back. He attacked the buttons of his waistcoat.

Eliza's tongue traced the curve of her bottom lip. "Take your time."

"You like to watch."

"I like to watch *you*," she amended. "You are everything I find beautiful, and sexual, and desirable."

He had no idea what to say to that, how to tell her what her candor meant to him. He could only slow the process of undressing, maintaining eye contact with her, allowing her to see how much he loved her. When the last stitch was shed, he straightened and waited for her to tell him what to do next. He'd taken what he needed earlier, and she'd given it to him without hesitation. Only the second time in her life that she'd had a man inside her and he'd been too overwrought to show her the gentleness she deserved. Now, it was his turn to give her what she needed.

"I'm overdressed," she said, toeing off her slippers. Her slim legs dangled off the end of the bed.

"What would you like me to do about that?"

"Undress me. But much more quickly than you bared yourself."

Jasper set his hands at her waist and helped her off the mattress. He resumed his task of unfastening her buttons, working quickly. The wedding gown was set aside with reverence, but the sheer chemise and pantalettes were left to puddle on the floor. Enamored with her softly freckled skin, he wrapped himself around her, his arms tucked under hers and his knees bent to accommodate her shorter stature. With one hand cupping a breast and the other tangling with the dark red curls between her legs, he owned her passion completely.

She purred with pleasure, her head falling back against his shoulder. "I love your hands on me. They are so big and strong, callused and warm."

"A tradesman's hands." He traced the delicately pink shell of her ear with his tongue.

"The only hands that will ever touch me this way."

Scissoring his fingers, he parted the lips of her sex, exposing the hood shielding her clitoris. "Will I find you wet?"

She began to pant as he rolled her nipple between his fingers. Her stance widened in invitation for a deeper caress. "Yes . . . You linger in me from earlier."

The thought of her drenched in his semen swelled his already heavy erection. He pushed his cock between her thighs, growling at the slickness that coated him.

"Let me," he coaxed, urging her to fold forward over the edge of the bed.

There was a slight tension in her lithe frame. Then she relaxed and lay facedown, presenting the lush curve of her beautiful buttocks. He cupped them, squeezing their fullness.

Reaching between her legs, he urged her to pull one leg up and onto the mattress, her thigh perpendicular to her body, opening her completely. He cupped her there, too, possessively. "I love you."

She rested her cheek on the counterpane and closed her eyes. "Say it again."

He took himself in hand, notching his cockhead into the tiny entrance to her silken cunt. "I love you."

With a slow roll of his hips, he pushed the fat crown into the fist-tight glove of her. Her fingers dug into the velvet and her low moan stirred his blood.

"My wife," he breathed, pushing inexorably deeper.

Eliza arched her back like a cat, which caused the tiny little muscles inside her to squeeze him. The pleasure of those rippling embraces, the sensation of being lured deeper into her . . . A deep groan escaped him. Hunching over her, Jasper worked his cock into her with quick shallow judders, sliding through quivering tissues until he hit the end of her, refusing to risk either of them climaxing until they were completely connected.

Her breath hitched.

"So deep . . ." she slurred.

He withdrew a few inches, then thrust, going even deeper. She hugged him at the root, clasping his throbbing cock in liquid heat. Catching her by the shoulder, he held her in place and rode her with long, leisurely thrusts. His bollocks smacked against her damp cleft in a steady, erotic rhythm. Eliza whimpered with every weighty tap against her clitoris, her nails leaving visible trails in the counterpane, the curls around her face growing damp with perspiration.

When the pressure to blow grew dangerously high, Jasper would pause at the deepest point of her and grind, whispering soothing words as she climaxed around him. Sweat soaked his hair and matted his chest, a visible sign of the restraint required to remain rock hard and full to bursting to please her.

Time passed, and Jasper lost track of it, as he always did when he was with Eliza. He knew only that she came so many times her fingers no longer had the strength to clutch the counterpane, and the cries she made as the pleasure hit were weak-as-a-kitten mewls.

It was her hoarse-voiced "I love you" that finished him.

With his cheek pressed against her glorious hair and his arms wrapped beneath her, he filled her with hot, wrenching pulses of the lust that sprang from a deeper source. From a well of hope and love inside him he hadn't known was there until she made him whole.

Chapter 17

Eliza was perusing the morning's papers at the breakfast table when Vanessa Chilcott appeared. Her stepsister was dressed in the housekeeper's clothes—a high-neck shirt that was slightly too snug around the breasts and a skirt that was a tad too long—but she carried herself with unassailable dignity.

"Good morning," Eliza greeted her, before returning to reading the reports of the fire the day prior.

"Good morning, Miss Martin."

It took a few moments for Eliza to realize the other woman was rooted to one spot. Frowning, she peeked over the top of the page. She gestured toward the console against the wall where plates and covered platters waited. "The food is there. Please help yourself to whatever you like."

As if all she'd needed was permission, Vanessa nodded and moved to serve herself. When she was finished and settled at the table, she said, "Congratulations on your wedding yesterday."

Eliza bit her lower lip and set the paper down. "Should I have asked you to attend? I was unsure after the events at the store and the discovery of our . . . relation to one another, whether I should or not."

Vanessa blinked. She stared at Eliza in the manner most people did when they comprehended how little she knew about etiquette.

"Good morning, ladies," Jasper said as he entered the room. His stride was easy and inherently sensual, with a touch of leisure as if time was no concern. "My wife is blessed with an extraordinarily pragmatic nature, Miss Chilcott. She rarely means offense when she observes—or does not observe, as the case may be—certain social mores."

Nodding, Vanessa watched as Jasper walked the length of the room to where Eliza sat at the far end. There was blatant appreciation in the blonde's eyes, a knowing understanding of what type of man he was—ruthlessly deliberate and dangerously sexual. Eliza imagined it would be impossible for any red-blooded woman to be immune to him. After all, as oblivious as she'd personally been toward men, she hadn't failed to want him either.

"I took no offense," Vanessa assured. "I'm grateful to have had a roof over my head last night."

Eliza shrugged. "It was the most reasonable course of action to have you stay here. You lost more than I did in the fire."

Jasper set one hand on the table and the other on the back of Eliza's chair. Bending, he kissed her temple and whispered, "I had need of you this morning, madam. In the future, you should order a tray brought to our rooms."

Her breath caught. Jasper had displayed a marked insatiability throughout the night, waking her repeatedly to take her again and again. On her back. Sprawled on her stomach. Arranged on her side. With her heels in the air or her thighs between his. Deep and shallow, hard and soft, pounding possessions and slow, endless glides . . . His repertoire of sensual delights was vast, and she suspected he'd shown her only a smidgeon of what he was capable of.

As he straightened, she turned her head, impulsively

pressing her lips to his. He stiffened in surprise, then gave an encouraging hum, remaining still as she kissed him sweetly. When she withdrew, Jasper's smile curled her toes. He traced the bridge of her nose with his fingertip, then he stepped away to fetch his own plate.

Bolstered by his presence and verbal support, Eliza took a deep breath and turned her focus to her stepsister. Vanessa's attention was firmly on her food, her eyes downcast as if to say she couldn't possibly be aware of the scandalous behavior taking place at the other end of the long room.

Vanessa cleared her throat. "Whether or not it was reasonable to provide lodging to a tenant who lied on her application is debatable, I think. I doubt many would have done so."

"But you are not simply a tenant," Eliza pointed out. "You are my stepsister."

A wry smile twisted Vanessa's lips. "Which is more of a detriment than an endorsement, is it not?"

Jasper pulled out the chair at the foot of the table, which was directly to Eliza's right, and sat.

Eliza nodded, seeing no point in being untruthful.

"Unfalteringly candid," Vanessa said. "My father quite enjoyed that about you, Miss Martin. He said it was freeing. It inspired him to be a better man."

"I don't mean to be rude, but he never mentioned you."

One blond brow rose. "When did you give him the opportunity?"

Eliza opened her mouth, then shut it again.

"Exactly." Vanessa carefully sliced into her black pudding with her knife. "I don't blame you. You are astute, and you knew straightaway that he pursued your mother for the fortune left by your father. It's all true what they say about us Chilcotts."

Nonplussed, Eliza glanced at Jasper, whose face was austere and gave away none of his thoughts.

"See this?" Vanessa set down her utensils and held out her hand. She pointed to a reddish birthmark that rested over the back of her wrist. "My grandmother once told me you could spot the rotten fruit in our family tree because we all bear this 'bruise.' "

"I see," Eliza said.

"What you do not see, however, is that even bruised fruit sometimes has salvageable parts. In my father's case, it was his heart. He courted your mother for her money; he married her because he loved her."

Eliza's hands linked together on the table. "If he'd truly cared for her, he would have been a positive influence."

"That sounds reasonable," Vanessa agreed. "But love is not reasonable. Love is wanting to see the other person as happy as possible as often as possible. Leastwise that's how my father viewed love. As you know, it wasn't an easy task keeping Lady Georgina happy. If he cared for her not at all, he could have had her committed. Or he could have taken her to the country and left her there. Or the Continent. Perhaps she might have taken a liking to America—"

"I understand what you're saying."

Jasper reached over and set one hand atop both of Eliza's.

"I think you should know," Vanessa continued, "*you* were a positive influence on my father, who in turn extolled the virtues of respectable living to me. He's the one who convinced me I could make an honest living."

Eliza was at a loss as to how to handle the conversation. What could she say that wasn't already known to Vanessa? "I'm sorry my difficulties with Mr. Reynolds spilled over into your life."

Vanessa shrugged. "I blame my surname for Mr. Reynolds's actions against my shop, not you. I believe he rented the space to me with the intention of extorting from me whatever money he thought I intended to extort from you. When

I caught him igniting the paraffin, he said, 'Don't worry. I can still ensure you see a profit from your plans.' That was when I hit him with the poker."

"Dear God."

"I must have seemed like the kindest of fates to him, falling so neatly into his lap through no effort on his part. A Chilcott to use as another means to garner more of your money."

Jasper looked at Eliza. "By distracting you with the fire and removing me with a bullet, Reynolds likely hoped his services would seem even more valuable. In the process, he would have discredited Mr. Bell and cast suspicion on Montague, ensuring those avenues no longer seemed viable to you."

"He had no way of knowing," she murmured, loving him all the more, "that you would forsake a chance to thwart Montague in favor of me."

He squeezed her hand.

Eliza glanced at Vanessa. "What will you do now?"

"I've spent much of my life making decisions based upon my surname. Even when taking a new direction, I did so by comparing it to the known alternative, which is still allowing the name to define me. No more. The store was a lovely dream, but I'm not certain it was *my* dream."

"I should like for you to stay here in the interim," Eliza said, startling herself.

"Another Martin inviting another Chilcott to live under her roof?"

"The parallel did not even occur to me." She'd made the decision impulsively and from the heart.

Jasper offered an encouraging smile.

"When you're finished," she said to him, "I would like to speak to you privately."

"Of course."

Robbins appeared in the open dining room doorway, bearing a calling card. He crossed the length of the room and set the silver salver in the space between Eliza and Jasper. "The Earl of Westfield has come to call."

"Send him in," Jasper said.

A moment later, Westfield entered the room, looking windblown and dashing for it.

"Good morning," he called out to the room at large, but his eyes were on Vanessa. "How fortunate. I haven't yet eaten."

"You're late, my lord," Jasper drawled.

"I cannot remember the last time I was out of bed at this hour. Only for you would I be conscious."

"Perhaps you should consider retiring to bed earlier, my lord," Vanessa said.

"What fun is there in that, Miss Chilcott?"

Vanessa kept her gaze on her plate. "That would be dependent upon who else is in the bed."

Jasper glanced at Eliza. His dark eyes were laughing. "My wife and I must adjourn, but please, enjoy yourself."

Westfield smiled. "I intend to."

"I wonder if I should warn Miss Chilcott about Westfield," Jasper said, as he and Eliza ascended the steps to her rooms.

"And here I was wondering if Westfield needed a similar warning." She smiled and there was an openness to the gesture that nearly caused Jasper to miss a step. "However, I think they are well-matched. Neither will gain much advantage with the other, I suspect. Although it's clear Westfield is hoping otherwise."

"He has an eye for beautiful women."

She looked aside at him. "Just so long as you do not."

"I cannot agree to that, I'm afraid. You see, there is a beautiful woman who shares my life, and I could never agree not to have an eye for her."

They entered her boudoir, and Jasper expected they would retire to the bedroom. They were newly wedded, after all. But Eliza sat on one of the sitting-room settees and arranged her striped skirts as if settling in for a not inconsiderable length of time. Her assertive nose was lifted high and her jaw was set.

Recognizing the signs of determination, Jasper shrugged out of his coat. "I'm impressed with how the conversation between you and Miss Chilcott progressed."

"I understand what she means in regards to allowing exterior forces to define us. For so long, I allowed my frustration with my mother to define me and my choices." She took a deep breath and said, "Even when it came to marrying you."

He took a seat beside her. "Whatever concerns you had about repeating your mother's mistakes were bravely managed. You would not be wearing my ring otherwise."

Eliza watched him lift her hand to his lips and press a kiss to her ruby and diamond wedding ring. "But you see, as determined as I was not to marry because of my mother, when I reversed my position it was also because of her. I became so determined that she wouldn't be the reason I refused you, that she became the reason I accepted you."

Unsure of where the conversation was going and certain he didn't like hearing she'd wed him for any other reason than loving him, Jasper retained his light hold on her hand. "What are you saying?"

"Mr. Reynolds attempted to sway me against you, and even when he relayed information meant to incite doubt and concern, I dismissed my own disquiet because not marrying you had taken on the meaning of giving my mother a victory." Her fingers tightened on his. "Do you understand?"

"I think I do. Do you still have those concerns and doubts?" He rubbed his chest with his free hand, fighting the restriction he'd begun to feel.

She smiled. "No."

Jasper had to focus on relaxing his jaw. "Did you ever believe, for even a moment, that I wanted to marry you solely to prevent Montague from attaining your fortune? Did you believe I might utilize your fortune to ensure he could not climb out of the hole he dug for himself?"

"I want you to take whatever amount is required to achieve your aims," she said quietly. "Use whatever you need."

He stared at her, speechless.

"What nearly happened yesterday," she went on, "with Anne Reynolds and the failed ambush . . . It was your past defining you. I couldn't give myself fully to our marriage until I released myself from my mother's influence. The same applies to you."

Jasper stood in a rush. "My mother came to London for the Season. She was a diamond of the first water. She had her pick of husbands."

"But she fell prey to the late Earl of Montague?"

Her gentle tone nearly undid him. He'd never shared his mother's tale with anyone. Lynd knew it only because he'd borne witness to it.

"Yes." Jasper shoved a hand through his hair. "Unlike the young lady we heard in the Cranmores' garden the other night, my mother went willingly to Montague's bed."

"Jane Rothschild," she supplied.

"But like Jane Rothschild, my mother became pregnant." He began to pace. "When Montague refused to offer for her, she had to tell her brother. Lord Gresham's response was to disown her."

"Her own sibling . . . Is that why you don't bear his name?"

"I changed it legally. He left her in the city when he retired to Ireland, Eliza. She had nowhere to turn."

"I cannot imagine." Her voice was barely a whisper. "Being so helpless."

He spoke more harshly than he intended. "And yet you freely offer me the means by which you are independent?"

She met his gaze unflinchingly. "You're angry with me for offering my support?"

"No. Damnation. I'm angry at Montague for placing money between us!" He reached the wall and pivoted. "My mother turned to him. Begged him. He made her his mistress, then boasted to one and all that he'd reduced the Season's brightest star to being his whore. When his luck in the gambling hells ran out and his debts mounted, someone offered to take a night with my mother as payment."

"Oh, Jasper," she breathed. "Where were you in all of this?"

"I was in the schoolroom during the day, and locked in my bedchamber at night. Some of the men Montague sent to her brought gifts and tokens of esteem. They remembered how promising her future had been and took pity on her. She pawned them all and used the money to fund my education . . . and her growing dependence on opium."

Jasper didn't look at Eliza as he spoke, knowing if he saw pity in her eyes he wouldn't be able to continue.

"As Montague's financial situation declined," he went on, "so did the quality of my mother's lodging, the men who came to her, and the gifts they brought her. She wasn't willing to allow my education to suffer, so she began to earn money the only way she could . . . through whatever acts and degradation were required."

His voice hardened. "Meanwhile, I learned all I could from my tutors, so that one day I could ruin Montague the way he ruined my mother. I was furious when he passed on before I was ready."

There was a length of silence, during which all he heard was Eliza's elevated breathing. Finally, she said, "What happened to your mother is unconscionable, Jasper. A cruelty so vile I could never have imagined it possible. And his son is cut of the same cloth."

She stood and came to him, catching him around the waist mid-stride and forcing him to accept the comfort she offered. He stood stiffly for a long moment, breathing hard, his mind filled with scenes from a past he wished desperately to forget. Then the scent of her perfume penetrated through the fog of memories and brought him back to the present. Back to the wife he'd never expected to have, yet could no longer imagine living without.

He pressed his cheek to her crown. "I know what you sacrifice with your offer. As consumed as I've been by vengeance, I could easily squander everything you and your father have built. You know this, but you love me enough to put my needs first."

"I do love you." Her arms banded tightly around him. "I want you to be happy."

"And I love you. I understood when I sent Lynd to deal with Mrs. Reynolds's assignment that what I wanted most was to spend time with you. I also realized Montague could rob me of that, if I allowed him to." He leaned back to look at her. "If I allowed him to define me and my actions."

She swallowed. "What will you do?"

"I intend to ask Westfield to return the deed to Montague, and I will wash my hands of him. That's why Westfield is here this morning. You see, my mother wins if I enjoy a life of happiness with a beautiful wife and rambunctious, extremely bright children. The victory would be hers."

Her hands cupped his face, her blue eyes shining with unshed tears and a love that humbled him. She was about to speak when a knock came at the door.

"Don't move," Jasper admonished.

Eliza's dimple flashed, and he almost told whoever was bothering them to return in a few hours. Or days . . .

He pulled the door open.

Robbins stood in the gallery. "Forgive me, Mr. Bond. There is a Runner here to see you and Mrs. Bond. A Mr. Bell."

"Right. Thank you. We'll be down in a moment."

Jasper collected his coat. Eliza accepted his arm when he was ready and they descended to the ground floor. As they passed the parlor, Westfield could be heard speaking with Miss Chilcott. He sounded affronted.

They met with Mr. Bell in Eliza's study.

The Runner declined to take a seat and looked grim. "Yesterday, Mrs. Reynolds mentioned the Earl of Montague multiple times."

Jasper kept his expression neutral, but shot a quick look at Eliza, who nodded.

"Right," Bell said. "I've no notion—yet—of how his lordship is connected to yesterday's events, but I thought it might be relevant to tell you he was murdered an hour ago."

Eliza lost the color in her cheeks, but said nothing. Jasper, too, needed a moment to absorb the news. He was surprised, then relieved to realize he felt no regret or anger, as he'd felt when his father died. Montague's escape into death robbed him of nothing. Everything he needed was standing right beside him.

"How?" Jasper asked finally.

"Miss Jane Rothschild did the deed," the Runner relayed. "Shot his lordship in the heart with her father's pistol."

Epilogue

Eliza stood in the middle of her uncle's study and wondered how she would find a slender journal amid the multitude of books.

"Are you quite certain it's not in your bedchamber?" she asked.

Melville's wild head of hair appeared on the other side of a high table. His face was seen shortly after, his cheeks red and eyes bright. "I'm certain I looked for it there."

"Can we not purchase a new journal for your use on the island?"

"I require the information in the journal," he said. "Not simply blank pages on which to write."

"Are we ready?"

Eliza jumped at the sound of Jasper's voice, startled as ever by how silently he moved. He stood directly beside her. "Not quite. We're still searching for his lordship's journal."

"In the barren desert of my heart,
you bloom with radiance
and fill the air with heaven's scent."

Jasper's brows rose as Lady Collingsworth entered the room while reading from a thin-spined book.

"I'm delighted, Burgess," Regina said, with a telltale blush. "Who knew you were a poet?"

Eliza was of the mind that her uncle was less than proficient in poetry, by any estimation, but she'd learned that the sentiment behind a gift or gesture was the most important aspect. Practicality came a distant second.

"Now may we set off?" Jasper held out his hand to Eliza. "I, for one, would prefer not to miss the ship carrying our luggage."

"I'm ready," Regina said, closing the journal and holding it out to Melville. When he accepted it, she took his arm.

"It will sound better when I read it to you," his lordship whispered, leading Regina out to the waiting carriage.

Setting her hand in Jasper's, Eliza wondered if the vibrating excitement reverberating through her was obvious on the exterior. He squeezed her fingers and smiled. "I can feel how anxious you are."

"Not anxious. Eager." She followed him back out to the foyer, where Robbins held her pelisse and bonnet. "I love the ocean and temperate weather. I cannot wait to be surrounded by both."

"There's nothing like falling asleep to the sound of crashing waves," he murmured. "I intend to lay a blanket on the sand and ravish you in the moonlight."

"Jasper." Eliza was scandalized . . . and intrigued. "Outdoors?"

"In sunlight, and in rain. On the beach, and beneath the trees. Also indoors, in every room in the house."

Her smile was wry as he helped her up into their carriage. Melville and Regina were in a separate equipage behind them. Although the two claimed to be no more than friends, it was clear there was a connection between them. Eliza had initially been surprised to learn of their affection, until Regina explained that Melville had courted her long ago. In the end, he felt it would be best for her to marry a man who spent the majority of his time connected to the rest of the world, and Regina had assumed Melville simply didn't love her. Eliza and Jasper's delayed wedding provided the time and opportunity for the two sweethearts to reconnect. So far, their renewed relationship seemed highly promising.

"I don't see how you expect to schedule all these hours of sexual congress," Eliza said, as the carriage lurched into motion, "while attempting to make a success of a sugarcane plantation."

"Is that a challenge, madam?"

"Could be . . ."

"There is a guesthouse. Melville and Lady Collingsworth will be no deterrent. With unhindered access to you, the possibilities are endless."

Eliza smiled. "Melville intends to cultivate a variety of seeds while he's with us, taking advantage of the warmer weather."

The light in Jasper's dark eyes was wicked. "I suspect it will be Lady Collingsworth he will be cultivating and tending."

"You have a lascivious mind."

"I do," he purred. "But my claim is bolstered by the indefinable magic of the tropics that stirs a man's blood."

"Ah." She nodded sagely. "Now your true intentions are revealed."

He leaned back into the squab and watched her with slumberous eyes. "Didn't I tell you the first day we met that seduction was my method of choice with you?"

"Yes. I'd forgotten." She hadn't, but in the weeks since they wed, she learned that teasing him led to delicious results.

"Shall I remind you?"

She licked her lower lip. "You are welcome to make the attempt."

He moved quickly, grabbing her by the waist and dragging her over him. "Wifely satisfaction is a point of pride with me, Mrs. Bond."

"I fear you may be too handsome for the task."

"Oh?" Jasper grabbed fistfuls of her skirts. "Considering the shortness of the distance to the docks, that's likely a boon."

"In addition," she went on, her voice growing husky, "it's impossible to disguise the air about you which distinguishes you."

"Pray tell me what that is." He reached into the opening of her pantalettes and parted the lips of her sex. He found her slick and hot for him.

"You are a predator. A dangerous man."

"Dangerously aroused," he agreed. "And madly in love."

She reached for the placket of his breeches and pressed her lips to his. "And mine."

"Always."

Don't miss *Ask for It*, the first book in Sylvia Day's Georgian series.

London, April 1770

"Are you worried I'll ravish the woman, Eldridge? I admit to a preference for widows in my bed. They are much more agreeable and decidedly less complicated than virgins or other men's wives."

Sharp gray eyes lifted from the mass of papers on the enormous mahogany desk. "*Ravish*, Westfield?" The deep voice was rife with exasperation. "Be serious, man. This assignment is very important to me."

Marcus Ashford, seventh Earl of Westfield, lost the wicked smile that hid the soberness of his thoughts and released a deep breath. "And you must be aware that it is equally important to me."

Nicholas, Lord Eldridge, sat back in his chair, placed his elbows on the armrests, and steepled his long, thin fingers. He was a tall and sinewy man with a weathered face that had seen too many hours on the deck of a ship. Everything about him was practical, nothing superfluous, from his manner of speaking to his physical build. He presented an intimidating presence with a bustling London thoroughfare as a backdrop. The result was deliberate and highly effective.

"As a matter of fact, until this moment, I was not aware. I wanted to exploit your cryptography skills. I never considered you would volunteer to manage the case."

Marcus met the piercing gray stare with grim determination. Eldridge was head of the elite band of agents whose sole purpose was to investigate and hunt down known pirates and smugglers. Working under the auspices of His Majesty's Royal Navy, Eldridge wielded an inordinate amount of power. If Eldridge refused him the assignment, Marcus would have little say.

But he would not be refused. Not in this.

He tightened his jaw. "I will not allow you to assign someone else. If Lady Hawthorne is in danger, I will be the one to ensure her safety."

Eldridge raked him with an all-too-perceptive gaze. "Why such passionate interest? After what transpired between you, I'm surprised you would wish to be in close contact with her. Your motive eludes me."

"I have no ulterior motive." At least not one he would share. "Despite our past, I've no desire to see her harmed."

"Her actions dragged you into a scandal that lasted for months and is still discussed today. You put on a good show, my friend, but you bear scars. And some festering wounds, perhaps?"

Remaining still as a statue, Marcus kept his face impassive and struggled against his gnawing resentment. His pain was his own and deeply personal. He disliked being asked about it. "Do you think me incapable of separating my personal life from my professional one?"

Eldridge sighed and shook his head. "Very well. I won't pry."

"And you won't refuse me?"

"You are the best man I have. It was only your history that gave me pause, but if you are comfortable with it, I have no objections. However, I will grant her request for reassignment, if it comes to that."

Nodding, Marcus hid his relief. Elizabeth would never ask for another agent; her pride wouldn't permit it.

Eldridge began to tap his fingertips together. "The journal Lady Hawthorne received was addressed to her late husband and is written in code. If the book was involved in his death . . ." He paused. "Viscount Hawthorne was investigating Christopher St. John when he met his reward."

Marcus stilled at the name of the popular pirate. There was no criminal he longed to apprehend more than St. John, and his enmity was personal. St. John's attacks against Ashford Shipping were the impetus to his joining the agency. "If Lord Hawthorne kept a journal of his assignments and St. John were to acquire the information—bloody hell!" His gut tightened at the thought of the pirate anywhere near Elizabeth.

"Exactly," Eldridge agreed. "In fact, Lady Hawthorne has already been contacted about the book since it was brought to my attention just a sennight ago. For her safety and ours, it should be removed from her care immediately, but that's impossible at the moment. She was instructed to personally deliver the journal, hence the need for our protection."

"Of course."

Eldridge slid a folder across the desk. "Here is the information I've gathered so far. Lady Hawthorne will apprise you of the rest during the Moreland ball."

Collecting the particulars of the assignment, Marcus stood and took his leave. Once in the hallway, he allowed a grim smile of satisfaction to curve his lips.

He'd been only days away from seeking Elizabeth out. The end of her mourning meant his interminable waiting was over. Although the matter of the journal was disturbing, it worked to his advantage, making it impossible for her to avoid him. After the scandalous way she'd jilted him four years ago she would not be pleased with his new appearance in her life. But she wouldn't turn to Eldridge either, of that he was certain.

Soon, very soon, all that she had once promised and then denied him would finally be his.

Sylvia Day's Georgian series continues with
Passion for the Game.

"If all angels of death were as lovely as you, men would line up to die."

Maria, Lady Winter, shut the lid of her enameled patch box with a decisive snap. Her revulsion for the mirrored reflection of the man who sat behind her made her stomach roil. Taking a deep breath, she kept her gaze trained on the stage below, but her attention was riveted by the incomparably handsome man who sat in the shadows of her theater box.

"Your turn will come," she murmured, maintaining her regal façade for the benefit of the many lorgnettes pointed in her direction. She had worn crimson silk tonight, accented by delicate black lace frothing from elbow-length sleeves. It was her most-worn color. Not because it suited her Spanish heritage coloring so well—dark hair, dark eyes, olive skin—but because it was a silent warning. *Bloodshed. Stay away.*

The Wintry Widow, the voyeurs whispered. *Two husbands dead . . . and counting.*

Angel of death. How true that was. Everyone around her died, except for the man she cursed to Hades.

The low chuckle at her shoulder made her skin crawl. "It will take more than you, my dearest daughter, to see me to my reward."

"Your reward will be my blade in your heart," she hissed.

"Ah, but then you will never be reunited with your sister, and she almost of age."

"Do not think to threaten me, Welton. Once Amelia is wed, I will know her location and will have no further need for your life. Consider that before you think to do to her what you have done to me."

"I could sell her into the slave trade," he drawled.

"You assume, incorrectly, that I did not anticipate your threat." Fluffing the lace at her elbow, she managed a slight curve to her lips to hide her terror. "I will know. And then you will die."

She felt him stiffen and her smile turned genuine. Ten and six was her age when Welton had ended her life. Anticipation for the day when she would pay him in kind was all that moved her when despair for her sister threatened paralysis.

"St. John."

The name hung suspended in the air between them.

Maria's breath caught. "Christopher St. John?"

It was rare that anything surprised her anymore. At the age of six and twenty, she believed she had seen and done nearly everything. "He has coin aplenty, but marriage to him will ruin me, making me less effective for your aims."

"Marriage is not necessary this time. I've not yet depleted Lord Winter's settlement. This is simply a search for information. I believe they are engaging St. John in some business. I want you to discover what it is they want with him, and most importantly, who arranged his release from prison."

Maria smoothed the bloodred material that pooled around her legs. Her two unfortunate husbands had been agents of the Crown whose jobs made them highly useful to her stepfather. They had also been peers of great wealth, much of which they left to her for Welton's disposal upon their untimely demise.

Lifting her head, she looked around the theater, absently noting the curling smoke of candles and gilded scrollwork that shone in firelight. The soprano on the stage struggled for attention, for no one was here to see her. The peerage was here to see each other and be seen, nothing more.

"Interesting," Maria murmured, recalling a sketch of the popular pirate. Uncommon handsome he was, and as deadly as she. His exploits were widely bandied, some tales so outrageous she knew they could not possibly be true. St. John was discussed with intemperate eagerness, and there were wagers aplenty on how long he could escape the noose.

"They must be desperate indeed to spare him. All these years they have searched for the irrefutable proof of his villainy, and now that they have it, they bring him into the fold. I daresay neither side is pleased."

"I do not care how they feel," Welton dismissed curtly. "I simply wish to know who I can extort to keep quiet about it."

"Such faith in my charms," she drawled, hiding how her mouth filled with bile. To think of the deeds she had been forced into to protect and serve a man she detested . . . Her chin lifted. It was not her stepfather she protected and served. She merely needed him alive, for if he were killed, she would never find Amelia.

Welton ignored her jibe. "Have you any notion what that information would be worth?"

She gave a nearly imperceptible nod, aware of the avid scrutiny that followed her every movement. Society knew her husbands had not died natural deaths. But they lacked proof. Despite this morbid certainty of her guilt, she was welcomed into the finest homes eagerly. She was infamous. And nothing livened up a gathering like a touch of infamy.

"How do I find him?"

"You have your ways."

Read on for an excerpt from the third of Sylvia Day's Georgian books, *A Passion for Him*.

London, 1780

The man in the white mask was following her.

Amelia Benbridge was uncertain of how long he had been moving surreptitiously behind her, but he most definitely was.

She strolled carefully around the perimeter of the Langston ballroom, her senses attuned to his movements, her head turning with feigned interest in her surroundings so that she might study him further.

Every covert glance took her breath away.

In such a crush of people, another woman most likely would not have noted the avid interest. It was far too easy to be overwhelmed by the sights, sounds, and smells of a masquerade. The dazzling array of vibrant fabrics and frothy lace . . . the multitude of voices attempting to be heard over an industrious orchestra . . . the mingling scents of various perfumes and burnt wax from the massive chandeliers . . .

But Amelia was not like other women. She had lived the first sixteen years of her life under guard, her every movement watched with precision. It was a unique sensation to be examined so closely. She could not mistake the feeling for anything else.

However, she could say with some certainty that she had never been so closely scrutinized by a man quite so . . . compelling.

For he *was* compelling, despite the distance between them and the concealment of the upper half of his face. His form alone arrested her attention. He stood tall and well proportioned, his garments beautifully tailored to cling to muscular thighs and broad shoulders.

She reached a corner and turned, setting their respective positions at an angle. Amelia paused there, taking the opportunity to raise her mask to surround her eyes, the gaily colored ribbons that adorned the stick falling down her gloved arm. Pretending to watch the dancers, she was in truth watching him and cataloguing his person. It was only fair, in her opinion. If he could enjoy an unhindered view, so could she.

He was drenched in black, the only relief being his snowy white stockings, cravat, and shirt. And the mask. So plain. Unadorned by paint or feathers. Secured to his head with black satin ribbon. While the other gentlemen in attendance were dressed in an endless range of colors to attract attention, this man's stark severity seemed designed to blend into the shadows. To make him unremarkable, which he could never be. Beneath the light of hundreds of candles, his dark hair gleamed with vitality and begged a woman to run her fingers through it.

And then there was his mouth . . .

Amelia inhaled sharply at the sight of it. His mouth was sin incarnate. Sculpted by a master hand, the lips neither full nor thin, but firm. Shamelessly sensual. Framed by a strong chin, chiseled jaw, and swarthy skin. A foreigner, perhaps. She could only imagine how the face would look as a whole. Devastating to a woman's equanimity, she suspected.

But it was more than his physical attributes that intrigued her. It was the way he moved, like a predator, his gait purposeful and yet seductive, his attention sharply focused. He did not mince his steps or affect the veneer of boredom so esteemed by Society. This man knew what he wanted and lacked the patience to pretend otherwise.

At present it appeared that what he wanted was to follow her. He watched Amelia with a gaze so intensely hot, she felt it move across her body, felt it run through the unpowdered strands of her hair and dance across her bared nape. Felt it glide across her bared shoulders and down the length of her spine. *Coveting* . . .

Don't miss the book that inspired *Bared to You*.
Read *Seven Years to Sin*, available now!

"And this," the captain said, turning slightly to gesture at the gentleman, "is Mr. Alistair Caulfield, owner of this fine vessel and brilliant violinist, as you 'eard."

Jess swore her heart ceased beating for a moment. Certainly, she stopped breathing. Caulfield faced her and sketched a perfectly executed, elegant bow. Yet his head never lowered and his gaze never left hers.

Dear God . . .

What were the odds that they would cross paths this way?

There was very little of the young man Jess had once known left in the man who faced her. Alistair Caulfield was no longer pretty. The planes of his face had sharpened, etching his features into a thoroughly masculine countenance. Darkly winged brows and thick lashes framed those infamous eyes of rich, deep blue. In the fading light of the setting sun and the flickering flames of the turpentine lamps, his coal-black hair gleamed with health and vitality. Previously his beauty had been striking, but now he was larger. More worldly and mature. Undeniably formidable.

Breathtakingly male.

"Lady Tarley," he greeted her, straightening. "It is a great pleasure to see you again."

His voice was lower and deeper in pitch than she remembered. It had a soft, rumbling quality. Almost a purr. He walked with equal feline grace, his step light and surefooted despite his powerful build. His gaze was focused and intense, assessing. Challenging. As before, it seemed he looked right into the very heart of her and dared her to deny that he could.

She sucked in a shaky breath and met him halfway, offering her hand. "Mr. Caulfield. It has been some time since we last met."

"Years."

His look was so intimate she couldn't help thinking of that night in the Pennington woods. A rush of heat swept up her arm from where their skin connected.

He went on. "Please accept my condolences on your recent loss. Tarley was a good man. I admired him and liked him quite well."

"Your thoughts are appreciated," she managed in spite of a suddenly dry mouth. "I offer the same to you. I was deeply sorry to hear that your brother had passed."

His jaw tightened and he released her, sliding his hand away so that his fingertips stroked over the center of her palm. "Two of them," he replied grimly.

Jess caught her hand back and rubbed it discreetly against her thigh, to no avail. The tingle left by his touch was inerasable.

"Shall we?" the captain said, tilting his head toward the table.

Caulfield took a seat on the bench directly across from her. She was discomfited at first, but he seemed to forget her the moment the food was brought in. To ensure a steady flow of conversation, she took pains to direct the discussion to topics addressing the ship and seafaring, and the men easily followed. No doubt they were relieved not to have to focus on her life of limited scope, which was of little interest to men. What followed was a rather fantastic hour of food and conversation the likes of which she'd never been exposed to before. Gentlemen did not often discuss matters of business around her.

It quickly became clear that Alistair Caulfield was enjoying laudable financial success. He didn't comment on it personally, but he participated in the discussion about the trade, making it clear he was very involved in the minutiae of his business endeavors. He was also expertly dressed. His coat was made with a gray-green velvet she thought quite lovely, and the stylishly short cut of the shoulders emphasized how fit he was.

"Do you make the trip to Jamaica often, Captain?" Jess asked.

"Not as often as some of Mr. Caulfield's other ships do." He set his elbows on the table and toyed with his beard. "London is where we berth most often. The others dock in Liverpool or Bristol."

"How many ships are there?"

The captain looked at Caulfield. " 'Ow many are there now? Five?"

"Six," Caulfield said, looking directly at Jess.

She met his gaze with difficulty. She couldn't explain why she felt as she did, but it was almost as if the intimacies she had witnessed that night in the woods had been between Caulfield and herself, not another woman. Something profound had transpired in the moment they'd first become aware of each other in the darkness. A connecting thread had been sewn between them, and she had no notion how to sever it. She knew things about the man she should not know, and there was no way for her to return to blissful ignorance . . .

Ask For It

ALSO BY SYLVIA DAY

Bad Boys Ahoy!

The Stranger I Married

Passion for the Game

A Passion for Him

Don't Tempt Me

Pride and Pleasure

Seven Years to Sin

SYLVIA DAY, WRITING AS LIVIA DARE

In the Flesh

ANTHOLOGIES

Perfect Kisses

Published by Kensington Publishing Corp.

Ask For It

SYLVIA DAY

KENSINGTON PUBLISHING CORP.
www.kensingtonbooks.com

KENSINGTON BOOKS are published by

Kensington Publishing Corp.
119 West 40th Street
New York, NY 10018

All Kensington titles, imprints, and distributed lines are available at special quantity discounts for bulk purchases for sales promotions, premiums, fund-raising, educational, or institutional use.

Special book excerpts or customized printings can also be created to fit specific needs. For details, write or phone the office of the Kensington special sales manager: Kensington Publishing Corp., 119 West 40th Street, New York, NY 10018, attn: Special Sales Department; phone 1-800-221-2647.

KENSINGTON and the k logo are Reg. U.S. Pat. & TM Off.

ISBN-13: 978-0-7582-9042-7
ISBN-10: 0-7582-9042-X

First Kensington Trade Paperback Printing: August 2006

10 9 8

Printed in the United States of America

To my mother, Tami Day, for fostering my love of romance novels and being such an awesome PR person. (She promotes my books like mad!) I love you, Mom.

Acknowledgments

Many thanks go to the judges of the 2004 IRW Golden Opportunity and the 2004 Gateway to the Rest contests for awarding this story First Place and Best of the Best rankings. Being named a winning finalist in the contests gave me confidence in both the story and my writing abilities.

Huge hugs go out to my critique partners—Sasha White, Annette McCleave, and Jordan Summers. Their assistance, support, and friendship helped me (and the story!) immeasurably.

My undying gratitude goes to my fabulous editor, Kate Duffy. She's absolutely wonderful. I'm so very, very lucky to write for her.

And to the Allure Authors (*www.AllureAuthors.com*), my friends and colleagues, for their support, encouragement, and ambition. You are an awesome group of women, and I'm so glad to be a part of Allure!

Prologue

London, April 1770

"**A**re you worried I'll ravish the woman, Eldridge? I admit to a preference for widows in my bed. They are much more agreeable and decidedly less complicated than virgins or other men's wives."

Sharp gray eyes lifted from the mass of papers on the enormous mahogany desk. "*Ravish*, Westfield?" The deep voice was rife with exasperation. "Be serious, man. This assignment is very important to me."

Marcus Ashford, seventh Earl of Westfield, lost the wicked smile that hid the soberness of his thoughts and released a deep breath. "And you must be aware that it is equally important to me."

Nicholas, Lord Eldridge, sat back in his chair, placed his elbows on the armrests, and steepled his long, thin fingers. He was a tall and sinewy man with a weathered face that had seen too many hours on the deck of a ship. Everything about him was practical, nothing superfluous, from his manner of speaking to his physical build. He presented an intimidating presence with a bustling London thoroughfare as a backdrop. The result was deliberate and highly effective.

"As a matter of fact, until this moment, I was not aware. I wanted to exploit your cryptography skills. I never considered you would volunteer to manage the case."

Marcus met the piercing gray stare with grim determination. Eldridge was head of the elite band of agents whose sole purpose was to investigate and hunt down known pirates and smugglers. Working under the auspices of His Majesty's Royal Navy, Eldridge wielded an inordinate amount of power. If Eldridge refused him the assignment, Marcus would have little say.

But he would not be refused. Not in this.

He tightened his jaw. "I will not allow you to assign someone else. If Lady Hawthorne is in danger, I will be the one to ensure her safety."

Eldridge raked him with an all-too-perceptive gaze. "Why such passionate interest? After what transpired between you, I'm surprised you would wish to be in close contact with her. Your motive eludes me."

"I have no ulterior motive." At least not one he would share. "Despite our past, I've no desire to see her harmed."

"Her actions dragged you into a scandal that lasted for months and is still discussed today. You put on a good show, my friend, but you bear scars. And some festering wounds, perhaps?"

Remaining still as a statue, Marcus kept his face impassive and struggled against his gnawing resentment. His pain was his own and deeply personal. He disliked being asked about it. "Do you think me incapable of separating my personal life from my professional one?"

Eldridge sighed and shook his head. "Very well. I won't pry."

"And you won't refuse me?"

"You are the best man I have. It was only your history that gave me pause, but if you are comfortable with it, I have no objections. However, I will grant her request for reassignment, if it comes to that."

Nodding, Marcus hid his relief. Elizabeth would never ask for another agent; her pride wouldn't permit it.

Eldridge began to tap his fingertips together. "The journal Lady Hawthorne received was addressed to her late husband and is written in code. If the book was involved in his death . . ." He paused. "Viscount Hawthorne was investigating Christopher St. John when he met his reward."

Marcus stilled at the name of the popular pirate. There was no criminal he longed to apprehend more than St. John, and his enmity was personal. St. John's attacks against Ashford Shipping were the impetus to his joining the agency. "If Lord Hawthorne kept a journal of his assignments and St. John were to acquire the information—bloody hell!" His gut tightened at the thought of the pirate anywhere near Elizabeth.

"Exactly," Eldridge agreed. "In fact, Lady Hawthorne has already been contacted about the book since it was brought to my attention just a sennight ago. For her safety and ours, it should be removed from her care immediately, but that's impossible at the moment. She was instructed to personally deliver the journal, hence the need for our protection."

"Of course."

Eldridge slid a folder across the desk. "Here is the information I've gathered so far. Lady Hawthorne will apprise you of the rest during the Moreland ball."

Collecting the particulars of the assignment, Marcus stood and took his leave. Once in the hallway, he allowed a grim smile of satisfaction to curve his lips.

He'd been only days away from seeking Elizabeth out. The end of her mourning meant his interminable waiting was over. Although the matter of the journal was disturbing, it worked to his advantage, making it impossible for her to avoid him. After the scandalous way she'd jilted him four years ago she would not be pleased with his new appearance in her life. But she wouldn't turn to Eldridge either, of that he was certain.

Soon, very soon, all that she had once promised and then denied him would finally be his.

Chapter 1

Marcus found Elizabeth before he even set foot in the Moreland ballroom. In fact, he was trapped on the staircase as impatient peers and dignitaries sought a word with him. He was oblivious to those who vied for his attention, arrested by a brief glimpse of her.

She was even lovelier than before. How that was possible he couldn't say. She had always been exquisite. Perhaps absence had made his heart grow fonder.

A derisive smile curved his lips. Obviously, Elizabeth did not return the sentiment. When their eyes met, he allowed his pleasure at seeing her again to show on his face. In return, she lifted her chin and looked away.

A deliberate snub.

The cut direct, exactly administered but unable to draw blood. She had already inflicted the most grievous laceration years ago, making him impervious to further injury. He brushed off her disregard with ease. Nothing could alter their fate, however she might wish it otherwise.

For years now he'd served as an agent to the crown, and in that time he had led a life that would rival the stories written in any sensational novel. He'd fought numerous sword fights, been shot twice, and dodged more than any man's fair share of cannon fire. In the process, he had lost three of his own ships and sunk a half dozen others before he'd been forced to remain in England by the demands of his title. And yet the sudden fiery lick of awareness along his nerve endings only ever happened when he was in the same room as Elizabeth.

Avery James, his partner, stepped around him when it became obvious he was rooted to the spot. "There is Viscountess Hawthorne, my lord," he pointed out with an almost imperceptible thrust of his chin. "She is standing to the right, on the edge of the dance floor, in the violet silk gown. She is—"

"I know who she is."

Avery looked at him in surprise. "I was unaware that you were acquainted."

Marcus's lips, known widely for their ability to charm women breathless, curved in blatant anticipation. "Lady Hawthorne and I are . . . old friends."

"I see," Avery murmured, with a frown that said he didn't at all.

Marcus rested his hand on the shorter man's shoulder. "Go on ahead, Avery, while I deal with this crush, but leave Lady Hawthorne to me."

Avery hesitated a moment, then nodded reluctantly and continued to the ballroom, his path clear of the crowd that besieged Marcus.

Tempering his irritation with the importunate guests blocking his path, Marcus tersely acknowledged the flurry of greetings and inquiries directed at him. This melee was the reason he disliked these events. Gentlemen who did not have the initiative to seek him out during calling hours felt free to approach him in a more relaxed social setting. He never mixed business with pleasure. At least that had been his rule until tonight.

Elizabeth would be the exception. As she had always been an exception.

Twirling his quizzing glass, Marcus watched as Avery moved through the crowd with ease, his gaze drifting past his partner to the woman he was assigned to protect. He drank in the sight of her like a man dying of thirst.

Elizabeth had never cared for wigs and was not wearing one tonight, as most of the other ladies did. The effect of stark white plumes in her dark hair was breathtaking, drawing every eye inexorably toward her. Nearly black, her hair set off eyes so stunningly colored they brought to mind the luster of amethysts.

Those eyes had locked with his for only a moment, but the sharp shock of her magnetism lingered, the pull of it undeniable. It drew him forward, called to him on the primitive level it always had, like a moth to a flame. Despite the danger of burning, he could not resist.

She had a way of looking at a man with those amazing eyes. Marcus could almost have believed he was the only man in the room, that everyone had disappeared and nothing stood between where he was trapped on the staircase and where she waited on the other side of the dance floor.

He imagined closing the distance between them, pulling her into his arms, and lowering his mouth to hers. He knew already that her lips, so erotic in their shape and plumpness, would melt into his. He wanted to trail his mouth down the slim column of her throat and lick along the ridge of her collarbone. He wanted to sink into her lush body and sate his driving hunger, a hunger that had become so powerful he was very nearly mad with it.

He'd once wanted everything—her smiles, her laughter, the sound of her voice, and the view of the world through her eyes. Now his need was baser. Marcus refused to allow it to be more than that. He wanted his life back, the life free of pain, anger, and sleepless nights. Elizabeth had taken it away and she could damn well give it back.

His jaw clenched. It was time to close the distance between them.

One look had shaken his control. What would it be like when he held her in his arms again?

* * *

Elizabeth, Viscountess Hawthorne, stood for a long moment in shock, heat spreading across her cheeks.

Her gaze had locked on the man on the staircase for only a moment and yet during that brief time her heart had increased its rhythm to an alarming pace. She was held motionless, arrested by the masculine beauty of his face, a face which had clearly shown pleasure at seeing her again. Startled and disturbed by her reaction to him after all these years, she had forced herself to cut him, to look away with haughty disregard.

Marcus, now the Earl of Westfield, was still magnificent. He remained the handsomest man she had ever encountered. When his gaze met hers, she felt the spark that passed between them as if it were a tangible force. An intense attraction had always existed between them. She was profoundly disturbed to discover it had not abated in the slightest.

After what he'd done, he should repulse her.

Elizabeth felt a hand at her elbow, jolting her back into the conversation. She turned to find George Stanton at her side, his concerned gaze searching her face. "Are you feeling unwell? You look a bit flushed."

She fluffed the lace at the end of her sleeve to hide her unease. "It is warm in here." Snapping her fan open, she waved it rapidly to cool her hot cheeks.

"I think a beverage is in order," George offered and she rewarded his thoughtfulness with a smile.

Once George had departed, Elizabeth directed her attention toward the group of gentlemen who surrounded her. "What were we discussing?" she asked no one in particular. Truthfully, she hadn't been paying attention to the conversation for most of the past hour.

Thomas Fowler replied. "We were discussing the Earl of Westfield." He gestured discreetly to Marcus. "Surprised to see him in attendance. The earl is notorious for his aversion to social events."

"Indeed." She feigned indifference while her palms grew

damp within her gloves. "I had hoped that predilection of the earl's would hold true this evening, but it appears I am not so fortunate."

Thomas shifted, his countenance revealing his discomfort. "My apologies, Lady Hawthorne. I had forgotten your past association with Lord Westfield."

She laughed softly. "No need for apologies. Truly, you have my heartfelt appreciation. I'm certain you are the only person in London who has the sense to forget. Pay him no mind, Mr. Fowler. The earl was of little consequence to me then, and is of even less consequence now."

Elizabeth smiled as George returned with her drink and his eyes sparkled with pleasure at her regard.

As the conversation around her continued, Elizabeth slowly altered her position to better secure furtive glimpses of Marcus navigating the clogged staircase. It was obvious his libidinous reputation had not affected his power and influence. Even in a crowd, his presence was compelling. Several highly esteemed gentlemen hurried to greet him rather than wait for him to descend to the ballroom floor. Women, dressed in a dazzling array of colors and frothy with lace, glided surreptitiously toward the staircase. The influx of admirers moving in his direction shifted the balance of the entire room. To his credit, Marcus looked mostly indifferent to all of the fawning directed toward him.

As he made his way down to the ballroom, he moved with the casual arrogance of a man who always obtained precisely what he desired. The crowd around him attempted to pin him in place, but Marcus cut through it with ease. He attended intently to some, offhandedly to others, and to a few he simply raised an imperious hand. He commanded those around him with the sheer force of his personality and they were content to allow him to do so.

Feeling the intensity of her regard, his gaze met hers again. The corners of his generous mouth lifted upward as perception passed between them. The glint in his eyes and the warmth of his smile made promises that he as a man could never keep.

There was an air of isolation about Marcus and a restless energy to his movements that had not been there four years ago. They were warning signs, and Elizabeth had every intention of heeding them.

George looked easily over her head to scrutinize the scene. "I say. It appears Lord Westfield is heading this way."

"Are you quite certain, Mr. Stanton?"

"Yes, my lady. Westfield is staring directly at me as we speak."

Tension coiled in the pit of her stomach. Marcus had literally frozen in place when their eyes had first met and the second glance had been even more disturbing. He was coming for her and she had no time to prepare. George looked down at her as she resumed fanning herself furiously.

Damn Marcus for coming tonight! Her first social event after three years of mourning and he unerringly sought her out within hours of her reemergence, as if he'd been impatiently waiting these last years for exactly this moment. She was well aware that that had not been the case at all. While she had been crepe-clad and sequestered in mourning, Marcus had been firmly establishing his scandalous reputation in many a lady's bedroom.

After the callous way he'd broken her heart, Elizabeth would have discounted him regardless of the circumstances but tonight especially. Enjoyment of the festivities was not her aim. She had a man she was waiting for, a man she had arranged covertly to meet. Tonight she would dedicate herself to the memory of her husband. She would find justice for Hawthorne and see it served.

The crowd parted reluctantly before Marcus and then regrouped in his wake, the movements heralding his progress toward her. And then Westfield was there, directly before her. He smiled and her pulse raced. The temptation to retreat, to flee, was great, but the moment when she could reasonably have done so passed far too swiftly.

Squaring her shoulders, Elizabeth took a deep breath. The glass in her hand began to tremble and she quickly swallowed the whole of its contents to avoid spilling on her dress. She passed the empty vessel to George without looking. Marcus caught her hand before she could retrieve it.

Bowing low with a charming smile, his gaze never broke contact with hers. "Lady Hawthorne. Ravishing, as ever." His voice was rich and warm, reminding her of crushed velvet. "Would it be folly to hope you still have a dance available, and that you would be willing to dance it with me?"

Elizabeth's mind scrambled, attempting to discover a way to refuse. His wickedly virile energy, potent even across the room, was overwhelming in close proximity.

"I am not in attendance to dance, Lord Westfield. Ask any of the gentlemen around us."

"I've no wish to dance with them," he said dryly, "so their thoughts on the matter are of no consequence to me."

She began to object when she perceived the challenge in his eyes. He smiled with devilish amusement, visibly daring her to proceed, and Elizabeth paused. She would not give him the satisfaction of thinking she was afraid to dance with him. "You may claim this next set, Lord Westfield, if you insist."

He bowed gracefully, his gaze approving. He offered his arm and led her toward the dance floor. As the musicians began to play and music rose in joyous swell through the room, the beautiful strains of the minuet began.

Turning, Marcus extended his arm toward her. She placed her hand atop the back of his, grateful for the gloves that separated their skin. The ballroom was ablaze with candles, which cast him in golden light and brought to her attention the strength of his shoulder as it flexed. Lashes lowered, she appraised him for signs of change.

Marcus had always been an intensely physical man, engaging in a variety of sports and activities. Impossibly, it appeared he had grown stronger, more formidable. He was power personified and Elizabeth marveled at her past naiveté in believing she could tame him. Thank God, she was no longer so foolish.

His one softness was his luxuriously rich brown hair. It shone like sable and was tied at the nape with a simple black ribbon. Even his emerald gaze was sharp, piercing with a fierce intelligence. He had a clever mind to which deceit was naught but a simple game, as she had learned at great cost to her heart and pride.

She had half expected to find the signs of dissipation so common to the indulgent life and yet his handsome face bore no such witness. Instead he wore the sun-kissed appearance of a man who spent much of his time outdoors. His nose was straight and aquiline over lips that were full and sensuous. At the moment those lips were turned up on one side in a half smile that was at once boyish and alluring. He remained perfectly gorgeous from the top of his head to the soles of his feet. He was watching her studying him, fully aware that she could not help but admire his handsomeness. She lowered her eyes and stared resolutely at his jabot.

The scent that clung to him enveloped her senses. It was a wonderfully manly scent of sandalwood, citrus, and Marcus's own unique essence. The flush of her skin seeped into her insides, mingling with her apprehension.

Reading her thoughts, Marcus tilted his head toward her. His voice, when it came, was low and husky. "Elizabeth. It is a long-awaited pleasure to be in your company again."

"The pleasure, Lord Westfield, is entirely yours."

"You once called me Marcus."

"It would no longer be appropriate for me to address you so informally, my lord."

His mouth tilted into a sinful grin. "I give you leave to be inappropriate with me at any time you choose. In fact, I have always relished your moments of inappropriateness."

"You have had a number of willing women who suited you just as well."

"Never, my love. You have always been separate and apart from every other female."

Elizabeth had met her share of scoundrels and rogues but always their slick confidence and overtly intimate manners left her unmoved. Marcus was so skilled at seducing women, he managed the appearance of utter sincerity. She'd once believed every declaration of adoration and devotion that had fallen from his lips. Even now, the way he looked at her with such fierce longing seemed so genuine she almost believed it.

He made her want to forget what kind of man he was—a heartless seducer. But her body would not let her forget. She felt feverish and faintly dizzy.

"Three years of mourning," he said, with a faint note of bitterness. "I am relieved to see grief has not unduly ravaged your beauty. In fact, you are even more exquisite than when we were last together. You do recall that occasion, do you not?"

"Vaguely," she lied. "I have not thought of it in many years."

Wondering if he suspected her deception, she studied him as they changed partners. Marcus radiated an aura of sexual magnetism that was innate to him. The way he moved, the way he talked, the way he smelled—it all boasted of powerful energies and appetites. She sensed the barely leashed power he hid below the polished surface and she recollected how dangerous he was.

His voice poured over her with liquid heat as the steps of the minuet returned her to him. "I am wounded you are not more pleased to see me, especially when I braved this miserable event solely to be with you."

"Ridiculous," she scoffed. "You had no notion I would be here this evening. Whatever your purpose, please go about it and leave me in peace."

His voice was alarmingly soft. "My purpose is you, Elizabeth."

She stared a moment, her stomach churning with heightened unease. "If my brother sees us together he will be furious."

The flare of Marcus's nostrils made her wince. Once he and William had been the best of friends, but the end of her engagement had also brought about the demise of their friendship. Of all the things she regretted, that was paramount.

"What do you want?" she asked when he said nothing more.

"The fulfillment of your promise."

"What promise?"

"Your skin against mine with nothing in between."

"You're mad." She breathed heavily, shivering. Then her eyes narrowed. "Don't toy with me. Consider all the women who have graced your sheets since we parted. I did you a good turn by releasing you to—"

Elizabeth gasped as his gloved hand spun about beneath hers and his fingers squeezed with crushing force.

With darkened gaze, he bit out, "You did a great many things to me when you broke your word. A good turn is not one of them."

Shocked at his vehemence, she fought back. "You knew how I felt about fidelity, how strongly I desired it. You could never have been the type of husband I wanted."

"I was exactly what you wanted, Elizabeth. You wanted me so badly it scared you away."

"That's not true! I am not afraid of you!"

"If you had any sense, you would be," he muttered.

She would have retorted, but the steps of the dance led him away. He flashed a brilliant smile at the woman who minced steps around him and Elizabeth grit her teeth. For the rest of the dance he spoke not a word, even while he charmed every other woman he came into contact with.

Elizabeth's hand burned from Marcus's touch and her skin was flushed from the heat of his gaze. He'd never hidden the blatant sexuality of his nature. Instead he'd encouraged her to release her own. He'd offered her the best of both worlds—the respectability of her station and the passion of a man who could turn her blood to fire—and she'd believed he could make her happy.

How naive she'd been. With a family such as hers, she should have known better.

The moment the dance was over Elizabeth fled with rapid steps. A slightly raised hand caught her eye, and she smiled at the sight of Avery James. She cleared her thoughts, knowing immediately he was the man she awaited. Avery would only attend a social event such as this at Lord Eldridge's behest.

Eldridge had assured her that as the widow of a trusted agent if she ever required anything she was only to ask. Avery had been assigned as the man for her to contact. Despite his cynically world-weary appearance, he was in fact a gentle and considerate man who had been indispensable to her in the first few months after Hawthorne's death. The sight of him reminded her again of why she was here.

Elizabeth picked up her pace as, behind her, Marcus called out her name.

"The dance you requested is over, Westfield," she threw over her shoulder. "You are free to bask in the glow of your hard-earned reputation and the amorous attentions of your admirers."

She hoped he understood the obvious. Whatever the cost, she would not be seeing him again.

Marcus watched Elizabeth move gracefully toward Avery. With her back to him, he no longer had to suppress his grin. She had given him the cut direct. Again.

But alas, his sweet Elizabeth would soon discover that he was not so easily dismissed.

Chapter 2

"Mr. James," Elizabeth greeted him with genuine affection. "It is a pleasure to see you again." She held out her hands and they were swiftly engulfed in his much larger ones, his face lit with a rare smile. Tucking her hand under his arm, he led her through nearby French doors to an indoor atrium.

She squeezed his forearm. "I thought perhaps I had arrived too late and missed my appointment."

"Never say it, Lady Hawthorne," he replied with gruff fondness. "I would have waited all evening."

Tilting her head back, Elizabeth sucked in a deep breath of the lushly scented air. The heady redolence contained within the vast space was a pleasant and most welcome relief after the smells of smoke and burnt wax, powders and heavy perfumes that had overwhelmed the ballroom.

As they strolled casually through the paths, Elizabeth turned to Avery and asked, "Would I be correct in assuming that you are the agent assigned to assist me?"

He smiled. "I will be partnering another agent in this matter, yes."

"Of course." Her mouth curved ruefully. "You always work in pairs, don't you? As did Hawthorne and my brother."

"The order of things works well, my lady, and has saved lives."

Her steps faltered. Saves *some* lives. "I lament the existence of the agency, Mr. James. William's marriage and sub-sequent resignation is a blessing I treasure. He almost died the night I lost my husband. I eagerly await the day when the agency is no longer a part of my life."

"We will do our best to resolve this with the utmost haste," he assured her.

"I know you will," she sighed. "I'm pleased you are one of the agents Lord Eldridge chose."

Avery squeezed her hand where it draped over his forearm. "I was grateful for the opportunity to meet with you again. It has been several months since we last met."

"Has it truly been that long?" she asked, frowning. "Time is running away from me."

"I wish I could say the same . . ." a familiar voice inter-jected from behind her. "Unfortunately, the last four years have seemed an eternity to me."

Elizabeth tensed, her heart stopping before quickening its pace.

Avery turned them both to face their visitor. "Ah, here is my partner now. I understand you and Lord Westfield are old acquaintances. Hopefully such a fortuitous arrangement will expedite matters."

"Marcus," she whispered, her eyes widening as the import of his presence struck her like a physical blow.

He bowed. "I am in your service, madam."

Elizabeth swayed on her feet, and Avery tightened his grip to steady her. "Lady Hawthorne?"

Marcus reached her in two strides. "Don't faint, love. Take a deep breath."

It seemed an impossible task as she gasped like a fish out of water, her corset suddenly unbearably constricting. She waved him off, his proximity and the scent of his skin mak-ing it even more difficult to expand her lungs.

She watched as Marcus shot a telling glance to Avery, who then turned and walked away, suddenly finding interest in the fronds of a distant fern.

Lightheaded but recovering, Elizabeth shook her head rapidly. "Marcus, you have truly lost your mind."

"Ah, feeling better, I see," he drawled with a sardonic tilt to his lips.

"Find your amusement in some other venture. Resign your commission. Leave the agency."

"Your concern is touching albeit confusing, after your own callous disregard for my well-being in the past."

"Save your sarcasm for another day," she snapped. "Have you no notion of what you've involved yourself in? It's dangerous to work for Lord Eldridge. You could be hurt. Or killed."

Marcus released a deep breath. "Elizabeth, you are overwrought."

She glared at him and glanced quickly at Avery, who maintained his discretionary study of the fern. She lowered her voice. "How long have you been an agent?"

His jaw tightened. "Four years."

"*Four years?*" She stumbled backward. "Were you an agent when you paid your addresses to me?"

"Yes."

"Damn you." Her voice was a pained whisper. "When were you planning on disclosing this to me? Or was I never to know until you came home in a coffin?"

He scowled and crossed his arms over his chest. "I don't see that it much matters now."

She stiffened at his icy tone. "All these years I feared reading the banns announcing your marriage. Instead I should have been perusing the obituaries." Turning away, Elizabeth sheltered her racing heart with her hand. "How I wish you had stayed far, far away from me." She gathered her skirts and hurried away. "I wish to God I'd never met you."

The sharp tapping of his heels on marble was the only warning she had before her elbow was caught and she was spun about.

"The feeling is bloody damn mutual," he growled.

He towered over her, his sensual mouth drawn taut with

anger, his emerald gaze sparkling with something that made her shiver.

"How could Lord Eldridge assign you to me?" she cried. "And why did you accept?"

"I insisted on taking this mission."

At her astonished gasp, his lips thinned further. "Make no mistake. You fled from me once. I will not allow it to happen again." He tugged her closer and the air sweltered between them. His voice turned rough. "I don't care if you marry the King himself this time. I *will* have you."

She struggled to escape, but his grip was firm. "Good heavens, Marcus. Haven't we inflicted enough damage on one another?"

"Not nearly." He thrust her away as if the feel of her against him was distasteful. "Now let us dispatch this matter regarding your late husband so Avery can retire."

Shaking, Elizabeth moved swiftly toward Avery. Marcus followed behind her with the predatory gracefulness of a jungle cat.

There was no doubt she was the one being hunted.

She stopped beside Avery and took a shuddering breath before turning.

Marcus watched her with an unreadable expression. "I understand you received a book written by your late husband." He waited for her answering nod. "Is the sender familiar to you?"

"The handwriting on the parcel was Hawthorne's. It was obviously addressed some time ago, the wrapping was yellowed and the ink faded." She had puzzled over the package for days, unable to determine its origin or its purpose.

"Your husband addressed a package to himself and it arrives three years after his murder." Marcus narrowed his gaze. "Did he leave any grilles[1], any cards with odd holes in them, anything written that struck you as unusual?"

[1]The grille method was developed by the French Cardinal Richelieu in the 1600s. Its purpose was to create secret messages that could only be deciphered by a special card punched with holes in strategic locations.

"No, nothing." She reached into her reticule, withdrawing the slim journal and the letter she'd received just a few days ago. She handed both to Marcus.

After a cursory perusal he tucked the book into his coat and then glanced through the letter, a frown gathering between his brows as he read. "In the history of the agency only Lord Hawthorne's murder remains unsolved. I had hoped to keep your involvement to a minimum."

"I will do whatever is necessary," she offered quickly. "Hawthorne deserves justice and if my involvement is required, so be it." Anything to finish this.

Marcus folded the missive carefully. "I dislike exposing you to danger."

Her emotions on edge, Elizabeth bristled. "So you seek to withhold me from harm while risking your own neck? I am more heavily invested in the outcome of this than you or your precious agency."

Marcus growled her name in warning.

Avery cleared his throat loudly. "It appears you two will not work well together. I would suggest bringing this difficulty to Lord Eldridge's attention. I'm certain there are other agents who—"

"No!" Marcus's voice cracked like a whip.

"Yes!" Elizabeth nearly collapsed in relief. "An excellent suggestion." Her smile was heartfelt. "Surely Lord Eldridge will see the sense in the request."

"Running again?" Marcus taunted.

She glared. "I am being practical. You and I quite obviously cannot associate with one another."

"Practical." He gave a derisive snort. "The word you seek is craven."

"Lord Westfield!" Avery frowned.

Elizabeth waved him off. "Leave us for a moment, Mr. James. If you would, please." Her gaze remained locked on Marcus as Avery hesitated.

"Do as she says," Marcus murmured, glaring back at her. Avery grunted, then spun on his heel and moved away with angry strides.

Elizabeth cut straight to it. "If I'm forced to work with you, Westfield, I will simply refuse to share any further information with the agency. I will handle the situation alone."

"Like hell you will!" The muscle in Marcus's jaw began to tick. "I will not allow you to place yourself in jeopardy. Attempt something foolish and see what happens. You won't like the outcome, I assure you."

"Truly?" she goaded, refusing to cower in the face of a temper that frightened most men. "And how do you propose to stop me?"

Marcus approached her menacingly. "I am an agent of the Crown—"

"We've established that."

"—on an assigned mission. Should you think to hinder my investigation I will view your actions as treasonous and treat you accordingly."

"You wouldn't dare! Lord Eldridge would not allow it."

"Oh but I would, and he wouldn't stop me." He came to a halt before her. "This volume looks suspiciously like a journal of Hawthorne's assignments and it could be related to his death. If so, you are in danger. Eldridge will not tolerate that any more than I."

"Why not?" she challenged. "Your feelings toward me are obvious."

He stepped closer, until the tips of his shoes disappeared beneath the edge of her hem. "Apparently not. However, plead your case to Eldridge if you must. Tell him how I affect you and how you long for me. Tell him about our sordid past and how even the memory of your dearly departed husband is not enough to overcome your desire."

She stared, and then her mouth fell open as a dry laugh escaped. "Your arrogance is stunning." She turned away, hiding the way her hands shook. He could have the damn journal. She would seek out Eldridge in the morning.

His mocking laughter followed her. "*My* arrogance? You are the one who thinks this is all about her."

Elizabeth stopped and spun about. "You made this personal with your threats."

"You and I becoming lovers is not a threat. It is a foregone conclusion and has nothing to do with your late husband's journal." He held up his hand when she attempted to argue. "Save your breath. This mission is important to Eldridge. I insisted for that reason alone. Having you in my bed does not require working with you."

"But . . ." She paused, recalling what he'd said to her earlier. He never stated his insistence was about her. Her face heated.

Marcus strolled casually past her, heading in the direction of the ballroom. "So feel free to disclose to Eldridge why you cannot work with me. Just be certain he understands that *I* have no difficulty at all working with *you.*"

Gritting her teeth, Elizabeth bit back every expletive that fought to blurt from her mouth. No fool she, she understood his game. She also understood he would not leave her be until he decided he'd had enough, mission or not. The only part of this debacle that was within her power to control was whether she survived this encounter with her pride intact.

Her stomach tightened. Now that she had rejoined society she would have to watch his seductions. She would be forced to associate with the women who caught his fancy. She would see the smiles he shared with them, but not with her.

Damnation. Her breathing quickened. Against every shred of self-respect and intelligence she had, she took the first step to follow him.

The soft touch upon her elbow reminded her of Avery's presence. "Lady Hawthorne. Is everything well?"

She gave a jerky nod.

"I will speak with Lord Eldridge as soon as possible and—"

"That won't be necessary, Mr. James."

Elizabeth waited until Marcus rounded the corner and disappeared from her view before facing Avery. "My role is simply to deliver the journal. Once that is accomplished the rest remains up to you and Lord Westfield. I see no need to change agents."

"Are you certain?"

She nodded again, anxious to finish the conversation and return to the ballroom.

Avery's look was clearly skeptical, but he said, "Very well. I will assign two armed outriders to you. Take them with you everywhere and send word to me as soon as you receive details about the meeting."

"Of course."

"Since we've finished here, I shall depart." His smile held a touch of relief. "I never cared much for these affairs."

He lifted her hand and kissed the back.

"Elizabeth?" William's booming voice rang through the vast space.

Eyes wide, she clutched Avery's fingers. "My brother must not see you. He'll suspect immediately that something is amiss."

Avery, appreciating her concern and trained to think on his feet, nodded grimly and ducked swiftly behind a rounded bush.

Turning, she caught sight of William approaching. Like Marcus, he didn't mince his steps. He walked toward her with casual grace, his leg bearing no outward sign of the injury that had almost taken his life.

Although they were siblings they could not have been more disparate in appearance. She had the raven hair and amethyst eyes of their mother. William had the fair hair and bluish-green eyes of their father. Tall and broad-shouldered he had the look of a Viking, strong and dangerous but prone to mirth as witnessed by the fine laugh lines that rimmed his eyes.

"What are you about?" he queried, casting an overly curious glance around the atrium.

Elizabeth tucked her hand in the crook of his elbow, and steered him toward the ballroom. "I was merely enjoying the view. Where is Margaret?"

"With her acquaintances." William slowed and then stopped, forcing her to halt with him. "I was told you danced with Westfield earlier."

"Gossip already?"

"Stay away from him, Elizabeth," he warned softly.

"There was no polite way to refuse him."

"Do not be polite. I don't trust him. It's odd that he is in attendance tonight."

She sighed sadly at the rift she'd caused. Marcus made poor husband material, but he'd been a good friend to William. "The reputation he's established these last few years has justified my actions of long ago. I'm in no danger of being swept away by his charms again, I assure you."

Tugging William toward the ballroom, Elizabeth was relieved when her brother gave no further resistance. If they hurried, she might be able to see where Marcus was headed.

Marcus stepped out from his hiding place behind a tree and brushed a stray leaf from his coat. Kicking dirt off his shoes, his gaze remained riveted on Elizabeth's retreating back until she disappeared from his sight. He wondered if it was obvious, this maddening desire he had for her. His heart raced and his legs ached with the effort he exerted not to follow her and snatch her away for his pleasure.

She was infuriatingly stubborn and obstinate, which is how he'd known she was perfect for him. No other woman could arouse his passions thusly. Furious or consumed with lust, only Elizabeth made his blood heat with the need to have her.

He wished to God it was love he felt. That emotion faded

eventually, burning out once the fuel was gone. Hunger only grew worse with time, aching and gnawing until it was fed.

Avery appeared at his side. "If that is what you call an 'old friend,' my lord, I would hate to see what your enemies are like."

His smile held no humor. "She was to be my wife." Stunned silence was the reply. "Have I rendered you speechless?"

"Damnation."

"An apt description." Girding himself inwardly, Marcus asked, "Does she plan to speak with Eldridge?"

"No." Avery shot him a sidelong glance. "Are you certain your involvement is wise?"

"No," he admitted, relieved his ploy had worked and grateful that, despite the years, he still knew her so well. "But I'm certain I have no other choice."

"Eldridge is determined to catch Hawthorne's murderer. In the course of our mission we may be forced to deliberately put Lady Hawthorne in danger to achieve our aims."

"No. Hawthorne is dead. Risking Elizabeth's life will not bring him back. We will find other ways to carry out our mission."

Avery shook his head in silent bemusement. "I trust you know what you are about, even if I do not. Now if you will excuse me, my lord, I shall make my egress through the garden, before anything else untoward occurs."

"I believe I'll accompany you." Falling into step beside his partner, Marcus laughed at Avery's raised brow. "When engaged in prolonged battle, a man must be prepared to retreat on occasion so that he may return refreshed to seize the day."

"Good God. Battles and brothers and broken engagements. Your personal history with Lady Hawthorne will only lead to trouble."

Marcus rubbed his hands together. "I look forward to it."

Chapter 3

"I am under siege!" Elizabeth complained as another obnoxiously large display of flowers was carried into the sitting room.

"There are worse fates for a woman than being courted by a devilishly handsome peer of the realm," Margaret said dryly, as she smoothed her skirts and sat upon the settee.

"You are a hopeless romantic, you know." Rising to her feet, Elizabeth collected a tiny brocade pillow and tucked it behind her sister-in-law's back. She deliberately kept her gaze diverted from the gorgeous and obviously costly flower arrangement. Marcus had implied that his interest was both professional and carnal, and she'd been as prepared as possible for such engagement. This soft assault on her feminine sensibilities was a surprise attack.

"I'm *enceinte*," Margaret protested as she was arranged more comfortably. "Not an invalid."

"Allow me to fuss a little. It brings me such pleasure."

"I'm certain I will appreciate it later, but for the moment, I am quite capable of seeing to myself."

Despite her grumbling, Margaret settled into the pillow with a sigh of pleasure, the soft glow of her skin displayed to perfection by the dark red of her curls.

"I beg to differ. You look more slender at five months pregnancy than you did before."

"*Nearly* five months," Margaret corrected. "And it is difficult to eat when you feel wretched most of the time."

Pursing her lips, Elizabeth reached for a scone, set it on a plate, and offered it to Margaret. "Take it," she ordered.

Margaret accepted with a mock glare, then said, "William says the betting books are filled with wagers on whether Lord Westfield still has matrimony in mind or not."

In the process of making tea, Elizabeth gaped. "Good God."

"You are a legend for jilting him—an earl so handsome and desired that every woman wants him. Except for you. It is simply too juicy to ignore. A tale of a rake's love thwarted."

Elizabeth snorted derisively.

"You've never told me what Lord Westfield did that caused you to break off your engagement."

Her hands shook as she spooned the tea leaves into the steaming pot. "It was long ago, Margaret, and as I've said many times before, I see no reason to discuss it."

"Yes, yes, I know. However, he clearly is desirous of your company, as witnessed by his repeated attempts to call on you. I admire Westfield's aplomb. He does not even blink when he is turned away. He simply smiles, says something charming, and takes his leave."

"The man has charm in bushels, I agree. Women flock to his side and make fools of themselves."

"You sound jealous."

"I am not," she argued. "One lump or two today?" Nevermind. You need two."

"Don't change the subject. Tell me about your jealousy. Women found Hawthorne attractive as well, but it never appeared to bother you."

"Hawthorne was steadfast."

Margaret took the offered cup and saucer with a grateful smile. "And you've said Westfield was not."

"No," Elizabeth said with a sigh.

"Are you certain?"

"I could not be more certain if I'd caught them in the act."

Margaret's mossy green eyes narrowed. "You took the word of a third party over that of your fiancé?"

Shaking her head, Elizabeth took a fortifying sip of her tea before answering. "I had a matter of grave urgency to discuss with Lord Westfield, grave enough that I ventured to his home one evening—"

"*Alone?* What in heaven's name would goad you to act so rashly?"

"Margaret, do you wish to hear the tale or not? It's difficult enough to talk about this without you interrupting."

"My apologies," came the contrite reply. "Please continue."

"I waited several moments after I arrived for him to receive me. When he appeared, his hair was damp, his skin flushed, and he was attired in a robe."

Elizabeth stared into the contents of her cup and felt ill.

"Go on," Margaret prodded when she didn't speak.

"Then the door he'd come through opened and a woman appeared. Dressed similarly, with hair as wet."

"Good grief! That would be difficult to explain. How did he attempt it?"

"He didn't." Elizabeth gave a dry, humorless laugh. "He said he was not at liberty to discuss it with me."

Frowning, Margaret set her cup and saucer on the end table. "Did he attempt to explain later?"

"No. I eloped with Hawthorne, and Westfield left the country until his father passed on. Until the Moreland ball last week, we've never again crossed paths."

"Never? Perhaps Westfield has collected his error and wishes to make amends," Margaret suggested. "There must be some reason he's pursuing you so doggedly."

Elizabeth shivered at the use of the word "pursuing." "Trust my judgment. His aim is nothing as noble as making amends for past wrongs."

"Flowers, daily visits—"

"Discuss something less distasteful, Margaret," she warned. "Or I will take my tea elsewhere."

"Oh, fine. You and your brother are a stubborn lot."

But Margaret was never one to be denied, which is how she'd convinced William to give up his agency life and marry her. Therefore, Elizabeth anticipated the moment when Margaret would return to the subject of Marcus and was not surprised when it came later that evening.

"He is such a beautiful man."

Elizabeth followed Margaret's gaze across the crush of guests at the Dempsey rout. She found Marcus standing with Lady Cramshaw and her lovely daughter, Clara. Elizabeth pretended to ignore him even as she studied his every move. "After hearing about our past, how can you be taken by the earl's pretty face?"

She'd deliberately avoided social events for the last week, but in the end had accepted the Dempsey invitation, certain the Faulkner ball up the street would be more likely to attract Marcus. The annoying man had found her anyway, and dressed so beautifully. His deep red coat fell to his thighs and was liberally decorated with fine gold embroidery. The heavy silk gleamed in the candlelight as did the rubies that adorned his fingers and cravat.

"Beg your pardon?" Margaret turned her head, her eyes wide with bemusement. She pointed her fan across the room. It was then that Elizabeth saw William and she blushed furiously at her mistake.

Margaret laughed. "They make a stunning couple, your Westfield and Lady Clara."

"He is not mine and I pity the poor girl if she's caught his eye." She lifted her chin and looked away.

The telltale swish of heavy silk skirts announced a new participant in their conversation. "I agree," murmured the elderly Duchess of Ravensend as she completed their circle. "She's just a child and could never hope to do that man justice."

"Your Grace." Elizabeth dipped a quick curtsy before her godmother.

The duchess had a mischievous gleam in her soft brown eyes. "Unfortunate that you are now widowed, my dear, but it does present you and the earl with renewed opportunities."

Elizabeth closed her eyes and prayed for patience. From the very beginning her godmother had championed Marcus's suit. "Westfield is a scoundrel. I consider myself fortunate to have discovered that fact before saying my vows."

"He is quite possibly the handsomest man I have ever seen," observed Margaret. "Next to William, of course."

"And attractively formed," added the duchess as she peered at Marcus through her lorgnette. "Prime husband material."

Sighing, Elizabeth fluffed her skirts and fought the urge to roll her eyes. "I wish you both would set aside the notion that I marry again. I will not."

"Hawthorne was barely more than a boy," noted the duchess. "Westfield is a man. You will find the experience to be quite different should you choose him to share your bed. No one said marriage was required."

"I have no desire to be added to that libertine's list of conquests. He is a voluptuary. You cannot deny that, Your Grace."

"There is something to be said for a man with experience," Margaret offered. "Married to your brother, I would know." She waggled her brows suggestively.

Elizabeth shuddered. "Margaret, please."

"*Lady Hawthorne.*"

Turning quickly, she faced George Stanton with a grateful smile. He bowed, his handsome face awash in a friendly grin.

"I would be pleased to dance with you," she said before he could ask. Eager to get away, she placed her fingertips upon his sleeve and allowed him to lead her away.

"Thank you," she whispered.

"You appeared to be in need of rescue."

She grinned as they took their places in line. "You are re-markably astute, my dear friend."

With a sidelong glance, she watched as Marcus bowed over the young Clara's hand and escorted her to the dance floor. As he moved toward her, Elizabeth couldn't help but admire his seductive gait. A man who moved as he did would be an expert lover, there was no doubt. Other women watched him as well, coveted him as she did, lusted for him . . .

When he lifted his head to catch her gaze, Elizabeth looked away quickly from his knowing smile. The man knew just how to rile her and was ungentlemanly enough to use that knowledge to his advantage.

As the steps of the *contredanse* brought the dancers to-gether and then moved them apart she followed his progress out of the corner of her eye. The next step would bring them together. Heated anticipation coursed through her veins.

She withdrew from George and turned gracefully to face Marcus. Knowing the encounter would be fleeting she per-mitted herself to enjoy the sight and smell of him. She drew a deep breath and set her palms against his. Desire flared in-stantly. She saw it in his eyes, felt it in her blood. She re-treated with a sigh of relief.

As the music for the dance concluded, Elizabeth rose from her low curtsy. She couldn't resist smiling. It had been so long since she'd danced, she had almost forgotten how much she enjoyed it.

George returned her smile and deftly moved them into po-sition for the next dance in the set.

Someone stepped in front of them, blocking their way. Before she looked up, she knew who it was. Her heart rate quickened.

Obviously, she'd miscalculated the lengths Marcus would go to to achieve his ends.

He nodded curtly in greeting. "Mr. Stanton."

"Lord Westfield." George looked to Elizabeth with a frown.

"Lady Clara, may I present to you Mr. George Stanton?" Marcus asked. "Stanton, the lovely Lady Clara."

George collected Clara's hand and bowed. "A pleasure."

Before Elizabeth could guess his intent, Marcus had reached for her. "An excellent pairing," Marcus said. "Lady Hawthorne and I, being *de trop*, shall leave you two to finish the set."

Tucking her hand firmly around his arm, he pulled her toward the open doors that led to the garden.

Elizabeth offered an apologetic smile over her shoulder, while inside, her heart leapt at the primitive display. "What are you about?"

"I thought that would be obvious. I'm causing a scene. You goaded me into this course of action by avoiding me the last sennight."

"I have not been avoiding you," she protested. "I've yet to receive another demand for the journal, therefore there was no reason to see you."

Exiting to the balcony, they found several guests enjoying the cool night air. Held so closely to his side, the sheer force of Marcus's presence once again surprised her.

"Your behavior is atrocious," she muttered.

"You may insult me at your leisure when we are alone."

Alone. A ripple of awareness brushed across her skin.

His gaze traveled over her face and searched her eyes. His own narrowed and though she tried to discern his thoughts his handsome features were set in stone. As they took the stairs into the garden, his pace quickened. She followed breathlessly, wondering what he meant to do, what he meant to say, startled to discover an unknown remnant of girlish romanticism thrilling at his determination.

Tucking her into a small alcove off the bottom of the staircase, Marcus eyed their surroundings carefully. Seeing they were alone, he moved swiftly. With gentle fingertips, he lifted her chin.

A kiss, she thought too late as his mouth covered hers. Then she couldn't think at all.

His lips were unbelievably gentle as they melded with hers but the sensations they elicited were brutal in their intensity. Elizabeth could not move, arrested by the powerful response of her body to his. Only their lips touched. A simple step backward would have broken the contact but she could not manage even that. She stood frozen, her senses reeling from the taste and scent of him, every nerve firing to life at his bold advance.

"Kiss me back," he growled, his fingers circling her wrists.

"No . . ." She tried to turn her head away.

Cursing, he took her mouth again. He did not kiss her sweetly as he had a moment before. This was an assault driven by bitterness so sharp she could taste it. His head tilted slightly, deepening the kiss, and then his tongue thrust forcefully between her parted lips. The depth of his ardor frightened her, and then fear flared into something far more powerful.

Hawthorne had never kissed her like this. This was more than just the joining of lips. It was a declaration of possession, of unquenchable need, a need Marcus built within her until she could no longer deny it. With a whimper, Elizabeth surrendered, tentatively touching her tongue to his, desperate for the intoxicating taste of him.

He growled his approval, the erotically charged sound causing her to sway unsteadily on her feet. Releasing her wrists, he supported her waist while a warm hand gripped the back of her neck, holding her still for his ravishment. His mouth moved skillfully over hers, rewarding her response with deeper flicks of his tongue. Her fists clutched his coat, pulling and tugging, trying to win some control but in the end unable to do more than just take what he gave her.

Finally he tore his mouth away with a tortured groan and buried his face in her perfumed hair. "Elizabeth." His voice was thick and unsteady. "We must find a bed. Now."

She gasped out a laugh. "This is madness."

"It has always been madness."

"You must stay away."

"I have. Four bloody years. I've paid the price for my imagined sins." He pulled back and stared down at her with eyes so hot they burned. "I've waited long enough to have you. I refuse to wait any longer."

The reminder of their past was sobering for both of them. "There is far too much between us to ever enjoy a liaison."

"I damn well intend to enjoy one regardless."

Shaking, she pulled back and, to her surprise, was released immediately. She pressed her fingers to her kiss-swollen lips. "I do not want the pain you bring. I do not want you."

"You lie," he said harshly. His finger traced the edge of her bodice. "You have wanted me since the moment we met. You want me still, I can taste it."

Elizabeth cursed her traitorous body, still so enamored of him it refused to listen to the dictates of her mind. Hot and aching all over, she was no better than any of the other besotted women who fell so easily into his bed. She backed away, but was stopped by the cold marble railing. Reaching behind her, she wrapped her hands around the baluster, gripping it so tightly the blood left her hands.

"If you had any care for me at all you would leave me be."

Flashing a smile that stopped her heart, Marcus stepped toward her. "I will show you the same care you once showed to me." His gaze smoldered with seductive challenge. "Give in to your desire for me, sweet. I assure you, doing so will not be something you regret."

"How can you say that? Have you not already wounded me once? Knowing how I feel about my father, you still acted as you did. I loathe men of your ilk. It's despicable to promise love and devotion to bed a woman only to cast her aside when you weary of the sport."

Marcus stopped abruptly. "It was *I* who was cast aside."

Elizabeth backed up tighter against the railing. "For good reason."

His lips twisted in a cynical smile. "You will receive me when I come to call, Elizabeth. You will drive out with me in the afternoons and accompany me to events such as these. I will not be turned away again."

The cold marble baluster froze her hands through her gloves and sent shivers up her arms. Despite the chill she felt hot, flushed. "Are you not satisfied with the numbers of women who fawn over you?"

"No," he replied with his habitual arrogance. "Satisfaction will come when you burn for me, when I invade your every thought and every dream. One day your infatuation will be so consuming that every breath you take apart from me will sear your lungs. You will give me whatever I desire, whenever and however I desire it."

"I will give you nothing!"

"You will give me everything." He closed the small gap between them. "You will yield all to me."

"Have you no shame?" Tears welled and clung to her lashes. He was implacable and the direness of her situation struck home with cruel effect. "After what you did to me, must you seduce me as well? Is my utter destruction the only thing that will appease you?"

"Damn you." His head dropped down to hers, his mouth brushing across her lips in a feather-light kiss. "I never thought to have you," he breathed. "I never expected that you would ever be free of your marriage, but you are. And I will have what was promised to me long ago."

Releasing the baluster, Elizabeth placed her hands against his waist to ward him off. The firm ridges of his stomach beneath her palms brought a raw, sweet ache to her body. "I will fight you with everything I have. I urge you to desist."

"Not until I have what I want."

"Leave her alone, Westfield."

Sagging with relief at the sound of the familiar voice, Elizabeth glanced up and saw William descending the staircase.

Marcus backed away with a vicious curse. Straightening, he shot his old friend a fulminating glare. Elizabeth exploited his distraction, taking the opportunity to slip past him. Running into the garden, she disappeared around a corner of yew hedges. He stepped forward, determined to go after her.

"I wouldn't," William said with soft menace, "If I were you."

"Your timing is unfortunate, Barclay." Marcus swallowed a growl of frustration, knowing his old friend would relish any opportunity to fight with him. The situation worsened as spectators, alerted by the carrying tone of angry voices and the rigid set of William's body, lined the edge of the balcony anticipating noteworthy gossip.

"When you desire Lady Hawthorne's company in the future, Westfield, be aware that she is indisposed to you indefinitely."

A statuesque redhead pushed her way through the throng of curious onlookers and ran down the steps toward them.

"Lord Westfield. Barclay. Please!" She clutched William's arm. "This is not the venue for such private discourse."

William broke off eye contact with Marcus and glanced at his lovely wife with a grim smile. "No need to fret. All is well." Lifting his gaze, he gestured to George Stanton who left the balcony and moved quickly to join them. "Please find Lady Hawthorne and escort her home."

"I would be honored." Stanton inched his way carefully between the two angry men before picking up speed and melding into the garden shadows.

Marcus sighed and rubbed the back of his neck. "You intercede based on a false assumption, Barclay."

"I will not debate the matter with you," William countered, all trace of civility gone. "Elizabeth has refused to see you and you will respect her wishes." He gently removed

Margaret's hand from his sleeve and stepped closer, his shoulders taut with repressed anger. "This will be your only warning. Keep your distance from my sister or I will call you out." The crowd above erupted in a series of muted gasps.

Marcus steadied his breathing with effort. Level-headedness had seen him through many volatile situations, but this time he made no effort to defuse the tension. He had a mission, as well as his own agenda. Both would require a great deal of time spent in Elizabeth's company. Nothing could be allowed to stand in his way.

Meeting William's challenge head-on, he stepped the last few paces until they were only inches apart. His voice softened ominously. "Interfering in my association with Elizabeth would not be wise. There is much left to be resolved between us and I will not have you intruding. I would never deliberately harm her. If you doubt my word, name your second now. My position is firm and worth whatever risk you present to me."

"You would risk your life to proceed?"

"Without question."

A weighted pause fell between them as they each measured the other carefully. Marcus made his resolve clear. He would not be deterred, threats of death or otherwise.

In return, William's gaze penetrated with its intensity. Over the years they had managed an icy public association. With William's marriage a stark contrast to his own bachelor's life, they'd rarely had the occasion to exchange words. Marcus lamented that lack. He often missed the companionship of his friend, who was a good man. But William had passed judgment too easily and Marcus would not bruise his pride by pleading a case to deaf ears.

"Shall we return to the festivities, Lady Barclay?" William said finally, the set of his shoulders relaxing a tiny fraction.

"I believe the night has grown chilly," Marcus murmured.

"Yes, my lord," Lady Barclay agreed. "I was about to say the same."

Hiding his regret, Marcus nodded, and then turned on his heel and left.

Elizabeth crossed into the foyer of Chesterfield Hall with a silent sigh. Her lips still throbbed and tasted of Marcus, a heady flavor that was dangerous to a woman's sanity. Although her heart rate had slowed, she was left feeling as though she'd just run a great race. She was grateful when her butler removed her heavy cloak and, tugging off her gloves, she headed directly toward the stairs. There was so much to consider, too much. She hadn't expected Marcus to be so damned determined to have his way. How she would handle a man such as he would take careful planning.

"My lady?"

"Yes?" She paused and turned to face the servant.

In his hand he held a silver salver which supported a cream-colored missive. Innocuous though it appeared, Elizabeth shivered at the sight of it. The handwriting and parchment were the same as the letter demanding Hawthorne's journal.

She shook her head and released a deep breath. Marcus would call on her tomorrow, of that she was certain. Whatever demand the note contained could wait until then. Reading it alone held no appeal. She knew how dangerous the agency's missions were and she didn't take her new involvement lightly. Therefore, if Marcus was so determined to plague her, she would at least make use of him in some small way.

Dismissing the servant with a wave, Elizabeth lifted her skirts and ascended the stairs.

What a sad twist of fate it was that the man assigned to protect her was the very one who'd proven he was not to be trusted.

Chapter 4

U nlike Marcus's own townhouse in Grosvenor Square, Chesterfield Hall was a sprawling estate located a good distance from the nearest house. Standing in the visitor's foyer, Marcus handed over his hat and gloves to the waiting liveried footman, then followed the butler down the hall to the formal parlor.

The location of his reception was a slight not lost on him. At one time he would have been shown upstairs and received as a near family member. Now he was not considered worthy of such a privilege.

"The Earl of Westfield," the servant announced.

Entering, Marcus paused on the threshold and glanced around the room, noting with interest the portrait that graced the space above the fireplace. The late Countess of Langston stared back at him with a winsome smile and violet eyes like her daughter's. Unlike Elizabeth's, however, Lady Langston's eyes held no wariness, only the soft glow of a woman content with her lot. Elizabeth had witnessed only briefly the kind of happiness his own parents had fostered over a lifetime. For a moment, regret rose like bile in his throat.

Once he'd sworn to dedicate his life to making Elizabeth look that happy. Now he wanted only to be done with his craving and free of her curse.

Clenching his jaw, he looked away from the painful reminder and found the curvaceous form that afflicted his waking and sleeping thoughts. As the butler shut the door with a soft click behind him, Marcus reached around his back and turned the lock.

Elizabeth stood by the arched window that overlooked the side garden. Dressed in a simple muslin day gown and bathed in indirect sunlight, she looked as young as when they'd first met. As always, every nerve ending in his body prickled with the sharp current of awareness that arced between them. In all of his many encounters, he'd yet to meet a woman who appealed to him as deeply or as hotly as Elizabeth did.

"Good afternoon, Lord Westfield," she said in the low throaty voice which brought to mind tumbled silk sheets. She shot a pointed glance at his hand, which remained curved around the knob. "My brother is at home."

"Good for him." He crossed the broad expanse of Aubusson rug in a few strides and lifted her bare fingertips to his lips. Her skin felt exquisite, the scent of her arousing. His tongue darted out to lick between her fingers and he watched as her pupils widened and the irises darkened. Marcus brought her hand to his heart and held it there. "Now that your mourning is over, do you intend to return to your own residence?"

Her gaze narrowed. "That would ease matters for you, wouldn't it?"

"Certainly breakfast in bed and afternoon trysts would be facilitated by a more private arrangement," he replied easily.

Yanking her hand from his grip, Elizabeth turned her back to him. Marcus bit back his smile.

"Considering your obvious distaste for me," she muttered, "I cannot understand why you desire to become intimate."

"Physical proximity does not necessitate intimacy."

Her shoulders stiffened beneath the fall of her dark hair. "Ah yes," she sneered. "You have proven that fact again and again, have you not?"

Flicking an imaginary piece of lint from his ruffled cuffs, Marcus walked to the settee and adjusted his coat before sitting. He refused to show his irritation at the censure he heard in her tone. Guilt was something he didn't require, he felt it often enough on his own. "I became what you once accused me of being. What would you have had me do, love? Go mad thinking of you? *Longing* for you?"

He sighed dramatically, hoping to goad her into facing him. It was a simple pleasure, gazing upon her features, but after four years it was a delight he needed as much as air. "I am truly not surprised to learn that, given the choice, you would have denied me what little solace I could find, cruel-hearted creature that you are."

Elizabeth spun about, revealing cheeks stained bright with color. "You blame *me*?"

"Who else is there to blame?" He opened his snuff box and took a small pinch. "It should have been you in my arms all these years. Instead, every time I bedded another woman I hoped she would be the one to make me forget you. But they never did. Not one." He snapped the lid shut.

Her nostrils flared on a swiftly indrawn breath.

"Often I would turn down the lamps and close my eyes. I would pretend it was you beneath me, you with whom I shared sexual congress."

"Damn you." Her hands clenched into tiny fists. "Why did you have to become just like my father?"

"You would have me be a monk?"

"Better that than a libertine!"

"While you sated another man's needs and suffered not at all?" He strove to appear calm and unaffected while every fiber of his being stood tense and expectant. "Did you think of me, Elizabeth, in your marriage bed? Were you ever haunted by dreams of me? Did you ever wish it were my body covering yours, filling yours? My sweat coating your skin?"

She stood frozen in place for a long moment, and then suddenly her lush mouth curved in a come-hither smile that made his gut clench. He'd known when the butler allowed him entry that Elizabeth was no longer willing to hide or run.

He'd girded himself inwardly for a fight. A sexual assault, however, had never crossed his mind. *Would he never understand her?*

"Would you like me to tell you about my marriage bed, Marcus?" she purred. "Would you like to hear the many ways Hawthorne took me? What he liked best, what he craved? Hmmm? Or would you prefer to hear how *I* like it? How I prefer to be taken?"

Elizabeth strolled toward him with a deliberate sway to her hips that made his mouth dry. In all of his dealings with her she'd never been the sexual aggressor. He was profoundly disturbed at how it aroused him, especially considering the last four years had been spent indulging in liaisons instigated by his lovers and not the reverse.

It didn't help that his reluctant passion was engaged by her words and the images they evoked. He pictured her face down on the bed, spread and willing as another man thrust into her from behind. His jaw ached from the force with which he clenched it, primitive feelings of claiming and possessing nearly undoing him. Pulling open the flaps of his coat, Marcus revealed the straining length of his cock within his breeches. Her steps faltered and then, with a lift of her chin, she continued toward him.

"I am not an innocent to run screaming at the sight of a man's desire." Elizabeth stopped before him and set her hands on either side of his knees. Before him hung the voluptuous swell of her breasts, nearly spilling from the rounded cut of her satin-edged bodice. In evening attire, her bosom was pressed flat by her corset. In day wear, the restriction was far less severe and his gaze was riveted by the bounty displayed for his benefit alone.

Never one to miss an opportunity, Marcus reached up and cupped the upper swell with his hands, gratified to hear the sharp hiss of her breath through her teeth. Her body had changed from the virginal ripeness of a girl to the fully curved figure of a woman. Squeezing and kneading, he stared at the valley between her breasts and imagined thrusting his cock through it. He growled at the thought and looked up at her mouth, watching in an agony of lust as she licked her lower lip.

Then suddenly she straightened, turned her back to him, and reached down to the small table. Before he could order her return, she'd tossed a sealed missive at his chest and walked away. He knew already what he would find inside. Still, he waited for his breathing to slow and his blood to cool before turning his attention to it. He noted the paper, a popular weight and tint he'd seen before.

Breaking open the unmarked seal with care, he scanned the contents. "How long have you had this?" he asked gruffly.

"A few hours."

Marcus turned the paper over and then lifted his gaze to hers. Elizabeth's skin was flushed and her eyes glazed, yet her chin was lifted at a determined angle. He frowned and stood. "You weren't curious enough to open it?"

"I'm aware of what it must say. He is prepared to meet with me and retrieve the book. How he worded the demand doesn't much matter, does it? Have you perused Hawthorne's journal since I gave it to you?"

He nodded. "The maps were easy enough. Hawthorne had some detailed drawings of the English and Scottish coasts, as well as some colonial waterways I'm familiar with. But Hawthorne's code is nigh indecipherable. I was hoping to have more time to study it."

Refolding the missive, Marcus put it in his pocket. Cryptography was a hobby he'd acquired after Elizabeth's marriage. The task required intense concentration, which allowed him a brief respite from thoughts of her, a rare gift. "I know this spot he refers to. Avery and I will be close by to protect you."

Shrugging, she said, "As you wish."

He stood and stalked over to her. Grabbing her shoulders,

he shook her. Hard. "How the hell can you be so bloody calm? Have you any notion of the danger? Or have you no sense at all?"

"What would you have me do?" she snapped. "Fall apart? Cry all over you?"

"A little emotion would be welcome. Something, *anything* to tell me you have a care for your own safety." His hands left her shoulders and plunged into her hair, tilting her head to the angle he desired. Then he kissed her as hard as he'd shaken her. He backed her up roughly, forcing her to stumble until he'd pinned her to the wall.

Elizabeth's nails dug deeply into the skin of his stomach as she clutched at his shirt. Her mouth was open, accepting the thrusts of his tongue. Despite the lack of finesse, she trembled against him, whimpered her distress, and then melted into his embrace. She kissed him back with a frenzy that nearly undid him.

Suddenly unable to breathe, Marcus broke away. His forehead pressed to hers, he groaned his frustration. "Why do you only come alive when I touch you? Don't you ever tire of the façade you hide behind?"

Her eyes squeezed shut and she turned her face away. "And what of your façade?"

"Jesus, you are stubborn." Nuzzling against her without gentleness, he rubbed the scent of her onto his damp skin while leaving his own sweat upon her cheek. With a rough and urgent voice he whispered, "I need you to follow my instructions when I give them to you. You must not allow your feelings to interfere."

"I trust your judgment," she said.

He stilled, his fists clenching in her hair until she winced. "Do you?"

The air thickened around them.

"Do you?" he asked again.

"What happened . . ." She swallowed hard and her nails dug deeper into his skin. "What happened that night?"

He let out his breath in an audible rush. His entire frame relaxed, the tension of their past releasing its merciless grip. Suddenly exhausted, Marcus realized the cold fury he still carried over the demise of their betrothal was all that had fueled him these many years.

"Sit down." He pulled away and waited until she crossed over to the settee. Studying her for long moments, he relished the sight of her mussed hair and swollen lips. From the beginning, he'd pursued her with singular attention, stealing her away to quiet corners where he would take her mouth with rushed, desperate kisses, risking scandal for glimpses of the fire Elizabeth hid so well.

Her beauty was simply the wrapping on a complex and fascinating treasure. Her eyes gave her away. In them one could find no trace of a lady's expected docility or meekness. Instead there were challenges, adventures. Things to be explored and discovered.

He wondered again if Hawthorne had been fortunate enough to see all her facets. Had she melted for him, opened to him, become soft and sated by his lovemaking?

Clenching his jaw, Marcus thrust the torturous thoughts away. "You know of Ashford Shipping?"

"Of course."

"One year I lost a small fortune to a pirate named Christopher St. John."

"St. John?" She frowned. "My abigail has mentioned the name. He's quite popular. Something of a hero, a benefactor of the poor and underprivileged."

He snorted. "A hero he's not. The man is a ruthless cutthroat. He was the reason I first approached Lord Eldridge. I demanded St. John be dealt with. Eldridge offered instead to train me to manage the pirate myself." His lips curved wryly. "The prospect of exacting my own retribution was irresistible."

Elizabeth pursed her lips. "Of course. A normal life is so dreadfully boring after all."

"Some tasks require personal attention."

Crossing his arms over his chest, Marcus enjoyed this opportunity to have her undivided attention. The simple act of conversing with her was a pleasure he relished, regardless of her scornful remarks. He'd been fawned over and catered to his entire life. Elizabeth's refusal to treat him as anything other than an ordinary man was one of the traits he found most attractive in her.

"I will never understand the appeal of a dangerous life, Marcus. I want peace and quiet in my life."

"Understandable, considering the family in which you were raised. You've had no structure, left to do as you wished by male family members too preoccupied with the pursuit of pleasure to see to you."

"You know me so well," she said scathingly.

"I have always known you well."

"Then you admit how poorly we would have suited."

"I admit nothing of the sort."

She dismissed the topic with a wave of her hand. "About that night . . ."

He watched her chin lift, as if she awaited a punishing blow, and he sighed. "I learned of a man who offered potentially damning information about St. John. We agreed to meet at the wharf. In return for his assistance the informant had one request in return. His wife was with child and knew nothing of the activities he'd engaged in to provide for her. He asked me to see to her welfare should anything untoward befall him."

"That was his wife in the robe?" Her eyes widened.

"Yes. In the midst of the meeting we were attacked. The sounds of a scuffle drew her attention and she came closer to investigate, into harm's way. She was thrown into the water and I leapt after her. Her husband was shot and killed."

"You did not bed her." It was a statement, no longer a question.

"Of course not," he answered simply. "But we both were

covered in filth. I brought her to my home to bathe while I made arrangements for her."

Elizabeth stood and began to pace, her hands clenching rhythmically in the folds of her gown. "I suppose I have always known."

A humorless laugh broke from his throat. Marcus waited for her to say something further, wondering at his sanity in wanting her still. He'd long suspected his imagined infidelity was merely the excuse she'd sought to sever their ties. To his mind, this afternoon only proved that to be true. She did not run into his arms and beg his forgiveness. She did not ask for a second chance or make any attempt to reconcile, and her silence infuriated him to the point where he wished to do violence.

His hands clenched into fists as he fought the urge to grab her and tear her clothes from her skin, to press her to the floor and plunge his cock into her, making it impossible for her to disregard him. It was the one and only way he knew he could penetrate her protective shell.

But his pride would not allow him to reveal his pain. He would, however, effect some change in her, a tiny crack in her reserve at least.

"I was as stunned as you when she entered, Elizabeth. She assumed you were the woman assigned to care for her. There was no way for her to know that my betrothed would visit at such an hour."

"Her dishabille . . ."

"Her garments were soaked. She had nothing aside from the robe lent to her by my housekeeper."

"You should have followed me," she said in a low, angry tone.

"I attempted to. It took me a moment, I admit, to recover from your slap to my face. You were too quick. By the time the widow was settled and I was free to come for you, you had departed with Hawthorne."

Elizabeth stopped her fevered pacing, her skirts settling

slowly as she stilled. Her head turned, revealing eyes that hid far too much from him. "Do you hate me?"

"Occasionally." He shrugged to hide the true depth of his bitterness, a bitterness that gnawed at him from the inside and tainted everything in his life.

"You want revenge," she stated without inflection.

"That is the least of it. I want answers. Why the elopement with Hawthorne? Do the feelings you have for me scare you that much?"

"Perhaps he was always an option."

"I refuse to believe that."

Her lush mouth curved grimly. "Does the possibility prick your ego?"

He snorted. "Play whatever game you like. You may hate wanting me, but you *do* want me."

Moving toward her, Marcus was stopped by her outstretched hand. She appeared calm, but her fingers shook badly. Her arm dropped.

There was far more to their differences than he'd yet discerned. They were strangers, bound by an attraction that defied all reason. But he would learn the truth. Despite his fear that she would elude him again, his need for her outweighed his instinct for self-preservation.

She'd asked if he hated her. At moments like this, he did. He hated her for making him care, hated her for remaining so beautiful and desirable, hated her for being the only woman he had ever wanted in this manner.

"Do you remember your first Season?" he asked in a hoarse voice.

"Of course."

He walked to the intricately carved sideboard and poured a small libation. It was too early for alcohol, but at the moment, he didn't care. He felt cold inside and as the fiery beverage splashed down his throat he relished the warmth it brought.

Finding a bride had not been his aim that year or any year

thereafter. He'd made it a point to avoid debutantes and their marriage machinations, but one look at Elizabeth and his intentions had changed.

He'd arranged an introduction and she'd impressed him with a confidence that belied her age. Securing permission to dance with her, he'd been delighted when she accepted despite his reputation. The simple contact of her gloved hand on his elicited a powerful sexual awareness, one he had never experienced before or since.

"You impressed me from the first, Elizabeth." Staring at his empty glass, he rolled it back and forth restlessly between his palms. "You didn't stammer or look faint when I was overbold with you. Rather you teased me and had the temerity to scold me as well. You shocked me so deeply the first time you swore at me I missed a step. Do you remember?"

Her voice was soft as it floated across the room. "How could I forget?"

"You scandalized every matron there by making me laugh aloud."

After that memorable first dance, he'd made it a point to attend the same events she did, which sometimes necessitated stopping at several houses before finding her. Society dictated that he could claim only one dance per evening and every moment spent with her had to be chaperoned, but despite these restrictions they'd discovered a mutual affinity. He was never bored with her, was instead endlessly fascinated.

Elizabeth was genuinely kind but had a quick temper that rose in an instant and dissipated as rapidly. She had in abundance all of the things that made a girl a woman but retained a childishness that could be at once endearing and frustrating. He admired her strength, but it was the fleeting glimpses of vulnerability that pushed him far past infatuation. He longed to protect her from the world at large, to shelter her and keep her all to himself.

And despite the years and the misunderstandings between them he still felt that way.

Marcus cursed under his breath and then jumped as her hand touched his shoulder.

"I know your thoughts," she whispered. "But it can never be that way again."

His laugh was harsh. "I've no desire to have it that way a second time. I want simply to be rid of the craving I have for you. You won't suffer in the slaking, I can promise you that."

Turning, he stared into her upturned face, seeing the violet eyes so unfathomable and sad. Her lower lip quivered and he stilled the betraying movement with a soft stroke of his thumb.

"I must go and make preparations for the meeting tomorrow." He cupped her flushed cheek and then lowered his hand to her breast. "I will speak with the outriders Avery assigned to you. They'll follow at a discreet distance. Wear neutral colors. No jewelry. Sturdy shoes."

Elizabeth nodded and held still as a statue as he lowered his head and brushed his lips across hers. Only the racing of her heart beneath his palm told him how he affected her. He closed his eyes at the painful tightening of his loins and chest. He'd give up his fortune to be rid of this longing.

Sick with self-disgust he stepped past her and departed, hating the hours between now and the moment when he could see her again.

Chapter 5

Marcus stared through the cover of bushes, his jaw clenching as a droplet of sweat trickled between his shoulder blades. Elizabeth stood a few feet away in the clearing with her husband's journal clutched tightly in her tiny hands. The grass beneath her feet was trampled by her pacing, releasing the scent of spring into the air, but it didn't soothe him as it normally would.

He hated this. Hated leaving her out there, exposed to whoever it was that wanted Hawthorne's book. She shifted nervously from one foot to the other and he longed to go to her, longed to soothe her and take the burden of waiting from her slight shoulders onto his own.

He'd had precious little time to prepare. Surrounded by trees, the specified location made surveillance frustratingly difficult. There were too many places to hide. Avery and the outriders, who stood nearby watching the worn paths that led to the meeting place, were completely undetectable to him. He couldn't signal them, nor they him, and he felt helpless. Waiting patiently was not in his nature and he gripped the hilt of his small sword with barely restrained ferocity. What in hell was taking so damn long?

This mission was the most important of any he'd previously been assigned to; it required the presence of mind and unflappable calm that marked all of his dealings. But to his dismay, he was as far from level-headedness as he'd ever been in his life. Failure was never an option, but this . . . *this* was Elizabeth.

As if she sensed his turmoil, she glanced around furtively, searching for him. She chewed her bottom lip between her teeth and his breath caught in his throat as he watched her. It had been so long since he'd had the opportunity to study her at his leisure. He drank her in, every detail, from the uplifted chin that defied the world, to the restless way she shifted the journal. A slight breeze ruffled the curls at her nape, revealing the slender white column of her throat. Distracted momentarily by her courage and the fierce protectiveness it engendered, Marcus failed to see the dark-clad body dropping from the tree until it was too late. He leapt to his feet as the realization hit, his blood roaring so loudly he could scarcely hear past it.

Elizabeth was knocked to the ground, the book flying from her hands to land a few feet away. She cried out, the startled sound cut short by the crushing weight of the man atop her.

With a low growl of fury, Marcus lunged over the bushes and tackled the assailant away from her, his fists striking before they rolled to a halt. A quick blow to the man's masked face subdued him and Marcus continued pummeling him with punishing blows, his rage such that he couldn't think beyond the instinct to kill anyone who threatened Elizabeth. He fought like a man possessed, snarling with the need to ease the fear that gripped him.

Elizabeth lay immobile, her mouth agape. She'd known Marcus was a physically powerful man, but he had always controlled himself with a confident air of self-mastery. She had romanticized him in her thoughts, imagining the self-assured rogue brandishing a sword or a pistol with careless arrogance, taunting his opponents with a few cutting remarks before making quick work of the matter with nary a bead of sweat on him. Her imagination had not pictured the Marcus before her—a vengeful beast, easily able to kill a man with his bare hands and at this moment quite willing to do so.

She scrambled to her feet, eyes wide, as he wrapped his hands around the man's throat, a man who was their only clue to the importance of Nigel's book. "*No!* Don't kill him!"

Marcus loosened his grip at the sound of Elizabeth's voice, the haze of bloodlust retreating. With amazing strength after such a beating, the assailant bucked upward, effectively garnering his release by throwing Marcus to his back.

Rolling quickly to his stomach, Marcus pushed himself up, prepared to fight, but the attacker scooped up the book and fled.

There was the barest glint of sunlight off the muzzle of a gun as the fleeing man turned and took aim, but it was warning enough. Marcus rose from the ground, his only goal to reach Elizabeth and shield her from harm. But he couldn't move fast enough. The report of the pistol bounced off the trees around them. He yelled a warning and turned, his heart stopping at the sight that greeted him.

Elizabeth stood by her mount, her hair in disarray about her shoulders. In her outstretched hands was the smoking muzzle of a gun.

Realizing where the shot originated, he turned his head and watched in confounded wonder as the assailant stumbled to his feet from where he'd fallen, his dropped gun skittering away across the dewy grass. The man's left hand was limp, the red journal abandoned, while his right hand pressed against a wound to his shoulder. Swearing, he ducked between two bushes and disappeared into the trees.

Stunned by the series of events, Marcus was startled as Avery ran past him in pursuit.

"Bloody everlasting hell," he snapped, furious at himself for allowing the situation to go so awry.

Elizabeth took his arm, her voice shaky and urgent. "Are you hurt?" Her free hand drifted over his torso.

His eyes widened at her obvious concern.

"Damn you, Marcus. Are you injured? Did he hurt you?"

"No, no, I'm fine. What the devil are you doing with that?" He stared, dazed by the sight of the pistol she held at her side.

"Saving your life." Her hand to her heart, she released her breath in a rush and then walked to the fallen journal to retrieve it. "You may thank me when you recover your wits."

Marcus sat silently in the sitting room of his London townhouse. Divested of his coat and waistcoat, he lounged with his feet propped up on the table, and watched the play of light from the window behind him as it moved through the brandy in his snifter.

To say the morning had been a disaster would be an understatement, and yet Elizabeth had retained the book and wounded her attacker. Marcus was not surprised. His friendship with William had given him rare insight.

Her mother lost to illness, Elizabeth had been raised by a father and older brother who were both notorious voluptuaries. Governesses never lasted long, finding the young Elizabeth to be incorrigible. Without the calming influence of a woman in the house, she'd been allowed to run wild.

As children, William had taken his sister with him everywhere—galloping neck-or-nothing through the fields, climbing trees, shooting pistols. Elizabeth had been blissfully unaware of the societal rules women were expected to follow until introduced to them at boarding school. Years of rigorous training in deportment had given her the tools she used to hide herself from him, but he paid them no mind. He would know her, all of her.

The mystery of the book was proving to be far more dangerous than any of them had previously realized. Steps had to be taken to ensure Elizabeth was kept safe.

"Thank you for allowing me to repair myself here," Elizabeth said softly from the doorway that led to the bedroom.

She'd used the room that was meant to be hers—that of the lady of the house. Turning to face her, he saw her staring down at her clasped hands. "William would have known something was amiss if I'd returned home looking a mess."

Marcus studied her, noting the dark circles that rimmed her eyes. Was she having trouble sleeping? Was he tormenting her dreams the way she tormented his?

"Is your family not in residence?" she asked, looking about as if she could find them. "Lady Westfield? Paul and Robert?"

"My mother writes that Robert's latest experiment is delaying their arrival. So that leaves you and me quite alone."

"Oh." She bit her lower lip.

"Elizabeth, this matter has become extremely dangerous. Once the man who attacked you recovers, he will come after you again. If he has associates, they won't wait."

She nodded. "I'm aware of the situation. I will be on my guard."

"That's insufficient. I want you to be guarded night and day, not just outriders when you go out. I want someone with you at all times, even when you sleep."

"Impossible. William will grow suspicious if I have guards at the house."

Marcus set the glass down. "William is more than capable of making his own decisions. Why don't you allow him to decide if he can be of assistance to you?"

She rested her hands on her hips. "Because *I* have made the decision. He is finally free of that damned agency. His wife is with child. I refuse to risk his life and Margaret's happiness for nothing."

"*You* are not nothing," he growled.

"Consider what happened today."

He stood. "I cannot stop considering it. It rules my thoughts."

"You were almost killed."

"You don't know that."

"I was there . . ." Her voice broke and turning on her heel, she strode toward the door.

He moved swiftly to block her egress. "I've not finished speaking, madam."

"I am finished listening." She attempted to step around him, but he sidestepped quickly into her path. "Damn you. You are so bloody arrogant."

She poked him in the chest with her finger and he stilled the movement with his hand. It was then he noticed her trembling.

"Elizabeth . . ."

She stared up at him, so tiny and delicate, yet formidable in her fury. The thought of her injured made his stomach clench. Deep in her eyes, he saw fear and his heart went out to her.

"Spitfire," he murmured, pulling her toward him. His fingertips tingled from the touch of her ungloved hand. Her skin was so soft, like satin. His thumb brushed over the pulse at her wrist and it leapt to match his own quickened heartbeat. "You were so brave today."

"Your charm won't work on me."

"I'm sorry to hear that." He tugged her closer.

She snorted. "Despite everything I say, you still insist on attempting to seduce me."

"Merely attempting? Not succeeding?" He laced his fingers with hers and found her hand cold. "I must try harder then."

Violet eyes glittered dangerously, but then he'd always liked a bit of danger. At least she was not thinking about the assailant anymore. Her hand was quickly warming within his. He intended to warm the rest of her as well.

"You are trying quite hard enough." Elizabeth took a step back.

He followed, directing her backward steps toward his bedroom, which waited on the other side of the private sitting room.

"Have women always fallen all over themselves for you?"

Arching a brow, he replied, "I'm not certain how I should answer that."

"Try the truth."

"Then yes, they have."

She scowled.

He laughed and squeezed her fingers. "Ah . . . Jealousy was always the emotion most easily inspired in you."

"I am not jealous. Other women can have you with my blessing."

"Not yet." He smiled when her scowl deepened. Stepping nearer, he slipped their joined hands around her back and tugged her to him.

Her gaze narrowed. "What are you about?"

"I'm distracting you. You are overwrought."

"I am not."

Her lips parted as his head lowered. He smelled gunpowder and her heady vanilla rose scent beneath that. Her palm grew damp within his and he nuzzled his nose against hers.

"You were magnificent this afternoon." He brushed his mouth across hers and felt her sigh against his lips. He nibbled gently. "Although it disturbs you to have shot a man, you don't regret it. You would do it again. For me."

"Marcus . . ."

He groaned, lost in the sound of her voice and the sweetness of her taste. His entire body was hard and aching from holding her so closely. "Yes, love?"

"I don't want you," she said.

"You will." He sealed his mouth over hers.

Elizabeth sank into Marcus's hard chest with a sob. It was not fair that he could overwhelm her—by touching her, caressing her, seducing her with his low, velvety voice and rich masculine scent. His emerald gaze burned, half-lidded with a desire she'd done nothing to arouse.

Against her will, her hands slipped around his lean waist

and caressed the powerful length of his back. "You're horrid to be so tender."

His sweat-misted forehead rested against hers. He groaned, his fingers slipping under the long hem of her riding jacket. "You're wearing too many damned clothes."

He took her mouth again, his tongue caressing with lush, deep licks. Lost in his kiss, she didn't realize he'd lifted and moved her until he kicked the door to his bedroom closed behind them, shutting them away from the world.

Protesting, she attempted to pull away. Then his hand cupped the curve of her breast, bringing aching pleasure even through the barrier of her garments. She moaned into his mouth and he tilted his head in response, deepening an already drowning kiss.

Elizabeth stood rigid, her arms at her sides, her thoughts warring with the dictates of her body. Her blood was on fire, her skin hot and painfully tight.

"I want you." His voice was a rough-edged caress. "I want to bury myself inside you until we forget ourselves."

"I don't want to forget."

His tone deepened. "I must think of this mission and the events that took place today, but I cannot. Because all I can think of is you. There isn't room for anything else."

Placing her fingers over his lips, Elizabeth silenced the seductive words that should have sounded practiced and confident, but didn't.

He tossed the counterpane back, revealing decadent silk sheets. With soft, tender kisses, he attempted to distract her from his fingers, which worked with deft skill to free the row of buttons that barred him from her skin. Slipping his hands under the open flaps, he pushed the jacket to the floor. She shivered even though she was flushed and he crushed her to his chest.

"Hush," he murmured against her forehead. "It's just you and me. Leave your father and Eldridge out of our bed."

She buried her face in the linen of his shirt and breathed him in. "I hate it when you leave me no privacy at all."

Turning her head to rest her cheek against his chest, Elizabeth took a shuddering breath. The bed was massive, easily big enough to sleep four large men side by side with room to spare. It waited . . . *for them.*

"Look at me."

Her gaze found his again, discovering a deep needy emerald hunger. Her lips quivered softly and Marcus leaned over, brushing his mouth across hers. "Don't be afraid," he whispered.

Remaining in a bedroom with him was the worst sort of danger. Far more dangerous than the attacker in the park. That man struck swiftly, like a viper. Marcus was more of a python. He would wrap himself around her and squeeze the life from her slowly until nothing of her independence remained.

"I'm not afraid." She shoved him backward as her stomach clenched tight. Caring nothing for her jacket, longing only to be away from him, she walked quickly to the door. "I am leaving."

Escape was seconds away when he grabbed her roughly and threw her face down upon the bed. "What are you doing?" she cried.

Marcus held her down, his grip tight as he bound her hands together with his cravat. "You would leave here half-dressed," he growled, "in your eagerness to put distance between us. This fear you have of me must be banished. You have to trust me implicitly, in every way, without question or you could be killed."

"This is the way you win trust?" she snapped. "By holding me against my will?"

He came over her, his knees straddling her hips, his large body caging hers to the bed. His teeth nipped her ear and his voice, low and angry, made her shiver all over. "I should have done this years ago. But I was lost in your charms and failed to see the signs. Even until this moment, I thought you so skittish that a gentle hand was necessary not to frighten you. Now I realize you need a good, hard riding to be broken properly."

"Bastard!" Heart pounding, Elizabeth struggled beneath him. In response he sat on her, effectively crushing her protest.

Nimble fingers tugged at the fastenings to her skirts and bustle. Then his weight left her. Standing at the edge of the bed, Marcus yanked the garments down. She briefly considered rolling on her back to conceal her buttocks, clearly visible beneath the thinness of her chemise, but didn't, deciding the front of her was far more needy of protection. "You won't get away with this," she warned. "You cannot keep me bound forever and when you release me, I'll come after you. I'll—"

"You won't be able to walk," he scoffed.

He reached for her boots and she lashed out at him, kicking with all her might. She screamed at the sudden sharp sting to her arse. The first spank was quickly followed by several more, each drop of his hand burning more than the last until she buried her face in the counterpane and cried with the pain of it. Only when she stopped flailing, and took the abuse without movement did he cease.

"Your father should have taken you over his knee long ago," he muttered.

"I hate you!" She turned her head to look at him, but couldn't reach around far enough.

Marcus's sigh was loud and resigned. "You protest too much, love. You will thank me eventually. I've given you the freedom to enjoy me. You can fight all you want and still get what you desire. All the pleasure and none of the guilt."

His hands cupped the flaming curves of her derriere and stroked gently, soothingly. The gentleness of his touch aroused her, the contrast startling after his previous treatment. "So beautiful. So soft and perfect." His voice deepened, became cajoling. "Let yourself go, sweet. If you must be forced, why not relish the experience?"

When his hands moved lower to the hem of her chemise and then slipped under it, she moaned in anticipation, her skin prickling with goosebumps at the feel of bare skin on bare skin. Her blood heated, her anger melting into something intoxicating as his thumbs moved higher, massaging either side of her lower back. Deep inside, her body softened at his skillful touch. The feel of air directly on her burning flesh coaxed a whimper of relief from her.

"You would fight me to the death, my stubborn temptress, if you were able, but tied up for my needs brings unexpected rewards, does it not?" He rolled her to her back before gripping her shoulders and pulling her into a seated position.

Elizabeth bit her lower lip to hide the pout of disappointment she felt at the unwanted distance between them. Her nipples ached, peaked hard and tight, eager for the pinch of his fingers to ease their torment. Marcus's dark green gaze narrowed on her flushed face. There was no tenderness, no sign of possible mercy, just stark intent and she knew he would not be swayed. Her stomach flipped as moisture pooled between her thighs at her helplessness.

He assisted her to her feet and moved her to the nearby chair whose wooden arms curved so beautifully. Pressing her down to the seat, he then tugged his shirt from his breeches, before pulling it over his head.

Elizabeth stared, arrested by his virility which was displayed so beautifully by rippling muscles beneath golden skin. His left shoulder was marred by a circular scar left by a bullet and silver ribbons on his flesh betrayed nicks from the sharp edge of a sword. As magnificent as he was, the sight of his past injuries reminded her that he was not meant for her. Even as her blood heated, her heart chilled.

"The agency has left its mark on you," she said snidely. "It's revolting."

Marcus arched a dark brow. "That explains why you cannot take your eyes from me then."

Peeved, she forced herself to look away.

He crouched before her and cupped the backs of her knees, spreading her legs wide and hooking them over the carved arms of the chair. Her face heated in embarrassment as the damp lips of her sex were opened to his view. "Close the curtains."

Frowning, he stared at the apex of her thighs. "God, no." He brushed across her curls with his fingers. "Why would you wish to hide this? It's heaven you hold here. A sight I've longed to see for far too long."

"Please." She squeezed her eyelids tightly together, her body tense and then trembling.

"Elizabeth. Look at me."

Tears accompanied the lifting of her lids.

"Why are you so frightened? You know I would never hurt you."

"You leave me nothing, you take everything."

He ran a blunt fingertip through her cream and then dipped a bit inside. Against her will, she arched into the caress, despite the painful tension the angle placed on her arms.

"You shared this with Hawthorne, but you won't with me? Why?" His voice was rough and abrasive. "Why not me?"

Her reply was shaky, betraying the depth of her distress. "My husband never saw me like this."

The wicked finger stilled, just barely entering her. "What?"

"Such things are done at night. One must—"

"Hawthorne made love to you in the darkness?"

"He was a gentleman, one who—"

"Was certifiable. Good God." Marcus snorted and removed his finger. He stood. "To have you for his own, to fuck as he wished, and not appreciate your beauty? What a waste. The man was an idiot."

Elizabeth lowered her head. "Our marriage was no different from any other."

"It was completely different than it would have been with me. How often?"

"How often?" she repeated dumbly.

"How often did he take you? Every night? Every few days?"

"What does it matter?"

His nostrils flared on a deep breath, his frame taut beside her. Running an agitated hand through his hair, he was silent for a moment.

"Release me, Marcus, and forget this." Her shame was complete, there was no more he could do to her.

Hard fingers lifted her chin to meet his gaze. "I'm going to touch you everywhere. With my hands, my mouth. In the light of day and long into the night. I'll take you in whatever manner I choose, wherever I choose. I will know you as no one else in your life has known you."

"Why?" She struggled again, completely at his mercy and unbearably aroused. Spread for him, she felt the emptiness inside her and hated how badly she needed him to fill it.

"Because I can. Because after today you will crave me and the pleasure I can give you. Because you'll trust me, damn you." He growled low in his throat. "All these years, married to him and then mourning him, when you could have been mine."

Dropping to his knees, he held her hips and dropped his head. Elizabeth held her breath as he closed his mouth full upon her breast, soaking through the fabric of her shirt and chemise. Startled at first, she was soon moaning and arching her back in silent encouragement. Sharp pangs of sensation radiated outward, moving in rhythm with his suction, her womb contracting in spasms of need.

Marcus's warm fingertips stroked from her waist to the ebony curls below. Painful tension seared her senses and Elizabeth gasped in surprise.

"I will touch you here," he warned. "With my fingers, my tongue, my cock."

She bit her bottom lip, eyes wide.

"You will enjoy it," he promised, his thumb tugging her lip free from her teeth.

"You want to treat me like a whore. That is your revenge."

His smile was devoid of humor. "I want to give you pleasure, I want to hear you beg me for it. Why should you be deprived?"

Marcus stood and freed the placket of his breeches. Reaching inside, he withdrew his cock, and a heretofore unknown level of wanting had her writhing in the chair. He was long and thick, the head broad and dark with the blood that engorged it. He jerked his hand along the length and creamy moisture leaked from the tip.

"See what the sight of you does to me, Elizabeth? How much power you wield? You are tied and helpless, yet it is *I* who is at *your* mercy."

Swallowing hard, her gaze was riveted to his display.

"Trust, Elizabeth. You must trust me, in all ways."

She looked up and ached at the sight of him. So beautiful, and yet harsh and rugged as only a man could be. "Is this about your mission?"

"This is about *us*. You and me." He stepped closer, and then closer still. "Open your mouth."

"*What?*" Her lungs seized.

"Take me in your mouth."

"No . . ." She recoiled.

"Where is the minx who said she was not one to run from the sight of a man's desire?" Marcus widened his stance until his powerful thighs bracketed the side of the chair and the glistening head of his cock rested directly before and slightly below her mouth.

"This is trust," he whispered. "Think how you can hurt me, how vulnerable I am. You can bite me, love, and unman me. Or you can suckle me and bring me to my knees with pleasure. I ask this of you, knowing the risk, because I trust you. Just as I expect you to trust me."

Elizabeth stared at him, fascinated by the abrupt change in the balance between them. She met his eyes again and saw the longing there, the need. For now there was no bitterness. He looked so much as he had before, when they'd been promised to one another and free of past injuries. He was so breathtakingly handsome, appearing younger without the burden of his enmity.

It was that openness that decided her mind. Taking a deep breath, Elizabeth followed the urging of her heart and opened her mouth.

Chapter 6

Marcus stood in an agony of lust as Elizabeth's lips parted and she leaned forward to take him into her mouth. As she scalded him with wet heat, his breath hissed out between his teeth. His knees buckled and he gripped the high back of the chair with his free hand to remain upright.

She pulled away with wide-eyed horror. "Did I hurt you?"

Incapable of speech, he shook his head rapidly. She swallowed hard and his cock leapt in his hand. Licking her lower lip, she opened her mouth and tried again, this time engulfing the whole of the crown.

"Suck," he gasped, his head falling so that he hovered over her, watching as her cheeks hollowed and she tugged with soft suction. His legs trembled and he groaned a low, tortured sound.

Encouraged, she took him deeper, her tongue swirling in tentative exploration. Her mouth was stretched wide to accommodate his girth and the sight was enough to wipe his brain of any rational thought.

"I'm going to move," he bit out. "Don't be frightened." His hips began to thrust forward, fucking her mouth with gentle, shallow strokes. Her eyes widened, but she didn't pull away or protest, instead she responded with less and less hesitation.

Watching her, Marcus was certain he'd passed on to his

reward and been given the realization of his deepest longing. He was afraid to believe it was Elizabeth who serviced him so well.

"God, Elizabeth . . ."

Releasing his cock, he dropped his hand between her legs and caressed her through the open folds of her sex. She moaned and he stroked with more intent, determined to concentrate on her in an effort to hold off his own imminent release. Slick and hot, she melted into his touch. She felt so good, like satin, and he grit his teeth as he slipped a finger inside her. Tight as she was, she'd be a snug fit. His chest ached. His sac weighed heavily, then drew up. He stepped back on shaky legs, his cock slipping from her mouth with a soft, wet pop.

She worked her jaw and licked her lips, her violet eyes dark and questioning.

His voice like gravel he whispered, "It's time."

Elizabeth shivered. Marcus had always looked at her as if she were a meal laid before a starving man. At the moment however, his gaze was . . . *desperate.* The tip of his cock leaked profusely, and she swallowed, her mouth flavored with his essence.

He'd felt so different from what she'd expected. She'd thought herself beyond the innocence of a virginal girl. Now she realized how little she knew. With the thick, pulsing roping of veins that etched his erection she'd imagined he would be hard, textured. Instead the skin had been as soft as the finest silk, slipping over her tongue in a rhythm that awakened a matching pulse between her legs.

The act was not what she had expected, not at all. She'd thought she'd feel used, nothing more than a receptacle for his lust. But he was devastated, she could see it and she'd felt it in the way he trembled. The way his voice had grown so hoarse. There was power to be had in possessing a man's passion.

"Release me," she ordered breathlessly, wanting to see how far she could take this.

He shook his head and pushed the back of the chair onto its hind legs. Caught off balance, she screeched until he stopped. It was then she understood his aim. Resting the top of the chair against the nearby damask-covered wall angled her perfectly, presenting her spread sex to his cock. His grin stole her breath, filled as it was with wicked promises. He reached between them and pressed his erect shaft down, bending his knees until he breeched her. He stroked up and down, coating her with the semen that continued to dribble from the flushed head.

She couldn't hold back the half-sob of anticipation. The blatant, deliberate teasing had her sweating and gasping for air. She ignored the voice that urged her to fight, choosing instead to enjoy him . . . just this once.

"Do your arms pain you?" he asked, never ceasing his movements, soaking her with the evidence of his excitement.

"*You* pain me."

"Should I stop?" From the catch in his voice, she knew the thought was torturous.

"I shall shoot you if you stop."

With a groan, he positioned and thrust deep, forging through her in a relentless drive. She writhed against the invasion, the size of him far too much for her long unused flesh. The tip of him rubbed inside her, stretching her, stroking her far better than his magical fingers had done.

Both hands to the wall, Marcus gasped as he slipped deep. "Ah, Christ." He shuddered. "You're hot as hell and tight as a fist."

"Marcus . . ." She whimpered. There was something undeniably erotic in the way he took her, still partially dressed with his boots on. It should have offended her. But it didn't.

All these years she'd spent consoling the women discarded by her father and listening to the gossip of women left disillusioned by Marcus's inconstancy. How had they failed to see their own influence? Marcus had nearly killed a man with his bare hands, yet here he stood before her, weakened in his need.

He pulled out, his head down bent. "Watch me fuck you, Elizabeth." His powerful thighs flexed beneath his breeches as he pressed back inside. She gazed, eyes riveted to the sight of the thick, proud shaft slick with her cream withdrawing, only to return in a painfully slow glide.

Her arms ached, her legs stretched uncomfortably, and her tailbone was growing numb from bearing the brunt of her weight, but she didn't care. Nothing mattered beyond the apex of her thighs and the man who rutted there.

"This is trust," he said, his hips pumping his cock into her with a precise, unfaltering rhythm.

Trust. Tears slipped past her lashes as the divine torment continued, his skill undeniable. He knew just how to stroke her, dipping with bent thighs to rub his cock in just the right spot to pleasure her to madness. She was panting with it, and then begging for it. Her blood roared, her nipples peaked so tightly beneath her garments they ached. "Please . . ."

Marcus was panting too, his chest heaving so forcefully it shook the sweat from his hair to drip onto her face. Her heart swelled at the intimacy.

"Yes," he growled. "Now." He dropped one hand between her legs and rubbed gently. Like a spring coiled too tightly, she broke free with a sharp cry. Her back bowed and Marcus moved in slow, deep strokes, drawing out her pleasure, keeping her taut and breathless and tearful beneath him.

"No more . . ." she cried, unable to bear another moment.

He thrust his cock deep and held it there, allowing the fading ripples of her orgasm to milk him. He sucked in a sharp breath and then began to shudder with such force the chair back tapped against the wall. He groaned, a long, low, pained sound as his cock jerked inside her filling her with his seed.

Gasping, he finally stilled. He tilted his head and stared

into her eyes. The frank bemusement in the emerald depths soothed her somewhat, lost as she was in her own devastation.

"Too fast," he muttered. One of his hands left the wall and cupped her cheek, his thumb following the curve of her cheekbone.

"Are you mad?" She swallowed hard to ease the hoarseness of her voice.

"Yes." He pulled away slowly, carefully, but she still winced from the loss. With great care he unhooked her legs from the arm of the chair and helped her to her feet. Weakened, she crumpled against him. He caught her up, and carried her to the bed.

Laying her on her side, Marcus untied her hands, rubbing her shoulders and arms when they tingled as the blood returned. Then he reached for the bow at her throat.

Elizabeth pulled back. "I must leave now."

Chuckling, Marcus took a seat next to her. He bent low to tug off his boots, removing a blade hidden there and setting it on the nightstand. "You are exhausted, and can barely walk. You are in no condition to seat a horse."

Elizabeth's hand drifted across his back, a finger swirling curiously around the bullet wound scar that marred his hard flesh. Turning his head, he kissed her fingertips as they traveled over the top of his shoulder, stunning her with the tender gesture. He stood, quickly doffing his breeches and she looked away as heat flared within her, staring out the window at the afternoon sky partly-hidden behind filmy sheers.

"Look at me," he said gruffly, a plea hidden under a rough command.

"No."

"Elizabeth, there is no shame in wanting me."

Her mouth curved ruefully, the view of the window fading from her perception. "Of course not. Every woman does."

"I am not thinking about other women, you shouldn't be

either." He sighed with the exasperation one would display over a recalcitrant child. "Look at me. Please."

She turned her head slowly, her heart hammering in her chest. Impossibly broad shoulders tapered to a rippled stomach, lean hips, and long, powerful legs. Marcus Ashford was perfection, the scars that marred his torso only serving to make him human and not some ancient god.

She'd intended to keep her gaze high, but she was unable to stop herself from looking lower. Long and thick, his impressive erection made her swallow hard.

"Heavens. How can you . . . ? You're still . . ."

He gave her a wicked smile. "Ready for sex?"

"I am exhausted," she complained.

Marcus tugged at the tie at her neck, using her distraction with his cock to lift her shirt over her head. "You don't have to do anything." But when he reached for her chemise she slapped his hand away, needing some barrier, however sheer, between them.

He strolled with casual ease to the corner and went behind the screen, returning a moment later with a damp cloth. He pushed her back into the pillows and reached for her knee. She rolled away.

"It's a little late for modesty, wouldn't you say, sweet?"

"What are you about?"

"If you come back here, I'll show you."

Elizabeth thought for long moments, guessing his intent and not certain if she could grant him that level of intimacy.

"My body has been inside yours." His voice was low and seductive. "Can you not trust me to bathe you?"

The hint of challenge in his tone decided her. She turned onto her back and spread her legs with more than a hint of defiance. His lopsided smile made her blush.

Gently he swept the cloth across her curls before parting her with reverent fingers and cleansing her folds. Sore as she was, the cool dampness felt wonderful and she breathed a soft sound of pleasure. She forced herself to relax, to close her eyes and release the tension brought on by Marcus's proximity. On the verge of drifting to sleep, she shot up with a startled cry when molten heat drenched her sex.

She stared down the length of her torso with wide eyes, her heart racing to see Marcus's dark smile.

"Did you just . . . *lick* me?"

"Oh yes." Tossing the washcloth carelessly to the rug, he crawled over her with potent grace. "I see I've scandalized you. Since you've already suffered enough today, I shall grant you a short reprieve. But be prepared to accept my future attentions in whatever manner I choose."

Shivering as his furred chest brushed across her chemise-covered nipples, Elizabeth sank farther into the pillows, overwhelmed by the sheer force of his presence.

This she knew—the feeling of a hard male body atop hers. But the feelings that rioted within her were all new. She had welcomed Hawthorne to her bed as she should, she'd appreciated his haste and solicitousness. Aside from the first painful time, the rest had not been unpleasant. He'd been quiet, clean, careful. Never had it been raw and primitive as it was with Marcus. Never had it caused this gnawing, aching need and heady desire. Never had it resulted in a blinding flash of pleasure that left her sated to her soul.

"Easy," he murmured against her throat as she rubbed impatiently against him.

Her husband's body had been a mystery, known to her only as a shadowy form that ventured into her room under the cover of darkness and a warm hand that pushed up her night rail. Marcus had begged her to look at him, had wanted her to know him and see him as he was, in all his glory. He was magnificent naked. The mere sight of him was enough to make her wet between her legs.

She refused, however, to be the only one left shaken from this afternoon dalliance.

"Tell me what you like, Marcus."

"Touch me. I want to feel your hands on my skin."

Her hands roamed across his back, down his arms, discovering scars and lengths of muscle so hard they felt like stone. Marcus moaned as she found especially sensitive areas, urging her to linger. His body was a tapestry of textures—soft and hard, fur and satin. He closed his eyes, his arms supporting his weight above her, allowing her to explore him at her leisure. The rigid length of his cock pulsed against her thigh, the warm trail of moisture it leaked telling her how much he enjoyed her unschooled touch.

This was power.

Groaning, he lowered his head, his silky hair drifting across her breasts filling the air around her with his scent. "Touch my cock," he commanded gruffly.

Taking a breath of courage, Elizabeth reached between their bodies and stroked the silken length, amazed at the hardness and the way it jumped under her touch. It was obvious he found pleasure in the caress, the crests of his cheekbones flushing, his lips parting with panting breaths. Encouraged, she experimented. Rough and soft, quick and teasing, she attempted to find the rhythm that would drive him to madness.

"Do you want me?" he asked. He stayed her hand by covering it with his own and she frowned in confusion. Then his hand drifted lower, catching her knee and spreading her wide.

"I'm surprised a libertine such as yourself needs to ask," she retorted, refusing to give him the capitulation he requested.

With no further warning he thrust into her, sliding through swollen tissues until there was no farther he could go.

She whimpered in surprise. Lovemaking in the bright light of day was something she wondered if she could ever learn to accept. She looked up at him, eyes wide.

Pinning her with his hips, Marcus gripped the straps of her chemise and rent the garment in half to the waist.

"You think you can build barriers between us with words

and clothing?" he asked harshly. "Every time you attempt it, I will take you just like this, become a part of you so that all your efforts will be for naught."

There was no place to hide, nowhere to run.

"This will be the last time," she vowed.

She was stunned that she had allowed him this close, a man whose beauty and charm had always weakened her. Then he lowered his mouth to hers, kissing her with a ravenous hunger. Gripping her hips possessively, Marcus held her still as he withdrew and then thrust again, shuddering as she did at the exquisiteness of it.

Elizabeth shifted restlessly, awed that her body had stretched to accommodate him, was even now stretching to hold him more comfortably. It was amazing, his hardness inside her, filling her completely, bringing a feeling of connection so deep she couldn't breathe.

"Elizabeth." His voice was deeply sexual as he wrapped his arms beneath her, pulling her tightly against him in a full body embrace. He nuzzled against her throat. "Only when I'm sated will you be rid of me."

With the ominous threat he began to move, a sinuous glide of his body upon and within her own.

"Oh!" she cried, startled as the sensations built higher with every slide. She'd meant to withhold her pleasure from him, meant to lie there and deny him what he wanted. But it was impossible. He could melt her with a heated glance. To fuck him, as he so crudely called it, was an act she was helpless to resist.

She tried to increase the pace, wrapping her legs around his hips, her hands grasping his buttocks and pulling him into her, but he was too strong and too determined to have his own way.

"Fuck me," she gasped, trying to regain the feeling of control by stealing some of his. "Faster."

Marcus groaned as she writhed beneath him. His voice

came, slurred with pleasure. "I knew it would be this way with you . . ."

In response, Elizabeth dug her nails into the flesh of his back. She loved feeling his damp skin against hers, his warm scent surrounding her. Slipping a little in his control, he slammed into her, hard and impossibly deep. Her toes curled.

Liquid heat traversed her veins, pooled in her core, and then convulsed in climax. She tightened around his thrusting cock, crying out his name, holding onto his flexing body as the only anchor in a swirl of incredible sensation.

And Marcus held on, drenched in sweat, heat radiating from every pore. He growled her name as he spilled into her and the brand of possession burned deep.

Closing her eyes, she cried.

Elizabeth felt as if her limbs were weighted with lead. It took all the effort she had to turn her head and look at Marcus sleeping next to her. His long, black lashes cast peaceful shadows upon his cheeks, the austere beauty of his features soft in repose.

She managed to roll onto her side, which was no easy task with his heavy arm thrown casually across her torso. Lifting onto one elbow, she studied him silently. Boyishly innocent while sleeping, he was so gorgeous she could hardly breathe.

Slowly, she traced her finger along the generous curve of his mouth, then his eyebrows and the length of his jaw. She squealed in surprise as his arm tightened, drawing her body over his.

"What do you think you are doing, madam?" he drawled lazily.

Sliding off him, Elizabeth sat on the edge of the bed, struggling for the nonchalance she was certain she should display. "Is this not when lovers part ways?" She needed to think and she couldn't do that with him lying naked beside her.

"There is no need for you to go." Leaning back against a

pillow, Marcus patted the space next to him. "Come back to bed."

"No." She slid off the mattress and gathered up her clothes. "I am sore and tired."

As she came around, his arm shot out and grabbed her, hauling her closer. "Elizabeth. We can take a nap and have tea later. Then you can go."

"That's not possible," she murmured without looking at him. "I must go home. I want a hot bath."

He rubbed her arm and grinned playfully. "You can have a bath here. I'll attend you myself."

Standing, Elizabeth hastily pulled on her stockings. She struggled with the tapes of her skirts, having difficulty tightening them. Marcus rose from the bed, heedless of his nakedness and crossed the room to her, brushing her fingers aside.

She turned away quickly, her face flushed. *Lord, he was handsome!* Every part of him was perfect. His muscles rippled with power just beneath golden skin. Recently sated, she still felt the renewed stirrings of desire.

He made quick work of dressing her, adjusting her garters, and securing her tapes. Jealous at his obvious experience, she stood stiffly until he turned her to face him.

He sighed, pulling her against his bare chest. "You are so determined to keep to yourself, to allow no one to get close to you."

She rested her head against his chest for a moment, savoring the smell of him now mixed with her own scent. Then she pushed him away.

"I gave you what you wanted," she replied, irritably.

"I want more."

Her stomach clenched. "Find it elsewhere."

Marcus laughed. "Now that I've shown you pleasure, you'll crave it, crave me. At night, you will remember my touch and the feel of my cock in you, and you will ache for me."

"You conceited—"

"No." He caught her wrist. "I will be craving you as well. What happened today is singular. You won't find the same elsewhere, and you will need it."

She lifted her chin, hating the idea that, deep inside, she suspected he was right. "I am free to look."

His fingers tightened painfully. "No. You are not." He tugged her hand down to his rampant erection. "When you need this, you will come to me. Don't doubt that I would kill any man who touches you."

"Does such forced fidelity work both ways?" She held her breath.

"Of course."

Marcus stood for a moment in the tense silence, before turning away to retrieve his discarded breeches.

Expelling the air from her lungs in a silent sigh of relief, Elizabeth took a seat in front of the mirror and attempted to fix her hair. She was amazed at the visage that stared back at her. Cheeks flushed, lips swollen, eyes bright—she looked nothing like the woman she'd been that morning. Looking away, she caught Marcus's reflection. She watched him dress, weighing his words and damning her foolishness. He was even more determined now than he'd been before bedding her.

When she was ready, she stood quickly, a little too quickly for legs still shaky from the afternoon's events. She stumbled, but Marcus was there, his arms warm bands of steel around her. He had been observing her as well.

"Are you all right?" he asked gruffly. "Did I hurt you?"

She waved him away with her hand. "No, no, I'm fine."

He stepped back. "Elizabeth, a discussion is in order."

"Why?" She fluffed her skirts nervously.

"Bloody hell. You and I. Just made love. In that bed." He gestured with an impatient thrust of his chin. "And the chair. And the floor in a moment, if you don't cease irritating me."

"We made a mistake," she said softly, icy fear settling in her stomach.

"Damn you." His sidelong glance was scathing and she flinched. "Play your games and bury your head in the sand if you must. I will have my way regardless."

"It was not my intent to play games, Marcus." She swallowed hard and moved toward the door. He made no move to stop her so she was startled when she turned and found him directly behind her.

"Don't be frightened about what happened in the park today," he murmured, once again all charm and honeyed drawl. "I will protect you from harm."

Her eyes slid closed. Suddenly the thought of leaving held less appeal. "I know you will."

"Where will you be this evening?"

"The Dunsmore musicale."

"I shall meet you there."

She sighed and opened her eyes. His determined gaze and dogged persistence warned her that he would not allow the matter between them to rest.

He brushed his mouth softly across hers before stepping back and offering his arm. Wary at what she perceived to be his far too easy capitulation, she took it and allowed him to lead her to the main floor.

The butler stood ready with her hat and gloves. "My lord, a Mr. James has called."

"The study? Excellent. You need not wait."

The butler bowed and retreated.

Elizabeth searched Marcus's face as he settled her hat on her head and deftly tied the ribbons. "I pray I can leave here unseen."

His mouth moved to her ear, and he spoke in a seductive whisper. "Too late. Even now the servants are watching us. It won't be long before every household in London knows we're lovers. Avery will learn of us, whether you are seen or not."

The color drained from her face. She hadn't considered that. Servants were the worst gossips. "I would think a man with a secret life such as yours would have discreet servants in his employ."

"I do. However, this is one bit of news I suggested they spread."

"Are you mad?" Then her eyes widened. "Is this about the wager?"

Marcus sighed. "You wound me. Losing is odious, love, but I would never use you in such a callous manner."

"Lose?" she cried, her mouth agape. "You didn't!"

"I did." He shrugged with nonchalance. "How foolish to avoid a bet in which the outcome is decided by my own actions."

She frowned. "Which way did you lean?"

His grin was blinding and made her heart skip a beat. "As if I'd tell you."

His hand at her elbow, Marcus escorted her through the rear garden and out a side gate that led to the stables beyond. He looked on grimly as she mounted her horse. The two armed outriders waited a discreet distance up the mews.

He sketched a quick bow. "Until this evening."

The burning between her shoulder blades told her he watched her until she rounded the corner and blended into the street beyond. The ache in her chest made breathing difficult and she knew it would only get worse the more time she spent with him.

And she knew what must be done about it.

Chapter 7

"Why does it smell like a perfumery in here?" William grumbled as he walked the upstairs hallway of the Chesterfield mansion with Margaret.

"The scent comes from Elizabeth's rooms."

He glanced at her with a frown and saw her eyes shining in mischievous anticipation.

He paused at the open doorway of his sister's sitting room and blinked rapidly. "It looks like a damned florist shop!"

"Isn't it sweet?" Margaret laughed, her fiery hair swaying softly with the movement.

William could not resist touching one of the swinging curls. His sweet, wonderful wife. Those who did not know her well thought her a rare redhead of even temperament. Only he knew how she saved the wild, passionate side of her nature just for him. As desire tightened his loins, he sucked in a breath, and was assaulted with the overpowering smell of flowers.

"Romantic?" he barked. Entering the room he dragged Margaret behind him. Riotous bouquets of expensive, richly scented floral arrangements covered every flat surface in the room. "Westfield," he growled. "I'll kill him."

"Calm yourself, William," she soothed.

He surveyed the scene grimly. "How long has this been going on?"

"Since the Moreland ball." Margaret sighed, the soft sound making him scowl. "And Lord Westfield is so handsome."

"You are a hopeless romantic," he grumbled, choosing to ignore her last comment.

Stepping closer, she wrapped her arms around his lean waist. "I have a right to be."

"How so?"

"I have found true love, so I know it exists." She stood on tiptoe, brushing her lips across his. William immediately increased the pressure, kissing her until she was breathless.

"Westfield is a scoundrel, love," he warned. "I wish you would believe me."

"I believe you. He reminds me of you."

He pulled back with a grunt. "And you would want that for Elizabeth?"

Margaret laughed. "You are not so wicked as all that."

"Because you have reformed me." He nuzzled against her.

"Elizabeth is a stronger woman than I. She could easily bring Lord Westfield to heel, if she were of the mind to do so. Allow her to handle him."

William backed out of the room, pulling her with him. "I have duly noted your opinion."

She attempted to dig in her heels, but he lifted her easily and turned in the direction of their bedchamber.

"You don't intend to listen to me, do you?"

He grinned. "No, I don't. I will handle Westfield and you will cease talking about it." He kissed her soundly as they reached their room. It was only by a twist of fate that he turned his head at that moment and saw Elizabeth reach the top of the stairs. He frowned, and lowered Margaret to her feet. She gave a soft murmur of protest.

"Give me a moment, sweet." He started off down the hall.

"You're meddling," she called after him.

Something was wrong with Elizabeth. That was obvious even from a distance. Flushed and mussed, she looked feverish. His stomach clenched as he neared her. The color of her cheeks deepened upon seeing him, and she looked for a moment just as their mother had before she died, burning with fever. The brief flash of remembered pain quickened his steps.

"Are you unwell?" he asked, placing a hand to her forehead.

Her eyes widened, and then she shook her head quickly.

"You look ill."

"I'm fine." Her voice was low and huskier than usual.

"I will send for the doctor."

"That's not necessary," she protested, her spine straightening.

William opened his mouth to speak.

"A nap, William. It's all I need. I swear it." She sighed and placed her hand on his arm, her violet eyes softening. "You worry too much."

"I always will." He placed his hand over hers, and then turned to escort her to her room. Since their mother had passed on and their father withdrew emotionally, Elizabeth had been all he'd had for most of his life. She'd been his only emotional connection during the time before Margaret when he'd been determined never to fall in love and risk the same misery as their father.

As they neared her room, his nose reminded him of the organic eruption that awaited them. "Why didn't you tell me Westfield was harassing you? I would have dealt with him."

"*No!*"

Her abrupt cry gave him pause, the fierce protectiveness he'd always felt for her rearing up in suspicion. "Tell me you are not encouraging him."

Elizabeth cleared her throat. "Haven't we had this discussion before?"

Closing his eyes, William released a deep breath and prayed for patience. "If you assure me that you will come to me for assistance if you have a need, I will refrain from asking you questions you don't want to answer." He opened his eyes and looked down at her, frowning at the sight of the high color of her skin and glazed eyes. She didn't look well at all. And her hair was disheveled. The last time her hair had looked like that . . .

"Have you gone racing again?" he barked. "Did you take a groom with you? Good God, what if you were thrown—"

"William." Elizabeth laughed. "Go see to Margaret. I'm tired. If you insist on interrogating me, you can do so once I've rested."

"I am not interrogating you. I just know you well. You are stubborn to a fault and refuse to listen to good sense."

"Says the man who worked for Lord Eldridge."

William released a frustrated breath, recognizing from her sudden rigid tone that she was finished talking. All well and good. He intended to manage Marcus on his own terms anyway. "Very well. Find me later." He bent and kissed her forehead. "If you still look flushed when you wake, I'm sending for the doctor."

"Yes, yes." Elizabeth shooed him away.

William went, but his concern would not be dismissed so easily, and they both knew it.

Elizabeth waited in the hallway just outside the office of Lord Nicholas Eldridge, pleased with herself for having snuck out of the house while William was occupied. Because she arrived unannounced, she anticipated cooling her heels. To his credit, Eldridge did not keep her waiting long.

"Lady Hawthorne," he greeted her in what she imagined to be a customarily distracted manner. Rounding the desk, he gestured to her to have a seat. "To what do I owe the pleasure of your visit?" Though the words were polite, the tone held an undercurrent of impatience. He resumed his seat and arched a brow.

She'd forgotten how austere he was, how serious. Yet despite the drabness of his attire and the gray of his wig, his presence was arresting. He bore the weight of his power with consummate ease.

"I apologize, Lord Eldridge, for the importunate nature of my visit. I've come to offer you a trade."

Gray eyes assessed her sharply. "A trade?"

"I would prefer to work with another agent."

He blinked. "And what are you offering in return?"

"Hawthorne's journal."

"I see." He leaned back in his chair. "Has Lord Westfield done something in particular, Lady Hawthorne, which would cause you to seek his replacement?"

She could not prevent her blush. Lord Eldridge pounced on the telltale sign immediately. "Has he approached you in some manner that would not befit his duties? I would take such an accusation seriously."

Elizabeth shifted uncomfortably. She did not want Marcus reprimanded, simply removed from her life.

"Lady Hawthorne. This is a personal matter, is it not?"

She nodded.

"I had valid reasons for assigning Lord Westfield to you."

"I'm certain you did. However, I cannot continue to work with him, regardless of your motives. My brother is growing suspicious." That was not her only reason, but it would suffice.

"I see," he murmured. He remained silent for a long time, but she did not waver under his intimidating scrutiny. "Your husband was a valuable member of my team. Losing him and your brother has been difficult. Lord Westfield has done an excellent job of shouldering a great deal of responsibility despite the demands of his title. He is truly the best man for this assignment."

"I don't doubt his ability."

"Still, you are determined, are you not?" He sighed when she nodded. "I will consider your request."

Elizabeth nodded, understanding he had conceded as much as he was going to. Standing, she smiled grimly at his assessing gaze. He escorted her to the door, pausing a moment before turning the knob.

"It is not my place, Lady Hawthorne, but I feel I should point out to you that Lord Westfield is a good man. I am aware of your history, and I'm certain the ramifications are uncomfortable. However, he is genuinely concerned for your safety. Whatever happens, please keep that in mind."

Elizabeth studied Lord Eldridge silently, and then nodded. There was something else, something he was not telling her. Not that she was surprised. In her experience, agents were always tight-lipped, sharing little of themselves with others. She was greatly relieved when he opened the door and allowed her to escape. While she held no ill will toward Eldridge, she nevertheless looked forward to the day when he and his damned agency were no longer a part of her life.

Marcus entered the offices of Lord Eldridge just before ten in the evening. The summons had arrived just as he prepared to depart for the Dunsmore musicale. While he was impatient to see Elizabeth, he had some thoughts to share about the investigation and this unexpected audience was highly opportune.

Marcus adjusted his tails and dropped into the nearest chair.

"Lady Hawthorne came to see me this afternoon."

"Did she?" Settled, Marcus took a pinch of snuff.

Eldridge continued to work without looking up, the papers before him lit by the candelabra on his desk and the shifting glow from the nearby fireplace. "She offered Viscount Hawthorne's journal in exchange for removing you from your duties."

The enameled snuff box snapped shut decisively.

With a sigh, Eldridge set aside his quill. "She was adamant about it, Westfield, even threatening to become uncooperative if I refused her."

"I'm certain she was most persuasive." Shaking his head, he asked, "What do you intend to do?"

"I told her I would look into it, and so I have. The question is—what do you intend to do?"

"Leave her to me. I was on my way to her when I received your summons."

"If I discover you are using your position with the agency to further your own personal agenda, I will deal with you harshly." Eldridge's expression was grim.

"I would expect nothing less," Marcus assured him.

"How is the journal coming along?"

"I'm making headway, but the going is slow."

Eldridge nodded. "Soothe her concerns then. If she comes to me again, I will have no choice but to honor her request. That would be lamentable since you are making progress. I would prefer you to continue."

Marcus pursed his lips and said what was on his mind. "Avery related today's events to you, yes?"

"Of course. But you have something to add, I see."

"I've thought of this situation ceaselessly. Something is amiss. The assailant was too aware of our preparations, as if he'd gained the knowledge beforehand. Certainly he would have expected her to contact the agency considering her husband's involvement and the relevance of the book, but the way he'd hidden himself, the escape route he had planned . . . Damn it, we were not incompetent! Yet he evaded four men with little effort. He *knew* how the men were arranged. And Hawthorne's journal. How did he learn of it?"

"You suspect internal perfidy?"

"How else?"

"I trust my men implicitly, Westfield. The agency couldn't exist otherwise."

"Consider the possibility. It's all I ask."

Eldridge arched a gray brow. "Avery? The outriders? Who can you trust?"

"Avery bears an obvious fondness for Lady Hawthorne. So you, Avery, myself—that is the extent of my trust at this moment."

"Well, that certainly negates Lady Hawthorne's request, does it not?" Eldridge pinched the bridge of his nose and sighed wearily. "Let me reflect on who might have been told about Hawthorne's journal. Return tomorrow and we'll discuss this further."

Shaking his head in silent commiseration, Marcus departed, gazing about the empty outer offices before moving down the hall with its towering ceilings and dimly lit chandeliers. For a brief moment, he'd been furious with Elizabeth and then the feeling passed. She would never have involved Eldridge unless she felt the need was dire. She'd been affected this afternoon, shaken enough to set aside her formidable pride.

A crack had appeared in her armor. He hoped it wouldn't be long before the shell was removed and he could once again see the vulnerable woman who hid inside.

"You look the fittest I've seen you in years," Margaret said, her sweet smile revealing a charming dimple. "You are radiant this evening."

Elizabeth flushed and fluffed the pale blue silk of her overskirts. She looked ravished. There was no other way to describe it. "It is *you* who is radiant. Every woman here pales in comparison. Pregnancy agrees with you."

Margaret's hand moved to cover the slight protrusion of her lightly corseted stomach. "I'm pleased you are making the effort to socialize and be seen. Today's ride in the park did wonders for your complexion. William is concerned about those formidable looking outriders you hired, but I explained how difficult it must be for you, reemerging alone after the death of your spouse."

Elizabeth bit her bottom lip. "Yes," she agreed softly. "It has been difficult."

Just then, the tiny hairs on the back of her neck began to rise. It was not necessary to turn around to discern why.

Marcus had arrived. She refused to face him. Her blood

still thrummed with the pleasure he'd given her, and a man as perceptive as he was would know it.

Margaret leaned closer. "Heavens. The way Lord Westfield looks at you could start a fire. Fortunate for you that William did not attend this evening. Can you imagine if he had? I'd wager they'd come to fisticuffs. You should have heard Westfield say you were worth the risk of death in a duel. Every woman in London is green with envy."

Elizabeth could feel the burning emerald gaze from across the crowded room. She shivered, her senses acutely attuned to the man who approached her.

"Here he comes." Margaret arched a copper brow. "The gossips will go mad over this, crazed as they've been over that row with William at the Morelands'. This will only add fuel to the fire." Her voice tapered off.

"Lady Barclay," purred the velvet voice, as Marcus bowed low over Margaret's proffered hand. His shoulder brushed deliberately against Elizabeth's arm, leaving goose bumps in its wake.

"Lord Westfield, a pleasure."

He turned and the intensity of his gaze robbed her of breath. Dear heaven. He looked as if he meant to toss up her skirts at any moment. Dressed in a dark blue coat and breeches, he made every other man fade to insignificance.

"Lady Hawthorne." He captured her hand, which hung limply at her side, and lifted it, meeting it halfway with the descent of his mouth. His kiss was anything but chaste, melting through her glove as his fingers caressed the center of her palm.

Instantly she was aroused, on edge, wanting those fingers to caress her everywhere as they'd done mere hours ago. He watched her with a knowing smile, well aware of her reaction.

"Lord Westfield." She tugged her hand, but he would not release it. Her stomach fluttered as his fingertips continued their gentle stroking.

Her Grace, the Dowager Duchess of Ravensend, announced the start of the musicale, and all the guests left the formal parlor to move into the ballroom where chairs had been assembled to face the musicians. Marcus tucked her hand around his arm and led her out to the foyer, deliberately falling behind.

"The man escaped," he said for her ears only.

She nodded, unsurprised.

He stopped, and turned to face her. "More must be done to protect you. And I will not be handing this assignment over to someone else, so your efforts this afternoon were for naught."

"This entanglement offers no benefit to either of us."

His hand reached up to touch her face, and she stepped back quickly.

"You forget yourself," she scolded. She shot a wary look around the foyer.

With one warning glance, Marcus sent the attending footman fleeing with haste. Then he turned all of his attention upon her. "And you forget the rules."

"What rules?"

His gaze narrowed and she took another step back. "I can still taste you, Elizabeth. I can still feel the silky clasp of your cunt on my cock and the pleasure you gave me still warms my blood. The rules haven't changed since this afternoon. I can have you however and whenever I wish."

"To hell with you." Her heart racing, her chest tight, she stumbled backward until the wall prevented further escape.

He bridged the gap between them, enveloping her in his rich, warm scent. Music poured from the ballroom and she shot a startled glance toward the sound. When she looked back at Marcus, he stood directly before her.

"Why do you insist on driving us both to madness?" he asked gruffly.

Her hand went to her throat, nervously fingering the pearls that rested there. "What can I do to satisfy your interest?"

she asked bluntly. "There must be something I can do or say, that will cool your ardor."

"You know what you can do."

She swallowed hard, and stared up at him. He was so tall, so broad of shoulder that he dwarfed her until she could see nothing around him. But her fear did not come from that. In fact, it was only when she was with Marcus that she felt truly safe. No, her fear came from inside, from a cold and lonely place she preferred to forget existed. And there he stood, so damn confident and predatory. He felt none of the uncertainty that she felt. Libertines never did, shielded as they were by the knowledge of their undeniable charm and appeal. If only she could boast such assured sexuality.

A slow smile curved her lips as the solution to her dilemma presented itself in a flash of comprehension. How could she have missed the obvious? Here she'd been floundering and unsure how to respond in the face of such an overwhelming sensual onslaught when she'd grown up with the best examples of how to manage these situations in her own household. She would simply do what William or her father or Marcus himself would do.

"Very well, then. You can meet me in the bachelor quarters of Chesterfield Hall for your fuck." The crude word stumbled over her tongue and she lifted her chin to hide her discomfort.

He blinked. "Beg your pardon?"

She arched a brow. "That's what I can do, correct? Spread my legs until you sate your lust? Then you'll tire of me and leave me in peace." Just speaking the words reignited the heat in her veins. Images from the afternoon filled her mind, and she bit her lower lip against the sudden rush of desire.

The intense predatory look of his features softened. "Christ, when you present it in that manner—" His brows drew together in a rueful frown. "What an ogre I must seem to you at times. I cannot remember the last time I felt so chastened."

The faintest trace of a smile touched her lips. She took a step closer, her hand coming up to press against the elaborately embroidered silk of his waistcoat before drifting down, caressing the rippling expanse of his stomach beneath. Her hand tingled through her glove, reminding her of how delicate the balance of power was.

Marcus caught her wandering fingertips and tugged her closer. Staring down into her face, he shook his head. "I presume you've conceived of some mischief."

"Not at all," she murmured, stroking his palm with her fingers and watching his gaze darken. "I intend to give you what you want. Surely you won't complain about that?"

"Hmmm. Tonight then?"

Her eyes widened. "Good heavens. Again today?"

Laughing, he relented, his mouth curving in a smile that made her breathless. The change in him was startling. Gone was the brutish arrogance, replaced by a boyish allure she found hard to resist. "Very well then." He stepped back, and offered his arm. "And you are correct, I surely won't complain."

Chapter 8

Marcus paced before the fire in the Chesterfield guest-house and tried to recollect his first sexual encounter. It had happened a long time ago and the rushed tumble in the Westfield stables had passed in a blur of sweaty skin, prickly hay, and gasping relief. Still, despite the less than clear remembrance of that afternoon, he was certain he'd never been as anxious as he was at the present moment.

Having escorted Elizabeth home from the Dempsey Ball over an hour ago, he'd rushed home and changed, only to return on horseback. He'd been waiting ever since.

Doubt twisted his stomach into knots, a sensation wholly unfamiliar to him. Would Elizabeth come to him, as she'd promised? Or would he wait here all night, desperate to taste her and feel her beneath his hands?

Standing, Marcus tossed more coals into the grate before glancing around the beautifully appointed bachelor quarters. While he would have preferred to have Elizabeth once again in his own bed, he would take what he could get and gladly.

The Aubusson rug was soft under his bare feet as he moved back to the chair facing the fire. He'd removed every garment but his breeches, astonished and not a little disconcerted by his haste to press his bare skin to Elizabeth's.

The outer door opened, and then shut quietly. Marcus stood, and moved to the hallway, lounging against the jamb in an effort to appear nonchalant and less needy than he felt. Then Elizabeth turned the corner and his breath caught. Against his will, his feet moved, one in front of the other. She paused, her luscious bottom lip caught between her teeth. Dressed in simple muslin, her hair free of its previous evening elaborateness, her face scrubbed clean of both powder and patch, she was a vision of casual youthful beauty.

"Where have you been?" he growled as he reached her, his hands gripping her waist and lifting her against him.

"I—"

He crushed her response with a kiss. She stiffened at first, and then suddenly she opened for him. A groan escaped, as the heady taste of her flooded his mouth. Fierce but sweet, her kisses had always driven him to madness.

A loud thump momentarily distracted him, and he pulled back to discern the source of the sound. Lying at their feet was a small volume covered in red leather.

"Your returning Hawthorne's journal?"

"Yes," she said, in the breathy voice that betrayed her arousal.

As he gazed at the book on the floor, Marcus was surprised at the jealousy that rose up within him. Elizabeth carried another man's name. She had once been physically joined to someone else. He still stung from the pain of it, much to his chagrin. He was not some foolishly besotted lad, selfish in his desire for the affection of a fair maid.

But he felt like one.

Marcus linked his fingers with hers, and tugged her into the bedroom.

"I came as quickly as I could," she said softly.

"Liar. You debated internally for a moment, at least."

She smiled, and his entire body hardened. "Maybe a moment," she conceded.

"But you came, regardless." He wrapped his arms around her, and fell back into the bed.

She laughed, the cold wariness of her features instantly

transformed. "Only because I knew if I didn't, you would probably come up and collect me yourself."

Burying his face in her neck, he chuckled and groaned at the same time. Under other circumstances, as painfully aroused as he was, he would have rolled his lover over and mounted her. In this instance, however, he was determined to find a way past Elizabeth's defenses. Sexual satisfaction was not his only aim.

Not any longer.

"You are correct." He stared up at her. "I would have fetched you."

Her hand touched the side of his face, one of the rare tender gestures she bestowed on him. Any touch of hers, any melting look, stunned him and moved him.

"You are far too arrogant. You do realize that, don't you?"

"Of course." He sat up and settled her against the pillows. Then he reached for the bottle of wine he'd set on the nightstand, and poured her a full glass.

Elizabeth licked her bottom lip and her lashes lowered, hiding her gaze as she accepted the libation. "You are half naked. It's . . . disconcerting."

"Perhaps if you disrobed it would be less so," he suggested.

"Marcus . . ."

"Or drink. That should relax you." It was why he'd brought two bottles with him. He remembered her giddy on champagne during their courtship, laughing and mischievous. He was eager to see her that way again.

As if she thought the same, Elizabeth lifted the goblet to her lips and took a large swallow. Normally, he'd chastise such an abuse of excellent vintage, but in this case he was pleased. A small droplet clung to the corner of her lips and he leaned forward and licked it away, closing his eyes briefly in contentment. He was startled when she turned her head and pressed her lips more fully to his.

Eyes wide, she pulled back and drank the rest of the wine down. She thrust the empty glass at him. "More, please."

Marcus smiled. "Your wish is my command." He studied her furtively as he poured, noting the way her fingers brushed restlessly over her thighs. "Why are you so nervous, love?"

"You are accustomed to this sort of . . . arrangement. For me, however, sitting here with you half-dressed and knowing the entire purpose of being here is for . . . for . . ."

"Sex?"

"Yes." She opened her mouth and then closed it, shrugging delicate shoulders. "It makes me nervous."

"That's not the only reason we are here."

Elizabeth frowned, and took another large drink. "It's not?"

"No. I'd like to talk with you as well."

"Is that how these things are normally done?"

He chuckled ruefully. "Nothing about this is like anything in my experience."

"Oh." Her shoulders sagged just a little.

Catching her free hand, he laced his fingers with hers. Her cheeks were already flushed, betraying the effects of the wine. "Could you grant me one small favor?" he asked, even though he had promised himself he wouldn't.

She waited expectantly.

Tamping down the sudden apprehension he felt, he rushed ahead. "Could you find it in your heart to tell me what happened the night you left me?"

Her gaze lowered to stare into the contents of her glass. "Must I?"

"If you would be so kind, love."

"I'd really rather not."

"Is it so dreadful?" he coaxed softly. "The deed is done and cannot be undone. I ask only to be relieved of my confusion."

Elizabeth released a deep breath. "I suppose I owe you that much."

When her silence stretched out he prodded, "Go on."

"The tale starts with William. One night, about a month before the start of my first Season, I couldn't sleep. I often had that trouble over the years after my mother died. Whenever I was restless I would visit my father's study and sit in the dark. It smells like old books and my father's tobacco—I find the combination soothing.

"William entered shortly after, but he failed to see me lying on the settee. I was curious so I remained quiet. It was very late and he was dressed in dark clothing, he'd even covered his golden hair. It was obvious he was going somewhere where he didn't wish to be seen or recognized. He carried himself so strangely, all chained up-ferocity and energy. He left and did not return until dawn. That was when I first suspected he was involved in something dangerous."

Elizabeth paused to take another drink. "I began to watch him when we were out. I studied his activities. I noticed he sought out Lord Hawthorne with regularity. The two of them would detach themselves from the gathering and have heated discussions in quiet corners, sometimes trading papers or other items."

Marcus sprawled across the counterpane and rested his head on his hand. "I never noticed. Eldridge's expertise at subterfuge never ceases to amaze me. I certainly never suspected William was an agent."

"Why would you?" she asked simply. "Had I not been watching them so closely, I would never have suspected anything either. But eventually William began to look exhausted, drawn. I was worried about him. When I asked him outright to tell me what he was doing, he refused. I knew I needed help." She glanced at him then, her violet gaze tortured.

"That is why you came to me that night." The bitter irony was not lost on him. He took the glass of wine from her fingers and washed the taste of it from his mouth. "Eldridge keeps the identities of his agents a closely guarded secret. In the event one of us is captured or compromised we have little information to share. I personally know very few."

The tight line of her normally lush mouth betrayed her distaste for the agency. Right now he was not feeling too charitable toward Eldridge himself. William's assignment, as well as his own, had contrived to bring his engagement to such a tragic end.

Elizabeth breathed a forlorn sigh. "When I returned from your home I was too upset to retire, so I went to my father's study. Nigel called for William later that morning and he was shown into the room, unaware I was there. I vented my rage on him. I accused him of leading William on a path to destruction. I threatened to tell my father."

Marcus smiled, imagining the scene. "I have learned to respect your temper, sweet. You become a veritable termagant when angered."

She returned a weak smile, devoid of life or humor. "I had assumed their activities were degenerate. I was shocked when Nigel explained that he and William were agents for the Crown." Her eyes shone with withheld tears. "And it was all suddenly too much . . . what I thought you had done, the danger William was in. I told Hawthorne about your infidelity in a moment of weakness. He said marriages of high passion were not the stuff of longevity or true happiness. I would have been discontented eventually, he said. Best I learned your true nature when I did, rather than after it was too late. He was so kind, so gentle in my distress. He provided an anchor at a time when I was adrift."

Marcus rolled onto his back and stared at the red velvet canopy above him. After her mother's death and her father's decline into emotional apathy, Hawthorne's words must have sounded like the veriest wisdom to Elizabeth. Tense and frustrated, his anger toward a dead man had no outlet. It should have been *he* who was her anchor, not Hawthorne. "Damn you," he swore vehemently.

"When I returned from Scotland I inquired about you."

"I had left the country by then." His voice was distant, lost in the past. "I called on you that morning, once I'd settled the widow. I wanted to explain, and make things right between us. Instead, William met me at the door and threw your note in my face. He blamed me for your rashness. I blamed him for not going after you."

"*You* could have come after me."

Marcus turned his head to meet her gaze. "Is that what you wanted?"

When Elizabeth shrank back into the pillows, he knew his rage and pain must be evident on his face.

"I . . ." Her voice choked off.

"Part of me held on to the hope that you would fail to go through with it, but somehow I knew." His eyes narrowed. "I *knew* you had done it—married someone else. And I couldn't help but wonder how it was that he was there for you, when the events of that night could not have been predicted. Perhaps, as you said, he was always an option. I could not remain in England after that. I would have stayed away longer if my father had not passed on. When I returned, I discovered you were widowed. I sent you my condolences so you would know I was home. I waited for you to come to me."

"I heard about your liaisons, your endless string of women." Her spine stiffened and she swung her legs over the side of the bed.

"Where in hell do you think you're going?" he growled.

He set the empty glass on the nightstand and yanked her into a sprawl across his chest. Holding her instantly soothed the restlessness that was his constant companion. Despite everything, she was his now.

"I thought the mood was ruined," she said with a pout.

He arched his hips upward, pressing his erection into her thigh. Her gaze darkened, the irises fading as desire quickened her breathing.

"Don't think," he said gruffly. "Forget the past."

"How?"

"Kiss me. We'll forget everything together."

She hesitated only a moment before lowering her head and pressing her moist lips to his. Frozen, he lay aching beneath her, the soft pressure of her curves burning his skin, her vanilla scent intoxicating him. He tightened his grip on her hips to hide the trembling of his hands. Why she affected him like this, he couldn't guess, though he'd spent endless hours trying.

She lifted her head, and he groaned at the loss.

"I'm sorry," she murmured, color washing across her cheeks. "I'm not good at this."

"You were doing beautifully."

"You're not moving," she complained.

He gave a rueful laugh. "I'm afraid to, love. I want you too badly."

"Then we are at an impasse." Her smile was sweet. "I don't know what to do."

Capturing her hand, he placed it on his chest. "Touch me."

She sat up, straddling his hips. Several curls framed the beauty of her face. "Where?"

Marcus doubted he could survive it, but he would expire a contented man. "Everywhere."

Smiling, her finger drifted tentatively through the hair on his chest leaving tingling paths in their wake. Her fingertips swirled around the scar that marred his shoulder and then brushed across his nipples. He shivered.

"You like that?"

"Yes."

Elizabeth hummed, her palms coming to rest against his stomach, which tautened in response. "Fascinating."

Choking out a laugh, he said, "I pray your interest is more than curiosity."

She giggled, a bit tipsy he suspected. "You are quite the handsomest man I've ever seen." Reaching up, she caressed the tops of his shoulders and then down his arms to entwine her fingers with his. The moment was simple and yet achingly complex. On the surface, they appeared to be two lovers, hopelessly smitten with one another, but the heavy undercurrent of wariness ran both ways.

"I'd hoped you would think so."

"Why? So you can seduce me with ease?"

He brought their joined hands to his lips and kissed her knuckles. "You are doing the seducing."

Elizabeth snorted. "There is no help for you, Lord Westfield. You are a rogue through and through. When this affair is over—"

With a firm tug, he yanked her down and kissed her breathless. He didn't want to hear about the end or even think of it.

Releasing her hands, his fingers moved along her spine, loosening her dress. He murmured his pleasure at finding nothing beneath it, no corset or chemise. As frightened as she was of the way he made her feel, she'd still come prepared. He'd also say she was eager, if the near frantic way she was caressing him was any indication. Parting the back of her gown, he tugged down the front and exposed her breasts, full and heavy with arousal. They were lovely, so pale, tipped with rosy nipples. He hadn't had the pleasure of fondling them before, a neglect he planned to correct posthaste.

When she lifted her hands, he brushed them away. "No. Don't hide, sweet, I enjoy looking at you as much as you enjoy looking at me."

"After all the women—"

"No more," he admonished. "No more talk of that." Sighing, he dropped his hands to her thighs. "I cannot change my past."

"You cannot change what you are." All the softness in her face fled. Only Elizabeth could sit bare breasted on a man and be so remote.

"Damn it, my sexual history is not who I am. And if I were you, I would think twice before complaining, since without my experience I would not be able to pleasure you so well."

"Grateful?" she snapped. "I would have been more grateful had you turned your attentions elsewhere."

She attempted to slip away, but he restrained her. Marcus pumped his hips upward, pushing the heated length of his erection into the burning dampness between her thighs. When she gasped, he did it again, watching as she ground herself onto his cock. Her immediate helpless response cooled his irritation.

"Why does my past anger you so?"

A finely arched brow rose.

"Tell me," he urged. "I truly want to know." He would get nowhere with her if she kept these barriers between them. Certainly he could have her body, but he wanted more than that during the length of their affair.

She wrinkled her nose. "Do you really care nothing for the women whose hearts you break?"

"Is that what this is about?" He held his exasperation in check. "Elizabeth, the women who entertain me are vastly experienced."

Her look was clearly disbelieving.

Sliding his hands beneath the hem of her gown, he caressed the lithe length of her thighs, his thumbs coming to rest against the soft curls of her sex. His cock hardened further at the realization that only the material of his breeches separated his torment from her sweet relief.

"Women are a bit more susceptible to elevated feelings after a pleasurable sexual encounter," he admitted. "But in all honesty, rarely has a woman become overly attached to me and even then, I doubt it was love."

"Perhaps you simply didn't notice the extent of their attachment. I vow, William was always taken aback when one of my female acquaintances would no longer receive me because of their unrequited feelings for him."

Marcus flinched. "I'm sorry, love."

"You should be. I suffer from a deplorable lack of companionship because of men like you and William. Thank heavens he married Margaret."

He brushed the tips of his thumbs across the soft, damp lips of her sex and her hips canted forward in unmistakable invitation.

"I shall be like your jaded paramours," she said suddenly.

Moving his hands, he spread her with his fingers and brushed against her clitoris. It hardened as he circled it. "In what way? I can conceive of no way you are like any woman I've ever met."

"*I* will discard *you*."

Gently, he pressed his thumb against the gathering slickness and slipped inside her. This was his. She would not deny him the pleasure of it. "Perhaps I'll overwhelm you, drench you in rapture until you cannot conceive of a night passing without my cock here, deep inside you."

Her soft plaintive moan was the death of him. Reaching between them, he tore open the placket of his breeches. Glancing up, he watched Elizabeth's eyes melt. Discard him, indeed. She would surrender that icy control that chilled him, he would see to it.

"I wanted to savor you, Elizabeth."

She stiffened when he gripped her hips and positioned her over his cock. "What—" Her voice strangled to silence as he pulled her down, sheathing himself.

He groaned as the molten heat of her clasped him like a velvet fist. Twisting rapture coiled in his loins and stiffened his spine, causing Marcus to grit his teeth and arch off the bed.

"Christ," he gasped. If he breathed wrong, he would come.

Elizabeth writhed around him, finding a position of comfort that lodged him more securely within her. Sweat beading his brow, he relaxed his hold on her waist and sank back into the pillows.

With her lovely face flushed, eyes huge and hot with need, she stared at him in silent inquiry.

"I'm all yours, love," he encouraged, needing to see her make the effort. Wanting to lie still and be fucked mindless by the woman who'd jilted him so long ago.

Biting her lower lip, she rose, lifting herself from his cock until only the tip remained inside. When she lowered again, her movements were awkward, tentative, but devastating nonetheless. His hands fell to the bed and fisted in the counterpane. Elizabeth moved again, panting, and the cool air on his cock followed by the heated grip of her cunt tore a groan from him.

She paused.

"Don't stop," he begged.

"I don't—"

"Faster, sweet. Harder."

And to his delight, she obliged, moving over him with her natural grace. The sight of her, barely dressed, with breasts bouncing, arrested him. He watched her, eyes half lidded with drugging pleasure, remembering her standing across the Moreland ballroom, a vision of regal unattainable beauty. Now she was his, in the basest way possible, her whimpered cries betraying how much she enjoyed him despite everything.

When he couldn't take any more, when the need to come was so overwhelming he feared leaving her behind, he held her in place and lunged his hips upwards, fucking her suspended body with rapid impatient drives.

"Yes . . ." Her hands covered his and her head fell back, the gesture one of blatant surrender. "Marcus!"

He knew that cry, understood the command, *Take me.* And rolling, he did just that, thrusting into her so hard he shoved her up the bed. Still he couldn't get deep enough. He growled, frustrated that even this primal act was not enough to slake the need that grew stronger the more he tried to satisfy it.

Elizabeth arched her neck, her breasts lifting to press hard nipples into his chest. With a sharp broken cry she tightened around him before dissolving into the rippling caresses that felt like nothing he'd ever experienced before.

He fucked through them like a mad man, forcing his cock into grasping depths, dipping into the scalding cream that bathed her inner thighs and lured his seed. He roared when he came, his semen spewing until he thought he would die of it. Lowering his head he bit her shoulder, punishing her for being the bane of his existence, the source of his highest pleasure and deepest pain.

The soft sound of pages turning woke her. Elizabeth sat upright, startled and a bit embarrassed to find herself completely unclothed and uncovered by the sheets. Searching the room, she discovered an equally naked Marcus seated at the small escritoire with Nigel's journal open before him. His gaze was riveted on her.

Bared and far too vulnerable, she pulled the sheet over her. "What are you doing?"

Giving her a heart-stopping smile, he stood and moved to the bed. "I'd intended to puzzle out Hawthorne's code, but was repeatedly distracted by the view."

She bit back a smile. "Lecher. There should be a law forbidding the ogling of sleeping women."

"I'm certain there is." He leapt onto the bed. "But it does not apply to lovers."

The way he said the word "lovers" made her shiver. Staking a claim to his passion, however briefly, made her blood heat. And then chill. It was too much, too fast.

"You say that so smugly." Glancing briefly into fire, her fingers picked restlessly at the eyelet work bordering the sheets. "No doubt you are pleased with your easy conquest of me."

"Easy?" he scoffed, flopping backward into the pillows and tossing his arms wide. "Was bloody damn difficult." Turning his head to look at her, he frowned and his voice lost its teasing edge. Rolling to his side, Marcus propped his head in his hand. "Tell me about your marriage."

"Why?"

"Why not?"

She shrugged, wishing she could find the control she'd felt earlier. "There's nothing of note to relay. Hawthorne was an exemplary spouse."

Pursing his lips, Marcus stared pensively into the fire. Before she could resist the impulse, she reached over and brushed a tumbled lock from his forehead.

He turned to press a kiss into her palm. "You had an accord then?"

"We enjoyed similar activities and he was content to allow me my freedom. He was so preoccupied with his agency work, I rarely saw him, but the distance suited us both."

He nodded, appearing deep in thought. "You didn't mind the agency so much then?"

"No. I hated it even then, but I was naïve and had no notion that anyone would be killed."

When he said nothing, Elizabeth looked at him under her lashes, wondering what he was thinking and why she was staying. She should go.

Then he said, "I believe some of what is written in that journal is about Christopher St. John, but until I have an opportunity to peruse the volume at leisure, I won't be certain."

"Oh." She twisted the edge of the sheet around her finger. Here was her opportunity to depart without awkwardness. "I'm sorry to have disturbed you." Sliding her legs to the edge of the mattress, she attempted to leave the bed and was stopped by his hand at her elbow. She glanced over her shoulder.

Emerald eyes filled with banked fire met hers. "You are a distraction I welcome," he murmured in the deeply sexual voice she'd come to anticipate.

Marcus pulled her back, crawling over her, pressing her down, his mouth nuzzling her stomach through the bedclothes. "You have no notion of how it affects me to be in your company like this, to work in the moments when you are otherwise occupied."

Gasping as his mouth surrounded her nipple through the sheet, Elizabeth's hand drifted to the warm skin of his shoulders and arms, feeling the power within them as they held his weight from her. With rhythmic laps of his tongue, he abraded the stiff peak, intuitively knowing how to make her mad for him.

"Marcus . . ." She struggled, knowing it was wrong to give in, fighting to regain control.

With a low growl, he released her breast and yanked the sheet out of the way. He covered her body with his, his mouth claiming hers, the heat and hardness of his frame causing her to melt into him helplessly. His hands moved with tender skill, knowing her so well, ravishing her senses, coaxing away her tension.

Until she dissolved in pleasure, falling from grace with a cry of surrender, knowing even as she did so that the climb back up grew longer by the moment . . .

Chapter 9

Elizabeth entered the main house through the study's garden doors. Although not yet dawn, the kitchen staff would already be preparing for the day's meals and she didn't want to chance crossing paths with one of them. Not with her hair a fright and her skin so flushed.

"Elizabeth."

Startled, she jumped. Finding William in the open doorway, her stomach tightened.

"Yes, William?"

"A moment, if you please."

Sighing, she waited as he stepped into the room and closed them inside. She braced herself.

"What in hell are you doing with Westfield? In our guesthouse? Have you lost your wits?"

"Yes." There was no point in denying it.

"Why?" he asked, clearly confused and hurt.

"I don't know."

"I'll kill him," he growled. "To treat you like this, to use you so callously. I told you to stay away from him, that his intentions were dishonorable."

"I tried, truly I did." Turning away, Elizabeth sank into a nearby chair.

Muttering an oath, William began to pace in front of her.

"You could have had anyone. If you were so set against marriage, you could have chosen a more suitable companion."

"William, I love you for your concern, but I am a grown woman and I can make my own decisions, especially about something as personal as taking a lover."

"Good God," he bit out. "To have to speak of such matters with you—"

"You don't, you know," she said dryly.

"Oh yes, I do." He rounded on her. "After suffering through your endless lectures about my licentious behavior—"

"Yes, you see, I learned from the best."

William stilled. "You've no notion. You are in over your head."

Elizabeth took a deep breath. "Perhaps. Or perhaps it is Westfield who is out of his depth." If not, he soon would be.

He snorted. "Elizabeth—"

"Enough, William, I'm tired." She stood and moved toward the hallway. "Westfield will call this evening to escort me to the Fairchilds' dinner." She'd tried to argue, but Marcus insisted her safety was in question. It was either with his escort or she couldn't attend. He'd been adamant, in his charming, drawling way.

"Fine," William snapped. "I'll have a word with him when he arrives."

She waved her hand nonchalantly over her shoulder. "Be my guest. Send for me when you're done."

"This is odious."

"I gathered you think so."

"An abomination."

"Yes, yes." She moved out into the hallway.

"I will thrash him if he hurts you," William called after her.

Elizabeth stopped and turned to face him. As meddling as he was, he was acting out of love, and she adored him for it. With a tender smile, she returned to him and hugged his waist. He crushed her close.

"You are the most vexing sibling," he said into her hair. "Why could you not be more pliable and even-tempered?"

"Because I would bore you to tears and drive you insane."

He sighed. "Yes, I supposed you would at that." He pulled back. "Be careful, please. I couldn't bear to see you hurt again."

The sadness evident on his handsome features tugged at her heart, and reminded her of the precariousness of her situation. Playing with Marcus was playing with fire.

"Don't worry so much, William." Linking her arm with his, Elizabeth tugged him toward the staircase. "Trust me to take care of myself."

"I'm trying, but it's damned difficult when you engage in stupidity."

Laughing, Elizabeth released his arm and ran up the stairs. "First one to the vase at the end of the gallery wins."

Easily reaching the vase first, William escorted Elizabeth to her bed chamber. Then he returned to his own room and wasted no time changing. He left a bewildered Margaret still abed and traveled into town to the Westfield townhouse. Taking the steps two at a time, he pounded the brass knocker that graced the door.

The portal opened, revealing a butler dripping in chilly hauteur as he gazed down the length of his nose.

Handing over his card, William barreled his way through the doorway and entered the foyer. "You may announce me to Lord Westfield," he said curtly.

The butler glanced at the card. "Lord Westfield is from home, Lord Barclay."

"Lord Westfield is abed," William snapped. "And you will rouse him and bring him to me or I will seek him out myself."

With a disdainful arch of his brow, the servant led him to the study, and then retreated.

When the door opened again, Marcus entered. William lunged at his old friend without a word.

"Bloody hell," Marcus cursed as he was tackled to the rug. He cursed again when William's fist connected with his ribcage.

William continued to rain blows as they rolled across the study floor, bumping into the chaise and knocking over a chair. Marcus made every effort to deflect the attack, but not once did he fight back.

"Son of a bitch," William growled, made more furious by being denied the fight he'd come for. "I'll kill you!"

"Damned if you're not doing an admirable job of it," Marcus grunted.

Suddenly, there were more arms in the fray, intervening and pulling them apart. Yanked to their feet, William fought off the unyielding grip that held his arms behind him. "Damn you, Ashford. Release me."

But Paul Ashford held tight. "In a moment, my lord. No offense intended. But Mother is home, and she does not care much for brawls in the house. Always made us go outside, you see."

Marcus stood opposite him and a few feet away, shrugging off the helping hand of Robert Ashford, the youngest of the three brothers. The resemblance between the two was uncanny. Only Robert's gold-rimmed spectacles and slighter frame distinguished the two. Unlike the brother behind William, who was raven-haired and dark-eyed.

William ceased his struggles, and Paul released him.

"Truly, gentlemen," Paul said, straightening his waistcoat and wig. "Much as I love a good fracas in the morning, you should at least be dressed for the occasion."

Holding a hand to his side, Marcus ignored his brother and said, "I trust your spirits have improved, Barclay?"

"Slightly." William glared. "It would have been more sporting if you'd participated."

"And risk angering Elizabeth? Don't be daft."

William snorted. "As if you have a care for her feelings."

"No doubt of that."

"Then why this? Why use her in this manner?"

Robert pushed up his spectacles, and cleared his throat. "I think we're done here, Paul."

"I hope so," Paul muttered. "Not the type of conversation I prefer to have at this time of morning. Now be good, gentlemen. Next time, it may be Mother who intercedes. I would pity you both then."

The brothers shut the door behind them as they retreated.

Marcus ran a hand through his hair. "Remember that chit you dallied with when we were at Oxford? The baker's daughter?"

"Yes." William remembered her well. A young, nubile thing. Beautiful and worldly, she was free with her favors. Celia loved a good hard fuck more than most and he'd been hot to give it to her. In fact, they'd once spent three days in bed, taking time only to bathe and eat. She'd been enjoyable with no strings.

Suddenly he caught the implication.

"Do you *want* to die?" William growled. "You are talking about my sister for God's sake!"

"And a woman grown," Marcus pointed out. "A widow, no innocent maid."

"Elizabeth is nothing like Celia. She hasn't the experience to engage in fleeting liaisons. She could be hurt."

"Oh? She seemed able to jilt me well enough and she shows no remorse for her actions."

"Why would she? You were an absolute cad."

"We are both to blame." Marcus moved to one of the wingbacks that flanked the dark fireplace and lowered himself into a weary sprawl. "However, things appear to have worked out for the best. She was not unhappy with Hawthorne."

"Then leave well enough alone."

"I cannot. There is something remaining between us. We've both agreed, as consenting adults, to allow it to run its course."

William moved to take the seat opposite. "I still cannot understand that Elizabeth could be so . . ."

"Nonchalant? *Laissez faire?*"

"Yes, exactly." He rubbed the back of his neck. "She was devastated at what you'd done, you know."

"Ah yes. So devastated she married another man post-haste."

"What better way to run?"

Marcus blinked.

"You think I don't know her?" William asked, shaking his head. "Have a care with her affections," he warned as he stood and moved toward the door. He paused on the threshold and looked back. "If you hurt her, Westfield, I'll see you on a field at dawn."

Marcus tilted his head in acknowledgment.

"In the meantime, come early this evening. We can await the women together. Father still has a fine collection of brandy."

"An irresistible invitation. I will be there."

Somewhat mollified, William made his egress. He also made a mental reminder to clean his pistols.

Just in case.

The ball was a massive success, as witnessed by the over-flowing ballroom and the beaming face of the hostess, Lady Marks-Darby. Elizabeth wove her way through the crush, escaping onto a deserted balcony. From her vantage point, she could see couples wandering through the intricate maze of hedges in the garden below. She closed her eyes and took a deep, cleansing breath.

The last week had been both heaven and hell. She went to Marcus every night in the guesthouse and while he'd never promised anything in return, she'd had her own expectations.

When she suggested the affair, she assumed he would pounce on her immediately upon her arrival, carry her off to bed, and when finished with her body take his leave. Instead, he drew her into conversation or fed her sumptuous cold suppers he brought with him. He encouraged discourse on a variety of topics and appeared genuinely interested in her opinions. He asked her about her favorite books and purchased the ones she mentioned that he had not yet read. It was all so very strange. She was completely unaccustomed to such intimacy, which seemed much more pervasive than their physical connection. Not that Marcus ever allowed her to forget that.

He held her in a constant state of physical turmoil. An erotic master, Marcus used the entirety of his formidable skill to make certain he never left her mind for even a moment. He found ways to surreptitiously brush against her shoulder or slip his hand down the curve of her spine. He bent far too close when speaking, breathing in her ear in a way that made her quiver with longing.

Laughter from the maze below brought a thankful respite from her thoughts. Two women came to a halt directly beneath the balcony, their melodious voices floating up to be heard clearly.

"The marriageable men are slim in number this Season," said one to the other.

"That is unfortunately true. And it's hideous luck that Lord Westfield should be so determined to win that wager. He practically hovers over Hawthorne's widow."

"She seems not to care much for him."

"Fool is unaware of what she is missing. He is glorious. His entire body is a work of art. I must confess, I am completely besotted."

Elizabeth gripped the railing with white-knuckled force as one of the women giggled.

"Lure him back, if you miss him so keenly."

"Oh, I shall," came the smug reply. "Lady Hawthorne may be beautiful, but she's a cold one. He's merely in it for the sport. Once he has redeemed himself, he'll want a little more fire in his bed. And I'll be waiting."

Suddenly, the women gasped in surprise.

"Excuse me, ladies," interrupted a masculine voice. The two women continued further into the maze, leaving Elizabeth to fume on the balcony.

The unmitigated gall! She grit her teeth until her jaw ached. The damned wager. How could she have forgotten?

"Lady Hawthorne?"

She turned at the sound of her name murmured in a deep, pleasantly raspy voice behind her. She eyed the gentleman who approached, taking in his appearance in an effort to identify him. "Yes?"

The man was tall and elegantly dressed. She could not know his hair color, covered as it was by a wig that was long in the back and tied at his nape. He wore a mask that wrapped around his eyes, but the brilliant blue color of his irises refused to be contained by it. Something about him arrested her gaze, tugging at her memory in a vaguely familiar way, and yet she was certain she had never met him before.

"Are we acquainted?" she asked.

He shook his head and she straightened, studying him closely as he emerged from the shadows of the overhang. What she could see of his face was well deserving of such beautiful eyes. He was, quite frankly, beyond handsome.

His lips, though thin, were curved in a way that could only be described as carnal, but his gaze . . . his gaze was coldly intent. She sensed he was the type of man who trusted no one and nothing. But that observation was not what caused her shiver of apprehension. Her misgiving was due entirely to the way he approached her. The subtle cant of his body toward hers was decidedly proprietary.

The raspy voice came again. "I regret I must be importunate, Lady Hawthorne, but we have an urgent matter to discuss."

Elizabeth shielded herself in her iciest social deportment. "It is the rare occasion, sir, when I find myself discussing urgent matters with complete strangers."

He showed a leg in a courtly bow. "Forgive me," he replied, his voice deliberately low and soothing. "Christopher St. John, my lady."

Elizabeth's breath halted in her throat. Her pulse racing, she took a preservative step backward. "What is it you wish to discuss with me, Mr. St. John?"

He took the position next to her, resting his hands on the wrought iron railing as he looked out over the maze. His casual stance was deceptive. Much like Marcus, he used an overtly friendly demeanor to reassure those around him, subtly urging others to lower their guard. The tactic had the opposite effect on Elizabeth. She tried not to tense visibly as her insides twisted.

"You received a journal that belonged to your late husband, did you not?" he asked smoothly.

The color drained from her face.

"How do you know of it?" Her eyes widened as her gaze swept over him. "Are you the man who attacked me in the park?" He did not appear to be suffering from any injury.

"You are in grave danger, Lady Hawthorne, as long as that book remains in your possession. Turn it over to me, and I will see to it you are not disturbed again."

Fear and anger blended inside her. "Are you threatening me?" Her chin lifted. "I take leave to tell you, sir, I am not without protection."

"I am well aware of your prowess with a pistol, but that skill is no proof against the type of danger you find yourself facing now. The fact that you have involved Lord Eldridge only complicates matters further." He looked at her and the barrenness in the depths of his eyes chilled her to the bone. "It is in your best interests to give me that book."

St. John's voice was laced with soft menace, his eyes piercing from behind the mask. His casual pose was unable to hide the vibrant energy that distinguished him as a dangerous man.

Elizabeth couldn't stop her shudder of fear and revulsion. He cursed under his breath.

"Here," he murmured gruffly, reaching into a small pocket that graced his white satin waistcoat. He withdrew a small object, and held it out to her. "This belongs to you, I believe."

Refusing to take her eyes from his face, she closed her hand around it.

"You must—" He stopped and swiveled quickly. She followed his gaze and relief flooded her to find Marcus standing in the doorway.

Pure ferocious rage radiated from him in waves. The lines of his face were harsh, reflecting murderous intent. "Back away from her," he ordered. His tension was palpable, coiled like a tight spring, ready to lash out at the slightest provocation.

St. John faced her unperturbed, and bowed again. His casual deportment fooled no one. A profusion of ill will and resentment poisoned the air around the two men. "We will continue our conversation some other time, Lady Hawthorne. In the meantime, I urge you to consider my request. For your own safety." He walked past Marcus with a taunting smile. "Westfield. Always a pleasure."

Marcus sidestepped, halting St. John's escape to the ballroom. "Approach her again, and I'll kill you."

St. John grinned. "You've been threatening me with death for years, Westfield."

Marcus bared his teeth in a feral smile. "I was merely biding my time until the proper excuse presented itself. I have it now. Soon I shall have what I need to see you hanged. You cannot evade justice forever."

"No? Ah, well . . . I await your convenience." St. John glanced at Elizabeth one more time before circumventing Marcus and melting into the crowded ballroom beyond.

She looked down at the object in her hand and the shock

of recognition forced her to grip the railing for support. Marcus was beside her instantly.

"What is it?"

She held out her open palm. "It's my cameo brooch, given to me by Hawthorne as a wedding gift. I broke the clasp. See? It is still broken. He offered to return it to the jeweler's for repair the morning of his death."

Marcus plucked the pin from her hand, and examined it. "St. John returned it? What did he say? Tell me everything."

"He wants the journal." She stared up at his grim features. "And he knew of the attack in the park."

"Bloody hell," Marcus growled under his breath, pocketing the brooch. "I knew it." Wrapping her hand around his arm, he led her from the balcony.

Within moments, Marcus had retrieved their cloaks and called for his carriage, assisting her inside as soon as it rolled to a halt. Ordering the outriders to guard her, he turned back toward the manse, his stride lengthening with purpose.

Leaning out the window, Elizabeth called after him. "Where are you going?"

"After St. John."

"No, Marcus," she begged, her fingers gripping the sill, her heart racing madly. "You said yourself he's dangerous."

"Don't worry, love," he called over his shoulder. "So am I."

Elizabeth waited endlessly, devastated to her very soul. For the first time since starting the affair, she acknowledged how little control she had. Marcus cared nothing for her worry or her distress. Knowing how she must feel, he'd left anyway, deliberately courting danger. And now she waited. He'd been gone so long. Too long. What was happening? Had he found the pirate? Had they exchanged words? Or fought? Perhaps Marcus was hurt . . .

She gazed sightlessly out the window as her stomach roiled. Certain she was about to cast up her accounts, Elizabeth thrust open the door and stumbled down. The outriders moved to her side just as Marcus appeared.

"Sweet." He pulled her close. The heavy silk of his coat was cold from the night air, but inside she was far more chilled. "Don't be frightened. I will protect you."

Elizabeth gave a choked, half-mad laugh. The most pressing peril came from Marcus himself. He was a man who thrived on reckless behavior and lived for the thrill of the chase. He would forever be placing himself in jeopardy, because taking risks was ingrained in his nature.

The agency . . . St. John . . . Marcus . . .

She had to get away from them all.

Far, far away.

Chapter 10

Marcus paused in his prowling of the guesthouse foyer to stare at the Persian rug beneath his feet. He searched for signs of wear caused by his relentless tread.

This damned affair was beyond frustrating. His desire for Elizabeth showed no signs of waning, his body constantly hard and aching for her touch. His physical reaction alone was irritating, but even more troubling was her ceaseless occupation of his every thought.

In all of his other affairs, he'd never spent the night with his paramours. He never brought women to his home, never shared his bed, never gave more than a brief use of his body. He'd never wanted to.

The situation with Elizabeth was entirely different. He had to tear himself away from her, waiting until the cursed rising of the sun forced him to leave. He returned to his home with her scent on his skin, to lie in the bed she had once occupied and relive the memories of her, naked and begging beneath him. It was torture of the most delicious kind.

And it was not just when he was alone that he was maddened by his need. When he'd stepped onto the balcony and recognized the man with whom she conversed, his heart had stopped beating altogether. Then it had raced with the primitive instinct to protect what was his.

He wanted to be closer, damn it all. Elizabeth wanted distance. She was perfectly happy to keep things simple and un-complicated by feelings or emotions. In past entanglements, he would have been pleased. This time, this affair, he was not.

Elizabeth was not immune. Her gaze lingered when she thought he was not aware, and when he held her in his arms, he could feel the racing of her heart against his chest. She curled around him when she slept and sometimes murmured his name, telling him he invaded her dreams as surely as she invaded his.

As the door opened and Elizabeth entered, Marcus spun about quickly. She offered a half-hearted smile, and then glanced away.

Evasion, façades, shields—he despised all of the tools she used to keep him at bay. Anger quickened his blood.

"Hello, my love," he muttered.

She frowned at his tone.

His eyes raked her from head to toe. When his gaze returned to hers, she was blushing.

Good. Better than indifferent.

"Come closer," he ordered arrogantly. There were some barriers between them he could remove, her clothing being one of them.

"No." Her voice was threaded with steel.

"No?" He arched a brow. There was something different about her, a stiffness to her demeanor that caused his stomach to tighten.

Her eyes softened. Wondering what she saw, Marcus glanced over her head to the mirror that hung on the wall behind her and was startled by the fierce longing that was reflected in his face. His hands clenched into fists.

"Marcus. I will not be staying tonight. I've come only to tell you that our affair is over."

He felt as though all of the oxygen had been sucked from the room. To be so easily discarded . . . *Again.*

"Why?" was all he could manage to say.

"There is no need for us to continue seeing each other."

"What about the passion between us?"

"It will fade," she said with a careless shrug.

"Then remain my lover until it does," he challenged.

Elizabeth shook her head.

He moved toward her, his heart thundering in a desperate rhythm, drawn to her scent and the need to feel her skin beneath his hands. "Convince me why we should end the affair."

Violet eyes widened, melting, and she backed away from him. "I don't want you anymore."

Stepping closer, Marcus didn't stop until he had her pressed against the wall, his thigh between hers, his hand curling around her nape. Burying his face in her neck, he breathed in her fragrance of warm, aroused woman.

She trembled in his arms. "Marcus . . ."

"You could have said anything else and I might have believed you. But to say you don't want me is so blatant a lie, I cannot credit it." He tilted his head and brought his lips to hers.

"No," she said, turning her head. "A physical response means nothing, as you well know."

Licking her lips, Marcus waged a battle of seduction, attempting to penetrate the defenses she'd erected against him. "Nothing?" he breathed.

She opened her mouth to retort and his tongue slipped inside, thrusting slow and deep, drinking in the taste of her. A moan escaped her. Then another.

His hand held her head still when she tried to pull away, his other wrapped around her hip, molding her into the heat of his erection. Marcus groaned, his body aching for her, his insides twisting as her hands remained at her sides, rejecting him silently even as her body responded helplessly to his touch. With a curse, he pulled away.

He didn't want her like this, bent to his will against her own. He wanted her warm and willing, as eager for him as he was for her.

"As you wish, Elizabeth," he said coldly, his gaze hard. He reached for his greatcoat, which hung on the rack beside the mirror. "You will crave me soon enough. When you do, come to me. Perhaps I'll still be available for your pleasure."

When she flinched and looked away, Marcus hardened his heart. He was hurting, a new and vastly unwelcome turn of events.

He left with a slam of the door, vaulting onto the back of his horse in his haste to leave. With a curt movement of his hand, he ordered the guards watching the guesthouse to remain behind.

As he rode away, his thoughts stayed with Elizabeth. Finding her on the balcony with St. John had nearly brought him to his knees. She had stood so bravely, with her spine straight and proud. She was no fool; he'd warned her of the danger, but she would not be cowed.

Damn her! Was there no way to rattle her? The still surface of her deportment was deceptive. The depths of her nature roiled with currents he longed to explore, yet he could never reach them.

She was tortured, he knew, and yet it was he who trolled the streets of London while she lay safe in Chesterfield Hall. It was he who suffered, and he had only himself to blame.

Why was it whenever she should be reaching for comfort, like tonight, she chose instead to turn away? Mere hours ago, she had been warm and passionate, her body arching beneath his, her thighs spread to welcome the thrusts of his cock. He could still hear the sound of his name on her lips and feel the bite of her nails in the flesh of his back. She'd been on fire, burning with passion. Over this last week together, he could have sworn the intimacy he felt with her went both ways. He refused to believe he was mistaken.

Feeling the chill of the late night air, he forced his mind

away from thoughts of Elizabeth to catch his bearings. Dazed, he was startled to see the front of Chesterfield Hall. Unconsciously, he had returned, driven by a part of him that was screaming to be recognized.

He ignored it.

Drawing to a halt before the now darkened guesthouse, Marcus glancing around, spotting the mounts of the guards tied nearby. They were either patrolling on foot or had followed her to the manse. He faced the guesthouse and wondered if the door remained unlocked, if Elizabeth's wonderful scent of vanilla and roses still lingered in the foyer. He dismounted and tested the knob, which turned easily. Entering, he closed his eyes to sharpen his sense of smell and inhaled deeply.

Ah, there it was—the faint alluring smell of Elizabeth. Slowly, he followed it, his eyes closed and stinging, his memory of the place guiding him through the darkness.

As he wandered silently through the house, Marcus allowed his mind to wander, replaying bits and pieces of their stolen moments together. He remembered her laughter, the throaty sound of her voice, the silken touch of her skin . . .

He paused, listening.

No, he was not mistaken. He heard the muffled sounds of crying. Tense, he walked cautiously toward the bedroom. With eyes now open, he could see the faint light of a fire dancing through the gap under the door. He turned the knob and stepped into the room. Elizabeth was there, seated in front of the grate. In much the same state as he was.

She was right—it was time to end the affair. He'd been a fool to press for one to begin with.

They were not meant to be lovers.

He couldn't think, could barely function, his work suffered along with his sleep. It was no way to carry on.

"Elizabeth," he called softly.

Her eyes flew open, and she brushed furiously at the wetness on her cheeks.

His heart softened. The crack in her shell was open wide and he could see the woman she hid so well, fragile and very much alone. He longed to go to her and offer the comfort she so obviously needed, but he knew her too well. She would have to come to him. Any overture on his part would only force her to flee. And he didn't want that. In fact, he couldn't bear the thought. He wanted to hold her, care for her. He wanted to be what she needed, if only just this once.

Saying nothing more, Marcus removed his clothing, his movements deliberately casual. He threw aside the counterpane and slipped into the bed. Then he watched her, waiting. As she did every night, she gathered his garments and folded them neatly. She was biding her time, collecting herself, and his chest tightened with his understanding.

When she came to him and presented her back, he said nothing, simply loosened her dress in response to her silent command. His cock twitched and then hardened as she shrugged out of it, revealing her body naked, as always, beneath. Sliding over, he allowed her the room to slip into the bed next to him, into his arms. Marcus tucked her against his chest and gazed at the gilt-framed landscape that hung above the mantel.

This is contentment, he thought.

Her face pressed against his chest, Elizabeth whispered, "It must end."

Marcus caressed the length of her spine with long soothing motions. "I know."

And as simple as that, their affair was over.

Marcus entered Lord Eldridge's offices a little past noon. Sinking into the worn leather chair in front of the desk, he waited for Eldridge to acknowledge him.

"Westfield."

"Lady Hawthorne was approached by St. John at the Marks-Darby ball last night," he said without preamble.

Gray eyes shot up to his. "Is she well?"

Marcus shrugged, his fingertips rubbing across the brass tacks along the arms. "By all outward appearances." Other than that he couldn't say. He'd been unable to coerce her into speaking about the subject. Despite his most passionate persuasion, she'd said not another word to him the rest of the night. "He knew of the book and the meeting in the park."

Eldridge pushed away from the massive desk. "A man matching St. John's description was treated for a bullet wound to the shoulder the same day."

Marcus released a deep breath. "So your assumptions about St. John's involvement in Lord Hawthorne's murder appear to be correct. Did the physician relate anything of value?"

"Nothing beyond the description." Eldridge stood, and stared out the window at the thoroughfare below. Framed by the dark green velvet of the curtains and the massive windows, the agency leader seemed smaller, more human and less legend. "I'm concerned for Lady Hawthorne's safety. To approach her at such a crowded event is an act of desperation. I would never have considered St. John would be so bold."

"I was surprised as well," Marcus admitted. "I intend to call on her now. Frankly, I'm afraid to leave her alone. St. John had a brooch of Elizabeth's, a piece she says Hawthorne had upon his person the night he was killed."

"So it's that way, is it?" Eldridge sighed. "The pirate has never lacked for boldness."

Marcus grit his teeth, remembering the vastly unpleasant encounters he'd had with St. John over the years. "Why do we tolerate him?"

"A reasonable question. I've often considered the alternative. However he is so popular I'm afraid his disappearance might make him a martyr. Hawthorne's work was a secret. We cannot reveal it, even to justify a criminal's death."

Cursing, Marcus stood.

"It chafes, Westfield, I know. But a public trial and hanging will do much to dispel his myth."

"You hope." He began to pace. "I've worked on the journal every day. The cryptic code changes with every paragraph, sometimes every sentence. I cannot find a pattern and I've learned nothing of value."

"Bring it to me. Perhaps I can be of assistance."

"I would rather continue my examination. I think I've learned enough to continue."

"Maintain a level head," Eldridge warned, turning around as Marcus growled low in his throat.

"When have I not?"

"Whenever Lady Hawthorne is involved. Perhaps she has information of import. Have you discussed any of this with her?"

Marcus sucked in his breath, not wanting to admit that he disliked talking about her marriage.

Eldridge sighed. "I had hoped it wouldn't come to this."

"I am the best agent to protect her," Marcus retorted.

"No, you are the worst, and I cannot tell you how it pains me to say so. Your emotional involvement is affecting this mission, just as I warned you it might."

"My personal affairs are my own business."

"And this agency is mine. I'm replacing you."

Marcus stopped and turned so swiftly the tails of his coat whipped about his thighs. "My services are required. Or have you forgotten? You have very few agents in the peerage."

Eldridge stood with both hands clasped behind his back. The somber tones of his garments and wig were matched by his grim features. "I admit, when you walked into my office that first time and knew what it is I do here, I was impressed. Brash, headstrong, certain your father would live forever and you could do as you pleased, you were perfect to send after St. John. The youthful delusion of immortality has never left you, Westfield. You still take risks others refuse. But never doubt there are more like you."

"Be assured, it has never once left my mind how expendable I am."

"Lord Talbot will take over."

Marcus shook his head and gave a wry, humorless laugh. "Talbot takes orders well enough, but he lacks initiative."

"He does not need initiative. He simply has to walk in your footsteps. He works well with Avery James, I've paired them often."

Cursing, Marcus spun on his heel and moved toward the door. "Replace me if you like. I won't leave her to the care of another."

"I am not giving you a choice, Westfield," Eldridge called after him.

Marcus slammed the door behind him. "I'm not giving you a choice either."

Marcus mounted his horse and headed straight to Chesterfield Hall. He'd planned to go there regardless, but now his need was more urgent. Elizabeth was certainly in the spirit of having nothing to do with him. He had to convince her otherwise and quickly. The affair was over, and good riddance. Now it was time to manage the rest of it.

He was immediately shown into the study where he forced himself to sit rather than pace in agitation. When the door opened behind him, he stood and turned with a charming smile for Elizabeth, only to scowl when he faced William.

"Westfield," came the terse greeting.

"Barclay."

"What do you want?"

Marcus blinked and then released a frustrated breath. Two steps forward and one back. "The same thing I want every time I call here. I wish to speak with Elizabeth."

"She does not wish to speak with you. In fact, she left specific instructions that you were no longer welcome."

"A moment of her time and all will be well, I assure you."

William snorted. "Elizabeth is gone."

"I will await her return, if you don't mind." He'd wait out by the street if he must. He had to talk with her before Eldridge did.

"No, you misunderstand. She has left Town."

"Beg your pardon?"

"She's gone. Packed up. Left. She came to her senses and realized what a cretin you are."

"She said that?"

"Well," William hedged. "I didn't actually speak with her, but Elizabeth mentioned her desire to leave London to her abigail this morning, although she left without the girl. Which is a good thing considering the mess she left behind."

Warning bells went off in Marcus's head. One of the many things he'd learned about Elizabeth in their short time together was that she was fastidiously tidy. Marcus strode toward the door. "Did she state her destination?"

"She mentioned only that she needed distance from you. Once she's calmed and sent word, I will go after her if she does not return on her own. This isn't the first time something you've done has goaded her into acting rashly."

"Show me to her rooms."

"Now see here, Westfield," William began, "I'm not lying to you. She's gone. I will see to her, as I always have."

"I will locate her boudoir myself, if I must," Marcus warned.

With a great deal of grumbling, cursing, and complaining, William led him upstairs to Elizabeth's suite of rooms. Marcus's gaze lifted from the rugs which were wildly askew and strewn with crushed flowers, to the armoire doors which were flung open and the contents scattered. Drawers were pulled out and the bed linens tossed about in a scene that came straight out of a nightmare.

"Seems she was in high temper," William said sheepishly.

"So it appears." Marcus kept his face impassive, but inside

his gut was clenched tight. He turned to the abigail. "How many of her garments did she take with her?"

The girl dipped a quick curtsy and replied, "None that I can tell, milord. But I've not finished yet."

Marcus wouldn't wait to find out. "Did she say anything of import to you?"

"No need to bark at the poor chit," William snapped.

Marcus raised a hand for silence and pinned the servant with his stare.

"Only that she was restless, milord, and eager to travel. She sent me into town on an errand and left whilst I was gone."

"Has she traveled without you often?"

The girl gave a jerky shake of her head. "It's the first time, milord."

"See how eager she was to flee you?" William asked grimly.

But Marcus paid him no mind. This was not the scene of a flared temper. Elizabeth's room had been ransacked.

And she was missing.

Chapter 11

"Sit down, Westfield," Eldridge ordered curtly. "Your frenzied pacing is driving me mad."

Marcus glared as he took a seat. "*I* am going mad. I need to know where Elizabeth is. God only knows the ordeal . . ." He choked, his throat too tight to speak.

Eldridge's normally stern features softened with sympathy. "You mentioned the outriders you assigned to her are gone as well. It's a good sign. Perhaps they were able to follow and will report her whereabouts when the opportunity presents itself."

"Or else they are dead," Marcus retorted. He stood and began pacing again.

Eldridge leaned back in his chair and steepled his fingers together. "I have agents checking all possible roads leading from Chesterfield Hall and questioning everyone who lives near enough to have seen or heard anything. Information is bound to surface."

"Time is a luxury we don't have," Marcus growled.

"Go home. Wait for word."

"I'll wait here."

"Your outriders may attempt to contact you. Perhaps they've already tried. You should return to your home. Keep yourself occupied. Pack and make preparations to leave."

The thought of a message waiting for him gave Marcus a sense of purpose. "Very well, but if you hear anything—"

"Anything at all, yes, I will send for you posthaste."

For the all too brief ride back to his home Marcus felt productive, but the moment he arrived and discovered nothing new had been reported his near ferocious agitation returned in full measure. With his family in residence, he could not give vent to his feelings, and was forced instead to retreat from their curious eyes.

He prowled the lengths of his galleries in his shirtsleeves, his skin damp with sweat, his heart racing as if he were running. Constant rubbing at the back of his neck left the skin raw, but he couldn't stop. The pictures in his mind . . . torturous thoughts of Elizabeth needing him . . . hurting . . . afraid . . .

His head fell back on a groan of pure anguish. He couldn't bear it. He wanted to yell, to snarl, to tear something apart.

An hour passed. And then another. Finally he could take the waiting no more. Marcus returned to his room, shrugged into his coats, and moved to the staircase, his intent to hunt St. John down. The pressure of his knife sheathed in his boot fueled his bloodlust. If Elizabeth were harmed in any way there would be no mercy.

Halfway down the stairs, he spotted his butler at the door and a moment later it opened, revealing one of the outriders. Covered in dust from his rapid return, the man waited in the foyer and bowed as Marcus's boot hit the marble floor.

"Where is she?"

"On the way to Essex, my lord."

Marcus froze. *Ravensend*. Seat of her late godfather, the Duke of Ravensend.

Elizabeth was running. Damn her.

He grabbed his packed valise, and turned to Paul who stood in the doorway of the study. "I will be in Essex."

"Is everything all right?" Paul asked.

"It will be shortly."

Within moments, Marcus was on the road.

The wheels of the Westfield travel coach crunched through the gravel on the final approach to Ravensend Manor before reaching the cobblestones that lined the circular driveway. The moon was high, its soft glow lighting the large manse and the small cottage beyond.

Marcus stepped down wearily and ordered his men to the livery. Turning away from the main house, he took rapid strides toward the cliff edge where the guesthouse and Elizabeth waited. He'd make his presence known to the duke in the morning.

The small residence was dark when he entered through the kitchen. He closed the door quietly, shutting out the rhythmic roar of the waves that battered the coast just a few yards away. Making his way through the house in darkness, Marcus checked every bedroom until he found Elizabeth.

Leaving his valise on the floor by the door, Marcus undressed silently and crawled into the bed next to her. She stirred at the feel of his cold skin beside hers.

"Marcus," she murmured, still fast asleep. She spooned into his chest, unconsciously sharing her warmth.

Despite his anger and frustration, he snuggled against her. Her trust while sleeping was telling. She had become accustomed to spending the nights next to him during the short duration of their affair.

He was still furious with her for running away, but his relief in finding her well and out of danger was foremost on his mind. Never again would he go through this torment. There could be no doubt that she was his. Not in Eldridge's mind, or hers.

Exhausted by worry, he buried his face in the sweetly scented curve of her shoulder and fell asleep.

* * *

Elizabeth woke and burrowed deeper into the warmth of the bed. Slowly rising to consciousness, she stretched out fully, her legs brushing along Marcus's hair-dusted calf.

With a sudden flare of awareness, she sat upright and shot a startled glance at the pillow beside her. Marcus slept peacefully on his stomach, the sheet and counterpane straddling his hips, leaving his muscular back exposed.

She jumped out of the bed as if it were on fire.

His eyes opened sleepily, his lips curving in a languid smile, and then he fell back asleep, obviously finding her angered surprise to be of no danger.

Grabbing her clothes, Elizabeth retreated to the next room to dress, wondering how he'd found her so quickly. She'd deliberately avoided any of her own family holdings so that it would be difficult, if not impossible to locate her. But Marcus had found her before even a day had passed.

Furious and flustered at finding him in her bed, Elizabeth left the house and made her way to the roped path on the cliffs that led to the beach below.

She picked her way carefully down the somewhat steep and rocky decline. The cliff rose some distance above the shore and Elizabeth ignored the stunning view in favor of studying the ground at her feet. She didn't mind the concentration it took. Instead she relished the temporary distraction from her confusion.

Finally reaching the beach, she dropped onto the damp sand and hugged her knees to her chest. She prayed for the sound of the waves lapping on the beach to soothe her.

She vividly recalled the first moment she'd laid eyes on Marcus Ashford, then the Viscount Sefton. She remembered how her breath had caught in her throat and how hot her skin had suddenly become, how her breathing and heart rate had quickened until she thought she might swoon. Those had not been singular reactions. She had felt them many times since then and even just that morning when he had smiled at her, all sleep-tousled masculine beauty.

She couldn't live like that, couldn't see how anyone could live consumed by a lust that seemed insatiable. Unschooled as she was, she hadn't known a body could crave the touch of another the way it did food or air. Now, finally, she understood an inkling of the hunger her father must feel every day. Without her mother he would always be ravenous, always searching for something that could appease the emptiness left by her loss.

Tilting her head, Elizabeth closed her eyes and rested her cheek against her knees.

Why couldn't Marcus simply stay away?

Marcus paused on the small porch and took in his surroundings. The bite of the salty morning air was sharp. He wondered if Elizabeth had collected a wrap before venturing out. To say she'd looked horrified to discover him in her bed would be an understatement. Knowing her as he did, he suspected she'd run out without forethought.

Where the devil had she gone?

"She's gone down to the beach, Westfield," came a dry tone to his left. Marcus turned his head to greet the Duke of Ravensend.

"Your Grace." He dipped his head in a bow. "It was my intent to present myself this morn and explain my presence. I trust you don't find my stay an imposition."

The duke led a black stallion by the reins and came to a halt directly before him. They were of an age, His Grace being the youngest after four older sisters, but Marcus was nearly a head taller. "Of course not. It's been too long since we last exchanged words. Walk with me."

Unable to refuse, Marcus reluctantly left the shadow of the guesthouse.

"Watch the horse," the duke cautioned. "He's a biter."

Heeding the warning, Marcus took the opposite side. "How fares Lady Ravensend?" he asked as they fell into step. He cast a longing glace over his shoulder at the roped path that led to the beach.

"Better than you. I thought you wiser than to chase more abuse. But I concede the appeal. Lady Hawthorne remains one of the most beautiful women I've ever had the fortune to cross paths with. I fancied her myself. As did most peers."

Nodding grimly, Marcus kicked a pebble out of his path.

"I wonder who she'll take up with once she's finished with you? Hodgeham, perhaps? Or Stanton again? A young one, I'm certain. She's as wild as this brute." The duke gestured to his horse.

Marcus grit his teeth. "Stanton is a friend in the chastest sense of the word and Hodgeham . . ." He snorted in disgust. "Hodgeham couldn't manage her."

"And you can?"

"Better than any other man."

"You should marry her then. Or perhaps that's your intent. Either you or some other poor chap. You leapt into that cage once before."

"She has no wish to marry again."

"She will," Ravensend said with a confident nod. "She has no children. When she's of the mind, she'll pick someone."

Marcus came to an abrupt stop. Eldridge, William, and now Ravensend. He'd be damned if another individual meddled in his affairs. "Pardon me, Your Grace."

He spun on the heel of his boot and made rapid strides toward the roped walk. He would put a stop to all their intrusions once and for all.

Elizabeth prowled the coastline restlessly, picking up small pebbles and stones along the way. She tossed them over the water, trying to skip them and failing miserably. William had once spent an entire afternoon attempting to teach her how to skip rocks. Although she'd never acquired the skill, the repetitive swing of her arm was calming. The music of the English coastline—the lapping waves and the cries of seagulls—brought her a measure of peace from her fevered thoughts.

"A calm surface is required, love," came the deeply luxurious voice behind her.

With shoulders squared, she turned to face her tormenter.

Dressed casually in a worn sweater and wool breeches, Marcus had never looked more virile, the roughness of his edges unblunted by any social veneer. His hair was tied back at his nape, but the salty breeze tugged the silken strands free and blew them softly across his handsome face.

Just looking at him made her feel like crying.

"You shouldn't have come," she told him.

"I had no choice."

"Yes, you did. If you had any sense you would allow this . . ." She gestured wildly. ". . . thing between us to die out gracefully, instead of dragging it out to its inevitable bad end."

"Damn you." A muscle in his jaw ticked as he took a step toward her. "Damn you to hell for throwing away what exists between us as if it does not signify. Risking your life—"

Her hands clenched into fists at his wounded tone. "I took the outriders with me."

"The only bit of sense you've shown since I met you."

"You are a bully! You have been from the first. Seducing, scheming, and manipulating me however you wish. Go back to London, Lord Westfield, and find another woman's life to ruin."

Turning from him, Elizabeth stalked toward the cliffs. Marcus caught her arm as she attempted to pass, pulling her to a stop. She struggled with a frightened cry, alarmed by the possessiveness of his gaze.

"I was content before you came along. My life was simple and orderly. I want that back. I don't want you."

He thrust her away with such force she stumbled. "Regardless, you have me."

She hurried toward the rope-lined path. "As you wish. *I* shall leave."

"Craven," he drawled after her.

Eyes wide, Elizabeth turned to face him again. Like the time he'd asked her to dance at the Morelands', his emerald eyes sparkled with challenge. This time though, she would not be goaded into acting foolishly.

"Perhaps," she admitted, lifting her chin. "You frighten me. Your determination, your recklessness, your passion. Everything about you scares the wits from me. It's not how I wish to live my life."

His chest expanded on a deep breath. Behind him the waves continued to beat upon the shore, the relentless driving rhythm no longer soothing. It urged her to flee. *Run. Run far away.* She took a backward step.

"Give me a fortnight," he said quickly. "You and I alone, here in the guesthouse. Live with me, as my partner."

"Why?" she asked, startled.

His arms crossed his chest. "I intend to wed you."

"*What?*" Suddenly dizzy, Elizabeth backed away with hand to throat. Tripping on her skirts, she fell to her knees. "You've gone mad," she cried.

His mouth curved in a bitter smile. "It seems so, yes."

Her breath coming in unsteady pants, Elizabeth leaned forward, her fingers sinking into the damp sand. She didn't look at him. She couldn't. "Whatever made you conceive of such a ridiculous notion? You've no wish to marry, nor do I."

"Not true. I must wed. And you and I suit."

She swallowed hard, her stomach roiling. "Physically, perhaps. But lust fades. In no time at all you'll grow weary of a wife and seek your pleasures elsewhere."

"If you are equally bored, you won't be disturbed."

Furious, she grabbed handfuls of sand and threw them at his chest. "Go to hell!"

He laughed, shaking out his sweater with maddening nonchalance. "Jealousy is a possessive emotion, love. You'll have to wed me if you want the right to feel that way."

Elizabeth searched his face, looking for deceit and found nothing but cool impassivity. His face, so breathtaking, revealed nothing of his thoughts. The determined line of his jaw, however, was achingly familiar. "I don't wish to marry again."

"Consider the benefits." Marcus held out his hand and ticked off with his fingers. "Elevated rank. Great wealth. I will afford you the same independence you enjoyed with Hawthorne. And you'll have me in your bed, a prospect you should find vastly appealing."

"Conceited rogue. Allow us to discuss the negatives as well. You thrive on danger. You are eager to die. And you're too bloody damn arrogant."

Grinning, he held out his hand and helped her to her feet. "I ask for a fortnight to change your mind. If I cannot, I'll leave you in peace and never bother you again. I'll resign from this mission and another agent will protect you."

She shook her head. "The situation here is far different than our life would be under normal circumstances. There is little danger for you around here."

"True," he admitted. "But perhaps I can make the rest of your life so pleasant that my work with Eldridge will be of less consequence."

"Impossible!"

"A fortnight," he urged. "It's all I ask. You owe me that much, at least."

"No." The gleam in his eye could not be mistaken. "I know what you want."

Marcus met her gaze squarely. "I won't touch you. I swear it."

"You lie."

His brow rose. "You doubt I can restrain myself? I shared a bed with you last night and didn't make love to you. I assure you, I have control over my baser needs."

Elizabeth chewed her lower lip, weighing her options. To be free of him forever . . .

"You will find another room?" she asked.

"Yes."

"You promise not to make any advances?"

"I promise." His mouth curved wickedly. "When you want me, you'll have to ask me."

She bristled at his arrogance. "What do you hope to accomplish by this?"

He came toward her and when he spoke, his voice was tender. "We already know you enjoy me in your bed. I intend to prove you will enjoy having me in the rest of your life as well. I'm not always so tiresome. In fact, some would say I'm quite pleasant."

"Why me?" she asked plaintively, her hand sheltering her racing heart. "Why marriage?"

Marcus shrugged. "'The time is right' would be the simplest answer. I enjoy your company, despite how often you are obstinate and disagreeable."

When she shook her head, he frowned. "You said yes once before."

"That was before I knew about the agency."

His tone deepened, became cajoling. "Don't you wish to manage your own household again? Wouldn't you like to have children? Build a family? Surely you don't wish to be alone forever."

Startled, she stared at him with wide eyes. Marcus Ashford discussing children? The longing that washed over her so unexpectedly scared her to death.

"You want an heir." She looked away to hide her reaction.

"I want you. The heir and other progeny would be added delights."

Her eyes flew to meet his again. Flustered by his nearness and his determination, Elizabeth turned toward the path in the cliffs.

"Do we have an agreement?" he called after her, remaining behind.

"Yes," she threw over her shoulder, her voice carried by the wind. "A fortnight, then you are out of my life."

His satisfaction was a palpable thing and she ran from it.

Elizabeth reached the top of the cliff and fell to her knees. *Marriage.* The word choked her throat and made her dizzy, leaving her panting for air like a swimmer too long under water. Marcus's will was a force to be reckoned with. What the devil was she to do now that he'd set his mind on marriage again?

Lifting her head, she looked toward the livery with aching longing. It would be such a relief to go, to leave the turmoil behind.

But she discarded the idea. Marcus would come for her, he would track her down as long as she still wanted him. And no matter how hard she tried, she was unable to hide the depth and breadth of her attraction.

Therefore, the only way to be rid of his attentions was to accept the bargain he offered. Marcus would have to end his pursuit of his own accord. There was no other way the obstinate man would quit.

Wearily resolved, Elizabeth stood and made her way toward the guesthouse. She would have to move carefully. He knew her too well. The slightest intimation that she was uneasy and he would pounce, pressing his advantage with his customary ruthlessness. She would have to be relaxed and indifferent. It was the only solution.

Satisfied she had a reasonable plan of action, she quickened her pace.

Meanwhile, Marcus lingered on the beach and wondered at his sanity. God help him, he wanted her still. Wanted her more than before. He'd once hoped to satisfy his need and finally be done with her. Now he prayed his aching need would never end, the pleasure was too great to forfeit.

If only he'd known the trap that awaited him in her arms. But there had been no way to know. With all his experience, he still could never have imagined the searing rapture of Elizabeth's bed or the ever-growing need he had to tame her and pin her beneath him, as lost to his desire as he was.

Picking up a rock from the pile Elizabeth left behind, he tossed it into the water. He'd created quite a challenge for himself. Her one vulnerability had always been their desire for each other. Naked and sated, Elizabeth was soft and open to discussion. Now he was denied seduction to achieve his ends. He would have to woo her like a gentleman, something he'd never managed even the first time.

But should he succeed, he would thwart Eldridge's plan to replace him and prove to one and all that Elizabeth was his. There would be no doubt.

Marriage. He shuddered. It had finally happened. The woman had driven him insane.

"I want to see where you're taking me."

"No," Marcus whispered in her ear, steadying her with his hands on her shoulders. "It would not be a surprise if you knew."

"I'm not fond of surprises," Elizabeth complained.

"Well, you will have to become accustomed, sweet, because I am full of them."

She snorted and he laughed, his heart as light as the afternoon breeze. "Ah, love. Much as you wish it weren't so, you adore me."

Her lush mouth curved in a smile, the ends of her lips touching the underside of the blindfold that blocked her vision. "Your conceit knows no bounds."

She shrieked as he hefted her into the air, and then sank to his knees. He set her down on the blanket he'd spread earlier and removed her blindfold, watching expectantly as she blinked against the sudden bright light.

With the help of the duke's staff, he'd arranged a picnic, selecting a field of wild grass just over the rise from the main manor. She'd been unnaturally tense since their talk on the beach that morning and he knew something unexpected was warranted if he wished to make headway.

"This is lovely," she exclaimed, her eyes wide and filled with pleasure. Sans the assistance of an abigail and unwilling to let him help her dress, Elizabeth was forced to attire herself in a startlingly simple gown. With her hair uncoiffed and tied back from her face, there was nothing to compete with the singular beauty of her features.

Basking in the glow of her surprise, Marcus silently agreed with her sentiment. Elizabeth was breathtaking, her fine features lovingly shielded by the wide brim of her straw hat.

Smiling, he reached into the basket and withdrew a bottle of wine. He filled a glass and handed it to her, the touch of her fingers against his sending a frisson of awareness up his spine.

"I'm pleased you approve," he murmured. "It's only my second attempt at formal courtship." His gaze lifted to hers. "I'm a bit nervous, truth be told."

"You?" She arched a brow.

"Yes, love." Marcus lay on his back and stared up at the summer sky. "It's distressing to think I may be refused. I was more confident the first time around."

Elizabeth laughed, a soft joyful sound that brought a smile to his face. "You shall find another, far more suitable candidate. A young woman who will worship your remarkable handsomeness and charm, and be far more biddable."

"I would never marry a woman such as you describe. I much prefer passionate, uneven-tempered seductresses like yourself."

"I am not a seductress!" she protested, and he laughed with delight.

"You certainly were the other evening. The way you arched your brow and bit your lip before fucking me senseless. I vow, I've never seen anything as seductive. And the way you look when you—"

"Tell me about your family," she interrupted, her cheeks flushing. "How are Paul and Robert?"

He glanced sidelong at her, relishing the view of her against the natural backdrop, freed from the constraints of society. The tall grass around them flowed like waves of water in the gentle breeze, filling the air with the scent of warm earth and salty sea. "They are well. They inquire about you, as does my mother."

"Do they? I am surprised, but pleased they don't resent me overmuch. They should venture out more. It has been almost a fortnight since they arrived, and yet they've not attended one social function."

"Robert still has no interest whatsoever in social pursuits. Paul prefers his club. He spends most of his time there. And my mother has to order new gowns every Season, and refuses to be seen until they are finished." His grin was fond. "Heaven forbid that she be seen in a gown from last year."

She smiled. "Is Robert still the spitting image of you?"

"So I've been told."

"You don't think so?"

"No. The resemblance is there, but no more than one would expect. And Paul remains as different from me as you are from your brother." He reached for her hand and linked his fingers with hers, needing the physical connection. She tugged, but he held fast. "You will see for yourself soon enough."

She wrinkled her nose. "You seem quite confident in your ability to win my hand."

"I cannot think otherwise. Now tell me you wrote Barclay about your location."

"Yes, of course. He would be frantic, and unbearable company for Margaret if I had not."

They lapsed into silence and Marcus enjoyed their rare accord, content to experience the daylight hours with her.

"What are you contemplating so seriously?" he asked after a time.

"My mother." She sighed. "William says she loved the coast. We used to visit here often and play in the sand. He tells stories of her lifting the hem of her skirts and dancing across the beach with our father."

"You don't remember?"

Her fingers tightened fractionally on his and lifting her glass, she took a large swallow of wine. Her gaze moved to the distant cliffs and her voice, when it came, was soft and faraway. "Sometimes I think I recall her scent or the tone of her voice, but I cannot be certain."

"I'm sorry," he soothed, rubbing his thumb across the back of her hand.

She sighed. "Perhaps it's for the best that she's only a fleeting impression. William remembers her, and it saddens him. It's why he's so protective, I think. Her illness progressed so quickly, it took us all by surprise. My father especially."

There was an unusual edge to Elizabeth's voice when she referred to her father. Marcus rolled to his side and rested his head in his hand, maintaining his casual pose while studying her intently. "Your father never remarried."

She returned his gaze, a small frown marring the space between her brows. "He loved my mother too much to ever take another wife. He still loves her."

Marcus considered the Earl of Langston's libidinous reputation. This in turn led him to consider his own dislike of romantic entanglements.

"Tell me about your father," he urged, curious. "As often as I've spoken with him, I still know precious little about him."

"You are probably better acquainted with him than I. My resemblance to my mother is painful, so he avoids me. I often think he would have been best served by never falling in love. Lord knows the sentiment brought him precious little happiness and a lifetime of regret."

There was a sadness in her eyes and a firmness to her lips that betrayed her distress. He wanted to pull her into his arms and comfort her, so he did just that, rising to a seated position and pulling her against his chest. Tossing aside the obtrusive hat, he pressed a kiss to her neck and breathed in her scent. Together, they faced the ocean.

"I worried about my mother when my father passed on," Marcus murmured, his hands caressing the length of her arms. "I was not certain she could live without him. Like your parents, mine also had a love match. But she is a strong woman and she recovered. While she most likely won't marry again, my mother has found contentment without a spouse."

"So have I," Elizabeth said softly.

Reminders of how she didn't need him would not benefit his cause. He had to win her before she learned of Eldridge's decision. Reluctantly pulling away, Marcus removed her glass from stiff fingers and topped it up. "Are you hungry?"

Elizabeth nodded, obviously relieved. Then she gave him a dazzling smile that made his breath catch and his blood heat.

At that moment, he knew. She was his, and he would protect her. Whatever the cost.

A cold tingle crawled up his spine as he remembered the sight of her ransacked room. What would have happened if she'd been home? Clenching his jaw, he vowed to never find out.

Marriage seemed a small price to pay to keep her safe.

Chapter 12

"The servants from the main house brought supper." Elizabeth looked up from Hawthorne's journal to see Marcus lounging in the doorway. With a sigh, she snapped the book closed and pushed aside the blanket she had wrapped around her legs. Rising from the chaise, she took the arm he offered her. Once they were seated in the small formal dining room, he tucked into his veal with his usual fervor.

She watched him with a soft smile. Marcus's appetite for life amazed her. He did nothing in half measure.

"I suppose the outriders told you my destination," she said dryly.

"Which is another reason we should wed," he replied around a bite. "You are a troublesome baggage. You require a great deal of watching over."

"I am perfectly capable of taking care of myself."

He frowned, his gaze piercing beneath his drawn brows. "Your room was ransacked after your departure, Elizabeth."

"Beg your pardon?" The color drained from her face.

His mouth twisted grimly. "You look as I felt when I saw it. I thought you had been kidnapped." He lifted his knife and shook it at her. "Don't ever scare me like that again."

Elizabeth barely registered his words. Her room. *Ransacked.* "Was anything missing?" she whispered.

"I'm not certain." Marcus set aside his utensils. "If anything is amiss, I'll replace it."

Bristling at the offer, which was entirely too proprietary, Elizabeth was struck with a terrifying thought. "William? Margaret?"

"Everyone is well," he soothed, his features softening.

"William must know about the journal, then?"

"Your brother assumed it was your doing, that I had driven you into a rage. He knows nothing more."

Her hand to her chest, Elizabeth tried to imagine what the scene must have looked like. "All of my things sorted through." She shuddered. "Why did you not tell me earlier?"

"You were already distressed, love."

"Of course I'm distressed, it's too dreadful."

"You've every right to feel violated. I thank God you weren't home at the time. Although that's not encouragement for you to run off whenever the urge strikes you."

"Sometimes a respite is a necessity," she retorted, her palms damp with her unease and disquiet.

"How well I know it," he murmured, reminding her of how he'd left England after her marriage. "But I need to know where you are, every minute of every hour."

Flustered by his news and stung by guilt she snapped, "*You* are why I need respite!"

Marcus heaved a clearly frustrated breath. "Eat," he ordered.

She stuck her tongue out at him, then gulped down her wine in an effort to warm the chill within her.

They finished the rest of the meal in silence, both absorbed in their own thoughts. Afterwards, they retired to the front parlor. Elizabeth resumed perusing the journal while Marcus took off his boots and began to polish them.

Using the book to hide behind, she watched him engaged in his task, the light from the fireplace casting a golden halo around him. As the powerful muscles of his shoulders shifted with his exertions, Elizabeth felt a familiar longing spread through her. She couldn't help but be reminded of his powerful body flexing over and inside hers, dissolving her will in decadent pleasure. After years of equanimity, she was inundated with feelings too strong to control.

With great effort, she returned her attention to the journal, but the endless pages of code were unable to engage her mind.

Shifting in his chair, Marcus was achingly aware of Elizabeth's heated gaze. He wished he could lift his head and return it, but she would be embarrassed to be caught staring and that would destroy the comfortable silence they were sharing. Rubbing furiously over the worn leather of his boots, he stealthily perused her.

Dressed like a peasant, she lay on the chaise with her legs curled up beside her and covered with a blanket. Her hair was unbound as it had been all day. He loved her hair. He loved to touch it and wrap it around his fist. Soft and unfettered in clothing and demeanor, Elizabeth aroused him just by breathing.

He smiled in spite of himself. As always, he was both soothed and excited by her presence. The world could go to hell around them and he would pay no mind, tucked away with no servants, no family. Just the two of them.

In separate beds.

Christ. He was certifiable.

Elizabeth shut the journal with a soft thump. Lifting his head, he gazed at her expectantly. Desire coursed through his veins when he saw her eyes, dark and melting. Hope welled. She wanted him.

"I believe I'll retire," she told him, her voice husky.

He took a deep breath to hide his painful disappointment. "So early?"

"I'm tired."

"Goodnight, then," he said, his voice studiously nonchalant as he returned his attention to his boots.

Elizabeth paused in the doorway, and watched Marcus for a moment, hoping he would break his word and ravish her. But he ignored her. His attention was fixed entirely on his task as it had been for the last hour. She might as well not have been there. "Goodnight," she said finally before drifting down the hallway to her room.

Pressing her back against the door, she closed it with a sharp click. She stripped and dressed in her night rail, then climbed into bed. Closing her eyes, she willed herself to sleep.

But oblivion was elusive. Her mind jumped from one lascivious thought to the next, remembering the coarseness of Marcus's callused palms as they caressed her skin, the feel of his strength over her, and the sound of his guttural cries as he reached his climax within her. Knowing he was hers for the asking and yet depriving herself was driving her mad.

Groaning into her pillow, she wished desperately for her body to cease its throbbing, but she couldn't forget Marcus, who sat by the fire, breathtakingly virile. Her skin became too tight, too hot . . . her breasts heavy and swollen, her nipples puckered tight and aching.

He'd come to her every night, sated her hunger long enough to make it through the brief hours until she could have him again. Now it had been two days and she was starved for his touch and the caress of his mouth. She tossed and turned, her movements making her hot. She threw back the covers, her skin and hair damp with sweat, her thighs squeezed tight in an attempt to dull the emptiness there.

Marriage. The man was mad. When he tired of her he would dally and she would lie at home, as she was doing now, and burn for him.

Damn him to perdition! She could do without him, didn't need him. She cupped her breasts in her hands and squeezed, a low moan escaping at the sudden flare of heat between her legs. Embarrassed and knowing it was wrong, she still couldn't prevent rolling her nipples between her fingertips and imagining it was Marcus. Her back arched, her legs spread against her will, her body desperate for the nightly fucking it had grown addicted to.

Near desperation, her hand moved down her torso and slipped between her legs. Her own juices coated her fingers as she found the source of her torment. Her head tilted back and she cried out softly, determined to find her own relief.

The door flew open with such force it slammed against the wall. Startled, she screamed and sat upright.

Marcus stood in the doorway in silent fury, a single taper held aloft in his hand. "Stubborn, contrary, maddening wench! I can hear you," he growled, striding into the room as if he had every right to. "You would punish us both rather than admit the truth."

"Get out!" she yelled, mortified to be caught in such a compromising position.

He set the taper on the nightstand and snatched up her hand, lifting it to his nose. His eyes closed and he breathed in the scent of her sex. Then he parted his lips and suckled her fingertips.

Eyes wide, Elizabeth whimpered as the hot velvet of his tongue swirled around and between her fingers, lapping her cream. Relief flooded her, making her limp and pliant. Thank God he'd come for her. She couldn't have borne another moment without his touch, his scent . . .

"Here." He shoved her wet fingers unceremoniously between her legs.

"Wh-what are you doing?" she asked breathlessly, yanking her hand to her waist to clutch at her night rail.

In the light of the candle and backlit by the fire in the grate, Marcus looked like Mephistopheles himself, austere and filled with a palpable dark energy. There was no softness to him, no seduction, just a silent irrefutable command. "Finding the relief you've refused me."

He tore open the placket of his breeches and pulled out the magnificent length of his cock. Elizabeth's mouth watered at the sight of it. Hard and thick, it pulsed with starkly etched veins. Her legs spread wider in invitation.

Marcus tilted his head arrogantly. "You shall have to ask

me, if you want this." His hand gripped at the root and stroked to the tip.

She groaned her anguish. He was merciless. Why couldn't he simply take what he wanted?

"You want me to take you," he said hoarsely, all the while holding his cock out to her like a gift. "You want me to take the decision from you, so there will be no guilt. Well, I won't, love. You set the rules and I gave my word."

"Bastard!"

"Witch," he threw back at her. "Tempting me, offering me heaven with one hand while taking it away with the other." He pumped his hand and a drop of cum beaded the tip of his erection.

"Must you always have your way?" she whispered, trying to collect how she could want him and hate him with equal ardor.

"Must you always deny me?" he retorted, his voice low and deep, brushing across her skin like rough silk.

Elizabeth curled into a ball and turned away from him . . . and a second later was flipped onto her back and dragged to the end of the mattress, kicking and screaming. "You are a brute!"

He bent over her with hands on either side of her head, the silky smooth head of his erection pressing into her thigh. His emerald eyes narrowed and burned. "You will lie here with your legs spread while I take my pleasure." Thrusting along her thigh, Marcus teased her with what she desired, leaving a trail of wetness behind. "If you move or otherwise attempt to evade me, I will tie you down."

Furious, Elizabeth lifted her hips and almost caught him. He slipped into her for a moment, just the tip, and she gasped with relief.

He pulled away with a curse. "If my goal were less worthy, I'd fuck you properly. Lord knows you need it."

"I hate you!" Tears welled and slid down her temples, yet still her body ached for him. If her pride meant any less to her she'd be begging.

"I'm certain you wish you did."

With far from gentle hands, he arranged her to his liking on a pile of pillows. Elizabeth found her hips on the edge of the bed, her legs hanging down the side and spread as wide as comfort would allow. She was completely exposed from the waist down, her glistening sex displayed in the candlelight. As always, Marcus held all the power and left her with nothing.

Her gaze rose to his face, and then traveled the length of his body, watching the play of muscles across his powerful torso as he moved. Curling his long fingers around his cock, Marcus swirled his hand down the length of his shaft, his strokes fluid and graceful despite his obvious lust. His heavy sac was tight and hard, his gaze locked between her thighs.

She lay motionless, arrested by the sight of him. She'd never witnessed anything so erotic in her life, could never have imagined it. One would think a person would be vulnerable in such a pose, and yet Marcus stood proudly, his stance wide for support as he pleasured himself. In an effort to see him better she tried to sit up, but his hands stilled.

"Stay where you are," he ordered tersely as he squeezed the engorged head of his cock in his fist. "Put your heels on the mattress."

Elizabeth licked her lips and the gesture made him groan. She lifted her legs as he'd demanded and watched a flush creep over the crests of his cheekbones. His pupils dilated, the brilliant emerald retreating until it was only a faint rim around the black.

It was then she realized that the power was hers. She so often forgot how he craved her, how he had always craved her, taking his harsh words as the truth when his every action belied what he said. Filled with renewed confidence, she spread her legs wider. His lips parted on a hiss of air. She plucked her nipples and he moaned. All the while she watched his hands, pumping his cock with a strength that looked painful, but gave him obvious pleasure. Her hands wandered down her torso toward her sex and his motions became more urgent.

She felt the moisture leaking between her legs and she dipped her fingers inside. Marcus growled. Elizabeth wondered if he knew she was there or if she was merely an inspiring view.

"*Elizabeth*."

Her name was a tormented cry from his lips as he spurted, his hot seed splashing in creamy bursts through her fingers and mingling with her own arousal. Startled by the stunning intimacy, she shivered and came, her neck arching back into the pillows with a gasping breath.

Feeling wicked and wonderful and some other warm emotion she couldn't name because she'd never felt it before, she slipped her fingers into her mouth and sucked the tangy saltiness of his release.

Marcus stood for a moment watching her with eyes so heated her cheeks flushed. Then he moved behind the screen and she heard him pour water from the pitcher and wash his hands. With breeches fastened he returned to her and cleansed his release from her stomach and thighs. She moaned at his touch, arching into his hand. He bent and pressed a firm, quick kiss to her forehead.

"I shall be next door, if you want me."

And he made his egress without another word or even a backward glance.

She stared at the closed portal with mouth agape and waited. Surely he would return? He couldn't be finished. The man was insatiable.

But he didn't return, and she refused to grovel for his attentions.

Sweating under the covers, but too cold without them, Elizabeth gave up trying to sleep a few hours before dawn. She pulled her cloak around her and returned to the parlor.

Marcus had banked the fire in the hearth, but the room was still warm. Tucking the chaise blanket around her feet, she picked up the journal, hoping it would bore her to sleep.

* * *

The sun was just beginning to light the sky when Marcus discovered Elizabeth fast asleep with Hawthorne's journal open on her lap. He shook his head and grimaced.

One sleepless night passed, thirteen left to survive.

Confused by his soul-deep disquiet, he tugged on his boots and left the small residence. He crossed the circular cobblestone drive that swung by both the main manse and the house he shared with Elizabeth, and headed toward the stables beyond. Below the cliff face he heard the rhythmic roaring of the waves upon the shore and felt the misty breeze as it swelled over the ledge and permeated his sweater. Once inside the warmth of the stables he sucked in the scent of sweet hay and horseflesh, such a stark contrast to the salty bite of the air outdoors.

He bridled one of his carriage bays and led the gelding out of the stall. With a singular determination to work himself to exhaustion so he could sleep at night, Marcus set to the task of grooming his horses. As the heat of his exertions made him sweat, he discarded his sweater in favor of comfort. Lost in thoughts of the night before and the remembrance of Elizabeth displayed erotically in the candlelight, he was startled by a gasp behind him.

Turning about swiftly, he faced the winsome lass who delivered their meals. "Milord," she said, dipping a quick curtsy.

Eyeing the groomsmen's quarters behind her, he quickly deduced her worry. "Don't fret," he assured her. "I've been known to be dumb and blind on occasion."

The servant studied him with obvious curiosity, her appreciative gaze taking in his bare chest. Surprised to find himself a bit flustered by a woman's sensual perusal, Marcus turned to retrieve his sweater. As his hand closed around the garment, which was slung over the nearest stall, the temperamental beast inside had the temerity to bite him.

Cursing, Marcus snatched back the injured appendage and glared at the duke's stallion.

"'e's a bit testy that one," the girl said with sympathy. She reached his side and held out a rag, which Marcus accepted quickly and wrapped around his hand to staunch the trickle of blood.

The girl was a pretty thing with soft brown curls and passion-flushed cheeks. Her dress was disheveled, betraying her recent activities, but her smile was genuine and filled with good humor. Marcus was about to return that smile when the stable door slammed open, startling his horse who then sidestepped anxiously, knocking Marcus into the servant and tumbling them both to the floor.

"You rutting beast!"

Marcus lifted his head from the girl's shoulder and met a violet gaze of such fury he couldn't breathe for a moment. Elizabeth stood with her hands on her hips in the stable doorway.

"I wouldn't wed you for any reason!" she shouted, before spinning in a swirl of skirts and running away.

"Christ." Marcus leapt to his feet and then yanked the servant girl to hers. Without another word, he was in pursuit, rushing past the gaping, sleep-mussed groomsman and out to the rapidly lightening dawn.

Elizabeth, a woman well accustomed to physical exertion, was several feet ahead of him and he lengthened his stride.

"Elizabeth!"

"To hell with you," she yelled back.

Her pace was frantic and her path too close to the cliff's edge for Marcus's comfort. His heart racing madly in his chest, he leapt, tackling her and twisting to land on his bare back. Small rocks and the coarse wild grass cut at his back as he slid some distance in the morning dew, Elizabeth's squirming body clutched tightly to his.

"Stop it," he growled, rolling to pin her beneath him and deflecting her flailing fists.

"Constancy is beyond you, you horrid man." Her face, so heartrendingly perfect, was flushed and tearstained.

"It's not what you think!"

"You were half dressed atop a woman!"

"A mishap, nothing more." He pinned her arms above her head to prevent sustaining any further injury. Despite the chill of the morning, the pain of his back and hand, and the consternation that drew his brows together, he was still intensely aware of the woman who thrashed beneath him.

"A mishap you were caught." Elizabeth turned her head and bit his bicep. Marcus roared and shoved his knee between her legs, sinking betwixt them intimately.

"Bite me again and I will turn you over my knee."

"Spank me again and I'll shoot you," she retorted.

Having no other notion of what to do, he lowered his head and captured her lips, his tongue slipping briefly inside before he yanked his head back from her snapping teeth.

He snarled. "If you worry so much about my fidelity you should ensure it."

Her mouth fell open. "Of all the arrogant utterances."

"Selfish wench. You don't want me, but God forbid if any other woman does."

"Another woman can have you, with my pity!"

He pressed his forehead to hers and muttered, "That chit is dallying with one of the groomsmen. You spooked my horse and caused a tumble."

"I don't believe you. Why was she standing so close to you?"

"I was injured." Marcus held her wrists with one hand and displayed his makeshift bandage. "She was attempting to assist me."

Frowning, but softening, Elizabeth asked, "Why are you bare-chested?"

"It was hot, love." Marcus shook his head at her disbelieving snort. "I'll present the libidinous parties to you for a confession."

A tear slid down her temple. "I will never trust you," she breathed.

He brushed his lips across hers. "More the reason to wed me. I vow marriage to you would exhaust any man into finding the female gender unappealing."

"That was cruel." She sniffled.

"I'm frustrated, Elizabeth," he admitted gruffly, the soft pressure of her curves under his only exacerbating his discomfort. "What more must I do to win you? Could you give me some clue? Some inkling of the length of the road left to travel?"

Her reddened eyes met his. "Why won't you cease? Lose interest? Seek the attentions of someone else?"

Marcus sighed, resigned to the miserable truth. "I cannot."

The fight left her tense body with a silent sob.

He hugged her tighter. She looked as he did—tired, unhappy. Neither one of them was getting any sleep, tossing and turning, craving each other. Physically they were so close, shut off from the world and alone together, and yet the distance between them seemed unending.

For the first time since he'd met her, Marcus conceded that perhaps they weren't meant for each other.

"Do you . . . Do you have a mistress?" she asked suddenly.

Stunned by the quick change of topic, he blurted, "Yes."

Her mouth quivered against his cheek. "I won't share you."

"I wouldn't make that request of you," he promised.

"You must rid yourself of her."

He pulled back. "I intend to make her my wife."

Elizabeth lifted her eyes to his.

"Vexing wench." He rubbed his nose against hers. "I've

barely the energy required to pursue you. Think you I have the wherewithal to chase other skirts?"

"I need time to think, Marcus."

"You have it," he promised quickly. The hope that was near dying flared again.

She pressed her lips to his throat and gave a shaky sigh. "Very well then. I'll consider your address."

Chapter 13

Elizabeth paced the length of her bed. The drapes at the windows were open, as they had been since the third night of her stay, and the pearlescent light of the moon lit the path she paced. There was no point in closing them. Dark or not, she couldn't sleep, snatching only an hour or two of rest a night.

She covered her face with her hands. If she didn't get some relief from this miserable aching for Marcus she would surely go mad.

Over the last ten days she had collected hundreds of images of him in her mind—Marcus lying on a blanket on the beach, Marcus sprawled in his shirtsleeves on the settee reading aloud, Marcus at the hearth lit by the light of the fire as he banked it for the night.

She had memorized his smiles and the way he rubbed the back of his neck when he was tense. She knew the way the overnight growth of beard darkened his face in the morning, and the way his eyes gleamed wickedly when he teased her, and then darkened when he wanted her.

And he did want her.

The look in his eyes and the timbre of his voice told her daily that he wished he were holding her, touching her, making love to her. But he kept his promise, making no overt attempts to seduce her.

Sighing, she stared at her hands clenched in front of her. The truth of it was, no effort was required on his part to make her desire him. It was instinctual, uncontrollable.

So why was she here, pacing her room in fevered anguish, when the relief she sought was just a door away?

Because he was wrong for her, she knew. The epitome of everything she had never wanted. A libertine of some renown, he'd proven again in the stables that he was not to be trusted. She wanted to lock him away, keep him to herself, share him with no one. Only then would she find some measure of peace. Only then could she catch her breath and not feel this clawing ache that she would lose him.

Jealousy is a possessive emotion, love, he'd said to her that first day on the beach. *You'll have to wed me if you want the right to feel that way.*

The right. The right to keep him, to claim him. She wanted that. Despite the torture she knew it would be.

There would be no pleasure in binding herself to a man like Marcus, a man whose appetite for life and adventure would make taming him impossible. There would be only heartache and endless disappointment. And the craving. The craving that would never go away.

She stilled and stared at the bed, remembering the depth of that hunger.

Were not a ring, his name, and the right to his body better than nothing at all?

Before she could consider it further, Elizabeth left her room and walked directly into Marcus's without bothering to knock.

Heading straight toward the bed, she slowed when she saw it was empty, the covers tossed back and wildly askew. Startled, she glanced around and found Marcus in front of the window.

Naked, he stood immobile, bathed in moonlight, watching her with an unblinking stare.

"Marcus?"

"What do you want, Elizabeth?" he asked harshly.

She clutched the sides of her gown with damp fists. "I haven't been able to sleep in over a week."

"You won't find sleep in this room."

She shifted restlessly. Now that she was with him and he was naked, she found her courage had been an ephemeral thing. "I had hoped you would say that," she admitted, her head down.

"So tell me what you want."

Unable to say the words, Elizabeth pulled her night rail over her head and dropped it to the floor.

Marcus reached her in two strides. Wrapping his arms around her waist with a low growl, he clasped her naked body firmly against his. He took her mouth with breath-stealing hunger, his tongue thrusting in blatant imitation of what was to come.

Holding her secure with one arm, he lifted and anchored her leg with the other, his knowledgeable fingers tracing the curve of her buttocks before delving into the crevice and the damp curls of her sex. Moaning her relief and pleasure, Elizabeth clung to his broad shoulders, her breasts held tight to his furred chest as he teased through the slickness of her desire, and then slid upwards into her heat.

His cock, hard and hot, burned the skin of her belly. She reached for it, wrapping trembling fingers around it, her other arm gripping his waist to keep her balance. He throbbed in her palm, groaned into her mouth, his powerful frame trembling against hers.

Elizabeth could barely breathe, couldn't move as his fingers fucked with the expertise of a man who knew his lover well. Hard and fast, he stroked her desire, making her mindless with need. She buried her face against his skin, gasping in his scent, imprinting it all over herself.

"Please," she begged.

"Please what?"

She groaned, her hips undulating to match the movements of his hand.

"Please what?" he demanded, removing his touch.

Sobbing at the sudden dearth of sensation, she pressed desperate kisses against his skin. "Please, take me. I want you."

"For how long, Elizabeth? One hour? One night?"

Her tongue tasted the flat point of his nipple and his breath hissed between his teeth.

"Every night," she breathed.

Marcus lifted her feet from the floor and took the two steps to the bed, sinking into its disheveled softness over her. Elizabeth opened her legs with blatant eagerness.

"Elizabeth . . ."

"Hurry," she begged.

Settling between her thighs, he thrust into her with consummate skill. He was harder, thicker than he had ever been before, stretching her completely and she tore her mouth from his, crying out as she climaxed immediately, primed for pleasure by days of longing and the mastery of his touch.

Marcus buried his face in Elizabeth's neck and groaned hoarsely as the endless spasms of her release milked his aching cock. Against his will, he came, flooding her grasping depths with his seed. It was too much, too fast. His toes curled and his spine arched with pleasure so intense it was almost painful. Lost for a breathless moment, he clutched her body to his with near desperation.

It could only have been moments, but it seemed like hours before he could roll his weight from her. He draped her body across his chest, her legs straddling his thighs, their bodies still joined. Whatever doubts he might have harbored about marriage were burned away by the shudders that still wracked his frame.

"Christ." He crushed her to his chest. Their coupling had lasted all of two minutes. He hadn't thrust at all, yet he had never experienced anything as powerfully fulfilling in his life.

Elizabeth had surrendered to him, acknowledged his claim. There would be no turning back now.

Her fingers stroked through the hair on his chest, soothing him. "I want you to resign your commission with the agency," she whispered softly.

He stilled and released a deep breath. "Ah love, you don't ask for much, do you?"

Elizabeth sighed, her breath warm against his skin. "How can you ask me to marry you, knowing the danger you court?"

"How could I not ask you?" he retorted. "I will never have enough of you, enough of this." He thrust gently, showing her the power of his interest in his renewed erection.

"Lust," she said scornfully.

"Lust I know well, Elizabeth. It does not come near to resembling this."

She moaned as he nudged deeper inside her. "What would you name this then?"

"Affinity, love. We simply suit very well in bed."

Elizabeth rose above him, pushing him deeper still, until the slick lips of her cunt hugged the root of his cock. She studied him with the narrowed-eyed glance that told him trouble was afoot. Then she clenched her inner muscles, hugging his cock in the most intimate of embraces.

His hands fisted in the disheveled sheets and he grit his teeth. Scant moments before he'd felt like he was dying. Already he was eager to feel that way again.

She lifted from him, his cock slipping free from swollen, wet tissues. "Promise me you will consider leaving Eldridge." She slid back onto him slowly.

Sweat beaded his brow. "Elizabeth . . ."

She lifted and lowered again, caressing his cock with her silken cunt. "Promise me you will be careful while considering."

His eyes slid closed on a groan. "Damn you."

Elizabeth rose, withdrawing from him.

His entire body tensed, waiting for the exquisiteness of her body to sink and clasp tightly around him. When she hesitated, he looked at her. She waited, one finely arched brow lifted in challenge. She would continue to wait until he capitulated, he knew.

Unable to do otherwise, Marcus surrendered immediately. "I promise."

And his reward was sweet indeed.

"Good God!"

Elizabeth jumped awake at the familiar, albeit horrified cry. Marcus's outstretched arm pushed her back down and she gasped at the sight of the wicked knife in his hand. She lifted her head and looked toward the door, gaping at the sight of the beloved figure there. *"William?"*

Her brother stood with a hand clasped over his eyes. "I will await"—he choked—"you both in the parlor. Please . . . dress."

With her brain still sleep muddled, Elizabeth slipped out of bed, shivering as her bare feet hit the cold floor. "I often tell myself that William cannot possibly become more outrageous and yet somehow he manages it."

"Elizabeth."

She ignored the soft query in Marcus's tone and moved swiftly to her discarded night rail at the foot of the bed. It was awkward, this moment, recalling the intimacy of the night before and the brazen way she'd elicited his promise. To wake to the sight of a blade in his hand was sobering. She'd agreed to marry this man, for no other reason than sexual *affinity* and misplaced possessiveness. She was daft.

"You can stay abed, love," he murmured. "I can speak with your brother."

Straightening with her garment in hand, Elizabeth paused at the sight him pulling on breeches. As he moved, the ripple of honed muscle along his arms, chest, and abdomen arrested her gaze.

He glanced up, caught her staring, and smiled. "You are a fetching sight, all sleep mussed and ravished."

"I'm certain I look a fright," she said.

"Impossible. I've yet to see you look anything but delectable."

He rounded the bed, took the night rail from her hands, and dropped it over her head. Then he kissed the tip of her nose. "Nowise did I plan for us to be rushed this morning." Shaking his head, he moved to the armoire and finished dressing. "Keep the bed warm and wait for me."

"It would be best if you learned now that I won't be ordered about. William is my brother. I will speak to him."

Marcus sighed internally at Elizabeth's stubbornness, acknowledging to himself that he would have to grow accustomed to it, and went to the door. "As you wish, love."

He raked her barely clad body with an affectionate glance before closing the portal behind him and traversing the length of the hall. He really shouldn't be surprised they'd been discovered, but he was, and disappointed. Their agreement was too new, the tie too tentative to set his mind at ease.

The first time he'd proposed he'd sat in the study of Chesterfield Hall and discussed the marital disbursements in cold, hard facts with her father. The banns had been read, and the papers notified. Teas and dinners had been held. He could not have expected she would bolt. He could not have anticipated she would marry another man. And at this moment he had far less than he'd had then. At this moment he had only her promise and she had proven that was not to be trusted.

Years of frustration and anger rose like bile in his throat. Until she made restitution for what she'd done to him he would never find peace.

He entered the parlor. "Barclay, your timing leaves much to be desired. You are—quite lamentably—*de trop*."

William paced before the fireplace, his hands clasped at his back. "I am scarred for life," he muttered.

"A knock would have been wise."

"The door was open."

"Well it's moot in any case; you shouldn't have come."

"Elizabeth had run off." William stopped and glared. "After the tantrum in her room, I had to find her and see if she was well."

Marcus ran his hands through his tumbled locks. He couldn't fault the man for caring. "She sent word. I suppose I should have as well."

"At the very least. Debauching someone else's sister would also be preferable."

"I am not debauching her. I'm marrying her."

William gaped. "*Again?*"

"We never quite finished the business the last time, if you recall."

"Damn you, Westfield." William's fists clenched until the knuckles were white. "If this has anything to do with that idiotic wager, I will call you out."

Rounding the settee, Marcus sat and bit back the harsh words that longed to be freed. "Your sterling estimation of my character is most uplifting."

"Why in hell would you want to wed Elizabeth after what transpired before?"

"We have an affinity," Elizabeth said from the doorway, studying the two men who held such important places in her life—both of them so obviously restless. "Or so he attests."

"An *affinity?*" William pierced her with a narrowed gaze. "What the devil does that have to do with anything?"

Then he paled and held up his hands. "On further consideration, I don't wish to hear the answer to that."

She didn't move, simply stood in the doorway trying to decide whether to enter or not. The tension in the room was as thick as fog. "Where is Margaret?"

"At home. The journey wouldn't be wise for her now. She becomes ill easily."

"You should be with her," she admonished.

"I was worried about you," he said defensively. "Especially when Westfield conveniently disappeared at the same time. Your missive told me nothing of your mind-set or your location. You are both damned fortunate that Lady Westfield saw fit to give me direction." He crossed the room to her and gripped her elbow. "Come outside with me."

"It's too cold," she protested.

William shrugged out of his coat and tossed it about her shoulders. Then he dragged her outside.

"Are you daft?" he growled when they were alone. The chilly bite of the coastal morning was rivaled by the chill of her brother's tone.

"I thought so earlier," she said dryly.

"I understand. You've had a taste of . . ." he choked, "carnal pleasure, one denied you before. It can be heady and unduly influencing for women."

"William—"

"It's hopeless to deny it. A man can discern these things. Women look different when they are content with their lovers. You lacked that appearance with Hawthorne."

"This is a very uncomfortable conversation," she muttered.

"I am enjoying this as much as I would a visit to the tooth drawers. But I must beg you to consider this engagement further. There was a reason why you didn't proceed with the marriage before."

Elizabeth looked at the sky, seeing soft blue peeking from the heavy morning clouds. She wondered if she could learn to look for brightness in a marriage that would be rife with cloudy issues.

"You could refuse," he suggested, softening his tone to match her mood.

"Even I am not that cruel." She sighed and leaned into him, accepting the strength he'd always provided.

"You don't wed to alleviate guilt. And I'm not so certain his intentions are honorable. He has much to hold against you. Once you wed him, I would have very little recourse should things deteriorate."

"You know Westfield better than to attribute such thoughts to him." She returned his scowl. "Honestly, there are many times I cannot abide the man. He's arrogant to a fault, stubborn, argumentive—"

"Yes, I agree, he has his faults, all of which I know well."

"If he recovers some of his lost dignity by wedding me, I won't hold it against him. At worst, should he lose interest, he'll simply treat me with the faultless, albeit distant charm for which he's known. He would never physically hurt me."

William blew out a frustrated breath and tilted his head back to look at the sky. "I still cannot find comfort in this. I wanted you to find love the second time. You are free to choose whomever you like. Why settle for 'affinity' when you can have true happiness?"

"You are becoming as much of a romantic as Margaret." Elizabeth shook her head and laughed. "There are times when Westfield's company is quite pleasant."

"So, enjoy a liaison," William suggested. "Much less messy all around."

Her smile was bittersweet. The fact was, Marcus was one of the very few individuals strong enough to stand up to William. She needed to show her brother she was in safekeeping with a man he could trust to be capable. Then perhaps he would worry about her less. Margaret needed him now, as would their child. If there had been any doubt about her forthcoming marriage, it was dispelled by her brother's presence here. He could not continue to leave his wife to care for his sister.

"I want to marry him, William. I don't think I'll be unhappy."

"You are using him to hide. If you choose a man who dislikes you, you have no worries about something more coming of the relationship. Our father has done you a grave injustice with his decline. You are still afraid."

She lifted her chin. "I understand you don't approve of my choice, but that's no reason to malign me."

"I'm speaking the truth, something perhaps it would have been best to do long before now."

"No one knows what the future will bring," she argued. "But Westfield and I are of like station and pedigree. He is wealthy and solicitous of my needs. When this affinity fades, we will still have that foundation. It is no less than any other marriage."

William's gaze narrowed. "You are set in this course."

"Yes." She was glad he'd come after her now. Secure in the knowledge that she was benefiting someone other than herself gave her a peace of mind she'd lacked upon waking. Whether William would admit it or not, this would be good for him, too.

"No elopement," he warned, his frown unabated but unable to diminish the beauty of his features.

"No elopement," she agreed.

"Am I allowed no say in the matter?" Marcus asked, coming up behind them.

"I think you've said quite enough," William retorted. "And I'm famished. I spoke to His Grace when I arrived and he said to drag you both up to the manse. He hasn't seen enough of you since you arrived."

"That was by design," Marcus said dryly. He held out his hand to her, an affectionate gesture they'd never shared in front of others. Sans gloves it was undeniably intimate. The look in his eyes dared her to refuse.

He was always daring her to refuse.

And just as she'd always done, she met the dare and placed her hand in his.

Chapter 14

By any estimation, their betrothal ball was a smashing success. The ballroom of Chesterfield Hall was filled to overflowing, as were the card and billiards rooms. Overwhelmed and overheated, Elizabeth was grateful when Marcus led her out to the garden to enjoy the cool night air.

Realizing the importance of the occasion, she had chosen a burgundy shot silk taffeta gown. Panniers widened the skirt, which was split in the front revealing an underskirt of white lace. Matching lace frothed from the elbows and surrounded the low square neckline. The gown had given her a surface shell of composure, but inside, her stomach was knotted.

She was an expert at the common social pleasantries, but tonight had been so different from the interactions she was accustomed to. The men had been dealt with easily. It was the women and their often catty, spiteful natures that caught her by surprise. After an hour, she'd resorted to smiling while relying on Marcus to carry them through the prying questions and snide comments disguised as congratulations. His skilful handling of women set her on edge, making her jaw ache from the unnaturalness of her outward mien. Not for the first time, she lamented the loss of the quiet she'd enjoyed on the coast.

After William departed Essex for London, Marcus had insisted they remain another three days in the guesthouse. They had lived those days in a state of deep intimacy. He had assisted her with her bath, and demanded she do the same for him. He had helped her to dress, and showed her how to undress him, patiently showing her where every button was and how best to free it until she was as skilled as any valet. He had reinforced those skills at every opportunity—on the beach, in the garden, in almost every room of the guesthouse. With every touch, every glance, every moment, Marcus had weakened her resolve until she had accepted without reservation that she no longer wanted to be free of him.

Resigned to their joined future, she made the effort to learn more about the issues that were important to him. She asked questions about his views of the Townsend Act repeal, and was secretly relieved when he showed no hesitation in sharing them with her. Discussing weighty topics with women was heavily discouraged, but then Marcus was not a man to follow convention.

Pleased with her interest, he debated a variety of topics with her, challenging and pushing her to explore all sides of a subject, then smiling with pride when she reached her own conclusions, even if they were in opposition to his own.

Elizabeth sighed. The simple fact was, she enjoyed his company and the times when business or Parliament kept him away, she found she missed him.

"That was a melancholy sigh if I ever heard one," he murmured.

Lifting her chin, she met his gaze, made more brilliant in contrast to the pure white of his wig. In a pale gold ensemble, Marcus outshone every other gentleman present.

"You look beautiful," she said.

His mouth tilted upward on one side. "I believe I am supposed to say that to you." The heat in his eyes left her no doubt as to what he was thinking.

William had forbade any further meetings in the guesthouse. She suspected Marcus had so readily agreed to that demand to ensure her continued cooperation. Achey and restless, her body craved his and the constant reminder of her need negated changing her mind about their approaching nuptials.

"You're flushed," he said. "And not for the reason I'd prefer."

"I'm thirsty," she admitted.

"We must find a drink for you then." With his hand over hers where it rested on his sleeve, he turned her back toward the manse.

She resisted. "I would rather await you out here." The thought of returning to the crush after so recently escaping was vastly unappealing.

Marcus began to protest. Then he spotted William and Margaret descending the stairs and led her to them. "I shall leave you in capable hands," he said with a kiss to the back of her hand. Moving away, he ascended the steps to the house with a grace she found hard to look away from.

Margaret linked arms with her and said, "The ball is an unequivocal triumph, as we all expected. Much more entertaining to gossip about you than any other topic."

William looked over their heads. "Where is Westfield going?"

Elizabeth hid a smile at his curt tone. "To the drink tables."

He frowned. "Wish he would have said something before he went in. I could use some libation myself. If you will excuse me, ladies, I believe I'll join him."

As William moved away, Margaret gestured toward the garden and they set off at a sedate stroll.

"You look well," Elizabeth said.

"Regardless, a clever modiste cannot hide this belly any longer, so this ball will be my last social event of the Season." Margaret smiled. "Lord Westfield seems quite taken with you. With luck, you will be having children of your own soon." Leaning closer, she asked, "Is he as skilled a lover as they say?"

Elizabeth blushed.

"Good for you." Margaret laughed, and then winced. "My back aches."

"You have been on your feet all day," Elizabeth scolded.

"A respite in the retiring room is long overdue," Margaret agreed.

"Then we must hasten to get you there."

Turning around, they headed away from the garden.

As they neared the house, they saw more guests filtering out into the cool night air. Elizabeth took a deep breath, and prayed for the patience she'd require to endure 'til morning.

"Yours will not be an easy pairing, you are aware of that?"

Marcus glanced at William as they descended the garden steps, drinks in hand. "Truly?" he drawled. "And here I'd been led to believe marriage was a tranquil institution."

William snorted. "Elizabeth is by nature quite feisty and downright argumentative, but around you, she is not herself. She's almost withdrawn. Lord only knows how you convinced her to accept your addresses, but I've taken note of her marked reticence around you."

"How obliging of you." Marcus clenched his jaw. He was a proud man. It did not sit well with him that Elizabeth appeared less than enthusiastic to wed him.

Margaret approached, her arched brows drawn tight with discomfort.

William rushed to her. "What pains you?" he asked gruffly.

She waved his concern away with a lift of her hand. "My back and feet ache is all. Nothing to worry yourself over."

"Where is Lady Hawthorne?" Marcus asked, searching the winding path behind her.

"Lady Grayton had an unfortunate mishap with an unruly climbing rose and needed more assistance than I." She wrinkled her nose. "Frankly, I think Elizabeth simply didn't want to return to the house yet."

Marcus opened his mouth to reply, but was silenced by a distant female scream.

William frowned. Marcus, however, was almost crippled with fear, his entire body tensing to the point of pain.

"Elizabeth," he whispered starkly, his well-trained senses telling him the danger that stalked her was right there in the garden. He dropped the glasses he held in his hands, paying no mind to the delicate flutes shattering on the stone pathway. With William fast on his heels, Marcus ran in the direction of the disturbing sound, his stomach clenched and frozen with dread.

He'd left her with family when he should never have left her at all. He knew his job, knew the rules, knew she was not safe anywhere after the ransacking of her room and he'd ignored all of it simply because she asked him to. He'd been a fool and now he could only hope fright from an overactive imagination would be the extent of his punishment.

Perhaps it was not Elizabeth. Perhaps it was a minor incident of a stolen kiss and a woman with a flair for dramatic outcries . . .

Just as panic began to overwhelm him, he saw her up ahead, sprawled on the pathway next to a rose-covered arbor in a flood of displaced panniers and endless skirts.

He dropped to his knees beside her, damning himself for lowering his guard. Lifting his head, he searched for her attacker, but the night was still and quiet except for her labored breathing.

William crouched on her other side. "Christ." His hands trembled as he reached for her.

Because the darkness made sight difficult, Marcus felt along her torso, searching for injury. Elizabeth groaned as his fingers lightly skimmed across her ribs, finding an object protruding from her hip. Moving her arm aside carefully, he exposed a small dagger.

"She's been stabbed," Marcus said gruffly, his throat tight.

Elizabeth opened her eyes at the sound of his voice. Her skin was pale beneath her powder, the rouge she wore unnatural in comparison. "Marcus." Her voice was a gasped whisper as her fingers curled weakly over the hand that touched the hilt. He gripped them tightly, willing some of his vitality into her, willing her to be strong.

This was his fault. And Elizabeth had paid the price. The extent of his failure was crushing, a brutal fall from the heights of satisfaction he'd felt when the evening started.

William stood, his body tense as he searched their surroundings much as Marcus had done a moment earlier. "We need to move her to the house."

Marcus lifted her, careful to avoid unduly jarring the knife. She cried out, then lost consciousness, her breathing slipping into a rapid but measured rhythm. "Where can I go?" he asked in near desperation. Through the ballroom was obviously not an option.

"Follow me."

Moving like shadows through the garden, they entered through the bustling kitchen. Then they took the cramped servants' staircase, which caused a laborious ascent hampered by Elizabeth's panniers.

Once safely in her room, Marcus shrugged out of his coat and reached into an inner pocket, withdrawing a small dagger not unlike the one lodged in Elizabeth's side. "Send for a doctor," Marcus ordered. "And ring for towels and heated water."

"I will instruct a servant on my departure. It will be faster if I collect the doctor myself." William left with reassuring haste.

With careful, tentative movements, Marcus used his knife to cut through the endless material that made up her dress, stays, and underskirts. The task was torturous, this sight of his blade next to precious ivory skin a nightmare, and he was drenched with sweat before she was free of the pile.

A steady steam of blood leaked from around the dagger.

She was still unconscious, but he whispered soothingly as he worked, trying to calm himself as well as her.

The door opened behind him, and he cast a quick glance over his shoulder to see the entry of Lord Langston and Lady Barclay. A maid entered directly behind, carrying a tray weighted with hot water and cloths.

The earl took one look at his daughter and shuddered violently. "Oh God," he breathed. He swayed unsteadily, his face a stark mask. "I cannot go through this again."

Marcus felt his stomach knot. The pain he witnessed on her father's face was what tormented Elizabeth so. That same pain had pushed Elizabeth away and every other woman who'd had the misfortune to care for the dashing, but endlessly grieving widower.

"Come. Let's get you settled somewhere quiet to wait, my lord," Margaret said softly.

Langston did not hesitate to agree, fleeing the room as if the hounds of hell were on his heels. Marcus cursed under his breath, fighting the urge to chase him and thrash some sense into him, to make the man care for his daughter.

Lady Barclay returned a quarter hour later. "I must apologize for Lord Langston."

"No need, Lady Barclay. It's long overdue that he answer for his own actions." He released a deep breath and rubbed the back of his neck.

"Tell me what to do," she said softly.

With silent efficiency, Margaret helped him clean the blood from Elizabeth's skin. As they were finishing, William returned with the doctor who removed the blade, examined the puncture, and announced the fine boning of her stays had deflected the dagger away from any vital organs, and into the fleshy part of her hip. Stitches and bed rest would be all that was required.

Nearly dizzy with relief, Marcus steadied himself against the post of the bed and tugged off his wig. Had Elizabeth been uncorseted, the wound might have been fatal, and his destruction assured.

He glanced at William and his wife. "I will remain with her, you both should return to the guests below. It's bad enough Elizabeth and I will be absent from our own betrothal celebration. Your absence will only worsen the situation."

"You should go below, Lord Westfield," Margaret said gently. "It would be less awkward if at least one of you were in attendance."

"No. Let them think what they like, I won't leave her."

Margaret nodded though her eyes were still troubled. "What tale should I relate to your family?"

Rubbing the back of his neck, he said, "Anything aside from the truth."

William turned to the maid. "Say nothing of this to anyone if you wish to remain employed."

"And ready the other bedroom in this suite for Lord Westfield," Margaret added, ignoring the glare from her husband. The maid left swiftly.

Margaret gestured William toward the door. "Come, dear. Lord Westfield has everything well in hand. I'm certain he will call for us if needed."

Still pale and clearly stricken, William nodded and followed Margaret out.

Elizabeth woke only a moment later, thrashing as the doctor began the first stitch. Marcus lay across the bed and held her down.

"Marcus!" she gasped, her eyes flying open. "It hurts."

She began to cry.

His throat aching with her pain, he bent low to kiss her forehead. "I know, love. But if you can find the strength to be still, it will be over all the sooner."

Marcus watched with much pride and admiration as Elizabeth did her best to remain unmoving while her wound was closed. She writhed slightly, but she did not cry out again. Fine beads of sweat dotted her brow and mingled with the steady flow of tears as she clung to his torso with bruising fingers. He was grateful when she lost consciousness again.

When the doctor finished, he cleaned his instruments carefully and returned them to his bag. "Keep an eye on that, my lord. If it festers, send for me again." He left as quickly as he'd come.

Marcus paced restlessly, his gaze never straying far from Elizabeth. An overwhelming well of protectiveness rose up within him. Someone had tried to take her away from him. And he had made that task too easy.

Far more than affinity was involved here. That relatively simple state could not account for the madness that threatened his sanity. To see her so pale and wounded, to think of what might have happened . . . He clutched his head in his hands.

For the rest of the night, he watched over her. When she stirred, he went to her, murmuring softly until she settled. He tended the fire in the hearth and checked her bandages regularly. He could not be still, could not sleep, feeling so helpless he wanted to howl and tear something apart.

Dawn lit the sky when the Earl of Langston returned to the room. Looking briefly at Elizabeth, his reddened eyes drifted to Marcus. Reeking of stiff drink and flowery perfume, the earl was disheveled, his wig askew as he stumbled in on his heels.

"Why don't you retire, Lord Langston?" Marcus asked with a disgusted shake of his head. "You look nigh as bad as she does."

Langston leaned heavily against a side table. "And you look far too collected for a man who nearly lost a bride."

"I prefer to be of sound mind," Marcus said dryly. "Rather than drowning in my cups."

"Were you aware that Elizabeth is the reflection of her mother? Rare beauties, the both of them."

Marcus released a weary breath and prayed for patience. "Yes, I am aware, my lord, and there are many things I wish to say to you, but now is not the time. If you don't mind, I have much to consider and would prefer to do it in silence."

Turning bleary eyes toward the bed, the earl winced at the sight of Elizabeth, the paleness of her skin making the heart-shaped patch on her cheek stand out in stark relief.

"Lady Langston gave you a family," Marcus felt compelled to say. "You do no honor to her memory by neglecting them as you have."

"You don't care for me, Westfield, I've known this. But then you fail to understand my situation. You cannot, since you don't love my daughter as I did my wife."

"Do not presume to say that Elizabeth is not important to me." The steel of Marcus's voice snapped through the tension like a whip crack.

"Why not? You think the same of me."

With that, the earl left Marcus to the silence he'd wanted, a silence he found deafening with its unyielding accusations.

Why had he not been there for her?

How could he have been so careless?

And would the fragile trust he'd worked so hard to build be shattered by his broken promise to protect her from harm?

His head fell back, and his eyes closed on a bitter moan.

He'd never allowed himself to consider losing her again and now, confronted with it like this, he realized what he hadn't before.

She'd become necessary to him. Far too necessary.

Chapter 15

Elizabeth jolted awake with a breathless gasp. Her heart racing, it took a moment to register the familiar canopy above her bed, and then a moment more before a heady floral scent teased her senses. She turned her head, her bleary gaze wandering and finding every flat surface in her room covered in a riotous display of hothouse roses. Amidst the flowery profusion, Marcus slumbered with careless grace in a chair beside her bed. He was dressed in a linen shirt open at the neck and soft tan breeches, his rich sable hair tied back at the nape. With his bare feet propped on a footstool, he looked very much at home.

Studying him in repose, Elizabeth felt a possessive pride that both alarmed and pleased her. A feeling so strong she was instantly comforted, the panic she'd felt upon waking dissipating with his proximity.

She raised her hands to rub gritty eyes, then attempted a seated position. She cried out at the pain that burned through her hip, and Marcus was instantly at her side.

"Wait." He pulled her up gently, propping pillows behind her. When she was comfortable, he sat next to her on the bed and poured her a glass of water from the nearby pitcher. With a grateful smile, she took a sip to clear her parched throat.

"How do you feel?" he asked.

She wrinkled her nose. "My hip throbs dreadfully."

"I expect it would." Marcus looked away.

Curious about his somber mood, she reached out to touch his hand. "Thank you for the flowers."

The curve of his mouth was intimately tender, though his thoughts were shuttered in a way she'd not seen in weeks. He looked very much like he had at the Moreland ball so many nights ago, remote and guarded.

"I'm sorry to have disturbed you," she said softly. "You looked very comfortable."

"With you, always." But the tone of his voice was practiced, far too smooth to be genuine, and he gently removed his hand from under hers.

She shifted nervously and pain lanced through her side.

"Stop that," he ordered with a chastising squeeze to her shin.

She shot him a narrowed glance, dismayed by the newly erected barrier between them.

The slight rap on the door broke the moment. Marcus bade the person to enter and Margaret walked in with William directly behind her.

"You're awake!" She greeted Elizabeth with a relieved smile. "How are you feeling?"

"Awful," Elizabeth admitted ruefully.

"Do you recall anything about what happened the other night?"

Everyone looked at her expectantly.

"The other night?" Her eyes widened. "How long have I been asleep?"

"Two days, and you needed every minute of that rest."

"Good heavens." Elizabeth shook her head. "I don't remember much. It all happened so quickly. Lady Grayton stalked off in a bit of a temper, blaming our slovenly gardeners for allowing the climbing rose to grow. Then I was accosted from behind and pulled away."

"How dreadful!" Margaret covered her mouth in horror.

"It was. Still, it could have been much worse."

"You were stabbed," William growled. "It does not get any worse."

She lifted her gaze to meet his. "I believe the assault was not meant to go that far. But the other man—"

Marcus stiffened at Elizabeth's words. *More than one.* He would expect as much from an organized effort, but the knowledge still struck a sharp blow. "What other man?"

Elizabeth sank back into the pillows, frowning at his harsh tone. "I could be mistaken, but I think the man who attacked me was frightened away by someone else."

"Most likely by Westfield and Barclay," Margaret suggested.

"No, someone else. There was a shout, a masculine voice, and then the . . . rest."

Margaret rounded the bed, and sat on the other side. William, however, strode purposefully toward the open door to the sitting room. "Westfield, a word, if you would."

Wanting to hear more of Elizabeth's recollection, Marcus shook his head. "I would rather—"

"If you please," William insisted.

With a curt nod, he rose and followed William, who shut the door behind them.

When William gestured to the nearest chair, Marcus realized this would not be a short conversation. "Barclay, I really must—"

"Elizabeth's stabbing is my fault."

Marcus stilled. "What are you talking about?"

William again gestured for him to sit as he moved to a nearby chair to do the same. "Hawthorne's death was not the result of highway robbery, as everyone has been led to believe."

Feigning surprise, Marcus sank onto the settee, and waited for more.

William hesitated a moment, studying him with disquieting intensity. "I cannot say much, I'm sorry. But since Elizabeth will soon be residing with you, I feel you should know something of what you will face as her husband." He paused for a deep breath, and then said, "Hawthorne was privy to sensitive information that led to his murder. It was not an accident."

Marcus kept his face impassive. "What information?"

"I cannot tell you that. I can only tell you that my own safety and the safety of my wife has been a point of tortuous care for the last four years, and with your marriage it will become likewise for you with Elizabeth. She and I are the only ones who knew Hawthorne well enough to be a danger to those who killed him."

"I can see that. However, I fail to see how her stabbing would be your fault."

"I knew of the danger and should have been more cautious."

Marcus sighed, knowing full well how the other man felt. William, however, had no knowledge of the journal or the attack in the park. Barclay's failure to foresee the events in the garden was excusable. Marcus's was not. "You have been dogged in your protection of her. You could not have done any more than you have."

"I don't believe the disarray we saw in her room was her doing," William continued. "Although she claims it was."

This time Marcus's shock was genuine. "You don't?"

"No. I think her room was ransacked. That is why I tracked her to Essex. I was terrified for her." William leaned his head back, and closed his eyes. Against the burgundy leather of the wingback chair the exhausted strain of his features was even more striking. "Those ten days were the worst of my life. When I found the two of you together, I wanted to thrash you both for allowing me to worry myself into an early graying."

"Barclay . . ." Marcus sighed, his guilt weighing heavily. "I am sorry."

William opened his eyes and scowled. "I have no notion how you found her before I did. I have connections—"

"A fortunate guess," Marcus said quickly.

"Yes, well, what she has in her possession that is so important I haven't a clue, though obviously Elizabeth does. I don't know if they've threatened her in some manner or if she simply wants to protect me. She's been skittish since Hawthorne passed on."

"It would be difficult to lose a spouse, I'm sure."

"Of course. I don't discount that." His voice lowered. "Although Hawthorne was an odd fellow, he was a good man."

Marcus leaned forward, resting his forearms on his knees. "Odd?"

"Hawthorne was an excitable sort. One moment he'd be as calm as you and I at this moment, then the next he'd be pacing and muttering. The damnedest thing, I tell you. Annoying at times."

"I know a few gentlemen such as you describe," Marcus said dryly. "The king, for one."

"In any case." William's gaze narrowed. "You are taking this rather well for a man discovering someone wishes to harm his future wife."

"That discovery was made a few days ago. I've had time to consider it. Of course this cannot be allowed to continue. No one can live like this, reacting after the fact. The threat has to be dealt with."

"I should have told you sooner." William grimaced. "I assumed I had some time to find the best way to present it. What does one say in a situation such as this? Too many questions and not enough answers. But things have been hectic, and you both are so bloody popular. You are always in a crowd. I thought the sheer volume of witnesses would keep her safe, but she's not inviolable anywhere. A *ball* for Christ's sake! One would have to be mad to attempt absconding with the guest of honor at such a well attended event. And the knife!"

Marcus stilled. "What of it?"

William flushed. "Nothing of importance, just—"

Rising, Marcus moved through the door to his chamber and retrieved the knife. He turned it over in his hands and examined it in the light of day. He'd meant to do this earlier, but the need to watch over Elizabeth was a lure he couldn't resist. The blade could wait, it was not going anywhere.

Now he studied it carefully. It was well made and costly. The gold handle was intricately designed with vines and leaves, which gave the hilt a textured grip. The base of the handle was monogrammed with the initials *NTM*. Nigel Terrance Moore, the late Viscount Hawthorne.

Marcus looked up as William entered the room. "Where has this been?"

"I assume whoever killed Hawthorne took all of his valuables. He always carried that, and it was with him the night he was killed."

Lost in thought, Marcus attempted to put the pieces of the puzzle together, but they didn't fit—no matter how many various ways he assembled it.

Christopher St. John had returned Elizabeth's brooch to her, the brooch Hawthorne had been carrying when he was killed. Now another item from that night had reappeared.

The clues laid blame at St. John's feet, but the attacks on Elizabeth were out of character. St. John was successful because of his cleverness and pinpoint precision. Both of the assaults against Elizabeth had resulted in failure, something the pirate would never have allowed to happen once, let alone twice. While it was possible St. John was the culprit, Marcus could not shake the feeling that something else was amiss.

Why take the risk of attacking Elizabeth at a ball where hundreds of people were in attendance? She would not be carrying the journal during such an event.

But if St. John was innocent, a possibility that infuriated Marcus, there was someone else who was aware of the journal, and desired it enough to kill for it. Acknowledging that his own efforts were not enough, he regretted he could not confide in William, but he would honor Elizabeth's wishes for the moment. In the end, her safety was paramount, and he would elicit all the help he needed to ensure it.

Elizabeth's gasp from the doorway startled them both. Dressed in a simple night rail and dressing robe, she stared at the dagger in shock, all color draining from her face. She looked so tiny, so childlike with her disheveled hair and fidgeting fingers.

His chest tightened, and Marcus shoved the feeling aside ruthlessly. His deepening affection for her could only bring more trouble, as had already been proven. Dropping the knife back into the drawer, he hurried to her side. "You should not be walking around yet."

"Where did you find that?" she asked in a barely audible whisper.

"It was the blade used to stab you."

Her knees buckled, and Marcus supported her gently in his arms, paying careful attention to her wounded hip. He walked her back to her room with William close on their heels.

"That was Hawthorne's," she whispered as he returned her to the bed.

"I know."

William moved to the other side. "I will explore this matter further, Elizabeth. Please don't worry, I—"

"You will do no such thing!" she cried.

He squared his shoulders. "I will do what is best."

"No, William. It is no longer your duty to protect me. You must look after your wife. How could I ever face Margaret were something to happen to you on my account?"

"What can Westfield do?" he scoffed. "I am in a much better position to acquire the information we need."

"Lord Westfield is a powerful and influential man," she argued. "I'm certain he has important connections as well. Leave this business to him. I will not have you involved in any way."

"You are being ridiculous," he grumbled, his hands on his hips.

"Stay out of this, William."

Leaving the side of the bed, he stalked toward the door. "I must do something or go mad. You would do no less for me." He slammed the door on his way out.

Elizabeth stared at the portal with mouth agape. When she lifted her gaze, she was crying. "Marcus, you must stop him."

"I will try my best, love." He stared grimly at the door, trying to ignore the way her tears tore at his conscience. "But your brother is as stubborn as you are."

After a light meal with Elizabeth, Marcus took his carriage and collected Avery James. Together, they traveled through town to meet with Lord Eldridge.

Staring pensively out the coach window, Marcus barely registered the bustle of the London streets or the calls of vendors to sample their wares. There was too much to consider, too much awry. He didn't say a word until they reached Lord Eldridge's office, and then he filled in the details he'd been unable to expand upon through the post.

"First of all, Westfield," Eldridge began when he'd finished, "I cannot leave you on this assignment. Your impending marriage destroys any hope for objectivity."

Marcus drummed his fingers on the carved wooden arm of his chair. "I maintain I am in the best position to protect her."

"At this point we know so little about the danger. The best protection would be to keep her locked away. But her safety is not our only aim. And before you protest, consider the alternatives. How else can we apprehend the culprit, other than to draw him out?"

"You want to use her as a lure." It was not a question.

"If need be." Eldridge moved his gaze to Avery. "What say you about the attack on Lady Hawthorne, James?"

"The reasoning eludes me," he admitted. "Why attack

Lady Hawthorne when she does not have the book with her? What purpose does that serve?"

Marcus stilled his fingers, and shared his conclusion. "Ransom. Lady Hawthorne for the journal. They know the agency is involved. The brooch and dagger suggest they were at the site where Hawthorne was murdered so they know Barclay is involved as well. The move against her was rash, yes. But it was truly the only time since Hawthorne's journal surfaced that she has been without escort."

"After the incident with the brooch I am certain St. John is involved," Eldridge said, rising from his seat and turning to take in the view of the thoroughfare. "The men assigned to watch him have a gap in their accounts of his whereabouts the evening of the betrothal ball, an hour of time close enough to the stabbing to be suspicious. Although underlings could have performed the deed, I would think something of this delicacy would be a task he would perform himself. He's a bold one."

"I agree," Marcus said gruffly. St. John was not averse to doing his own dirty work. In fact, he seemed to prefer it.

"There is one person who can help us," Avery suggested. "The individual who scared away Lady Hawthorne's attacker."

Marcus shook his head. "No one came forward at the ball, and I certainly cannot interview everyone on the guest list without revealing the nature of my inquiry."

Eldridge clasped his hands behind his back and rocked on his heels. "Troubling to be sure. I wish we understood the contents of that journal. The key to this whole affair is locked away in there." He fell silent a moment and then, casually, he mentioned, "Lord Barclay came by this morning."

Marcus stifled a groan. "I cannot say I'm surprised."

"He came looking for James."

Avery nodded. "I will speak with him when he comes to

me. Hopefully, he will allow me to research the matter on his behalf."

"Ha!" Marcus laughed. "Those Chesterfields are a stubborn lot. I would not count on his easy complacency."

"He was a good agent," Eldridge mused. "I lost him when he married. If this would bring him back into the fold—" He shot a pointed glance over his shoulder.

"You once told me that young, foolishly adventurous agents are easy to acquire," Marcus reminded.

"Ah, but there is no substitute for experience." Eldridge returned to his chair with a slight smile. "But it's just as well. Emotional detachment is necessary to put the mission first. Barclay would lack that. As, I suspect, do you, Westfield. It is extremely possible that your emotional involvement with Lady Hawthorne will jeopardize her life."

Avery shifted nervously in his seat.

Marcus smiled grimly. "It already has. But it won't happen again."

Eldridge's gaze never wavered. "You are certain about that, are you?"

"Yes." He'd forgotten, for a few brief weeks, how deeply she could hurt him. He'd thought himself beyond that. Now he knew he was not. It was best, for both of them, that he keep his distance. He refused to need her to survive. She'd already proven she did not need him. First, with her elopement, and then with her ease in ending their affair. There was no doubt he was expendable to her.

"All men succumb eventually, Westfield," Eldridge said dryly. "You are in great company."

Marcus stood, effectively cutting off the line of discussion. "I shall continue to work on the journal. The wedding is only a fortnight hence, and then she'll be in my home, where she'll be far better protected."

Avery stood as well. "I will speak with Lord Barclay and see what can be done to allay his concerns."

"Keep me advised," Eldridge ordered. "As it stands, unless we learn more about the journal we can only wait, or use Lady Hawthorne to draw out her attacker. It won't be long before we must decide which course to take."

Sunlight sparkled in the puddles left by the early morning's light rain. The day was momentous, the day of his wedding, and Marcus turned from the window to finish dressing. He had ordered the creation of a jacket and breeches in a pearl grey with a silver waistcoat heavily embroidered with silk thread. From the top of his wigged head down to his diamond-studded heels, his valet took great pains to make Marcus's appearance perfect, and the act of dressing took well over an hour.

Once finished, he walked through the adjoining sitting room, then beyond into the lady's chamber. Most of Elizabeth's personal belongings had already arrived, and he'd scattered them about the room in an effort to make her feel welcome and less alienated. Touching her things had seemed so intimate, he hadn't allowed the servants to do it. He would keep his emotional distance as he had the last fortnight, but he had rights now and after all he'd been through for her, he would damn well enjoy them.

Glancing around the room one last time, Marcus made certain everything was where it should be. His gaze came to rest on the escritoire, where a small likeness of Lord Hawthorne sat. Marcus picked it up, the image bothering him as it always did. Not because of jealousy or misplaced possessiveness: No, the image disturbed him because of the niggling sense that he should be seeing something he was missing.

As often happened in recent days, his mood turned pensive. How different his future would have been had the handsome viscount lived. When Elizabeth married, Marcus had thought she would be forever out of his reach. Seduction had crossed his mind. Despite the Hawthorne title, he'd always thought of her as his, but when he'd returned to England she was already widowed, negating that course of action.

He returned the image to the escritoire, where it joined likenesses of William, Margaret, and Randall Chesterfield. The past was gone and best forgotten. Today, a great injustice that had been done to him would be righted, and then his life would return to some semblance of the normalcy he'd known before Elizabeth.

Moving downstairs, Marcus collected his hat and gloves before vaulting into his coach. He was one of the first people to arrive at the church and he breathed a sigh of relief to learn Elizabeth was already in the bride's ready room preparing for the ceremony. Truth was, he'd half feared she would fail to appear. Until she spoke her vows, he couldn't quite allow himself the satisfaction he longed to revel in.

Smiling, he spoke with family, friends, and important members of society as they arrived. With safety paramount, agents were spread out liberally among the guests. Aside from Talbot and James, who sat together, he was unaware of who they were, he knew only that they were there.

A curious sort by nature, he couldn't help cataloging the personages in the pews, wondering who amongst them lived an agent's life like he did. He also noted the marked reticence between peers and their wives, and wished he also felt such detachment from Elizabeth.

Would they have lost their minds, as he nearly had, if their spouses had been threatened? Was their every breath contingent upon the safety of their wives? He doubted it. It was unnatural, this fascination. Without its curse, his failure to protect Elizabeth would never have occurred, and he would not feel as restless as a caged animal.

Oddly, the only way he could conceive of finding peace was to wed himself to his torment. For four years, the loss of Elizabeth had been the thorn in his side. Now, he could pull it free. Now, he would be rid of the ache that plagued him.

From this moment on, his mission and his own sanity could take precedence. Elizabeth would be his, and the world would know it. Those who thought to harm her would know it. *She* would know it.

There would be no more running, no more chasing, no more frustration. He'd wanted closure.

Today he would have it.

Chapter 16

"You're trembling," Margaret murmured.

"It's cold."

"Then why are you perspiring?"

Glaring, Elizabeth met her sister-in-law's sympathetic gaze in the mirror.

Unperturbed, Margaret smiled. "You look beautiful."

Lowering her eyes, Elizabeth examined her appearance in the mirror. She'd chosen pale blue silk taffeta with elbow-length sleeves, matching skirt and open overskirt. The result was serene, an emotion she wished she felt at the moment.

She sucked in a shuddering breath and grimaced. Having sworn this day would never come, she was completely unprepared for the reality of it.

"Your spirits will improve once you stand with him," Margaret promised.

"Perhaps I'll feel worse," she muttered.

But a quarter hour later, as Elizabeth walked down the aisle on her father's arm, the sight of Marcus arrested her, lifted her, just as Margaret had predicted. He was resplendent in his finery and gazed at her so intensely she could see the emerald color of his irises even from a substantial distance.

There was more between them than just this physical space. Marcus's reputation and his work with Eldridge were great obstacles she wondered if they could surmount. He'd hinted at fidelity and agreed to consider leaving the agency, but he'd made no promises. If he failed to change his course on either account, she could grow to detest him. And if he married her for revenge, their arrangement was doomed before starting. She couldn't help but worry, couldn't help but be very afraid of the future.

"Are you certain this is the path you choose to take?" her father asked in a low tone.

Startled, Elizabeth glanced at him with wide eyes. He stared straight ahead, as aloof as ever, in much the same way Marcus had adopted in the last few weeks. "Why?" was all she could manage to say.

His lips pursed as he stared at the altar and the man who waited there. "I had hoped you would consider marrying for happiness."

If not for the multitude of observers she might have gaped. "I would not have expected such a statement from you."

He sighed and shot her a sidelong glance. "I would gladly suffer a thousand torments for the privilege of having your mother as long as I did."

Her heart ached for him and the emptiness she glimpsed in his eyes. "Father—"

"We can turn about, Elizabeth," he said gruffly. "Westfield's motives concern me."

As the doubts began to churn her stomach, she turned her head to study her groom. Marcus's mouth curved with blatant charm, a silent encouragement, and her heart stopped.

"Think of the scandal," she whispered.

He slowed his steps. "I care for nothing other than your well-being."

Her breath caught for a moment and her steps faltered. How long had she waited for some sign that she mattered at all to her pater? Long enough that she'd thought it an impossible dream. The unexpected support for a hasty retreat was not only astonishing, but very tempting. She studied him and the occupants of the church, then she looked at Marcus again. She saw the tiny step forward he took and the clenching of his fists, barely noticeable warnings that he would give chase should she flee.

It should have frightened her further, that almost imperceptible threat. Instead, she remembered how the sound of his voice in the garden had filled her with relief. She remembered the way he'd held her after the stabbing, and how the trembling of his arms and voice had betrayed the depths of his concern. And the nights in his arms, how she craved them. Her heart started to race, but it was not the urge to run that moved her.

She lifted her chin. "Thank you, Father. But I'm certain of my course."

Marcus glanced at his younger brother, who stood with him at the altar. Paul grinned, his brow arching in silent query. *Any doubts?* his look seemed to ask.

Marcus opened his mouth to whisper back when the sudden hush in the church drew his attention. Elizabeth entered beside her father and the sight of her took his breath away. Paul's low whistle just before the music swelled said his unspoken question had been answered.

Marcus had never seen a more beautiful bride.

His bride.

Muffled weeping moved his attention to his mother who sat tearfully in the front row. His youngest brother, Robert, held her fragile hand carefully in his and gazed at Marcus through gold-rimmed spectacles with a reassuring smile.

The soon-to-be Dowager Countess of Westfield was beside herself with joy. She'd adored Elizabeth upon their first meeting so many years ago, and now said that any woman who could move her eldest son to matrimony must be extraordinary indeed. Marcus had never quite managed to explain that *he* was dragging his fiancée to the altar, and not the reverse.

Even as he thought it, Elizabeth's steady steps faltered. She glanced around the church like a frightened doe. He stepped forward. She would not run. Not again. His heart raced with something akin to panic. Then she met his gaze, lifted her chin, and continued to approach him.

The ceremony began. And it was long. Too bloody long.

Eager to hasten the process, he repeated his vows with strength and conviction, his deep voice carrying across the packed pews. Elizabeth repeated her vows slowly and with great care, as if she were afraid to stumble over the words. He could see her trembling, felt how cold her hand was in his, and knew she was terrified. He squeezed her hand gently, reassuringly, but with unmistakable claim.

And then the deed was finally done.

Pulling her close, he kissed her, and was surprised at the ardor with which she kissed him back. Her taste flooded his mouth, intoxicated his senses, made him mad with desire. His forced abstinence weighed heavily between his legs, demanding the rights that were now his alone.

It was horribly scandalous.

He didn't care.

Marcus felt an anxious, unrestrained emotion well up inside of him as he stared at his wife. It was almost too much.

So he crushed it and looked away.

Elizabeth tried not to think too much while she prepared for her wedding night. Taking her time with her toilette, she glanced around the room, content to be surrounded by her own things even in a strange place. The chamber was beautiful and expansive, the walls lined with soft pink damask. Only two doors separated her from the room where she'd first made love to Marcus. The remembrance made her skin hot and her stomach clench. It had been so long since he'd taken her, just thought of the night to come made her shiver in anticipation.

Despite the endless desire she'd become accustomed to, it

was still terrifying to have married a man whose will was greater than her own. A man so determined to achieve the realization of his goals that nothing was allowed to stand in his way. Could she influence such a man? Convince him to change his ways? Perhaps change was not even possible and she was foolish to hope.

When she finished bathing, she instructed Meg to leave her hair down, then she excused her abigail for the night. Elizabeth walked to her bed where her night rail and robe awaited her. Both garments had been especially ordered for her trousseau. Admiring them, she brushed her fingertips over the gossamer-thin fabric and costly lace.

She paused as her wedding ring caught the candlelight. It was so different from the much simpler set chosen by Hawthorne. Marcus had given her a massive diamond ring, the large center stone surrounded by a multitude of rubies. It was impossible to ignore, a blatant claim to her, and if that was not enough, the Westfield crest was etched upon the band.

There was a quick rap at her bedroom door and Elizabeth moved to pick up the night rail, then thought better of it. Her husband was a man of voracious sexual appetite and his interest lately had been less than warm. If she hoped to keep him engaged, she would have to be more daring. She didn't have the experience his many lovers had, but she had enthusiasm. One could only hope that would be enough.

Disregarding the garments, she called for him to enter. She took a fortifying breath and turned around. Marcus opened the door and then came to a halt just inside. Dressed in a thick black satin robe, his body visibly tensed at the sight of her. Frozen on the threshold, his emerald eyes smoldered and a tingling awareness flared over her skin. Elizabeth fought back the urge to cover herself with her hands, lifting her chin in a display of courage she didn't feel.

His low and husky voice brought goose bumps to her skin. "Wearing no more than my ring, you are beyond beautiful."

He stepped inside and closed the door, his movements deceptively casual. But she was not deceived. She sensed the fine, taut alertness about him. She watched in fascination as the front of his robe twitched and then rose with his erection. Her mouth watered, her nails digging into her palms as she waited for the halves of the robe to part and reveal that part of him she coveted.

"You're staring, love."

His robe swirled gently around his legs as he crossed the room to her, his body drawing close enough that she could feel the warmth radiating from him. His scent of sandalwood and citrus surrounded her, and her nipples peaked tight and hard, spreading sharp tendrils of desire from her breasts to her sex. She bit back a moan. Her desire for him increased by the day, aggravated by the forced celibacy of the last month.

When had she become such a wanton?

"I—I've missed you," she exhaled, waiting desperately for his touch.

"Have you?" He stared down at her with a rapt expression and she returned the scrutiny, noting the rigidity of his jaw that belied the heat of his gaze. He'd grown so distant, a charming stranger. Then his hand was between her legs, his long middle finger slipping through the lips of her sex to glide through her cream. "Yes, I see you have."

She whimpered when he pulled away and Marcus soothed her with a soft murmur.

His hands moved without haste to the belt of his robe. He tugged the trailing ends free and parted the edges, revealing the rippling power of his abdomen and the hard, pulsing length of his cock. Framed by the ebony lining of his robe, his lean body was stunning.

Elizabeth tore her gaze upward and met his. She said what she needed him to know, needed him to understand. "You belong to me."

Wanting to break through the sudden chill in his features,

she lifted her hand, her fingertips drifting along the side of his throat and farther down his chest. He sucked in a breath, his skin heating under her touch.

Her mouth curved as she relished the power she held over him. She'd never known it could be like this, had never really wanted it to be like this, but he was hers now. That fact altered everything.

Marcus lifted her by the waist and took the one step to the bed. "Lady Westfield," he growled, setting her down on the very lip and surging forward, his cock piercing deep into her with a single heavy thrust.

Elizabeth cried out, writhing away from the unexpected and painful intrusion, but he held her fast. He forced himself over her, pressing her into the bed, his robe a silken cage around their joined bodies. His mouth captured hers in a devastating kiss, his tongue thrusting in a blatant rhythm that robbed her of her senses.

This was no careful, coaxing seduction, as their previous encounters had been. This was a claiming of the basest kind, one that left her momentarily stunned and confused. She knew his touch, her senses recognized his scent and the feel of his body, but the man himself was a stranger to her. So intent and brutally possessive, throbbing hot and hard inside her.

One large hand found her breast and squeezed roughly, breaking her temporary paralysis. His thighs tightened against hers as he slid a fraction deeper. She struggled beneath him, turning her head to gasp for air. His lips moved on, trailing down her cheek, his teeth nipping sharply at her earlobe.

"*You* belong to *me*," he said gruffly.

A threat. She stilled as realization hit.

He wanted her submission. The ring, his name, her desire . . . it was not enough to soothe him.

"Why take what I would give freely?" she whispered, wondering if perhaps it was the only way he could have her, the only way she'd ever given herself. She thought back, trying to remember a time when she'd tendered herself without duress.

He groaned and buried his face in her neck. "You've given me nothing freely. I've paid with blood for all that I have of you."

Elizabeth's hands slipped beneath his robe and caressed the rippling cords of his back. He arched into her touch, sweating in his need, grinding his hips desperately against hers until she soothed him with her voice. "Let me give you what you want."

Marcus clasped Elizabeth to his chest with a crushing grip, biting the top of her shoulder as her cunt rippled along his cock in a teasing caress. "Witch," he whispered, laving the indentions left by his teeth.

He'd come to her room with a singular purpose, to slake their mutual need and consummate the marriage so long in coming. It was meant to be a dance, one of which he knew all the steps, a carefully planned encounter without the unwanted abandoned intimacy. But she'd met him naked, gilded by firelight, hair tumbled about her shoulders and chin lifted with a Jezebel's pride. She'd stood there and said he belonged to her. All these years she'd cared nothing for him, and now, *now*, after all he'd suffered, she claimed the victory.

And she *had* won. He was ensnared, gripped tight by her lithe thighs and creamy depths, her fingers kneading and drifting across his back.

Lost in her embrace, he arched his spine upward and kissed a fiery trail down her throat to her breasts. He licked and savored the pale skin, stroking the sides with his hands, cupping their weight as they become heavy and taut. Her nipples peaked tight, an irresistible lure, and he bit one crest, worrying it with his teeth before laving the hardened flesh with leisurely laps of his tongue. Marking her. As he would mark her everywhere.

Only when she begged did his mouth open and engulf her completely. He suckled her with slow, deep, rhythmic pulls of his tongue and lips, shuddering as the sensation traveled through her body to milk his cock. He could come like this, just from the measured clench and release of her silky tissues. Enflamed by the thought, he hollowed his cheeks, increasing the suction. His eyes drifted closed, his body shuddered as his sac drew up. He swiveled his hips, rubbing her clitoris, and then groaned with her orgasm, releasing his need in burning hot streams of semen.

Gasping and only partially sated, he released her breast and rested his head upon it, wondering if he would ever have enough of her.

Her fingers drifted into his hair. "Marcus . . ."

He rose above her, his arms on either side of her shoulders, and Elizabeth stared up at her husband, attempting to gauge his odd mood. His handsome face was so austere, his eyes searching hers. And she quivered, almost afraid. He looked angry, with his narrowed emerald gaze and harshly drawn mouth. Then he pulled away, the warmth of his body leaving hers, and she was bereft. How could he be equally absorbed and distant?

Marcus stood above his wife, taking in the sight of her sprawled and flushed pink, her thighs spread wantonly, revealing all that he coveted. His erection, covered in her cream, grew cold, but didn't diminish. He watched, arrested, as his seed dribbled from between her legs. His hand reached forward, collected it on his fingertips, and spread it around the lips of her cunt, massaging the clitoris that peeped from its hood.

Mine, mine, mine . . . all mine . . .

Half mad with relief and pleasure and desire, he spread his semen around her sex, watching her arch and writhe, listening to her beg and plead with a detachment that was not detached at all.

Every inch of satin skin belonged to him, every raven hair on her head, every breath she took. For the rest of their lives he could touch her like this, own her like this.

All mine . . .

The thought made him hard as stone, swollen and heavy as if he hadn't just spent himself in her. He stepped forward again, took his cock in hand, and massaged her with the tip. "Take me inside you."

Half expecting her reticence, he groaned when she lifted her hips immediately, engulfing the sensitive head of his cock in liquid, burning heat. He arched his hips and filled her, falling onto his outstretched arms as he sank into the heart of her. It was heaven, the blazing clasp of her cunt around his cooled shaft. If only he could remain like this forever. But he couldn't. Despite how right it felt, it was all wrong.

Gripping her shoulders to pin her in place, Marcus pressed his face against the side of her neck and began to fuck her, his strokes fierce with his hunger, skin slapping against skin. Wrapping her legs around his hips, she rose to meet his every thrust, returning his ardor, holding nothing in reserve, shamelessly crying out on every downward plunge. He battered her with his lust, and she took it, accepted it as she'd promised she would.

"Yes," she cried, her nails in his back. "Marcus . . . Yes!"

It was like drowning, being sucked into a whirlpool, and he grit his teeth and fought against it. Yanking out of her encircling arms, he stood, feet flat on the rugged floor. One hand gripping the bed post, he withdrew from her body until only the tip remained encased, every nerve ending in his body screaming its protest.

Elizabeth burned. Everything burned—her skin, her sex, the roots of her hair. Frustrated tears wept from her eyes. "Don't deny me!"

"I should," he bit out. "For years I was denied."

Rising to brace on her elbows, she stared at the place where they joined, where she ached. She had no power in this, none.

And she would acknowledge that if she must. "You feel so good," she choked out. "I will do anything—"

"Anything?" He rewarded her with a scant inch.

"Yes. For God's sake, Marcus."

He thrust deep and withdrew. Swiveled his hips and plunged. A shallow dip and then gone. Teasing her. And she watched the erotic display, the rippling of his abdomen as he fucked with such skill, the tensing of his thighs as he used his thick, beautiful cock to drive her mad.

She wanted to scream. Her skin was damp with sweat, her limbs trembling, her sex weeping. "What do you want from me?"

Continuing to vary the pace and depth of his fucking, his eyes never left her face. "Everything."

"You have it! I have nothing left."

He took her then, like a ravening beast, gripping the bedpost with white-knuckled force for leverage, the thrusts powerful enough to move her up the bed. He followed, pumping hard and deep with little care for her comfort.

Unable and unwilling to deny him, Elizabeth gave herself up to the turbulence of her husband's passion, her orgasm breaking with a cry of relief.

Marcus held himself above her, watching her abandon, absorbing her trembling, feeling her body tighten exquisitely around him even as he continued to take her.

He could not remember any time when he had been more caught up in the sexual act. His entire body was covered in a slick sheen of sweat, his hips working tirelessly to prolong her pleasure and hurtle himself toward his own. He growled with the sheer animal enjoyment of making love to his wife, a fiercely passionate woman who goaded his desire and then met it with her own.

Feeling, emotion, need—they both worked together to take him to a level of sensation he had never experienced before. His heart aching, he gasped her name as he poured himself into her, wishing desperately for it to be enough, but knowing it would never be. The bottomless well of his need was terrifying. Even now, spewing into her, clutching her desperately, gritting his teeth until his jaw ached, he still wanted more.

Would always want more, even when there was no more to be had.

He rolled from her as if she burned him. His chest heaving, he stared at the canopy, waiting for his eyes to focus, waiting for the room to cease its spinning. The moment it did, he left his wife's bed.

Her scent on his skin, her soft protest behind him, Marcus belted his robe and left her room.

He didn't look back.

Chapter 17

Elizabeth woke to a bright ray of sunshine that snuck between the tiny gap in the curtains and slanted across her face. Stretching, she became aware of the soreness between her legs, a pressing reminder of her husband's rough lovemaking and even rougher departure.

She slid out of bed slowly and stood for a moment contemplating what she now knew to be true. Marcus had married her for his vengeance and he'd gotten it from her tenfold, because some time between the horrendous evening in the Chesterfield garden and yesterday, she'd grown to care for him. A foolish, painful error.

Resigned to the fate she'd walked into with eyes wide open, she called for Meg and the footmen to bring up hot water for her bath, determined to scrub her husband's scent from her skin.

She'd cried the first and last time over Marcus Ashford. Why she'd thought their marriage would be a deeper union was something she couldn't recollect in the bright light of day. She imagined it was the sex. Too many orgasms had rattled her brain. In all fairness, his boredom had been obvious for weeks. Marcus had made no effort to hide it. Still, he'd been solicitous and courteous up until the night previous, and she had no expectation that he would change now that he'd exacted his revenge. She would afford him the same courtesy in return. So her second marriage would be much like her first, distant personages sharing a name and roof. It was not unusual.

Despite these mental reassurances, she felt ill and weepy, and her chest ached badly. The thought of facing Marcus nauseated her. When she finished with her toilette, she looked in the mirror, further distraught to see the faint shadows under her eyes that betrayed her lack of sleep and hours spent crying. It was best she leave the house for a while. This was not home yet, it was very much Marcus's bastion, and the memories she'd made in her history with the house were not pleasant. She took a deep breath and headed down to the foyer.

Passing through the hall, she looked at the clock and saw it was still early morning. Because of the hour, she was surprised to find Marcus's family at breakfast. She felt dwarfed as her tall brothers-in-law rose at her entry. They were a pleasant lot, the Ashfords, but at the moment she wished only to be alone to lick her wounds.

"Good morning, Elizabeth," greeted the lovely Dowager Countess of Westfield.

"Good morning," she returned with the best smile she could manage.

Elaine Ashford was a beautiful and gracious woman with golden hair the color of fresh butter and eyes of emerald green that became translucent when she smiled. "You are up early this morning."

Paul grinned. "Is Marcus still abed?" When Elizabeth nodded, he tossed his head back and laughed aloud. "He's upstairs sleeping off his wedding night, and you are down here dressed flawlessly and ready to go out, unless I miss my guess."

Elizabeth blushed and smoothed her skirts.

Smiling affectionately, Paul said, "Now we see how our

beautiful new sister has led our bachelor brother to the altar. Twice."

Robert choked on his eggs.

"Paul," Elaine admonished, her eyes lit with reluctant amusement. "You are embarrassing Elizabeth."

Shaking her head, Elizabeth was unable to hide her smile. Due to her injury, and the need to hide the knowledge of it, she'd had precious little time to become reacquainted with Marcus's family. But she knew from her earlier association that they were a light-hearted, mirthful group with a wicked sense of humor, due considerably to Paul's penchant for good-natured teasing. That he chose to tease her so informally made her feel accepted into their tight circle, and relieved some of the tension that made her shoulders ache.

Although physically of the same height and breadth of shoulder as Marcus, Paul had black hair and warm, chocolate brown eyes. Three years younger than Marcus and equally handsome, Paul could take Society, and its eager debutantes, by storm if he wished, which he didn't. Instead, he preferred to remain in Westfield. Elizabeth had yet to discern why he chose to isolate himself in the country, but it was a mystery she intended to unravel at some point.

Robert, the youngest, was nearly the spitting image of Marcus with the same rich sable hair and emerald green eyes, which were charmingly enhanced by spectacles. He was an extremely quiet and studious fellow, physically just as tall as his brothers, but much leaner and less muscular due to his bookish nature. Robert was interested in all things scientific and mechanical. He could wax poetic about any number of dull and boring topics, but all of the Ashfords indulged him when he took his nose out of his books and deigned to speak with them. At the present moment, that nose was buried in the newspaper.

Paul stood. "If you will excuse me, ladies. I have an appointment with the tailor this morn. Since I rarely come to

Town, I must exploit the opportunity to keep abreast of the latest fashions." He glanced at Robert, still engrossed in the paper. "Robert. Come along. You require new clothes more than I."

Robert glanced up, eyes blinking. "For what purpose would I dress in the latest fashions?"

Shaking his head, Paul muttered, "Never met a more handsome chap who could care less about his appearance." He walked over to Robert's chair and slid it back easily. "You are coming with me, brother, whether you like it or not."

With a long suffering sigh and a covetous glance at the newspaper, Robert followed Paul out of the house.

Elizabeth watched the exchange with affectionate amusement, liking both of her new brothers immensely.

Elaine arched her brows as she lifted her teacup. "Don't let his surliness disturb you overmuch."

"Paul's?"

"No, Marcus's. Marriage is an adjustment, that's all. I still wish you would consider going away. Allow yourselves to settle in without the pressures you'll find here in Town."

"We intend to, once the Parliamentary session is over." It was the excuse Marcus had suggested they supply. With the journal a hanging weight over her head, they couldn't afford to leave London. Waiting until the end of the Season seemed the reply least likely to raise suspicion.

"But you are unhappy with this decision, are you not?"

"Why would you say that?"

Offering a sad smile, Elaine said, "You've been crying."

Aghast to have her torment known, Elizabeth took a step back. "A bit tired, but I'm certain a drive in the crisp morning air will cure that."

"A lovely idea. I'll join you." Elaine pushed back from the table.

Stuck in a position where refusal would be rude, Elizabeth released a deep breath and nodded. With a strict warning to the staff to leave the lord of the house undisturbed, Elizabeth and Elaine departed.

As the town coach lurched into motion, Elaine noted, "You have a fair number of outriders to accompany you. I believe you are more heavily guarded than the king."

"Westfield is a bit overprotective."

"How like him to be so concerned."

Elizabeth seized the opportunity to learn more about her husband. "I've wondered, is Marcus much like his father?"

"No. Paul is most like the late earl, in appearance and disposition. Robert is a bit of an anomaly, God love him. And Marcus is by far the most charming, but the more reserved of the lot. Always has been difficult to collect his aim until after he's achieved it. He hides his thoughts well behind that polished façade. I've yet to witness him losing his temper, but he has one I'm certain. He is, after all, his father's son and Westfield was a man of high passion."

Sighing inwardly, Elizabeth acknowledged the truth in the words spoken to her. Despite hours of physical intimacy, she knew little about the man she'd wed, an exquisite creature who drawled when he spoke and shared few of his thoughts. Only when they were alone did she see the passion in him, both his fury and desire. In her own way, she felt blessed to know those sides of him, when his beloved family did not.

Elaine leaned across the carriage and captured one of Elizabeth's hands with her own. "I knew the moment I saw you together how perfect you would be for him. Marcus has never appeared so engaged."

Elizabeth flushed. "I would not have thought you would endorse me after what transpired four years ago."

"I subscribe to the 'reason for everything' school of thought, my dear. Life has always come too easily for Marcus. I'd prefer to think your . . . *delay* contributed to his grounding these last few years."

"You are too kind."

"You wouldn't think so if you knew the things I said about you four years ago. When Marcus left the country I was devastated."

Riddled with guilt, Elizabeth squeezed Elaine's hand and was touched when her hand was squeezed in return.

"Yet you married him anyway and he has grown much from the man who first offered for you. I hold no ill will toward you, Elizabeth, none at all."

I wish Marcus felt the same, Elizabeth thought silently, and not a little sadly.

The coach slowed to a halt. Before they had the opportunity to alight from the carriage, the employees of the shops lined the curb to greet them. Having spied the crest emblazoned on the door, they were anxious to assist the new Countess of Westfield and reap the rewards of her husband's largesse.

The morning passed swiftly, and Elizabeth found a respite from her melancholy with Elaine, appreciating the older woman's suggestions and advice while relishing the maternal companionship she'd lacked all her life.

Elaine paused in front of a milliner's window and sighed at a lovely creation displayed in the window.

"You should try it on," Elizabeth urged.

Elaine blushed and confessed, "I have a fondness for millinery."

Waving her mother-in-law inside, Elizabeth strolled to the neighboring perfumery, leaving the two outriders who followed her at the door.

Once inside, she stopped before a display of bath oils and removed the stopper from a bottle to sample the fragrance. Disliking the scent, she put it down and picked up another.

"I hear congratulations are in order, Lady Westfield," rasped a masculine voice behind her.

Startled, she almost dropped the fragile bottle, her stomach tightening in recognition of the unique voice. She spun to face Christopher St. John, her heart racing and eyes wide.

In the light of day, without a mask or wig to hide his features, he was a splendid looking specimen, angelic in appearance with his dark blond hair and vivid blue eyes.

Arrested at first by his exceptional handsomeness, she quickly came to her senses and changed her mind. Fallen angel was a more apt description. The signs of hard living were etched on his countenance. Shadows marred the skin beneath those amazing eyes, betraying a life that had no place for restful slumber.

His lips curved derisively. "Has no one told you it's not polite to stare?"

"Do you intend to stab me again?" she asked curtly, taking a step back and bumping against the display. "If so, get on with it."

St. John threw his head back and laughed, drawing the attention of the clerk behind the counter who gazed at him with blatant admiration. "Feisty, aren't you? I can see why Nigel liked you so well."

Her eyes widened as the familiar address. "And how would you know how my husband felt?"

"I know a great many things," he replied arrogantly.

"Ah yes, I forgot." She was frustrated by his confidence in the face of her fear. "You somehow learned of Hawthorne's journal and have been threatening me for it ever since." Elizabeth gripped the bottle of bath oil so tightly her hands ached.

St. John glanced down. "Put the bottle aside before you hurt yourself."

"Don't worry about me. It's *you* who most stands to be hurt by it." She hefted the bottle in warning before dropping it carelessly onto the shelf, ignoring the roiling in her stomach. "What do you want?"

St. John stared at her, his face reflecting an odd mixture of emotions. "It took me all morning to lose those lackeys Westfield has hounding me."

Through the glass front of the store she saw the backs of the two outriders who stood guard. "How did you get in here?"

"Through the rear entrance. It has been extremely difficult to approach you with those damned outriders and Westfield guarding you at all times."

"That is the point."

He scowled. "The first time we met, I had only a few moments to speak with you. I couldn't explain."

"Explain now."

"First, you must know I would never hurt you." His jaw tightened. "I'm attempting to assist you."

"Why would you wish to do that?" she scoffed. "I am married to a man who would see you hanged if he could."

"You are my brother's widow," he said quietly. "That is all that matters to me."

"*What?*" Physically thrown off balance by his statement, Elizabeth reached behind her in an effort to steady herself and instead knocked over several bottles, which crashed to the floor and shattered, filling the room with the cloying scent of flowers and musk.

"You lie!" But the moment she denied it, she knew it was true.

Upon closer examination, the similarities were obvious. Nigel's hair had been the same dark wheat color and his eyes had been blue although not as brilliant as St. John's. The nose was the same, the shape of the jaw and chin, the placement of the ears.

"Why would I?" he asked simply.

She examined the pirate in greater detail. His mouth was not the same. Nigel's had been less wide, the lips thinner, and his skin had been softer, more pampered. Nigel had sported a mustache and Van Dyke. Christopher's face was clean-shaven. But the differences were minor. Had she known to look, she would have caught the resemblance earlier.

Brothers.

The color drained from her face.

Her lungs sought air, but the restriction of her corset made it difficult to breathe. She felt dizzy and her legs gave way, but St. John caught her to him before she fell. He dipped her over a steely arm, his hand tilting her head back to better open her airway. "Easy," he soothed in his raspy voice. "Take a breath. Now another."

"Damn you," she gasped. "Have you no tact? No sense to know better than to spring such news on me with no warning?"

"Ah, your charm is once again in evidence." He smiled and looked for a moment very much like Nigel. "Keep breathing as deeply as you can. I have no notion of how you women suffer your corsets."

The bells above the door chimed merrily.

"The dowager has arrived," he murmured in warning.

"Elizabeth!" Elaine cried, her voice growing louder as she rushed closer. "Unhand her immediately, sir!"

"I apologize, my lady," St. John replied with a smile that was charming even from Elizabeth's underside view. "But I am unable to oblige you. If I release Lady Westfield she will certainly collapse to the floor."

"Oh," said the shop girl as she joined the muddle. "Christopher St. John."

"St. John?" murmured Elaine, trying to place the name.

"'E's famous," supplied the girl.

"You mean infamous," grumbled Elizabeth as she struggled to right herself.

Christopher laughed.

Elaine frowned. Uncertain of how to handle the situation she fell back on her manners. "Thank you, Mr. St. John, for your assistance. I'm certain The Earl will be most appreciative."

The full lips curved with wry amusement. "I sincerely doubt that, my lady."

Elizabeth struggled against his thickly muscled chest. "Release me," she hissed.

He chuckled as he straightened her, making certain she was steady on her feet before dropping his arms away. Then he turned and paid the besotted shop girl for the broken items.

"Elizabeth, are you unwell?" Elaine asked with obvious concern. "Perhaps it is too soon after your illness for you to be out."

"I should have eaten this morning. I felt faint for a moment, but it's passed now."

St. John returned to their sides, gave a courtly bow, and made his excuses.

"Wait!" Elizabeth hurried after him. "You cannot simply walk away after telling me something like that."

Christopher lowered his voice, glancing over her head at the dowager countess. "Does your mother-in-law know of this affair?"

"Of course not."

"Then it's not wise to discuss this now." He collected his hat from atop the bin near the rear hallway where he'd left it. "I will find you again soon. In the meantime, please be careful and trust no one. I would never forgive myself if something untoward happened to you."

It was shortly before luncheon when Elizabeth and Elaine returned home. They parted on the second floor landing, both retreating to their rooms to change their gowns. Elizabeth was exhausted, hungry, and totally confused by St. John's revelations, a combination that gave her a splitting headache.

What was she to do now?

She couldn't share St. John's claims of kinship until she knew them to be true. And if they were, her marriage would be a disaster. Marcus truly hated St. John and had wed her for reasons best left unconsidered. What would he do if he knew? Despite how she wished it, she couldn't see him considering it of no consequence. Certainly it would mean something to him, and Eldridge as well, that the man they pursued with a vengeance was connected to her in so personal a way. And William. All these years it was St. John who bore the blame for nearly killing him. But was that true? Was the pirate so cold and calloused as she'd been led to believe? And Nigel . . . *Dear God, Nigel.* Working for Eldridge to hunt his own brother. Or perhaps he'd assisted St. John in his activities, which made him a traitor.

She needed time to think and contemplate the ramifications of what she'd learned today. As it was, she was barely able to walk, her steps dragging and her stomach growling. Later, once she was of firmer mind, she would reason out how to share the news with her husband.

Entering her room, she closed the door. She moved to collapse in the large wingback chair by the fireplace and started in surprise to find Marcus sitting there.

"Good heavens, Marcus! You gave me a fright."

He rose from the chair and Elizabeth wondered if it was her lack of sleep that made him appear taller and more menacing. "Surely not so much of a fright as I received when I discovered you had left the house," he drawled.

Her chin lifted in response to the sudden leap of her heart. Dressed for riding, he was impossibly handsome and she hated to discover that she still wanted him, even after crying over him all night. "Such care for my well-being. Unfortunate that you had none for me last night."

When she attempted to pass him, his hand whipped out and caught her upper arm, dragging her to him. "I heard no complaints," he growled.

"Perhaps if you'd stayed longer you would have."

"If I'd stayed longer, there would be no complaints at all."

She yanked free of his grip, her chin quivering at his words, which betrayed his understanding of the pain he inflicted. "Leave me and take your arrogance with you. I must change for luncheon."

"Despite being *de trop*, I believe I'll stay," he said softly, though the challenge in his eyes was hard.

"I don't want you here." His presence renewed the unhappiness she'd spent all morning trying to forget.

"And I did not want you venturing out without me. Sometimes we don't attain the things we desire."

"How well I know it," she muttered, ringing for her abigail.

He released a breath that could only be described as frustrated. "Why must you deliberately ignore the danger?"

"I took the outriders with me and as you can see, I am home and all in one piece. You didn't mind when I went out before. Am I to be a prisoner now that we're wed?"

"You have not been out since the stabbing. The danger is greater now, and well you know it."

Elizabeth dropped into her gilt vanity chair and gazed at his angry reflection in the mirror.

Marcus eyed her closely before resting his large hands on her shoulders and squeezing so tightly she flinched. He opened his mouth as if to speak and then a soft rap came at the door.

For the next half hour he watched as her abigail helped her to dress. He said nothing, but his stifling presence made both her and the servant uncomfortable. By the time she finished changing she was certain she was about to expire from hunger and the thick tension radiating from her husband. She was greatly relieved when they reached the main floor and joined his family for the meal. She settled into her seat and ate with as much decorum as she could manage considering how long she'd gone without food.

"I am relieved to see you feeling better, Elizabeth," Elaine said. "I thank the Lord you were caught by that St. John fellow before you fell to injury, although he did seem—"

"Could you repeat that, Mother?" Marcus said with dangerous softness.

Elizabeth winced and ate with greater haste.

"Surely your wife mentioned her near faint this morn?" Elaine shot a questioning glance down the table.

"As a matter of fact, she did not." Setting his knife and fork down with unnatural care, he offered a grim smile and asked, "Did you say St. John?"

Elaine blinked in obvious confusion.

Elizabeth's stomach clenched in apprehension. She should say something, she knew, but her throat was so tight she couldn't manage even one word.

The sudden pounding of Marcus's fist on the table startled everyone. Only the plates rattling sharply together broke the ensuing stunned silence. He slid his chair back and stood, placing his palms flat on the table. His glowering face had Elizabeth quaking in her chair. She held her breath.

"At what point did you intend to share this with me?" he roared.

The Ashfords sat with mouths agape, utensils paused in mid-air.

Galvanized by their horror, Elizabeth pushed back from the table and stood. Paul and Robert leapt to their feet.

"My lord," she began. "If you would prefer to—"

"Do not try to sway me with sudden docility, Lady Westfield." He walked around the table. "What did he want? By God, I'll kill him!"

She tried again. "Might I suggest the study?"

Paul sidestepped neatly into his path. Marcus glared, then moved to the sideboard and poured a hefty ration of brandy.

"I didn't mention it directly, because I knew it would upset you."

Marcus stared at her as if she'd grown two heads, then he downed his drink in one gulp and left the room, his handsome face set in harsh, unyielding lines. She heard the front door slam behind him.

Paul whistled softly.

"Good heavens," gasped Elaine, collapsing backwards in her chair. "He was *angry*."

Robert shook his head. "I would not believe it if I hadn't seen it with my own eyes. Can hardly believe it now."

All eyes turned, awestruck, to look at Elizabeth who stood trembling. She inhaled a shaky breath. "I apologize. I realize you are unaccustomed to seeing him in such a state. I regret you had to witness it today."

Robert frowned. "St. John. The name sounds familiar."

"I should explain." She sighed. "Marcus suspects St. John is responsible for the attacks on vessels belonging to Ashford Shipping, but there is no evidence to support that."

"Was it simply unfortunate that he happened to be in such close proximity to you?" asked Elaine. "I thought it odd for him to be perusing soaps and bath oils."

Elizabeth searched for an explanation. "He was a close friend of Hawthorne's. When our paths cross, he pays his respects."

Robert removed his spectacles and began to polish the lenses. "Is St. John aware of Marcus's suspicions about him?"

"Yes."

"Then he should bloody well stay away from you and keep his respects to himself," Paul growled.

Elaine tapped her fingers against her water glass. "You did not appear to care much for him yourself, Elizabeth."

"He is a stranger to me."

"And for Marcus to be goaded into such a temper over the whole affair," Elaine continued, "well, I've never seen the like."

"He was very angry," Elizabeth agreed, crestfallen. She'd never seen him so furious. That his fury had driven him to leave the house made her sick to her stomach. Certainly she was angry at him as well, but this gulf between them seemed as wide as when she'd been married to Hawthorne. She stepped away from the table. "I pray you will excuse me."

Climbing the stairs, Elizabeth considered the events of the

day with a heavy heart. Marcus was important to her. She'd known that when she chose to marry him, and though she'd tried to discount it when he'd treated her so coldly, it remained immutable. Now that their bond, as tentative as it was, was threatened, she understood the depth of her attachment.

This morning the distance between them had been entirely her husband's doing. Now she too contributed to their estrangement. Perhaps if he cared for her they could meet in the middle, but she'd destroyed whatever tenderness he'd felt for her four years ago.

And she finally understood just how much she had lost.

Chapter 18

Elizabeth woke to damp skin at her back and warm hands on her body, one wrapped in her hair and the other stroking her thigh. Her toes were curled, her nipples hard, her body already aware, even though her mind was not.

She whimpered. Marcus had been gone for hours, all through the afternoon and late into the night. She had cried herself to sleep again, after she'd sworn she wouldn't, and the feel and smell of him against her was both a balm and a barb. His cock, hard and hot, snuggled in the valley between her buttocks, a silent promise of his amorous intent.

"Hush," he said softly, his mouth nuzzling her throat, his wet hair cooling her suddenly feverish skin. Gripping her inner thigh, he lifted her leg and anchored it on his own, his fingers drifting to the curls between her legs. His touch was gentle, coaxing, once again the lover she craved and not the fiercely possessive husband who'd claimed her the night before.

With skill born of much practice and intimate knowledge, Marcus parted the lips of her sex with reverent fingers and dipped inside, swirling around her clitoris and the opening to her body with a callused fingertip, the roughness of which heightened her pleasure almost unbearably. Desperate, she undulated helplessly against his hard body. "Please . . ."

"My wife," he exclaimed, his tongue swirling around the

shell of her ear, his breath hot against the newly damp flesh. "Always on fire. Naked in her bed, and waiting for my attentions."

He stroked through her cream and then slipped inside her, thrusting into the drenched walls of her sex with maddening leisure. *In and out.* Just that one digit, not nearly enough to satisfy, but enough to make her beg for more.

"Marcus!" She struggled to turn, to move, to take what she wanted, but his arm tightened and pinned her still.

"Relax, and I'll let you come."

Elizabeth stilled a tremor shaking her body as his single finger was joined by another, the deep plunge and withdrawal sounding wetly over her panting breaths. She hitched her leg higher, opening herself wider, and he fisted his hand in her hair and arched her neck back.

Turning her head, she met his avid mouth with her own, her tongue thrusting along his in a frenzy of desire. Her eagerness goaded him, broke his rigid control. The shift was tangible, his frame tensing behind her, his cock swelling even further between them, his hips grinding forward.

She gasped as his thumb rubbed her clitoris, the barely-there pressure increasing her thrashing. At her back she felt the rapid rise and fall of his chest, in her mouth she caught his harsh exhalation. Her skin was coated with a fine sheen of sweat and she rode his thrusting fingers with greater and greater urgency.

"Please!" she cried, clenching around his fingers in her quest to orgasm. "I need you."

Marcus shifted, his fingers sliding free to reach for his cock. Then he was there, the wide flared head breaching her and pushing inside. His hand, drenched in her cream, cupped her breast, pinched her nipple. And deeper he slid, a thick pulsing possession.

"Yes," she hissed struggling to meet him, to hurry him, to take the long length of him.

His groan in her ear enflamed her. That she could bring him such pleasure while lost in her own was an intoxicating power.

And still he pressed into her.

But it was not enough. The curve of her buttocks kept him from the full depths she craved, and she wanted *him*, all of him. Not just his cock and his hand at her breast, but his body over hers, his eyes locked on hers. The gulf between them was there, widened by the hours he'd spent away from her today, but in this there was no division. In this, they could be one.

"You're not deep enough," she complained, wiggling her bottom against his pelvis, crushing the curls at the base of his shaft.

He growled. "Greedy vixen."

"You made me this way." She cupped her hand over his, kneading her breast with his hand, bearing down on his rigid cock with her hips. "Roll me over," she urged, her voice husky with want. "Fuck me deeply. Let me hold you."

It was the last that moved him. He yanked free of her with a curse, pulling her onto her back so he could loom over her. Elizabeth spread her legs wide in welcome and moaned aloud when he sank to the hilt inside of her.

He stilled then, staring down at her in the faint light from the banked fire. Backlit as he was, she couldn't see his features, but his eyes glittered with an unmistakable hunger.

Her heart ached with longing. Marcus Ashford belonged to her, and yet he would never truly be hers.

At least she had this. His passion, his desire. It would have to be enough since it was all he would give her. The feeling of his cock stroking in deep inner caresses, the clenching of his hard, muscular buttocks as he propelled himself into her, the scent of his skin, heated and damp with sweat, the sound of his guttural cries of pleasure.

She wrapped her arms around him and held him as if she would never let go, absorbing what she could of him, until finally, with silent tears, she sank into blissful relief with him.

*   *   *

Flat on his back, Marcus stared up through the darkness to the canopy above. Against his side Elizabeth curled, her thigh atop his, her arm across his waist. The warm, soft feel of her curves was heaven after the loneliness of their wedding night. Dawn had arrived without him sleeping a wink. He'd paced for hours, fighting the urge to return to her, to hold her, as he had during the nights of their affair. He'd thought the physical distance would help him find objectivity, but when he awoke to find her gone, he'd realized how hopeless that endeavor was.

Their row, and the gulf it created, had shown him the folly in pushing her away. Damn it, she was his *wife*! He'd waited all these years to have her, only to turn away from her once she was his.

Elizabeth stirred, and then sat up. Heedless of her nakedness, she settled back on her heels. She presented such a vision of loveliness Marcus almost forgot to breathe. Wanting to see her in all her glory, he slid from the bed to light the bedside taper.

"If you walk out that door, don't visit me again," she said coldly.

He stilled, fighting the urge to snap back. While her threat to bar him from her bed was not one he would accept, *ever*, he understood it was his own churlish behavior that prompted her to throw down the gauntlet.

"I simply wish to throw some light on the situation."

She made no sound, but he could sense her sudden relief and closed his eyes. He had every right to protect her, and his goal had been worthy, but the execution had been a terrible mistake. How much damage had he inflicted? *She said nothing of St. John to him . . . she didn't trust him . . .*

"Are you still angry?" she asked hesitantly.

He sighed aloud. "I haven't yet decided. What happened today? Tell me everything."

Behind him, she shifted uncomfortably and his hackles

rose. "St. John approached me. H-he claims to want to help me. I believe he—"

"In what way did he offer to help?"

"He didn't say. Your mother arrived. He was unable to finish speaking."

"Dear God," he exclaimed, horrified at the thought of St. John in such close proximity to his wife and his mother.

"He knows who desires Hawthorne's journal."

"Of course he does." His voice was gritty with renewed anger. He should have killed the pirate.

Leaving the bed, Marcus took a moment to stoke the fire and relight the extinguished taper. Then he returned to Elizabeth and eyed her suspiciously. "You are not the type of woman who succumbs to fits of vapors. You forget I have seen you shoot a man without a qualm. You are hiding something from me." He arched a brow in silent query.

Her gaze met his.

"Why didn't you tell me earlier, Elizabeth?"

"I was feeling cross."

Marcus narrowed his gaze. He knew she could be spiteful when angered, but she was not stupid. Anger alone would not prevent her from protecting herself. Something was amiss, he could feel it. She was attempting to conceal information and he considered all possibilities. Perhaps the pirate had threatened her in some manner. If so, he intended to discern the cause and attend to it directly. More than he already had.

"Where did you go?" she asked when the silence stretched out.

"To locate St. John, of course."

Her eyes widened and then dropped to his torso. She gaped. "Look at you! You've been hurt."

"He revealed even less information than you, dear wife. But I'm certain he now understands the foolishness of approaching you again."

"What did you do?" Her fingertips drifted with heartening concern to the spreading bruise that marred his ribs.

He shrugged, completely unaffected by her horrified gaze. "St. John and I simply engaged in casual discourse."

She poked brutally into the swelling and he winced. "*That* does not come from talking," she argued. "And look at your hand." She examined his swollen knuckles and shot him a chastising glance.

Marcus grinned. "Better you should look at St. John's face."

"Ridiculous. I want you to stay away from him, Marcus."

"I will," he agreed, "If he stays away from you."

"Aren't you curious as to what manner of help he's offering?"

Marcus grunted. "He made no offer of assistance to me. He is deceiving you, love. Attempting to win your trust so you will give the book to him."

Elizabeth opened her mouth to argue further, then thought better of it. It was best if Marcus didn't dig too far into Christopher St. John. It was miraculous that nothing more than blows were exchanged. She marveled at her husband's restraint. That the pirate continued his activities chafed Marcus, she had no doubt, but he forced himself to wait. For what, she was not certain. There must be something Eldridge wanted with St. John, or they would have disposed of him long ago.

She was startled when Marcus reached for her hand and tugged her face-first onto the bed. He rolled over her, caging her to the mattress. It was then she noted his erection, the tip of it pressing into the curve of her derriere.

"You are my wife," he growled in her ear. "I expect you to tell me of the things that happen in your life, to share things with me, even if they seem inconsequential, but most especially when the matter is so dire. I will not tolerate your lying to me or withholding things from me. Do I make myself clear?"

She pursed her lips. The brute.

He thrust his hips forward and his cock glided through the valley between her buttocks, his path eased by the weeping head. "I will not have you putting your life in danger. You should never leave the house without me. Can you understand how worried I was? Wondering if you were in danger . . . wondering if you needed me."

"You are aroused," she replied, surprised.

"You are naked," he said simply, as if only that was enough. "You must learn to trust me, Elizabeth." His lips moved against her shoulder as he stroked himself with her prone body. "I will try to be worthy of it."

Elizabeth's hands fisted in the sheets and she hid her sudden tears. "I'm sorry I made you angry."

Marcus nuzzled her throat. "I apologize to you, as well."

"I accept, on the condition you share my bed." Elizabeth moaned as he thrust again, a slow deliberate glide that left a damp trail behind. Heat blossomed instantly. With a forlorn sigh, she closed her eyes. She should have told him the truth when she had the chance. Now he would always wonder why she hid it from him.

"My bed is bigger," he drawled, slightly breathless.

Her heart swelled with tenderness. The urge to tell him about her kinship with St. John was nearly overwhelming. But now was not the time.

She arched her hips upward impatiently. "If we switched locations, would you hurry?"

Lifting enough to allow her to her knees, he entered her from behind with a single powerful stroke.

"Sweet Elizabeth," he groaned, his cheek to her back. "We can switch rooms tomorrow."

Elizabeth waited in the far reaches of the garden. Pacing with impatience, she spun about quickly as she heard approaching footsteps.

"Mr. James! Thank God, you've come."

Avery stopped before her, frowning. "Why have you sent for me?" He glanced around. "Where is Lord Westfield?"

She took his arm and tugged him behind a tree. "I require your assistance and Westfield must not know of it."

"I beg your pardon? Your husband is the agent assigned to assist you."

She gripped his arm tighter to convey her urgency. "Christopher St. John approached me yesterday. He claims to be brother to Hawthorne. I must know the truth."

Avery was stunned into silence.

Looking over his shoulder, she watched the path behind him. "Westfield was furious when he learned of the meeting. He left the house to search for St. John." She lowered her voice. "They exchanged blows."

Avery's mouth quirked with a rare smile. "Well, then. All was well."

"How can you say that?" she cried.

"Lord Westfield was merely making a point. And releasing some steam in the process."

"How can you condone such rash behavior?"

"I do not condone it, Lady Westfield, but I can understand his motivation. Your husband is an excellent agent. I am certain he did not go into the encounter without careful planning. He would never have allowed emotion to rule his actions."

Elizabeth snorted. "I assure you, he was highly strung when he departed."

Avery tried to look reassuring. "I believe Lord Westfield is more than capable of handling this matter, if you will just trust him to do so."

"I cannot go to him with conjecture." She clasped her hands together imploringly.

"What is it you would ask of me that you would not ask of your husband?"

"I need you to research St. John's story. If what he says is true, we must wonder at the irony of two brothers working on opposite sides of the law. Hawthorne was killed and my brother wounded while investigating St. John. That cannot be a coincidence." She clutched his hand. "And Lord Eldridge must remain ignorant of this development."

"Why?"

"Because he would certainly tell Westfield. I'm not certain how my husband will take the news. I need some time to sort this out."

"You sound as if you believe."

Elizabeth nodded miserably. "I have no reason not to. The resemblance between St. John and Hawthorne is startling, and the tale is so fantastic how can it not be true?"

"I fear you may be doing a disservice to his lordship."

"A little more time," she begged. "It's all I ask. I promise to tell him everything you discover."

He released a long-suffering sigh. "Very well. I will investigate, and keep my silence in the interval."

Elizabeth's heart gave a tiny leap of grateful relief. "Thank you, Mr. James. You have always been a dear friend to me."

Flushing a dull red, he said, "Don't thank me just yet. We may both end up regretting that I agreed to this business."

Over the next few weeks, Elizabeth accustomed herself to married life with Marcus. The Ashfords remained in residence at his insistence. He rested easier knowing she was not alone and Elizabeth appreciated the company while he attended to his affairs.

At Eldridge's insistence, they attended the occasional Society event, ones most likely to attract St. John. The pirate had managed to throw off the agents tracking his whereabouts and hadn't been seen in London since the afternoon he'd spoken with her. His sudden departure was a mystery that set them all on edge.

The threat to her was always on Marcus's mind. Guards were stationed in and around the house, dressed in Westfield livery to avoid arousing the suspicions of his family. The endless waiting made her husband as restless as a caged animal. She'd known from their very first dance together that he was a man who held a tight rein on his passions. He unleashed them fully on her.

He held nothing back. When he was angry, he yelled. When he was pleased, he laughed. When he was aroused, he made love to her, regardless of what time of day it was or where they were at the moment. Twice he left the Lords in the middle of the afternoon to seduce her. She had never felt so important to someone, so necessary. Blatantly possessive, he showed no hesitation in speaking harshly to any man who acted too familiarly with her.

For her own part, Elizabeth found that her jealousy did not ease with her new ownership. It was a miserable personality flaw to be cursed with in a society where dalliance was not only widespread, but expected. Marriage only increased Marcus's appeal to other women. His vibrant energy was now mellowed to the slow, languid grace of a man who was well-loved often by a passionate woman. It made him irresistible.

One evening, during a masked ball, Elizabeth's jealousy finally got the better of her. As Marcus moved toward the beverage tables, she noticed several women choosing the same moment to replenish their own glasses. Looking away in disgust, Elizabeth spied the Dowager Duchess of Ravensend coming toward her.

"Do you see the way women follow my husband?" she complained, rising from a quick curtsy.

Her Grace shrugged. "Masked events give license to cast off what little restraint Society clings to. Note the shaking palm tree in the far right corner? Lady Grenville and Lord Sackton have abandoned their spouses in favor of some exhibitionist sport. And Claire Milton returned from the garden with twigs in her hair. You should not be surprised they sniff after Westfield like mongrel bitches."

"I'm not," she announced curtly. "But I won't tolerate it. Excuse me, Your Grace." With rapid strides, she moved into the next room to find her husband.

She located him near the refreshment tables, a glass in each hand and surrounded by women. He shrugged innocently when he saw her, his lips curving wickedly beneath the edge of his half mask. Pushing through the small crowd, Elizabeth claimed one of the glasses, and then linked her arm with his. Her spine stiff, she led Marcus back to the ballroom, all enjoyment in the evening gone.

The duchess took one look at her face, and excused herself with a smile.

Marcus chuckled. "Thank you, Lady Westfield. To my recollection that is the first time I have ever been rescued."

"You have never wanted to be rescued," she snapped, hating that he could be so nonchalant in the face of her upset.

He lifted a hand to caress a powdered curl. "You're jealous!" he crowed.

She turned away, wondering, as she often did, how many women in the room knew him carnally as she did.

Marcus stepped around until he faced her. "What is it, love?"

"None of your affair."

Uncaring of their audience, Marcus traced the bottom curve of her lip with his gloved thumb. "Tell me what's wrong, or I cannot fix it."

"I detest every woman who knew you before." Blushing, she lowered her head and waited for his laughter.

Instead, his deep, velvety voice swirled around her, encasing her in warmth. "Do you remember when I said intimacy and sex can be mutually exclusive?" His head lowered to hers, his mouth brushing her ear as he whispered, "You are the only woman I have ever been intimate with."

A tear escaped. Marcus brushed it away.

"I want to take you home," he murmured, his emerald gaze hot behind the mask. "And be intimate with you."

She left with him, desperate to have him all to herself. That night he was so tender in his lovemaking, adoring her with his body, giving her everything she asked. His gentle ardor brought tears to her eyes and afterward he held her in his arms as if she were the most precious thing in the world.

Every day brought her closer to him. She was beginning to need him, not just with sensual craving but for so much more. It was a passion that would take a lifetime to sate.

She could only pray fate would give her that chance.

Chapter 19

"You should not have come to my home."

Christopher St. John vaulted into the unmarked Westfield town coach. The pirate's overwhelming presence dominated the interior and added a palpable energy to the air, forcing Elizabeth to retreat into the squabs. Glancing out the window, she remained surprised at the elegance of the small townhouse he resided in. It was conspicuous in the unfashionable part of town where it was located. However the two burly henchmen at the door betrayed the seediness of the goings-on within.

He took the seat opposite her. "It's not a fit place for a lady and this ostentatious equipage is attracting the kind of dangerous attention you don't want."

"You know I had no choice. As soon as I learned your direction, I had to come. I have no other way of reaching you." She arched a brow. "You, Mr. St. John, have questions to answer."

His full mouth curved wryly, as he leaned back and adjusted his coat. "No need to be so formal. We are related, after all."

"As if I could forget."

"So you believe me then."

"I had your claim investigated."

St. John glanced around, taking in the opulence of the dark

leather interior with one sweeping glance. "Such a shame you married Westfield. Looks as if the man could use a lightening of his purse."

"I strongly suggest you find other sport, if you don't wish to anger me. I am not pleasant when I'm cross."

St. John blinked, then threw his head back and laughed. "By God, I do like you. Rest assured, I am loyal to members of my family and Westfield is something of a family member, is he not?"

Rubbing between her brows in a vain effort to ward off a headache, she muttered, "Westfield knows nothing of this and I prefer to keep it that way."

St. John reached over and opened the small compartment door by his seat. Withdrawing a glass, he poured two fingers of brandy, which he then offered to her. When she refused, he put the decanter away. "I realized you hadn't told him about us when he came to see me. However, I did think you would have told him since then."

Studying him more closely, she noted the faint yellow of a healing bruise around his left eye and the small scab on his lip. "Are your injuries from Westfield?"

"No other man would dare."

She winced. "I apologize. I had no intention of telling him about our meeting, but I neglected to tell my mother-in-law to keep quiet about it."

St. John waved his hand in a dismissive gesture. "No lasting harm done. Quite stimulating, actually. After years of doing nothing more strenuous than exchanging barbs, it was time for us to get to business. I was glad he found me. I was curious to see how he felt about you. The man has never had a weakness in his life. I regret you are one I cannot exploit."

"What is your grievance with Westfield?"

"The man is too arrogant, too titled, too wealthy, too pretty—too everything. He's as rich as Croesus and yet he cries foul when I take a tiny bit of his blunt."

She snorted. "As if you would have a party should some-one steal from you."

He choked on his brandy.

"I must know about Hawthorne," she asked, leaning for-ward. "It's driving me mad not knowing who he was."

St. John removed his hat and ruffled his wavy blond locks with a large hand. "Nigel was your spouse. I prefer you to re-member the man you spent a year of your life with."

"But I don't understand. If you were close to one another, how could he work with Eldridge without harming you or . . . or . . ."

"Acting as traitor?" he finished softly. "Elizabeth, I pray you leave such concerns outside the scope of your recollec-tions. He was a good husband to you, was he not?"

"So I should only cling to the facets I knew and discard the others?"

He sighed and set his hat on the seat next to him. "Did your investigation reveal information about our father?"

Elizabeth sat back and bit her lip.

"Ah, I see it did. Touched, they call it. A bit off, half mad—"

"I understand."

"Do you?" He looked down and examined his jeweled heels with unnecessary focus. "Did you hear of the violence? The ravings? No? That's for the best. Suffice it to say that no steward would work for him and he was too daft to manage his finances properly. When he passed, Nigel discovered the title was bankrupt."

"How? We never wanted for anything."

"We met when I was ten. My mother had been raised in the village and when her condition became obvious, she was released from her position as scullery maid and returned to her family in shame. Nigel was two years younger than I, but even as children we knew. We looked too much alike, had certain mannerisms that were the same. Nigel would find ways to see me. I'm certain it must have been difficult living with our pater. He needed the escape of friendship and brother-hood.

"So when I learned of his financial difficulties, I came to London and learned what I needed to. I became friends with the people I had to, I did the things they asked me to do, I went to the places they told me to go. Whatever it took to make money, I did it."

There was no pride in his voice. In fact, his tone held no inflection at all.

"Nigel asked me how I was able to pay off his debts, which, I assure you, were exorbitant. When he learned of my activities, he was furious. He said he could not stand by and enjoy his newfound wealth and stability while I placed myself in danger. Later, when I realized I was being investigated, Nigel went to Lord Eldridge and—"

"—became an agent," she finished, her heart sinking as her worst fears were realized. "My brother was assigned to track you. Hawthorne used me to ingratiate himself with Barclay."

St. John leaned forward, but when she shrank away, he withdrew. "It's true that information learned through the agency allowed me to elude Westfield, but Nigel cared for you, don't doubt that. He would have offered for you re-gardless of your brother. He admired and respected you. He spoke of you often and was adamant that I continue to look after you if something should happen to him."

"The irony," she muttered. "Westfield prefers I not use my widow's pension and yet some of that settlement rightfully belongs to him, does it not?"

"In a way," he conceded. "Proceeds from the sale of Ashford cargos were used to pay off the Hawthorne debt."

Elizabeth felt the color drain from her face. This was worse than she could have ever possibly imagined. "There is so much I don't understand. How did you come to have my brooch?"

"I was nearby when Barclay and Hawthorne were attacked," he said sadly. "It was I who sent men to find help for your brother. I took the brooch because I was not certain I could trust anyone else to care for it and see it returned to you."

"Why were you there? Was his death because of you?"

He flinched. "Perhaps. In the end we must all pay for our sins."

"What is in the journal that makes it so important? Who wants it?"

"I cannot say, Elizabeth, for reasons I cannot explain."

"Why?" she cried. "I deserve to know."

"I'm sorry. For your protection, you must not know."

"He tried to kill me."

"Give the book to me," he urged. "It's the only way to spare you."

She shook her head. "Westfield has it locked away. I don't have access to it. It contains maps of various waterways in addition to the coded writings. He thinks the book may have detailed information about Nigel's missions. If I were to give the book to you, a known pirate, it would be considered treasonous. He would question me, discover our kinship, Eldridge would learn of it—"

"Westfield would protect you. I would manage Eldridge."

She swallowed hard. She couldn't lose Marcus. Not now. "After what transpired four years ago, my husband does not trust me. If I were to betray him this way he would never forgive me."

St. John cursed under his breath. "The book is worthless without Nigel. No one will be able to decipher it. If I take it off your hands, you can go away, have a honeymoon. Then I can draw the man out with it and end this."

"You know more about the journal than you are telling me," she accused. "If it were worthless, my life wouldn't be in danger."

"The man is mad," he growled. "Mad, I tell you. Think of

the attack on your person at your betrothal ball. Were those the actions of a rational person?"

Her lips pursed. "How did you learn of the stabbing?"

"I've had men watching out for you. One of them was there at your betrothal ball."

"I knew it!" There *had* been someone else in the garden, someone who chased away her assailant.

"I am doing my best to assist you—"

"You've been absent for weeks," she scoffed.

"On your behalf," he corrected. "I have been searching."

"Find him! Leave me out of this mess."

He dropped his glass carelessly inside the door panel. "I have been scouring England, and during those times you have been assaulted on two occasions. He knows me too well. He plans his attacks when I am out of Town." St. John grabbed her hands and held them tightly within his own. "Find a way to give me the book and this can all be over."

Shaking her head, Elizabeth pulled her hands away. "Tell me truthfully: Does the book have anything to do with Nigel's murder?"

St. John remained bent over, his elbows resting on his knees as he stared at her with clear eyes. "In a way."

"What does that mean?"

"Elizabeth, you already know too much."

Frustrated tears filled her eyes. There was no way to know if St. John was sincere or simply very cunning. She strongly suspected the information in the journal had something to do with him. If she were correct, her husband would want to use the information to bring the pirate to trial. For Marcus, it could be the chance for justice he'd waited years for.

"I must think about this. It is too much to absorb at once." She sighed wearily. "I have had little enough happiness in my life. My husband has been my one true joy. You and your brother's machinations could be the end of that."

"I am truly sorry, Elizabeth," he said, his sapphire gaze

dark with regret. "I have hurt a great many people in my life, but to have hurt you is a sincere lament of mine."

St. John opened the carriage door and began to descend. Suddenly he turned about. Hunching in the doorway, he kissed her on the cheek, his lips warm and gentle. Then he leapt from the carriage and reached for her hand. "You now know my direction. Come to me if you need anything. Anything at all. And trust no one but Westfield. Promise me that."

She gave a jerky nod and he backed away.

The footman waited patiently, too well trained to show any emotion.

"Return to the house," she ordered, her head throbbing painfully and her stomach twisting with dread.

She couldn't help feeling that St. John would be the end of her happiness.

Marcus studied Elizabeth from the doorway of his bedroom. She slept, her beautiful face innocent in slumber. Despite her betrayal, his heart swelled at the sight of her cuddled peacefully in bed. Next to her, on the small table, sat two open packets of headache powder and a glass of water, half full.

Slowly she stirred, the force of his presence and the heat of his gaze penetrating her sleep. She opened her eyes and focused on him, the instant tenderness of her gaze quickly shielded by guilt-heavy lids. He knew in that instant the reports were true. He held himself upright by will alone, when all he wanted to do was crawl to her and bury his pain in her arms.

"Marcus," she called in the soft, throaty voice that never failed to arouse him. Despite his anger and torment, he felt his cock stir. "Come to bed, darling. I want you to hold me."

Traitorously, his feet moved toward her. By the time he reached her, he had removed his coat and waistcoat. He stopped at the edge of the bed. "How was your day?" he asked, his voice carefully neutral.

She stretched, the movement of her legs pulling down the sheet so that her torso was exposed through the thin shift she'd worn to sleep. He grew hard, and hated himself for it when his thoughts drifted to the secrets she kept. Nothing could temper his response to her. Even now, his heart struggled to forgive her.

Wrinkling her nose, she said, "Truthfully? It was one of the most horrid days of my life." Her mouth curved seductively. "But you can change that."

"What happened?"

She shook her head. "I don't want to talk about it. Tell me about your day instead. It was certainly better than mine." Pulling back the covers, she silently invited him to join her. "Can we have dinner in our rooms tonight? I don't feel like getting dressed again."

Of course not. How many times would she want to dress and undress in one day? Maybe she hadn't undressed at all. Maybe St. John had merely pushed her skirts up and . . .

Marcus clenched his jaw and willed the image away.

Sitting on the bed, he yanked off his shoes. Then he turned to her. "Did you enjoy your trip into town?" he asked casually, but it didn't fool her.

Elizabeth knew him too well.

She made a great show of sitting up in the bed and fluffing the pillows into a comfortable pile. "Why don't you simply say what you mean?"

He tore his shirt over his head, then stood to remove his breeches. "Did your lover not bring you to orgasm, love? Are you anxious for me to finish what he started?" He slid into bed next to her, but found himself alone. She had slipped out the other side and stood at the foot of the bed.

With hands on her hips, she glared at him. "What are you talking about?"

Marcus leaned back against the pillows she had so recently arranged. "I was told you spent some time with Christopher St. John today, in my carriage with the curtains closed. He gave you a touching kiss goodbye and an open welcome to call on him for *anything* you might need."

The violet eyes sparked dangerously. As always, she was magnificent in her fury. He could barely breathe from the sight of her.

"Ah so," she murmured, her lush mouth drawn tight. "Of course. Despite your insatiable appetite for me, which often leaves me sore and exhausted, I find I still require further sexual congress. Perhaps you should commit me?"

Turning on her bare heel, she left.

Marcus stared after her, agape. He waited to see if she would return and when she did not, he pulled on his robe and followed her to her room.

She stood by the hall door in her dressing gown, telling a maid to bring up dinner and more headache powder. After sending the servant away, she slipped into her bed without looking at him.

"Deny it," he growled.

"I see no need. You are decided."

He stalked over to her, caught her by the shoulders, and shook her roughly. "Tell me what happened! Tell me it's false."

"But it's not," she said with arched brow, so damn collected and unruffled he wanted to scream. "Your men related the events exactly."

He stared at her in shock, his hands on her shoulders beginning to shake. Afraid to do violence, Marcus released her and clasped his hands behind his back. "You have been meeting with St. John and yet you won't tell me why. What reason would you have for seeing him?" His voice hardened ruthlessly. "For allowing him to kiss you?"

Elizabeth didn't answer his questions. Instead, she asked one of her own. "Will you forgive me, Marcus?"

"Forgive you for what?" he yelled. "Tell me what you've

done! Have you taken a fancy to him? Has he seduced you into trusting him?"

"And if he has?" she asked softly. "If I've strayed, but want you back, would you have me?"

His pride so revolted at the thought of her in the arms of another man that, for a moment, he thought he would be violently sick. Turning away, his fists clenched convulsively at his sides. "What are you asking?" he bit out.

"You know very well what I'm asking. Now that you are aware of my duplicity, will you discard me? Perhaps now you'll send me away. Now that you no longer want me."

"*Not want you?* I never cease wanting you. Every damned moment. Sleeping. Waking." He spun about. "And you want me too."

She said nothing, her lovely face a mask of indifference.

He could send her to the country with his family. Distance himself from her . . .

But the mere thought of her absence made him crazy. His ache for her was a physical pain. His pride crumbled beneath the demands of his heart.

"You will stay with me."

"Why? To warm your bed? Any woman can do that for you."

She was only an arm's reach away and yet her icy demeanor had her miles from him.

"You are my wife. You will serve my needs."

"Is that all I am to you? A convenience? Nothing more?"

"I wish you were nothing to me," he said harshly. "God, how I wish you were nothing."

To his amazement, her lovely face crumpled before his eyes. She slipped from the bed and sank to the floor. "Marcus," she sobbed, her head bowing low.

He stood frozen.

She wrapped her arms around his legs, her head resting on his feet, her tears slipping between his toes. "I was with St. John today, but I didn't stray from you. I could never."

Near dizzy with confusion, he lowered himself slowly to the floor and took her in his arms. "Christ . . . Elizabeth . . ."

"I need you. I need you to breathe, to think, to *be*." Her eyes, overflowing with tears, never left his face. Her hand moved to cup his cheek and he nuzzled into her touch, breathing in her scent.

"What is happening?" he asked, his voice hoarse from his clenched throat. "I don't understand."

She pressed her fingertips to his mouth. "I will explain."

And she did, her voice breaking and faltering. When she fell silent, Marcus sat stunned.

"Why didn't you confide in me before?"

"I didn't know the whole of the story until this afternoon. And when I did know it, I couldn't be certain how you would react. I was afraid."

"You and I, we are bound." He caught her hand and held it to his heart. "Whether we will it or no, we are in this to-gether—our life, our marriage. You may not have wanted me, but you have me all the same."

There was a rap at the door. Marcus cursed, then stood, pulling her up with him. Opening the portal, he accepted the dinner tray. "Tell the housekeeper to make preparations to pack."

The servant bowed stiffly and left.

Elizabeth frowned at him, her porcelain skin pinked from crying. "What are you about?"

Setting the tray aside, he grabbed her hand and pulled her through the sitting room to his room. "We are retiring to the country with my family. I want you out of London and tucked away for a while until I can make sense of this muddle." He closed the door behind them. "We have been concentrating on St. John. I felt secure enough staying in Town when he was the only perceived threat. Now I have no notion of whom to suspect. You are not safe here. It could be anyone. Someone we invited to our betrothal ball. An acquaintance who comes to call." He rubbed the back of his neck.

"But what of Parliament?" she asked.

He shot her an incredulous glance as he shrugged out of his robe. "Do you think I care more about Parliament than I do about you?"

"It is important to you, I know that."

"You are important to me." Moving to her, he loosened her dressing gown and pushed it to the floor, then divested her of her shift.

"I'm hungry," she protested.

"So am I," he murmured as he picked her up and carried her to the bed.

"I agree, leaving London would be wise." Eldridge paced in front of the windows, his hands clasped behind his back, his tone low and distracted.

"There was no way to know," Marcus said softly, understanding how difficult it must be to learn of a traitor in their midst.

"I should have seen the signs. St. John could not have eluded justice all these years without some assistance. I simply didn't want to credit it. My pride wouldn't allow it. And now, perhaps there is another among us, maybe more."

"I say the time has come for us to be more persuasive with St. John. So far, he is the only individual who seems to know anything about Hawthorne or the bloody journal."

Eldridge nodded. "Talbot and James can see to him. You see to Lady Westfield."

"Send for me if there's a need."

"I probably shall." Eldridge sank into his chair and sighed. "At the present moment, you are one of the few men I can trust."

For Marcus, there was only one man he could trust to care first and foremost for Elizabeth, and when he left Eldridge, he went straight to him, and told him everything.

William stared down at Hawthorne's book in his hands, and shook his head. "I never knew of this. I was not even aware that Hawthorne kept journals. And you." He raised his gaze. "Working for Eldridge . . . How alike we are, you and I."

"I suppose that is why we were once good friends," Marcus said without inflection. His gaze drifted around the study, remembering when he had sat in this very room and arranged marriage settlements. So long ago. He stood, and prepared to depart. "Thank you for guarding the journal."

"Westfield. Wait a moment."

"Yes?" He paused midstep, and turned about.

"I owe you an apology."

Every muscle in Marcus's body stiffened.

"I should have heard your version of events before passing judgment." Setting the book aside, William rose to his feet. "Explanations are perhaps worthless at this point, and in the end they are just excuses for why I failed you as a friend."

Marcus's anger and resentment ran deep, but it was a tiny spark of hope that prompted him to say, "I would like to hear them, in any case."

William tugged at his cravat. "I had no notion of how to feel when Elizabeth first mentioned her interest in you. You were my friend, and I knew you were inherently a good man, but you were also a scoundrel. Knowing my sister's fears, I thought you two would be a bad fit." He shrugged, a sign not of nonchalance, but of sheepishness. "You've no idea what it is like to have a sister. How you worry for them, and want to protect them. And Elizabeth is more fragile than most."

"I know." Marcus watched his old friend begin to pace nervously, and knew from experience that when William moved so restlessly, he was in deadly earnest.

"She was mad for you, you know."

"Was she?"

Snorting, William said, "Bloody hell, yes. She went on and on about you. And your eyes, and your blasted smiles, and a hundred other things I did not care to hear about. That is why, when I woke to her tearstained missive about your indiscretion, I took it to be true. A woman in love will believe anything her lover tells her. I assumed you were beyond redemption for her to run off as she did." He stilled, and faced him. "I am sorry I assumed. I am sorry I did not go after her, and talk some sense into her. I am sorry that later, when I knew I had done you an injustice, I did not come to you and make amends. I allowed my pride to dictate my actions, and I lost you, the only brother I have ever known. I am most sorry about that."

Marcus sighed inwardly, and walked to the window. He stared out at nothing, wishing he could give some glib rejoinder to defuse the tension. Instead, he gave the moment the attention it deserved.

"You are not entirely to blame, Barclay. Neither is Elizabeth. If I had told her about the agency, none of this would have happened. Instead, knowing how she longed for stability, I hid it from her. I wanted to have everything. I did not realize until too late that what I wanted and what I needed were two different things."

"I know it is my commitment to Elizabeth that brought you here today, Westfield, but I want you to know that I am equally committed to you. If you ever require a second, I will not fail you again."

Marcus turned, nodded, and welcomed the chance presented to him. "Very well, then," he drawled, "we can call it even, *if* you forgive me for stealing Lady Patricia from you, although I think we both agree that your offense was greater."

"You stole Janice Fleming, too," William complained. Then he smiled. "Although I thrashed you for that one."

"Your memory is faulty, old chap. It was you who ended up in the trough."

"Good God, I forgot about that."

Marcus twirled his quizzing glass by its ribbon. "You once took a dunking in the Serpentine, too."

"You fell in first! I was attempting to assist you when you pulled me in."

"You would not have wanted me to drown alone. What are friends for, if not to suffer together?"

William laughed. Then they shared a grin, and an unspoken agreement to truce. "Truly. What are friends for?"

Chapter 20

It was late afternoon on the second day of travel when they arrived at the ancestral home of the Ashford family. The compelling castle-like appearance of the massive mansion gave mute testimony to the perseverance of Marcus's lineage. Turrets rose at varying heights across the great expanse of the stone exterior that sprawled for some distance to the left and right of the front door.

The three carriages and luggage cart slowed to a stop. Instantly the front door of the mansion flew open and a multitude of servants in Westfield livery descended the steps.

Alighting from the carriage, Elizabeth stared in awe. Marcus set his hand at her waist and stood beside her. His voice was low and intimate in her ear. "Welcome home."

He kissed the sensitive part of her neck where her shoulder met her throat. "Wait until you see the inside," he said with obvious pride.

As they entered the foyer, Elizabeth sucked in her breath with wonder. The ceiling vaulted away from them to dizzying heights, where a large crystalline chandelier hung from an impossibly long chain. Tapers gently lit alcoves located along the walls on either side, and the stone floor was covered in several immense Aubusson rugs.

Elizabeth set the pace for the group, walking slowly as she struggled to take in her surroundings. The sound of their muffled footsteps echoed hollowly through the vast space. In front of them, at the other end of the foyer, was a wall of French doors. When opened, they led out onto the large expanse of lawn just beyond.

But the focal point of the room was the immense split staircase curving gracefully along either wall to join at a massive landing above. From there the ascent branched off to hallways on the left and right, which led to the east and west wings.

Paul looked at her with a proud smile. "It is impressive, isn't it?"

Elizabeth nodded with eyes wide. "To call it impressive wouldn't do it justice."

They made their way up the dual staircase on the left side while servants hauled up trunks on the right. Marcus drew to a halt in front of an open doorway and held out his hand to urge Elizabeth inside. Paul and Robert excused themselves, promising to see them at the evening meal.

The room she entered was massive and beautifully decorated in soft shades of light taupe and creamy blue. Striped silk curtains framed wide windows that overlooked the front circular drive. Two doorways flanked the sides of the room. Through the open door to the left she could see a sitting room and a decidedly masculine bedroom beyond that, and on the right, a nursery.

Marcus stood directly behind her. "Do you like it?"

"It's perfect," she acknowledged.

With a caressing smile and a mischievous wink, he left through the sitting room and headed to his room beyond.

Alone, Elizabeth took in the contents of the room with greater care, this time noting the little details. The small bookcase built into the bottom of the window seat held copies of her favorite books. The vanity drawers held her customary toiletries.

As he had for the nights they'd spent in the guesthouse, Marcus had thought of almost everything.

Removing her hat and gloves, she went in search of her husband. Stepping through the open double doors that led to his room, she found Marcus at the desk, sans coat and waistcoat. She approached him with a smile.

"Marcus," she started gently. "Must you charm me every day?"

Rounding the desk, he wrapped her tightly in his arms, his mouth pressing a hard kiss to her forehead. "Of course."

She hugged him back almost desperately, so grateful she couldn't help telling him so.

"I'm relieved the house pleases you," he said gruffly, his mouth nuzzling her skin. "I will give you a full tour before supper and in the morning the staff will line up for your inspection."

"It is not so much the house that pleases me, as your thoughtfulness and care for my comfort." Elizabeth kissed the sharp line of his jaw.

He squeezed her brutally close, and then set her away. Returning to his desk, he bent his head to the papers he pulled from a drawer.

Sighing at the loss of his embrace, she sank into a chair in front of the fireplace. "What are you doing?"

His gaze remained on the desktop. "Gathering my ledgers and notifying my steward that I'm in residence. I usually handle expenditures after the Season, but since we are here, I may as well begin now."

"You are not decoding the journal?"

He glanced up and hesitated a moment before answering. "Keeping you and the journal in one location is foolhardy."

She stilled, surprised. "Where is it? With Eldridge?"

"No." He took a deep breath. "I placed it in Barclay's care."

"What?" she asked, shooting to her feet. "Why?"

"Because he is the only person besides St. John to have worked with Hawthorne closely on matters regarding the agency. And, at this moment, he's one of the few people I can trust."

"What about Mr. James?"

"I would have preferred Avery, but Eldridge has him occupied at the moment."

Elizabeth's stomach dropped. "St. John."

Marcus's eyes narrowed. "Yes. We must know everything he knows."

"What of Margaret? And the baby? The time draws near, William cannot be embroiled in this now." Her hand lifted to shelter her racing heart. "What if they should be attacked, as I was? How could you do this, when I begged you not to?"

"Barclay has been prepared for attacks against himself and his wife since Hawthorne's death." He rounded the desk.

"And that is why my room was ransacked?" she snapped.

"Elizabeth—"

"Damn you. I trusted you."

His voice came low and angry. "You entrusted me with your safety and I am seeing to it."

"You don't care about me," she argued. "If you did, you would not have done something guaranteed to hurt me. They are all I have, to risk them this way—"

"They are not all that you have! You have me."

She shook her head rapidly. "No. You belong to the agency. Everything you do is for them."

"That's not true, and well you know it."

"I know I was wrong about you, wrong to trust you." She brushed aside a tear with the back of her hand. "You deliberately said nothing to me."

"Because I knew it would upset you. I knew you would not understand at first."

"You lie. You failed to tell me because you knew it was *wrong*. And I will never understand. Never."

Elizabeth swept around the settee toward the door.

"I am not done speaking, madam."

"Then continue, my lord," she threw over her shoulder, nearly running to her room to hide the tears that flowed freely. "I no longer wish to listen."

* * *

William paced the length of his sitting room.

Margaret sighed, squirming into the pillows on the chaise, trying to find comfort for her aching back. "You knew nothing of this journal?"

"No." He scowled. "But Hawthorne was an odd fellow. I'm not surprised to learn his father was mad. I'm certain Hawthorne was a bit touched as well."

"How does that pertain?"

"There is something odd about this. I've gone over Westfield's notes. He has already dedicated a great deal of his time to the study of the journal and all we've learned is some spotty descriptions of remote locations with no explanation. I cannot understand the purpose."

Margaret rested her hands on her protruding stomach and smiled at the feel of her child moving in response to her touch. "So let's set aside the contents of the book for the moment and concentrate on Hawthorne himself. How did he come to be your partner?"

"He was assigned to me by Eldridge."

"Did he ask for you in particular?"

"I don't believe so. If I recall correctly, he gave some tale about a grievance against St. John."

"So he could just as easily have been assigned to Westfield, who was also investigating St. John."

William plunged both hands into his golden hair. "Perhaps, but Westfield was frequently paired with Mr. James. I had not yet built a strong rapport with any other agents."

"And you and Westfield never knew of one another's activities, even though you were fast friends?"

"Eldridge does not—"

"—share such information, in case you are captured or tortured for information." Margaret shuddered. "I thank God you no longer amuse yourself in that manner. Heaven only knows how Elizabeth manages. But then she's far stronger than I. Is it possible Hawthorne married Elizabeth in the hopes he would learn something of Westfield's activities?"

"No." William sat next to her and placed his hand over hers. "He would not have known about Westfield. Just as I did not. I believe he married her to ensure he would remain my partner."

"Ah, yes, that would have been wise. So we have Hawthorne, working with you to investigate St. John, but all the while his aim is to thwart you. He is married to Elizabeth and keeping a journal of cryptic text that so far has been revealed to be nothing of import. But in fact, it must be important enough to kill for."

"Yes."

"I'd say the best option would be to capture St. John and pair him with the journal, make him tell you what it says."

His mouth curved ruefully. "According to Elizabeth, St. John claims only Hawthorne can decode it. But obviously that cannot be true, so Avery is tracking the pirate, who most inconveniently has fled London again. He is the key."

"I worry for Elizabeth, you know I do, but I cannot help but wish Westfield had taken the journal elsewhere."

"I know, love. If there had been another choice, I would have suggested it. But truly, despite his long-standing association with James and Eldridge, I am the only man he knows who can be trusted to care more for Elizabeth than the agency. And you and I have been cautious for so long. I couldn't bear for our children to live in fear. We must end this." His gaze pled for her understanding.

She cupped his cheek with her hand. "I'm glad you now know the truth about Hawthorne and St. John, to ease the guilt you've felt all these years. Perhaps Hawthorne's death was inevitable, with his life so deeply entrenched in the criminal." She moved her hand to place his against her belly and smiled as his blue eyes widened with awed pleasure at the feeling of a strong kick against his palm.

"Can you forgive me for accepting this task while you carry my child?" he asked hoarsely, bending to press an ardent kiss to her powdered forehead.

"Of course, my love," she soothed. "You could not have done otherwise. And truly, in light of your lost friendship, I think it is a hopeful sign that Westfield came to you for help. We shall solve this puzzle together. Maybe then we can all find some peace."

"Pray, tell me what is the matter, Elizabeth," Elaine asked with concern. "It pains me to see you so distressed."

"I should be in London now, not here."

Elizabeth moaned as they sat in the family parlor, her thoughts filled with worry for William and Margaret. Marcus may have done what he thought was best, but he should have discussed it with her, allowed her to come to terms with it. He should have given her the opportunity to speak to William and thank him for his assistance. Her chest tightened as she thought of her brother, who loved her so much.

"I'm so sorry you are not happy here—"

"No, it's not that," she assured quickly. "I love it here. But there are . . . things that require my attention."

Frowning, Elaine said, "I don't understand."

"I asked Westfield to do something important for me and he disregarded my wishes."

"He must have had good reason," Elaine soothed. "He adores you."

Paul entered the parlor. "Why so glum?" he asked. Taking one look at Elizabeth's tear-streaked face, he scowled. "Is it Marcus? Has he yelled at you again, Beth?"

Despite her misery, Paul's use of a pet name brought a reluctant smile to her face. No one had ever called her anything besides Elizabeth.

"No. I almost wish he would," she admitted. "He's been so civil toward me this last week I can barely stand it. A good row would do much to improve my spirits."

Paul laughed. "Well, reserved civility is what Marcus does best. I take it you've had a lovers' quarrel?"

"That's a rather tame description, but I suppose it is something similar."

His brown eyes lit with mischief. "I happen to be somewhat of an expert on lovers' quarrels. The best way to recover is not to mope. You'll find greater satisfaction in exacting a little revenge."

Elizabeth shook her head. She'd already denied Marcus her bed for the last six nights. Every night he tested the locked door to her chamber. Every night he turned away without a word. During the day, he was his customary charming self, polite and solicitous.

What was lacking were the heated looks and the familiar stolen caresses that told her he wanted her. The message was clear. He would not be the only one denied.

"I think I've gone as far as I dare to incite a response," she said.

"Cheer up then, Beth. Lovers' quarrels never last long."

But Elizabeth couldn't agree with that. She'd hold her own until Marcus apologized. He couldn't just run roughshod over her. Decisions of this magnitude had to be discussed.

And quite frankly, she could be as stubborn as he.

The coals in the hearth shifted and Elizabeth jumped, every muscle in her body tense with expectation. She waited almost breathlessly for Marcus to test the brass knob. Once he did so, she could relax and attempt sleep.

If he kept to his routine, she'd have only a few more moments to wait. Sitting upright in bed, she clutched the edges of the sheet in her lap with nervous fingers. The lace throat of her night rail seemed too tight, making it difficult to swallow.

Then the knob began a slow turn to the right.

She couldn't take her eyes from it, couldn't even blink.

It made a soft click as it reached the barrier of the lock.

Her jaw clenched until it ached.

The knob released, turning rapidly back to its previous position.

She closed her eyes and sighed with a confusing mixture of both disappointment and relief. She didn't get to appreciate the dichotomy, however, because a heartbeat later the door opened and Marcus walked in, spinning a looped ribbon around his index finger, the end of which dangled the key.

Biting her lower lip, she seethed, but held her tongue. She should have known not to expect fair play from a man used to gaining whatever he desired. At any cost.

He strolled to the nearest chair and turned it about to face the bed, rather than the grate. Then he sat, crossing one ankle over the opposite knee and adjusting his heavy silk robe with studious leisure. The traitorous key was slipped into his pocket.

"You are the most arrogant man I have ever met."

"You are welcome to discuss my perceived flaws at a later date. At the present moment, let's keep to the topic of why you've been barring me from your bed."

She crossed her arms beneath her breasts. "You know why."

"Do I? Well then I appear to have forgotten. Would you be so kind as to remind me? And be quick about it, if you please. I've done my best to allow you time to set aside your pique, but a sennight of waiting has stretched my patience."

Elizabeth growled. "I am not merely a cunt to rut in. If you need sex so badly, take yourself in hand."

His harshly indrawn breath was the only sign she'd struck effectively. "If all I needed was sexual release, I would have done just that. Now, the reason for the locked door?"

She sat there for a long time, thinking it would be best if he determined what was wrong on his own. But finally the pregnant silence was too much to bear. "You owe me an apology."

"I do?"

"Yes."

"For what, pray tell?"

"You know why. It was wrong to involve William when I asked you not to."

"I will not apologize for that." His large hands, with their long, elegant fingers, curled over the carved wooden arms of the chair.

She lifted her chin. "Then we have nothing more to discuss."

"Ah but we do," he drawled softly. "Because I'm sharing your bed tonight, my lovely wife, and I prefer it to be a pleasurable experience."

"I have feelings, Marcus, and a mind. You cannot just trample over those things and expect me to welcome you with open arms."

"I covet your feelings, Elizabeth, and I respect your mind. I could not have married you otherwise."

Her head tilted as she considered him, so tall and broad he dwarfed the chair he occupied. "If you speak the truth, why didn't you discuss your intent with me and allow me to offer my opinion? You belittle me by acting without my knowledge and then concealing your actions."

"I concealed nothing. When you asked, I told you. And your opinion was known to me. I am fairly clever," he said dryly. "You can tell me something once and I'll retain it."

"Then my opinion is of so little consequence it does not bear considering?"

He stood. "I will always consider your opinion, and give it as much weight as my own, but your safety will always come first. Always."

Feeling on unequal footing, Elizabeth slid from the bed. Although Marcus was far taller than she, it gave her some comfort to stand tall against him. "And what of William's safety? And his family?"

Marcus crossed to her, and lifting a hand, brushed the back of his fingers along her cheekbone. His eyes closed, as if he savored the touch of her. For her part, she shivered at the smell of him, that warm scent of sandalwood and citrus she knew and loved so well.

"I worry for him, yes. And I regret I was forced to involve him. Should something happen to him or his wife I would be forever wracked with guilt and I would mourn the loss of a man who was once, and hopefully will be again, as close to me as my brothers." His voice lowered, became almost wistful. "But I would survive. I could not say the same were I to lose you."

"Marcus . . ." Stunned by his words, her hand came up to catch his and hold it to her cheek.

"I don't know how I lived those four years without you. Looking back now, remembering the endlessness of days, the aching longing, the sense I was missing something vital . . ." He shook his head. "I couldn't go through that again. And that was before. Before I knew the many facets of your smiles, the warmth of your skin, the sounds of your pleasure, feeling you next to me both in public and private."

Suddenly, she felt overwhelmed and she gasped for breath.

He tugged her closer and embraced her within gentle arms. "I am sorry you are hurt by my decision, but I would make it again, a hundred times over. This is difficult for you, I know, and I understand you cannot collect how I feel. I would sacrifice my own life to protect yours, because none of it would be worth anything without you. And so I am resigning my commission, because my work jeopardizes you."

"Wh-why . . ." She swallowed hard and held him tight. "I never expected you would say such things to me. I-I don't know how to reply . . ."

"A week without you was enough to realize it was best to explain myself plainly, so there would be no doubt."

"I never thought you would love me. Not after all that I've done."

His cheek rested atop her head. "I used to wonder why it had to be you. I've met beautiful women, smart women, funny and bold women. Why Elizabeth? Why not someone who could open her heart to me? Perhaps it was the chase. Perhaps it's that you are wounded and I wish to heal you." He shrugged. "The Lord only knows."

"I still cannot help but wish you would have told me your intent," she grumbled, even though her upset was immeasurably soothed by his declaration of her importance.

"In the future, I hope I have more time to convince you of the merits of my opinion, but in this case I didn't have that luxury."

She leaned against his arms and narrowed her eyes. "How long could it have possibly taken?"

He laughed. "A sennight it seems, and we didn't have that."

Looking up at him, seeing the warmth in his eyes and the loving curve of his mouth, she wanted to sigh like a besotted schoolgirl. Time and intimate familiarity did not lessen the effect of his masculine beauty. She didn't have the words to say things like he did, so plainly and with such courage. But she would do the best she could.

Her hands slipped between them and parted the front of his robe, revealing the body that made her mouth dry and her sex clench in eagerness. Her fingertips drifted over taut, warm skin, across his abdomen, and down to his thighs.

"Feel what you do to me?" he asked, his eyes drifting shut as he quivered beneath her touch. He licked his lips and clutched her waist, the crests of his cheekbones flushing with arousal. "I ache for this, Elizabeth, burn for it." Reaching for her hand, he brought it to his cock, already hard and throbbing. He drew in his breath sharply when she curled her hands around it.

Awed, her gaze roamed the length of his body, helpless in the grip of only exploratory caresses.

Trust, he'd said to her once. *This is trust.*

She would have to trust that he would always do what was

best for her, even if she did not agree with his methods. Would she not do the same to protect him?

Filled with feelings that had no outlet, she sank to her knees and opened her mouth, giving him the pleasure she knew he desired.

Ahhh . . . how she loved it as well. The silky feel of him, his ravished gasp, those long fingers clenched in her hair.

"Yes," he cried as he thrust his hips gently, his buttocks like stone within her palms. "I would die for this."

A moment later he lifted her and carried her to the bed, her night rail drifting over her head to be cast aside. She sank into softness, covered by hardness and everything melted as he lifted her thigh and slid deep within her.

The strength of him, the hard length of his thrusting cock, the damp skin, the near unbearable intimacy, was diminished by the intensity of his gaze.

Awash in heat and consumed by the memory of his words, she wrapped her arms around his straining body and cried with joy. Her tears wet his shoulder, mixed with his sweat, bound them together. Her body seized beneath his, suspended in orgasm, held there by the steady plunge and withdrawal Marcus knew would prolong her pleasure.

And when he joined her, when he shuddered against her and cried out her name, she set her mouth to his ear and spoke her heart.

Chapter 21

"Mr. Christopher St. John has come to call, my lady." Elizabeth looked up from her novel and stared at the butler with mouth agape. She dropped the book on the settee next to her and rose. "Where did you put him?"

"In the lower parlor, my lady."

Marcus had departed with the steward to survey some tenant properties that required repair. Elaine had retired for an afternoon nap, and Robert and Paul had gone to the village only an hour past. She was alone, but unafraid, nodding at the two guards who stood on either side of the parlor door.

Taking a deep breath, she swept into the room. St. John rose when she entered, splendidly attired and angelically handsome. He smiled and the brief reminiscence of Nigel momentarily disconcerted her.

As she drew closer, she noted he appeared leaner, the ever-present shadows under his eyes were darker, and while his bearing was as proud as ever, she could sense the weariness beneath the façade.

"Rather daring of you to come calling here."

He shrugged. "I half expected to see Westfield charging through that door. I'm relieved it's you instead. I'm not worthy of a fight right now." He glanced over her head. "Where is his lordship?"

"Near enough."

His blond brows lifted, and his lips curved. "As long as he gives me a wide berth, I'll manage."

"Eldridge is searching for you."

Immediately the smile left Christopher's face. "I know."

"You say you want to help me, but you place my life in jeopardy by maintaining your silence."

He spun away, moving toward the window to brush aside the curtain and stare at the front circular drive. "I never wanted to involve you. I knew the man was vile, but to use you, to threaten you . . ." He growled. "I wish to God that bloody journal had remained hidden."

"I cannot say I feel the same. Perhaps if it had not arrived, Marcus and I would not have found each other again."

Facing her, he offered a sad smile. He looked around, taking note of the liveried guards who stood conspicuously by the doorway. "I see Westfield has you well-guarded. That eases my mind somewhat."

"I see you look worn," she retorted bluntly.

"Thank you for noticing," he grumbled, "after I took such pains to make myself presentable. I must remember to discharge my valet."

"The best valet in the world cannot hide the signs of hard-living," she retorted. "Have you ever considered a change of occupation? The way you live is sapping the life from you."

His full mouth thinned with displeasure. "I am not here to discuss my way of life."

Taking a seat, she waited for him to do the same. "Very well then. I no longer have the journal."

St. John cursed so foully Elizabeth blushed. "Is it in Eldridge's possession?"

She hesitated a moment, wondering how wise it would be to tell him anything further. "No," she said finally, the restlessness of her fingers was the only betraying sign of her unease.

"Thank God. Keep it from him."

"He has been content to allow Westfield to work on it. At the moment, he seems most interested in finding you."

"Yes, he would be. I'm surprised he waited this long, truth be told. I would venture to say he wanted all of his agents in a lather before he released them on me. He's nothing if not meticulous."

Elizabeth studied St. John carefully. "Why did you come?"

"Once I learned Eldridge was looking for me I understood how delicate this situation has become. I don't know what to do. In the end there is only one solution and yet it's nearly impossible to implement."

She opened her mouth to speak when a sudden disturbance outside drew their attention. Leaping to her feet, she ran with St. John to the window. Out front, a village cart tottered precariously on three wheels. "Stay here," she ordered, knowing Marcus would wish to speak with the pirate, perhaps even detain him.

Elizabeth took only a moment to ensure assistance was being offered and then turned back to the room. It was empty. She stood blinking.

"Where did he go?" she asked the two guards.

They rushed in and quickly searched the space.

St. John was gone.

Marcus leaned his shoulders against the headboard and adjusted the weight of his wife's sated body, which draped over his own. Even her grumbled protest failed to make him smile. He stroked his hand down the length of her spine, soothing her back to sleep, while finding his own elusive.

Why had St. John come? If his aim had been the journal, he would want more than just Elizabeth's verbal confirmation that it was no longer with her. And yet he'd learned no more than that before dropping out the window and fleeing. To have arranged the distraction of the broken cart in advance was typical. To have known the house was emptied of Ashford men meant he'd been watching them.

His arms tightened around Elizabeth and her face nuzzled his chest in response. The pirate's warning was clear, *You are not safe. Even in your own domain.*

Even as he thought it, Marcus stilled. He cocked his head, his ears straining to hear over the soft crackling coming from the grate. He was greeted by silence, but he couldn't relax. The hairs on his nape stood on end.

He'd long ago learned to trust his instincts, so he slid down to his back and rolled, settling Elizabeth into the pillows. Her arms surrounded him, accustomed to his habit of waking her for sex. Pressing a quick kiss to her mouth, Marcus disentangled himself and withdrew from the warmth of the bed.

"What are you doing?" she complained, blinking.

Her pout was flattering and he took a moment to relish it. There had been a time when he could only dream of having her in his bed, eager for him. His ring on her finger caught what remained of the firelight and his jaw tightened. He'd be damned if anyone or anything jeopardized her now.

Tugging on his discarded breeches, he whispered, "Hold that thought for a moment, love." He grabbed his small sword, which rested conveniently against a nearby chair, and withdrew the blade from its scabbard. Elizabeth's head came up from the pillow. With a finger to his lips, he warned her to silence, and then padded across the room on bare feet. Marcus took a deep breath before cracking open the door that led to the sitting room.

Through the tiny space between the door jamb he could see across to Elizabeth's chamber. From the gap beneath her door, candlelight was clearly visible. Once again, his instincts had stood him in good stead. Someone was in there. Marcus rolled his shoulders and slipped out of his bedroom. St. John hadn't given up. He'd come back, as Marcus had suspected he would.

He'd wanted to position a guard in the sitting room, but Elizabeth had been horrified that someone would be so close while they made love. She'd been adamant and, doubting his restraint, he'd acceded. Now he could only shake his head at his fascination for his wife, which overruled every other consideration. Moving rapidly, he reached the door and tested the knob. It was locked. Cursing himself, he returned to his room for the key.

Elizabeth was slipping on her dressing gown.

Marcus shook head and scowled. *Stay here*, he mouthed.

What is it? she replied.

For his answer he held up the key, and then he returned to the sitting room. Immediately he noted the light under her door was gone. Hindered by darkness, it took him a moment to reach it. The chill breeze that flowed from the gap over his bare feet betrayed the open window on the other side. He was not fool enough to enter an unlighted room. Stepping out to the dimly lit hallway, Marcus grabbed the taper from the alcove and lit the candelabra on the console.

When he turned about, he saw the hallway door to Elizabeth's room was ajar. He kicked it open with his foot, candelabra in one hand, small sword in the other. The drapes were spread wide, allowing the pale light of the moon to cast shadows. The sheers fluttered in the soft evening breeze, a ghostly presence that made his fists clench tight. High as they were on the second floor, he doubted anyone would make the effort to enter or exit from that venue. Which meant they were either still in the room, or had slipped down the hallway while he'd gone for the key.

Elizabeth.

All was quiet, but still his nerves sizzled with awareness.

"My lord?" murmured a deep voice behind him. "What is amiss?"

Marcus turned, and faced one of the guards. Behind him stood Elizabeth, who worried her bottom lip with her teeth. For a moment, his throat clenched tight at the thought of her traversing the unsafe galleries. But there was naught else she could have done and once again his heart swelled with admiration. She was a practical woman, and a brave one. He took a moment to collect himself and then answered, "Someone was trespassing in her ladyship's room. Wait with her until I can be certain the intruder is gone."

The guard gave a quick nod, and Marcus made a thorough sweep. The room was empty, but the sense of unease remained with him. "Wake the other guards," he ordered as he returned to the hall. "Search the vacant rooms and exits. Discover how he gained entry. And from this night on, I want one of you to stay in my sitting room."

Passing the candelabra to the grim-faced guard, Marcus caught Elizabeth's elbow and led her back to the bedroom.

"It's time to come out of hiding, Marcus."

"No."

"You know I must." She stopped abruptly to face him.

His jaw tightened, and he shook his head. "It's too dangerous."

"What else can we do? Look at the risk to your family, to your home."

Marcus took her face in his hands. "You are my family, my home."

"Please don't be obstinate."

"You ask too much, Elizabeth."

"I ask for freedom." Her eyes glittered up at him. "I weary of this. We make no progress with this endless waiting. We must take the initiative and force his hand. End this."

He opened his mouth, and she placed her fingers over his lips. "Don't argue further. I understand your position. Just consider it. That's all I ask of you."

Knowing she was correct did not ease his torment and when they returned to the bed he held her too closely, needing her physical proximity to warm the icy fear that tightened his chest.

"Please don't worry," she whispered, her soft lips moving

against the skin of his chest just before she drifted back to sleep. "I trust you."

He held her close, loving her for believing in him enough to propose such peril. She'd once said she would never trust him, and he had believed that without question. To discover he'd reached her so deeply was a soothing balm to the festering wounds that were healing with every day that passed.

But he had nothing but contempt for himself, unable to understand how she could display such unwavering faith when he continued to fail her at every turn.

For Elizabeth, the three days following the incident in her room were fraught with tension. Marcus withdrew to his study, where he worked tirelessly to find all vulnerabilities in his defense of her. The nights were worse. Because of the guard positioned on the other side of the bedroom door, she could not relax enough to enjoy lovemaking and Marcus refused to take her when she was so reluctant.

"I hate to see you so glum, dear Beth," Paul said one afternoon, as she gathered together the meal plans scattered across the dining table.

"I am not glum."

He arched a brow. "Are you bored then? I wouldn't blame you. You have been penned up for days."

Wrinkling her nose, she almost confessed how she missed Marcus, but that would not have been appropriate so she simply shook her head.

"Would you like to go to the village?" he asked.

"No. Thank you." Marcus wouldn't allow her out of the manse, but that was not her only consideration. Luncheon would be served shortly and that seemed to be the only time lately when she had a few moments of his charming discourse. She told herself it was silly to miss him when they were so physically close, but she could not change how she felt, and quite surprisingly, would not want to. She'd once dreaded needing him so much. It was now a bond she relished.

"Are you certain?" Paul pressed.

Waving him off with a reassuring smile, Elizabeth moved out to the foyer. A few moments more and then she could call Marcus away. Her step lightened as she thought of her husband and the smile he would bestow upon her when she called his name from the study doorway. Lost in the thought, she missed seeing the arm that reached out and snatched her into the space beneath the left side curving staircase. Her meal plans, which she'd been carrying to the kitchen to discuss with the cook, scattered across the marble floor.

Her startled protest was cut off by a passionate kiss, her husband's large body crowding her to the wall. Her hands, lifted to push her attacker away, slipped around his neck and held him close.

"Sweet wife," he breathed, his lips pressed to hers.

Her heart racing at the sudden fright, she gasped to catch her breath. "Wh-what are you about?"

"I need you." He nibbled at her throat. "It's been three damned days."

Eyes closed, she breathed him in. The warmth of his skin, the obviously aroused length of his frame, the large hands that moved feverishly over her curves . . .

"Why can you not remain naked?" he complained. "Too much material separates my touch from you."

Elizabeth noted their surroundings. The sunlight from the rear lawn poured in from the French doors displaying their ardor to any hapless passerby. Only from the foyer were they hidden from view. "You must stop."

"I cannot."

She gave a breathless laugh, so enamored with his attentions she wished she were naked as well. Her blood thrummed in her veins, her body softening and relaxing into his. "What are you doing?"

"Making up for my lack." Marcus pulled away only slightly, his hands occupied, one at her waist, the other fighting uselessly to feel her breast through her corset.

"We'll be seen," she cautioned.

"You cannot dissuade me." He licked her lips.

"You cannot mean to ravish me here."

"Can I not?" He tugged at her silk bodice and the threads popped in protest. "I'm nigh desperate."

"Marcus." She swatted his hands away.

"I want you." The look in his eyes gave proof to that statement.

"Now?" She bit her lower lip, pleased that he had no control over his desire. "I don't understand your mood. Can you not wait?"

He shook his head and the simple denial filled her heart with joy.

"I want you, too," she confessed.

His grip tightened and the scorching heat of his gaze made her blush. "I never thought you would, not truly." His voice lowered. "But you do, don't you?"

Nodding, Elizabeth pressed her lips to his chin. "I ache for you. I've missed you so much."

"I have been here." He drew her as close as her skirts would allow.

"I'm selfish, Marcus. I want the entirety of your attention."

"You have it." His smile was wicked. "Now, would you like the rest of me as well? We can slip away, find somewhere private."

"Can I bind you? Tie you down? Keep you to myself for hours, days?"

Marcus drew back with widened eyes. "Are you serious?" He couldn't hide the sensual interest that deepened the curve of his smile.

The image in her mind made her wet. "Oh yes."

"You have five minutes with which to find a bed and disrobe. Any longer and I will cut that dress from you with my blade."

"You wouldn't," she protested, laughing. "I adore this gown."

"Four and three-quarters."

Elizabeth turned and fled. "Don't forget to collect my papers," she called over her shoulder.

Lifting her hem, she hurried up the stairs. Halfway to the top, she saw the butler emerge from the upper floor gallery. He descended to meet her.

"My lady, the post has arrived."

She reached for the missive on the silver salver, recognizing the familiar Langston crest stamped in the wax. "Thank you."

Breaking the seal, Elizabeth scanned the brief contents, and then reread them.

"Margaret has had the baby early," she cried. "A boy!"

"Two minutes," Marcus drawled, his deep voice coming from just below her.

She stilled instantly. "Did you hear? I must go to them."

"Come here, Lady Westfield." His purr was ominous as he ascended the staircase with predatory grace. "You wanted my attention. I vow, you have it. Your nephew will have to wait."

Elizabeth laughed aloud. "You will have to catch me first," she challenged as she flew up the stairs. She gained the landing and ran down the hallway, the precious letter in one hand and her skirts held in the other. Marcus was fast on her heels.

Elaine watched the antics from the lower parlor doorway. She spoke to Paul who stood next to her. "I have never seen him so happy. Marriage has done wonders for him."

"So it has," he agreed.

She looked up with an affectionate smile. "You, dear son, are next."

Chapter 22

Because of the need for secrecy, it was after midnight when the hired hackney arrived at Chesterfield Hall. Exiting the carriage at the rear of the mansion, Elizabeth and Marcus then entered through the delivery door.

"Is this level of prudence truly necessary?" Elizabeth complained as she shivered in the chill night air.

Marcus tossed his cloak over hers and wrapped his arms around her, sharing his warmth. "I refuse to take chances with your life. You are too precious to me."

They made their way up to Elizabeth's former room by way of the servants' staircase. "How precious am I?" she asked softly, preceding him down the hallway.

"Priceless."

Closing the door behind them, Marcus removed both cloaks from her shoulders before turning her to face him. He lowered his head, his eyes staring deeply into hers. His kiss was soft and generous, his lips clinging with obvious affection.

"Do you love me, Marcus?"

She had promised herself never to ask him how he felt about her. He showed her in a hundred different ways every day how much she meant to him. But somehow the need to hear the words could not be denied.

His mouth smiled against hers. "Do you even have to ask?"

Elizabeth pulled back to search his face. "Would it pain you so greatly to say it?"

His mouth parted to speak just as a soft rap came at the door. "Come in," he called out, unable to hide his relief.

William poked his tousled blond head inside. "Lady Barclay heard you arrive. She would like Elizabeth to meet her nephew now. You will have to wait until morning, Westfield."

"Of course I'll come now." Elizabeth stood on tiptoe and waited until Marcus lowered his lips to hers. "I am not finished with this conversation, my lord."

He nuzzled his nose against hers. "I await your pleasure, Lady Westfield."

As Elizabeth left the room, William stayed behind.

Marcus regarded his brother-in-law carefully, noting the dark shadows under his eyes. "You look exhausted."

"The future Earl of Langston has a voracious appetite and Lady Barclay has refused a wet nurse. I attempted to dissuade her, but to no avail. She stands firm."

"Congratulations." Marcus extended his hand and William clasped it firmly. "You are a most fortunate man."

William ran his hands through his hair. "You should not have returned to London."

"I agree, but like your wife, Elizabeth could not be discouraged. Unfortunately, she has reached the point where she's willing to make herself a target to bring the situation to a head." Marcus sighed. "The woman shows a deplorable lack of fear."

"Yes, she always has. Don't look so grim, Westfield. I can see you are not in accord with her decision by way of your early morning arrival and avoidance of returning to your own residence. You don't want anyone to be aware of her return."

"Do you fault me for that? She is my wife. You must know how I feel. Have you not lived with the same fear these last four years?"

"It was not like this," William admitted. "There was no journal to worry over and no knowledge of a spy within the agency. The danger is greater now, I'm not blind to it or nonchalant. I love Elizabeth, as you well know, but I have a son. The time has come to conclude this chapter of our lives so we can all proceed."

"And what of my children? Should something befall Elizabeth I will be left with nothing. You both beg the impossible from me."

"Westfield . . ." William sighed heavily. "You and I will be prepared when the time comes."

"When the time comes for what?" Elizabeth asked from the doorway.

"For you to be *enceinte*," William said with a smile that hid the true nature of their exchange.

Elizabeth's eyes widened. "You were discussing children?" She looked at Marcus. "*Our* children?"

He smiled at the thought. Every day he forced himself to believe she was his. It was a gift he continued to marvel over.

William engulfed her in a quick hug.

"Your son is beautiful," she said with a soft smile. "He'd fallen asleep by the time I arrived. I look forward to holding him when we are both less weary."

Kissing her forehead, he yawned before making his egress. "'Til morning then."

The door shut with a quiet click and Elizabeth faced Marcus with shoulders squared. "We have never discussed children."

"There is no need." He moved toward her. "They'll come when they come, and not a moment sooner."

She looked away, biting her lower lip.

He frowned at the sudden chill of her features. "What pains you, love?"

"I don't wish to discuss it."

Chuckling softly, he ran a fingertip over her collarbone, feeling the flare of awareness flow from his touch to her skin.

"You often say that, and then force me to pry your thoughts from you. But the hour is late, so I pray you'll spare me."

Her eyes closed. "Can we not just retire? I'm tired."

"Tell me," he urged, his lips to her brow. He dropped his voice seductively. "There are ways I can make you. Would you like that?"

"Perhaps . . ." Her chin lowered, as did her volume. "Perhaps I'm barren."

He pulled away, stunned. "Where do you find these ridiculous notions?"

"Think of it. I was married a year to Hawthorne and—"

"He didn't put any effort into it," Marcus dismissed with a snort.

"You have put more than enough effort into it these last months," she argued. "And still my courses come with clockwork regularity."

Frowning, Marcus stared at Elizabeth's downcast head. Her tangible sadness caught his breath. "Ah, sweet." He reached behind her and began to loosen her garments. "You worry without cause."

"With every month that passes I fear I've failed you." She rested her cheek against the velvet of his coat.

"How odd. With every month that passes I'm thankful I can have you to myself for a little while longer."

"Please don't jest."

"Never. I have two brothers. The Ashford line is in no danger."

"Surely you want your own offspring and it is my duty to provide them."

"Enough." He spun her around to facilitate undressing her. "I only want you. In all my life, I've only ever wanted you."

"Marcus—" Her voice broke, as did his heart to hear it.

"I love you," he said gruffly, his throat tight. "I always have." Beneath his hands he felt her crying. "If it is meant to be just you and I alone, I would die the happiest man. Never doubt it."

She turned and caught him, tugging his mouth down to hers, pressing tear-covered lips to his. "I don't deserve you," she sobbed, her fingers frantic in his hair.

Marcus absorbed her assault with a crushing embrace, unable to speak now that he'd said the words he'd once sworn not to say, not to even think. She pressed forward, her movements so wild he stumbled backward. Her hands slipped into his coat, shoved it from his shoulders, tore at the ivory buttons of his waistcoat.

"Elizabeth."

She was everywhere, clawing at the many layers of his clothing and the placket of his breeches until all he could do was help her. He understood her, perhaps better than she understood herself. She was cornered, trapped by feelings she had run from since she'd met him, and she was running again, only this time it was *to* him, rather than *away* from him. And he would give her the solace she needed, and take what she offered in return, because he loved her with every breath in his body.

"Take this off," she cried, ripping at her bodice. "Get this off me."

He gripped the loosened back flaps, and rent the gown open. She stepped out of the remnants, then with corset and chemise and a pile of underskirts, his wife tugged him to the floor, pressed him down, and tossed her leg over his hips. Marcus laughed, adoring her in her concentration and near brutal need of him. Then he gasped, and arched upward as she took him in hand, and then took him inside her, clasping his cock in slick, silky tissues.

"Christ," he groaned, wondering, as he did every time he fucked her, if the pleasure would ever subside to where it was at least bearable. If this was all there was, if his seed never took root, he could live with that. He knew it in his soul.

Elizabeth stilled, panting, her waist and breasts squeezed tight by her undergarments. She gazed down at her husband, sprawled beneath her, so gorgeous in his disarray. Marcus Ashford, known for his unshakable implacability, was flushed, his eyes bright, his sensual mouth parted. Unable to resist, she cupped his nape in her hand and lowered her lips to his. The taste of him, dark and dangerous, and the feeling of his tongue, silken and hot, made her shiver and clench tight around the shaft that throbbed within her.

He moaned into her mouth, and wrapped gentle arms around her. He thrust his hips upward in deep lunges, stroking her depths with the broad head of his cock.

"Marcus . . ." Filled with heated, voluptuous yearning, she rose and swiveled her hips, then bore down as he pumped upward, taking him so deeply she writhed with the pleasure of it. Every touch, every growl from his throat told her how much he loved her and accepted her, how much he needed her. Despite all her faults.

The intensity of his gaze was a tactile caress. He loved to watch her, she knew. Loved to hear her cries, and feel her need. Her body undulated over his, a thing separate from her mind, lost to her desire. The unyielding grip of her corset altered the experience, made her both achingly aware and dreamily dizzy.

"Yes," he urged hoarsely. "Take what you need. Let me give it to you."

Her fingertips rested on his abdomen and beneath his linen shirt she felt the tight, hard lacing of muscles flex with his exertions. Her eyes locked with his. "Hold me."

He pulled her down, pressed his lips to hers, his tongue driving into her mouth in rhythm with the long, deep plunges of his cock. She was so wet, so aroused, every upward thrust sounded wetly through the room.

I would die for this, he'd said, and she knew it was true, because there in his arms, she did.

And was reborn.

* * *

Elizabeth woke late in the morning, and found herself alone. She bathed and dressed, eager to find Marcus before she spent the rest of the day with Margaret and the baby.

As she descended the main stairs, she spied Lord Eldridge and Avery standing with her husband in the visitors' foyer. She paused a moment, composing herself for whatever was ahead, and then proceeded.

Seeing her approach, Marcus met her at the bottom of the staircase. "Good morning, my love." His gaze, both warm and appreciative, spoke volumes.

"Has something transpired?" she asked.

"I must leave with Eldridge. St. John has been seen in London, and there are other things that need to be attended to."

She smiled briefly at Lord Eldridge and Avery. "Good morning, my lord. Mr. James," she called out.

Both gentlemen bowed in greeting.

Turning her attention back to Marcus, she searched his face, and noted the taut lines that etched his lips. "Is there something else? Something you are withholding from me?"

He shook his head. "I simply worry about leaving you. Avery will remain, but I would much prefer to guard you myself. Whenever I turn my back, something untoward happens and—"

Setting her fingers to his lips, Elizabeth silenced him. "Hush, I will be fine with Mr. James. And William is here."

"Even the King's guards could not ease my mind."

"So stay," she said simply. "Send Mr. James with Eldridge."

"I cannot. I have resigned my commission, and there are things I must resolve before I can be free."

Elizabeth covered her mouth with her hand, tears filling her eyes and threatening to fall from her lashes. He'd kept his promise.

"Tell me those are happy tears."

"I love you," she breathed.

His mouth curved in an intimate smile. "I shall return at my soonest. Stay out of trouble in the meantime. Please."

Making their egress from Chesterfield Hall, Marcus and Eldridge retrieved the reins from the waiting groomsmen and mounted their horses.

"Did you say anything to Lady Westfield?" Eldridge asked once they'd reached the road.

"No. It would only serve to unduly worry her."

"You don't believe a threat against your life is worth the worry?"

Marcus snorted. "St. John would have killed me before, if that was his true intent," he said dismissively. "He is aware that threats to Lady Westfield carry the greater weight. Still, the possibility exists that I would lower my guard of her to raise my own. A foolish attempt, but it costs him nothing more than the missive he sent you to try."

Marcus was so confident in his assessment that when the shot rang out and burning pain tore through his shoulder, he was caught completely unaware.

The horses reared, Eldridge yelled, and Marcus was thrown with stunning force to the ground. Dazed, he could not defend himself against the half dozen men who swarmed toward him in ambush. He could only realize, with horrified clarity, how far he had erred when Talbot loomed over him with small sword in hand. *He works well with Avery James,* Eldridge had said. Blind to the perfidy, he'd left Elizabeth in the care of the very man who wished her harm.

Now he lay on his back and noted that the trees, which shielded the lane, were a verdant backdrop to the steel of the blade swooping toward him with deadly precision.

But in the end, his greatest fear came not from his approaching death, but for his beloved wife, who needed him. And he would not be there.

Chapter 23

"You look beautiful."

Margaret blushed. "Good heavens, Elizabeth. How can you say such a thing? I must look a fright. I've not had a full night of rest since the birth, my hair is ever in disarray, I am—"

"Glowing," Elizabeth interjected.

Gazing with adoration at her infant son, Margaret smiled, "I did not believe it was possible to love someone as much as I do this child." She glanced at Elizabeth who stood by the door. "You shall see when you and Westfield have children of your own."

Elizabeth nodded sadly, and reached for the doorknob. "I will leave you to feed my nephew."

"It's not necessary for you to go," Margaret protested.

"We arrived so late yesterday, I find myself still weary. A small nap, and then I'll return."

"Where is Lord Westfield?"

"Attending to some matters. I expect he'll return shortly."

"Very well, then." Margaret nodded. "Come back to me refreshed. I miss female companionship."

Yawning, Elizabeth retreated to her room, her heart heavy with worry. Marcus was disturbed. Despite his denials to the contrary, she couldn't shake the feeling that something was terribly wrong.

She paused in the gallery outside her chamber, frowning when she noted the door was ajar. Entering cautiously, she saw the familiar figure digging in her escritoire drawers. He turned to face her.

It was then she saw the knife in his hand.

She froze, and swallowed hard. "What are you about, Mr. James?"

Inwardly steeled for the pain of being run through, Marcus jolted in surprise at the sound of gunfire. Talbot jerked, his eyes widening in horror. Deep crimson soaked through his waistcoat, spreading from the hole that bored through his chest. The downward swing of his sword arm faltered and he stumbled, forcing Marcus to roll away as he fell to the ground. Dead.

Surrounded by a grisly melee, Marcus leapt to his feet, staring at the battle that raged around him. A dozen men, none of whom he recognized, fought with deadly intent. Dust rose from the dry lane, choking his throat and gritting his eyes. Steel clashed in a macabre cacophony, and while his left arm was nigh useless, his right was serviceable. He withdrew his sword with lightning speed, prepared to defend himself.

"Stand down."

Spinning about with blade raised, he faced St. John.

"You are in no condition to fight," the pirate said dryly, tossing aside a now useless smoking pistol.

"How long have James and Talbot been in your employ?"

St. John continued to approach him. "They haven't been. That's not to say I lack eyes and ears within the agency. However, the men you mention are not associates of mine."

Marcus stilled, his thoughts quickly catching up to the reality he faced. He turned, searching for Eldridge, and found him nowhere. He did, however, note Talbot again, and came to the only conceivable conclusion. Nothing was as it seemed.

Snorting, St. John said, "So now you see the truth. I would have told you. However, you would not have believed me."

A man fell at their feet, and they both leapt quickly out of the way.

"Allow my men to handle this, Westfield. We must bind your wound, ere you bleed to death, and find Lady Westfield."

It was galling, the thought of working with St. John, and Marcus spit out the bile that coated his tongue. All this time, all these years . . .

Gradually the lane grew quiet, but Marcus's blood raged, drowning his hearing in roaring sound. He shrugged out of his coat, discarding the ruined garment in the blood-spattered dirt. St. John worked quickly and efficiently at binding his damaged shoulder while Marcus watched the pirate's lackeys drag the proliferation of bodies away with frightening nonchalance.

"How long have you been aware of this?" he asked gruffly.

"Years."

"And the journal?"

Tightening the binding until Marcus winced, St. John nodded at his handiwork and stepped back. "Can you seat a horse?"

"I have been shot, I'm not an invalid."

"Right. Let's go. I can explain on the way."

"Where is the journal, my lady?" Avery asked.

Elizabeth kept her gaze trained on the knife. "Safe."

"None of us are safe."

"What are you talking about?"

He came toward her quickly, and she recoiled. "Now is not the time to be skittish. I need you to think quickly and trust me implicitly, or you will not survive."

"I don't understand."

"I don't know that I do either. I watched several men approach from the rear garden and fan around the manse."

"A siege?" she cried in horror. "There are servants here, Lord and Lady Barclay . . . Oh God. The baby."

Avery gripped her elbow and led her toward the door. "Lord Langston is gone, as is Westfield and Eldridge. If there are enough of the brigands, they could take you with little effort. They've ransacked your room before, they know the way in."

"Who would be so daring?"

A trusted bewigged figure filled the doorway, blocking their egress.

Avery paused, his jaw tightening grimly. He jerked his chin toward door. "*He* would."

Marcus peered through the cover of bushes, and cursed under his breath. His heart raced in a panicked rhythm as he thought of his wife. In all of his near death encounters, had he ever been so afraid?

He counted four men at the front and three at the rear. If he were well, it would be a simple matter, but he had only one arm. Weakened by both blood loss and near crippling fear for Elizabeth, he knew he would be unable to fight them all. So he watched in frustrated helplessness as St. John's men tended to the distasteful matter, creeping stealthily along the perimeter, waiting for an opening to strike.

"Eldridge knew almost from the first moment," St. John said quietly, drawing Marcus's attention. "He noted the resemblance between Hawthorne and me immediately. He confirmed his suspicions and confronted Hawthorne, threatening to reveal his treasonous intent for joining the agency."

"Unless . . . ?"

"Unless we worked with him. He would provide the information, we would make use of it, and he would collect half the proceeds."

"Jesus." Marcus returned his gaze to Chesterfield Hall, barely registering the brick exterior with its climbing vines. Four years of his life had been dedicated to a lie. "I trusted him," he said grimly.

"Hawthorne didn't. Hence the creation of the journal."

"Which contains . . . ?"

"Nothing." St. John shrugged at his glare. "Hawthorne knew we were expendable, so he bartered with the journal, which was said to be an account of witnesses to Eldridge's guilt and locations of booty we'd hidden from him. In truth, we had nothing, but the book ensured our safety. If something befell us, Eldridge's perfidy would be revealed and he would lose what he thinks to be a fortune."

"You saved yourself, but risked my wife?" Marcus growled. "Look at all she has suffered, what she is suffering now."

"I am responsible for the search of her rooms. The attacks, however, were not my doing. They were a warning to me. I would have killed Eldridge long ago, but he swore Lady Westfield would pay with her life if his death came by my hand. He also threatened to reveal Hawthorne's treason. I could not allow that to happen. So we have waited, he and I, for the day when the balance would tip and free one of us to kill the other."

Standing from his low crouch, Marcus watched as the last of Eldridge's men were eliminated, their throats slit so that no sound was made. With the same precision they'd shown on the lane, St. John's lackeys quietly dragged the bodies away from the manse and into the nearby coppice. "Why not kill you when the journal surfaced? Once it was in his grasp, what use did he have for you?"

"He fears I am the only man alive who can decipher Hawthorne's code." St. John gave a mirthless laugh. "He has allowed you to try. I imagine if you had succeeded, he would have killed you and laid blame on me. He cannot simply do away with me, the people would riot."

They left the cover of the bushes, and ran toward the manse. "It's too quiet," Marcus muttered as they entered through the front door. Chills coursed down his spine, along with the sweat that dampened his skin and clothing. They moved cautiously, unsure of what traps awaited them.

"*Westfield.*"

Both men paused midstep. Turning their heads, they met the intense aqua gaze of Viscount Barclay who stood frozen in a nearby doorway.

"Is there something you wish to tell me?" he asked, but his casual words could not hide the tension that stiffened his frame or the pure hatred he directed at St. John with a scathing glance.

Swiveling to face his brother-in-law, Marcus revealed his injury.

"Good God. What happened to you?"

"Eldridge."

William's eyes widened, and he took the news with a visible shudder. "*What?* I cannot . . . *Eldridge?*"

Marcus moved not at all, but William knew him well enough to be answered. He released a deep breath, composing himself, setting aside questions that could wait in deference to matters that couldn't. "You cannot continue. You need a surgeon."

"I need my wife. Eldridge is here, Barclay. In this house."

"No!" William shot a horrified glance up the stairs, then he pointed at St. John. "And you think him worthy of your trust?"

"I don't know whom to trust, but he just spared my life. That will have to suffice for the time being."

Pale and obviously confused, William took a moment to collect his thoughts, but for Marcus it was a moment too long. Too much time had passed. Eldridge was ahead of them by some lead. Elizabeth was endangered, and he was nearly mad with the agony of it. Leaving the others behind, he threw caution to the wind and raced up the stairs.

"Lord Eldridge?" Elizabeth frowned in confusion as she looked past him. "Where is Westfield?"

"Lord Westfield is otherwise occupied. If you wish to be reunited, you will retrieve the journal and come with me."

She stared, attempting to make sense of what he was

about. Then she noted the tiny dark spatters on the gray velvet of his coat. The sick sense of foreboding intensified. Her hands clenched into fists, and she stepped forward. "What—have—you—done?"

Eldridge shifted, startled, and Avery took that slight advantage to launch himself the short distance and tackle him to the ground.

The two men hit the floor with a sickening thud and rolled out to the hallway, crashing into the opposite wall. Her mind dazed and her chest tight, Elizabeth wondered briefly if the noise would wake the baby. It was that thought which galvanized her.

She searched the room desperately with her eyes, seeking something, anything that could be used as a weapon.

"Run!" Avery grunted, his hands occupied with holding at bay the knife Eldridge wielded.

That single word forced her to move. Lifting her skirts, Elizabeth ran past the men locked in deadly combat and fled down the hall toward Margaret's rooms. She rounded the corner and rammed headfirst into a unyielding barrier. With a scream of terror, she fell, clutching desperately at the hard body that fell with her.

"Elizabeth."

The breath left her lungs as they hit floor.

Sprawled atop her husband, she lifted her head and caught sight of William's shoes as he ran to his rooms.

"Leave Eldridge to me," St. John rasped softly, as he stepped past them.

Elizabeth returned her gaze to her husband, but had trouble seeing him with the tears that streamed from her eyes. With gentle hands, Marcus rolled her from him. He was frighteningly pale, his mouth drawn, but the warmth and relief in his gaze was undeniable.

"He said you were captured!" she cried.

"I was very nearly killed."

She noted the blood-soaked bandage that wrapped his torso and shoulder. "Oh dear God, you've been hurt!"

"Are you well?" he asked gruffly, rising to his feet and then pulling her to hers.

She nodded, the tears flowing unchecked. "Mr. James saved my life by holding off Eldridge until I could escape, but I found him searching my room. He wanted the journal, Marcus. He had a knife . . ."

Marcus pulled her closer, absorbing her trembling with a one-armed embrace. "Hush. Go to your brother, love. Do not leave his side until I come for you. Do you understand?"

"Where are you going?" She gripped the waistband of his breeches in nerveless fists. "You need help. You're bleeding." Elizabeth straightened her spine. "Let me see you to William, then I can consider—"

His mouth took hers in a hard, quick kiss. "I do adore you, my fearless bride. But indulge me, if you will. Allow me to finish this. My masculine pride begs it of you."

"Don't be arrogant now! You are in no condition to chase criminals, and I can aim a pistol better than most men."

"I will not disagree." His voice firmed. "However, in this instance I'm afraid I must exert my husbandly right of command, despite the row I know that will cause. Go, my love. Do as I say. I will return to you shortly, and then you may both harangue and fuss over me to your heart's content."

"I do not harangue."

Steel clashed in the nearby hallway, and the look in his eyes hardened enough to make her shiver. Following the urging of the gentle shove he gave her, Elizabeth moved with shaky legs down the hall.

"Be careful," she admonished. But when she looked behind her, he was already gone.

Marcus watched Elizabeth retreat, and thanked God for her. Everything he'd believed in, everyone he'd thought solid and immutable had shattered in one fell blow. Except for her. Wanting desperately to take shelter in her, but needing to end this first, he turned about, running toward the sounds of conflict.

He rounded the corner, his jaw locked with grim resignation and discovered St. John, his body moving with loose-limbed grace, his sword arm thrusting so quickly it was difficult to track it. Eldridge opposed him, his wig lost, his hair wild, his face reddened from exertion. It was a losing battle he fought, but the agency leader was not Marcus's concern. Certainly Marcus had his grievances, but his wife was alive, and St. John's brother was not.

His attention was instead on Avery, who stood to the side with dagger in hand. Marcus waited, unobserved, wanting to give Avery the opportunity to do what was right. They had worked together for years, and Marcus had, up until an hour ago, thought of the agent as a friend. He couldn't prevent the tiny hope that his trust had not been completely misplaced.

St. John feinted, and then lunged forward on his right foot. A winded Eldridge could not move swiftly enough to deflect the hit, and Marcus watched as the blade sank home in his thigh and he fell to his knees.

The pirate loomed over the vanquished Eldridge with teeth clenched, his hand fisted around the other man's throat.

"You cannot kill me," Eldridge croaked. "You need me."

It was then that Avery made his move, approaching the distracted St. John from behind with his arm raised and knife ready to fall.

"Avery," Marcus growled.

Avery spun about and threw himself forward, forcing Marcus to return. Parrying the flashing dagger with his small sword, Marcus leapt back a step. "Don't do this," he grunted. But Avery would not desist.

"I have no choice."

Marcus attempted to draw out the confrontation, praying Avery would break through his panic and cease. He aimed his blade at less vulnerable areas, striking to wound and not to kill. Finally, however, exhausted by his own injury and depleted of options, he made a fatal thrust.

Panting, Avery sank to the floor, his back to the wall, blood drizzling from the corner of his lips. His hands were stained crimson, pressing against the spot on his chest where Marcus had impaled him. Eldridge lay at his feet, St. John's sword sunk so deep into his heart it gouged into the wood floor beneath.

Sighing, Marcus dropped into a crouch. "Ah, Avery. Why?"

"My lord," Avery gasped, sweat dripping from his brow. "You know the answer to that. Prison is not for the likes of me."

"You spared my wife, I might have helped you."

A translucent red bubble formed between Avery's lips and burst as he spoke. "I grew . . . I grew quite fond of her."

"And she of you." Marcus withdrew a handkerchief and wiped the sweat from Avery's brow. The agent's eyes closed at the touch of the cloth.

Marcus glanced at Eldridge. The scene was surreal, and heartrending.

"There were more . . . men," Avery wheezed. "Is she safe?"

"Yes, she's safe."

Avery nodded, his breath rattling in his lungs, and then he stilled, his body slumping into death's embrace.

Marcus stumbled to his feet, weary and disheartened. He glanced at St. John who said softly, "You saved my life."

"Consider my debt paid for your like service to me. What do you intend to do with Eldridge?"

"The poor man was a victim of highway robbery." St. John yanked his sword free. "My men will make certain he is found at the appropriate time and in the appropriate manner. If we are done here, I shall see to it."

Marcus could not prevent the twinge of guilt and sorrow he felt. He'd admired Eldridge, and would mourn the man he'd once thought him to be.

"Take the journal with you," he said gruffly. "If I never see the blasted thing again it will be too soon."

"My men will manage these two," the pirate said, gesturing over the bodies with the bloody tip of his sword. "We are liberated, Westfield. I trust the king will believe the tale when told to him by both you and Barclay. Then the bad seeds will be routed from the agency and Eldridge's threat to haunt me after death will be negated."

"Yes, I suppose that is true." But Marcus found little comfort in the ending. He knew he'd be haunted by this day forever.

"Marcus?"

He turned at the tentative sound of his wife's voice. Elizabeth stood a few feet away, a pistol weighting her arm and dangling at her side. The sight of her, so small but determined, eased the tightness in his chest, and he left the ugliness behind to find solace in her arms.

EPILOGUE

London, April 1771

The weather was perfect for a ride in the Park, and Marcus relished the day. His mount was spirited and pranced impatiently, but nevertheless, he managed the reins with one hand, while touching the brim of his hat in greeting with the other. It was the start of a new Season, his first complete Season with Elizabeth as his wife, and he could only call his mood elated.

"Good afternoon, Lord Westfield."

Marcus turned his head toward the landaulet that drew up beside him. "Lady Barclay." He smiled.

"May I inquire after Lady Westfield?"

"You may. She's presently napping, I am sorry to say. I pine for her company."

"She's not ill, is she?" Margaret asked, her brows drawn into a frown beneath her wide-brimmed hat.

"No, she's well. Weary and a bit achy at the moment, but then we just returned to Town, as you know. The journey can be tiring." Of course, he hadn't allowed her much sleep at the inn.

Elizabeth grew more beautiful by the day, and more irresistible. He often thought of the portrait of her mother, the one that hung above the fireplace in the formal parlor of Chesterfield Hall. He'd once wished to see such happiness re-flected in Elizabeth's countenance. Now he would say her contentment far surpassed it.

To think that a year ago he'd thought to sate his lust and end his torment. The former would never happen, not while he breathed, but the later was a distant memory. He thanked the Lord daily that he'd managed to slay her demons as well. Together, they'd found peace, and it was a state of being he cherished.

"I am relieved to hear it's nothing serious. My son is quite eager to see his aunt again, and she promised to call this week."

"Then I'm certain she shall."

They spoke for a few moments longer, but when his horse grew agitated, Marcus bade his farewell. He took a less trav-eled path than the Row, and freed his mount to run, then he turned toward Grosvenor Square, hoping he'd given Elizabeth enough time to sleep, but too impatient to dally any more, re-gardless.

As he rode up to the steps of his house, he caught sight of the man who departed and a heavy uneasiness settled over him.

He tossed the reins to the waiting groomsman and hurried inside.

"Good afternoon, my lord," the servant greeted as Marcus handed over his hat and gloves.

"Apparently not, since the doctor was here."

"Lady Westfield is ill, my lord."

"The dowager?" But he knew that was not the case. His mother had looked the picture of health at breakfast while Elizabeth had been out of sorts for over a sennight. Worried beyond measure, he took the stairs two at a time. Her mother had fallen ill and never recovered, a fact he could not forget since the scars from that loss had kept them apart for years.

He entered their rooms cautiously, hesitantly. Pausing on the threshold of Elizabeth's boudoir, he caught the scent of illness, which lingered, defying the windows which were flung wide open to entice the air to circulate. His wife lay still as death on the couch with unhealthy pallor, her skin lightly misted with sweat despite the fact she wore only her negligee and the temperature was more cold than warm.

The doctor was an idiot. Despite his lack of medical knowledge, it was obvious to Marcus that Elizabeth was gravely ill.

A maid bustled around the room, arranging flowers in an effort to scent the room with something pleasant. One look from Marcus, however, and she curtsied and hurried away.

"My love." He fell to his knees beside the couch and brushed the damp tendrils of Elizabeth's hair off her forehead. Her skin was clammy, and he fought the urge to snatch her to him and hold her close.

Elizabeth moaned softly at the touch of her husband's hand. Opening her eyes, she stared at Marcus, acknowledging, as she often did, that she would never tire of looking at him.

"What ails you?" he asked softly, his low velvety voice a soothing caress.

"I was just thinking of you. Where did you go?"

"For a ride in the Park."

"You wicked man. Tormenting all the women in London with the sight of you." The harsh cynicism that had once etched his features was gone, revealing a face of breathtaking masculine beauty. "I'm certain you set every female heart aflutter."

He made a valiant effort to smile through his worried frown. "You never become jealous anymore. I'm not certain how I should feel about that."

"You arrogant man. I trust you to behave yourself. Especially in the near future when I cannot be with you."

"Cannot be with . . . Dear God." He tugged her from the sofa into his arms. "Please spare me," he begged. "Tell me what's wrong. I am wretched over your illness. I will find the best specialists, research every medical volume, call upon—"

She pressed cool fingertips to his lips. "A midwife will suffice."

"A midwife?" His eyes widened and then shot to her belly. "A *midwife?*"

"You certainly put enough effort into it," she teased, adoring the wonder that slowly filled his eyes. "You should not be quite so startled."

"Elizabeth." He squeezed her gently. "Speech fails me."

"Tell me you are happy. That is all I ask."

"Happy? Bloody hell, I was beyond happy when it was just you and I. And content. Now . . . now there are no words for how I feel."

Elizabeth buried her face in her husband's throat and breathed him in, finding instant comfort just from the feel of him next to her. She had suspected pregnancy for weeks, as her breasts had grown more tender and her body had been plagued by weariness. Hiding her morning illness had not been easy, but she'd managed until today. She finally called for the doctor when she'd been inwardly certain she would hear the news she desired above anything.

"I know precisely what you mean to convey," she murmured against his skin. "I will never be able to tell you how it touches me that you loved me, even when it seemed we would not have children."

Settling more comfortably into his lap, Elizabeth thought of how different her life was now from how it had been only a year ago. She'd said she wanted equanimity, but what she had truly wanted was numbness, a respite from the knowledge that she was missing something vital. To have been so afraid, so sure that loving Marcus would weaken her, rather than strengthen her . . . She couldn't fathom it now.

"I love you," she murmured, perfectly happy for the first time since she was a child. Secure in his arms, she drifted to sleep and dreamed of the future.

Sylvia Day's Georgian series continues with *Passion for the Game*.

"If all angels of death were as lovely as you, men would line up to die."

Maria, Lady Winter, shut the lid of her enameled patch box with a decisive snap. Her revulsion for the mirrored reflection of the man who sat behind her made her stomach roil. Taking a deep breath, she kept her gaze trained on the stage below, but her attention was riveted by the incomparably handsome man who sat in the shadows of her theater box.

"Your turn will come," she murmured, maintaining her regal façade for the benefit of the many lorgnettes pointed in her direction. She had worn crimson silk tonight, accented by delicate black lace frothing from elbow-length sleeves. It was her most-worn color. Not because it suited her Spanish heritage coloring so well—dark hair, dark eyes, olive skin—but because it was a silent warning. *Bloodshed. Stay away.*

The Wintry Widow, the voyeurs whispered. *Two husbands dead . . . and counting.*

Angel of death. How true that was. Everyone around her died, except for the man she cursed to Hades.

The low chuckle at her shoulder made her skin crawl. "It will take more than you, my dearest daughter, to see me to my reward."

"Your reward will be my blade in your heart," she hissed.

"Ah, but then you will never be reunited with your sister, and she almost of age."

"Do not think to threaten me, Welton. Once Amelia is wed, I will know her location and will have no further need for your life. Consider that before you think to do to her what you have done to me."

"I could sell her into the slave trade," he drawled.

"You assume, incorrectly, that I did not anticipate your threat." Fluffing the lace at her elbow, she managed a slight curve to her lips to hide her terror. "I will know. And then you will die."

She felt him stiffen and her smile turned genuine. Ten and six was her age when Welton had ended her life. Anticipation for the day when she would pay him in kind was all that moved her when despair for her sister threatened paralysis.

"St. John."

The name hung suspended in the air between them.

Maria's breath caught. "Christopher St. John?"

It was rare that anything surprised her anymore. At the age of six and twenty, she believed she had seen and done nearly everything. "He has coin aplenty, but marriage to him will ruin me, making me less effective for your aims."

"Marriage is not necessary this time. I've not yet depleted Lord Winter's settlement. This is simply a search for information. I believe they are engaging St. John in some business. I want you to discover what it is they want with him, and most importantly, who arranged his release from prison."

Maria smoothed the bloodred material that pooled around her legs. Her two unfortunate husbands had been agents of the Crown whose jobs made them highly useful to her stepfather. They had also been peers of great wealth, much of which they left to her for Welton's disposal upon their untimely demise.

Lifting her head, she looked around the theater, absently noting the curling smoke of candles and gilded scrollwork that shone in firelight. The soprano on the stage struggled for attention, for no one was here to see her. The peerage was here to see each other and be seen, nothing more.

"Interesting," Maria murmured, recalling a sketch of the popular pirate. Uncommon handsome he was, and as deadly as she. His exploits were widely bandied, some tales so outrageous she knew they could not possibly be true. St. John was discussed with intemperate eagerness, and there were wagers aplenty on how long he could escape the noose.

"They must be desperate indeed to spare him. All these years they have searched for the irrefutable proof of his villainy, and now that they have it, they bring him into the fold. I daresay neither side is pleased."

"I do not care how they feel," Welton dismissed curtly. "I simply wish to know who I can extort to keep quiet about it."

"Such faith in my charms," she drawled, hiding how her mouth filled with bile. To think of the deeds she had been forced into to protect and serve a man she detested . . . Her chin lifted. It was not her stepfather she protected and served. She merely needed him alive, for if he were killed, she would never find Amelia.

Welton ignored her jibe. "Have you any notion what that information would be worth?"

She gave a nearly imperceptible nod, aware of the avid scrutiny that followed her every movement. Society knew her husbands had not died natural deaths. But they lacked proof. Despite this morbid certainty of her guilt, she was welcomed into the finest homes eagerly. She was infamous. And nothing livened up a gathering like a touch of infamy.

"How do I find him?"

"You have your ways."

Read on for an excerpt from the third of Sylvia Day's Georgian books, *A Passion for Him*.

London, 1780

The man in the white mask was following her.

Amelia Benbridge was uncertain of how long he had been moving surreptitiously behind her, but he most definitely was.

She strolled carefully around the perimeter of the Langston ballroom, her senses attuned to his movements, her head turning with feigned interest in her surroundings so that she might study him further.

Every covert glance took her breath away.

In such a crush of people, another woman most likely would not have noted the avid interest. It was far too easy to be overwhelmed by the sights, sounds, and smells of a masquerade. The dazzling array of vibrant fabrics and frothy lace . . . the multitude of voices attempting to be heard over an industrious orchestra . . . the mingling scents of various perfumes and burnt wax from the massive chandeliers . . .

But Amelia was not like other women. She had lived the first sixteen years of her life under guard, her every movement watched with precision. It was a unique sensation to be examined so closely. She could not mistake the feeling for anything else.

However, she could say with some certainty that she had never been so closely scrutinized by a man quite so . . . compelling.

For he *was* compelling, despite the distance between them and the concealment of the upper half of his face. His form alone arrested her attention. He stood tall and well proportioned, his garments beautifully tailored to cling to muscular thighs and broad shoulders.

She reached a corner and turned, setting their respective positions at an angle. Amelia paused there, taking the opportunity to raise her mask to surround her eyes, the gaily colored ribbons that adorned the stick falling down her gloved arm. Pretending to watch the dancers, she was in truth watching him and cataloguing his person. It was only fair, in her opinion. If he could enjoy an unhindered view, so could she.

He was drenched in black, the only relief being his snowy white stockings, cravat, and shirt. And the mask. So plain. Unadorned by paint or feathers. Secured to his head with black satin ribbon. While the other gentlemen in attendance were dressed in an endless range of colors to attract attention, this man's stark severity seemed designed to blend into the shadows. To make him unremarkable, which he could never be. Beneath the light of hundreds of candles, his dark hair gleamed with vitality and begged a woman to run her fingers through it.

And then there was his mouth . . .

Amelia inhaled sharply at the sight of it. His mouth was sin incarnate. Sculpted by a master hand, the lips neither full nor thin, but firm. Shamelessly sensual. Framed by a strong chin, chiseled jaw, and swarthy skin. A foreigner, perhaps. She could only imagine how the face would look as a whole. Devastating to a woman's equanimity, she suspected.

But it was more than his physical attributes that intrigued her. It was the way he moved, like a predator, his gait purposeful and yet seductive, his attention sharply focused. He did not mince his steps or affect the veneer of boredom so esteemed by Society. This man knew what he wanted and lacked the patience to pretend otherwise.

At present it appeared that what he wanted was to follow her. He watched Amelia with a gaze so intensely hot, she felt it move across her body, felt it run through the unpowdered strands of her hair and dance across her bared nape. Felt it glide across her bared shoulders and down the length of her spine. *Coveting.*

Enjoy more of Sylvia Day's Georgian series with *Don't Tempt Me*.

Paris, France—1757

With her fingers curled desperately around the edge of the table before her, Marguerite Piccard writhed in the grip of unalloyed arousal. Gooseflesh spread up her arms and she bit her lower lip to stem the moan of pleasure that longed to escape.

"Do not restrain your cries," her lover urged hoarsely. "It makes me wild to hear them."

Her blue eyes, heavy-lidded with passion, lifted within the mirrored reflection before her and met the gaze of the man who moved at her back. The vanity in her boudoir rocked with the thrusts of his hips, his breathing rough as he made love to her where they stood.

The Marquis de Saint-Martin's infamously sensual lips curved with masculine satisfaction at the sight of her flushed dishevelment. His hands cupped her swaying breasts, urging her body to move in tandem with his.

They strained together, their skin coated with sweat, their chests heaving from their exertions. Her blood thrummed in her veins, the experience of her lover's passion such that she had forsaken everything—family, friends, and esteemed future—to be with him. She knew he loved her similarly. He proved it with every touch, every glance.

"How beautiful you are," he gasped, watching her through the mirror.

When she had suggested the location of their tryst with timid eagerness, he'd laughed with delight.

"I am at your service," he purred, shrugging out of his garments as he stalked her into the boudoir. There was a sultriness to his stride and a predatory gleam in his dark eyes that caused her to shiver in heated awareness. Sex was innate to him. He exuded it from every pore, enunciated it with every syllable, displayed it with every movement. And he excelled at it.

From the moment she first saw him at the Fontinescu ball nearly a year ago, she had been smitten with his golden handsomeness. His attire of ruby red silk had attracted every eye without effort, but Marguerite had attended the event with the express aim of seeing him in the flesh. Her older sisters had whispered scandalous tales of his liaisons, occasions when he had been caught in flagrant displays of seduction. He was wed; yet discarded lovers pined for him openly, weeping outside his home for a brief moment of his attention. Her curiosity about what sort of shell would encase such wickedness was too powerful to be denied.

Saint-Martin did not disappoint her. In the simplest of terms, she did not expect him to be so . . . *male*. Those who were given to the pursuit of vice and excess were rarely virile, as he most definitely was.

Never had she met a man more devastating to a woman's equanimity. The marquis was magnificent, his physical form impressive and his aloofness an irresistible lure. Golden-haired and skinned, as she was, he was desired by every woman in France for good reason. There was an air about him that promised pleasure unparalleled. The decadence and forbidden delights intimated within his slumberous gaze lured one to forget themselves. The marquis had lived twice Marguerite's eight and ten years, and he possessed a wife as lovely as he was comely. Neither fact mitigated Marguerite's immediate, intense attraction to him. Or his returning attraction to her.

"Your beauty has enslaved me," he whispered that first

night. He stood near to where she waited on the edge of the dance floor, his lanky frame propped against the opposite side of a large column. "I must follow you or ache from the distance between us."

Marguerite kept her gaze straight ahead, but every nerve ending tingled from his boldness. Her breath was short, her skin hot. Although she could not see him, she felt the weight of his regard and it affected her to an alarming degree. "You know of women more beautiful than I," she retorted.

"No." His husky, lowered voice stilled her heartbeat. Then, made it race. "I do not."

The Stranger
I Married

ALSO BY SYLVIA DAY

Bad Boys Ahoy!

Ask for It

Passion for the Game

A Passion for Him

Don't Tempt Me

Pride and Pleasure

Seven Years to Sin

SYLVIA DAY, WRITING AS LIVIA DARE

In the Flesh

ANTHOLOGIES

Perfect Kisses

Published by Kensington Publishing Corp.

The Stranger
I Married

SYLVIA DAY

KENSINGTON PUBLISHING CORP.
www.kensingtonbooks.com

KENSINGTON BOOKS are published by

Kensington Publishing Corp.
119 West 40th Street
New York, NY 10018

All Kensington titles, imprints, and distributed lines are available at special quantity discounts for bulk purchases for sales promotions, premiums, fund-raising, educational, or institutional use.

Special book excerpts or customized printings can also be created to fit specific needs. For details, write or phone the office of the Kensington special sales manager: Kensington Publishing Corp., 119 West 40th Street, New York, NY 10018, attn: Special Sales Department; phone 1-800-221-2647.

KENSINGTON and the K logo are Reg. U.S. Pat. & TM Off.

ISBN-13: 978-0-7582-9039-7
ISBN-10: 0-7582-9039-X

First Kensington Trade Paperback Printing: January 2007
Fourth Printing: September 2012

10 9 8 7 6

Printed in the United States of America

This book is gratefully dedicated to Editorial Goddess Kate Duffy. There are numerous reasons why I think she's fabulous—from the biggies like being the first editor to buy my work, to the smaller (but no less important) things like being generous with her praise.

Kate,
How lucky I am to write for you.
Your enthusiasm for our work together is such a gift. I'm thankful every day to have found you right at the beginning of my career. You have taught me so much, and given me so many opportunities to grow. You allow me to write the stories in my heart, and you've shown me how wonderful the editor/author relationship can be.
Thank you so much.
Sylvia

Acknowledgments

As always, huge thanks and hugs go out to my critique partner, Annette McCleave (*www.AnnetteMcCleave.com*). She keeps me on my toes, and I love her for it.

Much love goes out to my agents Deidre Knight and Pamela Harty. I am blessed, honored, and grateful to work with you both.

And the Allure Authors (*www.AllureAuthors.com*) for supporting me and my work. The Allure gals have a true sisterhood, and it means a great deal to me.

Prologue

London, 1815

"Do you truly intend to steal your best friend's mistress?"

Gerard Faulkner, the sixth Marquess of Grayson, kept his eyes on the woman in question, and smiled. Those who knew him well also knew that look, and its wicked portent. "I certainly do."

"Dastardly," Bartley muttered. "Too low even for you, Gray. Is it not sufficient to cuckold Sinclair? You know how Markham feels about Pel. He's lost his head over her."

Gray studied Lady Pelham with a connoisseur's eye. There was no incertitude about her suitability for his needs. Beautiful and scandalous, he could not have designed a wife more suited to irritating his mother if he'd tried. Pel, as she was affectionately referred to, was of medium height, but stunningly curved, and built for a man's pleasure. The auburn-haired widow of the late Earl of Pelham had a brazen sultriness that was addicting, or so rumor said. Her former lover, Lord Pearson, had gone into a long decline after she ended their affair.

Gerard had no difficulty seeing how a man could mourn the loss of her attentions. Under the blazing lights of the massive chandeliers, Isabel Pelham glittered like a precious jewel, expensive and worth every shilling.

He watched as she smiled up at Markham with a wide curving of her lips, lips which were considered too full for conventional beauty, but just the right plumpness to rim a man's cock. All around the room, covetous male eyes watched her, hoping for the day when she might turn those sherry-colored eyes upon them, and perhaps select one of them as her next lover. To Gerard, their longing was pitiable. The woman was extremely selective, and retained her lovers for years. She'd had Markham on a leash for nearly two now, and showed no signs of losing interest.

But that interest did not extend to matrimony.

On the few occasions when the viscount had begged for her hand, she refused him, declaring she had no interest in marrying a second time. Gray, on the other hand, had no doubts whatsoever that he could change her mind about that.

"Calm yourself, Bartley," he murmured. "Things will work out. Trust me."

"No one can trust you."

"You can trust me to give you five hundred pounds if you drag Markham away from Pel and into the card room."

"Well, then." Bartley straightened his spine and his waistcoat, neither action capable of hiding his widening middle. "I am at your service."

Grinning, Gerard bowed slightly to his greedy acquaintance who took off to the right, while he made his way to the left. He strolled without haste around the fringes of the ballroom, making his way toward the pivotal object of his plan. The journey was slow going, his way blocked by one mother-and-debutante pairing after another. Most bachelor peers similarly hounded would grimace with annoyance, but Gerard was known as much for his overabundance of charm, as he was for his penchant for mischief. So he flirted outrageously, kissed hands freely, and left every female in his wake certain he would be calling on her with a formal offer of marriage.

Casting the occasional glance toward Markham, he noted the exact moment Bartley lured him away, and then crossed the distance with purposeful strides, taking Pel's gloved hand to his lips before the usual throng of avid admirers could encircle her.

As he lifted his head, he caught her eyes laughing at him. "Why, Lord Grayson. A woman cannot help but be flattered by such a single-minded approach."

"Lovely Isabel, your beauty drew me like a moth to a flame." He tucked her hand around his forearm, and led her away for a walk around the dance floor.

"Needed a respite from the ambitious mothers, I assume?" she asked in her throaty voice. "I'm afraid even my association will not be enough to make you less appealing. You are simply too delicious for words. You shall be the death of one of these poor girls."

Gerard breathed a deep sigh of satisfaction, an action which inundated his senses with her lush scent of some exotic flower. They would rub along famously, he knew. He had come to know her well in the years she had been with Markham, and he had always liked her immensely. "I agree. None of these women will do."

Pel gave a delicate shrug of her bare shoulders, her pale skin set off beautifully by her dark blue gown and sapphire necklace. "You are young yet, Grayson. Once you are my age, perhaps you will have settled down enough to not completely torment your bride with your appetites."

"Or I can marry a mature woman, and save myself the effort of altering my habits."

Arching a perfectly shaped brow, she said, "This conversation is leading somewhere, is it not, my lord?"

"I want you, Pel," he said softly. "Desperately. Only an affair will not suffice. Marriage, however, will take care of it nicely."

Soft, husky laughter drifted in the air between them. "Oh,

Gray. I do adore your humor, you know. It is hard to find men so deliciously unabashed in their wickedness."

"And it is lamentably hard to find a creature as blatantly sexual as you, my dear Isabel. I'm afraid you are quite unique, and therefore irreplaceable for my needs."

She shot him a sidelong glance. "I was under the impression you were keeping that actress, the pretty one who cannot remember her lines."

Gerard smiled. "Yes, that's true. All of it." Anne could not act to save her life. Her talents lay in other, more carnal activities.

"And honestly, Gray. You are too young for me. I am six and twenty, you know. And you are . . ." She raked him with a narrowed glance. "Well, you *are* delectable, but—"

"I am two and twenty, and could ride you well, Pel, never doubt it. However, you misunderstand. I have a mistress. Two, in fact, and you have Markham—"

"Yes, and I am not quite finished with him."

"Keep him, I have no objections."

"I'm relieved to have your approval," she said dryly, and then she laughed again, a sound Gray had always enjoyed. "You are quite mad."

"Over you, Pel, definitely. Have been from the first."

"But you've no wish to bed me."

He looked at her with pure male appreciation, taking in the ripe swell of her breasts above the low bodice. "Now, I did not say that. You are a beautiful woman, and I am an amorous man. However, since we are to be bound together, *when* we decide to fall into bed with one another is moot, yes? We shall have a lifetime to make that leap, *if* we decide it would be mutually enjoyable."

"Are you in your cups?" she asked, frowning.

"No, Isabel."

Pel stopped, forcing him to stop with her. She stared up at him, and then shook her head. "If you are serious—"

"There you are!" called a voice behind them.

Gerard bit back a curse at the sound of Markham's voice, but he faced his friend with a careless smile. Isabel's countenance was equally innocent. She truly was flawless.

"I must thank you for keeping the vultures at a distance, Gray," Markham said jovially, his handsome face lit with pleasure at the sight of his paramour. "I was momentarily distracted by something that proved not to be worth my time."

Relinquishing Pel's hand with a flourish, Gerard said, "What are friends for?"

"Where have you been?" Gerard growled a few hours later, as a hooded figure entered his bedroom. He paused his pacing, his black silk robe swirling to a halt around his bare legs.

"You know I come when I can, Gray."

The hood was thrown back revealing silvery blond hair and a beloved face. He crossed the room in two strides and took her mouth, lifting her feet from the floor. "It is not often enough, Em," he breathed. "Not nearly."

"I cannot drop everything to serve your needs. I am a married woman."

"You've no need to remind me of that fact," he grumbled. "I never forget it."

He buried his face in the curve of her shoulder, and breathed her in. She was so soft and innocent, so sweet. "I've missed you."

Emily, now Lady Sinclair, gave a breathless laugh, her lips swollen from his kisses. "Liar." Her mouth turned down morosely. "You have been seen with that actress more than a few times in the fortnight since I saw you last."

"You know she means nothing. It's you I love."

He could explain, but she would not understand his need for wild, unrestrained fucking, just as she had not understood Sinclair's demands. She was too slight of frame, and genteel in sensibility, to enjoy such fervency. It was his respect for her which led him to seek such release elsewhere.

"Oh, Gray." She sighed, her fingers curling into the hairs at his nape. "Sometimes I think you truly believe that. But perhaps you love me as much as a man like you is able."

"Never doubt it," he said ardently. "I love you more than anything, Em. I always have." Taking a moment to divest her of the cape, he tossed it aside and carried her to the waiting bed.

As he undressed her with quiet efficiency, he seethed inside. Emily was supposed to have been *his* bride, but he had gone away on his Grand Tour, and returned to find his childhood love married. She said her heart had been broken when he left, and rumors of his affairs had reached her ears. She had reminded him that he had never written, which led her to believe he had forgotten her.

Gerard knew his mother had helped to plant the seeds of doubt, and then had watered them daily. Emily had not been worthy in the dowager's eyes. She had wanted him to marry a bride of higher station, so he would do the opposite, to thwart her and pay her in kind.

If only Em had held on to her faith a little while longer, they could have been wed now. This could have been her bed, one she did not have to leave before the sun rose.

Naked, her pale skin glowing like ivory in the candlelight, Emily took his breath away, as she always had. He had loved her as long as he could remember. She was so beautiful. Not in the way Pel was. Pel had an earthy, carnal sensuality. Em was a different kind of beautiful, more fragile and understated. They were as opposite as a rose was to a daisy.

Gerard was very fond of daisies.

His large hand reached out and cupped the slight weight of her breast. "You are still maturing, Em," he said, noting the new fullness.

She covered his hand with her own. "Gerard," she said in her lilting voice.

He caught her gaze, and his heart swelled at the love he saw there. "Yes, my love?"

"I am *enceinte*."

Gerard gaped. He had been careful, and made use of French letters. "Em, dear God!"

Her blue eyes, those lovely eyes the color of cornflowers, filled with tears. "Tell me you are happy. Please."

"I . . ." He swallowed hard. "Of course, sweet." He had to ask the obvious question. "What of Sinclair?"

Emily smiled sadly. "I do not believe there will be a doubt in anyone's mind that the child is yours, but he will not refute it. He gave me his word. In a way, 'tis fitting. He released his last mistress due to pregnancy."

His stomach clenched tight with shock, Gerard laid her down upon the mattress. She looked so tiny, so angelic against the blood red color of his velvet counterpane. He discarded his robe and climbed over her. "Come away with me."

Gerard lowered his head, and sealed his lips over hers, moaning at the sweet taste of her. If only things were different. If only she had waited.

"Come away with me, Emily," he begged again. "We can be happy together."

Tears slid down her temples. "Gray, my love." She cupped his face in her tiny hands. "You are such a passionate dreamer."

He nuzzled the fragrant valley between her breasts, his hips grinding his erection into the mattress in an attempt to temper his desire. With an iron will, he controlled his baser demands. "You cannot deny me."

"Too true," she gasped, caressing his back. "If I had been stronger, how different our lives would have been. But Sinclair . . . the dear man. I have shamed him enough."

Gerard pressed loving kisses into her tight belly, and thought of his child who had taken root there. His heart raced in near panic. "What will you do then, if you will not have me?"

"I depart tomorrow for Northumberland."

"*Northumberland!*" His head lifted in surprise. "Bloody hell, why so far away?"

"Because that is where Sinclair wishes to go." With her

hands under his arms, she tugged him over her, her legs spreading wide in welcome. "Under the circumstances, how can I refuse?"

Feeling as if she were drifting away, Gerard rose over her, and slid his cock slowly into her, groaning his lust as she closed hot and tight around him. "But you will come back," he said hoarsely.

Emily's golden head thrashed softly in pleasure, her eyes squeezed shut. "God, yes, I will return." Her depths fluttered along his shaft. "I cannot live without you. Without this."

Holding her tightly to him, Gerard began to thrust gently. He stroked into her in the way he knew brought her the most pleasure, while restraining his own needs. "I love you, Em."

"My love," she gasped. And then she came apart in his arms.

Tink.

Tink.

Isabel awoke with a groan, knowing by the soft purplish color of the sky and her exhaustion that it must be just after dawn. She lay there a moment, her mind groggy, trying to determine what had disturbed her sleep.

Tink.

Running her hands over her eyes, Isabel sat up and reached for her night rail to cover her nakedness. She glanced at the large-faced clock on the mantel and realized Markham had departed only two hours before. She had hoped to sleep until late afternoon, and still intended to do so, once she dealt with her recalcitrant swain. Whoever he was.

She shivered as she made her way to the window, where tiny pebbles hitting the glass provided the annoying sound. Isabel pushed up the sash and looked down at her rear garden. She sighed. "I suppose if I must be disturbed," she called out, "it is best that it be for a sight as handsome as you are."

The Marquess of Grayson grinned up at her, his shiny brown hair disheveled and his deep blue eyes red-rimmed. He was

missing his cravat and the neck of his shirt gaped open, revealing a golden throat and a few strands of dark chest hair.
He appeared to be lacking a waistcoat as well, and she could
not help but smile back at him. Gray reminded her so much
of Pelham when she had first met him nine years ago. Those
had been happy times, short-lived as they were.

"O Romeo, Romeo!" she recited, taking a seat on the window bench. "Wherefore art thou—"

"Oh, please, Pel," he groaned, cutting her off with that
deep laugh of his. "Let me in, will you? It's cold out here."

"Gray." She shook her head. "If I open my door to you,
this incident will be all over London by supper time. Go
away, before you are seen."

He crossed his arms stubbornly, the material of his black
jacket straining to contain his brawny arms and broad shoulders. Grayson was so young, his face as yet unlined. Still a
boy in so many ways. Pelham had been the same age when
he'd swept her off her seventeen-year-old feet.

"I am not leaving, Isabel. So you may as well invite me in,
before I make a spectacle of myself."

She could tell by the stubborn set of his jaw that he was serious. Well, as serious as a man such as him could be.

"Go to the front, then," she relented. "Someone will be
awake to admit you."

Isabel rose from the window seat, and retrieved her white
satin dressing robe. She left her bedroom and walked into her
boudoir, where she opened the curtains to let in the now pale
pink light. The room was her favorite, decorated in soft shades
of ivory and burnished gold, with gilt-edged chairs and chaise,
and tasseled drapes. But the soothing color scheme was not
what most moved her. That distinction went to the only spot
of obtrusive color in the space—the large portrait of Pelham
that graced the far wall.

Every day she gazed upon that likeness, and allowed her
heartbreak and loathing to rise to the surface. The earl was
impervious, of course, his seductively etched mouth curved in

the smile that had won her hand in marriage. How she had loved him, and adored him, as only a young girl could. Pelham had been everything to her, until she had sat at Lady Warren's musicale and heard two women behind her discussing her husband's carnal prowess.

Her jaw clenched at the memory, all her old resentment rushing to the fore. Nearly five years had passed since Pelham met his reward in a duel over a paramour, but she still smarted from the sting of betrayal and humiliation.

A soft scratching came to the door. Isabel called out and the portal opened, revealing the frowning countenance of her hastily dressed butler.

"My lady, the Marquess of Grayson requests a moment of your time." He cleared his throat. "From the service door."

Isabel bit back a smile, her dark mood fleeing at the image she pictured of Grayson standing haughty and arrogant, as only he could be, while semi-dressed and at the delivery entrance. "I am at home."

A slight twitching of a gray eyebrow was the only indication of surprise.

While the servant went to fetch Gray, she went around the room and lit the tapers. Lord, she was weary. She hoped he would be quick about whatever was so urgent. Thinking of their earlier odd conversation, she wondered if he might not need some help. He could be a bit touched in the head.

Certainly they had been unfailingly friendly with one another, and beyond mere acquaintances, but never more than that. Isabel had always rubbed along well with men. After all, she liked them quite well. But there had been a respectful distance between her and Lord Grayson, because of her ongoing affair with Markham, his closest friend. An affair she had ended just hours ago, when the handsome viscount had asked her to marry him for the third time.

In any case, despite Gray's ability to arrest her brain processes for a moment with his uncommon beauty, she had no further interest in him. He was Pelham all over again—a man too selfish and self-centered to set aside his own needs for another's.

The door flew open behind her, startling her, and she spun about, only to be met head-on with over six feet of powerful male. Gray caught her around the waist and spun her about, laughing that rich laugh of his. A laugh that said he'd never once had a care in the world.

"Gray!" she protested, pushing at his shoulders. "Put me down."

"Dear Pel," he cried, his eyes alight. "I've had the most wondrous news told to me this morn. I'm to be a father!"

Isabel blinked, growing dizzy from lack of sleep and the spinning.

"You are the only person alive I could think of who might be happy for me. Everyone else will be horrified. Please smile, Pel. Congratulate me."

"I will, if you put me down."

The marquess set her on her feet and stepped back, waiting.

She laughed at his impatient expectation. "Congratulations, my lord. May I have the name of the fortunate woman who is to become your bride?"

Much of the joy in his blue eyes faded, but his charming smile remained. "Well, that would still be you, Isabel."

Staring up at him, she tried to discern what he was about, and failed. She gestured to a nearby chair, and then sat herself.

"You really are quite lovely with sex-mussed hair," Gray mused. "I can see why your lovers would mourn the loss of such a sight."

"Lord Grayson!" Isabel ran a hand over the tangles in her long tresses. The present fashion was close-cropped curls, but she preferred a longer length, as did her paramours. "Please, I must hasten you to explain the purpose of your visit. It has been a long night and I am tired."

"It has been a long night for me as well, I have yet to sleep. But—"

"Might I suggest you sleep on this wild idea of yours? Rested, I think you might see things differently."

"I will not," he said stubbornly, twisting to drape one arm over the back of the chair, a pose that was sultry in its sheer artlessness. "I've thought it through. There are so many reasons why we would be perfect for one another."

She snorted. "Gray, you have no notion of how wrong you are."

"Hear me out, Pel. I need a wife."

"I do not need a husband."

"Are you certain about that?" he asked, arching a brow at her. "I think you do."

Isabel crossed her arms, and settled into the back of the chaise. Whether he was insane or not, he *was* interesting. "Oh?"

"Think on it. I know you grow rather fond of your paramours, but you have to dismiss them eventually, and not due to boredom. You are not that type of woman. No, you have to release them because they fall in love with you, and then want more. You refuse to take married men to your bed, so all of your lovers are free and they all wish to marry you." He paused. "But if you were already married . . ." Gray let his words hang in the air.

She stared at him. And then blinked. "What the devil do you gain out of such a marriage?"

"I gain a great deal, Pel. A great deal. I would be free of the marriage-minded debutantes, my mistresses would understand that they will receive no more from me, my mother—" He shuddered. "My mother would cease presenting marital prospects to me, and I shall have a wife who is not only charming and likeable, but one who doesn't have any foolish notions of love and commitment and fidelity."

For some strange, unaccountable reason, Isabel found herself liking Lord Grayson. Unlike Pelham, Gray wasn't filling some poor child's head with declarations of undying love and devotion. He wasn't making a marital bargain with a girl who might grow to love him and be hurt by his indiscretions. And he was thrilled to have a bastard, which led her to believe he intended to provide for it.

"What of children, Gray? I am not young, and you must have an heir."

His famous, heart-stopping grin burst forth. "No worries, Isabel. I have two younger brothers, one of whom is already wed. They will have children, should we neglect the task."

Isabel choked out a half-crazed little laugh. That she would even consider the ridiculous notion . . .

But she had said good-bye to Markham, much as she regretted that end. He was mad for her, the foolish man, and she had selfishly tied him up for almost two years. It was time for him to find a woman worthy of him. One who could love him, as she could not. Her ability to experience that elevated emotion had died with Pelham on a field at dawn.

Looking at the earl's portrait again, Isabel hated that she had inflicted pain on Markham. He was a good man, a tender lover, and a great friend. He was also the third man whose heart had been broken by her need for physical closeness and sexual release.

She often thought of Lord Pearson, and how emotionally destroyed he had been by her dismissal. She was weary of the hurt feelings, and often berated herself for causing them, but knew she would go on as she had been. The human need for companionship would not be denied.

Gray was right. Perhaps if she were already married, she could find and enjoy a true sexual friendship with a man without him hoping for more. And she would never have to worry about Gray falling in love with her, that much was certain. He had professed a deep love for one woman, but maintained a steady string of paramours. Like Pelham, constancy and the ability to deeply love was beyond him.

But could she engage in similar infidelity after experiencing the pain it could bring?

The marquess leaned forward, and caught up her hands. "Say yes, Pel." His stunning blue eyes pleaded with her, and she knew Gray would never mind her affairs. He would be too occupied with his own, after all. This was a bargain, nothing more.

Perhaps it was exhaustion that stunted her ability to think properly, but within the space of two hours, Isabel found herself in the Grayson traveling coach on the way to Scotland.

Six months later . . .

"Isabel, a moment of your time, if you would, please."

Gerard watched the empty open doorway until his wife's curvaceous form, which had just passed by, filled it again.

"Yes, Gray?" Isabel stepped into his study with an inquisitively raised brow.

"Are you free Friday evening?"

She gave him a mock chastising look. "You know I am available whenever you need me."

"Thank you, vixen." He leaned back in his chair and smiled. "You are too good to me."

Isabel moved to the settee and sat. "Where are we expected?"

"Dinner at the Middletons'. I agreed to speak to Lord Rupert there, but Bentley informed me today that Lady Middleton has also invited the Grimshaws."

"Oh." Isabel wrinkled her nose. "Devious of her to invite your inamorata and her husband to an event you are attending."

"Quite," Gerard said, rising and rounding the desk to take a seat next to her.

"That smile is so wicked, Gray. You really should not let it out."

"I cannot restrain it." He tossed his arm over her shoulders and pulled her close, breathing in the exotic floral scent that was both familiar and stirring. "I am the luckiest man alive, and I am smart enough to know it. Can you imagine how many peers wish they had a wife like mine?"

She laughed. "You remain deliciously, unabashedly shameless."

"And you love it. Our marriage has made you a figure of some renown."

"You mean 'infamy,'" she said dryly. "The older woman starved for the stamina of a younger man."

"Starved for me." He fingered a loose tendril of fiery hair. "I do like the sound of that."

A soft knock on the open door had them both looking over the back of the settee at the footman who waited there.

"Yes?" Gerard asked, put out to be interrupted during a rare quiet moment with his wife. She was so often occupied with political teas and other female nonsense that he was hardly ever afforded the opportunity to enjoy her sparkling discourse. Pel was infamous, yes, but she was also unfailingly charming and the Marchioness of Grayson. Society may speculate about her, but they would never shut their doors to her.

"A special post arrived, my lord."

Gerard held out his hand and crooked his fingers impatiently. As soon as he held the missive, he grimaced at the familiar handwriting.

"Heavens, what a face," Isabel said. "I should leave you to it."

"No." He held her down by tightening his arm on her shoulder. "It's from the dowager, and by the time I am done reading it, I will need you to pull me out of the doldrums, as only you can."

"As you wish. If you want me to stay, I will. I am not due out for hours yet."

Smiling at the thought of hours to share with her, Gerard opened the letter.

"Shall we play chess?" she suggested, her smile mischievous.

He shuddered dramatically. "You know how much I detest that game. Think of something less likely to put me to sleep."

Turning his attention to the letter, he skimmed. But as he came to a paragraph written as if it were an afterthought, but which he knew to be a calculated strike, his reading slowed and his hands began to shake. His mother never wrote without the intent to wound, and she remained furious that he had married the notorious Lady Pelham.

> ...*a shame the infant did not survive the birthing. It was a boy child, I heard. Plump and well-formed with a dark mane of hair, unlike his two blond parents. Lady Sinclair was too slightly built, the doctor said, and the baby too large. She bled out over hours. A gruesome sight, I was told*...

Gerard's breathing faltered, and he grew dizzy. The beautifully handwritten horrors on the page blurred until he could no longer read them.

Emily.

His chest burned, and he started in surprise as Isabel thumped him on the back.

"Breathe, damn you!" she ordered, her voice worried, but filled with command. "What the devil does that say? Give it to me."

His hand fell slack, the papers falling to flare out on the Aubusson rug.

He should have been with Em. When Sinclair had returned his letters unopened, he should have done more to support her than merely sending friends with secondhand greetings. He had known Em his whole life. She was the first girl he'd kissed, the first girl he had given flowers to, or wrote poetry about. He could not remember a time when the golden-haired angel had not been in the periphery of his existence.

And now she was gone, forever, killed by his lust and self-ishness. His darling, sweet Emily, who deserved so much better than he had given her.

Faintly, he heard a buzzing in his ears, and thought it could be Isabel, who held one of his hands so tightly within her own. He turned and leaned against her, his cheek to her bosom, and cried. Cried until her bodice was soaked, and the hands that stroked his back shook with worry. He cried until he could not cry anymore, and all the while he hated himself.

They never made it to the Middletons'. Later that night, Gerard packed his bags and headed north.

He did not return.

Chapter 1

Four years later

"His Lordship is at home, my lady."

For a great many women such a statement was a common utterance and nothing of note, but for Isabel, Lady Grayson, it was so rarely heard, she could not remember the last time her butler had said the same to her.

She paused in the foyer, tugging off her gloves before handing them to the waiting footman. She took her time with the task, taking the extra brief moments to collect herself, and ascertain that her racing heart was not outwardly visible.

Grayson had returned.

Isabel could not help but wonder why. He'd rejected every missive she sent to his steward, and had sent none to her. Having read the dowager's letter, she knew what had broken him that day he'd left both London and her. She could imagine his pain, having seen his initial excitement and subsequent pride at becoming a father. As his friend, she wished Gray had allowed her to provide him more than just that one hour of comfort, but he'd turned away from her, and years had passed.

She smoothed her muslin skirts, and touched a hand to her upswept hair. When she caught herself checking her appearance, Isabel stopped with a muttered curse. This was Gray. He would not care how she looked. "The study?"

"Yes, my lady."

The scene of that day.

She nodded, and squared her shoulders, shoring up her nerve. As ready as she would ever be, Isabel passed the curving staircase and turned into the first open door on the right. Despite her mental and physical preparations, the sight of her husband's back struck her like a physical blow. He stood silhouetted in the window, appearing taller and definitely broader. His powerful torso tapered to a trim waist, beautifully curved ass, and long, muscular legs. Framed by the dark green velvet curtains, the perfect symmetry of his form stole her breath.

But there was a somber, oppressive air that surrounded him that was so distant from the carefree man she remembered. It forced her to take another deep breath before opening her mouth to speak.

As if he felt her presence, Gray turned before she managed a word. Her throat closed tight as a fist.

He was not at all the man she had married.

They stared at each other, both held motionless in the pregnant pause. Only a few years, and yet it seemed a lifetime had passed. Grayson was no longer a boy, not by any stretch of the imagination. His face had lost that faint remnant of youth, and time had etched its passing in the lines that bracketed his mouth and eyes. Not happy lines, she could see. Frown lines, lines of sorrow. The brilliant blue of his irises that had caused many women to fall in love with him were now a deeper, darker shade. They no longer smiled, and appeared to have seen far more than possible in only a four year span.

She raised a hand to her bodice, dismayed by the rapid lift and fall of her chest.

Gray had been beautiful before. Now, there were no words

to describe him. She forced her breathing to slow, and fought off a sudden, desperate flare of panic. She had known how to handle the boy, but this . . . this *man* was not tamable. Had she met him anew, she would know to stay far away.

"Hello, Isabel."

Even his voice had changed. It was deeper now, slightly raspy.

Isabel had no notion of what to say to him.

"You have not changed at all," he murmured, striding toward her. The previous cockiness of his bearing was gone, replaced by the type of confidence one gained from walking through hell and surviving it.

Sucking in a deep breath, she was inundated with the familiar scent of him. A little spicier, perhaps, but he smelled like Gray, nevertheless. Staring up at his impassive face, she could do no more than shrug helplessly.

"I should have written," he said.

"Yes, you should have," she agreed. "Not just to warn me of your intent to visit, but before, if only to say that you were well. I have been worried about you, Gray."

He gestured with his hand toward a nearby chair, and she sank into it gratefully. As he moved to the settee across from her, Isabel noted his quaint garb. While he wore trousers with jacket and waistcoat, the garments were plain, and of common materials. Whatever he had been doing these last years, it apparently had not required the latest fashions.

"I apologize for your worry." One side of his mouth curved upward in a ghost of his former smile. "But I could not tell you I was well, when I was far from it. I could not bear to look at letters, Pel. It was not because they were from you. For years I avoided any sight of correspondence. But now . . ." He paused, and his jaw tightened, as if with determination. "I am not visiting."

"Oh?" Her stomach fluttered. Their camaraderie was gone. Instead of the easy comfort she had once enjoyed with him, she now felt decidedly nervous.

"I have come here to live. If I can remember how to do that."

"Gray—"

He shook his head, his slightly-longer-than-fashionable locks drifting about his neck. "No pity, Isabel. I do not deserve it. What's more, I don't want it."

"What *do* you want?"

His met her gaze directly. "I want many things, but mostly I want companionship. And I want to be worthy of it."

"Worthy?" She frowned.

"I was a dreadful friend, as are most selfish people."

Isabel stared down at her hands and noted her gold wedding band—a symbol of her lifelong commitment to a veritable stranger. "Where have you been, Gray?"

"Taking stock."

So he was not going to tell her. "Very well, then. What do you want from me?" She lifted her chin. "What service can I provide?"

"First, I will need to be made presentable." Gray waved a careless hand down the length of his body. "Then I will need to hear the latest *on dit*. I have read the papers, but you and I both know that gossip is rarely the truth. Most importantly, I will require your escort."

"I am not certain how much assistance I can offer you, Gray," she said honestly.

"I am aware." He stood and moved toward her. "The gossips have been unkind to you in my absence, which is why I have returned. How responsible can I be, truly, if I cannot take care of my own wife?" He dropped to a crouch beside her. "It is a great deal to ask of you, Pel, I know. It was not what you agreed to when we made our bargain. But things have changed."

"*You* have changed."

"God, I can only hope that's true."

Gray caught up her hands, and she felt calluses against her fingertips. She looked down, and saw his skin dark from the sun and reddened from work. Next to her smaller, paler ones, the contrast was like night to day.

He gave a gentle squeeze. Isabel lifted her gaze, and was stunned again by the comeliness of his features.

"I will not coerce you, Pel. If you wish to live your life as you have been, I will respect that." That faint hint of his remembered smile shined through again. "But I am not above begging, I warn you. I owe you much, and I am quite determined."

It was that brief glimpse of the old Gray that soothed her. Yes, the outer shell had changed, perhaps even much of the interior, but there was still some of the scapegrace charmer she knew in there. For the moment, it was enough.

Isabel smiled back, and his relief was tangible. "I will cancel my engagements for this evening and we can strategize."

Grayson shook his head. "I need to gather my bearings, and familiarize myself with being home again. Enjoy yourself tonight. You shall be burdened with me soon enough."

"Perhaps you would agree to have tea with me, in an hour or so?" Maybe then she could compel him to tell her about his absence.

"I would enjoy that."

She stood, and he rose with her.

Heavens, he was tall. Had he always been? She could not recall. Pushing aside her surprise, Isabel turned toward the door, and found one hand still caught in his.

Gray released it with a sheepish shrug. "See you in an hour, Pel."

Gerard waited until Isabel departed the room before sinking onto the settee with a groan. During his absence, insomnia had been a recurring torment. Needing physical exhaustion to sleep, he'd worked the fields of his many properties and in doing so he had become accustomed to muscle aches and pains. Never had his body hurt in quite the manner it did now. He hadn't realized how tense he was until he was alone and the seductive floral fragrance that was his wife's alone had dissipated.

Had Isabel always been so beautiful? He could not remember. Certainly he had used the word "beautiful" to describe her in his thoughts, but the reality was beyond what the mere utterance could convey. Her hair had more fire, her eyes more sparkle, her skin more glow than he had remembered.

Over the last few years he had said "my wife" hundreds of times as he paid her accounts and handled other matters relating to her. However, until today, he had never actually put the appellation together with the face and body of Isabel Grayson.

Gerard ran a hand through his hair, and wondered at his sanity when he'd made this marriage bargain with her. When Pel had walked into the room, all the oxygen had left. How had he never noted that corollary before? He had not lied when he said she looked the same. But for the first time, he *saw* her. Truly *saw* her. Then again, during the last two years, he had begun to see a great many things he had been blind to before.

Like this room.

He glanced around and grimaced. Dark green with dark walnut paneling. What in hell had he been thinking? A man could not peruse accounts properly in this gloomy place. And reading was out of the question.

Who has time to read when there are drinks to be had, and women to woo?

The words of his youth came back to taunt him.

Rising to his feet, Gerard walked to the bookshelves and withdrew random volumes. Every one he opened creaked in protest at the bending of its bindings. None of them had ever been read.

What kind of man surrounded himself with beauty and life, and then never spared a moment to appreciate any of it?

Filled with self-disgust, he sat at his desk and began a list of things he wanted changed. Before long he had filled several sheets.

"My lord?"

He lifted his head to see the lackey in the doorway. "Yes?"

"Her ladyship inquired after you. She wishes to know if you have decided against tea?"

Gerard glanced at the clock in surprise, and then pushed away from the desk and stood. "The dining room, or the parlor?"

"Her ladyship's boudoir, my lord."

Every muscle tensed again. How had he forgotten that, too? He had enjoyed sitting in that bastion of femininity and watching her prepare for her evenings out. As he climbed the stairs, he thought back on what time they'd spent together and admitted it had been filled with very little meaningful discourse. But he knew he had liked her, and that she had been a confidant to him.

He needed a friend now, since he no longer had any. He determined that he would rekindle the friendship he had once enjoyed with his wife, and with that expectation in mind, he lifted his hand and knocked on her door.

Isabel took a deep breath at the sound of the soft knock, and then called out permission to enter. Gray came in, pausing on the threshold, a telling moment of hesitation she had not seen from him before. Lord Grayson never waited. He leapt into action the moment he thought of something, which is how he often landed into mischief.

He stared at her, long and hard. Enough to make her regret the decision to receive him in her dressing gown. She had debated internally for almost half an hour, and in the end had decided to act as much as possible like she had before. Surely, the sooner they settled into their usual routine, the more comfortable they both would be.

"I believe the water is most likely cold by now," she murmured, turning away from the gilded vanity to sit on the nearby chaise. "But then I was always the one who drank tea."

"I preferred brandy."

He closed the door, giving her a brief moment to savor the sound of his voice. Why she should notice its slight rasp now, when she hadn't before, puzzled her.

"I have it here." She gestured toward the low table where a china tea set, brandy decanter, and goblet waited.

Gray's mouth widened in a slow smile. "You are always thinking of me. Thank you." He looked around. "I am pleased to find the space exactly as I remember it. With the walls and ceiling draped with white satin, I have always felt like I am standing in a tent when I am in here."

"That was the effect I wanted," she said, relaxing into the low back and curling her legs next to her.

"Is that so?"

He sat across from her, tossing his arm across the back of the settee. Isabel could not help but remember how he used to do the same to her shoulders. At that time, she had thought nothing of it. That version of Grayson had merely been exuberant.

He also hadn't been quite so large.

"Why a tent, Pel?"

"You have no notion of how long I've waited for you to ask that," she admitted with a soft chuckle.

"Why didn't I ask before?"

"We did not talk about such things."

"No?" His eyes laughed at her. "What did we talk about then?"

She moved to pour him a brandy, but he shook his head. "Why, we talked about you, Gray."

"*Me?*" he asked with raised brows. "Surely, not all the time."

"Nearly all the time."

"And when we weren't talking about me?"

"Well, then we were talking about your inamoratas."

Gray grimaced, and she laughed, remembering how much fun she used to have in simple discourse with him. Then she noted how he looked at her, as if he could not quite put his finger on something about her. Her laughter faded away.

"How insufferable I was, Isabel. How did you ever tolerate me?"

"I quite liked you," she said honestly. "There never was any guessing with you. You always said exactly what you meant."

He looked past her shoulder. "You still hang Pelham's portrait," he mused. Gray returned his gaze to hers. "Did you love him so very much?"

Isabel turned, and looked at the painting behind her. She tried, truly tried to dredge up some remnant of the love she had once felt for him, but her bitter resentment was too deep. She could not reach below it. "I did. I cannot remember the feeling now, but once I loved him desperately."

"Is that why you avoid commitment, Pel?"

She looked back at him with her lips pursed. "You and I did not discuss personal things either."

Gray's arm left the back of the chair and he leaned forward, resting his forearms on his knees. "Could we not be better friends now, than we were then?"

"I am not sure that would be wise," she murmured, once again glancing at her wedding band.

"Why not?"

Isabel rose and stood at the window, needing to put distance between herself and his new intensity.

"Why not?" he asked again, following her. "Do you have other, closer friends who you share things with?"

He set his hands atop her shoulders, and it took only a moment for his touch to heat her skin, and his scent to reach her nostrils. When next he spoke, his voice came close to her ear. "Is it too much to ask that you add your husband to your list of trusted friends?"

"Gray," she breathed, her heart racing with her distress.

Her restless fingers brushed the satin billowing beside the window frame. "I do not have friends such as you describe. And you say the word 'husband' with an import we never gave to it."

"How about your lover, then?" he pressed. "Does he hear your thoughts?"

Isabel attempted to pull away, but he held her fast.

"Why a tent, Pel? Can you tell me that, at least?"

She shivered at the feel of his exhale against her nape. "I like to imagine it is a part of a caravan."

"A fantasy?" Gray's large hands slid down her arms. "Is there a sheik who occupies this fantasy? Does he ravish you?"

"My lord!" she protested, thoroughly alarmed by the way her skin was prickling with sensual awareness. There was no way to ignore the hard male body that bracketed hers.

"What do you want, Gray?" she asked, her mouth dry. "Have you suddenly decided to change the rules?"

"And if I have?"

"We would end up apart, our friendship ruined. You and I are not the type of people who find love ever after."

"How would you know what type of man I am?"

"I know you kept a mistress while professing to love another."

His hot, open mouth pressed against the side of her throat, and her eyes slid closed at the seductive touch.

"You said I have changed, Isabel."

"No man changes *that* much. Regardless, I . . . I have someone."

Gray turned her to face him. His hands around her wrists were hot, his gaze hotter. Lord, she knew that look. It was the look Pelham had brought her to heel with, the look she made certain none of her lovers gave to her. Passion, desire— she welcomed those. But carnal hunger was something to be avoided at all costs.

That famished gaze swept over her body from head to toe and back again. Her nipples ached and tightened as his heated examination passed them, until she knew they must be visible even through her gown. His perusal paused there on the upward journey, and a low growl rumbled in his throat. Her lips parted on a panting breath.

"Isabel," he rasped, his hand lifting to cup her breast, his thumb brushing across the tight peak. "Could you not give me a chance to prove my worth?"

She heard her own needy moan, felt her blood heat and grow sluggish. His mouth lowered to hers, and she tilted her head back, waiting.

And wanting.

A soft scratching at the door broke the moment. She stumbled backward, breaking free of his slackened hold. Her fingers covered her lips, pressing hard to hide their quivering.

"My lady?" came the soft query of her abigail from the hallway. "Should I return later?"

Gray waited, his breathing harsh, the crests of his cheekbones flushed. There was no doubt in Isabel's mind that if she sent her maid away, she would be flat on her back and mounted within moments.

"Come in," she called, wincing at the note of panic that she could not hide.

Damn him. He'd made her want him, this new spouse of hers. Want him with the type of need that made her ache, a need she had thought herself too old and too wise to ever feel again.

It was her worst nightmare come to life.

Her husband closed his eyes a moment, collecting himself, as Mary swept in and went straight to the armoire.

"Shopping tomorrow, Pel?" he asked, his voice maddeningly calm. "I do need new garments."

The most she could manage was a jerky nod.

Grayson sketched an elegant bow and retreated, but his presence lingered in her mind long after he had gone.

* * *

Gerard made it to the hallway that led to his rooms before pausing to rest against the damask-covered wall. He closed his eyes and cursed himself. His plan to renew relations with his wife had gone horribly awry the moment he had opened the door.

He should have been prepared, he should have known how his body would react to the sight of Pel draped in black satin, one creamy shoulder bared as she lounged on a chaise. But how could he have known? He had never felt that way about her before. At least, not that he could recollect. But during those previous meetings in her boudoir, he had been so in love with Em. Perhaps that was what had granted him immunity from his wife's abundant charms.

Banging the back of his head lightly against the wall, Gerard could only hope that it would knock some sense into him. To lust for one's wife. He groaned. For most men, that would be so convenient. Not for him. Isabel had been frightened by his interest.

Though not uninterested, a voice whispered in his mind.

Yes, his seduction skills were a bit dusty, but he hadn't completely forgotten everything. He knew the signals a woman's body gave when she lusted in return.

Isabel may be correct in saying they were not the type of people who found love ever after. Lord knows they had both stumbled badly in that pursuit before. But perhaps it did not have to be a grand love affair. Perhaps it could simply be an affair of indefinite duration. A marriage of friendship, and a shared bed. As much as he liked Pel, they had the foundation. He loved the sound of her laugh—that rich, throaty purr that warmed a man from the inside. And her smile, with its teasing hint of wickedness. The sexual attraction was there in bushels. Besides, they were married, after all. Surely that gave him a leg up.

Gerard pushed away from the wall, and went to his rooms. Garments tomorrow, then a slow reintroduction to Society, and a heated seduction of his wife.

Of course, there was her paramour to attend to.

He grimaced. That would be the most difficult part. Isabel did not love her amours, but she cared a great deal for them, and was fiercely loyal. Winning her would take cunning and time, the latter being something he was not accustomed to investing in the pursuit of women.

But this was Pel, and as many would attest, she was worth the wait.

Chapter 2

"You do not look happy, Isabel," John, the Earl of Hargreaves, whispered in her ear. "Perhaps you would care to hear a bawdy joke? Or move along to another party? This one *is* dreadfully boring."

Isabel sighed inwardly and offered a bright smile. "If you wish to leave, I have no objections."

Hargreaves set his gloved hand at the small of her back and gave a soft caress. "I did not say I wanted to leave. I suggested it as a cure for your ennui."

At the moment, she almost wished she were bored. To have her head filled with nothing of import would be infinitely better than having it filled with thoughts of Gray. Who was the man who had moved into her home today? She truly had no notion. She knew only that he was very dark, shadowed with torments she could not understand, because he would not share. He was also very dangerous. As her husband, he could demand anything of her that he desired and she would be helpless to deny him.

Deep in her heart, Isabel could not help but long for the Marquess of Grayson she had once known. The younger Gray with the ready wit and careless disdain. He had been so simple to manage.

"Well, Isabel?" Hargreaves pressed.

She hid her slight irritation. John was a kind man, and had

been her paramour for over two years, but he never voiced an opinion, never gave a hint of what he would prefer. "I would like you to decide," she said, turning to face him.

"Me?" He frowned, which did nothing to lessen his appeal.

Hargreaves was very handsome with his aquiline nose and dark eyes. His black hair was graying at the temples, a distinguishing feature that only served to increase his attractiveness. A renowned swordsman, his body displayed the lanky grace of one who was expert in the sport of fencing. The earl was well-liked and well-respected. Women wanted him, and Isabel was no exception. A widower with two sons, he had no need for a wife, and he was good-natured. She usually enjoyed his company. In bed, and out.

"Yes, you," she said. "What would you like to do?"

"Whatever you desire," he said smoothly. "As always, I live for your happiness."

"It would make me happy to know what you want," she retorted.

Hargreaves' smile faded. "Why are you so out of sorts this evening?"

"Asking for your opinion does not make me out of sorts."

"Then why are you snapping at me?" he complained.

Isabel closed her eyes, and tamped down her frustration. Her irritation with John was Gray's fault. She looked at Hargreaves, and caught up his hand in hers. "What would you like to do? If we could do anything at all, what would give you the most pleasure?"

His scowl lifted as his lips curved in a sultry smile. He reached out and stroked the tiny bit of skin that was visible between her short sleeve and long glove. Unlike Gray's touch, it did not make her burn, but it did spread a gentle warmth that Hargreaves could stoke into a fire. "Your company gives me the most pleasure, Isabel. You know this."

"Then I will join you at your home shortly," she murmured.

He departed immediately. Isabel waited a discreet amount of time, and then she made her egress as well. During the carriage ride to Hargreaves House, she brooded over her situation and considered what, if any, options she had. John noted her preoccupation the moment she entered his bedroom.

"Tell me what troubles you," he murmured as he removed her cloak.

She sighed and admitted, "Lord Grayson has returned."

"Bloody hell." Hargreaves circled her and faced her head-on. "What does he want?"

"To live in his home, to regain his social life."

"What does he want *with you*?"

She noted his distress, and sought to soothe him. "Obviously I am here with you, and he is at home. You know how Grayson is."

"I know how he *was*, but that was four years ago." He moved away, pouring himself a drink. When he held the decanter up to her, she nodded gratefully. "I do not know how to feel about this, Isabel."

"You should not feel anything. His return does not affect you." Not like it affected her.

"I would be foolish not to see how it could affect me in the future."

"John." She accepted the proffered glass and kicked off her slippers. What could she say? Perhaps Gray's advances toward her had not been an anomaly. It was possible her husband would still want her in the morning. Then again, perhaps the stress of returning had addled him in some way. She could only hope that the latter was true. A girl should only have to live with one man like Pelham in a lifetime. "No one knows what the future will bring."

"God, Isabel. Do not spout phrases like that." He tossed back his drink and poured another.

"What would you like me to say?" she asked, hating that she could offer no words of comfort and still tell the truth.

He set his snifter down so hard the reddish liquid sloshed

over the sides. Hargreaves ignored it, and came to her. "I want you to tell me it does not matter that he has returned."

"I cannot." She sighed, and lifted to her tiptoes to kiss the clenched line of his jaw. His arms came around her, and squeezed her tight. "You know I cannot. I wish I could."

Taking the glass from her, Hargreaves set it on the end table, and pulled her toward the bed. She shook her head.

"You deny me?" he asked, clearly incredulous.

"I am confused, John, and distressed. Both of which rather dampens my ardor. It is no reflection on you. I promise."

"You have never turned me away. Why did you visit? To torment me?"

Isabel pulled back, her lips pursed. "My apologies. I was unaware that I was only invited to fornicate." She tugged her hand from his, and moved away.

"Pel, wait." Hargreaves caught her about the waist, and buried his face in the curve of her neck. "Forgive me. I feel a gulf between us that was not there before, and I cannot bear it."

He turned her to face him. "Tell me truthfully. Does Grayson want you?"

"I don't know."

John released a frustrated breath. "How in hell can you not know, Isabel? You, of all women, should know if a man desires to be in your bed or not."

"You have not seen him. His garments are odd—coarse and overly simple. Wherever he has been, it has not been anywhere he would socialize. Yes, he lusts, John. I recognize that much. But is it *me* he lusts for? Or a woman in general? That is what I do not know."

"Then we must find your husband his own paramour," John said grimly. "So that he will leave mine alone."

She gave a weary laugh. "What an odd conversation to have."

"I know." Hargreaves grinned, and cupped her cheek in

his hand. "Shall we sit, and plan a dinner, then? We can make a list of all the women we think Grayson would enjoy, and invite them."

"Oh, John." Isabel smiled her first genuine smile since Gray had returned. "That is such an inspired enterprise. Why could I not have thought of it?"

"Because that's what you have me for."

Gerard read the morning's newspaper over coffee, and attempted to ignore his anxiousness. He would be seen today, Society would know that he had returned. Over the next few days, old acquaintances would come to call, and he would have to decide which friendships to renew, and which would remain in the past.

"Good morning, my lord."

He looked up at the sound of Isabel's voice, and took a sharp, quick inhale as he stood. She was dressed in pale blue, her bodice low and displaying the generous curves of her breasts, while the waist was high and banded with darker blue ribbon. Her gaze would not meet his directly until he returned her greeting. Then she looked at him, and managed a smile.

Pel was obviously nervous, and it was the first time that he had ever seen her less than utterly confident. She stared at him a moment. Then her chin lifted, and she approached him. She pulled out the chair next to him before he could unlock his muscles and do it for her. He cursed inwardly. He had not been a monk for four years, but it had been a good while since his last liaison. Too long.

"Gray," she began.

"Yes?" he prodded when she hesitated.

"You need a mistress," she blurted.

He blinked, and then dropped back into his chair, holding his breath to avoid smelling her. One whiff of her perfume, and he would be hard, no doubt. "A mistress?"

She nodded, and bit her luscious bottom lip. "I doubt you will have any difficulty acquiring one."

"No," he said slowly. Good God. "With the proper attire, and a reintroduction to Society, I could manage the task, I'm sure." Gerard stood again. He could not talk about this with her. "Shall we go, then?"

"Eager, are we?" She laughed, and he grit his teeth at the lusty sound. The wariness that had stiffened her frame when she first entered was gone, leaving behind the Pel of old. A Pel who expected him to contract a mistress, and leave her alone.

"You ate upstairs, did you not?" He backed up a step, and breathed through his mouth. How in hell would he make it through the afternoon? Or the next week, or month? Or—bloody hell—years, as she often invested in her affairs.

"Yes." She stood. "Let's be off then, Lothario. Far be it for me to delay the discovery of your next amour."

Gerard followed at a safe distance, but doing so was not effective in quelling his lust due to the lamentable fact that he now had an excellent view of Isabel's gently swaying hips and lush derriere.

The landau ride was a bit better, as the open top helped to dissipate the scent of exotic flowers. And the walk on Bond Street was better than that, since he could no longer think about his errant cock while being gaped and pointed at. Pel walked beside him, chatting merrily, her lovely face shaded by a wide-brimmed straw hat.

"This is ridiculous," he muttered. "You would think I had risen from the dead."

"In a way, you have. You left without a word, and kept in touch with no one. But I think they are just as interested in the changes to your appearance."

"My skin is sun-darkened."

"Yes, it is. I quite like it. Other women will like it, too."

He glanced down at her in the course of his reply, and realized that from his vantage he had a prime view of her breasts.

"Where is the damned tailor's?" he growled, frustrated beyond measure.

"You *do* need a woman," she said, shaking her head. "Here we are. This is the establishment you listed in your old schedule, is it not?"

The door opened inward with a soft ring of bells, and within moments they were in a private fitting room. He was divested of his clothing, which Pel ordered away with a toss of her hand and a wrinkling of her nose. Gerard stood there in his smalls, and laughed. Until she turned to face him. Then the way she looked at him tightened his throat and choked off his merriment.

"Good heavens," she breathed, while circling him. Her fingertips brushed lightly across the ridges of his abdomen. He bit back a groan. The entire room smelled like her. Now she was touching him intimately.

The tailor entered, and gaped a moment in surprise. "I believe I will have to take new measurements, my lord."

Isabel stepped back quickly at the intrusion, her cheeks flushed. The tailor began to work, and she recovered quickly, directing her attention to talking the tradesman into parting with finished garments ordered by another customer.

"Surely, you would not wish His Lordship to leave your establishment in any manner other than suitably attired?" she asked.

"Of course not, Lady Grayson," came the ready reply. "But these are the closest to finished that I have, and they will not fit His Lordship. But perhaps I could add some extra material here."

"Yes, and let it out a little more there," she said, when the tailor pinned the material at his shoulder. "Look how broad he is. You can remove the padding. First and foremost, he must be comfortable."

Her hand drifted down his back, and Gerard clenched his fists to fight off a shudder. He was anything but comfortable.

"Do you have smalls that will fit him?" she asked, her voice lower and huskier than usual. "This material is too coarse."

"Yes," the tailor said quickly, eager to sell as much as possible.

The jacket was whisked away, and Gerard pulled on the matching trousers. They stood behind him, the tailor and Isabel, and he was grateful. He was holding off a cockstand by dint of will alone. He could not help being aroused. Pel's gaze was so hot, he felt it, and she continued to touch him and say admiring things about his body. A man could only take so much.

"Do not alter this," she breathed, her breath hot against his bare back. Her hand cupped the curve of his ass. "Is it too tight back here, my lord?" she asked him softly, caressing him. "I hope not. It looks wonderful."

"No. The back is fine." Then he lowered his voice so only she could hear. "But you have made the front damned uncomfortable."

The curtain moved to the side, and an assistant entered with the smalls. Gerard closed his eyes in misery. Everyone would see his condition now.

"Thank you," Isabel murmured. "Lord Grayson will need a moment."

He stood in surprise as she shooed the others out. Only when they were alone did he turn to face her. "Thank you, Isabel."

Her eyes were riveted to the placket of his trousers. She swallowed hard, and hugged the smalls to her chest. "You should remove those before you burst the seams."

"Will you help me?" he asked gruffly, hoping.

"No, Gray." She handed him the smalls, and looked away. "I told you, I have someone."

Gerard was tempted to remind her that she also had a hus-

band, but that would not be fair, considering how he had co-
erced her into marriage. Selfishly, he had wanted her as his
wife to irritate his mother, and save himself from overly ambitious mistresses. He had paid no regard to the censure she
would face by taking lovers without first providing him an
heir. This was his repayment for his narcissism—to desire
what belonged to him, but was not his to take.

He nodded, swallowing the bitterness of his regret. "Give
me some privacy. If you would, please."

She did not look at him as she left.

Isabel stepped out of the fitting room, and closed the curtain behind her. Her hands shook terribly, incited by the sight
of Gray's body as he dressed and undressed, teasing her with
his male perfection.

He was in the prime of his life, retaining the power and
strength of youth, while adding the maturity of tough times
and a few years. He rippled with muscle everywhere, and she
knew from being held against him yesterday that he wielded
that power carefully.

Honestly, Gray. You are too young for me.

Why had she not stayed the straight course? Looking at
him now, seeing all of his vigor and vitality, Isabel collected
how wrong she had been to bind his life to hers.

He needed a lover to take up his time and attention. A
man of his age was bursting with lust, and the primal desire
to sow his oats. She was convenient and attractive, and so he
wanted her. She was the only woman he knew, for the time
being. But one does not have an affair with one's spouse.

Isabel groaned inwardly. God, why had she married again?
She had made the ultimate commitment to avoid commitment, and look where that foolishness had landed her.

Men who looked like Gray were not constant. She had
learned that lesson with Pelham. The dashing earl had needed
a wife, and he'd lusted for her. A perfect combination in his
mind. But once his infatuation had faded, he had moved on

to the next bed, completely disregarding how in love with him she was. Grayson would move on as well. Certainly, he was more somber now, more grounded than when they had wed, but his age was undeniable.

Isabel could bear the rumors of his sexual prowess, and the innuendoes that she was too old to satisfy him or provide him an heir, as long as she felt no claim to him. She was faithful to her lovers, and expected the same in return for the duration of the affair. And therein lay the rub. Affairs were meant to be ended, while marriages lasted until death.

Isabel walked away, determined to find something to distract her from her thoughts. Moving toward the main room, she was intent on looking at the latest renderings, but the sliver of open curtain caught her eye. She paused. Then took a step back.

Against her will, she peeped through that tiny gap, and was arrested by the sight of Gray's fine derriere. Why had God given so much beauty to one man? And that ass! It was fiendish to have a man who looked as good from the back as he did from the front.

The firm cheeks were pale, especially in contrast to the deep tan of his torso. Where had he been, and what had he been occupied with to have developed those muscles and gained that skin color? He was glorious—his back, buttocks, and arms flexing with rhythmic power.

She released her held breath. It was then she noted *why* he was making those repetitive motions.

Gray was masturbating.

Christ! Isabel sagged against the wall as her knees went weak. She could not look away, even as her nipples tightened into aching points, and a slow trickle of arousal began deep inside her. Had she pushed him to this with a simple touch and a heated glance? The thought of holding so much power over such a glorious creature made her ache. Customers and employees scuttled behind her, and there she stood, obviously a voyeur. A woman of the world, she was nevertheless devastated by lust.

He was panting, his thighs straining, and she wished she could see the front of him. What did that beautiful face look like in the heat of passion? Was the lacing of muscle on his abdomen taut with tension? Was his cock as well built as the rest of him? Her imaginings were worse than the watching.

His head fell back, his dark hair drifting across his shoulders, and then he shuddered with a low, pained moan. Isabel moaned with him, sweat misting her skin, and then she turned away before he saw her. Before she saw him, in all his glory.

What the devil was she to do now?

Yes, she was a sensual woman, and the sight of a man pleasuring himself would titillate her, regardless. But never to this extent. She could barely breathe, and the need to climax was near maddening. It would be foolish to tell herself otherwise.

She recognized the tendrils of heat that curled low in her belly. Some called it desire. She called it destruction.

"Lady Grayson?" he called, in that deep raspy voice.

She placed that tone now that she had heard it enough. It was a bedroom voice, the sound of a man who had just cried out his pleasure. Why he should have that voice all the time, to torment women with the desire to give him reason to sound that way, was simply wrong.

"Y—yes?" She took a deep breath, and entered.

Gray faced her wearing the new smalls. His cheeks were flushed, his eyes knowing. She had not gone undetected.

"I hope one day you do more than watch," he said softly.

She covered the lower half of her face with a gloved hand, mortified and anguished. Yet he was unashamed. He stared at her intensely, his gaze taking in the outline of her hardened nipples.

"Damn you," she whispered, hating him for coming home

and turning her life upside-down. She ached all over, her skin too hot and too tight, and she detested the feeling and the memories it brought with it.

"I am damned, Pel, if I must live with you and not have you."

"We had a bargain."

"This," he gestured between them, "was not there then. What do you propose we do about it? Ignore it?"

"Spend it elsewhere. You are young and randy—"

"And married."

"Not truly!" she cried, ready to tear out her hair in frustration.

Gray snorted. "As truly as marriage can be without sex. I intend to correct that lack."

"Is that why you came back? To fuck your wife?"

"I came back because you wrote to me. Every Friday the post would come and there would be a letter, written with soft pink parchment and scented of flowers."

"You sent them back, every one of them. Unopened."

"The contents were not important, Pel. I knew what you did and where you went without your recounts. It was the thought that mattered. I had hoped you would desist, and leave me to my misery—"

"Instead you brought the misery to me," she snapped, pacing the length of the small room to ease the feeling of confinement. "It was my obligation to write to you."

"Yes!" he cried, triumphant. "Your obligation as *my wife*, which in turn forced me to remember that I had a like obligation to you. So I returned to quell the rumors, to support you, to correct the wrong I did you by leaving."

"That does not require sex!"

"Lower your voice," he warned, grabbing her arm and tugging her closer. He cupped her breast, his thumb and forefinger finding her erect nipple, and rolling it until she whimpered in helpless pleasure. "*This* requires sex. Look how aroused you are. Even in your fury and distress, I would wager you are wet between the thighs for me. Why should I take someone else, when it is you I want?"

"I have someone."

"You persist in saying that, but he is not enough, obviously, or you would not want me."

Guilt flooded her that her body should be so eager for him. She never entertained the idea of another man while attached to one. Months passed between her lovers, because she mourned the loss of each one, even though she was the party who said good-bye.

"You are wrong." She yanked her arm from his grip, her breast burning where he had touched her. "I do not want you."

"And I used to admire your honesty," he jeered softly.

Isabel stared at Gray, and saw his determination. The slow, dull ache in her chest was so familiar, a ghost of the hell Pelham had left her in.

"What happened to you?" she asked sadly, lamenting the loss of the comfort she once felt with him.

"The blinders were torn from me, Pel. And I saw what I was missing."

Chapter 3

Once appropriately attired, Gerard moved aside the curtain and stepped out into the short hall. He caught sight of Isabel immediately. Standing by the window, her auburn hair caught stray rays of sunshine and turned to fire. The contrast of those silken threads of flame against the ice blue of her gown was stunning, and very apropos. The heat of her desire had scorched him, even as she chilled him with her words. In fact, he was surprised she had remained the two hours it had taken to alter the pilfered garments. Gerard had half-expected her to leave. But Pel was not one to hide from things unpleasant. She may avoid discussing them, but she would not actually run from them. It was one of the quirky traits he rather liked in her.

He sighed, damning himself for pushing too hard, but he could do nothing differently. He did not understand her, and he could not make amends without comprehension. Why was she so determined to have nothing of importance between them? Why desire him, know he craved her in return, and refuse to act upon it? It was not like Isabel to deny herself the pleasures of the flesh. Did she perhaps love her present amour? His hands clenched into fists at the thought. Gerard was well aware that it was possible to love one person, and yet physically require the attentions of another.

At that thought, he cursed inwardly. He had obviously not

changed all that much to have pawed and groped at his wife. What in hell was the matter with him? A gentleman did not treat his spouse in that fashion. He should be wooing her, not salivating to rut in her.

He called out as he approached so as not to startle her. "Lady Grayson."

Pel turned to face him with a winsome smile. "My lord. You look very dashing."

So it was that way, was it? Pretend as if nothing had happened.

He smiled with all the charm he possessed, and lifted her gloved hand to his lips. "A husband must, to escort a wife as fair as you, my lovely Isabel."

Her hand shook a little in his, and her voice when she spoke had a slight catch. "You flatter me."

He wished to do a great deal more to her, but that would have to wait. He tucked her hand around his arm, and led her to the door.

"Even I cannot do you justice," she said, as he retrieved her flowered straw hat from the clerk and set it on her head, pinning it in place with the ease of familiarity. The door chimes rang, and he stepped closer, his back to the street, to allow the new customer to pass. The air sweltered between him and Pel, flushing her skin and tensing his frame.

"You need a lover," she breathed, those sherry eyes wide and held by his gaze.

"I have no need of one. I have a wife who desires me."

"Good afternoon, my lord," the clerk called out, rounding the counter.

Gerard moved to her side, and offered his arm again. Now facing the doorway, he saw the distinguished-looking gentleman who wore an expression of such horror it did not take but a moment to register who it must be. And what he must have heard.

"Good afternoon, Lord Hargreaves." His fingers closed over Pel's on his arm, staking an irrefutable claim. Never having been a possessive man, he frowned and tried to examine why he should feel this way now.

"Good afternoon, Lord and Lady Grayson," the earl said tightly.

Isabel straightened. "Lord Hargreaves, a pleasure."

But it was not, not for any of them. The tension was palpable. "Excuse us," Gerard said when Hargreaves continued to block the doorway. "We were on our way out."

"Lovely to see you again, my lord," Isabel murmured, her voice unusually somber.

"Yes," Hargreaves muttered, stepping aside. "Quite."

Opening the door, Gerard gave one last studious look at his rival, and then led his wife out with a hand at the small of her back. They walked slowly down the street, both lost in their thoughts. Several pedestrians attempted to approach, but a narrowed glance was effective at keeping them away.

"That was awkward," he muttered finally.

"You noted that, did you?" she said, refusing to look at him.

In a way, he missed the overconfidence of his youth. Four years ago, he would have brushed off the encounter as amusing. In fact, he had done that very thing on several occasions, as social engagements had brought him face to face with Pel's lovers, and she with his. Now he was all too aware of his flaws and shortcomings, and to his knowledge the popular and respected Hargreaves had none.

"I've no notion of how I will explain your comment to him," she said, obviously upset.

"He knew the risks when he chose to dally with another man's wife."

"There were no risks! No one could predict that you would come home daft."

"It is not daft to desire your spouse. Pretending you don't, however, is ridiculous."

He stopped abruptly as a merchant door swung inward, and a customer ran out directly before them.

"My apologies, my lady!" the man cried to Pel, tipping his hat before he strode away quickly.

Gerard looked at the establishment, curious about the reason for the man's excitability. His mouth curved as he reached for the door.

"A jeweler's?" Isabel asked with a frown.

"Yes, vixen. There is something I should have attended to years ago."

He urged her inside, and the clerk lifted his head from the sales record book with a smile. "Good afternoon, my lord. My lady."

"That was a happy man who just departed," Gerard noted.

"Ah yes," the clerk agreed. "A bachelor embarking on an offer of marriage, which is strengthened by the lovely ring he purchased today."

In search of equal pleasure, Gerard perused the offerings in the glass cases.

"What are you looking for?" Pel asked, bending over beside him. Her scent appealed to him so deeply, he wished he could lay amongst satin sheets infused with it. With her graceful limbs entwined with his, it would be heaven.

"Have you always smelled so wonderful, Pel?" He turned his head to look at her, and found her almost nose to nose.

She pulled back with a blink. "Gray, really. Can we put off a discussion on perfumery, and find what you want?"

Smiling, he caught her hand, and glanced up at the hovering clerk. "That one." He pointed to the largest ring in the case—a massive ruby surrounded by diamonds, and supported by a filigreed band of gold.

"Heavens," Pel breathed, as it came out from behind its glass shield and sparkled in the light.

Gerard lifted her hand, and sized the ring on her finger, pleased to see it fit snugly, but not too tightly, over her glove. Now, she looked like a married woman. "Perfect."

"No."

He arched a brow, and discerned his wife's distress. "Why not?"

"It . . . it's too large," she protested.

"It suits you." He lounged against the case, and smiled, keeping her hand trapped firmly within his own. "While I was in Lincolnshire—"

"You were?" she asked quickly.

"Amongst other places," he said, stroking her palm. "I would watch the sunset, and think of you. There were times when a ribbon of red clouds in the sky would exactly match the highlights in your hair. When the light catches that ruby, it reflects almost the same color."

She stared at him as he lifted her hand to his mouth. He kissed first the stone, and then the middle of her gloved palm, relishing the opportunity to be close to someone again.

The sunrises, with all their warm golden beauty, had brought memories of Em. He'd dreaded them at first. Each morning reminded him that another day had come, and Emily would not be living it. Later, the warmth the sun brought had been a benediction, a reminder that he had another opportunity to become a better man.

The sunsets, however, had always belonged to Pel. The darkening sky and the welcoming blanket of night that disregarded his imperfections—that was Isabel, who never pried. The sensuality of a bed, and the moments when he could release the stress of the day—that was Isabel, too, lying on her chaise in her boudoir. How odd that her lighthearted companionship had come to mean so much to him, and yet he'd never noticed it when it had been his to enjoy.

"You should save your silver tongue for a woman less jaded than I."

"Dear Pel," he murmured, smiling. "I adore that you are jaded. You hold no illusions about my less-than-sterling character."

"I have no idea what your character is anymore." She

pulled away, and he released her. Straightening her spine, Isabel glanced around the small store. When she saw the clerk busy recording their transaction, she said, "I don't understand why you would say such things to me, Gray. You never had any romantic notions, nor sexual ones, to my knowledge."

"What color are the flowers in front of our house?"

"I beg your pardon?"

"The flowers. Do you know what color they are?"

"Certainly, they're red."

He arched a brow. "Are you certain?"

She crossed her arms, and arched her own brow. "Yes, I'm certain."

"And the ones in the planters by the street?"

"What?"

"The planters by the street have flowers in them. Do you know what color those blooms are?"

Isabel chewed her lower lip.

Gerard tugged off his glove, and then tugged that lush bottom lip out of her teeth. "Do you?"

"They are pink."

"They're blue."

He moved his hand to her shoulder, and stroked the creamy expanse of skin with his thumb. The heat of her flesh burned through his fingertips, and spread up his arm, igniting a hunger such as he had not felt in years. For so long he had been numb and frozen inside. To feel this heat, to desire to burn with her touch, to want so desperately to be scorched inside her . . . He relished all of it.

"Blue flowers, Pel." His voice was huskier than he'd like. "I've found people tend to take for granted the things they see every day. But just because one fails to see something, does not mean it isn't there."

Goose bumps prickled her skin. He felt them, even through the calluses on his fingertips.

"Please." She brushed his hand away. "Don't lie, and say

pretty things, and attempt to make the past into what you wish it to be in the present. We were nothing to each other, nothing. And I wanted it that way. I *liked* it that way." She tugged off the ring, and set it on the counter.

"Why?"

"Why?" she parroted.

"Yes, my lovely wife, why? Why did you like our marriage as a sham?"

Her eyes shot daggers at him. "You liked it as a sham, too."

Gerard smiled. "I know the reasons why I liked it, but we are talking about you."

"Here you are, Lord Grayson," the clerk said with a wide smile.

Cursing inwardly at the interruption, Gerard dipped the proffered quill in ink and signed the bill. He waited until the ring was boxed and tucked into his inner coat pocket before glancing at Isabel. As she had in the tailor's, she stood staring out the window with a ramrod straight spine, every inch of her voluptuous form betraying her anger. He shook his head, and could not help but think that all the restrained passion in her was untapped. What the devil was Hargreaves doing, or more likely *not* doing, that left her so volatile? Another man might see the rigidness of her spine, and be discouraged. Gerard took it as a sign of hope.

He walked to her, drawn to the vibrancy that attracted everyone. Coming to a stop directly behind her, he breathed her in, and then whispered, "Can I take you home with me?"

Startled by Gray's husky voice in her ear, Isabel spun about so quickly, he was forced to arch backward to avoid being whacked in the face with the brim of her hat. The near miss made him laugh, and once he started, he could not stop.

She gaped at him, awed by how young he looked when lost in merriment. His laugh sounded rusty, as if it had not been let out in awhile, and she loved the sound of it—deeper and richer than it had been before, and she had adored it even then. Unable to resist, she smiled, but when he grabbed his ribs and gasped, she had to laugh with him. Then he caught her about the waist, and spun her around, just like he used to do.

Setting her hands on his broad shoulders for balance, Isabel hung on, and remembered again how she enjoyed being with him.

"Put me down, Gray!" she cried.

With his head tilted back, he looked at her and said, "What will you give me if I do?"

"Oh, that's not fair. You are making a spectacle of us. Everyone will hear of this." She thought of Hargreaves' expression when he'd seen them in the tailor's, and her smile faded. How awful she was to cavort with Gray, when it would hurt John.

"A boon, Pel, or I will carry you around until you agree. I am quite strong, you know. And you are light as a feather."

"I am not."

"Are so." His lip made that little pout of his. It would look ridiculous on any other man, but on Gray it made women want to kiss him. It made Isabel want to kiss him.

"You think too much," he complained when she stared at him mutely. "You rejected my gift. Offering me a boon is the least you can do."

"What do you want?"

He considered it a moment, and then said, "Supper."

"Supper? Can you be more specific?"

"I want to have supper with you. Stay home tonight, and share a meal with me."

"I have commitments."

Gray moved to exit the shop. "My good man," he called out to the clerk. "The door, if you would please."

"You would not carry me outside like this."

"Do you truly believe I wouldn't?" he asked with a devilish smile. "I may have changed, but a leopard cannot completely lose its spots."

Isabel glanced over her shoulder, and saw the street approaching and the multitude of pedestrians who strolled there. "Yes."

He paused mid-step. "Yes, what?"

"Yes, I will have supper with you."

His grin was triumphant. "You are such a generous soul, Pel."

"Stuff," she muttered. "You are a blackguard, Grayson."

"Perhaps." He set her down, and then tucked her hand around his arm, leading her out to the street. "But really, would you want me any other way?"

Looking at him, seeing the lightening of the oppressive air that had surrounded him the day before, she knew she liked him best as a scoundrel. It was when he was most happy.

Just like Pelham.

Only a fool would make the same mistake twice.

Recognizing the voice of reason, Isabel reminded herself to heed it, and keep her physical distance from him. As long as he remained at least three feet away from her, she was fine.

"Lord Grayson!"

They both sighed as a rather large woman approached them wearing a monstrosity of a hat, and an even worse pink ruffled concoction of a dress.

"That is Lady Hamilton," Isabel whispered. "A lovely woman."

"Not in that garment," Gray replied through his smile.

It took everything she had not to laugh aloud.

"Lady Pershing-Moore told me she saw you with Lady Grayson," Lady Hamilton said, panting as she came to a halt before them. "I said she must be daft, but it seems she was correct." She beamed. "So wonderful to see you again, my lord. How was . . . wherever you were?"

Gray accepted the offered hand, bowed over it, and said, "Miserable, as any locale would be without the company of my charming and beautiful wife."

"Oh." Lady Hamilton shot Isabel a wink. "Of course. Lady Grayson accepted an invitation to my rout, which will be held the week after next. I do pray that you intend to accompany her."

"Certainly," Gray said smoothly. "After my extended absence, I intend to never be away from her side for even a moment."

"Wonderful! I now look forward to the event with even greater anticipation."

"You are too kind."

Saying her farewells, Lady Hamilton retreated quickly.

"Gray," Isabel began with a sigh. "Why stir up gossip in this way?"

"If you think there is any possibility that we will not be gossiped about, you are delusional." He continued down the street toward their waiting landau.

"Why add fuel to the fire?"

"Do they teach women how to speak in riddles in finishing school? I vow, you all do it so well."

"Damn you, I agreed to be your escort until you find your footing, but that will not take long, and once you go your own way—"

"We are going the same way, Pel," he drawled. "We're married."

"We can separate. After the last four years it would merely be a formality."

Gray took a deep breath, and looked down at her. "Why would I want to do that? Better yet, why would you?"

Isabel kept her eyes ahead. How could she explain, when she wasn't certain she knew the answer? She shrugged helplessly.

His hand over hers, he gave a soft squeeze. "A great deal

has happened in the last twenty-four hours. Give both of us some time to adjust to one another. I admit, things between us have not progressed the way I anticipated."

He assisted her into the landau, and then directed the driver home.

"What *did* you anticipate, Gray?" Perhaps if she knew his aim, she could find some understanding. Or at the very least ease some of her worry.

"I thought I would return, you and I would sit down with a few bottles of excellent vintage, and become reacquainted. I imagined slowly finding my way in this world, and settling into the comfort you and I once knew together."

"I would like that," she said softly. "But I doubt the possibility unless we can find a way to be like we were."

"Is that truly what you desire?" He twisted in the seat to face her, and her gaze dropped, noting how muscular and powerful his thighs were. She could not seem to cease taking note of such things now. "Do you love Hargreaves?"

Isabel's brows shot up. "Love him? No."

"Then there is hope for us." He smiled, but the determination in his voice was unmistakable.

"Not that I don't care quite a bit for him, because I do. We have many interests in common. He is of a like age. We—"

"Does my age bother you, Isabel?" He studied her from beneath the brim of his hat, his blues eyes narrowed and considering.

"Well, you *are* younger, and—"

Gray caught her about the neck, and pulled her close, tilting his head to duck under her hat. His mouth—that sculpted mouth that could dazzle or sneer with equal effectiveness—brushed across hers.

"Oh!"

"I will not accept a sham anymore, Pel." He licked across her lips, and groaned softly. "God, the way you smell drives me insane."

"Gray," she gasped, pushing at his shoulders and discovering just how hard he was. Her lips trembled and burned. "People can see us."

"I don't care." He swiped his tongue quickly into her mouth, and she shivered at the taste of him. "You belong to me. I can seduce you if I want to." As his hand at her nape stroked softly, his voice lowered. "And I definitely want to."

He sealed his lips over hers, a brief tease, and then he pulled away, whispering, "Shall I demonstrate what a younger man can do for you?"

Her eyes drifted shut. "Please . . ."

"Please what?" His free hand rested next to her thigh, and kneaded her, sending waves of yearning through her body. "Please show you?"

She shook her head. "Please don't make me want you, Gray."

"Why not?" He tugged off his hat, and set his mouth to her throat, licking across her racing pulse.

"Because I will hate you forever if you do."

He pulled back quickly in surprise, and she took the opportunity to shove hard, which effectively knocked him over. He fell to his back, his arms flailing outward in an attempt to halt his descent. She flinched as his shoulders hit the side with a loud thump, leaving him nearly prone.

"What the devil?" Gray stared at her, wide-eyed.

She scrambled over to the rear-facing squab.

"Yes, you can have your way, Gray," she said grimly. "Much to my shame. But while my body may be all too willing to indulge, I happen to have morals, and a care for Hargreaves, who does not deserve to be set aside after nearly two years of companionship just for a rut."

"A *rut*, madam?" he growled, cursing as he nearly fell off the seat in his attempt to sit up. "One does not 'rut' with their spouse."

Once he'd managed to resume his perch, the full extent of

his arousal was revealed by the stretching of material between his legs. Isabel swallowed hard, and looked away quickly. *Good God.*

"What else could it be?" she said crossly. "We know nothing of one another!"

"I know you, Pel."

"Do you?" She snorted. "What is my favorite flower? Favorite color? Favorite tea?"

"Tulips. Blue. Peppermint." Gray snatched his hat off the floorboards, shoved it on his head, and crossed his arms.

She blinked.

"Thought I wasn't paying attention?"

Isabel bit her lower lip, and rifled through her memories. What were his favorite flowers, color, and tea? She was ashamed to realize she did not know.

"Ha!" he said triumphantly. "All well and good, Isabel. I shall give you the time you require to come around, and during that time you can learn all about me, and I about you."

The landau rolled to a halt outside their home. She glanced at the planters by the street, and saw the blue flowers. Gray leapt down, and then assisted her. He walked her up the steps, bowed, and then turned about.

"Where are you going?" she called after him, her skin still tingling from his touch, her stomach clenched at the determined set of his shoulders.

He paused, and looked back at her. "If I go in the house with you, I will take you, whether you will it or no." When she said nothing, his mouth curved mockingly. Within moments, he was gone.

Where would he go? He was obviously aroused, and virile enough that his release in the tailor's shop would not affect his ability to perform again. The thought of him occupied in carnal pursuits prodded her in a horribly familiar way. She knew what he looked like unclothed, and she knew that any other woman who saw him similarly would be putty in his hands. An ache she had thought to never feel again gnawed at her belly. A twinge from the past. A reminder.

Entering her home of nearly five years, Isabel discovered, to her dismay, that it already felt almost empty without Gray's vital presence. She cursed him for the upheaval he had wrought in only a few scant hours, and she took the stairs to her room determined to rectify the matter. Detailed planning of her dinner party was in order. She also needed to study her spouse, and ascertain his likes and dislikes.

Then, once she knew him, she would find the perfect mistress for him. She could only hope that Hargreaves' plan would work, and work quickly.

Experience had taught her that men like Gray could not be resisted for long.

Chapter 4

As Gerard ascended the steps to the double doors of Remington's Gentleman's Club, he knew that if it weren't for his frustration, he would be nervous. Inside the popular establishment, there would be at least several gentlemen whose wives or paramours had been sampled by him. In the past, he would have felt no awkwardness. *Rules do not apply in love or war,* he would have said. Now, he knew better. Rules applied everywhere, and he was not exempt from following them.

He handed his hat and gloves to one of the two attending footmen, and passed through the main gaming areas to the great room beyond. Seeking a deep armchair and a libation of some sort, he glanced around the room as he entered. He found comfort in the familiar surroundings. The smell of leather and tobacco reminded him that some things were timeless. A pair of light blue eyes met his, and then they looked away in a deliberate snub. Gerard sighed, accepting his due, then moved forward to make the first of what he knew would be an endless number of apologies to an equally infinite number of recipients.

He bowed, and said, "Good afternoon, Lord Markham."

"Grayson." The man who was once his closest friend did not even look at him.

"Lord Denby, Lord William," Gerard greeted the other two gentlemen who sat with Markham. He turned his attention back to the viscount. "I beg a moment of your time, Markham. If you would grant me that much, I would be eternally grateful."

"I do not think I can spare it," Markham said coldly.

"I understand. I will have to apologize to you here, then," Gerard said, unwilling to be denied.

Markham's head swiveled toward him.

"I am sorry my marriage caused you discomfort. As your friend, I should have had a care for your interests in the matter. I also offer my felicitations on your recent marriage. That is all I wished to say. Good day, gentlemen."

Gerard tilted his head slightly, and then turned about. He found his own small table and leather armchair, releasing his pent up breath as he sat. A few moments later, he opened the paper brought to him, and attempted to relax, a task made more difficult by the stares directed his way, and the peers who approached with greetings.

"Grayson."

He stiffened, and lowered his paper.

Markham stared at him for a long moment, and then gestured to the seat opposite him. "May I?"

"Certainly." Gerard set aside his reading, as the viscount settled into his chair.

"You look altered."

"I would like to think I am."

"I would say so, *if* your apology was sincere."

"It was."

The viscount ran a hand through his dark blond locks, and smiled. "My marriage is pleasant, which eases the sting immeasurably. But tell me this, as I've wondered for years, did she set me aside for you?"

"No. Honestly, you were our only connection up until the moment we spoke our vows."

"I fail to understand. Why deny my suit, but accept yours, if there was nothing between you?"

"Does any man discuss the reasons why his wife married

him? Does any man ever know? Whatever her impetus, I am a most fortunate man."

"Fortunate? You have been absent for four bloody years!" the viscount cried, studying him. "I almost did not recognize you."

"A great deal can happen in that time span."

"Or *not* happen," Markham said. "When did you return?"

"Yesterday."

"I spoke with Pel the day before, and she said nothing to me."

"She was not aware." Gerard gave a mirthless laugh. "And, unfortunately, she is not as pleased as I would wish."

Markham settled more comfortably into the big chair, and gestured to a nearby footman for a drink. "I am surprised to hear that. You two always rubbed along famously."

"Yes, but as you noted, I have changed. My tastes are different, as are my goals."

"I wondered how it was that you were immune to Pel's charms," the viscount said, laughing. "Fate does have a way of balancing the scales, if given enough time. I would be lying if I said I wasn't pleased to see you suffer a bit."

Gerard gave a reluctant smile. "My wife is a mystery to me, which deepens my dilemma."

"Isabel is a mystery to everyone. Why do you think so many wish to possess her? The challenge is irresistible."

"Do you remember her marriage to Pelham?" Gerard asked, wondering why he had never bothered to inquire before. "I would like to hear of it, if you do."

Markham accepted the mug offered to him by the attendant, and nodded. "There is not a peer my age who has forgotten Lady Isabel Blakely as she was in her youth. She is Sandforth's only daughter, and he doted on her. Still does, as far as I know. It was known that her dowry was substantial, which attracted the fortune hunters, but she would have been popular, regardless. We all awaited her coming out eagerly. I had plans to offer for her even then. But Pelham was wily. He did not wait. He seduced her fresh out of the schoolroom, before any of us had a chance at wooing her."

"Seduced?"

"Yes, seduced. It was obvious to everyone. The way they looked at one another . . . Theirs was a grand passion. Whenever they were in close proximity, the heat was palpable. I envied him that, the worship of a woman so obviously ripe and willing. I had hoped to have that with her, but it wasn't to be. Even after he began to stray, she still adored him, although it was clear it pained her greatly. Pelham was a fool."

"Hear, hear," Gerard muttered, silently examining the flare of jealousy he felt.

Markham chuckled, and took a long drink. "You remind me of him. Or rather, you did before. He was two and twenty when he married her, and just as cocky as you. In fact, Pel used to note often how much you reminded her of Pelham. When you married, I assumed that was why. But then you kept on with your distractions, and she with hers. You confounded all of us, and angered more than a few. It seemed a waste to have Pel finally remarried, only to have it be to a man who had no interest in her."

Gerard stared down at his hands, which were reddened and callused from hard work. He twisted the thin gold band he wore, a piece of jewelry he and Pel had bought as a lark, jesting that it would never see the light of day. He wasn't quite sure why he wanted to wear it, but now that it was on, he found he liked it. It was an odd feeling, the feeling of belonging to someone. He wondered if Pel had felt it when she wore the ring he'd bought her this afternoon, and if that was why she had rejected it so summarily.

The viscount laughed. "I really should hate you, Gray. But you make it damn difficult."

Gerard's brows lifted into his hairline. "I've done nothing to stop you from hating me."

"You're thinking, and brooding. If those are not signs that you have changed, I've no notion what would be. Cheer up. She's yours now, and unlike myself or Pearson or any of the others, she cannot set you aside."

"But there is Hargreaves," he reminded.

"Ah yes, there is that," Markham said with a broad grin. "As I said, fate does have a way."

"I am horribly disappointed that your errant spouse is not at home," the Duchess of Sandforth complained.

"Mother." Isabel shook her head. "I cannot believe you hastened here simply to ogle Gray."

"As if I wouldn't." Her Grace smiled with the wide grin of a naughty cat. "Bella, you should know by now that over-whelming curiosity is one of my vices."

"One of many," Isabel grumbled.

Her mother ignored that. "Lady Pershing-Moore came to call, and you cannot imagine how dreadful it was that she knew every minute detail of Grayson's appearance, while I did not even know he was in town."

"The only dreadful thing is that woman." Isabel paced the length of her boudoir. "I'm certain she has filled as many gossip-hungry ears as she could manage in one day."

"Is he as fine as she says?"

Sighing, Isabel admitted, "Yes, I'm afraid so."

"She swore the way he looked at you was indecent, is that true as well?"

Isabel paused, and stared at her mother, gazing into eyes of rich, dark brown. The duchess was still considered a great beauty, though her auburn hair was now liberally shot with silver strands. "I am not discussing this with you, Mother."

"Why not?" Her Grace replied, affronted. "How delicious! You have a stunning lover, and a young husband who is even more stunning. I envy you."

Pinching the bridge of her nose, Isabel sighed. "You should not envy me. This is a disaster."

"Ah ha!" Her mother leapt to her feet. "Grayson does want you. About time, if you ask me. I was beginning to wonder if he wasn't a bit touched."

He *was* touched in the head, in Isabel's opinion. They had known one another for years, and lived together for six months with nary a spark. Now it was a conflagration whenever she merely laid eyes on him. On second thought, perhaps she was touched, too. "I need to find him a woman," she muttered.

"You are not a woman? I was certain the doctor assured me you were."

"Mother, good grief. Be serious, please. Grayson needs a mistress."

Moving to the window, Isabel moved aside the sheers, and stared out at the small side garden. She could not help but remember the morning he'd stood below the window of her townhouse, and begged her to admit him. Then begged her to marry him.

Say yes, Pel.

Another memory, one fresher in her mind, was from yesterday afternoon when Gray had stood behind her in this exact spot, and made her want him, which had ruined everything.

"How does his need for a mistress relate to his wish to bed you?" the duchess asked.

"You would not understand."

"You are correct about that." Her mother came over, and set her hands on her shoulders. "I thought you had learned something from Pelham."

"I learned *everything* from Pelham."

"Do you not miss that passion, that fire?" Her Grace

spread her arms wide, and spun around with the exuberant carelessness of a young girl, her dark green skirts twirling around her. "I live for it, Bella. I crave those indecent looks, and thoughts, and actions."

"I know you do, Mother," Isabel said dryly. Her parents had long ago decided to find their romances outside the marital bed, a state of living they both seemed quite content with.

"I thought perhaps you had set aside those silly dreams of lifetime love when you began to take your own lovers."

"I did."

"I don't believe so." Her mother frowned.

"Simply because I think fidelity is a sign of respect, does not mean I attach it to love, or the hope for love." Isabel moved back toward her escritoire, where she had been working on menus and a guest list for her upcoming dinner.

"Bella, my sweet." Her mother sighed, and returned to the chaise where she poured a cup of tea. "It is not in a husband's nature to be faithful, especially handsome and charming husbands."

"I wish they would not lie about it," Isabel said crossly, shooting a glance at the portrait on the wall. "I asked Pelham if he loved me, if he would be true to me. He said, '*All women pale in comparison to you.*' And foolish chit that I was, I believed him." She threw up her hands.

"Even if they have the best of intentions, it is impossible for them to resist all the light-skirts who fall into their beds. Wishing for beautiful men to act against their nature will only lead to heartbreak."

"Obviously I have no desire for Gray to act against his nature, or I would not be actively working toward procuring him a mistress."

Isabel watched her mother drop three lumps of sugar and a ridiculous amount of cream into her tea. She shook her head when her mother lifted the pot in silent query.

"I fail to see why you do not enjoy his attentions while he

is willing to give them to you. Good heavens, the way Lady Pershing-Moore persisted about his appearance, I think I would take him myself if he were interested."

Closing her eyes, Isabel released a long-suffering sigh.

"You should take lessons from your brother, Bella. He is far more practical about such matters."

"Most men are. Rhys would be no exception."

"He has made a list of marriageable females and—"

"*A list?*" Isabel's eyes flew open. "Now that is too much!"

"It's perfect. Your father and I did the same, and look how happy we are."

Isabel held her tongue.

"Is it tenderness for Hargreaves that holds you back?" her mother asked softly.

"I wish it were. This would be so much simpler." Then she could disregard Gray's sudden preoccupation with her, and deal with him the way she dealt with any overzealous swain— with a smile and a dash of humor. She found it very hard to smile and be humorous when her nipples ached and she was damp between the thighs.

"We rub along well, Gray and I. I like him, he's great fun. I could live with great fun, Mother. For a lifetime. I could not live with a man who had wounded me in some fashion. I am softer than you, and bear scars from Pelham."

"And you think finding Grayson a mistress will make him less appealing? No, don't answer that, darling. I know you find attached men unattractive. An admirable scruple." Her Grace rose, and came to her, setting her slender arm around her daughter's waist and perusing the notes. "No, no. Not Lady Cartland." She gave a delicate shudder. "I would wish a pox on a man before I'd wish her on him."

Isabel laughed. "Very well." She dipped the quill and drew a slash across the name. "Who then?"

"Was he not with someone when he left? Besides Emily Sinclair?"

"Yes . . ." Isabel thought for a moment. "Ah, I remember. Anne Bonner, an actress."

"Invite her. He left for reasons other than boredom, so perhaps there is still something there."

A sharp pang of loneliness took Isabel off guard, and her hand paused above the parchment long enough to create an ink drop. "Thank you, Mother," she said softly, grateful, for once, to have her parent with her.

"Of course, Bella." The duchess leaned over, and pressed their cheeks together. "What are mothers for, if not to help their daughters find mistresses for their husbands?"

Isabel lay on her bed and attempted to read, but nothing could hold her attention. It was just after ten, and she had remained at home as Gray had asked. The fact that he had not redeemed his requested boon was his error, and if he thought he could collect later, he was sorely mistaken. She would not be affording him the option again. Canceling her plans for one evening was enough of an imposition, especially when he didn't have the courtesy to show up.

This was, of course, what she had hoped for, that he would find his pleasures elsewhere. This was exactly what she wanted. Everything was going well. Perhaps she wouldn't need to hold a homecoming dinner after all. What a relief. She could set aside the planning, and direct her attentions to living her life as she had before her husband returned.

She released her breath, and considered retiring when she heard a sound from the boudoir. Surely it wasn't excitement she felt, as she tossed aside the book. She was simply investigating. Anyone would if they heard strange noises in their suite.

Isabel ran into the next room, and threw open the hallway door. Then gaped.

"Hello, Pel," Gray said, standing in the gallery in only his rolled-up shirtsleeves and trousers. Bare feet, bare throat, and bare forearms. With his thick, dark hair damp from a recent bath.

Dastardly.

"What do you want?" she grumbled, upset that he would come to her dressed, or undressed as the case may be, in that fashion.

He arched a brow, and lifted his arm, bringing a small basket up to her eye level. "Supper. You promised. You cannot withdraw now."

She stepped back to allow him entry, and attempted to hide her blush. Failing to see the obvious basket because she was ogling him was mortifying. "You missed dinner."

"I didn't believe you would want me." The double entendre was clear. He stepped into her room, and she could not help but breathe in his scent as he walked by. The size of her satin-draped boudoir shrank to embrace him, and enclosed them together. "Supper, however, was guaranteed."

"Are your only pursuits those that are guaranteed?"

"Obviously not, or I wouldn't be here." Gray sat on the floor by the low table, and opened the basket. "You shan't chase me away with your ill-humor, Isabel. I waited all day for this meal, and I intend to enjoy it. If you've nothing charming to say to me, put one of these pheasant sandwiches in your mouth, and just let me look at you."

She stared at him, and then he lifted his gaze and winked one of those blue eyes at her. Her descent to the floor was only partially due to courtesy. The rest was due to suddenly weak knees.

He pulled out two glasses and a bottle of wine. "You look lovely in pink satin."

"I thought you reconsidered." She lifted her chin. "So I changed."

"No need to worry," he said dryly. "I had no illusions that you dressed to entice me."

"Rogue. Where have you been?"

"You never used to ask me that."

Isabel had never cared before, but she would not say that aloud. "You used to volunteer information, now you share nothing."

"Remington's," he said around a bite.

"All evening?"

He nodded, and reached for his glass.

"Oh." She knew of the courtesans there. Remington's was a bastion of male iniquity. "D-did you enjoy yourself?"

"You aren't hungry?" he asked, ignoring the question.

Lifting her wine, she took a large swallow.

Gray laughed, the sound pouring over her like warm liquid. "That's not food."

She shrugged. "Did you enjoy yourself?" she asked again.

His look was pure exasperation. "I would not have stayed as long as I did if I were miserable."

"Yes, of course." He'd bathed, and changed his clothes. Isabel supposed she should be grateful that he did not come to her reeking of sex and perfume, as Pelham had done on several occasions. Her stomach roiled at the thought, though the image in her mind was of Grayson and not Pelham, and she moved up to the chaise, lying on her back to stare at the tented ceiling. "No. I am not hungry."

A moment later she was inundated with the smell of Gray—that of starched linen and sandalwood soap. He sat on the floor beside her, and caught up her hand in his own.

"What can I do?" he asked softly, his callused fingertips drifting over her palm, sending heated frissons across her skin. "It pains me that my presence distresses you so, but I cannot stay away, Pel. Do not ask me to."

"And if I did?"

"I could not oblige you."

"Even after tonight's amusements?"

His fingers stilled, and then he gave a low chuckle. "I should be a good husband, and set your mind at ease, but I have just enough of the rapscallion left in me to want you to suffer a bit, just as I will be suffering."

"Men who look like you never suffer, Gray," she retorted with a snort, turning her head to meet his gaze.

"There are men who look like me? How disheartening."

"See how our relationship alters when you change your role from friend to husband?" she complained. "Lies, evasions, things left unsaid. Why do you want us to live in that manner?"

Gray ran a hand through his hair, and groaned.

"Can you answer me that, Gray? Please help me to understand why you wish to ruin our friendship."

His eyes met hers, filled with the bleakness she had felt around him yesterday. Her heart swelled with emotion at the sight. "God, Pel." He set his cheek against her thigh, his dark hair dampening the satin. "I don't know how to discuss this, and not sound maudlin."

"Try."

He stared at her for a long time, his long eyelashes shielding his thoughts and casting shadows upon his cheekbones. The fingers that stroked her palm stopped, and entwined with hers. The simple intimacy was like a physical blow. For a moment, she found it difficult to breathe.

"After Emily died, I despised myself, Isabel. You've no notion of how I wronged her—so many ways, so many times. What a waste it was for a woman like her to perish due to a man like me. It took me a long while to accept the self-loathing, and realize that while I could not change the past, I could honor her by changing who I was in the future."

She tightened her grip on his hand, and he squeezed back. It was then she felt the unrelenting curve of a ring on his finger. Grayson had never worn his wedding band before. That he wore it now gave her a jolt that made her shiver violently.

He nuzzled his face against her, making her gasp at the resulting flare of longing. Misunderstanding her distress, he said, "This is dreadful. I apologize."

"No . . . Continue. Please. I want to know everything."

"It is a miserable task attempting to change one's charac-ter," he said finally. "I think whole years passed without find-ing anything worth smiling about. Until you walked into the study yesterday. Then, in that one moment, I saw you and felt a spark." He lifted their joined hands, and kissed her knuckles. "Then later, in this room, I smiled. And it felt good, Pel. That spark turned into something else, something I have not felt in years."

"Hunger," she breathed, her eyes riveted to his impas-sioned face. She knew the feeling, because it gnawed at her now.

"And desire, and *life,* Isabel. And that is from the outside. I can only dream about what it would be like from the in-side." Gray's voice deepened, and turned husky with want, his eyes now free of the abject torment she had witnessed in them when he'd first arrived. "Deep inside you, as far as I can go."

"Gray . . ."

His head turned, his hot, open mouth pressing against her upper thigh, burning through the pink satin of her robe and night rail. She tensed all over, her spine arching gently in a silent plea for more.

Tormented, Isabel pushed his head away. "After you have slaked that hunger, what happens to us then? We could not go back to what we had before."

"What are you talking about?"

"Have you never found that you can no longer eat a food you used to crave? Once hunger is appeased, the dish you gorged on becomes unappetizing." She sat up, and slipped past him. Rising to her feet, she began to pace, as was her wont when agitated. "We would be truly estranged then. I would most likely choose a different property in which to reside. Social events where we meet would become uncom-fortable."

He rose to his feet, and followed her with his gaze. A gaze that was tactile in its intensity. "You see your former lovers every day. They are sociable with you, and you with them. What makes me different?"

"I do not look at them over coffee in the morning. I do not rely on them to settle my accounts, and see to my welfare. They do not wear my ring!" She paused, and closed her eyes, shaking her head at the foolishness of her errant mouth.

"Isabel," he began softly.

She held up her hand, and stared at the portrait on the wall. A golden god stared back at her, forever arrested in his prime. "We will find you a paramour. Sex is sex, and another woman would be far less messy."

Her husband moved with such grace, she failed to hear him approach. Gray's encircling arms came as a surprise— one banding her waist, the other crossing her torso so a large hand could cup her breast possessively. She cried out as her feet left the floor, and he buried his face in her neck. The feel of his body was so hot and hard behind her, filled with strength, yet tender in its clasp.

"I do not require your assistance to find sex. I require *you*." He licked and nipped at the tender skin of her throat, and then he breathed her in, his arms tightening around her with a low groan. "I want messy. And sweaty and dirty. God give me strength, for I have been cursed with wanting that from my wife."

Isabel burned at the feel of his erection, and then melted in his embrace when he ground it against her in near desperation. "No."

"But I can be gentle, Pel. I can love you well." His grip lightened, his fingertips softly teasing her nipple. She writhed in his arms, the ache between her legs nearly unbearable.

"No . . ." she moaned, wanting him with every breath in her body.

"See your ring on my finger," he growled, obviously frustrated. "Know that I am yours. That I am different from the others." Gray licked the shell of her ear, and then bit the lobe. "Want me, damn you. The way I want you."

Grayson set her aside with a curse, and left the room, leaving Isabel to the warring halves within her—the part of her that knew an affair with Gray could not last, and the part of her that did not care if it didn't.

Chapter 5

Gerard stood in his parlor, and silently cursed the crowd that gathered there. The daylight hours were his time to spend with Pel and work on building their rapport. Tonight, he knew she would venture out and dazzle the peerage with her charm and beauty. Isabel was a social creature who enjoyed time spent in the company of others, and until he had acceptable garments he could not escort her. So he had determined to make the most of the time he was afforded, perhaps take her on a picnic. But then the callers had begun to arrive. Now their home swarmed with curious visitors who wanted to see both him, and the state of his scandalous marriage.

Resigned, he watched his wife pour tea for the women around her. Isabel sat in the middle of the settee, surrounded by blondes and brunettes who paled in comparison, her auburn hair striking and distinguishing. She wore a high-waisted gown of cream-colored silk, a shade uniquely suited to her pale skin and radiant tresses. In his parlor, which was decorated in striped blue damask, she was in her element, and he knew that despite the reasons why they had married, Pel had been an excellent choice as a bride. She was charming and gracious. He could find her easily, simply by following the sounds of laughter. People were happy in her presence.

As if she felt the weight of his regard, Isabel lifted her gaze and caught his eye. A soft pink flush swept up her chest to color her cheeks. He winked at her and smiled, just to watch her blush deepen.

How had it ever escaped his notice how she stood apart from all other women?

He could not help but note it now. Simply being in the same room with her made his blood thrum in his veins, a feeling he had once thought to never feel again. Isabel had attempted to keep her distance by moving from room to room, but he followed her, needing the flare of awareness he felt only in proximity to her.

"She is lovely, is she not?"

Gerard turned to the woman at his side. "Indeed, Your Grace." A smile curved his mouth at the sight of Pel's mother, a woman of renowned beauty. It was obvious his wife would age just as well. "She takes after her mother."

"Charming, and dashing," Lady Sandforth murmured, returning his smile. "How long will you be staying this time?"

"As long as my wife is here."

"Interesting." She arched a brow. "May I be so bold as to ask why you have had a change of heart?"

"The fact that she is my wife is not enough?"

"Men desire their wives in the beginning, my lord. Not four years later."

He laughed. "I am a little slow, but I'm catching up."

A movement caught his eye, and Gerard turned his head to discover Bartley at the door. He took a moment to think, trying to decide how he should proceed. They had once been friends, but only in the most mercenary sense of the word. He made his excuses, and moved to meet the baron, offering a genuine smile of welcome.

"Bartley, you look well." And indeed he did, having lost a good portion of the weight that had thickened his waistline.

"Not as well as you, Gray," Bartley returned. "Although I admit, you appear to have the chest of a laborer. Have you been working your own fields?" He laughed.

"Occasionally." Gerard gestured down the short hallway by the stairs. "Come. Have a cigar with me, and tell me what trouble you've occupied yourself with in my absence."

"First, I have brought you a present."

Gerard's eyebrows rose. "A gift?"

Bartley's florid complexion was mitigated by a broad grin. "Yes. Since you've just returned, and have yet to truly socialize, I knew you would be a tad . . . shall we say, lonely?" He gestured toward the front door with a jerk of his head.

Curious, Gerard's gaze followed the prodding, and he saw the dark-haired beauty by the front door—Barbara, Lady Stanhope. Her mouth curved in a smile so carnal, it could only be called wicked. He remembered that smile, remembered how it had incited his lust and a torrid nine-month affair. Barbara liked her fucking sweaty and messy, too.

He moved to greet her, lifting her proffered hand to kiss the back. Her long nails raked his palm with sensual deliberation.

"Grayson," she said, in a girlish voice that did not suit her disposition. That had turned him on, too, hearing that innocent angel's voice while he used her lush body. "You look divine, at least from what I can see of you with your clothes on."

"You also look well, Barbara, but then you knew that."

"When I heard you had returned, I came quickly, before another woman snatched you up."

"You should not have come to my home," he admonished.

"I know, darling, and I'm leaving. I just knew I would have a better chance at you if you saw me in person. A note is so impersonal, and not nearly as fun as touching you." Her eyes, clear as jade and just as beautifully colored, sparkled with amusement. "I would like us to be friends again, Gray."

Gerard arched a brow, and his mouth curved in an indulgent smile. "A lovely offer, Barbara, but I must decline."

She reached out and brushed a hand down his stomach,

giving a soft purr. "I heard the rumors of you and Lady Grayson reconciling."

"We were never estranged," he corrected, taking a small step backward.

Barbara gave a soft pout. "I do so hope you will reconsider. I've procured a room at our favorite hotel. I will be there for the next three days." She blew a kiss to Bartley, then she looked up again. "I hope to see you there, Grayson."

He bowed. "I wouldn't wait up."

As the footman closed the door behind his lascivious guest, Bartley came to his side. "You can thank me with brandy and a cigar."

"I have never required your services in this particular regard," Gerard said dryly.

"Yes, yes, I know. But you've just arrived, and I wanted to save you a spot of trouble. No need to keep her when you're done with her."

Shaking his head, Gerard led Bartley away from the door to his study. "You know, Bartley. I doubt there is a chance in hell of reforming you."

"Reforming me?" the baron cried, horrified. "Good God, I should hope not. How dreadful."

The hour was nearly six before their home was empty of visitors. As Isabel stood in the foyer beside Grayson and watched the last callers depart, she could not contain her sigh of relief. The entire day had been a study in misery and clenched teeth. She could swear that every one of Gray's former paramours had come calling today. At least the peeresses had, the ones who knew she could not turn them away. And Gray had been charming and witty, making every one of those odious women infatuated with him all over again.

"Well, that was trying," she muttered. "Despite what a scoundrel you are, you remain popular." She turned, and took

the stairs. "Of course, the majority of visitors were women."
Young women.

The soft chuckle beside her was maddeningly smug. "Well,
you do wish me to contract a mistress," Gray reminded.

She shot him a sidelong glance, and found that lusciously
etched mouth twitching with a withheld smile. She snorted.
"Shameless of them to come to *my* home, and ogle you
within my view."

"Perhaps scheduled interviews would please you better?"
he suggested.

Coming to an abrupt halt on the next-to-last stair, Isabel
set her hands on her hips and glared at him. "Why are you
deliberately trying to provoke me?"

"Sweetheart, I loathe being the one to point this out to
you, but you were already provoked." He let that smile out,
and she gripped the railing to support herself at the sight of
it. "I must admit, it warms my heart to see you so jealous."

"I am *not* jealous." Isabel took the last stair, and turned
down the hallway. "I simply require a little respect to be afforded to me in my own home. And, I learned long ago that
any man who makes a woman jealous is not worth having."

"I agree."

The softly spoken acknowledgment startled her, and her
steps faltered just before she reached her door.

"I hope you keep in mind, Pel," he murmured, "that I did
not enjoy those visitors any more than you did."

"Liar. You adore fawning women. All men do."

*It is not in a husband's nature to be faithful, especially
handsome and charming husbands,* her mother had said, and
Isabel knew that firsthand. Of course, Gray had not lied to
her. He made no promises to be faithful, only to be a good
lover, a fact she did not doubt.

"I adore fawning women only when they are temperamental marchionesses with satin-draped boudoirs." He reached
around her, turning the brass knob, his arm brushing against

the side of her breast. "What vexes you, Isabel?" he asked, his mouth to her ear. "Where is that smile I long for?"

"I am trying to be pleasant, Gray." She hated being ill-humored. It was not in her nature.

"I had other plans for today."

"You did?" She did not know why it bothered her that he had somewhere to go, a task to accomplish that did not include her.

"Yes." He licked the shell of her ear, his broad shoulders blocking out everything but him. "I had hoped to spend the day wooing you, and showing you my charming side."

Isabel pushed against his chest, tamping down the little quiver his words and nearness gave her. He leaned closer, resting one hand against the jamb, surrounding her with his scent and hard body. A thick lock of his dark hair fell over his brow, making him look relaxed and very much like a six-and-twenty-year-old man.

"I have seen quite enough of your charming side." And his passionate side. She shivered at the memory of his arms around her, and his lips at her throat.

"Are you cold, Isabel?" he asked, his voice low and intimate, his gaze half-lidded. "Shall I warm you?"

"Frankly," she whispered, her hands brushing over the top of his shoulders, which made him shudder. "I am very hot at the moment."

"Me, too. Stay home with me tonight."

She shook her head. "I really must go out." Stepping back into her room, she expected him to follow, but he did not.

"Very well." Gray sighed, and ran a hand through his hair. "Will you be taking dinner in your room?"

"Yes."

"I have some tasks to attend to, then I will return and watch you prepare. I hope you have no objections. A man must find his pleasures where he can."

"No, I have no objections." She was beginning to realize that the thought of him finding pleasure elsewhere was highly disturbing.

"Until later then." He pulled the door closed, and Isabel stared at the portal for long moments after he had departed.

Over the course of the next few hours, she bathed and ate a light meal. Normally she would gossip with Mary during her toilette. Servants knew the prime bits, and she liked to hear them. Today, however, Isabel was quiet. Her mind was occupied with the events of the afternoon. She knew some of the women in her home today were intimately familiar with her husband. Over the last four years, she had met those same women many times and thought nothing of it. Now it bothered her to such an extent, she could not stop thinking about it.

Worse than that, though, were the new women, the ones not in his past, but in his future. The ones who had come to bat their eyelashes, touch his arm, and smile with carnal promise. Every one of them so certain Isabel would not mind. Why would she? She had Hargreaves, and she had never minded before. Fact was, she did mind. Knowing one of those women would soon share Gray's bed made her blood simmer. Dressed only in her chemise and underbust corset, she was nevertheless overheated by her thoughts and frustration.

She closed her eyes as her abigail swept her hair up, and arranged it in the popular style of short curls around her face. There was a slight knock at the door, and then it opened without further ado. The presumptive move was slightly disturbing, but what bothered her most was the direction from whence the sound came. Opening her eyes, she looked to the side, and watched Gray enter from the adjoining bedroom.

"What . . . ?" she sputtered.

He took a deep breath, and then sprawled on her favorite chaise. "You look ravishing," he said, as if it were perfectly normal for him to enter from the master suite. "Or more aptly, ravishable. Is that a word, Pel? If not, it should be, with your likeness rendered next to it."

From the time they had married, he had kept a room down the hall and around the corner from hers. She had offered to take a suite in the guest area, since this was his home and their marriage a sham, but he had pointed out how much more time she spent at home than he did. Which was true. She slept in her bed every night. Gray sometimes did not sleep in his room for days on end.

The thought sparked her temper. "What were you doing in there?"

He blinked innocently. "Whatever I felt like. Why?"

"There is nothing in there besides empty furniture."

"On the contrary," he drawled. "Most of my possessions are in there. At least the ones I use on a regular basis."

Her fingers curled around the edge of her vanity. The thought of Gray sleeping mere feet from her, with only a door to separate them, was instantly arousing. She pictured his body nude, as she had seen it in the tailor's. She wondered if he slept facedown, with those powerful arms wrapped around a pillow and that luscious, tight ass bare to her view. Or perhaps faceup? The feel of his cock was imprinted on her derriere from last night. The long, hard heat of him . . . Bare . . . Gray's beautiful body sprawled in sleep . . . Tangled in sheets . . .

Oh Lord . . .

Swallowing hard, she looked away from him before he could read her thoughts or see her turmoil.

"Bartley inherited a chicken."

"Beg your pardon?" Isabel's eyes moved to her husband's again. As he had the night before, he was dressed in loose trousers and shirtsleeves, a tempting sight, which she was certain he knew. They would have to deal with his changing rooms eventually, but she did not have the heart to tackle the argument now. She already had an altercation ahead of her when she met with Hargreaves.

"Bartley's aunt was an eccentric," he replied, his voice directed upward as he moved to lie on his back. "She kept a chicken as a pet. When he last visited her, she was so pleased with her chicken he felt it best to agree and say that it was the handsomest chicken he had ever seen."

"A handsome chicken?" Her lips twitched.

"Quite." She could not miss the smile in his voice. "When she passed on, she bequeathed portions of her estate to her many relatives and—"

"Bartley was given the chicken."

"Yes." Gray's laughing eyes met hers in the mirror as she stood to don her gown. "No, don't laugh, Pel. This is serious, you know."

Her abigail smothered a giggle.

"Oh, of course," Isabel said gravely, schooling her features.

"The poor creature is mad for Bartley. But then I do believe chickens have pea-sized brains."

"Gray!" she cried, laughing.

"Apparently he cannot go into his rear garden any longer. The moment he steps outside, she begins screeching for him." Gray leapt to his feet in a fluidly graceful motion, and held out his arms. "She runs at him with her wings spread in joy, and flies into her lover's arms."

Both she and her abigail laughed aloud.

"You are fabricating that tale!"

"I am not. While I do admit to having a wild imagination," he said, coming toward her, "even I could not imagine any female mad for Bartley, poultry or otherwise."

Gray smiled at her maid. "I can take over from here."

Mary curtsied, and left.

Isabel's smile faded as he came up behind her, and began to

work on the tiny row of cloth-covered buttons that ran up her spine. She held her breath, trying not to smell him. "We were doing so well, Gray," she complained. "For a moment, I felt the friendship we had before. Why ruin it by reminding me of this damned attraction?"

His fingertips drifted over her chemise-covered upper back. "Gooseflesh. You have no notion of how difficult it is for a man to stand this close to a woman he desires, to feel that desire returned, and then not act upon it."

"Friends," she insisted, secretly amazed at the steadiness of her voice. "That is the only way to make this marriage work."

"I can be your friend, as well as your lover." His hot, open mouth pressed against the top of her shoulder.

"And what will become of us when we are no longer lovers?"

Wrapping his arms around her waist, Gray set his chin on her shoulder and stared at their reflection. He was so much taller than she was. He had to hunch over her, surrounding her completely.

"What do you want me to say, Isabel? That we will always be lovers?"

His hands pushed down her loose bodice and cupped her breasts, kneading gently, his hips swirling against her derriere. The fierce evidence of his desire was unmistakable, and heat spread instantly across her skin. She was primed for sex, her body repeatedly aroused by his seductions, and her eyes slid closed on a low moan.

"Look at us," he urged. "Open your eyes. See how flushed we are, how needy." Strong, nimble fingers tugged at her nipples. "I know I could make you come like this, still fully clothed. Would you like to come, Isabel?" He licked her sweat-misted skin. "Of course, you would."

Afraid to see herself in his arms, she shook her head.

Gray shifted, his hips aligning so he could rub his cock against her, up and down, the hard length making her sob in near desperation. He worked her nipples, elongating them, pulling and twisting until she cried out in pleasure. She felt every motion of his fingers as if they were between her legs, her cunt creamy and aching for him.

"I cannot say we will always be lovers." His gruff voice skittered across her skin, making her nipples tighten further. He groaned. "But I can tell you that if my lust for you were half the measure it is now, I would still want you desperately."

She knew he would still want someone else, too. Even when he'd been in love, he had not been steadfast. Despite this knowledge, her back arched, thrusting her breasts into his hands and her buttocks against his bone-hard erection. Gray growled—a deep, throaty warning. "Stay home with me."

The temptation to do so was nearly overwhelming. She wanted to push him to the floor, sink her body onto his cock, and ride out this agitation.

"I never once wanted you," she moaned, undulating in his embrace, every part of her straining. She was almost mad with desire, prepared to throw aside everything she held dear to take him. But some of her reasoning would not be denied. "Not once did I ever look at you, and think about sharing your bed."

Now she could not stop thinking about it.

Forcing her eyes to open, Isabel stared at the mirror and watched herself writhe between his skilled hands and hard body. At that moment she hated herself, hated seeing an echo of the girl she had been almost a decade ago, helpless in the grip of a desire skillfully crafted for a man's pleasure.

Gray's arms tightened, pinning her tightly to his chest. His mouth, hot and wet, nuzzled all over her throat and shoulder. "God, I want to fuck you," he rasped, the clasp of his fingers becoming a hard pinch. "I want that so badly I'm afraid I will tear you apart."

The crudeness of his speech was more than she could tolerate. With a cry, she climaxed, her cunt spasming so hard her knees nearly gave way. Gray held her upright, his hold strong and steady.

Panting, Isabel turned her gaze away from her wanton reflection and sought out Pelham's likeness. She looked into dark eyes that had once drawn her into sexual decadence, and she called to mind every one of his mistresses. She remembered every occasion where she had been forced to sit across from one of them at a social function or to smell their perfume on her husband's skin. She thought of all the women who had been in her home today with their come-hither smiles, and her stomach roiled violently, dousing her ardor instantly.

"Release me," she said, her voice low and determined. She straightened, shrugging him off.

He stiffened behind her. "Listen to your breathing, and the rapid beat of your heart. You want this as badly as I do."

"I do not." She struggled in near panic until he released her with a curse. Then she spun on him with her fists clenched, every cell in her body working to turn her raging desire into just plain rage. "Keep your distance from me. Move back to your room. Leave me alone."

"What in hell is the matter with you?" He ran both hands through his thick, dark hair. "I do not understand you."

"I don't want a sexual relationship with you. I have said that many times."

"Why not?" he said crossly, beginning to pace.

"Do not push me anymore, Grayson. If you continue forcing yourself on me, I will have to leave."

"*Forcing* myself on you?" He pointed a finger at her, a wealth of frustration betrayed by the rigidity of his body. "We will sort this out. Tonight."

Lifting her chin, Isabel held her gown to her breasts and

shook her head rapidly. "I have plans for this evening. I told you that."

"You cannot go out," he scoffed. "Look at you. You are shaking all over with the need for a hard tumble."

"That is not your concern."

"Damned if it isn't."

"Gray—"

Gray's eyes narrowed dangerously. "Do not bring Hargreaves into this, Isabel. Do not go to him to sate the needs I arouse."

She gaped. "Are you threatening me?"

"No. And well you know it. I am promising you, that if you go to Hargreaves to ease cravings brought on by *my* touch, I will call him out."

"I cannot believe this."

He threw up his hands. "Neither can I. There you stand, aching for me. Here I stand, ready to fuck you until neither of us can walk. What is the problem, Isabel? Can you tell me that?"

"I do not want to ruin our marriage!"

Gray took a deep, calming breath. "I must point out to you, dear wife, that marriage, by nature, includes sex. Between the spouses, not third parties."

"Not our marriage," she said firmly. "We had a bargain. You must find someone else."

"That blasted bargain! Christ, Pel. Things have changed." He stepped toward her with arms outstretched, the tense line of his jaw softening.

She ran to her escritoire, and put the piece of furniture between them. If he touched her, she would crumble.

His jaw clenched again. "As you wish," he bit out. "But this is not what you want. I saw you today, the way you looked at every woman who walked in the door. The truth is, whatever your reasoning is for not wanting me in your bed, you don't want me in any other woman's bed either." Gray bowed. "However, your wish is my command. You can collect your error on your own."

Before she could react, he was gone. And while she regretted her words immediately, she did not chase him down and tell him not to go.

Chapter 6

Gerard strode the length of the hallway that led to Lady Stanhope's hotel room, and cursed his stubborn wife.

There were benefits to doing as Isabel urged. His desire for her was nigh unbearable, causing him to push her too quickly and frighten her. He understood this, and he appreciated that he was not giving her enough time to become accustomed both to his new interest and his return to her life. It was true that fucking Barbara would take the edge off his hunger, but *damn it!* He did not want to take the edge off. He wanted to experience the aching, burning, intoxicating passion with Isabel, not a substitute for her.

But the thought of his wife with Hargreaves was so infuriating, his blood boiled. He would be damned if she eased her needs while he suffered with his own. Gerard knocked on Barbara's door, and walked right in.

"I knew you would come," she purred, nude on the bed, wearing only a black ribbon around her throat. He hardened instantly, as any man would at the sight of her. Barbara was a beautiful woman with a ravenous sexual appetite, enough to incite his anger and frustration into adulterated lust.

Shrugging out of his jacket and unfastening the buttons of his waistcoat, he approached the bed with grim determination.

Barbara came up on her knees, and moved to help him.

"Grayson," she breathed in her girlish voice, her eager hands shoving his garments off his shoulders to pool on the floor. "You are so hot for it tonight."

He crawled over her, pinning her to the bed, then rolled, bringing her over him.

"You know what to do," he muttered, then lay there, staring up at the ceiling, his mind completely disconnected from the meaningless sex that would soon follow.

Tugging his shirt free, Barbara ran her hands across his rippled abdomen. "I think I could orgasm just looking at you." She leaned over him, pressing her breasts against his thigh as she worked to open his trousers. "But, of course, I will do more than look."

Gerard closed his eyes, and longed for Isabel.

Isabel stepped down from her carriage and entered the Hargreaves residence by way of the mews. It was a path she had taken hundreds of times, and one that used to fill her with warm anticipation. Tonight, however, was completely different. Her stomach was knotted, and her palms damp. Gray had left on horseback, and she knew he had gone to another woman.

And she was the one who had driven him there.

At this moment, he was most likely buried deep inside someone, his gorgeous ass tightening and flexing as he thrust his cock into a willing body. She told herself their marriage was best this way. Better he find someone else now, than after she had succumbed. But even knowing this, she did not feel any better. The pictures in her mind tormented her, and the feeling of possessiveness did not abate. As she walked silently along the upper floor hallway, she could not fight her feelings of guilt and betrayal.

She knocked softly on John's bedroom door, then entered.

Hargreaves sat before the fire. Dressed in a multi-colored silk robe, and holding a snifter in his hand, he stared broodingly into the fire. "I did not think you would come," he said without looking at her. His voice was slightly slurred, and she noted the near-empty decanter on the table next to him.

"I am sorry," she murmured, sinking to the floor at his feet. "I know the gossip hurts you. It pains me deeply."

"Have you slept with him?"

"No."

"But you want to."

"Yes."

His eyes met hers, and he cupped her cheek in his hand. "Thank you for your honesty."

"I sent him away tonight." She nuzzled into his touch, relishing the peace and familiar comfort she found in his presence. "He went."

"Will he stay away?"

Leaning her cheek against his knee, she stared into the fire. "I'm not certain. He seems quite determined."

"Yes." John's fingers slipped into her hair. "I remember that age. The barest periphery of your mortality hits you, and the need to sire an heir becomes nearly overwhelming."

Isabel stiffened. "He has two younger brothers. He does not need an heir."

John's laugh held no humor. "When did he tell you this? When you married? When he was two and twenty? Of course he was not interested in children at that time. Most men are not. Fucking is primary, and pregnancy does put a damper on that."

She thought of Gray's boyish excitement over Emily's pregnancy, and her blood ran cold. He had shown a strong desire for children before.

"He is a marquess, Isabel," Hargreaves said, his lips on the rim of his glass, his fingers in her hair. "He needs an heir, and while he may have brothers, a man does like to produce his own issue. What other reason did he give you for returning?"

"He said he felt guilt for leaving me to face the rumors alone."

"I would not have thought Grayson was capable of such

altruism," Hargreaves said dryly, setting his empty glass aside. "He would have to be a completely different man than the one I knew of only four years ago."

Staring into the fire, Isabel suddenly felt very foolish and very hurt. She sat there for a long time watching the flames dance.

Later, John's hand drifted, weighing heavily on her shoulder. She turned her head, and found him sleeping. Torn, and terribly confused, she rose and fetched a blanket. Once she knew he was comfortable, she left.

Gerard turned his head away when Barbara attempted to kiss him. Her perfume was cloying, a musky scent he had once found attractive and now found sadly lacking. His cock was rock hard and aching in her hand, his body responding to her expert ministrations despite his emotional and mental disconnections. She whispered shocking, depraved things in his ear, and then she straddled him, preparing to mount him.

"I am so glad you came home, Grayson," she breathed.

Home.

The word swirled through his head, and made his stomach clench tight. He had never had a home. As a child, his mother's bitterness had poisoned everything around him. The only time he had felt relaxed and accepted was with Pel. That had changed with their new attraction, but he would do whatever was necessary to have that accord again.

And his present encounter was not the way to go about it.

This was not home. This was a hotel, and the woman preparing to fuck him was not his wife. Gripping her waist, Gerard turned quickly, tossing her to the bed next to him.

Barbara squealed in delight. "Yes!" she cried. "I wondered when you would enter into the spirit of things."

Gerard thrust his hand between her legs, and stroked her to orgasm. He knew just what she liked, and where she liked it. Within moments Barbara was coming, and he was free to depart this sordid encounter.

Releasing a frustrated breath, he rolled from the bed, re-fastened his trousers, and moved to the washstand in the corner.

"What are you doing?" she purred, stretching like a cat.

"Washing. Then leaving."

"No, you are not!" She sat up. With her flushed cheeks and pouty red mouth, she was lovely. But not at all what he wanted.

"Sorry, sweet," he said gruffly, scrubbing his hands in the basin. "I am not in the mood this evening."

"You lie. Your cock is hard as a poker."

Gerard turned, and collected his coat and waistcoat.

Barbara's shoulders slumped. "She's old, Grayson."

"She is my wife."

"That never bothered you before. Besides, she has Hargreaves."

He stiffened, his jaw clenching.

"Ah. A direct hit." Her smile was as wicked as always. "Is she with him now? Is that why you came to me?" Spreading her legs, she leaned against the pillows and ran her hands between her thighs. "Why should she have all the fun? I can offer the same entertainments."

Buttoning the last button, Gerard moved to make his egress. "Good night, Barbara."

He was only a few feet down the hall when he heard something fragile shatter against the door. Shaking his head, he descended the stairs quickly, eager to go home.

Comfortably ensconced in her own bedroom, Isabel dismissed Mary as soon as she had undressed. "But bring me some Madeira," she murmured as the abigail curtsied.

When she was alone, she sank into the wingback in front of the fire and thought of Hargreaves. This situation was so unfair to him. He had been good to her, she adored him, and she hated herself for being so confused. Her mother would say there was no monopoly on desire, and life had proved that to be true. The duchess would find nothing at all wrong with desiring two men at one time. Isabel, however, would always believe that a person should be strong enough to resist baser demands, if they cared enough.

Several minutes later, a knock drew her attention to the open door, and she gestured the maid in. The servant balanced the bottle of Madeira and a glass on a tray in one hand. The other was loaded with towels.

"What are those for?" Isabel asked.

"Forgive me, my lady, Edward requested them for His Lordship's bath."

Edward was Gray's valet. It was nearly dawn. Her husband was bathing away the scents of his carnal exertions and she sat here, morose and guilty. Suddenly furious at the unfairness, she stood and collected the towels. "I will see to this."

The girl's eyes widened, but she curtsied, and set down the bottle and glass before departing.

Isabel crossed her boudoir to the dressing room and then, without any warning, opened the door to the bathing room. Gray lay in steaming water, his head resting against the lip of the tub with his eyes closed. He did not move at all when she entered, and she took a brief moment to absorb the sight of his dark chest and long, powerful legs. All of his beauty was visible through the clear water, including the impressive cock she had felt only briefly. She was instantly aroused, which further incited her temper. A narrow-eyed glance at Edward sent the valet fleeing from the room.

Gray took a deep breath, and then stiffened all over. "Isabel," he breathed, his eyes drifting open. He stared at her with impossibly blue eyes framed with wet lashes, and made no effort to cover himself.

"Did you enjoy your evening?" she bit out.

His lips pursed at her tone. "Did you?"

"No, I did not, and I blame you entirely."

"Of course you would." The silence stretched out, the air between them thick with things left unsaid and a desire that went unappeased. "Did you fuck him, Pel?" he asked finally, his voice gruff.

Her gaze roamed over the length of his body.

"Did you?" he repeated when she said nothing.

"Hargreaves was deep in his cups, and miserable." *While Gray spent a pleasurable evening in some woman's bed.* The thought so enraged her, she threw the towels in his face, and spun on her heel. "I hope you fucked enough for all of us."

"Bloody hell. Isabel!"

Hearing a splash, she began to run. Her bedroom was near, she could make it . . .

Gray caught her by the waist, and lifted her feet from the floor. She flailed, kicking and elbowing, slipping in his wet grasp and her satin night rail.

"Cease," he growled.

"Release me!"

She reached back, and yanked on his wet hair.

"Ow, damn it!"

He stumbled, then dropped to his knees, pressing her face-down upon the floor and covering her body with his own. Her gown was soaked in the back, her breasts flattened into the rug. "I hate you!"

"No, you don't," he muttered, stretching her arms over her head.

She squirmed as much as she was able with his weight atop her. "I cannot breathe," she gasped. He slid to the side, keeping one heavy leg across hers and her arms pinned. "Desist, Gray. You have no right to accost me like this."

"I have every right. Did you fuck him?"

"Yes." She turned her head to glare at him. "I fucked him all night. In every way imaginable. I sucked his—"

Gray's mouth took hers so hard she tasted blood. His tongue slid into her mouth, thrusting in a brutal rhythm, his lips slanting across hers. He held both of her wrists in one hand, while the other reached for the hem of her gown and yanked it upward.

Her blood raced through her veins, her heart pounded furiously against her rib cage. Incited beyond bearing, she bit down on his bottom lip. His head jerked backward with a curse.

"Unhand me!"

Her night rail was trapped beneath her, halting its upward progress, and Gray moved his weight to finish the job. The slight ease in pressure gave her room to buck, and she did, knocking him off guard. She scrambled on her hands and knees.

"Isabel," he snarled, lunging toward her.

He caught the trailing end of her gown and held it tight, causing the thin ribbon ties at her shoulders to rip away. She crawled right out of the ruined garment, intent on reaching her room. Hope flared the moment before her ankle was caught in a vicelike grip. Kicking out with her free leg, she fought desperately, but Gray was too powerful. He climbed over her, subduing her arms, and shoving his thigh between her legs.

Tears of frustration coursed down her cheeks. "You cannot do this," she cried, writhing, fighting against the craving within her more than she fought against him. As she struggled, the heavy heat of his erection was an unmistakable weight against her buttocks.

He once again pinned her arms over her head with one hand. The other brushed gently down her side, and then between her legs. He parted the folds of her sex, slipping two fingers deep inside.

"You're wet," he groaned, his fingers drifting through the evidence of her excitement. She twisted her hips in an attempt to escape his probing. "Calm down." Gray buried his face in the back of her neck. "I fucked no one, Isabel."

"You lie."

"That is not to say that I failed to make the attempt. In the end, however, I only wanted you."

She shook her head, crying silently. "No. I do not believe you."

"Yes, you do. You know a man's body well enough. I could not be this hard if I had been coming all night."

His fingertips, slick with her cream, found her clitoris and circled over it. Her spine arched helplessly, her blood slowing and becoming sluggish with her desire. He was everywhere, completely surrounding her, his hard body caging hers to the floor. A finger dipped inside her until it was buried. She shivered all over, and drenched his hand.

"Hush," he soothed, his voice low and thick by her ear. "Let me ease you. We are both overwrought."

"No, Gray."

"You want this as much as I do."

"I don't."

"Who is lying now?" His finger left her, his damp hand clutching her thigh and lifting it out of the way. His arm slipped under her head, his biceps pillowing her cheek, his palm cupping her left breast. "I need you."

She attempted to close her legs, but then the tip of his cock was there, just at the slick rim of her sex. He stroked it against her, and pinched her nipple. She whimpered as lust misted her skin with sweat.

"You are hot and creamy for my cock." The edge of his teeth grazed her shoulder. "Tell me you don't want me."

"I don't want you."

His chuckle rumbled against her back. The thick head of his shaft entered her, stretched her, the pressure just what she needed, but still not enough. Her hips moved without volition, straining to take more, but he pulled back enough to keep just that tiny bit of him inside her.

"No," he admonished, suddenly much more in control, as if the carnal connection soothed him in some way. "You don't want me."

"Damn you." She ground her face against his arm, wiping away her tears.

"Tell me you want me."

"I do not." But a moan escaped her, and her hips swiveled restlessly, massaging him inside her.

"Isabel . . ." His teeth sank gently into her shoulder, his hips shifting to slide his cock deeper. "Stop that, before I blow without you."

"You wouldn't dare!" she gasped, the thought of being left in this agony was horrifying.

"Continue, and I will be unable to help myself."

She moaned her misery, and buried her face in his arm. "You want to breed me."

"*What?*" He stilled. "What the devil are you talking about?"

"Confess," she said hoarsely, her chest tight. "You have returned for an heir."

To her surprise, he shuddered against her. "Ridiculous. But I know you will not believe me, so I promise not to come in you. Not until you want me to."

"You are corrrect. I don't believe you."

"You shall drive me mad, stubborn wench. Cease making excuses, and simply admit you want me. Then I will give you this." He gave her a shallow thrust. "And not my seed."

"You are horrid, Grayson." She wiggled, desperate to stroke herself to orgasm.

"Actually, I am very good." His tongue entered her ear. "Allow me to prove it."

"Do I have a choice?" She shivered, her skin sticking to his with their sweat. "You will not let me go."

Gray sighed, and hugged her to his chest. "I *cannot* let you go, Isabel." He nuzzled against her throat, and swelled inside her. "Christ, I love the way you smell."

And she loved the way he felt, thick and hard, his cock as large and virile as the rest of him. Pelham had trapped her with this—this heated, drugging pleasure that made a woman want to languish in her bed and be fucked endlessly. A slave to desire.

She was too weak with craving to protest as his fingers found her clitoris and massaged the surrounding skin stretched wide to accommodate him.

"I am thicker at the root," he murmured wickedly. "Imagine how that will feel while I pump it into you."

Her eyes closed, her legs spreading in silent invitation. "Do it, then."

"Is that what you want?" His surprise was patent.

"Yes!" She thrust her elbow into his ribs, and heard him grunt. "You hateful, arrogant cretin."

Reaching up to lace his fingers with hers, Gray gave a low growl and began to thrust in shallow digs. He forced her to feel every inch, made her stretch to his width, acknowledging his power and possession. She cried out her pleasure and relief, the feel of him so devastating to her heightened senses.

It was a claiming, one she could say she fought until the very end.

Clenching her hands with his, Isabel surrendered to her new addiction with a sob of despair.

Chapter 7

Gerard grit his teeth as he worked his cock into slick, swollen tissues. Crushing Pel to his chest, he struggled to keep his wits while every cell in his body was focused on the heated pleasure of her cunt and the panting cries she welcomed him with. He burned all over, even the roots of his hair, his drying skin misting with sweat until it was damp again.

"Oh Pel," he crooned, pushing her leg aside so he could pump deeper. "It feels like heaven inside you."

She writhed beneath him, the gyrations of her hips a stimulation he could barely stand. "Gray . . ."

The breathy plea made him shudder hard against her. "Damn it, cease wiggling before I lose what little control I have."

"This is control?" she gasped, arching her hips up in silent demand. "What are you like when you have none?"

He released her hands, and hugged her slim body to his.

Many times in his life he had been witless with lust. Many times he had given those baser impulses free rein. Never had the need been as fierce as it was with Isabel. Her flamboyant beauty, blatant sexuality, and lush curves were made for a man as primitive in his desires as he was. She had been too much for him four years ago, though his arrogance would never have allowed him to admit it. Now he was worried he would be too much for her. And frightening her from his bed was not an option.

Releasing her hands, he thrust his hands beneath her, and rolled, bringing her over him.

"W—what?" she gasped, her unbound hair falling over his face and shoulders, drowning him in her scent. His cock grew impossibly harder.

"Ride me," he growled, his hands releasing her as if she burned him. Her ripe body draped over his was nearly his undoing. What he wished to do more than breathe was to pin her beneath him, and shaft her tight cunt without mercy until he was well and truly spent. And then do it again. But she was his wife, and deserved better than that. Since he could not trust himself to take the lead, he had to trust it to her.

Isabel hesitated, and he thought for a moment that she would change her mind and refuse him again. Instead she set her hands to the floor and raised her torso. She slid down, taking more of him inside her, until the drenched lips of her sex kissed the base of his cock. His hands fisted as she moaned plaintively. The positioning of her body angled his cock deliciously.

"God, Gray. You feel so . . ."

Squeezing his eyes tightly shut, Gerard sucked in his breath at her unspoken praise. He understood what went unspoken. There were no words for this.

Perhaps it was simply that she had aroused and rejected him repeatedly, as no other woman ever had. Perhaps it was because she was his wife, and that added bit of true ownership increased the moment's poignancy. Whatever it was, sex had never been like this, and they hadn't even begun.

"You must move, Pel." Opening his eyes, he swallowed hard as she extended her arms straight behind her, the ends of her hair pooling on his chest. He wondered how they would do this. Would she dismount and face him? Watching her come would give him great pleasure, but the thought of separating his cock from her was nigh unbearable.

"Must I?" she purred in a taunting tone, and while he could not see her face, he knew her look would be sly. She lifted one hand, her weight settling more firmly on the other arm, her ass cradled by his loins. He lay frozen with bated breath as she reached between her legs, first giving his drawn up balls a teasingly soft squeeze before stroking higher.

Oh hell. If she masturbated on his cock, he would explode.

"Are you going to—?" he began.

She did.

He grunted as her cunt clenched tight as a fist around him. "Bloody hell!"

Clutching her hips in almost panic, Gerard held her slightly aloft as he thrust upward violently, fucking through her gasping depths like a man possessed.

"Yes!" she cried, her head falling back, burying his throat and mouth in fiery tresses. All the while her body milked his cock, luring his seed, the pulsating spasms nearly brutal in their intensity.

It went on forever, her first heated release, but he bit his lip bloody and held on. Only when she went limp in his arms, did he yank himself free, coming hard, spurting scalding streams of lust and longing across her thigh and the rug.

He had wanted to take the edge off.

They had barely scratched the surface.

Pel lay back over him, gasping for air, and he cupped her breasts and kissed her temple. The scent of her mixed with sex was intoxicating. He pressed his nostrils against her skin and breathed it in.

"You are a horrid, dreadful man," she whispered.

Gerard sighed. Of course, he would have to marry the most obstinate woman in the world. "*You* rushed the business. But I shall be certain to lengthen the process the next time around. Perhaps then you will be more agreeable." He levered them both up to a seated position.

"Next time?"

He could tell she was poised to argue, so he reached between her legs and stroked her clitoris with a soft glide of his fingertips. When she moaned, he grinned. "Yes, next time, which will commence momentarily, once I have cleaned us up a bit and moved this arrangement to a more comfortable venue."

She scrambled to her feet, spinning to face him, a whirl of auburn hair and flushed, creamy skin. Staring up at her, Gerard was struck by the absolute carnal perfection of her form. Purely, beautifully naked, Isabel Grayson was a Venus, a siren—full-breasted with generously curved hips, and a wide mouth framed by full kiss-bruised lips. His cock responded with admirable haste. Isabel's eyes dropped to it, and then widened.

"Good grief. We just attended to that thing."

He shrugged, and bit back a smile as she continued to stare, her gaze blatantly appreciative and only slightly intimidated. Rising to his feet, he caught up her hand and tugged her back into the bathing chamber. "I cannot help but respond. You are quite simply a stunningly attractive woman."

Isabel snorted, but followed him without protest, although she lagged slightly behind. He glanced over his shoulder to see why, and caught her ogling his ass with a riveted gaze. She was too preoccupied to realize he'd taken note, so he flexed his buttocks and then laughed when she blushed. Whatever her objection to marital sexual intimacy, it was certainly not due to lack of interest in him.

"Care to tell me about your night?" he asked solicitously, treading new ground. He was not accustomed to casual conversation in the middle of an amorous interlude. His fully engorged erection was not helping him concentrate either. Not that he could help it. His wife's gaze was burning his skin.

"Why?"

"Because you are upset about it." Gerard turned and pushed her into a chair, taking a moment to brush the lovely hair he so admired over her shoulders.

"This is so awkward," she complained, her arms crossing

over her chest modestly as he reached into the tub and pulled out one of the soaked towels. "What are you doing?" she asked, watching him squeeze out the excess water.

"I told you." He dropped to a crouch before her, and with a hand on each knee, forced her legs apart.

"Stop that!" Isabel slapped at his hands. He arched a brow and slapped her back, although with far more gentleness. "Brute," she gasped with wide eyes.

"Wench. Allow me to clean you up a bit."

Sherry-colored eyes shot fire at him. "You have done quite enough, thank you. Now leave me in peace, and I will care for myself."

"I haven't even started," he drawled.

"Nonsense. You've had what you wanted. Let's forget this happened, and go on as we were."

Gerard rocked back on his heels. "Had what I wanted, eh? Don't be daft, Pel." He shoved her clenched thighs apart and thrust the cloth between them. "I have yet to do the things I want. You have not been bent over a piece of furniture and fucked from behind. I have not sucked your nipples or your—" He ran the cloth gently through the lips of her sex, and then followed it with a teasing glide of his tongue, pausing a brief moment to tease her clitoris from its hood. "You have not been flat on your back and ridden properly. In short, we are nowhere near finished."

"Gray." She surprised him by cupping his cheek with her hand. Her gaze was earnest and direct. And very hot. "We started this with a bargain. Let us end this with one."

His eyes narrowed in suspicion. "What kind of bargain?"

"A pleasurable one. If I give you one night, and promise to do whatever you wish, will you in turn promise to keep to our original agreement from the morning onward?"

His blasted cock raised its head in eager agreement, but Gerard was not so keen. "One night?" She was mad if she thought that would be enough for either of them. He was as hard at this moment as he had been before he'd come, she affected him that much.

He returned his attentions to his ministrations, spreading her lips and cleaning her gently. She was lovely, flushed and glistening, and blessed with a dazzling frame of dark mahogany curls.

Her fingers sifted through his hair, tugging it to draw his gaze back up to her face. Her fingertips glided over his features, following first the arch of his brows before caressing his cheeks, and then his lips. She seemed wearily resigned. "These lines around your eyes and mouth . . . they should age you, diminish your beauty. Instead, they do the opposite."

"It is not a bad thing to want me, Isabel." He dropped the cloth, and embraced her waist, his face buried between her breasts where the scent of her was so strong. She was naked in his arms, and yet a barrier was between them. No matter how tightly he held her, he could not get close enough.

Turning his head, he caught her nipple with his mouth, suckling, seeking intimacy. He licked the distended tip, stroked his tongue around it and relished the velvety softness. She moaned, her hands gripping his head, pulling him closer.

He was aching for her, physically hurting. He released her breast, and caught her up. Her legs wrapped around his waist, her arms around his neck, and he grunted his approval at her longed-for acquiescence. His pace quickened as he walked straight through to his bedroom, a chamber he had stood in only hours before, despondent that he had changed rooms to be closer to Pel and had instead pushed her away.

Now she would scent his sheets, warm his blood, and sate his hunger. As he set her down carefully on the bed, his throat tightened. Above her, the headboard displayed his crest, below her lay his red velvet counterpane. The thought of indulging in his wife's charms in such a proprietary setting aroused him beyond bearing.

"One night," she murmured against his throat.

Gerard shuddered, both from the feel of her breath across his skin, and from the realization that he could not take her as he truly desired. He would have to woo her with his body and show her how gentle he could be, because he had to change her mind and make her crave him.

And she was giving him only one night in which to do it.

Isabel sank into linen-covered pillows on Gray's bed and noted again how much he had changed. He had once preferred silk sheets, she knew. What the change signified, she didn't know, but she wanted to. She opened her mouth to ask, but he took it, his lips firm against hers, his tongue sweeping inside with a slow, deliberate glide. Moaning, she welcomed his weight over hers.

He was hard all over, every inch of his golden skin stretched taut over rippling muscle. In all of her life, she had never seen a masculine body as beautifully formed as her husband's. Considering that Pelham had been exquisite in his own right, it was not a compliment she bestowed lightly.

"Pel." Gray breathed into her mouth, a low seductive burr of sound. "I am going to lick you all over, kiss you everywhere, make you come all night."

"And I will do the same to you," she promised, her tongue swiping soothingly across his damaged lower lip. Having decided on the goal of exhausting their mutual lust, she was now prepared to give her all to the endeavor.

Pulling away slightly to look at her, Gray gave her the opportunity she needed to take the upper hand. She hooked her heel over the back of his calf, and rolled, rising above him. Then she laughed when he rolled again and reclaimed the advantage.

"Oh no, vixen," he chastised, staring down at her with laughing blue eyes. "I gave you the top previously."

"I did not hear you complaining at the time."

His mouth twitched with a withheld smile. "It was over so quickly I didn't have a chance to protest."

She arched a brow. "I think you were simply speechless with pleasure."

Gray laughed aloud, the sound teasing her as it vibrated from his chest to hers. Her nipples peaked tighter in response. The lowering of his lids told her he noticed.

"Whatever I wish," he reminded, as he moved his hand down to lift her leg and spread her wide. With a roll of his hips, the tip of his cock breached her, forced her to open, the size of him almost uncomfortable but highly tantalizing.

Immediately she melted, her cunt softening, growing slick, crowning the broad head of his cock with her cream. Her toes curled, and her chest grew tight. He smelled wonderful, the bergamot that scented his soap diminished by the primitive scent of his sweat and the recent bout of sex.

"Gray." His name was both a request for more and a plea for less. She didn't know how to fight the sudden feeling of connection. In the years since Pelham had passed on, sexual congress had been about gratification, satiation. This, on the other hand, was pure surrender.

His large hands slipped beneath her shoulders, his forearms holding his weight aloft enough to prevent crushing her. "You are handing Hargreaves his congé."

It was a statement, an order, and while she wished she could argue with him just for his arrogance, she knew he was right. To be so attracted to Gray was proof that her interest was not as engaged by John as it once had been.

Still the knowledge saddened her, and she turned her head to hide her stinging eyes.

Gray brushed his mouth across her cheekbone, and pressed a scant inch into her. She groaned and arched upward, eager to forget her hazardous decision to indulge.

"I can make you happy," he promised against her skin. "And you will never lack pleasure, I can assure you of that."

Perhaps he could make her happy, but she could not do the same for him, and once he strayed, contentment would rapidly deteriorate into misery.

She wrapped her legs around his hips and pulled herself upward from the mattress, slowly engulfing his cock. Her eyes slid closed, her focus shifting to her blossoming enchantment with Grayson's lovemaking. He was so long, so thick. No wonder his mistresses tolerated his indiscretions. He would be hard to replace.

"Do you prefer a slow fucking, Pel?" he asked in a strangled whisper, his arms trembling as he sank in a bit more. "Tell me what you like."

"Yes . . . Slow . . ." Her voice was slurred, her nails digging into his broad back. She liked it any way and every way, but was rapidly losing the ability to think coherently.

She sank downward as he took over, his buttocks clenching as he slowly worked his way into her. Despite his recent penetration, her cunt forced him to earn the right to enter again. His cock pushed in and pulled out in a steady rhythm, every downward plunge taking him a little bit deeper.

Sweat from him dripped onto her throat and chest. "God, you are tight," he groaned.

She flexed her inner muscles just to increase his torment.

"Push me too far and you will regret it," he warned darkly. "I don't want to come in you, but I won't stop. Not for any reason. You gave me one night, and I am damn well taking it."

Isabel shivered. *I won't stop.* He would take her whether she willed it or no. The thought aroused her, as evidenced by the sudden rush of cream that allowed him to sink home in one deep glide.

"Open wider." His lips touched her ear. "Take all of me."

She was already so full it was hard to breathe, but she shifted slightly and he slipped in to the root.

"Beautiful," he praised, nuzzling his damp cheek against hers. "Now we can go as slow as you like."

Beginning to move, Gray took her with breathtaking leisure, moving in deliberate undulations of his entire body—his chest flexing against hers, his thighs buffeting hers, his fingers kneading almost restlessly against the tops of her shoulders.

She fought the sounds that struggled to be freed until she was unable to bear it any longer, her head tilting back on a plaintive whimper.

"That's the way," he encouraged, his voice gravelly and strained. "Let me hear how much you like it." He swiveled his hips and thrust, stroking her deep inside. She was so wet it was audible and she cried out, raking his back. He arched into her touch, and ground into her. "My God, Isabel . . ."

She matched his tempo, throwing her hips upward as he came down, the tip of his cock striking some tender spot she hadn't known existed. She mewled and writhed, growing desperate at his steady pace. "More . . . Give me more . . ."

Gray rolled to his side, and anchored her thigh on his hip, the tight roping of his abdominal muscles rippling as he pumped harder, not faster, his pelvis slapping against hers. The position was intimate, their bodies pressed together, their faces just inches from each other. Their panting breaths mingled between them as they strained in unison toward their mutual goal. One bicep pillowed her head, one large hand cupped her buttock holding her in place to take his thrusts. His bright blue gaze stared at her, glittering with his lust, his jaw locked and teeth grinding together. He looked like he was in pain, his cock rigid and impossibly thick.

"Come," he grit out. "Come now!"

The harsh bite of command in his tone was a delicious threat, one that shoved her off the edge with brutal force. She cried out, nearly screamed, her orgasm so powerful her entire body shook with each clenching spasm.

His fingers dug into her, bruising her, his cock slamming deep. Only when she was finished did he pull out, shoving her leg off his hip so he could fuck through her closed thighs.

She held still, awed as he came, his cock jerking between her legs, each pulse met with a grunt, his open lips pressed to her forehead.

Even as Gray emptied himself onto the counterpane, she knew she was ruined. She wanted *this,* longed for this depth of feeling during sex.

She hated him for reminding her of what it could be like, of what she was missing, of what she had avoided for the last several years. He had given her an addicting taste of what he would soon take away.

Already she missed it, and ached for its loss.

It was the sounds of industrious servants in the bathing chamber that first raised Gerard's eyelids, but it was the scent of sex and exotic flowers that raised the rest of him. With a soft grumble at the intrusion, he took a quick inventory of his present circumstance.

His left arm was asleep from acting as a pillow for Pel's head. He lay sprawled on his back, his wife's buttocks against his hip, her back curved into his side. She wore a sheet, he was bare. He had no notion of what time it was, and it did not matter. He was still tired, and if the sound of Isabel's soft snoring was any indication, she was too.

He had been having his way with her for hours, his need slaked only slightly with each successive encounter. Even now his cock stuck straight up in the air, aroused by the feel and smell of her. Although he was exhausted, he knew there would be no sleep with an erection like he had. He rolled into Pel, casting off the sheet that covered her with his working arm and lifting her leg over his. Using gentle fingers, he reached between her legs, cupping her sex, feeling how swollen she was.

He licked the tip of his middle finger and then stroked her clitoris, circling it, rubbing it, teasing it. She whimpered and halfheartedly attempted to push his hand away.

"No more, damn you," she muttered, her voice husky

with sleep and disgruntlement. But when he reached deeper, he found her wet.

"Your cunt disagrees."

"Blasted thing is daft." She pushed his arm again, but he only cuddled closer. "I am exhausted, you horrid man. Allow me to sleep."

"I will, vixen," he promised, kissing the top of her shoulder. He circled his hips against her so that she felt how needy he was. "Let me take care of this, and we can sleep all day."

Isabel groaned into his numb arm. "I am too old for you, Gray. I cannot keep pace with your appetite."

"Nonsense." He reached between her legs and positioned his cock. "You don't have to do anything." He bit her shoulder gently as he forged his way into her with soft, shallow strokes. Half-asleep and intoxicated by the rapturous feel of her, he moved languidly, his fingers circling her clitoris, his face buried in the wild tangle of her hair. "Just lie there and come. As many times as you want."

"Oh God," she breathed, creaming in welcome. She moaned softly, her hand coming to rest on his flexing wrist as he pleasured her.

Too old for him. Even as he scoffed at the notion, the tiny part of his brain not presently lost to their lazy fucking wondered if it was as much of an issue for her, as it was for Society. It was not one for him, certainly. Did that have something to do with her reticence? Did she believe herself unable to satisfy him? Was that why she insisted he acquire a mistress? If so, his constant sexual demands were not helping his cause any. Perhaps he should—

Her cunt fluttered around him, and the thought was lost. He increased the pressure on her clitoris and growled as she fell into orgasm with a soft, startled cry. He would never have his fill of that feeling. Tight as a glove to begin with, when Isabel came, it was in hard, clenching spasms. Like a fist tightening rhythmically. He swelled in response, and her back arched into his chest.

"Christ, Gray. Do not get any bigger."

He bit a little deeper into her soft flesh.

He wanted to drive into her, fuck her senseless, roar out his pleasure. He wanted her nails in his back, her hair soaked with sweat, her nipples marked by his teeth. She drove him insane, and until that ravenous animal within him was freed and fed, he would never be fully sated.

They would quite simply have to fuck a great deal, he thought, his tortured grimace hidden in her tresses. It was a goal he suspected would not be an easy one to attain, given her present state of soreness and exhaustion. Plus her obstinate nature and the ridiculous thought that he was too young for her. And he had no clue as to what any of her other objections might be. There was the bloody bargain, of course. And Hargreaves . . .

As the obstacles between them stacked up, he groaned. It shouldn't be this damned difficult to seduce his own wife.

But as she came apart in his arms, her body shivering against his own, his name on her lips as she cried out, he knew, as he had known from the moment he first saw her, that Isabel was worth it.

Chapter 8

Isabel shut her boudoir door quietly behind her, and made her way to the staircase. Gray remained sprawled in the bathtub, his beautifully etched mouth curved in a triumphant, contented smile. He thought she was well and truly seduced, and perhaps she was. Certainly she moved differently, her body was relaxed and languid. Sated. *Demented.*

She wrinkled her nose. What a dreadful mire.

Now keeping him at bay would be difficult at best. He knew what he could do to her, how to touch her, how to speak to her to make her mindless with lust for him. He would be insufferable from here on out, no doubt. Merely removing herself from the bed had been a chore. The man was insatiable. If Gray had his way, she was certain they would never leave it.

Her sigh came out like a low, pained moan. The first few months of her marriage to Pelham had been similar. Even before they said their vows, he had snared her in a web of seduction. The rakishly handsome earl with the golden hair and wicked reputation had appeared to be everywhere, showing up at all the venues she did. Later, she realized those had not been random acts of fate, as her stupid heart had believed. At the time, however, it seemed they were destined for one another.

The smiles and winks he had given her created a feeling of

familiarity, a sense that they shared some secret. She had assumed it was love, silly girl that she was. Fresh from the schoolroom, Pelham's amorous attentions completely overwhelmed her, sweet gestures such as paying her abigail to deliver notes to her.

Those single lines written in a bold masculine scrawl had been devastating.

> *You look ravishing in blue.*
> *I miss you.*
> *I thought of you all day.*

After they wed he fucked her abigail, but at the time Isabel had taken the girl's adoration of the dashing peer as a sign that he was the right choice for a husband.

The week before her coming-out ball, he climbed the elm outside her bedroom balcony, and snuck boldly into her room. She was sure only pure love could goad him to take such a risk. Pelham had whispered to her in the darkness, his voice raw with lust as he stripped away her night rail, and loved her with his mouth and hands. *I hope I am caught. Then you will for certain be mine.*

Of course, I'm yours, she whispered back, awash in the glory of orgasm. *I love you.*

There are no words for what I feel for you, he returned.

A sennight of midnight liaisons and decadent pleasure had garnered her total supplication. The consummation on the seventh night had guaranteed she was his. She had entered her first Season completely off the market, and while her father would have preferred a peer of higher station, he did not gainsay her choice.

Only enough time for the reading of the banns was allowed before they married, and then they'd fled the city for a blissful honeymoon in the countryside. There she had been overjoyed to lie in bed with Pelham for days on end, rising only to bathe and eat, wallowing in carnal delights as Gray wished to do now. The similarities between the two men could not be ignored. Not when the thought of both men made her heart race and her palms damp.

"What the devil are you doing, Bella?"

Isabel blinked, quickly regaining her awareness of her surroundings. She stood at the top of the staircase, her hand on the rail, lost in thought. Her mind was sluggish from lack of sleep, and her body was sore and tired. Shaking her head, she stared down into the foyer and met the scowling countenance of her older brother, Rhys, Marquess of Trenton.

"Is it your intention to hang about up there all day? If so, I consider my obligation to you met, and I will be off to find more pleasant adventures."

"Obligation?" She descended to him.

He smiled. "If you have forgotten, do not look to me to remind you. It's not as if I wish to go."

Rhys' hair was a dark mahogany, an absolutely glorious color that set off his tan skin and hazel eyes. The ladies went a bit batty around him, but occupied with his own pleasures, he scarcely paid them any mind. Unless he found them sexually attractive. The simple fact was, he was very much like their mother when it came to the opposite sex. A woman to him was a physical convenience, and when she was no longer convenient, she was easily discarded.

Isabel knew that neither her mother nor brother had any malicious intent. They simply could not see why any of their lovers would fall in love with an individual who did not return the sentiment.

"Lady Marley's breakfast," she said, as she remembered. "What is the time?"

"Nearly two." His jaded gaze raked her from head to toe. "And you are just rolling out of bed." His mouth curved knowingly. "Apparently, the rumors of your reconciliation with Grayson are true."

"Do you believe everything you hear?" Reaching the marble foyer, she tilted her head back to look up at her brother.

"I believe everything I see. Reddened eyes, bruised mouth, clothing you chose without thinking clearly."

Isabel glanced down at her somewhat simple muslin day gown. It was not what she would have selected had she remembered her schedule for the day. Of course, thinking back on it now, Mary had questioned the garment, but Isabel had been so anxious to leave the room before Gray accosted her again that she had waved off the soft query.

"I will not discuss my marriage with you, Rhys."

"Thank God for that," he said with a shudder. "Deuced annoying when women start discussing their feelings."

Rolling her eyes, she requested her pelisse from the nearby servant. "I do not have feelings for Grayson."

"Quite sensible."

"We are just friends."

"Obviously."

As she secured her hat with a hat pin, she shot him a side-long glance. "What did I promise you again, in return for your escort? Whatever it is, it is worth more than your company."

Rhys laughed, and Isabel silently acknowledged his appeal. There was something about men who could not be tamed. Thankfully she had grown out of the fascination for such hopeless sport long ago.

"You are introducing me to the lovely Lady Eddly."

"Ah, yes. Under normal circumstances I wouldn't agree to such a blatantly obvious pairing, but in this case I think you two are perfect for one another."

"I definitely agree."

"I am having a dinner party . . . eventually. You and Lady Eddly are both invited as of this moment." Having Rhys there would help to calm her nerves. And she would need all the assistance in that regard as she could muster. The mere thought of surviving a dinner with Gray and a bevy of his former paramours made her stomach roil.

Sighing at her predicament, Isabel shook her head. "Horribly uncouth of you to use your sister in this manner."

"Ha," Rhys scoffed, collecting her pelisse from the returning maid and holding it out for her. "Dreadful of you to drag me along to a breakfast, and at the Marley residence no less. Lady Marley always smells of camphor."

"It is not as if I wish to go either, so cease your whining."

"You wound me, Bella. Men do not whine." With his hand on her shoulder, he spun her to face him. "Why are we attending if you doubt your enjoyment of the event?"

"You know why."

He snorted gently. "I wish you would disregard what others thought about you. I personally find you the least annoying woman I know. Straightforward, pleasant to look upon, and capable of witty discourse."

"I suppose your opinion is the only one that matters."

"Is it not?"

"I wish I could ignore the gossip," she grumbled, "but the Dowager Lady Grayson feels the need to bring it to my attention as often as possible. Those horrid notes she sends infuriate me. I wish she would just spit her venom out, rather than attempt to hide it beneath a thin layer of civility." Isabel stared into her brother's resigned features. "I have no notion how Grayson grew up sane with that harridan as a mother."

"You do realize that women who look as you do often have trouble with other females? Catty creatures that you are. You cannot bear it when one woman attracts excessive masculine attention. Not that you have ever experienced that particular kind of jealousy," he finished dryly. "You are always the woman attracting the regard."

She had experienced other kinds of jealousy though, such as the kind a wife experiences when the bed her husband ruts in is not her own.

"Which is why I associate with men more so than women, though that has its pitfalls, too." Isabel was aware that other women found her appearance off-putting, but there was nothing she could do about that. "Let's be off then."

Both of Rhys' brows rose into his hairline. "I must pay my respects to Grayson. I cannot simply abscond with his wife. The last time I did that, he gave me a brutal pummeling in the pugilist rings at Remington's. The man is much younger than I, take pity on me."

"Write him a note," she said curtly, shivering at the image of her husband with his hair still damp. Just thinking of it reminded her of the night before and the way he had taken her.

"Don't have feelings for Grayson, indeed." Rhys' hazel gaze was blatantly skeptical.

"Wait until you marry, Rhys. The need to escape occasionally will become all too clear." With that in mind, she gestured impatiently toward the door.

"I've no doubt about that." He offered his arm, and retrieved his hat from the waiting butler.

"You are not getting any younger, you know."

"I am aware of my advancing years. Therefore, I have made a list of suitable spousal prospects."

"Yes, Mother told me of your 'list,'" she said dryly.

"A man must be sensible about choosing a bride."

Isabel nodded with mock severity. "Of course, feelings should never be considered."

"Did we not already agree to avoid a discussion of feelings?"

Smothering a laugh, she asked, "And who is at the top of your list, may I ask?"

"Lady Susannah Campion."

"The Duke of Raleigh's second daughter?" Isabel blinked.

Lady Susannah was indeed a sensible choice. Her breeding was exceptional, her deportment flawless, and her suitability for the rank of duchess could not be denied. But the delicate blonde girl had no fire, no passion. "She would bore you to tears."

"Come now," he demurred. "She cannot be as bad as that."

Her eyes widened. "You have yet to meet the girl you are considering marrying?"

"I've seen her! I would not marry a chit sight unseen." He cleared his throat. "I simply have not had the pleasure of speaking with her yet."

Shaking her head, Isabel felt again like she did not quite fit in with her *sensible* family. Yes, falling out of love was a dreadful experience, but falling into it wasn't so bad. She was certainly a far wiser and better-rounded individual than she had been before meeting Pelham. "Thank heaven you are coming with me today, for Lady Susannah will certainly be at the breakfast. Be certain you speak with her."

"Of course." As they left the house and approached his waiting phaeton, Rhys adjusted his long-legged stride to hers. "This might be just the thing to make dealing with an angry Grayson worthwhile."

"He will not be angry."

"Not with you perhaps."

Her throat tightened. "Not with anyone."

"The man has always been a trifle touchy where you are concerned," Rhys drawled.

"He has not!"

"Has, too. And if he has truly decided to exert his husbandly rights, I pity the man who intrudes. Step lightly, Bella."

Releasing a deep breath, Isabel kept her thoughts to herself, but the butterflies in her stomach took flight again.

Gerard gazed at his reflection, and heaved a frustrated breath. "When is the tailor scheduled to arrive?"

"Tomorrow, my lord," Edward replied with obvious relief.

Turning to face his longtime valet, Gerard asked, "Are my garments truly that dreadful?"

The servant cleared his throat. "I did not say that, my

lord. However, removing dirt clods and repairing torn knees are not exactly a full utilization of my many talents."

"I know." He sighed dramatically. "I did consider dismissing you on several occasions."

"My lord!"

"But since tormenting you was often my only entertainment, I resisted the urge."

The valet's snort made Gerard laugh. Leaving the room, he mentally arranged his schedule for the day. His plans started with a discussion with Pel about redecorating his study and ended with her once again sharing his bed. He was content with that schedule until his foot met the marble floor of the foyer.

"My lord."

He faced the bowing footman. "Yes?"

"The Dowager Marchioness has arrived."

His hackles rose. He had managed a blessed four years without seeing her, but he would have gone a lifetime if that had been possible. "Where is she?"

"In the parlor, my lord."

"And Lady Grayson?"

"Her Ladyship departed with Lord Trenton a half hour past."

Normally, Gerard would take exception with Trenton, as he did with anyone who deprived him of his wife's company without telling him first, but today he was relieved to spare Isabel his mother's visit. There could be a hundred excuses for why his mother had come, but the truth was simply that she wished to berate him. She took such pleasure in it, and now she had four years' worth of bile to vent. It would be unpleasant, no doubt, and he steeled himself inwardly for the trial ahead.

He also took a moment to acknowledge what he'd avoided seeing before, that he had always been slightly jealous of those who stole Pel's attentions. The feeling of possessiveness was only exacerbated by his deepened interest in her.

But he did not have time to contemplate what that meant at the moment, so Gerard nodded to the servant, took a deep breath and headed in the direction of the parlor. He paused a moment in the open doorway, studying the silver strands that were now weaved liberally through the once dark tresses. Unlike Pel's mother, whose love for living preserved her beauty well, the dowager marchioness simply looked tired and worn.

Sensing his presence, she turned to face him. Her pale blue gaze raked him from head to toe. Once, that look would have withered him. Now, he knew his own value. "Grayson," she greeted, her voice tight and clipped.

He bowed, noting that she still wore widow's weeds even after all these years.

"Your clothes are a disgrace."

"It is lovely to see you, too, Mother."

"Do not mock me." She sighed loudly, and sank onto the sofa. "Why must you vex me so?"

"I vex you just by breathing, and I'm afraid I am not willing to go to the extent of stopping to please you. The best I can do is to give you a wide berth."

"Sit, Grayson. It is rude of you to stand and force me to strain my neck looking up at you."

Gerard sank into a nearby wooden-armed chair. Sitting directly across from her, he was able to study her in depth. Her back was ramrod straight, painfully so, her hands clenched in her lap until the knuckles were white. He knew he took after her in coloring—his father's portrait was of a man with brown hair and eyes—but her bone-deep rigidity was far removed from his own ability to bend when necessary.

"What ails you?" he asked, only superficially concerned. Everything ailed his mother. She was simply a miserable woman.

Her chin lifted. "Your brother Spencer."

That caught his attention. "Tell me."

"Completely lacking in any sort of male authority, he has

decided to adopt your way of living." Her thin lips pursed tighter.

"In what way?"

"In every way—whoring, drinking to excess, complete irresponsibility. He sleeps all day and is out all night. He has made little effort to support himself since leaving school."

Scrubbing his hand across his face, Gerard struggled to reconcile the image she presented with the fresh-faced brother he had known four years ago. It was his fault, he knew. Leaving any child in the care of their mother was bound to lead to a preoccupation with the pursuit of oblivion.

"You must speak with him, Grayson."

"Talking will accomplish nothing. Send him to me."

"I beg your pardon?"

"Gather up his possessions, and send him to me. It will take some time to straighten him out."

"I will not!" His mother's spine stiffened further. How that was possible, he could not say, but it did. "I will not have Spencer under the same roof as that harlot you married."

"Watch your tongue," he warned with ominous softness, his fingers curling around the carved arms of his chair.

"You have made your point and embarrassed me utterly. End this farce now. Divorce that woman for adultery, and do your duty."

"*That woman,*" he bit out, "is the Marchioness of Grayson. And you know as well as I that a successful petition for divorce would include evidence of marital harmony prior to the adultery. It could also be said that my own inconstancy drove her to hers."

His mother flinched. "To wed a mistress. For heaven's sake, could you not have wounded me alone, and not the title as well? Your father would be so ashamed."

Gerard hid the way that statement cut him with an impassive face. "Regardless of my reasons for choosing Lady Grayson, it is a choice I am quite content with. I hope you can learn to live with it, but I am not overly concerned if you do not."

"She has never once honored her vows to you," the dowager said bitterly. "You are a cuckold."

His breath was harshly drawn, his pride stung. "Am I not culpable for that? I have not been a husband to her in anything but a fiduciary capacity."

"Thank God for that. Can you imagine what kind of mother that woman would be?"

"No worse than you."

"Touché."

Her quiet pride made him feel guilty. "Come now, Mother." He sighed. "We are so close to ending this lovely visit without bloodshed."

But as always, she could not quit while they were ahead.

"Your father has been dead for decades, and yet I have been true to his memory."

"Is that what he would have wanted?" he asked, genuinely curious.

"I am certain he would not have wanted the mother of his sons to fornicate indiscriminately."

"No, but a genuine companion, a man who could offer the comforts women long for—"

"I knew what I promised when I said my vows—to do honor to his name and title, to give him and raise fine sons who would make him proud."

"And yet we never do," Gerard said dryly. "As you so often point out to us, we are constantly shaming him."

Her brows drew together in a glower. "It was my responsibility to be both a mother and father to you all, to teach you how to be like him. I realize you think I have failed, but I did the best I could."

Gerard held his retort, his mind filling with memories of whippings with leather straps and hurtful words. Suddenly eager to be alone, he said, "I am more than willing to take

Spencer in hand, but I will do so here, in my house. I have my own affairs to attend to."

"'Affairs' is an apt description," she muttered.

He put his hand to his heart, deflecting her sarcasm with his own. "You disparage me unjustly. I am a married man."

Her gaze narrowed as she assessed him. "You have changed, Grayson. Whether that is a good thing or not remains to be seen."

With a wry smile, he rose. "I have a few arrangements to make in anticipation of Spencer's arrival, so if we are done . . . ?"

"Yes, of course." His mother fluffed out her skirts as she stood. "I have my doubts about this, but I will present your solution to Spencer and if he agrees, so will I." Her voice hardened. "Keep that woman away from him."

His brow arched. "My wife does not have the pox, you know."

"That is debatable," she snapped, departing the room in a flounce of dark skirts and chilly hauteur.

Gerard was left with both relief and a sudden longing for the comfort of his wife.

"I warned you."

Rhys looked down at the top of his sister's head. Standing beneath a tree on the Marley rear lawn, they were alone and apart from the other milling guests. "She is perfect."

"Too perfect, if you ask me."

"Which I did not," he said dryly, but silently he agreed with Isabel's assessment. Lady Susannah was poised and collected. She was a beauty, and yet when he had spoken to her, she reminded him of a moving statue. There was very little life in her.

"Rhys." Isabel turned to face him, her dark red brows drawn together beneath her straw hat. "Can you see yourself being a friend to her?"

"A friend?"

"Yes, a friend. You will have to live with your future wife, sleep with her on occasion, discuss issues relating to your children and household. All of these things are much easier to accomplish when you are friends with your spouse."

"Is that what you have with Grayson?"

"Well . . ." The line between her brows deepened. "In the past, we were close acquaintances."

"Acquaintances?" She was blushing, something he had rarely seen her do.

"Yes." Her gaze drifted, and she suddenly seemed very far away. "Actually," she said softly. "He was a very dear friend."

"And now?" Not for the first time, Rhys found himself wondering what the arrangement was between his sister and her second husband. They had always seemed happy enough before, laughing and sharing private looks that said they knew each other well. Whatever their reasons for seeking sex outside of their marriage, it was not because of lack of charity with each other. "The rumors suggest that you may soon have a marriage that is more . . . traditional."

"I do not want a traditional marriage," she grumbled, her arms crossing beneath her bosom, her attention coming back to the present.

He held up his hands in self-defense. "No need to snap at me."

"I did not snap."

"You did so. For a woman who just rolled out of bed, you are remarkably testy."

Isabel growled. He raised his brows.

Her glare lasted a moment longer and then it faded into a sheepish pout. "I am sorry."

"Is Grayson's return so trying?" he asked softly. "You are not yourself."

"I know it." She released a frustrated sounding breath. "And I have not eaten since supper."

"That explains a great deal. You were always grumpy when hungry." He held out his arm. "Shall we brave the throng of dour biddies, and fetch you a plate?"

Isabel covered her face with a gloved hand and laughed.

Moments later she stood opposite him at the long food tables, loading her small plate unfashionably high. He shook his head and looked away, hiding his indulgent smile. Moving a short distance from the others, Rhys pulled out his pocket watch and wondered how much longer he would have to bear this odious affair.

It was only three o'clock. He closed the golden door with a click and groaned.

"It is the height of bad taste to look as if you cannot wait to depart."

"I beg your pardon?" He spun about, searching for the owner of the lyrical feminine voice. "Where are you?"

There was no reply.

But the hair at his nape was suddenly on end. "I will find you," he promised, studying the low hedges that lined his left and rear sides.

"To find implies that something is hidden or lost, and I am neither."

Gads, that voice was sweet as an angel's and sultry as a siren's. Without care for his tan-colored breeches, Rhys plunged through the hip-high shrubs, rounded a large elm, and found a small sitting area on the other side. There, on a half-circle-shaped marble bench sat a petite brunette with a book.

"There was a pathway a little further down," she said without looking up from her reading.

His gaze raked her trim form, noting the worn toes of her slippers, the slightly faded hem of her flowered gown, and the too-tight bodice. He bowed and said, "Lord Trenton, Miss . . . ?"

"Yes, I know who you are." Snapping the book closed, she lifted her head and studied him with the same thorough perusal he had given her.

Rhys stared. He could not do otherwise. She was no great beauty. In fact, her delicate features were unremarkable. Her nose was pert and covered with freckles, her mouth just as any other female mouth. She was not young or old. Nearing thirty would be his guess. Her eyes, however, were as pleasing as her voice. They were large and round and a startling blue with yellow flecks. They were also filled with keen intelligence, and even more intriguing, a mischievous sparkle.

It took him a moment to realize she said nothing.

"You are staring," he pointed out.

"So are you," she retorted with a straightforwardness that reminded him of Bella. "I have an excuse. You do not."

His brows raised. "Share your excuse with me. Perhaps I can make use of it as well."

She smiled, and he suddenly found himself uncomfortably hot. "I doubt that. You see, you are quite the handsomest man I have ever seen. I confess it took my brain a moment to reclassify my previous notions of manly beauty, in order to fully process yours."

He returned her smile in full measure.

"Stop that," she said with a chastising wag of an ink-stained finger. "Go away."

"Why?"

"Because you are affecting my ability to think properly."

"Don't think." He moved toward her, wondering what she smelled like and why her clothes were worn and her fingertips stained. Why was she alone, reading, in the midst of a gathering? The sudden flood of questions and the overpowering need to know the answers puzzled him.

As she shook her head, glossy dark curls drifted across her pink cheeks. "You are every bit the rake they say you are. If I did nothing to sway you, what would you do?"

The impertinent chit was flirting with him, but he suspected it was unintentional. She was truly curious, and that unabashed quest for knowledge piqued his jaded interests. "I am not certain. Shall we find out together?"

"Rhys! Damn you," Isabel muttered from a short distance away. "You will not collect from me if you have run off."

He stopped mid-step and cursed under his breath.

"Saved by Lady Grayson," the girl said with a wink.

"Who are you?"

"No one important."

"Is that not for me to decide?" he asked, entirely too reluctant to leave her.

"No, Lord Trenton. That was decided long ago." She stood, and collected her book. "Have a good day." And before he could think of a reason for her to stay, she was gone.

Chapter 9

Isabel paused in the foyer of her home at the sound of masculine voices. One was rushed and urgent. The other, her husband's, was low and unwavering. The door to Gray's study was closed or she would have peeked, out of curiosity. Instead, she looked at the butler who was collecting her hat and gloves. "Who is with Lord Grayson?"

"Lord Spencer Faulkner, my lady." The servant paused a moment, then added, "He arrived with luggage."

She blinked, but in no other way did she betray her surprise. With a nod of dismissal, Isabel went to the kitchen to make certain the cook was aware of the extra mouth to feed. Then she went upstairs to take a short nap. She was exhausted, both from a night spent with very little sleep and an afternoon of chatting inanities with women who spoke unkind things about her behind her back. Rhys was supposed to have been both support and a distraction, but he himself had seemed distracted, his gaze wandering restlessly over the guests as if he were looking for something. Like a way to escape, she imagined.

With the help of her abigail, Isabel stripped down to her stockings and chemise, then took down her hair. Within moments after lying on her bed, she was asleep and dreaming of Gray.

Isabel, he breathed in a voice filled with sin. His mouth, hot and wet, moved across her exposed shoulder. His stroking hand was equally hot, the callused palm causing a delicious friction even through the silk that covered her legs.

Her heart warned her to refuse him, and her arm lifted to push his touch away.

I need you, he said roughly.

Her blood thrummed with eagerness and she whimpered, every nerve ending alive and waiting for the pleasure he could bring. She could smell him and feel his warmth. His ardor radiated outward, igniting hers. It was a dream, and she did not want to wake up. Nothing she did here would affect her.

Her hand dropped away.

Good girl, he praised, his lips to her ear. He lifted her thigh and set it over his. "I missed you today."

She came to consciousness with a start.

And found a very hard bodied, very aroused Grayson at her back.

"No!" Struggling, Isabel squirmed out of his embrace and sat up. She glared at him. "What are you doing in my bed?"

He rolled to his back and tucked his hands under his head, completely unabashed about his obvious erection. Dressed in an open-collared shirt and trousers, his blue eyes sparkling with both devilry and lust, he was unbearably handsome. "Making love to my wife."

"Well, cease." She crossed her arms under her bosom and his eyes dropped to her breasts. Her blasted nipples replied with enthusiasm. "We had a bargain."

"Which I never agreed to."

Her mouth fell open.

"Bring that mouth over here," he murmured, his eyelids lowering.

"You are dreadful."

"That is not what you said last night. Or this morning. I believe you said, 'Oh God, Gray, that is *so* good.'" His lips twitched.

Isabel threw a pillow at him.

Gray laughed and shoved it under his head. "How was your afternoon?"

She sighed and shrugged, her body achingly aware of the man who sat so close to her. "Lady Marley had a breakfast."

"Was it pleasant? I confess, I'm surprised you managed to lure Trenton to such an event."

"He wants a favor."

"Ah, extortion." He smiled. "I love it."

"You would, you wicked man." Catching up one of the pillows, she reclined opposite him. "Perhaps you could fetch my robe?"

"Damnation, no," he said, shaking his head.

"I have no wish to incite your already considerable appetite for sexual congress," she said dryly.

He caught up her hand and kissed her fingertips. "The mere thought of you incites me. At least this way, I also have a charming view."

"Was your day better than mine?" she asked, making every effort to ignore how his touch burned her.

"My brother has come for an extended visit."

"I heard." Gooseflesh spread across her skin as he stroked her palm. "Is something wrong?"

"Wrong? Not precisely. Apparently, he is running amok."

"Hmm . . . Well, he is the age for it." But studying Gray, she could see he was disturbed. "You look so grave. Is he in trouble?"

"No." Gray fell onto his back again and stared up at the ornate ceiling. "He has not yet run up any great debt or angered someone's husband, but he is certainly on a steady course in that direction. I should have been here to guide him, but once again my own needs came before anyone else's."

"You cannot blame yourself," she protested. "Any wildness on his part is natural for boys his age."

Her husband stilled, his head turning to reveal narrowed eyes. "Boys his age?"

"Yes." She recoiled slightly, suddenly wary.

"He is the same age as I was when we wed. Did you think I was a boy then?" He rolled on top of her, pinning her to the bed. "Do you think I am a boy now?"

Her heart raced. "Gray, really—"

"Yes, really," he purred, his jaw set ominously as he thrust his hand under her buttocks and tilted her pelvis to cradle his. He rolled his hips, rubbing his cock against the perfect spot between her legs. "I want to know. Do you think me less than a man because I am younger than you?"

She swallowed hard, her body tense and straining beneath his. "No," she breathed. Her subsequent inhale filled her lungs with his luscious scent. Grayson was virile, temperamental, and most definitely a man.

He stared down at her for a long moment, his cock hardening and swelling between her thighs. Lowering his head, he took her mouth, his tongue licking between her parted lips. "I have wanted to do this all day."

"You did do this all day." Her hands fisted in the counterpane to prevent herself from touching him.

Gray rested his forehead against hers and laughed. "I hope you have no objection to Spencer's visit."

"Of course not," she assured him, managing a smile through her near painful attraction. What the devil was she to do with him? With herself? She could only hope that Lord Spencer would distract him from his single-minded seduction. How long could she truly expect to resist?

"Thank you." He brushed his mouth across hers, then twisted to drape her body over his.

She frowned, puzzled. "No need to thank me. This is your home."

"This is *our* home, Pel." He settled into the pillows. When she tried to slide off him, he caught her waist. "Stay here."

When she opened her mouth to argue, he grimaced, which arrested her. "What is it?" Before she could think better of it, her hand was cupping his cheek. He leaned into her touch and sighed.

"Spencer told me that I am his hero."

Her brows rose. "What a lovely thing to say."

"But it's not. Not at all. You see, to him, I am the brother he knew before. That is the man whom he and his friends emulate. They are drinking in vast quantities, associating with questionable people, and showing no concern whatsoever for the effect of their behavior on others. He said he has yet to manage two mistresses, but he is giving it his best effort."

Isabel winced, her stomach clenching at the reminder of how wild her husband was. His edges might have smoothed some, but he was no less dangerous. So far he had been cocooned with her while awaiting his garments, but soon he would be out and about. Once that happened, everything would change.

He nipped the fleshy part of her palm with his teeth, and held her gaze with his. "I told him he was better off finding a wife such as you. You are more expensive than two mistresses, but worth every shilling."

"Grayson!"

"It's true." His smile was wicked.

"There is no hope for you, my lord." But she had to bite her lip to keep a straight face.

His hands left her waist and followed the curve of her spine. "I missed you, dear Pel, these last four years." He gripped her shoulders, and pulled her gently but firmly to his chest. "I must begin anew. You are all I have at the moment, and I am grateful that you are more than enough."

Her heart welled with tenderness for him. "Whatever you need—" He chuckled, and her eyes widened in horror. "As far as your brother is concerned, you understand. Not for . . ." She wrinkled her nose as he laughed. "Odious man."

"Not for sex. I collect what you meant." His mouth nuzzled into her hair, and his chest expanded beneath her. "Now, you must understand what *I* mean." Cupping her buttocks, he rocked her against his rigid cock. His lips to her ear, he whispered, "I ache for you—for your body, your scent, the sounds you make when we're fucking. If you think I will deny myself those pleasures, you are mad. A raving lunatic."

"Stop that." Her voice was so thready it had no substance. He was like warm marble beneath her—hard, ridged, solid. She could almost believe he would support her, provide her an anchor, but she knew men of his ilk too well. She did not hold it against him, she simply accepted it.

"I will make a bargain with you, dear wife."

Lifting her head, she caught her breath at the heat that burned in his eyes and flushed his cheeks. "You do not honor your bargains, Grayson."

"I shall honor this one. The day you stop wanting me is the day I will no longer want you."

She stared at him, taking in the wicked arch of his brow, before sighing dramatically. "Can you grow a wart?"

Gray blinked. "Beg your pardon?"

"Or overeat? Perhaps cease to bathe?"

He laughed. "As if I would do anything to make myself less attractive to you." The fingers that combed through her hair were gentle, the smile he gave her tender. "I find you irresistible as well."

"You never paid me any mind before."

"That is not true, and you know it. I am no more immune to your charms than any other man." His jaw firmed. "Which is why Spencer will accompany you when you go out tonight."

"Your brother has no interest in the tame social affairs I attend," she said with a laugh.

"He does now."

Isabel took a moment to absorb the sudden quiet intensity of her husband's tone, before sliding off of him and leaving the bed. The fact that he let her go without argument made her wary. "Must I be home at a certain time as well?" she asked tightly.

"Three." He sat up further on the pillows and crossed his arms. The unspoken challenge was evident in his tone and posture.

She picked up the gauntlet. "And if I fail to return by that time?"

"Why, I will come after you, vixen," he replied with ominous softness. "I've no wish to lose you, now that I have found you."

"You cannot do this, Gray." She began to pace.

"I can, and will, Pel."

"I am not chattel."

"You do belong to me."

"Does that possession apply to you in like fashion?"

He frowned. "What are you asking?"

She paused next to the bed and set her hands on her hips. "Will you always return at three when I am not with you?"

His frown deepened.

"When you do not return in a timely manner, will I have the right to hunt you down? Shall I barge into whatever den of iniquity you happen to be gracing and rip you from the arms of your lover?"

Gray rose from the bed with slow, predatory grace. "Was that your intent? A lover?"

"We are not talking about me."

"Yes. We are." Rounding the bed, he came toward her on bare feet. Somehow she found the sight arousing, which only goaded her temper. The man was everything she did not want, and yet she wanted him more than anything.

"I am not a sex-obsessed female, Grayson, which is what your question implies."

"You can be as sex-obsessed as you like. *With me.*"

"I cannot keep up with you," she scoffed, backing away. "Eventually, you will fill the lack elsewhere."

"Why worry about '*eventually*' now?" His gaze penetrated

as he stalked her. "Forget the past and the future. If there is one thing I learned over the last four years, it is that *this* moment is the one that matters."

"How is that any different than how you lived before?" Sidestepping quickly, Isabel nearly ran to the door that led to her boudoir. She gasped as Gray caught her about the waist. The feel of him behind her—hard, aroused—flooded her with memories.

"Before," he said harshly in her ear, "everything in my life could wait until another day. Visiting my estates, meeting with my stewards, seeing Lady Sinclair. Sometimes that other day never comes, Pel. Sometimes today is all there is."

"See how different we are? I will always think of the future and how my actions today will come back to haunt me."

With one arm banded around her waist, he used his free hand to knead her breast. Against her will, she moaned.

"*I* will haunt you." Gray surrounded her, dominated her, teased her with his seductive touch. "I am not fool enough to cage you in, Isabel, not when we are already leg-shackled together." With a curse, he released her. "I will remind you of that as often as is necessary."

She spun to face him, her skin missing the touch of his. "I will not be guarded like a prisoner."

"I've no wish to lessen your freedom."

"Then why?"

"Soon others will know you have dismissed Hargreaves. They will sniff after you, and for the moment, I am unable to do aught about it."

"Staking your claim?" she asked coldly.

"Protecting you." Linking both arms behind his neck, he stretched and suddenly looked weary. "I returned for the express purpose of being a husband to you, I have said that from the first."

"Please. We have run this into the ground."

"Indulge me, vixen," he said softly. "One day at a time, that is all I ask. Surely you can spare that much?"

"I have already—"

"How else can we live together? Answer me that." His voice roughened as his arms fell to his sides. "Each craving the other . . . hungry . . . I am famished for you. Starving."

"I know," she whispered, feeling the great distance between them, even though they stood so close. Shivering with lust, her nipples hardened. She grew moist for him despite her soreness. "And I cannot sate you."

"I did not sate you either. We spent mere hours together. Not nearly enough time." Gray moved toward the door to make his egress.

"We have not finished discussing your three o'clock rule, Grayson."

He stilled, but did not face her. In the candlelight, his hair gleamed with the vitality that defined him. "You stand there clad only in chemise and stockings, your body creamy and begging for a fucking. If I stay here a moment longer, that is what you will get, Pel."

She hesitated, her arm lifting toward his tense back, a momentary sign of weakness before she could control it.

How else can we live together?

They couldn't. Not for much longer.

Her hand dropped. "I shall be home by three."

Gray nodded and left without looking back.

Gerard looked across his desk at Spencer and released a weary breath. There was too much turmoil in his life at the moment. The only time he felt remotely at peace with his return to London was when he was talking with Pel.

Not arguing. Talking.

He wished to God he understood her. Why was she so focused on the unraveling of a relationship that had yet to truly begin? To him that made as much sense as wearing a fur-lined coat in warm weather just because it would one day rain.

"This is not what I anticipated when I agreed to come

here," Spencer grumbled, shaking his head. His hair was over-long, and a thick lock fell over his forehead in a way Gerard knew would urge women to touch it. He knew because it was a style he once sported for that very reason. "I thought you and I would be going about town together."

"And we shall, once I am suitably attired. In the mean-time, I envy you an evening spent in Lady Grayson's company. You will enjoy yourself, I can assure you."

"Yes, but I was hoping to spend my evening with a woman I can fuck."

"You will escort my wife home no later than three, and after that you are free to do as you please." Gerard almost advised him to enjoy himself, since it was the last such late night Spencer would have in a while. But he held his tongue.

"Mother hates her, you know," Spencer said, pausing briefly in front of the desk. "Truly detests her."

"And you?"

Spencer's eyes widened. "Do you truly wish to hear my opinion?"

"Certainly." Gerard leaned back in his very uncomfortable chair and reminded himself to toss it out when the study was overhauled. "I'm curious to learn how you feel about my wife. You will be sharing a residence with her. Your thoughts, therefore, concern me."

Spencer shrugged. "I cannot decide if I envy you or pity you. I've no notion how a peeress came to have a body like that. Pel's beauty is not genteel in any fashion. That hair. Her skin. Her breasts. And for God's sake, where in hell did she get those lips? Yes, I would give up a fortune for a woman like that in my bed. But to take one to wife?" He shook his head. "And yet both you and Pelham sought your pleasures outside the marriage bed. Can you tell me why?"

"Idiocy."

"Ha!" Spencer laughed and strolled to the array of de-canters. After pouring himself a drink, he turned and rested his hip against the mahogany table. His body was lean with youth, and Gerard studied him, trying to see how Pel must have seen him when they'd wed. Perhaps the contrast between himself and Spencer would facilitate his cause with his wife. Surely she could not fail to note how different he was now.

"And I've no wish to provoke you, Gray, but I prefer women who prefer me."

"Perhaps that would have been possible, had I been here to see to her."

"True." Tossing back his drink, Spencer set his glass down and crossed his arms. "Will you be bringing her into line now?"

"She was never out of line."

"If you say so," Spencer said skeptically.

"I do. Now, I expect you to stay with Lady Grayson for the duration of your evening. Stay out of the card rooms and rein in your libidinous inclinations until she is home safely."

"What, exactly, do you expect to happen to her?"

"Nothing, because you will be there."

Gerard rose as Pel's lush form filled the doorway. She wore pale pink, a color that should have made her look sweetly innocent; instead it emphasized her worldliness and vibrant sensuality. Her full breasts were beautifully showcased in the loving embrace of her high-waisted gown. The overall effect, to him, was of a sugar-coated treat. One he wished to nibble and consume until he was gorged.

He blew out his breath; his response to the mere sight of her was both primitive and instinctual. He wished to toss her over his shoulder, run up the stairs, and fuck like rabbits. The image was so absurd, he could not help but chuckle through a tortured groan.

"Come now," she murmured with a slight smile. "I cannot look as bad as all that."

"Good God," Spencer cried out, moving forward to capture her hand and lift it to his lips. "I shall need a small sword to hold them off. But never fear, my dearest sister-in-law, I shall serve you until the very end."

Isabel's soft, husky laughter drifted through the study and weakened Gerard's already shaky resolution to allow her to go. He was not a jealous man by nature, but Isabel resisted the connection he sought and his tenuous position in her life caused him a rare level of anxiety.

"How gallant of you, Lord Spencer," she rejoined with a blinding smile. "It has been some time since I've enjoyed the company of a brazen rake."

The warm appreciation in his brother's eyes made Gerard grit his teeth. "I take it as my personal duty to fill that lack."

"And you shall do so admirably, I have no doubt."

His throat tight, Gerard cleared it, drawing their attention to him. Somehow he managed a smile that sparked a hot flicker in Pel's eyes. Words were caught and held on his tongue, squelched before they could be freed. He was desperate to say things that would make her stay—anything and every-thing, so he would not have to spend the evening alone. The night before had been hell while she was gone. The air in their rooms was scented of her skin, making it more obvious how cold and lonely the house was without her vibrant pres-ence.

He sighed in resignation and held out his hand, every mus-cle hardening when her gloved fingertips pressed lightly into his palm. He escorted her to the door, draped her in her cloak, and returned to his study window to watch his car-riage carry her away.

She belonged to him, as surely as his entailed estates. Nothing and no one could take her away. But he had no wish to keep her by force. He wished to earn her regard, just as he had earned the respect of his tenants. Pride in ownership worked both ways, and until he'd worked side by side with his tenants on his many holdings—until he'd worn their clothes, attended their celebrations, and eaten at their tables—they'd had none for him, an errant lord who paid them no mind and felt no loyalty.

His methods had been extreme by any measure, and every time he moved his attentions to a new estate, he had to begin the process of building trust and respect anew. But it had been healing for him. A chance for him to find a home, a place to belong, things he'd never had before.

Now he knew it had been training for this. This was his true home. And if he could find a way to share it with Isabel, in every way, if he could cool his ardor enough and rein in the base needs that clawed at him, perhaps contentment with her could be his.

It was a goal worth striving for.

"She has thrown you over, has she, Lord Hargreaves?" asked a girlish voice beside him.

John turned his head away from the sight of Isabel across the ballroom, and bowed to the lovely brunette who spoke to him. "Lady Stanhope, a pleasure."

"Grayson has ruined your cozy little arrangement," she purred, her eyes leaving his to find Pel. "Look how zealously Lord Spencer guards her side. You know as well as I that he would not be here if Grayson had not ordered him to be. Makes one wonder why he is not here to see to the matter himself."

"I have no wish to discuss Lord Grayson," he said tightly. Unable to help himself, he stared at his former mistress. He still could not collect how everything could change so drastically in so short a time. Yes, he had noted Pel's increasing restlessness, but their friendship had been strong and the sex as satisfying as always.

"Even if discussing him could return Lady Grayson's attentions to you?"

His head whipped toward her. Dressed in blood red satin, Stanhope's widow was hard to miss, even amongst the crowd. He had noted her several times over the course of the evening, especially since she seemed to be spending a great deal of her time studying him. "What are you saying?"

Lady Stanhope's rouged mouth curved in a portentous smile. "I want Grayson. You want his wife. It would be to both of our benefits to work together."

"I've no notion of what you are talking about." But he was intrigued. And it showed.

"That's fine, darling," she drawled. "You can leave all the notions to me."

"Lady Stanhope—"

"We are allies. Call me Barbara."

The determined tilt of her chin and eyes as hard as the jade they resembled told John she knew what she was about. He glanced at Pel again and caught her staring back at him with her full bottom lip worried between her teeth. His pride smarted.

Barbara's hand slipped around his arm. "Let's walk, and I shall tell you what I have planned . . ."

Chapter 10

Sitting at her boudoir desk, Isabel addressed the last of her dinner invitations with a flourish that belied the apprehension she felt. Grayson had never been the type of man who would brush off such machinations. He was devious and lacked the morals that restrained most, and while he admired similar cunning in others, he did not feel as charitable to those who would try their trickery on him.

Fully cognizant of the fact that she was, in effect, poking a sleeping lion with a stick, she hesitated a moment, staring at the tidy stack of cream-colored missives at her elbow.

"Would you like these sent out immediately?" her secretary asked, hovering nearby.

She hesitated a moment, and then shook her head. "Not just yet. You may go for now."

Rising from her seat at the escritoire, Isabel knew she was only prolonging the inevitable by failing to set in motion her search for a mistress for Gray, but she needed a bit more inner strength to manage the task. The tension and heated awareness between them was anathema to her mental health.

She'd slept fitfully the night before. Her body, while sore, craved the feel of his. If only she knew what had caused their relationship to alter so drastically, perhaps she could find a way to change it back.

As Gray had requested earlier, she moved over to the adjoining door to speak with him, her stomach fluttering at the mere thought of seeing him. She had barely cracked the portal open when the sound of angry voices stilled her.

"What concerns me is the talk, Gray. Since I avoid those types of preening social events, I had no notion of how bad it is. It is truly dreadful."

"What is said about me is no concern of yours," Gray rejoined tightly.

"Damned if it isn't!" Spencer cried. "I am a Faulkner, too. You chastise me for running wild, and yet Pel has a far worse reputation. They wonder if you have the wherewithal to bring her to heel. They whisper about why you left, that perhaps your recalcitrant wife is too much for you. That you are not man enough to—"

"I suggest you say no more." Gray's interjection was fraught with menace.

"Turning a deaf ear does nothing to correct the damage. She was in the retiring room for no more than a few minutes, and in that time I overheard things that made my blood run cold. Mother is right. You should petition Parliament to be rid of her. You quite easily have two witnesses to her adultery. Hundreds, in fact."

"You tread on thin ice, brother."

"I will not tolerate the disparagement of our name, and I am aghast that you would do so!"

"Spencer." Gray's voice dropped in warning. "Do not do anything idiotic."

"I will do what is necessary. She is a mistress, Grayson. Not a wife."

There was a loud grunt, and the wall beside her shook violently. Isabel covered her mouth to stifle a cry.

"Say another unkind word about Pel," Gray bit out, "and I will not restrain myself. I will not tolerate any slander of my wife."

"Bloody hell," Spencer gasped. His surprised voice was so close to the gap in the door she was certain she would be discovered. "You attacked me! What has happened to you? You have changed."

Stumbling footsteps told her that Gray had pushed his brother away.

"You say I have changed. Why? Because I choose to honor my promises and commitments? That is maturity."

"She does not afford a like respect to you."

The low growl from Grayson frightened Isabel. "Get out. I cannot be near you now."

"We are well met, then, for I cannot bear to be near you either."

Angry-sounding footfalls preceded the slamming of the hallway door.

Her heart racing madly, Isabel slumped against the wall and felt ill. She was well aware of the talk, which had started when they wed and grew worse as they lived separate lives. Gray's title held enough power that no one would dare cut her, and she had considered the gossip the price she must pay for her decisions and the freedom she desired. Gray had seemed immune, and so she had assumed he did not care. Now she knew he did care. A great deal. To learn that she had hurt Gray was so painful she could barely catch her breath.

Unsure of what to do or what to say to minimize the damage she had caused, Isabel stood motionless until she heard Gray's weary sigh. That soft sound touched her deeply, melting something that had long been frozen. She gripped the knob, pulled the door open . . .

. . . and was arrested by the sight that greeted her.

Gray was clad in only trousers, a new garment by the look of it, which reminded her of the tailor's earlier call. He stood by the bed, his hand on the carved post, his back and beautifully curved buttocks hard with tension.

"Grayson," she called quietly, her blood hot from the mere sight of him.

He straightened, but did not face her. "Yes, Pel?"

"You wished to speak with me?"

"I apologize. Now is not a good time."

She took a deep breath, and stepped further into the room. "It is I who owes you an apology."

He turned to face her then, causing her to reach for a nearby chair and grip the back of it. The sight of his bare torso stole her wits.

"You overheard," he said flatly.

"It was not my intent."

"We are not discussing this now." His jaw tightened. "I am not fit company at the moment."

Shaking her head, Isabel pushed away from her support and moved forward. "Tell me how I can help you."

"You won't like my answer, so I suggest you leave. Now."

Heaving out her breath, she fought back the urge to cast up her accounts. "How could we have erred so greatly?" she asked, almost to herself.

Veering off course, she walked toward the other side of the room. "Ignorance, I suppose. And arrogance. To think that we could live as we pleased and expect Society to accept us."

"Go away, Isabel."

"I refuse to come between you and your family, Gray."

"My family be damned!" he retorted. "As you will be, if you stay here any longer."

"Don't growl at me." She shot him a narrowed glance. "You once shared your problems with me. Now that *I* am the problem, I think that habit is even more important. And cease looking at me like that . . . What are you doing?"

"I warned you," he said grimly. Moving so quickly she had no time to evade him, Gray caught her about the waist with his hands and carried her to the bathing chamber. His skin was hot, his grip too tight. He set her down, shoved her inside, and slammed the door shut between them.

"Gray!" she shouted through the portal.

"I am feeling violent, and your scent is making me lustful. Persisting with your inane prattle will see you tossed on your back and your mouth put to much better uses."

Isabel blinked in shock. His rudeness was meant to drive her away, to scare her, and it very nearly succeeded. She'd never had a man speak to her so crudely and in such anger. It did odd things to her insides, making her quiver and her breath shorten.

Standing with her hand pressed against the door, she listened for sounds of him. She had no notion of what she should do, but walking away when he was so inflamed seemed cowardly. And yet . . . She was no fool. She knew men far better than women, and the best thing to do with a surly man was stay out of his way. She was well aware of what would happen should she choose to enter his rooms again. "Grayson?"

He did not reply.

There was nothing she could do for him, nothing that could change the facts or make him feel better beyond the temporary release of orgasm. But perhaps that was what he needed after hearing the disparagement of his virility. Perhaps it was what she needed, to forget for a short time that both of her marriages had failed. The first time, she had been young and naïve. But this time she had known better. How foolish to have thought Gray would not mature with age, which he appeared to have done by taking responsibility for Lord Spencer. Which left her wondering if perhaps Pelham also would have changed, had he been given the time.

"I can hear you thinking through the door," Gray said wryly, his voice directly opposite the barrier.

"Are you still angry?"

"Of course, but not with you."

"I *am* sorry, Grayson."

"For what?" he asked in a low tone. "Marrying me?"

She swallowed hard, the word "no" trapped in her throat because she refused to give it voice.

"Isabel?"

Sighing, she moved away. He was right. Now was not the time to discuss this, not when she couldn't think clearly. She hated the door between them. It blocked his scent and his touch and the hunger in his eyes—things she should not want. Why could she not be more practical about her wedded state, like the rest of her family? Why did her emotions have to become so tangled up and ruin everything?

"Just so we are clear," he said gruffly. "I am not sorry, and out of all the things said to me in the last hour, hearing you say we have done something wrong disturbs me the most."

Her steps faltered. How could he not regret the marriage that caused him such grief? If this was not enough to lessen his determination to have a true conjugal relationship, nothing would be.

Anger filled her at the sudden softening she felt toward him. She should not be melting over him. Her mother would not melt. Neither would Rhys. They would enjoy the great sex until they were sated and be done with it. Her chin lifted. That was what she should do also, if she were practical about such matters.

She left the bathing chamber, and walked slowly into her boudoir. The fact was, she could be practical about her affairs because the rules were set from the beginning and the end was anticipated. There was no ownership, such as she had felt for Pelham and was beginning to feel for Gray.

Drat the man! They had been friends. Then he had returned as a stranger, and took the place of her spouse.

A husband was a possession. A lover was not.

Her stomach flipped.

She is a mistress, Grayson. Not a wife.

Lord Spencer's angry words were, quite simply, the solution.

Yanking on the bellpull, Isabel waited impatiently for her abigail to come up and then, with the servant's help, she undressed. Completely. And unpinned her hair. Then she squared her shoulders and quickly crossed the distance back to Gray's room. She threw the door open, saw her husband reaching for a shirt that lay on the bed, and with a running start, jumped onto his back.

"What in—"

Caught off balance, he tumbled face-first into the bed. Isabel hung on. Reaching behind him, Gray flipped her onto the counterpane with a deep growl.

"Finally, you come to your senses," he muttered, before lowering his head and sucking a nipple into his mouth.

"Oh," she cried, startled by the feel of drenched heat. Heavens, the man recovered quickly! "Wait."

He grunted and went on suckling.

"I have rules!"

Heated blue eyes met hers, and he released her nipple with a loud pop. "You. Naked. Whenever I want you. Wherever I want you. Those are the only 'rules.'"

"Yes." She nodded, and he stilled, his large body turning hard as stone. "We will draft an agreement, and—"

"We have a written agreement, madam—a marriage certificate."

"No. I will be your mistress and you will be my lover. The arrangement will be clear and on paper, since I cannot trust you to keep to your end of bargains."

"Just for curiosity's sake," he began, pushing up from the bed to stand over her. His hands went to the placket of his trousers. "Are you deranged?"

She pushed up onto her elbows, her mouth watering as he shoved his garments to the floor and was suddenly, gloriously naked and impressively aroused.

He pounced on her with little finesse. "Your mental malady will not dampen my ardor, so you needn't worry about that. You can spout all the gibberish you like while I ride you. I will not mind a bit."

"Gray, really."

Catching her knee, he shoved her thighs wide and settled his lean hips between them. "A wife is cherished and treated with a gentle hand. A mistress is a convenient cunt to rut in. Are you certain you wish to alter your status in our bedroom?"

It was then she realized he was still angry, his jaw clenched dangerously. The heavy heat of his erection was like lightning striking her skin. Gooseflesh spread over her body, and her breasts swelled painfully. "You don't frighten me."

His body was so hard and hot to the touch, it burned her. "You do not heed warnings very well," he murmured in a low tone, and before she could process it, he'd thrust his cock into her. Not quite creamy for him and still a bit sore, she cried out and arched upward, the entry both painful and unexpected.

His hand fisted in the length of her hair, keeping her head back and her throat exposed. It also kept her helpless and rigidly in place as he began to fuck her with fierce, powerful lunges.

"When we are through with each other," she gasped, her determination unwavering, "we will separate. I will return to my old residence. We will be friends, and you can regain face."

He rammed into her, striking so deep she lost her breath.

"You can have only me," she managed a moment later, moisture flooding her sex as he took what he wanted and excited her by doing so. "Slide between another woman's sheets and you void our arrangement."

Gray lowered his head and sucked hard on her neck. He grunted with every deep plunge of his cock, his heavy balls slapping against her with each downward stroke. The result of having her head held back was her breasts thrusting upward, and the coarse hairs on his chest scraped across her nipples. She whimpered at the feeling, her wits slipping rapidly.

She should not feel so good. Her position was uncomfortable, his touch bruising, his mouth and teeth hurtful against her tender throat. His hips pummeled hers, his shaft a thick intrusion that pumped through swollen tissues . . . And yet the absolute certainty in his touch, the complete lack of hesitation, his supreme arrogance in using *her* body for *his* pleasure was nearly rapturous.

"Yes . . ." As her body shivered on the verge of climax, she moaned a low plaintive sound. She clawed at his sides, dug her heels in his ass, and gave as good as she received.

"Isabel," he growled, his mouth pressed to her ear. "Brazen enough to tackle a man naked, but so swiftly mastered by a hard cock."

It would not be like it was before! "My rules," she reminded, then she sank her teeth into his chest.

"Damn your rules." Gray yanked out of her, his free hand gripping his cock and pumping, guttural sounds accompanying the spurting of his cum across her belly. It was base and raw, very different from his lovemaking of just a day before, and it left her writhing in an agony of lust.

"Selfish bastard."

Tossing his leg over her hips, he rolled and came over her, straddling her. His beautiful mouth was hard, his face flushed and eyes glazed. "A man is not required to pleasure his mistress."

"So you accept the arrangement," she bit out, her teeth clenched together. She was in control, regardless of how he might wish it otherwise.

As his hands began to rub his seed into her skin, his smile was cold and tight. "If you have a wish to make a devil's bargain, so be it." He caught her nipples between damp fingertips and rolled them.

Isabel slapped at him. "Enough!"

"I should allow you to leave, all angry and hot and wet. Maybe then you would feel a little of what I do."

"Spare me," she scoffed. "You had your pleasure."

He hummed a soft chastising sound. "Do you truly believe I could be sated while you are not?"

"Do I misunderstand the semen on my stomach?"

Gray leaned back to give her an unhindered view of the

hard length of his cock. The sight of it was nearly too much for her overheated body. Even his arrogant smile did nothing to dampen her desire. He was built for a woman's pleasure, and he damn well knew it.

"I believe we have already established your stamina,.Grayson."

His gaze narrowed, which aroused her suspicions. She could see his mind at work. Considering something devious, no doubt. "Any man kneeling over your creamy cunt would be ready to rut in it."

"How poetic," she murmured dryly. "Be still my heart."

"I save my poetry for my wife." He slid downward, his smile wicked enough to make her tense in apprehension. "If it were she in my bed, I would not leave her so distressed."

"I am not distressed."

He licked the edge of skin that prefaced the damp curls of her sex. She gasped.

"Of course not," he said, grinning. "Mistresses do not expect orgasms."

"I always have."

Ignoring her, he dipped his head and swiped his tongue through the lips of her sex. Her hips arched involuntarily. "I would tell my wife how I love the taste of her and the feel of her petal soft skin. How the scent of our combined lust arouses me further, and keeps me hard despite the many times I come on her."

She watched his strong hands with their neatly trimmed nails and unfashionable calluses press her legs open wider. The sight of his dark skin against her paler flesh was erotic, as was the lock of dark hair that fell over his brow and tickled her inner thighs.

"I would tell her how much I love the color of her hair here, the rich chocolate with glints of fire. It is like a beacon that lures me to her, promising untold delights and hours of pleasure." Gray pressed a kiss against her clitoris, and when she keened softly, he suckled, stroking his tongue leisurely back and forth across it.

Releasing the counterpane she held so tightly, she reached for him, her fingertips sliding through the thick silk of his hair to caress the sweat-dampened roots. He made that noise she adored, a cross between an arrogant grunt and a groan of encouragement, and then he rewarded her with faster licks.

Draping her legs over his shoulders, she tugged him closer, lifting her hips to swivel against his expert mouth. Any moment she expected him to stop, to tease her cruelly by leaving her wanting. Desperate to come, she begged, "Please . . . Gray . . ."

He mumbled reassurance, his large hands gentling her as he brought her to orgasm with the gentle fucking of his tongue. She froze, every muscle and sinew locked with the pleasure that unfurled slowly and increased in intensity until she shivered uncontrollably.

"I love that," he murmured, shrugging carefully out from under her and crawling up the length of her body. "Almost as much as I love this." He surged into her spasming depths with a growl.

"Oh my God!" She could not open her eyes, even to look at him, something she enjoyed so much she often stared. She was drunk on him—the smell of him, the feel of him.

The sight of him would ruin her.

"Yes," he hissed, sinking deep, his cock as hard as stone and hot enough to melt her. Curling his arms beneath her shoulders, Gray embraced her from head to toe. His mouth to her ear he whispered, "I would tell my wife how she feels to me, so hot and drenched, like dipping my cock into warm honey."

She felt the tight roping of his abdomen flex against her belly as he withdrew in a slow, torturous glide and then pumped back inside.

"I would love her body the way a husband should, with care for her comfort and an eye toward her pleasure."

Her hands caressed the curve of his spine, cupping his steely buttocks. She moaned as they clenched on a perfect stroke. "Keep doing that," she whispered, her head falling to the side.

"This?" He withdrew, and then, circling his hips, screwed back into her.

"Mmmm . . . A little harder."

The next pump of his hips struck deep. Delicious.

"You are a demanding mistress." As his mouth followed the curve of her cheekbone, he chuckled.

"I know what I want."

"Yes." His hand stroked her side, cupped her hip, and angled her perfectly for his measured thrusts. "Me."

"Gray." Her arms tightened, her body awash in lustful longing.

"Say my name," he urged hoarsely, his cock shafting her cunt in long, rhythmic plunges.

Isabel forced her heavy eyelids to open, and met his gaze. The request was not frivolous. His handsome features were open, boyish, stripped of their usual arrogant assurance. A mistress would not use his name. Neither would most wives. The intimacy was telling. And with his body riding hers with unfailing skill, devastating.

"Say it." Now it was a command.

"Gerard," she cried, as he made her come in a white hot flare of heat.

And he held her, and made love to her, and crooned praise to her.

Just as a husband would.

Chapter 11

"What have I done?"

Although he heard Pel's whisper, Gerard remained still with his eyes closed, feigning sleep. Her head rested on his bicep and the soft curve of her ass pressed against his hip. The air around them was redolent of sex and exotic flowers, and he felt like he was in heaven.

But obviously, his wife did not.

She heaved a forlorn sigh, and pressed her lips to his skin. The urge to roll and embrace her tightly was nearly overwhelming, but he resisted it. Somehow, he needed to puzzle her out. There was a key to her, if only he could find it.

To bargain with him for his fidelity . . . That was what she had done. He was flattered and touched, but decidedly curious as to her motives. Why not simply ask him to be true to her? Why go to such lengths—threatening to leave him—to accomplish her aim?

Constancy toward one woman was unknown to him. His needs were sometimes violent as they had been today, and while some women served such a purpose, others, such as his wife, were made for lovemaking. Opening his eyes was not required to know that Isabel's body was bruised by his ardor. If he subjected her to such treatment often she would grow to fear him, and that was something he could not bear.

But for now, she was his and promised to his bed. That would bide him some time to do a bit of research. He needed to learn more about her, so he could understand her. With understanding would come the ability to keep her happy. Or so he hoped.

Gerard waited until Pel was asleep before leaving the bed. Despite how he wished to linger, it was time to find Spencer and attempt to explain. Perhaps Spencer would understand, perhaps he would not, but Gerard could not allow the situation between them to remain as it was for a moment longer.

He blew out his breath. A temper was something he was still becoming accustomed to. Prior to four years ago, he had never felt deeply enough about anything to become angry over it.

Walking past the full-length mirror, Gerard paused, having caught a glimpse of himself as he passed by. He turned, and stared at his reflection, noting the bite mark on his chest. Swiveling at the hips, he perused his back and the scratches that laced either side of his spine. Just above his buttocks, two round shadows hinted at bruises to come, marks left by his wife's heels as she spurred him on.

"I'll be damned," he breathed, his eyes wide. He looked nigh as bad as Pel. No passive lover was she. He was well met.

Something wondrous tingled in his chest, and then burst forth as a low chuckle.

"You are an odd creature," came the sleep-husky voice behind him. "Laughing is not the first thing I think of doing when I see you naked."

Heat rushed over his skin. He moved back toward the bed, and as he did so, he could not help but notice the marks of his teeth on her neck. His blood heated and rushed at the sight. He was a primitive beast, but at least he knew it. "What *is* the first thing, then?"

Pel pushed herself up to a seated position. Disheveled and

flushed, she looked ravished and it was an air of satiation that would linger around her throughout the evening, an unspoken claim.

"I think your ass is divine, and I wish to bite it."

"*Bite* it?" He blinked. "My ass?"

"Yes." She tucked the sheet beneath her arms, her face devoid of the humor that would have revealed she was teasing.

"Why on earth would you wish to do such a thing?"

"Because it looks taut and firm. Like a peach." Licking her lips, she arched a challenging brow. "I wish to see if it's as hard when clenched between my teeth."

His hands moved without volition to cover his rear. "You're serious."

"Quite."

"Quite." Gerard studied his wife with a narrowed glance. It never occurred to him that Isabel might also have some . . . *quirks* in the bedroom. Since she had indulged his anomalous cravings, he supposed it was only fair that he indulge hers, even if his flesh did tighten warily at the thought.

Her amber eyes darkened and heated, a sensual invitation to dally, and he could not refuse. Not when her capitulation was so fresh. He had wanted this, wanted her willing, and if that meant allowing her to bite his ass, he would bear it. It would only take a moment. Then he would dress and speak to Spencer.

"Odd, this," he muttered, lying facedown beside her.

"I did not suggest this very moment," she said dryly. "Or even that I wished to make the thought a reality. I simply answered your question."

He heaved out a relieved breath. "Thank God." But when he moved to leave the bed, she dropped the sheet and bared her breasts. Groaning, he asked, "How in hell is a man expected to go about his business when you tempt him so?"

"He isn't." Wiggling her courtesan's body out from under his sheets, she stunned him with her beauty so that he lost the sense to move as she crawled over him. "Or are you comfortable only when you are the biter?"

Isabel straddled his back in reverse—her feet by his hands, her hips at his shoulders, her breasts at the small of his back. The lush feel of her curves and the seductive heat of her sleep-warmed body made him hard again.

And he had thought himself spent for a while.

Encircling her ankles with an apprehensive grip, Gerard waited. Then he felt her hands, so tiny and soft, stroking along the curve of his buttocks before squeezing gently. That he could not see her actions only increased the surprising eroticism of the act. Ridiculous though it was, the thought of her admiring another man in such a manner unnerved him.

"Have you always had this fascination?"

"No. You have a singular ass."

He waited for more, but she said nothing further. Instead she began to hum a soft appreciative sound, and his cock grew so hard it hurt to be prone. The tips of her fingers kneaded his flesh, rubbing and pressing in a way that made every hair on his body stand at attention. Gooseflesh dotted his skin. Closing his eyes, he buried his face in the bed.

A soft touch followed the crease where his buttocks met his thighs. Then he felt the heat of her breath gust across his skin. He tensed all over—starting at his rear and then spreading outward. The wait was endless.

And then she kissed him.

First one cheek, and then the other. Soft, open-mouthed kisses. He felt her nipples grow stiff against his back, and took some comfort knowing he was not alone in this. Whatever *this* was.

Then his wife bit him, ever so gently, and his toes curled.

His bloody toes curled!

"Christ, Isabel," he said hoarsely, his hips moving restlessly, pressing his aching cock into the bed. He knew for a certainty that no other woman could bite his ass and actually arouse him unbearably while doing so. He was positive that if another female were to take Pel's place he would be laughing now. But this was no laughing matter. This was torture of the most sensual kind.

Something hot and wet slid across his skin, and he jerked. "Did you *lick* me?"

"Shhh," she murmured. "Relax. I won't hurt you."

"You are killing me!"

"Should I cease?"

Gerard grit his teeth and considered. Then said, "Only if you wish to stop. Otherwise, no. However, I feel I should remind you that my body is yours to take whenever you desire."

"I desire it now."

He grinned at the steel that laced her bedroom voice. "Then by all means."

Time passed and he lost track of it, lost in the sultry scent of his wife and the masculine satisfaction derived from being so thoroughly admired. Eventually, she moved away from his rear and moved onto his legs. When she reached his feet, he laughed at her soft ticklish touch. When she reached his shoulders and her hair drifted over his back, he sighed.

One morning, not too long ago, he had sat on the short stone wall that surrounded one of his terraces and tried to remember what it felt like to smile with true contentment. What a godsend it was to have found that here, in his home. With Pel.

Then Isabel urged him to roll over, straddled his hips, and took him inside her, slowly. She was burning hot and drenched, and he watched, shaking, as his cock was engulfed inch by throbbing inch between the flushed, glistening lips of her sex.

"Oh God . . ." she breathed, her thighs trembling, her eyes heavy-lidded and locked with his. The soft whimper turned into rapid pants. That she enjoyed his cock to the extreme was not only obvious, but more than enough to make his balls crawl into his body.

"I won't last," he warned, his hands tugging her downward impatiently. He'd taken her several times now, but never had she taken him, and she was a mature woman with a comfortable understanding of her own desires. From the moment they had been introduced, he'd admired her poise and confidence. Now he found it both mesmerizing and satisfying to share the control of their bedsport with her. "I am ready to blow."

"But you won't."

And he didn't. Fear for her held him back, because she was his wife—his to please, his to enjoy, his to protect. He would not lose her like he lost Em.

His. She was his.

Now he need only convince her of that.

When Gerard finally found the strength of will to leave his bed, he went directly to Spencer's rooms, but did not find him there. A cursory search of the house turned up nothing. It was then he discovered his brother had departed soon after their row. To say he was worried would be an understatement. He had no notion of what Spencer had overheard the night before or who had spoken the words that so angered him.

I will not tolerate the disparagement of our name . . . I will do what is necessary.

Growling, Gerard went to his office and penned two quick notes. One waited for Isabel, while the other was dispatched immediately. He had planned to escort his wife to whatever events she had agreed to attend, and he'd looked forward to both her company and the chance to dispel the rumors that plagued them. Now he was forced to scour clubs, brothels, and taverns to be certain Spencer did not land firmly into a puddle of trouble, as their mother claimed was his wont to do.

Damn and blast, he thought, as he waited for his horse to be saddled and brought around. An entire afternoon of physical exertion had made him somewhat jellied in the legs and should the need come for fisticuffs, he was certain he would not be at his best. Because of this, he prayed Spencer was not pursuing a fight, but simply drinking or whoring. And of those two choices, Gerard preferred the latter. Sated, perhaps, his brother would be more amenable to listening to reason.

Vaulting into the saddle, he urged his mount away from the house that was now a home and wondered how many more decisions of his past would hurt those he cared for.

"What are you doing here, Rhys?" Isabel asked as she entered the parlor. Try as she might, she could not hide the irritated note in her voice. To wake up without Gray was bad enough; to read his curt and vague missive only compounded her disgruntlement.

> *I must see to Spencer.*
> *Yours,*
> *Grayson*

She knew how men related to one another—they argued, and then made up over ale and women. Well acquainted with her husband's stamina, she could not put the indulgence past him.

Her brother rose from his seat on the blue velvet settee and sketched a quick bow. Dashingly dressed in evening black, he was a remarkable sight. "I am at your service, madam," he intoned in a comical imitation of an upper servant.

"My service?" She frowned. "Whatever am I supposed to need you for?"

"Grayson sent for me. He wrote that he was unable to accompany you this evening and suggested I might like to. For if I did, surely I would be too weary to meet him in the rings at Remington's in the morning. And in his gratitude for my escort, he would excuse me. Indefinitely."

Her eyes widened. "He threatened you?"

"I warned you he would give me a thrashing for taking you away from him yesterday."

"Ridiculous," she muttered.

"I agree," he said dryly. "However, fortuituously I had plans to attend the Hammond ball regardless, as Lady Margaret Crenshaw will be there."

"Another victim on your list? Have you, at the very least, spoken to this one before?"

Rhys shot her a dark glance. "Yes, I have, and she was very pleasant. So, if you are ready . . . ?"

Although she had dressed for an evening out, she'd actually considered remaining at home to wait for Gray. But that would be foolish. He obviously wished her to go, since he went to such lengths to see her escorted. She was not a young girl any longer, nor naïve. It should not bother her one whit that Grayson had spent hours finding pleasure in her body, only to leave her behind for the evening. A mistress would find nothing untoward, she told herself.

And she continued to remind herself of that fact as the course of the evening progressed. But when she caught a glimpse of a familiar face in the crowded Hammond ballroom, the knowledge was discarded. Mistress or not, a knot formed in her belly, only to be quickly replaced by a cold flare of anger.

"Lord Spencer Faulkner is here," Rhys noted casually, as the young man entered the ballroom just a few feet away from where they stood along the edge of the dance floor.

"So he is." But Grayson was not. So he had lied to her. Why was she surprised?

She studied her brother-in-law carefully, noting both the similarities to her husband and the differences. Unlike her close resemblance to Rhys, Gray and Lord Spencer had only a passing physical familiarity, which gave her a small glimpse of what their father must have looked like.

As if he felt her perusal, Spencer turned his head and met her gaze. For one brief, unguarded heartbeat she saw something decidedly unpleasant, and then it was shielded with studious impassivity.

"Well, well," Rhys murmured. "I believe we have finally met a man who is truly immune to your charms."

"You saw that?"

"Unfortunately, yes." His gaze raked the throng before them. "I can only hope that you and I were the only ones who—Good God!"

"What?" Alarmed by his shock, Isabel rose to her toes and looked around. *Was it Gray?* Her heart raced. "What is it?"

Rhys thrust his champagne at her with such haste the sloshing liquid nearly overwhelmed the flute, which would have ruined her satin gown. "Excuse me." And then he was off, leaving Isabel blinking after him.

Rhys followed the trim form that weaved easily through the guests. Almost as if she were a wraith, she went by unnoticed, an unremarkable woman wearing an unremarkable dress. But Rhys was arrested. He knew that dark hair. He had dreamt of that voice.

She left the ballroom, and moved swiftly down the hall. He followed. When she exited the manse through a study door, he gave up any effort to hide his pursuit and he caught the knob just as it swung away from him. Her small, piquant face tilted up to his, the wide eyes blinking.

"Lord Trenton."

He stepped out onto the terrace, and shut out the sounds of the ball with a click of the latch. Sketching a short bow, he caught up her gloved hand and kissed the back of it. "Lady Mystery."

She laughed, and his grip tightened. Her head angled to the side in what looked to be puzzlement. "You find me attractive, don't you? But you cannot reason why. Quite frankly, I am equally puzzled."

A soft chuckle escaped him. "Will you allow me to investigate a little?" He bent slowly, giving her time to pull away before he brushed his lips across hers. The soft touch affected him strangely, as did her scent, which was so soft it was a mere hint in the cool night air. "I think a few experiments might be in order."

"Oh my," she breathed. Her free hand moved to shelter her stomach. "That just gave me a little flutter right here."

Something warm expanded in his chest, and dropped to settle between his legs. She was not his type of female at all. Mousy. A bluestocking. Certainly he found her discourse refreshing in its frankness, but why he wished to toss up her skirts was a matter he could not reconcile. She was too slender for his tastes, and lacked the full womanly curves he appreciated. Still, he could not deny that he wanted her, and he wanted to know her secrets. "Why are you out here?"

"Because I prefer here to there."

"Walk with me, then," he murmured, tucking her hand in the crook of his elbow and leading her away.

"Will you flirt shamelessly with me?" she asked as she fell into step beside him. They found a winding garden path and strolled. The way was unlit so they progressed slowly.

"Of course. I will also discover your name before we part."

"You sound so certain of that."

He smiled down into her moonlit eyes. "I have my ways."

She harrumphed skeptically. "You shall have fun matching wits with me."

"I've no doubt your brain is formidable, but that is not the part of you I would use my wiles on."

She gave a chastising push to his shoulder with her free hand. "You are wicked to speak thusly to a woman of my inexperience. You are making me light-headed."

Rhys winced, slightly chagrined. "Sorry."

"No, you're not." Her hand brushed across where she had touched him a moment before and his blood heated, his step faltered. How could the brush of a gloved hand over the material of his coat and sleeve arouse him?

"Is this sort of bantering the way men speak to women they feel an intimacy with? Lady Grayson laughs often at things that are said to her by men I find to be quite dull."

Coming to an abrupt halt, Rhys glared down at her.

"I meant no offense!" she said quickly. "In fact, Lady Grayson is a woman I find to be multifaceted in only the most flattering sense."

Studying her carefully, he concluded she was sincere and began walking again. "Yes, once you become friends with a member of the opposite sex and you are comfortable with them, your conversation can become intimate."

"Sexually intimate?"

"Oftentimes, yes."

"Even though the end goal is not sexual, merely for temporary amusement?"

"You are a curious kitten." His smile was indulgent. To think that such a mundane act as flirtation could become exciting when seen through her eyes. He wished he could sit for hours with her and answer all of her questions.

"I'm afraid I lack the knowledge required to banter in the manner to which you are accustomed. So I hope you forgive me when I just ask you outright to kiss me."

He stumbled, scattering the gravel on the path. "I beg your pardon?"

"You heard me, my lord." Her chin lifted. "I would very much like you to kiss me."

"Why?"

"Because no one else ever will."

"Why not? You underestimate yourself."

Her smile was impish and filled him with delight. "I estimate myself just fine."

"Then certainly you know that another man will kiss you." Even as he said it, Rhys realized how deeply the thought disturbed him. Her lips were soft as rose petals and sweetly plump. They had cushioned his when he kissed her, and he found them to be the prettiest lips he'd ever seen. The image in his mind of another man sampling them made his fists clench.

"Another man may like to, but he won't." She stepped forward, and rose to her tiptoes, offering her mouth to him. "Because I will not allow him to."

Against his will, Rhys caught her to him. She was slender as a reed, her curves slight, but she fit to him. He held still for a moment, absorbing that fact.

"We fit," she breathed, her eyes wide. "Is that usual?"

He swallowed hard and shook his head, lifting one hand to cup her cheek. "I've no notion what to do with you," he admitted.

"Just kiss me."

Rhys bent his head, hovering only a hair's breadth away. "Tell me your name."

"Abby."

He licked her lower lip. "I want to see you again, Abby."

"So we can hide in gardens and be scandalous?"

What could he say? He knew nothing about her, but her attire, her age, and the fact that she ran about unescorted told him of her lack of consequence. It was time to marry, and she was not a woman he could court.

Her smile was knowing. "Just kiss me and say good-bye, Lord Trenton. Be content that you have given me the fantasy of a handsome, dashing suitor."

Words failed him, so he kissed her, deeply and with feeling. She melted into him, became breathless, gave a soft whimper that stole his wits. He wanted to take liberties with her. Strip her bare, share with her all the things he knew, see the sexual act as she would, with wonder.

So when she left him in the garden, the farewell he should have spoken would not come. And later, when he returned to the manse with a sham exterior of normalcy, he realized she had not said it either.

Chapter 12

"How interesting that she should arrive without Grayson," Barbara murmured, her hand tucked lightly over Hargreaves' arm. Turning her head, she perused the throng again.

"Perhaps he intends to join her later," the earl replied, with far more nonchalance than she would like. Should he suddenly decide he no longer wanted Isabel Grayson, she would be alone in her attempts to lure Grayson back to her bed.

She released him and stepped back. "Trenton has left her side. Now would be the time to approach her."

"No." He shot her an arch look. "Now is *not* the time. Think of the talk that would ensue."

"Gossip is our aim," she argued.

"Grayson is not a man to be toyed with."

"I agree, but neither are you."

Hargreaves stared across the ballroom, his narrowed gaze arrested by his former love.

"Look how morose she is," Barbara goaded. "Perhaps her decision is one she already regrets. But you will never know if you don't speak with her."

It was this last thought that garnered the results she wanted. With a muttered oath, Hargreaves moved away, his broad shoulders squared in determination.

She smiled and turned in the opposite direction, seeking and then finding the young Lord Spencer. Feigning an attempt to move past him, Barbara brushed her breasts along his forearm and when he turned to her with wide eyes, she blushed.

"I do apologize, my lord." She looked up at him through her lashes.

He offered an indulgent smile. "No apologies necessary," he said smoothly, catching up her proffered hand. He moved to step out of her way, but she held tight. He arched a brow. "My lady?"

"I would like to reach the drink tables, but the crush is rather daunting. And I am so very parched."

His half smile was knowing. "I would be honored to offer my services."

"How gallant of you to come to my aid," she said, falling into step beside him. She studied him furtively. He was quite handsome, though in not the same way as his older sibling. Grayson had a dangerous edge that could not be ignored, despite his outward appearance of insouciance. Lord Spencer's nonchalance, however, was not a façade.

"I endeavor to make myself useful to beautiful women as often as possible."

"How fortunate for Lady Grayson to have two such dashing Faulkner men at her beck and call."

His arm stiffened beneath her gloved touch and she could not hold back her smile. Something was amiss in the Grayson household, a circumstance that could only work to her advantage. She would have to ply the youngest Faulkner with her wiles to discover what the issue was, but that was a prospect she found most appealing.

With a quick glance over her shoulder to be certain Hargreaves had gone to Isabel Grayson, Barbara wiggled her shoulders in anticipation and determined to enjoy the rest of Lord Spencer's evening.

* * *

"Isabel."

John halted a discreet distance away. His gaze raked her from head to toe, taking in the pearls weaved through her auburn tresses and her lovely dark green gown, the deep color of which set off her creamy porcelain skin to perfection. Her three-strand choker of pearls did an admirable job of attempting to hide the faint bruising around her neck, but he took note of it nevertheless. "Are you well?"

Her smile was both fond and sad. "As well as can be expected." She canted her body toward him. "I feel dreadful, John. You are a good man who deserved to be treated better than I have treated you."

"Do you miss me?" he dared to ask.

"I do." Her amber gaze met his directly. "Though perhaps not in the way that you might miss me."

His mouth curved. As always, he admired her candor. She was a woman who spoke without artifice. "Where is Grayson this evening?"

Her chin lifted slightly. "I will not discuss my husband with you."

"Are we no longer friends, then, Pel?"

"We certainly will not be if your aim is to pry into my marriage," she snapped. And then she blushed, her gaze dropping.

He opened his mouth to apologize, then stopped. Isabel's ill-humor had grown more and more frequent as their affair progressed. He now began to wonder if their relationship had been winding down prior to Grayson's return and he had simply been too dense to realize it.

Releasing a deep breath, he attempted to turn his thoughts inward in consideration of this possibility. However, a sudden disturbance and Pel's subsequent stiffness beside him drew his attention. He looked up and found the Marquess of Grayson standing across the room. Grayson's gaze was first riveted on Isabel, then it moved to rest on him.

Chilled by that stare, John shivered. Then Grayson turned away.

"Your husband has arrived."

"Yes, yes. I know. Excuse me."

She had already traveled a short distance from him when he remembered Barbara's plan. "I will escort you to the terrace, if you like."

"Thank you," she replied with a nod that set her fiery curls in motion. He had always loved her hair. The combination of dark chocolate and reddish glints was striking.

The sight of it was almost enough to distract him from the icy blue gaze piercing between his shoulder blades.

Almost.

"Grayson!"

Gerard stared after his wife and tried to discern her disgruntlement. She was quite obviously put out by something he'd done, though he had no notion of what it could be. However, he was not surprised. Aside from his afternoon of wondrously satisfying bedsport, the rest of his day had been hellish.

He heaved a sigh and turned away. "Yes, Bartley?"

"It appears your brother was serious when he mentioned coming here. He arrived over an hour past and according to the footman stationed at the door, he has yet to depart."

Looking back over the crush, Gerard failed to see Spencer anywhere, but he watched as Isabel stepped onto a crowded outer terrace with Hargreaves. He wished he could speak with her, but he'd learned it was best to tackle one problem at a time, and Spencer was the graver issue at the moment. He trusted Pel. He could not say the same for his hotheaded brother.

"I shall start with the card room," he murmured, grateful to have run into Bartley as the man was exiting Nonnie's Tavern. This ball was the last place he would have searched for Spencer.

"Is that not Hargreaves with Lady Grayson?" Bartley asked, scowling.

"Yes." Gerard turned away.

"Should you not say something to him?"

"What would I say? He is a good man and Isabel a sensible woman. Nothing untoward will happen."

"Well, even I know that," Bartley said with a laugh. "And how like you not to pay any mind. But if you are serious about courting your wife, I would suggest at least the pretense of jealousy."

Gerard shook his head. "Ridiculous. And I am certain Pel would say the same."

"Women are odd creatures, Gray. Perhaps there is something about the fairer sex I know that you do not," Bartley chortled.

"I doubt that." Gerard moved away to find the card room. "You say my brother was only slightly out of sorts?"

"So it seemed to me. However, he is certainly aware of my friendship with you. That might have sufficed to keep his mouth shut on the matter."

"One can only hope he showed such discretion all evening."

Bartley followed fast on his heels. "What will you do when you find him?"

Gerard came to a halt, easily absorbing the impact of Bartley against his back.

"What the devil?" Bartley mumbled.

Turning, Gerard said, "The search will progress far more swiftly if we part ways."

"Won't be near as fun."

"I am not here to have fun."

"How will I find you, if I manage to find him?"

"You will manage, clever chap that you are." Gerard continued on, leaving Bartley behind. The starch in his cravat was chafing, Pel was close and yet so far away, the upcoming confrontation with his brother weighed heavily . . . Altogether, his mood was not the most charitable.

And as his search lengthened, his mood only grew worse.

Isabel stepped onto the crowded balcony and attempted to ignore how Grayson's cut had wounded her. She thought it would be a difficult task, but as she spied a familiar head of graying hair, her thoughts were immediately directed elsewhere. She sighed. Releasing Hargreaves, she said, "We should part ways now."

Following her gaze, he nodded and quickly retreated, leaving her to make her approach to the Dowager Countess of Grayson. The older woman met her halfway and linked arms, leading her away from the other guests.

"Have you no shame?" the dowager whispered.

"Do you truly expect me to reply?" Isabel retorted. Four years and she still had not learned to tolerate the woman.

"How a woman of your breeding can show so little concern for the title she bears is beyond my collection. Grayson has always done his best to irritate me, but marriage to you is beyond the pale."

"Can you please find something new to harp about?" Shaking her head, Isabel pulled away. Now that they were no longer in sight of anyone, the pretense of familiarity could be dropped. The dowager's fervent desire to maintain the esteem of the Grayson name and lineage was understandable, but the manner in which she sought to achieve her aim was not one Isabel could champion.

"I will see him rid of you before I take my last breath."

"Good luck," Isabel muttered.

"I beg your pardon?" The dowager drew herself up.

"I have spoken to Grayson about separation many times since his return. He refuses."

"You have no wish to be married to him?" The dowager's complete astonishment would have amused Isabel if she were less distressed over Gray's behavior since leaving her bed. To be set aside so easily . . . To be ignored so directly . . . To have trusted a man who lied to her . . .

It hurt, and she had promised herself that no man would ever hurt her again.

"No, I do not." She lifted her chin. "The reasons for our marriage seem foolish and ill-conceived now. I'm certain they always have been and we were both too obstinate to take note."

"Isabel." The dowager pursed her lips and fingered her weighty sapphire necklace with a narrowed, thoughtful glance. "You are serious?"

"Yes."

"Grayson insists that a petition for divorce will meet with failure. In any case, the scandal will be dreadful for all."

Tugging off one of her long gloves, Isabel reached out and fingered the petals of a nearby rose. So Gray had been considering severing their bond. She should have known.

How unfortunate for her that she was a woman who relished the companionship of others. She thrived on it. Perhaps if she did not, she would not feel such a need to be held and cared for, and she would not be in this position now. Many women abstained. She could not.

She sighed. The censure heaped on them for a divorce petition would be devastating, but how much more devastating would marriage to Grayson be? She'd nearly been destroyed by her last spouse and her attraction to the man Gray had become was just as powerful as what she had once felt for Pelham.

"What do you want me to say?" she asked bitterly. "That I am prepared for and accepting of a future as a woman divorced for adultery? I am not."

"But you are resolved, I can see it in the set of your shoulders. And I will help you."

Isabel turned at that. "You will *what?*"

"You heard me." A slight smile softened the dowager's

harshly drawn mouth. "I am not sure *how* I will help you. I only know that I will, in whatever manner I can. Perhaps I will even see you well settled."

Suddenly, the events of the day were too much for Isabel. "Excuse me." She would find Rhys and ask him to escort her home. Faulkner scratches wounded her on all sides, and she wished for her room and a decanter of Madeira more than she wished for her next breath.

"I shall be in touch, Isabel," the dowager marchioness called after her.

"Lovely," she muttered, speeding up her steps. "I cannot wait."

Frustrated by his lack of success in finding Spencer, Gerard was about to do violence to someone, when he turned a corner and came to an abrupt halt, his way blocked by a woman backing out of a dark room.

She turned and jumped. "Good heavens," Lady Stanhope cried, her gloved hand sheltering her heart. "You frightened me, Grayson."

He studied her with an arched brow. Flushed and slightly disheveled, she was obviously fresh from some assignation. When the door opened again and Spencer stepped out with crumpled cravat, Gerard's other brow rose to match the first. "I have been looking for you for hours."

"You have?"

His brother was clearly far more relaxed than he had been earlier. Intimately familiar with Barbara's sexual appetite, Gerard was not surprised. He smiled. This was exactly how he had hoped to find Spencer.

"I would like to speak with you."

Spencer straightened his coat and shot a glance at Barbara, who hovered. "Tomorrow perhaps?"

Studying him carefully, Gerard asked, "What are your plans for this evening?" He would not wait if his brother was still intent on some trouble.

Another pointed glance at Barbara settled Gerard's worries. If Spencer was fucking, he would not be fighting. "Breakfast in my study, then."

"Very well."

Lifting Barbara's bare hand to his lips, Spencer sketched an elegant bow and moved away, most likely to arrange their departure.

"I will be along in a moment, darling." Barbara's eyes remained locked on Gerard.

When they were alone, he said, "I am grateful for your association with Lord Spencer."

"Oh?" She made a moue. "A tiny flare of jealousy would be welcome, Grayson."

He snorted. "There is nothing between us to warrant jealousy, and there never has been."

Her hand came up to rest against his abdomen, her green eyes sparkling mischievously through her lashes. "There could be, if only you would warm my bed again. Although our liaison the other evening was lamentably short, it reminded me of how beautifully you and I suit each other."

"Ah, Lady Stanhope," Pel said tightly behind him. "Thank you for locating my husband for me."

Gerard did not have to turn around to know that his evening had, impossibly, taken a turn for the worse.

As the obviously rumpled countess moved away, Isabel stood silently, her fists clenched. Grayson eyed her warily, his powerful frame tense with expectation while she considered what she wanted to do. She had once fought hard for Pelham, and the effort had been draining and pointless. Husbands lied and strayed. Practical wives understood this.

With her heart encased in the icy shell she had learned to rely on, she simply turned her back to Gray with the intent to leave—the ball, his house, *him.* In her mind she was already packing, her brain quickly sorting through her belongings.

"Isabel."

That voice. She shivered. Why must he have that raspy bedroom voice that dripped lust and decadence?

Her steps did not falter, and when he caught her elbow to stay her egress, her thoughts shifted to her previous home and how all of her furniture would be sadly out of date.

Gray's gloved hand cupped her cheek. Forced her gaze to meet his. She registered blue eyes of a striking color and thought of her parlor settee, which was of a similar tone. She would have to throw it out.

"Christ," he muttered harshly. "Don't look at me like that."

Her gaze dropped to where his large hand gripped her forearm.

Before she realized it, he had pulled her into a dark room that reeked of sex and closed the door behind them. Her stomach roiled, and feeling the overwhelming urge to flee, she hurried across the moonlit space toward a room on the other side. It was a library where windowed doors led outside. There she paused and leaned her hands upon the back of a leather wingback chair, sucking in deep breaths of untainted air.

"Isabel." Gray's hands gripped her shoulders, moved down to tug her grip free of the chair back, and then linked his fingers with hers. His body was feverishly hot against her back. She began to sweat.

Green, perhaps? No, that wouldn't do. Gray's study was green. Lavender, then? A lavender settee would be a change. Or pink. No man would want to visit a pink parlor. Wouldn't that be lovely?

"Would you talk to me, please?" he coaxed. He was very good at coaxing. And wheedling and charming and fucking. A girl could lose her head over him if she lowered her guard.

"Tassels."

"What?"

He turned her to face him.

"Pink with gold tassels in the parlor," she said.

"Fine. Pink flatters my coloring."

"You will not be invited to my parlor."

His lips pursed, his frown deepened. "The hell I won't. You are not leaving me, Pel. What you overheard does not mean what you think."

"I do not think anything, my lord," she said evenly. "If you will excuse me . . ." She sidestepped.

He kissed her.

Like candle-warmed brandy the kiss hit her stomach first, then spread outward. Intoxicating. Making her thoughts and blood run sluggishly. Needing air, she took a deep breath through her nose and smelled Gray. Starched linen. Clean skin.

His embrace tightened, lifting her slightly until only the tips of her curled toes brushed against the Aubusson rug beneath them. Against her belly she felt his cock stir, but his mouth connected sweetly with hers, his tongue tasting and licking, not plunging. As the ice inside her melted under the heat of his ardor, she moaned. His lips were so beautiful, so soft against hers. The lips of an angel . . . with the skill and ability to deceive like the devil.

Clean skin.

Gray's mouth traveled along her cheekbone until he nuzzled against her ear.

"As impossible as it is, I want you again." He rounded the chair and sank into it, holding her in his lap as if she were a small child. "After this afternoon, my hunger should have settled down to a minor craving, yet at this moment it seems worse than before."

"I know what I heard," she whispered, refusing to believe what her nose suggested was the truth.

"My brother is brash," he continued, ignoring her. "And I wasted hours looking for him tonight. Still, despite the knowledge that he could be wounded, or could seriously wound someone else, it was the desire to be with you that created my unholy impatience."

"You have been with that woman intimately. Recently."

"I was relieved to learn he'd vented his earlier anger with a quick rut in the next room."

Isabel stilled. "Lord Spencer?"

"I was even more pleased to see him departing with Lady Stanhope to continue their activities in a more appropriate venue. His doing so frees the rest of my evening to seduce you."

"She wants you."

"So do you," he said smoothly. "I am an attractive man with an attractive purse and an attractive title." He pushed her gently away so he could meet her gaze. "I also have an attractive wife."

"Have you fucked her since you returned?"

"No." His mouth brushed across hers. "And I know you find that hard to believe."

Strangely, she didn't.

"If I were you, Pel, I am not certain I would believe a scoundrel like me either, especially with your past."

Her spine straightened. "My past does not signify." She'd had enough pity to last a lifetime, she did not require any more. Certainly she did not want any from Gray.

"Ah, but it does, as I am beginning to see." His face was stark in its perfection, his eyes narrowed and considering. The hard edges to his lips and mouth he'd shown when he first returned were back. Signs of a deep sadness.

"I am not a good man for you, Pel. I am not good at all. All men have faults, but I'm afraid I am nothing but faults. Still, I am yours and you must learn to bear with me, because I am selfish and refuse to let you go."

"Why?"

She held her breath, but it was his next words that made her dizzy.

"You heal me."

His eyes closed and he pressed his cheek to hers, the tender gesture startling her to the very marrow of her bones. The Marquess of Grayson was known for a great many things, but tenderness was not one of them. The fact that these displays were becoming more frequent in number terrified her. She could not be the salve that mended him for another woman.

"Perhaps I can heal you, too," he whispered against her mouth. "If you allow me to."

For a brief moment, she pressed her lips to his. Exhausted by the stresses of the day, she longed to curl into his chest and sleep for days. Instead, she wiggled off his lap and stood. "If healing means forgetting, I want no part of it."

He heaved out a breath as weary in sound as she felt.

"I have learned from my past mistakes, Gray, and I am glad to have learned." Her fingers twisted together restlessly. "Forgetting is not my aim. I *never* want to forget."

"Then teach me how to live with my mistakes, Pel." He stood.

She looked at him. Studied him.

"We should leave London," he said urgently. Coming to her, he caught up her hands.

"What?" Her eyes widened and she shivered. *Alone with Gray.*

"We cannot function together as a couple here."

"A couple?" Her head shook violently.

The door opened, startling them both. Gray pulled her to him with lightning speed, protecting her in an all-encompassing embrace.

Lord Hammond, the owner of the library in which they stood, blinked in the doorway. "I beg your pardon." He began to back out, and then stopped. "Lord Grayson? Is that you?"

"Yes," Gray drawled softly.

"With Lady Grayson?"

"Who else would I be consorting with in a darkened room?"

"Well . . . Ah . . ." Hammond cleared his throat. "No one else, of course."

The door began to swing closed again, and Gray took the opportunity to cup her breast. His mouth lowered toward hers, taking ruthless advantage of her inability to pull away.

"Er, Lord Grayson?" Hammond called out.

Gray sighed and raised his head. "Yes?"

"Lady Hammond has arranged a house party this weekend at our country estate near Brighton. She would be beyond pleased if you and Lady Grayson would attend. And I would relish the opportunity to reacquaint myself with you."

Isabel gasped as Gray's grip flexed rhythmically around her breast. Without the aid of candlelight or a fire, they could not be seen clearly. Still, the fact that another individual stood inches away from where she was being fondled so intimately made her heart race.

"How large is the party?"

"Not large I'm afraid. A dozen at last count, but Lady Hammond—"

"Sounds perfect," Gray interjected, his fingers tugging at her hardened nipple. "We accept your invitation."

"Truly?" Hammond's portly frame drew up to the limits of its inconsiderable height.

"Truly." Clutching her hand, Gray dragged her from the room, squeezing past the viscount, who was too surprised to move quickly enough.

Her emotions a morass, Isabel followed with only a slight drag.

Hammond followed quickly behind them. "Friday morning we set off. Is that acceptable?"

"It's *your* party, Hammond."

"Oh, yes . . . That's true. Friday, then."

With a deliberate flick of his wrist, Gray signaled a nearby footman to fetch cloak and carriage, and turned to another servant who hovered nearby. "Tell Lord Trenton I said his obligation has been met."

It was not lost on Isabel how easily her husband had managed to achieve his aim to spirit her away. She almost wished she could be angry about it, but she was too stunned.

Her husband had not lied or strayed.

But whether that was a blessing or a curse, she could not yet say.

Chapter 13

As the Grayson carriage pulled into the crowded drive of the Hammond residence, Isabel could not bite back her groan. One guest in particular filled her with dread.

Sitting across from her, Gray arched his brow in silent query.

Your mother, she mouthed, showing caution so as not to anger Lord Spencer, who shared a squab with her husband.

Gray pinched the bridge of his nose with a loud sigh.

Suddenly all the anticipation she'd had for the upcoming long weekend party fled. Stepping down from the carriage with Gray's assistance, she managed a smile and took inventory of the assembled guests. She shuddered when the Dowager Lady Grayson gifted her with a conspiratorial wink. There was no avoiding the fact that Isabel had liked the woman better when they had been at odds.

"Bella."

The relief she felt at the sound of the voice behind her was dizzying. Turning, she caught Rhys' outstretched hands like a lifeline thrown to a drowning woman. His smile was brilliant, his rich mahogany hair capped by a dashing hat.

"What are you doing here?" she asked, well aware that tame country parties were not his preference.

He shrugged. "I feel the need for a little respectable company."

Her eyes narrowed. "Are you ill?"

Laughing, he shook his head. "No, though I do believe I've caught a bit of melancholia. Something I'm certain a few days of fresh country air will do wonders to cure."

"Melancholia?" Tugging off her glove, Isabel pressed her wrist to his forehead.

Rhys rolled his eyes. "Since when does a bad mood cause fevers?"

"You have never been in a bad mood in your life."

"There is a first for everything."

A firm grip at her waist drew her attention.

"Grayson," her brother greeted, his gaze lifting above her head.

"Trenton," Gray returned. "I would not have expected to find you here."

"A temporary bout of insanity."

"Ah." Gray tugged her closer, a motion which had her gazing up at him with wide eyes. They'd had an unspoken accord to avoid touching each other in public, since it seemed to spark a flare of lust neither could control. "I appear to be suffering from the same ailment."

"Grayson. Isabel. Lovely to see you both here," the dowager said as she approached.

As Isabel opened her mouth to reply, Gray squeezed the upper swell of her buttock. She jumped, startling his mother. Reaching behind her, she swatted at his hand.

"Are you unwell?" the dowager asked, frowning in disapproval. "You should not have come if you are ill or out of sorts."

"She is perfectly healthy," Gray said smoothly. "As I can well attest."

Isabel stomped on his booted foot, although doing so caused no damage at all. *What was his intent?* She could not collect. To tease her so openly . . .

"Crudity is common," his mother reproved. "And beneath a man of your station."

"But, Mother, it is so enjoyable."

"Lord and Lady Grayson! How lovely of you to come."

Turning her head, Isabel found Lady Hammond descending the stairs from her front door. "We are delighted to be invited, of course," she replied.

"Now that you have arrived," the viscountess continued, "we can set off. What a lovely day to make the trip, don't you agree?"

"I do," she murmured, eager to return to their carriage.

"I shall ride with you, Grayson," the dowager said.

Isabel winced, suddenly finding the prospect of the day-long drive a torment.

Gray gave a soothing caress down the length of her spine, but the comfort it offered did not last. The rest of the morning and afternoon was spent in the tight confines of their traveling coach listening to his mother chastising them all for one transgression or another. She could only imagine the horror of living with a parent who found fault with everything, and she surreptitiously stroked Gray's thigh with the back of her hand in sympathy. He sat deathly silent the entire ride, coming to life only when they stopped to change horses and take luncheon.

It was with great relief that they arrived at the Hammonds' lovely country estate late in the day. As soon as the carriage rolled to a halt, Grayson leapt out and assisted her down. That was when she caught sight of Hargreaves, and realized why Grayson had been acting as possessive as he had. Even now, despite his outward appearance of boredom, she sensed his alertness in the proximity he kept to her and the slow sweep of his gaze across the drive.

"What a lovely estate," the dowager cried, bringing the pleased smile of the viscountess her way. It was indeed a praiseworthy property with its lovely golden brick exterior and profusion of colorful flowers and climbing vines.

A week here under other circumstances would be a joy. Considering the personages in attendance, including Lady

Stanhope who was presently ogling Gray in a manner that riled Isabel, she doubted that would be the case in this instance. "We should have remained in London," she muttered.

"Shall we go?" Gray asked. "I have an estate not far from here."

She turned wide eyes to him. "Are you mad?" But she could see in the intensity of his blue eyes that he was quite willing to leave. While it seemed sometimes that no trace of the Grayson she once knew remained, flashes of the one she recalled occasionally appeared. He was more polished, more somber, but no less ruthless than he always had been. "No."

He sighed and offered his arm. "I knew you would say that. I hope you are amenable to spending a great deal of time in our rooms."

"We could have spent time in our rooms at home. Here it will be rude."

"You should have mentioned that earlier and saved us the trip."

"Don't foist the blame for this on me," she whispered, shivering slightly at the feel of his powerful forearm flexing beneath her fingertips. "This was entirely your doing."

"I wanted to travel away," he said dryly, his sidelong glance revealing his knowledge of his affect on her, "and spend some time with you and Spencer. I had no notion this would turn into a gathering of all the people we most wished to avoid."

"Isabel!"

Rhys' cry caught their attention. Walking backward with his gaze directed elsewhere, her brother nearly ran her over. Grayson, however, stepped in as a formidable buffer and saved her.

"Beg your pardon," her brother offered quickly, then he looked at her with a tangible excitement about him. "Do you know who that woman is over there?"

Looking around his tall frame, she saw a small group of women speaking with Lady Hammond. "Which one?"

"The brunette to the right of Lady Stanhope."

"Oh . . . Yes, I know her, although at the moment, her name eludes me."

"Abby?" he prompted. "Abigail?"

"Ah, yes! Abigail Stewart. Niece to Lord Hammond. His sister and her entrepreneurial American husband have passed on, leaving Miss Stewart orphaned, though quite wealthy I've been told."

"An heiress," Rhys said softly.

"Poor thing," Isabel said with a commiserating shake of her head. "She was hounded to death last season by every scapegrace and destitute man in England. I spoke with her briefly once. She is very bright. A bit rough around the edges, but charming."

"I never noticed her."

"Why would you? She hides herself well and she is not your type of female at all. Too smart for you," she teased.

"Yes . . . I'm certain that is true." He walked away frowning.

"I think you were correct," Gray said, his voice low and near enough to make her senses leap to attention. "I do believe he's ill. Perhaps we can follow his lead. You and I can feign poor constitutions and lie abed for a week. Together. Unclothed."

"You are incorrigible," she said, laughing.

With quiet efficiency, they and the other guests were settled in their rooms to freshen up before the evening meal. Gerard made certain that Isabel was well established and tended by her abigail, before excusing himself to meet with the other gentlemen below.

Despite the unfortunate choice of guests, he found some slight convenience in it. The odd menagerie created by the presence of his mother and Hargreaves allowed him to dispense with whatever remaining illusions they had about his marriage to Pel. His affairs were not to be interfered with. Foolish of them, really, to forget how few qualms he had. However, it was no great burden to remind them.

Entering the lower parlor, he took in the design of the room, noting the large windows framed with dark red, tasseled drapes, and the proliferation of burgundy leather chairs. A man's retreat. Just the type of setting he required to say what needed to be said.

He gave a curt nod to Spencer, refused the cheroot offered to him by Lord Hammond, and then strode across the Aubusson rug toward the window where Hargreaves stood studying the view outside. As he approached, Gerard examined the proud bearing and impeccable attire of the earl. This man had shared two private years with Pel and knew her far better than he himself did.

He remembered how she had been with Markham, lit like a candle with confidence and sparkling eyes. The contrast to the purely mercenary sexual regard with which she held him was striking and disturbing. The casual friendship they had once shared was now marred by tension. He missed the ease he'd once felt with her, and longed to bask in the kind of affectionate attentions she shared with others.

"Hargreaves," he murmured.

"Lord Grayson." The earl turned cool dark eyes on him. They were almost of a height, with Gerard having only a slight advantage. "Before you try to waylay attempts on my part to woo back Isabel, allow me to tell you I have no intentions in that regard."

"No?"

"No, but if she comes to me I will not turn her away."

"Despite the hazard such an action would place you in?" Gerard was a man of action, not empty threats. By the slight nod Hargreaves gave him, he could see the other man knew it.

"You cannot cage a woman like Isabel, Grayson. She values her freedom more than anything. I am certain it chafes her to realize she married you to be free, and yet finds herself trapped." His shoulders lifted in a shrug. "Besides, you will tire of her eventually or she of you, and this desire you have to claim her so primitively will fade."

"My *claim*," Gerard said dryly, "is not merely primitive. It is also legal and binding."

Hargreaves shook his head. "You have always wanted women who belong to someone else."

"In this case, the woman I want belongs to me."

"Does she? Truly? Odd you should discover that after five years of marital oblivion. I have seen you together since your return, as has everyone else. In truth, it appears you barely tolerate one another."

Gerard's mouth curved in a slow smile. "We definitely more than tolerate one another."

The earl's face flushed. "I do not have time to school you on women, Grayson, but suffice it to say that orgasms are not all a woman requires to be content. Isabel will not grow an attachment to you, she is incapable of it, and even if she were open to elevated feelings, an inconstant man such as yourself will never appeal. You are much like Pelham, you know. He, too, failed to see the prize that was his. I cannot count the number of times Isabel would tell me some humorous tale of your exploits and finish with, 'Just like Pelham used to do.'"

A blow to his gut could not have struck Gerard harder. Outwardly impassive, his insides knotted with apprehension. Markham had said the same. There could be no worse mark against him than to remind his wife of her late husband. If he could not, at the very least, prove himself better than Pelham, he would never win Isabel's affections.

But she had written him faithfully every week, and held on to that tenuous tie. Surely, there was some hope to be found in that?

Damn it! Why had he disregarded those letters?

"You say she is incapable of deep affections, and yet you think she may return to *you,* when she has never been known to revisit a paramour once finished with him?"

"Because we are friends. I know how she likes her tea, what her favorite books are . . ." Hargreaves straightened. "She was happy with me before you returned—"

"No. She was not. You know this as well as I." Isabel would not have been tempted away if Hargreaves had been what she wanted. She was not a fickle woman. But she *was* a woman who bore wounds, and Gerard was determined to heal them.

The earl's jaw tightened. "I think we understand each other. There is nothing left to be said. You are aware of my position. I am aware of yours."

Gerard tilted his head slightly in acknowledgment. "*Are* you aware? Be certain, Hargreaves. I am easily irritated and frankly, I will not have this conversation again. Next time I feel the urge to remind you of my marriage, I shall demonstrate the finer points of this discourse with the tip of my blade."

"Gentlemen, can I regale you with my tales of India?" Lord Hammond intruded, his gaze shifting nervously between them. "A fascinating country, I must say."

"Thank you, Hammond," Gerard said. "Perhaps over port this evening."

He withdrew and crossed the room to Spencer, who raised both brows as he approached.

"Only you, Gray, would be so brazen."

"Time is precious I've learned. I see no point in squandering it when directness works so well."

Spencer laughed. "I must admit, I was resigned to a week of lassitude. I am pleased to see there won't be a dull moment."

"Certainly not. I intend to keep you busy."

"Do you?"

Spencer's eyes lit up bright enough to compete with his

grin. Gerard realized again how much influence he had on his younger brother. He only hoped he made full and positive use of it.

"Yes. There is a Grayson property only an hour's ride from here. We will go there tomorrow."

"Smashing!"

Gerard smiled. "Now, if you will excuse me . . ."

"Can't stay away from her for long, can you?" Spencer shook his head. "You are more randy than I will ever be, I think. Much as it pains me to admit that."

"You assume when we are alone we only stay abed."

Spencer snorted. "Are you saying that is not the case?"

"I refuse to say anything at all."

Sinking deeper into her cooling bathwater, Isabel knew she should finish, but could not seem to manage the strength to do so. Despite how often she serviced him, Grayson's sexual appetite for her had not abated at all. Sleep was a luxury she snatched when she could.

She almost wished she could complain, but she was too sated to make the effort. It was difficult to muster true irritation when the man ensured she had a few orgasms for every one of his. And he had quite a lot.

He had begun to use French letters, no longer capable of withdrawing before he came. The lessening of sensation for him meant that he could fuck longer, a circumstance she had appreciated previously with the lovers she saw only once or twice a week. With her amorous husband it was very nearly too much. He enjoyed her writhing and begging for mercy beneath him, continuing the sensual torment until she could do nothing but whimper in pleasure and take what he gave her.

The man was an animal, nipping with his teeth, bruising with his hands, and she loved every moment of it. Grayson's passion was real, not practiced like Pelham's had been.

Isabel sighed. Against her will, memories of the last house

party she'd attended with her late husband filled her mind, bringing with them the all too familiar roiling in her stomach. He had been in top philandering form then, dallying with other women in alcoves and slipping from his room at night. The entire fortnight had been hell, the time spent wondering which of the women drinking tea with her had serviced her husband the night before. By the time they left, she was fairly certain all the attractive ones had.

From that occasion onward, she'd denied Pelham her bed, which he had the temerity to protest until he realized she would cause him bodily injury if he insisted. Eventually, they had ceased to travel together at all.

The adjoining door opened and Gray's delicious voice dismissed her abigail. His footfalls as he approached were as sure and confident as always. There was a rhythm to them, a cadence, the sound of dominance. Grayson took for granted that every time he entered a room he owned it.

"You're chilled," he noted, his voice coming so close to her ear she knew he must be crouching beside her. "Let me assist you out."

Opening her eyes, she saw his outstretched hand, saw his face so close to hers, so intent on her. The way he examined her always took her off guard. Of course, she often found herself staring at him in the same manner.

As was happening more often, the sudden flare of possessiveness the sight of him aroused was painful and piercing. He was a man any woman would beg to claim as her own private property, but she, the only woman who had the right to do so, could not. Would not.

He had removed his clothes and now wore only a thick silk robe. Before she could stop herself, Isabel touched his shoulder and watched the blue of his eyes turn to icy fire. A touch, a smile, a lick of her lips—all could stoke his ardor in the space of one breath.

"I'm weary," she warned.

"You start it, Pel. Every damn time." As he stood, he pulled her up with him and then held a towel out for her.

"I do not!"

As he wrapped her, he kissed the tender spot where her shoulder met her throat—a gentle press of his lips to her flesh, not the heated open-mouthed kisses she had grown used to. "Yes, you do. On purpose. You want me panting for you."

"Your 'panting' is inconvenient."

"I have come to realize you like it inconvenient. You like me hard and aching for you in public, and in private. You like me mindless with lust until I would fuck you anywhere, in front of anyone, at any time."

She snorted, but shivered at his tone and the feel of his breath gusting across her damp skin.

Was it true? Was her aim to provoke him?

"You are always mindless with lust, Gray. You always have been."

"No. Lustful, yes. Mindless with it, never. Sometimes, I actually think I could take you in public, Isabel, the craving is so provoking. Deny me now, and I may bend you over the dinner table and provide the evening's entertainment." He nibbled her earlobe.

She laughed. "There is no hope for you. You are a beast."

He growled playfully and nuzzled against her. "You know how to tame me."

"Do I?" Turning in his arms, she faced him with a smile and brushed one fingertip across the bare skin revealed by the part in his dressing robe.

"Yes. You do." Gray caught her hand and thrust it lower, between the parting of his robe at his thighs so that she felt how hard he was.

"It is nearly ridiculous how quickly you rouse," she chastised with a shake of her head.

And he was so base about it, so blatant. Yes, she was seduced by him, but he was not a seducer. Perhaps his outrageous handsomeness had made the need for coaxing unnecessary. Or perhaps it was the size of the cock that throbbed against her palm. That would accomplish the task for him nicely.

He flexed inside her clasp and smiled with wicked arrogance.

She smiled back, admitting to herself that she quite liked primitive. No games, no insincerity, no guessing.

"You don't *feel* tamed." She moved in a way that caused the towel about her to puddle on the floor. Stroking the heated length of his shaft, she licked her lips.

"Witch." He stepped forward, pushing her back, catching her hips when she stumbled in surprise. "You enslave me with sex."

"Not true." He rarely allowed her the lead, preferring to remain in control.

"I came in here with the express purpose of taking a nap. You instigated everything I must now do to you to slake my craving enough to catch some sleep."

The backs of her thighs hit the high bed, and he lifted and tossed her upon the turned-down mattress. Then he shed his robe and crawled over her.

Staring up at him, she found herself smitten with his smile, with the gleam in his eyes, with the dark silky hair that fell over his brow. How different he was from the brooding, gloomy man who had stood in her drawing room so recently. *Had she wrought this change? Did she hold that much sway over him?*

Her eyes drifted lower.

"That look," he said dryly, "is the reason we spend so much time in this position."

"What look?" Isabel batted her lashes mischievously, enjoying the renewed teasing banter she'd missed. There always seemed to be so much tension between them. Its absence was a pleasure.

Gray dipped his head and licked the tip of her nose, then pressed his mouth to hers. "It says, *Fuck me, Gerard. Spread my thighs, mount me, make me hoarse and limp from pleasure.*"

"Good heavens," she purred. "It's a wonder I manage a word in edgewise with such chatty eyes."

"Hmmm . . ." His voice lowered to the tone she recognized as the immediate herald to troublemaking. "I certainly cannot manage speech when you look at me like that. Drives me insane."

"Perhaps you shouldn't look at me, then," she suggested, her hands coming up to stroke his lean hips.

"You would never allow me to ignore you, Pel. You foster my infatuation at every turn."

Infatuation. She shivered. *Could he care for her? Did she want him to?* "Why would I do such a thing?"

"Because you don't want my attention to wander." He kissed her before she could digest what he said.

Isabel lay still, her mouth ravished by a kiss that curled her toes, Gray's tongue licking across hers, gliding under it, drinking from her as if she were some delicacy. All the while in her mind, she considered what he had said. *Was she attempting to bind him to her with sexual extortion?*

When Gray lifted his head, his breathing was as disturbed as hers. "You do not afford me even half a moment to think of another woman." His eyelids lowered, shuttering his thoughts. "You take me to your bed at every opportunity. You exhaust me—"

"Ha. Your appetite is inexhaustible." But the rejoinder that was meant to be dismissing, was instead shaky and inflected with a question. *Had she gone from wanting him to stray, to wanting to keep him all to herself?*

In one graceful, fluid movement, he rolled and brought her over him. "I require as much sleep as any other human." He pressed his fingers over her mouth to silence a coming protest. "I am not so young as to forgo sleep altogether, so discard any attempt to use that excuse again. You are not too old for me. I am not too young for you."

Catching his wrist, she tugged his hand away. "You could always sleep apart from me."

"Don't be daft. You mistake my observation for a complaint, which it is not." Gray stroked the curve of her spine, applying pressure so that her breasts connected more fully to his chest. "Perhaps once or twice it has crossed my mind that I should manage my cock, instead of allowing it to lead me. But then I remember the feel of your cunt in orgasm, the way it clutches me, the way you arch up and cry out my name. And I tell my brain to cease prattling and leave me alone."

Dropping her forehead to his chest, Isabel laughed.

He tucked her into his side. "If you require a physical display of my affections at this moment, I am more than prepared to oblige you. We can't have you worried about waning interest and all that. Whatever you need, Pel, to make it possible to believe in me, I will do it. I suppose I should have stated that bluntly earlier so there would be no doubt. I am not Pelham."

The look in his eyes was fond, with banked lust—the look of a man who was just as content to hold her as he was to ride her.

Her throat tightened, her eyes stung.

"Where did you find these sudden insights into my behavior?" she asked softly. The Grayson she'd married had never looked far enough beyond himself to see such things.

"I told you, you have my undivided attention." His fingers plunged into her hair, loosening and then pulling out the pins that held it up, before tossing them to the floor. "There is no other person I would wish to be with more than you, female or otherwise. You make me laugh, you always have. You never allow me to become too full of myself. You see all of my faults and find most of them charming. I've no need of any other companions. In fact, you and I will remain in our rooms this evening."

"Now who's daft? Everyone will think we are up here having sex if we skip dinner."

"And they will not be wrong," he murmured, his lips to her forehead. "We are honeymooners, they should expect nothing less from us."

Honeymoon. Just that one word brought back the dreams she'd once had of a passionate, monogamous marriage. How hopeful she had been then. How naïve. She should be too old to experience that kind of eager anticipation for the future.

Should be. But was finding the opposite was true.

"But we shall also take our meal together up here," he continued, "and play chess. I will tell you of my—"

"You hate chess," she reminded, pulling back to look at him.

"Actually, I have learned to enjoy it. And I am quite good. Be prepared to suffer defeat."

Isabel stared up at him. So many times, she felt as if a stranger had returned to her. A man who looked very much like the man she married, but wasn't. *How much had he changed?* He was so mercurial. Even now he seemed different from the man who had left her room just an hour before.

"Who are you?" she breathed, her hand reaching up to touch his face, to trace the arch of his brow. So much the same. So very different.

His smile faded. "I am your husband, Isabel."

"No, you are not." She pressed him back, sliding over him again. The texture of his hard body was so wonderful to her—the hard ridges and planes, the dusting of hair over his sun-darkened skin.

"How can you say that?" he asked, his voice turning husky as she moved upon him. "You stood next to me at the altar. You said the vows, and heard mine."

Lowering her head, she took his mouth in a lush kiss, suddenly wanting him. Not because she was physically unable to resist the temptation he presented, but because she saw something in him she had failed to see before—commitment. He was committed to her, to learning about her and understanding her. The knowledge made her shiver, made her sink into his embrace, made her relish the feel of his strong arms encircling her back.

He turned his head, evading her questing mouth. Panting, he said, "Don't do this."

"Do what?" She caressed the length of his torso, cupped his hip, shifted so she could reach between his legs.

"Don't tell me I am not your husband and then silence me with sex. We will have this out, Pel. No more of this nonsense about mistresses and the like."

She stroked his cock with a firm, sure hand. If anything proved that Gray had changed it was his resistance to lovemaking while seeking a deeper connection. Despite every bit of her brain that said her life experiences were correct in their dismissal of lasting marital affection, some tiny voice inside her urged her to believe otherwise.

He caught her wrist and bucked with a curse, taking the advantage. Looming over her, he pinned her arms to the bed. His face above her was hard as stone, his eyes glittering with the determination that was mirrored by his tense jaw.

"You've no wish to fuck me?" she asked innocently.

Growling, he said, "There is a heart and mind attached to the cock you enjoy so well. Altogether they form a man—your spouse. You cannot fragment the whole and take only the pieces you want."

His declaration shook her, then decided her. Pelham . . . the Grayson she once knew . . . Neither would ever say such a thing. Whoever this man was above her, she desired to know him. To discover him, and the woman she felt like when she was with him.

"You are not the husband I said my vows to." She saw him

prepared to protest, and rushed ahead. "I did not want him, Gerard. You know that."

The sound of his name sent a visible ripple through the length of his frame. His gaze narrowed. "What are you saying?"

She arched beneath him, stretching, enticing. Spreading her thighs, she welcomed him. Opened to him. "I want you."

"Isabel . . . ?" He pressed his damp forehead to hers, his hips settled against hers, his heavy cock finding her slick for him through no physical manipulation on his part. "Christ, you will be the death of me."

Her head fell to the side as he entered her slowly. So slowly. Bare skin to bare skin. She had missed the feel of him this way, without a barrier between them.

The difference between this and their usual coupling was marked. When he'd first returned, he had been gentle, but the strain of that control had been obvious. Now, as he rocked deeper and deeper into her eager body, she knew he moved leisurely because this moment was one he wished to lengthen.

His mouth to her ear, he whispered, "Who do you want?"

Her voice came slurred with pleasure. "*You . . .*"

Chapter 14

There were a thousand excuses for why Rhys was standing in the Hammond garden late in the evening. There was only one true reason. And she was presently moving toward him with a shy smile.

"I was hoping I would find you out here," Abby said, holding out her bare hands.

He bit the tip of his gloved finger and yanked off his glove, so that when he caught her hands he could feel them. The simple, chaste contact flared heat across his skin, and he did the last thing a gentleman would do—he pulled her closer.

"Oh my," she breathed, eyes wide. "I do enjoy it when you act the scoundrel."

"I will do much more than act," he warned, "if you continue to seek me out."

"I thought it was *you* seeking *me* out."

"You should stay away, Abby. I seem to have lost my senses where you are concerned."

"And I am a woman who desperately enjoys, perhaps even needs, having a handsome man lose his senses over her. It never happens to me, you know."

His conscience losing the battle, Rhys lifted his hand, cupped her nape and fitted his mouth to hers. She was so slight, so slender, but she lifted to her tiptoes and kissed him back with such sweet ardor that she nearly knocked him off his feet. The soft scent of her perfume mixed with the scents of evening flowers, and he longed to bask in it, roll around a bed in it.

She had dressed differently tonight, in beautiful golden silk that hugged her body perfectly. Understanding how hounded she was by fortune hunters, he appreciated her need to fade into the woodwork with ill-fitting, unattractive garments and hide in dark gardens.

Lifting his head, he murmured, "You are aware of where these meetings are leading?"

She nodded, her chest rising and falling against his with panting breaths.

"Are you also aware of where this can*not* lead? There are limits imposed by my station. I should accept them gracefully and walk away, but I am weak—"

She silenced him with her fingers over his lips, her piquant face lit with a dazzling grin. "I do love that you have no wish at all to marry me. To me, that is not a weakness, but a strength."

Rhys blinked. "Beg your pardon?"

"There is no doubt in my mind that you want *me*, and not my money. It is quite remarkable really."

"Is it?" he choked out, his cock as hard as a poker. Why the devil this woman had such an effect on him he could not collect.

"Quite. Men who look like you never find anything at all appealing about women who look like me."

"Fools, the lot of them." The conviction in his voice was genuine.

Abby leaned her cheek against his chest with a soft laugh. "Of course. Why men like Lord Grayson are so taken with women who look like Lady Grayson when I am around is an absolute mystery."

He stiffened, shocked at the undeniable flare of jealousy he felt. "You are attracted to Grayson?"

"What?" She pulled back. "I find him attractive, certainly.

I doubt there is a woman alive who wouldn't. But I am not attracted to him personally, no."

"Oh . . ." He cleared his throat.

"How will you begin my ravishment?"

"Little one." He shook his head, but could not restrain his indulgent smile. Brushing the back of his hand along the curve of her cheekbone, he admired the way the moon was reflected in her eyes. "Understand, I mean to have more than a few kisses and some improper fondling. I will bare your skin, spread your thighs, steal what should be a gift for your husband."

"That sounds wicked," she breathed, gazing up at him raptly.

"It will be. But I assure you, you will enjoy every moment."

He, however, will probably wallow in guilt for the rest of his life, but he wanted her desperately enough to make that future torment worthwhile.

He pressed his lips very softly to hers, his hand at her waist slipping to cup what felt to be a fine derriere. "Are you certain this is what you want?"

"Yes. I have no doubts. I am seven and twenty. I have met hundreds of gentlemen over the course of my life and none of them have affected me as you have. What if no man ever will but you? I will regret forever that I did not enjoy what I could of your attentions."

His heart clenched painfully. "Losing your virginity to a cad such as myself will make your wedding night very awkward."

"No, it will not," she assured him confidently. "If I do marry, it will be with a man who is smitten enough with me to skip dinner like Lord Grayson has done for Lady Grayson."

"What Grayson feels is not 'smitten,' love," he said dryly.

Abby waved a careless hand. "Whatever name you give to it, he grants no significance to anything in her past. My future spouse will feel the same about me."

"You sound so certain."

"I am. You see, he would have to love me desperately to win my hand, and a little matter of a torn piece of flesh would not matter to him. In fact, I intend to tell any future spouse of mine all about you, and—"

"Good God!"

"Well, not literally," she hastened to say. Her gaze turned dreamy, her smile fond. "I would simply tell him of the man who made my stomach flutter and my heart race when he smiled. How wonderful that man was to me, what happiness he brought me after the death of my parents left my life a misery. And he will understand, Lord Trenton, because when you love someone that is what you do. You understand."

"What a dreamer you are," he scoffed in an attempt to hide how deeply her words touched him.

"Am I?" Frowning, she pulled away. "I suppose you are correct. My mother warned me once that affairs are practical endeavors, not the stuff of romance."

Rhys arched a brow, then linked their fingers and pulled her toward a nearby bench. "Your mother said that?"

"She said it was foolish of women to think that affairs were grand passions and marriages a duty. She said it should be the opposite. Affairs should be nothing more than a satiation of needs. Marriages should be lifelong commitments to deep-seated desires. My mother was a forward-thinking woman. After all, she *did* marry an American."

"Ah yes, that's true." Sitting, he pulled Abby into his lap. She weighed nearly nothing and he tucked her close, resting his chin on her head. "So she is the one responsible for filling your head with all that love nonsense."

"It's not nonsense," she chided. "My parents were mad for each other and very, very happy. The smiles on their faces when they were together again after an absence . . . The glow they had when they shared a smile over the dining table . . . Wonderful."

Licking the exposed column of her throat, he reached her ear and whispered. "I can show you wonderful, Abby."

"Oh my." She shivered. "I swear my stomach just turned a flip."

He loved how he affected her, how open and innocent she was in her responses. She was so pure of character. Not because she was naïve—she saw the workings of the world clearly—but because the less admirable facets of mankind did not disillusion her. Yes, she had been hunted by disreputable gentlemen, but she saw that for what it was—the stupidity and greed of a few men. The rest of the world was given the benefit of her doubt.

It was that quality of hopefulness which he found so irresistible. He would most likely be damned to perdition for taking her, but he could do nothing else. The thought of never having her, never experiencing her joy in passion was unbearable.

"What wing of the manse are you in?" he murmured, wanting to lie with her *now*.

"Let me come to you."

"Why?"

"Because you are the more experienced and jaded of the two of us."

"What does that have to do with anything?" *Would the woman ever cease confounding his wits?*

"You have this scent about you, my lord. Your cologne and soap and starch. It is quite delicious and when your skin heats up, the smell sometimes makes me feel as if I could swoon. I can only imagine how much more pronounced the effect will be after the physical exertions of lovemaking. I doubt I would be able to sleep a wink with that scent all over my bed linens. For you, however, the odor of sex would be nothing of note. Therefore, *I* should smell up *your* sheets, rather than you smell up mine."

"I see." Before he knew what he was doing, he had her bent over the cool stone bench and he was kneeling over her, taking her mouth with a need he had not felt since . . . since . . . *blasted!* Who in hell cared when it had been. It was damn well happening now.

His hands cupped the slight curves of her breasts and squeezed, eliciting a moan from her that swelled upward and filled the area of the garden they occupied. Discovery was a very real hazard and yet he could not find the will to cease. He was drunk on *her* scent, her response, the way she arched upward into his embrace and then shrank back, frightened.

"My very skin aches," she whispered, writhing.

"Hush, love," he soothed, his lips moving against hers.

"I—I feel so hot."

"Shhh, I will ease you." He stroked down the length of her side trying to gentle what was quickly becoming a wild passion.

Her hands slipped between his coat and waistcoat, clawing at his back. The scratching made his cock throb and he paid her in kind by scraping the tips of his short nails across her hardened nipples. With one hand gloved and the other not, he knew the dual sensations would madden her.

"Christ almighty," she gasped. Then she grabbed his ass and yanked their hips together.

His breath hissed between his teeth. She cried out.

"Abby. We must find a room."

She turned her face into his throat, her lips moving feverishly across the sweat-dampened skin. "Take me here."

"Don't tempt me," he muttered, certain he was only minutes away from doing just that. If anyone were to stumble upon them now, there would be no way to explain. He was crouched over her like an obvious lecher. She was the innocent, who hadn't the wherewithal to deny a seasoned rake's advances.

How had they ended up like this? A stolen moment or two of her company, and he was about to break his one cardinal rule: no deflowering virgins. What fun was there in that? No quick rut, this. There would be blood, tears. He would have to seduce her properly, take his time, delay his own gratification . . .

"My lord, please!"

Hell and damnation. It sounded like heaven.

"Abigail." He meant to hurry her off so they could meet naked—er, properly. But he was having the hardest time removing his fingers from around her nipples. Yes, her breasts were small, but her nipples were not. He couldn't wait to—

Her lovely gown tore as he yanked the shoulder down and bared her breast. She cried out again as he lowered his mouth and suckled her. Such long, delicious nipples. They rolled over his tongue like berries and were just as sweet.

"Please, oh please, my lord." She arched upward into his mouth and he almost came, that silken undulation an unbearable tease to his near-to-bursting cock.

It was only the sound of approaching laughter that saved her from ruination on a garden bench.

"Bloody hell." He moved swiftly, pulling her up and straightening her bodice. The nipple he had been sucking poked wantonly through the silk and he rubbed his thumb over it, unable to help himself.

"Don't stop!" she protested loudly, forcing him to cover her mouth with his hand.

"Someone is coming, love." He waited until she nodded her understanding. "Do you know where my room is?" She nodded again. "I will be there shortly. Don't dally. I will hunt you down if you do."

Her eyes widened. Then she nodded emphatically.

"Go."

Rhys watched her take a side path toward the manse and disappear from sight. Then he ducked behind a nearby vine-covered arbor and waited. It wouldn't do for both of them to return to the house too closely to each other. Even if neither or only one were seen, it was best to be overly cautious.

"But to petition Parliament, Celeste?" came Lady Hammond's voice from a nearby intersecting lane. "Think of the scandal!"

"I have thought of nothing but that for nearly five years," retorted the dowager Lady Grayson. "I have never been so mortified as I was when they did not attend dinner this evening. Which was an excellent repast, I must say."

"Thank you." There was a long pause, then, "Grayson seems quite taken with his wife."

"In only the most superficial sense, Iphiginia. Besides, she has no wish to be married. Not only has she proven that over the last four years, she has also said as much to me."

"She did not!"

Blinking, Rhys thought exactly the same thing. Isabel would never say such a thing to Grayson's mother.

"She did," the dowager replied. "She and I have agreed to assist each other."

"You jest!"

Good God! Rhys growled low in his throat. Bella would not be pleased when he saw her again. Damned if he wouldn't be pulling her out of another scrape.

Waiting until the women moved further along, he then left his hiding spot and moved surreptitiously through the garden toward the manse, where sinful pleasures awaited him.

Abby paused a moment at Trenton's doorway, wondering if one was supposed to knock before an assignation, or if she now had the right to just walk in unannounced. She was still debating this when the door flew open and she was yanked inside.

"What the devil took you so long?" Trenton complained, turning the lock and scowling down at her adorably.

Her stomach performed its little somersault again.

He was dressed in a burgundy silk robe, which revealed dark curling hair on his chest and hair-dusted calves that betrayed his nakedness beneath. With his arms akimbo, he was missing only the tapping foot to be a perfect picture of impatience.

Over her.

Her stomach flipped again.

How beautiful he was. What perfection! She sighed audibly. He was, of course, a bit hyperopic to miss her lack of physical charms, but she would not complain about that.

He reached for her and she sidestepped quickly. "Wait!"

"For what?" His scowl deepened.

"I—I have something to show you."

"If it's not you naked and writhing," he grumbled, "I am not interested."

She laughed.

She had watched him during dinner, noting his ready charm and droll discourse. The females seated on either side of him had been captivated, but she had felt his regard return to her often.

"Grant me a moment." She arched a brow when he opened his mouth to protest. "This is *my* deflowering. Once we reach the bed, I will cede command of this affair to you. Until then, however, I would like the preliminaries to be under my control."

Trenton's lips twitched and his eyes sparkled with a heat that made her shiver with anticipation. If his behavior in the garden was any indication, he was going to devour her. "As you wish, love."

Moving behind the privacy screen, she began to undress. This was not at all how she had imagined losing her virginity. There was no tender, patient husband waiting to treat her like fine porcelain. There was no ring on her finger or name attached to hers.

"What the devil are you doing?" he muttered, as if she were the most beautiful woman in the world and worthy of such avid interest.

He did have a way of looking at her that made her *feel* beautiful.

"I am almost done." She had dressed in the gown that was the simplest to remove without assistance, but it was still a chore. Finally, though, she was free and prepared. Taking a deep breath, Abby stepped out from behind the screen.

"About bloody . . ." His words faded into silence as he ceased pacing and turned to face her.

She shifted nervously under the sudden overwhelming heat of his gaze. "Hello."

"Abby." Just one word, but it was filled with awe and pleasure. "My God."

The fingers of her right hand fluttered nervously along the low neckline of her red gown. "My mother was blessed with a larger bosom, so I am afraid I cannot do the garment justice."

Trenton approached with his innate elegant grace, his cheekbones flushed, his lips slightly parted on rapid breaths. "If you did any more justice to that garment, I would be on my knees."

Blushing, she looked away, relishing the flutters she felt as he drew closer and then touched her gently. "Thank you."

"No, love," he murmured, his voice husky and deep, rippling down her spine. "*I* thank *you*. I cherish the gift you are giving to me."

With a finger beneath her chin, he angled her mouth and fitted his lips to hers. The kiss started softly, but quickly built until his mouth was slanting feverishly over hers, stealing her breath, making her dizzy. She quivered against him and was caught close to his hard body, lifted, and laid upon the bed.

Then he was everywhere. Stroking, kneading. His fingers tugging, pinching. His mouth wet and suckling. Nipping teeth. Hoarsely voiced words of encouragement and praise.

"Trenton!" she begged, certain she would die as her body shuddered with longing he seemed determine to stoke, but not appease. For all his impatience earlier, he was not rushed now.

"Rhys," he corrected.

"*Rhys . . .*"

Unsure of what to do, what to say, she could only touch his shoulders, his beautiful hair, the straining and sweat-dampened length of his muscular back. What a work of art he was, his body able to arouse her just by sight. All men were not as blessed as he was and she knew she was beyond fortunate to share her bed with such an incomparable masculine creature.

"Tell me how to please you."

"If you pleased me any more, love, we would both regret it."

"How is that possible?"

"Trust me," he murmured before taking her mouth and sliding his hand up from the back of her knee to her hip. Before she could protest his fingers were parting the lips of her sex.

He groaned as his touch slipped through the slickness that gathered there. "You're dripping."

"I—I'm sorry." She felt herself blush to the roots of her hair.

"Dear God, do not be sorry." Rhys came over her, nudging her thighs wider. "It's perfect. You are perfect."

She wasn't. Not nearly. But the reverent way he touched her told her that for the moment at least, he truly thought she was.

Because of this, she bit her lip and held back her sobs as the broad head of his cock breached her, then pierced her and stretched her unmercifully. Despite her resolve to be a lover he would enjoy, she struggled.

Rhys pinned her hips, held her in place, slid inexorably into her. " . . . Hush . . . a little more . . . I know it hurts . . ."

And then something inside her made way for him and he was seated fully, a thick throbbing presence.

His palms cupped her cheeks, his thumbs brushed away her tears, his mouth worshipped hers. "Little one. Forgive me the pain."

"Rhys." She clung to him, grateful for him, knowing the trust she had in him was a rare, precious gift. Why this man, this stranger, should affect her the way he did, Abby could not collect. She was simply glad to have him for the little time he would be hers.

He held her, soothed her with praise. How soft she felt, how perfectly she fit him, how touched he was by the moment. She doubted a husband could have appreciated her more.

When she calmed, Rhys began to move, a torturously slow glide of his rock hard flesh from her swollen sex and then a sleek return. What pain there was faded and pleasure blossomed, unfurling like a flower so that she did not realize how she arched up to meet his downward thrusts until he spoke.

"Just like that," he growled, his skin dripping sweat. "Move with me."

Following his urgently voiced commands, she wrapped his pumping hips with her legs and felt him slide impossibly deeper. Now every perfect stroke struck a place inside her that made her toes curl, made her writhe and claw at his back.

"Thank God," he grunted when she dissolved into blissful release with a startled gasp.

Then he shuddered brutally and flooded her with liquid heat. Clutching her so tightly it was hard to breathe, he gasped, "*Abby!*"

She held him to her heart and smiled a woman's smile.

No, it was not at all how she had dreamed of losing her virginity.

It was so much better.

Rhys woke to a softly muttered curse and opened his eyes. Turning his head, he could barely discern Abby hopping on one foot while holding the other.

"What the devil are you doing stumbling about in the dark?" he whispered. "Come back to bed."

"I should go." With the poor light provided by the banked fire, he noted that she was dressed as she had been when he'd opened the door to her.

"No, you should not. Come here." He pulled the counterpane and linens back invitingly.

"I shall fall asleep again and never make it back to my room."

"I will wake you," he promised, already missing her slight body against his.

"It's simply not practical for me to fall asleep again, only to be woken up in a few hours to move to my room where I shall fall asleep again and be woken up again by my abigail."

"Love." He sighed. "Why be practical alone when we can be impractical together?"

He barely made out the shaking of her head. "My lord—"

"Rhys."

"Rhys."

Ah, that was better. That softly dreamy quality that entered her voice when she said his name.

"I want to hold you a little longer, Abby," he coaxed, patting the bed beside him.

"I must go." She moved to the door and Rhys lay stunned, feeling bereft and put out by her ease in leaving him when he so desperately wished she would stay.

"Abby."

She paused. "Yes?"

"I want you." His voice was sleep-husky, which he hoped hid the tightness of his throat. "Can I have you again?"

The pause that stretched out made him grind his teeth. Finally she replied in a tone one would use to accept an invitation to tea. "I would like that."

Then she was gone, as any sensible light-o-love would go. Without a lingering kiss or longing touch.

And Rhys, a man who had always been sensible about his affairs, found himself insensibly piqued.

* * *

"This is not at all what I envisioned when you asked me to accompany you," Spencer grunted, hefting a boulder into place.

Gerard smiled and stepped back to note the progress they were making on the low stone wall. His intention had not been to labor, but when they'd come across a large number of his tenants working on the endeavor, he appreciated the opportunity. Hard work and aching muscles had taught him a great deal about looking inward for satisfaction and relishing the simple things, like a job well done. It was a lesson he was determined to pass on to his brother.

"Long after you and I are gone, Spence, this wall will remain. You are a part of something lasting. If you consider your past, can you think of anything else you have done that leaves a mark on this world?"

Straightening, his brother frowned. With their shirtsleeves rolled up, and dusty, scuffed hessians, they looked very little like the peer and family they were. "Please don't tell me you have become philosophical as well. 'Tis bad enough you are doting on your own wife."

"I suppose doting on someone else's wife would be better?" Gerard said dryly.

"Damned if it wouldn't be. That way, when you have had your fill, she becomes another man's teary puddle and not your own."

"What faith you have in me, little brother, considering my wife's ability to bring men to tears."

"Ah yes, messy, that. I don't envy you." He wiped the sweat off his forehead with the back of his hand and then burst into a grin. "However, when Pel's crushed you beneath her heel like an annoying bug, I will be at the ready to help you recover. A little wine, a little women, and you shall be good as new."

Shaking his head, Gerard looked away with a laugh and

found his attention caught by a scuffle between two young men just a short distance down the grassy hill. Concerned, he left his spot.

"No need to worry, my lord," came a gruff voice beside him. He turned to find the largest of the men standing at his side. "'Tis only my boy Billy and his friend."

Gerard returned his attention to the scene and found the boys racing each other off the hill to the flat land below. "Ah, I remember days like that in my youth."

"I think we all do, my lord. See the young girl sitting on the fence?"

Following the pointing finger, Gerard's heart stilled at the sight of the pretty blonde who laughed at the two boys running toward her. Silvery hair caught the sunlight, competing in brilliance with her smile.

She was lovely.

And very much like Emily in appearance.

"The two of them 'ave been competing for her affections for years. She 'as 'erself a soft spot for my boy, but in truth, I 'ope she's wise enough to pick the other."

Gerard tore his riveted gaze away from the young beauty, and arched both brows. "Why?"

"Because Billy only *thinks* 'e fancies 'er. 'E's got to compete with everyone, be better than everyone, and even though 'e knows she's not the one for 'im, 'e just cannot bear to lose 'er adoration. 'Tis purely selfish. But the other boy, 'e really loves 'er. 'E's always 'elping 'er with 'er chores, walking with 'er to the village. Caring for 'er."

"I see." And Gerard did, in a way he never had before.

Emily.

He had not thought of her at all on his Grand Tour. Not once. Too busy whoring to think of the adoring girl back home. Only upon his return and discovery of her marriage did he make any effort. Had he been like Billy? Simply jealous of attentions he hadn't appreciated until they were given to another?

You have always wanted women who belong to someone else.

Dear God.

Gerard turned, moved to the finished portion of the low wall, and sat, his gaze sightless as he looked inside instead of outward.

Women. He suddenly thought of them all, all the ones who had crossed his path.

Was it only competition with Hargreaves that had driven him to want Pel so desperately?

Warmth built in his chest and spread outward as he thought of his wife. *I want you.* The way those words had made him feel had nothing to do with Hargreaves. It had nothing to do with anyone but Isabel. And now that a mirror had been set before him, he realized that she was the only woman who had ever made him feel that way.

"Are we done?"

Raising his gaze, he found Spencer standing before him. "Not nearly."

Flooded with guilt for what he had done to Emily, Gerard set to work, doing what he had done for four long years—exorcised his demons by exhausting them.

"Lady Grayson."

Lifting her gaze from the book before her, Isabel saw John approaching where she sat on the rear Hammond terrace and offered him a gentle smile. Nearby to the right, Rhys sat with Miss Abigail and the Hammonds. To the left, the Earl and Countess of Ansell were enjoying afternoon tea with Lady Stanhope.

"Good afternoon, my lord," she greeted in return, admiring his trim form dressed in dark gray, and his sparkling eyes.

"May I join you?"

"Please do." Despite the things left unspoken between them, she was grateful for his company. Especially after sharing tea with the dowager, who had thankfully just departed.

Closing her novel, she set it aside and gestured to a servant for more refreshments.

"How are you, Isabel?" he asked with a searching glance, once he settled in the seat across from her.

"I am well, John," she assured him. "Very well. How are you?"

"I, too, am well."

She glanced around, then lowered her voice. "Please tell me truthfully. Have I hurt you?"

His smile was so genuine it soothed her immeasurably. "My pride smarts, yes. But truthfully, we were slowly approaching the end of our association, were we not? I was oblivious to it, as I have been oblivious to most things since Lady Hargreaves passed on."

Her heart welled with tenderness. Having lost a love once, she knew partly how it felt. It must have been much worse for John, since he had been loved in return.

"My time with you meant a great deal to me, John. Despite the horridly abrupt way our liaison ended, you do know that, don't you?"

Leaning into the backrest, he held her earnest gaze and said, "I do know that, Isabel, and your feelings for me made it much easier to see the purpose of our liaison and give it the closure it deserves. You and I came together for solace, the both of us wounded by our marriages—me, by the death of my beloved wife, and you, by the death of your not-so-loved husband. No strings, no demands, no goals . . . just companionship. How could I ever resent you for moving forward when something deeper came into your life?"

"Thank you," she said fervently, taking in every aspect of his handsome features with renewed affection. "For everything."

"In truth, I envy you. When Grayson came to me, I—"

"What?" She blinked in surprise. "What do you mean 'he came' to you?"

John laughed. "So, he didn't tell you. My respect for him has increased two-fold."

"What did he say?" she asked, nearly overrun with curiosity.

"What he said is not important. It is the passion with which he said it that I envied. I want that, too, and I think I am finally ready for it, thanks in no small part to you."

She wished she could reach out and squeeze his hand, which rested casually on the table, but she could not. Instead, she urged, "Promise me that we shall always be friends."

"Isabel." His voice held a smile. And a thread of steel. "Nothing on this earth could prevent me from being your friend."

"Truly?" She arched a brow. "What if I play matchmaker? I have a friend . . ."

John gave a mock shudder. "Now, that might do it."

As soon as Gerard and Spencer returned to the Hammond manse, they went straight to their rooms to bathe away the odors, sweat, and grime of the day.

Gerard longed to go to Isabel and had to fight the powerful urge to do so. He needed to talk with her, and share his discovery. He wanted to find comfort in her and soothe her fears with the knowledge that she was above all women to him. Most of all, he suspected she always would be and he wanted her to know that.

But then he wished to hold her, too, and he needed to be clean to do that.

So he sank into a hot bath, rested his head against the lip, and dismissed Edward.

When the door opened long moments later, he smiled, but kept his eyes closed. "Good evening, vixen. Did you miss me?"

A throaty murmur of assent made his smile broaden.

Isabel drew closer and his blood quickened with anticipation. Languid from exhaustion and the warmth of the bath, it took him precious moments to register the scent of a foreign perfume as she bent over him, then the re-opening of the door . . .

What in—

. . . just before an equally foreign hand thrust into the water and wrapped around his cock.

He jerked in surprise, sloshing water over the rim of the tub as he opened his eyes and met Barbara's startled gaze. He'd noted the inviting glances she sent his way, but he had thought her wise enough to heed his returning scowl and warning at the Hammond's ball in town. Apparently not.

He caught her wrist just as her gaze lifted and then filled with abject horror.

"If you wish to keep that hand," came Pel's voice from the adjoining doorway. "I strongly suggest you remove it from my husband's bath."

Dripping with ice, the words chilled him despite the warmth of the water he sat in.

Bloody everlasting hell!

Chapter 15

Why does my wife have such an unfortunate way of finding me in the most compromising positions?

Baring his teeth, Gerard growled at his intruder, who stumbled back in fright. Rising from the water, he caught up the towel that had been draped over a chair by his valet and watched Pel stalk Barbara out of the room.

Isabel shouted down the hallway after Barbara's retreating figure. "I am not done with you, madam!"

Squaring his shoulders, Gerard waited for his lioness to turn and face him. When she did, he flinched at her thundercloud expression. She stared at him a moment with unreadable amber eyes, her hair loose and flowing about her torso, her lush body covered in a dressing gown. Then she turned away, moving quickly to her room.

"Isabel."

He fumbled for his robe and followed her, holding his hand out to prevent the rapidly closing door from smacking him in the face. Once inside, he studied her warily as he dressed, watched her pacing, wondered how to begin the conversation. Finally, he said, "I did not instigate nor participate in that advance."

She shot a sidelong glance at him, but did not still her pacing.

"I think you want to believe me," he murmured. She was not hurling invectives at him, or objects for that matter.

"It is not that simple."

Walking toward her, he caught her shoulders, forcing her to still. It was then he felt her labored breathing, which caused his heart to race desperately. "It *is* that simple." He shook her slightly. "Look at me. See *me*!"

Isabel's gaze lifted and bore that same dazed, unfocused film he had seen at the Hammond's ball.

Cupping her cheeks with his hands, he tilted her face up. "Isabel, my love." He pressed his cheek to hers and breathed deeply, inhaling her scent. "I am not Pelham. Perhaps, before . . . when I was younger . . ."

She clutched his robe in clenched fists.

He sighed. "I am no longer that man, and I have never been Pelham. I have never lied to you, never hidden anything from you. From the moment we met, I have opened myself to you like I have with no other. You have seen me at my worst." Turning his head, he kissed her cold lips, licking the seam, coaxing them softly to open. "Can you not find it in your heart to see me at my best?"

"Gerard . . ." she breathed, her tongue brushing tentatively along his, making him groan.

"Yes." He pulled her closer, taking ruthless advantage of that tiny show of weakness. "Trust me, Pel. I have so much I wish to entrust in you. So much to share. Please, give me— give *us*—that chance."

"I am afraid," she admitted, baring what he had known, but was waiting for her to say.

"How strong you are to reveal that," he praised, "and how lucky I am to be the man you share your fears with."

She tugged at the loose belt of his robe, undid her own, and pressed her bare skin to his. No barriers between them. Her cheek to his chest, he knew she listened to his heart, heard its steady beat. He reached beneath her dressing gown and stroked the length of her spine.

"I don't know how to do this, Gray."

"Neither do I. But surely, using our combined experience with the opposite gender, we can manage. I was always able to tell when a paramour was tiring of me. Surely—"

"You lie. No woman has ever lost interest in you."

"No *sane* woman," he corrected. "Did you see no warning signs with Pelham? Or did he just wake up one morning without his brain?"

Isabel rubbed her face in his chest and laughed. It was a shaky sound, but true mirth, nevertheless. "There were signs, yes."

"So we shall make another bargain, you and I. You tell me the moment you see what appears to be a sign, and I promise to reassure you in a way that leaves no doubt."

She pulled back and looked up him, her mouth lush and wide, her eyes fringed with chocolate-colored lashes. He stared, enraptured by her features, which were nowhere near refined or delicate. Isabel was a raving, brazen beauty.

"God, you are so lovely," he murmured. "It hurts sometimes to look at you."

Her creamy skin flushed, that telltale touch of color speaking volumes. Pel was a woman of the world if ever there was one, but he could make her blush like a schoolgirl.

"Do you think your plan will work?" she asked.

"What? Talking to each other? Never allowing doubts to fester?" He sighed dramatically. "Too much work perhaps? I guess we will simply have to stay abed and fuck like rabbits."

"Gerard!"

"Oh, Pel." Lifting her, Gerard spun in a circle. "I am mad for you. Can you not see that? As much as you worry about holding my interest, I worry about holding yours."

Isabel wrapped her slender arms around his neck and pressed a kiss to his cheek. "I am mad for you, as well."

"Yes," he said, laughing. "I know."

"Conceited rake."

"Ah, but I am *your* conceited rake, which is just how you

want me. No, don't pull away. Let's make love, and then talk."

She shook her head. "We cannot skip dinner again."

"You dressed to seduce me, and now that your curves are pressed to my skin, you withdraw? What torture is this?"

"Considering how no provocation is required to lure you to sex, that was not my intent. I am undressed in this fashion because I napped." Her mouth curved in that wicked smile he adored. "And dreamt of you."

"Well, now I am here. Use me as you wish. I beg of you."

"As if you are deprived." She stepped back, and he made a great show of struggling to release her.

Growling, he muttered, "I wish I could say coming here was an error, but I think not."

"I think not either." She shot him a seductive glance over her shoulder. "And . . . good things come to those who wait."

"Do tell me more," he purred, following her.

"I shall tell you while you help me dress. But first things first, you keep that woman away from you, Grayson. If I find you with her again, I will definitely take that as a sign."

"Never fear, vixen," he murmured, wrapping his arms about her waist as she paused in front of the armoire. "I believe your point was well and truly made."

She laced her fingers with his at her abdomen. "Hmmmph. We shall see about that."

"I thought she intended to scratch my eyes out!"

Spencer shook his head and looked across the Hammond lower parlor to where Isabel stood off to the side, speaking with Lady Ansell. "What the devil were you thinking?"

Barbara wrinkled her nose. "When I exited my rooms and saw Grayson entering his, I assumed Pel was still below with the other guests."

"It was daft of you, however you look at it." He caught the eye of his brother, whose glowering look spoke volumes. *Rein her in,* it said.

"I know," she said morosely.

"And really, you know, I've tried to tell you—one Faulkner cock is as good as another."

"Yes, I suppose that's true."

"Have you learned your lesson? Stay away from Grayson."

"Yes. Yes. Will you promise to save me from her wrath?"

"Perhaps . . ."

She understood. "I will make my excuses in a moment." Barbara moved away.

Anticipating a night of carnal gratification, Spencer watched her sashay away with a smile.

"Did I hear Lady Stanhope correctly?" bit out a voice from behind him.

"Mother." He rolled his eyes. "You really must stop eavesdropping."

"Why did you warn her away from Grayson? Let her have him."

"Apparently, Lady Grayson took exception to that idea, to the point where Lady Stanhope fears for her person."

"*What?*"

"And Lord Hargreaves has gracefully withdrawn from the field. The newly reunited Graysons no longer have any impediments to marital bliss."

Glaring across the room, she muttered, "That woman agreed to cast him aside. I should have known she was lying."

"Even if she had not been, Gray is so taken with her, I doubt anything would keep him away. Look how he devours her with his gaze. And truth be told, I spoke with him a great deal today and she makes him happy. Perhaps you should concede this particular battle."

"I will not!" she retorted brusquely, brushing her dark gray skirts with gloved hands. "I will not live forever and before I take my dying breath I wish to see Grayson with a suitable heir."

"Ah . . ." He shrugged. "Well, perhaps it will be that which decides events in your favor. Pel has never struck me, or anyone else for that matter, as the maternal type. Had she longed for children, she would have increased long ago. Now her age is advanced and likely prohibitive to conception."

"Spencer!" His mother caught his arm and turned bright eyes to meet his. "You are a genius! That is exactly it."

"What? Which part?"

But his mother had already moved away, her slight shoulders straightened with a determination that made him glad to be exempt from its direction. He did, however, feel bad for his brother and so he moved to Gray's side as Lord Ansell left it.

"Sorry," Spencer murmured.

"Why did you bring her with you?" Gray asked, misunderstanding the apology.

"I told you. I was certain this trip would be a bore of heinous proportions. You cannot expect that I would be celibate in addition to that. I would offer to exhaust her from her meddling, but I ache all over, damn it. My arse, legs, arms. Some good I shall be to her, though I am determined to make my best effort."

Laughing, his brother clapped him on the back and said, "Well, her 'meddling' may have been fortuitous."

"*Now* I am certain you want a trip to Bedlam. No man possessed of all his mental faculties would say that being caught by his wife with his cock in another woman's hands was fortuitous."

Grayson smiled, and Spencer grumbled, "Well, out with it, man. You must explain, so that I may use a like circumstance to my advantage."

"I would not recommend a like circumstance to anyone. However, in this particular case it allowed me the opportunity to set my wife's greatest fear at ease."

"And that is?"

"For only I to know, brother," Gray said cryptically.

* * *

"My dear guests, your attention please!" Lady Hammond called out, tinkling a few keys on the pianoforte for greater effect.

Gerard looked at their hostess and then allowed his gaze to drift to Pel, just as hers moved to meet his. Her wide smile filled him with contentment. An hour or two more, and they could be alone.

"As a bit of training for tomorrow's scavenger hunt, Hammond and I have hidden two items somewhere in the manse—a gold pocket watch and an ivory comb. Unless the door is locked, or it is one of your bedchambers, any room is a possible hiding place. Please, if you find an item, make it known. I have a treat in store when the hunt is over."

Moving to his wife, Gerard was preparing to take her arm when she arched a wicked brow and stepped back. "If you hunt me instead, my lord, we will enjoy ourselves more than we would the watch or comb."

Instantly, Gray's blood both quickened and heated. "Minx," he whispered so as not to be overheard. "Put me off before dinner and then make me chase you for it afterwards."

The curve of her lush mouth deepened. "Ah, but I am *your* minx, which is just how you want me."

The low growl that escaped him could not have been contained if he'd tried. Everything primitive in him responded to her verbal acquiescence to his ownership. The desire to toss her over his shoulder and find the nearest bed was both embarrassing and arousing. The sudden darkening of her eyes told him that she understood what beast she'd stirred and welcomed it. Welcomed him. How was it possible that he had found a wife both genteelly raised and a tigress in bed?

His smile was feral.

She winked and turned on her slippered heel, strolling out of the room with the other guests, her hips moving with an exaggerated swing.

He gave her a few moments head start, and then he pursued her in earnest.

*   *   *

Isabel followed Gray surreptitiously, avoiding both his gaze and the other guests. She should have allowed him to catch her half an hour ago, but she so enjoyed watching his sultry stride and flexing ass. Lord, her husband had the most beautiful ass. And that walk. It was the walk of a man absolutely certain he would be fucking shortly. It was languid and loose-limbed. Irresistible.

He was coming back around again and this time she would draw him in, her blood as hot as she was certain his must be. Focused as she was on Grayson, she failed to register the form behind her until a hand was clamped over her mouth and she was dragged back into hiding.

Only when Rhys spoke and she knew her abductor did she cease her startled struggling, her heart still racing. He released her and she rounded on him.

"What the devil are you doing?" she whispered crossly.

"I was about to ask the same of you," Rhys retorted. "I overheard the dowager Lady Grayson telling Lady Hammond about your pact."

Isabel winced. *How had she forgotten about that?* "Dear God."

"Exactly." He glowered down at her, every inch the chastising older brother. "Bad enough you would even speak aloud of leaving Grayson, but to say it to his mother who is now spreading the tale. What were you thinking?"

"I was not thinking," she admitted. "I was distressed and spoke rashly."

"You chose to marry him. You must now live with that choice as all women of your station do. Can you not find a way to coexist?"

She nodded rapidly. "Yes, I think we can. We have agreed to make the attempt."

"Oh, Bella." Rhys sighed and shook his head, his disappointment tangible, flooding her with guilt. "Did you not learn to be practical with Pelham? Carnal craving is not love or even the prelude to it. Why must you be so set on romance?"

"I am not," she argued, looking away.

"Hmmm . . ." He caught her chin and dragged her gaze back to his. "You lie, but you are a grown woman and I cannot make your decisions for you. We shall just leave it at that. But I worry over you. You are too sensitive, I think."

"We cannot all have hearts of steel," she grumbled.

"Gold." His smile faded as he expressed his concern. "The dowager is not a woman to take lightly. She is determined, although I do not know why. You are a duke's daughter and a fine pairing for any peer. If you make a true match with Grayson, I cannot see the objection."

"No one makes her happy, Rhys."

"Well, she will find her path damned uncomfortable if she thinks to tangle with our pater, and he *will* intercede, Bella."

Isabel sighed. As if their pasts and personal issues were not dilemma enough, she and Grayson had external combatants as well. "I shall speak to her. For all the good it will do."

"Good."

"There you are," Gray purred behind her, the moment before his hands cupped her waist. "Trenton. Do you not have a watch to hunt?"

Rhys sketched a slight bow. "I believe I do." His parting glance at Isabel spoke volumes, and she gave a slight nod before he turned about and moved down the gallery.

"Why do I feel as if the mood for play is lost?" Gray asked when they were alone.

"It is not."

"Then why are you so tense, Pel?"

"You could correct that." She turned in his arms.

"If I knew the cause," he murmured. "I'm certain I could."

"I wish to be alone with you."

Nodding, he led her toward their wing, but when she heard voices approaching, Isabel pulled him into the nearest room. "Lock the door."

With the drapes closed, the room they entered was so dark she could not see, which was just what she wanted at the moment. She heard the lock click into place.

"Gerard." Turning, she surged into him, her hands slipping beneath his jacket to embrace his lean waist.

Caught off guard, Gray stumbled backward until he hit the door. "Christ, Isabel."

She lifted to her tiptoes and buried her face in his neck. *How she loved the feel of him!*

"What is it?" he asked gruffly, his arms coming around her.

"Is this all we have? This craving?"

"What the devil are you talking about?"

She licked along his throat, consumed by a fever for him in her blood. She had never surrendered to him. Not completely. Perhaps it was that last bit of resistance which goaded his pursuit. If so, she needed to know that now. Before it was too late.

Cupping his ass, Isabel rubbed her body against his.

He shuddered. "Pel. Do not provoke me thusly here. Let's go to our room."

"You seemed game for the chase earlier." She kneaded along his spine through the thin satin back of his waistcoat. All the while she pressed into him, her breasts to his chest, her belly to the rigid length of his cock.

The darkness was freedom. All there was in her world at the moment was the large body she desired, the smell of Gray, the deliciously raspy voice, warmth. Heat. Need.

"You were playful then. I anticipated a bit of fondling, stolen kisses." He gasped as she stroked him through his trousers, but he did not stop her. "Now you are . . . you are . . . Bloody hell, I've no notion what you are, but it requires our bed, my cock, and uninterrupted hours."

"What if I cannot wait?" she breathed, squeezing the thick head of his shaft through her glove and his broadcloth.

"You would have me take you here?" His voice was thick

with lust. "What if someone should come? We've no idea what room we are in."

Her fingers worked at the placket of his trousers. "Someplace unused, since there is no fire in the grate." She hummed her pleasure as he sprang free, hard and straining. "I am offering you the opportunity to take me in a public arena, as you said you were quite capable of doing."

He caught her wrist, but undeterred, her other hand reached around and squeezed his ass. Enflamed, he growled before twisting swiftly so that she was against the door. "As you wish."

As his hands delved beneath her skirts, he bit hard at her shoulder.

Her head drifted to the side as he parted her and stroked her clitoris. She widened her stance shamelessly and reveled in his expertise. He had once spent hours fucking her with his fingers and his tongue, determined to know every nuance of her body's ability to orgasm.

"What has possessed you? What did Trenton say to you?" His long fingers slipped inside her, stroking skillfully. Wetness spread across her flesh at the point where his bared cock thrust impatiently against her. "Jesus, Pel. You are soaked."

"And you are dripping semen down my leg." She shivered with the first stirrings of release, every part of her aching for more than just this. "Take me. Please. I want you."

As she had hoped, it was the last words that moved him. He cupped the back of her thighs and lifted her effortlessly. Isabel reached between them and guided him to her, moaning in near delirium as he lowered her onto his jutting cock.

Gray leaned forward, his chest moving against hers in harsh, uneven breaths. She held him, breathed him in, absorbed the feel of his weight against her, his thickness inside her.

Did you not learn to be practical with Pelham?

"Is this all that we have?"

"Isabel." He nuzzled against her throat, his open mouth

hot and wet against her. A hard shudder coursed through his frame when she tightened around him. "I pray this is all we have, for I cannot survive any more than this."

Pressing her cheek to his, she moaned softly as he moved. Withdrawing. Sliding back inside. Slowly. Savoring.

"More." It was not a request she made.

He paused, tensing.

"Damn you," Gray muttered finally, his fingers digging painfully into her flesh. "Can I ever pump deep enough? Can I ever fuck you enough? Sate you enough? Will I ever be *enough?*"

Bending his knees, he increased his pace, thrusting high and hard and deep, until she felt him in her throat. Startled by his sudden vehemence, she could say nothing.

"Is this all we have, you ask? Yes!" He rammed her into the door, bruising her spine, pinning her there. Making her cry out softly with pleasure and pain, unmoving except for the heated length throbbing inside her. She writhed and scratched at him, on the edge. She clung to his shoulders, his hips, trying to move, but there was no way. "You and I and no one else, Isabel. If it drives me into the grave, I will find a way to be what you need."

In her heart, warmth unfurled. Gray was not like Pelham. He was open and honest. His passion was real and truly heartfelt.

Perhaps she was not practical when it came to marriage, but with her husband she had no need to be. "I want to be what you need, as well. Desperately." She made the admission without fear.

"You are." He pressed his sweat-dampened face against hers. "For God's sake, you are everything."

"Gerard." Her fingers tangled in his silky hair. "Please."

He moved, building a steady rhythm and maintaining it. She allowed him the lead, becoming limp except for the inner muscles she tightened around his pumping cock. He grunted at every tight squeeze. She moaned with every deep plunge.

There was no race to the finish, only a giving, one to the other, using their knowledge to ensure the greatest pleasure.

When he set his mouth to her ear and panted, "Christ! I cannot . . . Pel! I cannot stop! I'm going to come . . .", she gasped, "Yes! Yes . . ."

His hands at her thighs spread her wide, he thrust to the hilt and groaned, a tortured sound so loud she heard him over the roaring of blood in her ears. His orgasm was violent, his powerful body shaking, his cock jerking, his chest heaving as he gave her what she'd once spurned. Filled with him, overflowing with the essence of him, she held tight and came around him in a breathless, burning release.

"Isabel. My God, Isabel." He crushed her to him. "I'm sorry. Let me make you happy. Let me try."

"Gerard . . ." She pressed kisses across his face. "*This* is enough."

Chapter 16

As he left Bella behind, Rhys was so lost in thought he failed to look ahead. Turning the corner, he ran into a hastily moving body and had to reach out swiftly to prevent her fall.

"Lady Hammond! My apologies."

"Lord Trenton," she replied, straightening her skirts and touching a hand to her golden curls, which showed a faint trace of gray. When she looked up at him with a bright smile, he was startled, considering how he had very nearly run her over. "I apologize, as well. I was not minding my path in my haste to ensure my guests' enjoyment."

"Everyone is having a fine time of it."

"I am so relieved! I must thank you for the attention you paid to Hammond's niece this evening. The poor dear is so beleaguered by destitutes. I am certain discourse with a non-marital-minded man was refreshing. She was in as fine a mood as I have ever seen, which pleases me greatly. I appreciate your forbearance in speaking with her for such a length of time."

He held back a grunt. The image of him as a benign figure who had no sincere interest in Abby irked him in a way he could not understand. He longed to retort and refute, to say she was unique and desirable for more than her purse. But why he wished to defend her so fiercely eluded him. Perhaps it was guilt.

"No thanks are necessary," he assured her with practiced smoothness.

"Are you enjoying the scavenger hunt?"

"I was, yes. Now though, I will bow out and leave the rest of the guests to the glory."

"Is anything amiss?" she asked, the concerned hostess.

"Not at all. I am simply very good at such pursuits, and it would not be very sporting of me to win tonight, when I have every intention of winning tomorrow." He winked.

She laughed. "Very well. Good eventide to you, my lord. We shall see you over breakfast."

They parted ways and Rhys took the shortest route to his rooms. Once he'd undressed, he dismissed his valet for the evening and settled before the fire with a decanter and glass. Shortly, he was in his cups and somewhat eased of his regret over Abby, at least until the door opened.

"Go away," he muttered, making no effort to cover his legs, which were bared by the part in his robe.

"Rhys?"

Ah, his angel.

"Go away, Abby. I am not in any condition to receive you."

"You look perfectly conditioned to me," she said softly, coming over and circling the chair until she stood between him and the fire.

Divested of her underskirts for ease in undressing, he could see the outline of her lithe legs through her gown. He grew hard, a condition he was unable to hide, dressed as he was.

She cleared her throat, her gaze riveted.

Feeling the urge to shock her, Rhys yanked aside one edge of his robe and bared his upthrust cock. "Now that you have seen what you came here to see, you can go."

Abby sat in the chair across from him, her back ramrod straight, her gaze curious and capped with a studious frown. She was so damned adorable, he had to look away.

"I did not come here to simply gaze at what I want and not have it," she said primly. "A sillier concept I've never heard of."

"I have something sillier for you," he retorted gruffly, shifting his half empty glass to create prisms from the firelight. "You working so industriously toward an unwanted pregnancy."

"Is that the impetus behind this mood you are having?"

"My 'mood' is called 'guilt,' Abigail, and since I've not felt that particular emotion before, I am not comfortable with it."

She was silent for long moments. Long enough for him to drain his drink and refill it. "You regret what happened between us?"

He did not look at her. "Yes."

A lie, for he could never regret the time he had spent with her, but it was best if she did not know that.

"I see," she said softly. Then she stood and came toward him. She paused beside his chair. "I am sorry you regret it, Lord Trenton. Know that I never will."

It was the wavering undercurrent in her voice that made him move lightning quick to capture her wrist. When he forced himself to look at her, he saw tears, which cut him so deeply he dropped the glass in his other hand, the thud of its impact drowned by the roaring of blood in his ears. The feel of her, just that slight, fragile piece of her, set off memories of touching other parts. Impossibly, he began to sweat.

She tried to pull herself free, but he held fast, rising to his feet, gripping the back of her neck roughly. "See how I hurt you? How I can do nothing but hurt you?"

"It was heaven," she cried, swiping furiously at her tears. "The things you did . . . the way you felt . . . the way *I* felt!"

Abby struggled, but he maintained his grip. She glared at him through her weeping, her cheeks flushed, her lips red and parted. "I see my mother was correct. Affairs are physical release, nothing more. I suppose sex must feel this way for everyone. *With* anyone! Why else would so many indulge?"

"Cease!" he barked, his heart racing as he saw the path of her logic.

Her voice rose. "Why else would the experience mean so little to you? Stupid of me to think you and I are unique. I am so easily replaceable for similar intimacy. I conclude that any other man could provide a like orgasmic event for me!"

"Damn you. No other man."

"To hell with you, my lord!" she cried, glorious with indignant fury. "I am no great beauty, but I am certain there are men who could make love to me without regret."

"Let me assure you," he bit out, "any other man who touches you will regret it immensely."

"Oh." As she blinked up at him, her free hand fluttered to her throat. "Oh my. Are you being possessive?"

"I am never possessive."

"You threaten any man who might touch me. What do you call that?" She shivered. "Never mind. I love it, whatever you call it."

"Abby," he growled, furious at the tightening he felt in his gut. *Would she forever drive him insane?*

"That growl . . ." Her eyes widened, then softened. "Your roguish tendencies turn my insides to jelly, did you know that?"

"I did not growl!" Against his will, his arm drew into his body, pulling her with it.

"Yes, you did. What are you doing?" she gasped when he licked the very edge of her lips. "You intend to ravish me, do you not?"

His half-drunken brain was inundated with the warmth of her slender body, the soft scent of her, and the voice he loved.

Her cries in orgasm were enough to make his cock weep with joy. It was leaking even now, he was so aroused, and she had done nothing to make him feel this way. It was simply *her*. Something indefinable about her.

"No," he murmured in her ear. "I intend to *fuck* you."

"Rhys!"

When he released her wrist and reached for her breast, he was not surprised to find her nipple hard against his palm. Those long, delicious nipples. He pulled her to the floor.

"What? Here?" Her shock would have made him laugh, if he weren't concentrating so fiercely on yanking her skirts out of the way. "On the *rug*? What about the bed?"

"Next time."

Finding her slick and hot, Rhys began to work his cock into her with a groan of surrender. Abby whimpered softly.

"Will you regret this, too?" she asked, squirming beneath him.

He knew she was sore, could feel how swollen her tissues were, but could not desist. Watching her as he forced her body to take him, he nearly drowned in those blue eyes with their golden flecks. "Never," he vowed.

"You lied earlier." Her smile was brilliant and watery with renewed tears. "I have never been so happy to have been lied to."

He had never been so happy either.

Which was a torment worse than hell itself.

Unwilling to leave Isabel after her apparent upset the night before, Gerard found himself walking several feet behind her as the Hammond party left their horses with grooms and walked to a location prepared for an alfresco picnic. Dressed in flowered muslin with a large satin bow at the back and a wide-brimmed straw hat upon her upswept auburn tresses, his wife looked both elegant and young. The latter effect was enhanced by her sparkling eyes and wide smile.

That he was responsible for her look of contentment was astonishing to him. Prior to four years ago, he had never pleased anyone but himself, and he'd never in his life made a woman happy outside of sexual intercourse. He had no notion how he'd managed the deed. He knew only that he would continue to keep her so blissful if it killed him.

To wake to Isabel pressing kisses to his chest with laugher in her eyes was beyond heavenly. To feel her turn to him, snuggle with him, reach for him when she grew cold . . . It was a type of intimacy he hadn't known existed, and he had found it with his wife, the most beautiful and wonderful woman in the world. He deserved it less than anyone, but he had it. And he would cherish it. Spilling his seed inside her had been a foolhardy lapse, one he would not repeat. He could not risk impregnating her.

Glancing aside, he studied Trenton and said, "You still look morose. The country air not working its wonders on you?"

"No," Trenton grumbled, frowning. "My ailment cannot be cured by fresh air or anything else."

"What kind of ailment is that?"

"The female kind."

Laughing, Gerard said, "I hope to be slowly developing a cure for that myself. Unfortunately, I doubt it would help you if I do."

"Once Isabel discovers a dalliance on your part," Trenton warned ominously, "the saints above will not be able to cure you."

Gerard came to an abrupt halt and waited for Trenton to face him. The rest of the party continued on until they were quite alone. "Is that what you told my wife last night? That I would stray?"

"No." Trenton stepped closer. "I merely told her to be practical."

"Isabel is one of the most pragmatic women I know."

"Then you do not know her well."

"Beg your pardon?"

Trenton smiled wryly and shook his head. "Isabel is a romantic, Grayson. She always has been."

"Are we talking about *my wife*? The woman who discards men who become too attached to her?"

"Lovers and spouses are two very different things, would you not agree? She will become attached to you if you continue on your present course. And women can be positively demonic when their affections are rebuffed."

"Attached to me?" Gerard asked softly as wonder filled him. If this morning's playful affection was any indication of what Pel was like when attached, he wanted more of it. All of it. Today was the best day of his life. What if all of his days could be like this one? "I've no intention of rebuffing her. I want her, Trenton. I intend to keep her happy."

"To the exclusion of all others? Nothing less will content her. For some unknown reason, she has odd delusions of love and fidelity in marriage. She certainly did not learn that in our family. From faery tales, perhaps, but not from a firm grounding in reality."

"No others," Gerard said, distracted. He looked ahead, wishing he could see his wife from this vantage. As if she felt his silent demand for the sight of her, she appeared and waved, causing him to take an involuntary step toward her.

"You are champing at the bit," Trenton observed.

"How should I win her heart?" Gerard asked. "With wine and roses? What do women consider romantic?"

Wildflowers picked as afterthoughts and off-the-top-of-his-head poems had lured Em, but his goals were different now, more important. He could not leave this to chance. Everything for Isabel had to be perfect.

"You are asking *me*?" Trenton's eyes widened. "How the devil would I know? I've never in my life wanted a woman to fall in love with me. Damned inconvenient when they do."

Gerard frowned. Pel would know and he longed to ask her, just as he had always turned to her for advice and her opinions. But in this instance, he was quite definitely on his own. "I will puzzle it out."

"I am glad you appreciate her, Grayson. I often wondered what Pelham was looking for outside of wedlock when he had Isabel so smitten within it. He was a god to her in the beginning."

"He was an idiot. I am no god to Pel. She is well aware of all my shortcomings. If she can see past them, it will be a miracle." He began walking and Trenton fell into step beside him.

"I would think that to love a person in spite of their faults, rather than because you cannot see those faults, would be the deeper of the two attachments."

Considering that thought a moment, Gerard broke out in a grin. Which faded as they rounded a large tree and he saw Hargreaves speaking with Isabel. She laughed at something said to her, and the earl's returning look was both open and fond. They stood together with an obvious familiarity.

Inside him, something twisted and churned. His fists clenched. Then she saw him, and excused herself, moving toward him swiftly.

"What delayed you?" she asked, taking his arm with blatant ownership.

The writhing thing inside him quieted and he exhaled audibly. He wished he were alone with her, talking with her as they had last night when they'd returned to their rooms. Lying in bed with Pel curled to his side and their fingers linked over his chest, he had told her about Emily. Told her about what he had discovered about himself, and listened to her assurances and voice of reason.

"You are not a bad man," she had said. "Merely one who was young and in need of adoration after living with a mother who could do nothing but chastise you."

"You make it sound so simple."

"You are complicated, Gerard, but that does not mean it is not something simple that goads you."

"Such as?"

"Such as saying farewell to Emily."

Puzzled, he asked, "How am I to do that?"

She rose to hover above him, her eyes glowing with the reflection of the firelight. "In your heart. In person. In any way at all."

He shook his head.

"You should. Perhaps during a long walk. Or you could write her a letter."

"Visit her grave?"

"Yes." Her smile took his breath away. "Whatever you need to do to say good-bye and set aside your guilt."

"Will you go with me?"

"If you wish me to, of course I will."

In the space of an hour, she changed his self-loathing to self-awareness and acceptance. She made everything seem right, made every challenge bearable, made the completion of difficult tasks seem possible. He longed to provide the same for her, to be as valuable a partner to her as she was to him.

"And you?" he asked. "Will you allow me to help you make peace with Pelham?"

She lowered her cheek to his chest, her hair spilling over his shoulder and arm. "Anger at his memory has strengthened me for so long," she said softly.

"Strengthened *you*, Pel? Or your barriers?"

Her sigh blew hot across his skin. "Why do you pry at me?"

"You said this was enough, but it isn't. I want all of you. I am not inclined to share parts of you with any man—dead or living."

Her breathing stilled until he almost shook her in alarm.

Then she gasped and clung to him, her legs tightening around his, her hands clutching his shoulders. He embraced her just as fiercely in return.

"You can hurt me," she whispered. "Do you understand that?"

"But I will not," he vowed, his lips to her hair. "Eventually, you will come to believe that."

After a time, they drifted into sleep, the deepest slumber Gerard had known in many years, because he was no longer trudging through his day waiting for it to end. He had something to look forward to upon waking.

"Isabel," he said now, leading her a short distance away from the other guests. Ways to win her deeper affections sifted through his brain. "I should like very much to take you to my estate tomorrow."

She glanced aside at him from beneath her hat, the jaunty angle revealing the curve of her lips and not much more. "Gerard, you may take me anywhere."

The double entendre was not lost on him. It was a beautiful day, his marriage was on the mend, he had romance on his mind and in his heart. Nothing could steal his contentment. He was about to reply, his heart light at Pel's teasing banter . . .

"*Grayson.*"

The crossly voiced intrusion could not have come at a worse time.

Heaving out a disappointed breath, he turned reluctantly to face his mother. "Yes?"

"You cannot continue to avoid the other guests. You must attend this afternoon's treasure hunt."

"Certainly."

"And supper this evening."

"Of course."

"And the ride scheduled for tomorrow."

"My apologies, madam, but I cannot oblige you there," he said smoothly, finding her overbearing tendencies lacking their usual irritating effect. Even his mother could not ruin his day. "I have the time reserved for Lady Grayson."

"Have you no shame?" the dowager snapped.

"Scarcely any, no. I thought you knew that."

Isabel bit off a laugh and looked away quickly. He somehow managed to keep his face impassive.

"What is so important that you would abandon your hosts again?"

"We travel to Waverly Court tomorrow."

"Oh." His mother frowned at him a moment, an expression so common to her countenance that lines permanently etched its passing. "I should like to go. I've not been there in many years."

Gerard was silent a moment, remembering suddenly that his parents had spent some time in residence there. "You are welcome to join us."

The smile she bestowed on him startled, the transformation of her features was so unnerving. But it disappeared as quickly as it came. "Now come join the rest of the party, Grayson, and behave yourself as is appropriate to your station."

Watching his mother walk away, he shook his head. "I hope you can disregard her gloom."

"I can with you at my side," Isabel replied offhand, as if she were not saying something that completely rocked him to the core.

He took a brief moment to catch his bearings, and then allowed his grin to break free.

No doubt about it. Nothing could ruin his day.

"Lady Hammond would have to pair us together," Rhys muttered, moving rapidly up the wooded path.

"The thought of hunting treasure with you made me giddy," she teased. "I am dreadfully sorry if you do not feel the same about being with me."

The side glance he shot at her was so hot, her skin felt burned. "No. I would not call what I feel 'giddy.'"

The dead leaves along the trail crunched beneath every heavy step of his hessians. Dressed in dark green, he was stunningly handsome. Once again, she marveled that such a bold, masculine creature would find anything arousing about her, but it was clear the marquess did. And was very upset by that fact.

"If I had any say in the matter," he grumbled, "I would pull you into that clearing over there and lick you from head to toe."

Staring straight ahead, Abby had no idea what a woman was supposed to say in reply to such a statement. So she looked at the paper in her unsteady grip and said, "We need a smooth stone. There is a river around the bend up there."

"That dress you are wearing is distracting."

"Distracting?" It was one of her most flattering, a soft pink muslin with burgundy satin ribbon edging the low-cut bodice. She had selected it just for him, even though she hadn't the bosom to make it truly fetching.

"I know with a quick tug, your nipples will pop free and I can suck on them."

Her empty hand sheltered her racing heart. "Oh my. You are being very naughty."

He snorted. "Not as naughty as I would like to be. Pinning you to a tree and lifting your skirts would do nicely."

"Lifting my—" She stumbled to a halt as every cell in her body responded to the picture his words evoked. "It is the middle of the day."

Rhys, lost in his own thoughts, took several steps forward before realizing she remained behind. He turned to face her, his rich hair glinting in the filtered light of the overhead canopy. "Are your nipples different in the sunlight? Is your scent altered? Your skin less soft? Your cunt less tight and wet?"

She shook her head rapidly, unable to speak.

His gaze bore intensely into hers. "I have to depart in the morning, Abby. I cannot remain here and debauch you further. That I am trusted to be alone with you is like trusting the wolf to guard the lamb. It's perverse."

Try as she might to keep her mother's advice firmly in her mind, she could not do it. Her heart ached. She could only hope her exterior did not betray her.

"I understand," she said tonelessly, all her previous enjoyment in the day gone.

Why did this man appeal to her so deeply?

She had lain in her bed after leaving him and pondered that question for hours. In the end, she decided it was a combination of many things, some external, like his attractiveness and charm. And others internal, like his tendency to find new joy in her discoveries about how men and women related with one another. With him, she did not feel gauche. She was desirable, witty, and wise. Rhys thought it was "wonderful" that she enjoyed puzzling out scientific equations. He had even kissed the ink stains on her fingers as if they were a thing of beauty.

He was known for his ennui and jaded views, but Rhys was only dormant, not dead. She longed to be the catalyst that revived him, but she knew his sense of duty to his title would never allow her to be.

It would be best if he left.

"It would be best if you left."

He stared at her for a long moment, unmoving, so when he lunged at her and grabbed her roughly, she was caught completely unawares. His hands in her hair, he kissed her with unrestrained passion, his thrusting tongue stealing her breath and her wits.

"You make me forget myself," he said harshly against her

bruised lips. "To see you dismiss me so summarily drives me insane."

"*Something* has obviously driven you insane," snapped a familiar female voice.

Rhys groaned. "Bloody hell."

"Leave it to you, Trenton," drawled Lord Grayson, "to ruin my day."

Chapter 17

"I've no notion what to say to you, Rhys," Isabel scolded, glaring up the narrow path at her brother.

Gray leaned over and murmured, "I will see Hammond's niece back to the manse so that you may speak with Trenton in private."

"Thank you." Her eyes met his for a moment and she squeezed his hand in gratitude. She watched as he collected the obviously flustered girl and led her away. Then she rounded on Rhys. "Have you lost your mind?"

"Yes. God, yes." His countenance was gloomy as he kicked at a tree root that rose slightly above the dirt.

"I know you were out of sorts when we left London, but to use that child as salve for your—"

"That 'child' is the same age as your husband," he pointed out dryly, making her gasp in horror.

"Ooohhh . . ." She chewed her lower lip and began to pace.

Lately, she often forgot about the age difference in her marriage. After she'd first wed Grayson, the gossips had salivated over her superior years, but she managed to ignore them. Now, however, she was most definitely entertaining a younger man in her bed.

But she could not think of that now.

"Do not dare make that comparison." Her chin lifted. "Grayson is far more experienced in such matters, whereas it is quite obvious that Miss Abigail is not."

"It was almost effective in distracting you," he muttered.

"Ha!" She shook her head and then said more somberly, "Please tell me that you have not taken her to your bed, Rhys."

His shoulders drooped.

"Dear God." Isabel paused her pacing and stared at her brother as if he were a stranger. The Rhys she knew would have no interest in an innocent bluestocking. "How long has this been progressing?"

"I first made her acquaintance at that blasted breakfast you forced me to attend." He growled. "This is all *your* doing."

She blinked. Weeks. Not merely the last couple of days. "I am attempting to understand. Not to sympathize, mind you," she added hastily. "But simply to comprehend it. I cannot."

"Do not ask me to enlighten you. All I know is that I cannot be within a few feet of her without my brain ceasing to function. I become some boorish rutting beast."

"Over *Abigail Stewart*?"

The glare he shot her spoke volumes. "Yes, over Abigail. Damn it, why can no one see her worth? Her beauty?"

Wide-eyed, she studied him in detail, noting the flush at the crest of his cheekbones and the brightness of his eyes. "Are you in love with her?"

His look of astonishment would have been comical if she weren't so disturbed. "I am in lust with her. I admire her. I enjoy talking with her. Is that love?" He shook his head. "I will be Sandforth eventually and must consider the dukedom before considering my own desires."

"Then what were you doing with her alone in the garden? This path is well-trodden. Any one of the other guests could have happened upon you. What of Hammond? What would you have said to him in return for abusing his hospitality and trust this way if he had been the one to discover you embracing?"

"Damnation, Bella! I do not know. What more can I say? I erred."

"You *erred*?" Isabel blew out her breath. "Is that why you came? To be with her?"

"I had no notion she would be here, I promise you that. I meant to distract myself from thoughts of her. Remember when we arrived? I had to ask you who she was."

"Are you expecting the girl to become your mistress?"

"No! Never," he said emphatically. "She is much like you—filled with dreams of romance and love in marriage. I've no wish to take that away from her."

"But you took the virginity meant for that great love?" She arched a brow. "Or was she not a virgin?"

"Yes! Of course she was. I am her only lover."

Isabel said nothing. The notes of pride and possession in his tone were clear to both of them.

Rhys groaned and rubbed the back of his neck. "I am departing in the morning. The best thing I can do at this point is stay away."

"You never heed my advice, but I will share it with you anyway. Consider your feelings for Miss Abigail carefully. Having known both happiness and despair in my marriages, I strongly recommend you find a spouse you enjoy spending time with."

"You would have an American as the Duchess of Sandforth?" he asked incredulously.

"Alter your thinking, Rhys. She is the granddaughter of an earl. And frankly, there must be something exceedingly extraordinary about her for you to lose your head as you have done. If you put your mind to it, I am certain you can help reveal that side of her to the world."

He shook his head. "Romantic nonsense, Bella."

"Certainly being practical in one's choices is wise when the heart is not involved, but when it is, I think you should weigh those additional concerns carefully."

Frowning, he stared up the path in the direction Gray and Abigail had taken. "How furious was our pater when you selected Pelham?"

"Nowhere near as furious as he was when I wed Grayson, but he adapted." Stepping closer, Isabel set her hand on his shoulder. "I don't know if you will find comfort in this, or pain, but it was quite clear to me that she adores you."

He winced and held out his arm to her. "I don't know how I should feel about that either. Come. Let's return to the house. I must set my valet to packing."

A depressive air hung about the Hammond party in the parlor that evening. Rhys lacked his customary charm and quick wit, and retired early. Abigail put on a brave face, and to the casual eye, one would find nothing amiss, but Isabel could see the strain that tightened the other woman's mouth. Beside her on the settee, Lady Ansell was equally despondent, despite having won the treasure hunt earlier.

"Your necklace is a lovely piece," Isabel murmured, hoping to cheer the viscountess.

"Thank you."

They had known each other casually for years, though after her recent marriage to the viscount, Lady Ansell had spent a great deal of her time traveling abroad with her husband. Not quite pretty, the viscountess nevertheless was a handsome woman, tall and proud in bearing. It was clear to many that her match with Ansell was a love match, which gave the woman a sparkle to her eyes that more than made up for her lack of classical beauty. Tonight, however, that sparkle was missing.

Lady Ansell turned to face her, revealing a reddened nose and quivering lips. "Forgive my importunateness, but would you walk in the garden with me? If I go alone, Ansell will come and I cannot bear to be alone with him now."

Startled by the request, and concerned, Isabel nodded and rose to her feet. She shot a placating smile at Gray before exiting out the open glass-paned doors to the terrace and leaving him behind. Strolling along the lighted gravel paths with the statuesque blonde, Isabel maintained her silence, having learned long ago that sometimes it was best simply to be present, no discourse necessary.

Finally, the viscountess said, "I feel dreadful for poor Lady Hammond. She is certain that despite her careful planning, her party is a crashing bore. I have tried my best to enjoy myself, I truly have, but I am afraid no amount of festivities can enliven my mood."

"I will reassure her again," Isabel murmured.

"I'm certain she would appreciate it." Sighing, Lady Ansell said, "I miss wearing the glow you bear. I wonder if I will ever reclaim it for myself."

"I have found that contentment moves in cycles. Eventually, we rise above the depths. You will, too. I promise you."

"Can you promise me a child?"

Blinking, Isabel had no notion of what to say to that.

"I'm sorry, Lady Grayson. Forgive my curtness. I do truly appreciate your concern."

"Perhaps speaking your troubles aloud will help ease your mind?" she offered. "I will lend you my ear, and my discretion."

"I have regret. I do not think there is ease from that."

From her own experience, Isabel knew this was true.

"When I was younger," the viscountess said, "I was certain I would never find a spouse who would suit me. I was too eccentric, and eventually I became a spinster. Then I met Ansell, who loved to travel as much as my parents had. All of my originality appealed to him. We are quite evenly matched."

"Yes, you are," Isabel agreed.

A faint smile softened the other woman's palpable sadness. "If only we had found each other sooner, perhaps we could have conceived."

Icy fingers wrapped around Isabel's heart. "I am sorry." It was inadequate, but all she could manage.

"At nine and twenty, the physician says perhaps I have waited too long."

"Nine and twenty . . . ?" Isabel asked, swallowing hard.

A suppressed sob rent the still night air. "You are near my age; perhaps you understand."

All too well.

"Ansell assures me that even if he had known I was barren, he would still have wed me. But I have seen the way he looks at small children, the longing in his eyes. There comes a time when a man's need to produce issue is strong enough to be felt by others. My one duty as his viscountess was to bear his heir and I have failed him."

"No. You mustn't think that way." Isabel hugged her waist to ward off a sudden chill. All the joy she had once felt in the day slipped away from her. Could happiness be hers when the age for new beginnings belonged to women much younger than she was?

"This morning my courses started and Ansell was forced to leave our rooms to hide his dismay. He claimed he wished to ride in the early morning air, but in truth, he could not bear to look at me. I know it."

"He adores you."

"You can still find disappointment in those you adore," Lady Ansell argued.

Taking a deep breath, Isabel acknowledged that her time for childbearing was slipping rapidly through the hourglass. When she barred Pelham from her bed, she had ended what dreams she'd had of having a family of her own. She had mourned the loss deeply for many months, and then she'd found the strength to move past that dream.

Now, with her future filled with renewed possibilities, time was running away from her and circumstances forced her to wait even longer. Propriety and common sense dictated that she refrain from pregnancy until there could be no public doubt the child was Grayson's.

"*Lady Grayson.*"

The deep, raspy voice of her husband behind her should have startled her, but it did not. Instead, she was assailed with a longing so intense it nearly brought her to her knees.

Turning, both she and Lady Ansell found their spouses and host rounding a corner flanked by yew hedges. With his hands held behind his back, Gray was the picture of coiled predatory grace. He had always carried his power with envious ease. Now, with his dangerous edge blunted by her ability to sate his desires, he was even more compelling. The sultriness of his stride and half-lidded eyes made her mouth water, as she knew they would most women. That he was hers, that she could keep him and bear children with him made tears well. It was simply too much after going so long without.

"My lords," she greeted hoarsely, remaining rooted to Lady Ansell's side by good manners and nothing else. Had she the choice, she would have moved into Gray's arms immediately.

"We have been sent to find you," Lord Hammond said with a tentative smile.

After a quick perusal of her companion reassured her of the viscountess' renewed composure, Isabel nodded and was grateful to return to the manse where concerns of babies and regrets could be momentarily set aside.

The sound of crunching gravel alerted Rhys to the approaching figure. If he'd had any doubt that he was making the right decision, it was dispelled when Abby came into view, bathed in moonlight. The racing of his heart and nearly overwhelming need to crush her to him proved Bella's words true—Abby was the person he wished to make his life's journey with.

"I went to your rooms," she said softly, as direct as always.

How he adored that about her! After a lifetime of saying what was expected and hearing equally worthless discourse in return it was a joy to spend time with a woman who had no social artifice at all.

"I suspected you would," he replied gruffly, backing up when she stepped forward. The color of her eyes was not visible in the near darkness, but he knew it as well as he knew the color of his own. He knew how they darkened when he filled her, and how they glistened when she laughed. He knew every ink stain on her fingers, and could tell her which ones hadn't been there the last time he saw her. "And I knew that if you did, I would take you to bed."

She nodded her understanding. "You are departing tomorrow."

"I must."

The determined finality in Rhys' tone pierced Abigail like a rapier thrust.

"I shall miss you," she said.

Though the words themselves were the truth, the casual tone she used to impart them was a lie. The thought of the endless days before her without Rhys' touch and his hunger, was devastating. Even having known it would end like this, she was still unprepared for the pain of separation.

"I will come back for you as soon as possible," he said softly.

Her heart stilled before leaping. "Beg your pardon?"

"I travel to visit my father tomorrow. I will explain the situation between you and me, and then I will return to London and court you as I should have done from the beginning."

The *situation.*

"Oh my." Abby walked slowly over to a nearby marble bench and sat, her gaze lowering to her twisting fingers. The moment Grayson's voice had interrupted their kiss, she had dreaded this result. What had been nothing but joy and love for her, was now a lifetime duty for Rhys. She could not allow him to make the sacrifice, especially considering how obviously he resented his craving for her.

She looked at him and managed a soft smile. "I thought we agreed to approach our affair pragmatically."

He frowned. "If you think I have done anything pragmatically since meeting you, you are daft."

"You know what I mean to convey."

"Things have changed," he argued gruffly.

"Not for me." She held out her hands to him, then caught the gesture and clasped them back together. Any sign of weakness and he would note it. "Surely Lord and Lady Grayson will afford you their discretion if you ask it of them."

"Of course." He crossed his arms. "What are you saying?"

"I don't want to be courted, Rhys."

He gaped at her. "Why the devil not?"

She affected a shrug. "We had an agreement. I am not inclined to alter the rules at this point."

"Alter the rules . . . ?"

"I enjoyed our time together immensely and I will always be grateful to you."

"Grateful?" Rhys parroted, staring at Abby in confounded wonder. He longed to go to her, to hold her and break through the wall that was suddenly between them, but it was too dangerous. Ravishment was a very real hazard.

"Yes, quite." Her smile was a thing of beauty that shattered him.

"Abby, I—"

"Please. Say no more." Rising to her feet, she approached him and rested her fingertips over his tense arm. Her touch burned through the velvet of his coat. "I will forever count you as a dear friend."

"A friend?" He blinked furiously as his eyes burned. Releasing his breath, Rhys soaked up the sight of her—the tightly coiled dark tresses, the high waist of her pale green gown, the gentle swell of her breasts above the scooped neckline. All his. Nothing, not even her outrageous dismissal, would ever convince him otherwise.

"Always. Will you promise me a dance when next we meet?"

Rhys swallowed hard. There were a hundred things he wished to say, questions to ask, assurances to give . . . but they were all dammed up behind the lump in his throat. Here he had been falling in love, while Abby had merely been falling into bed? He refused to believe that. No woman could melt for a man the way she did for him and not feel something deeper than friendship.

A harsh laugh erupted without thought. If that wasn't a perfect comeuppance for a seasoned rake, he had no notion what was.

"Farewell until then," Abby said, before turning and walking away with undue haste.

Crushed and confused, Rhys sank onto the bench still warm from her body heat and dropped his head in his hands.

A plan. He needed a plan. This could not be the end. Every labored breath protested the loss of his love. There was something he was missing, if only he could think well enough to discover it. He had been with enough women to know that Abby cared for him. If what she felt wasn't love, surely there was a way to make it turn into love. If Isabel could be swayed, so surely could Abigail.

Lost in the process of thinking while fighting abject despair, he failed to register his lack of privacy until Grayson stumbled out from behind a tree. Disheveled and sporting leaves in his hair, the Marquess of Grayson was an odd sight.

"What are you about?" Rhys muttered.

"Do you know that in the whole of this garden I cannot find one red rose? There are pink roses and white roses, even an orange shade of rose, but no true red."

Running his hands through his hair, Rhys shook his head. "Is this part of your wooing of Isabel?"

"Who else would I be doing this for?" Grayson heaved out his breath. "Why could your sister not be the practical sort I thought she was?"

"I have discovered that practicality in women is exceedingly overappreciated."

"Oh?" Grayson arched a brow and dusted himself off as he moved closer. "I take it the situation between you and Miss Abigail is not proceeding satisfactorily?"

"Apparently, there is no situation," he said dryly. "I am a 'dear friend.'"

Grayson winced. "Good God."

Rhys rose to his feet. "So, considering the ruination of my own love life, if you reject my offer to help yours I would understand completely."

"I will take all the assistance I can get. I've no wish to spend the whole of my night gardening."

"And I've no wish to spend the whole of my night pining, so the distraction will be welcome."

Together, they moved deeper into the garden. Thirty minutes and several pricks of rose thorns later, Rhys grumbled, "This love business is dreadful."

Tangled in a climbing rose, Grayson growled, "Here, here."

Chapter 18

Standing in the doorway that separated his room from the adjoining sitting room, Gerard watched his wife glance at the small walnut clock on the mantel, tap her foot impatiently, and then mutter an oath under her breath.

"Such language from a lady," he drawled, relishing the warmth he felt at the knowledge that she missed him. "Puts me in the mood for sex."

She spun to face him and set her hands on her hips. "Everything puts you in the mood for sex."

"No," he argued, entering the room with a wicked smile. "Everything *about you* puts me in the mood."

She arched a brow. "Should I take your disheveled appearance and long absence as a sign? You look as if you've been tumbling a serving maid in the bushes."

Lowering his hand to rub the hard length of his cock, he said, "Here is a sign you can take. Proof that my interest is only for you." Then he pulled out the hand he had hidden behind his back, revealing a perfect red rosebud atop a very long stem. "But I think you will find this one more romantic."

Gerard watched Pel's eyes widen and knew that as far as roses went, the one he held aloft was a prime specimen. After all, nothing but the absolute best would do for his wife.

Her smile shook slightly, and her amber eyes glistened, making the itchy scratches on the backs of his hands pale to insignificance.

He knew that look. It was the smitten glance young debutantes had been giving him for years. That it now came from Isabel, his friend and the woman he lusted for so desperately, made everything he did not understand about courting come into clarity. Finesse may be something his primitive brand of claiming lacked, but he had always been able to be honest with Pel. "I want to woo you, win you, dazzle you."

"How is it that you can be so crude one moment and yet so appealing the next?" she asked with a shake of her head.

"There are moments when I am unappealing?" He clasped a hand over his heart. "How distressing."

"And impossibly, you look delectable with twigs in your hair," she murmured. "All that effort spent on me, and outside of bed, no less. A girl could swoon."

"Feel free, I'll catch you."

Her laugh made everything in the world right again. Just as it had done from the moment he met her.

"Do you know," he murmured, "that the sight of you—dressed or undressed, sleeping or waking—has always calmed me?"

She tugged the rose free of his grasp and lifted it to her nose. "'Calm' is not a word I would select to describe you."

"No? What would you choose, then?"

As she moved to add the rose to a nearby vase, he shrugged out of his coat. The knock that interrupted her reply surprised him. Then he listened to Isabel instruct the servant to bring hot water for his bath and he nodded to himself. His wife had always been one to anticipate a man's comfort.

"Stunning," she said when they were alone again. "Overwhelming. Determined. Relentless. Those descriptors suit you best."

Pausing before him, she slowly undid the carved buttons of his waistcoat. "Brazen." Pel licked her lower lip. "Seductive. Definitely seductive."

"Married?" he suggested.

She lifted her gaze to meet his. "Yes. Definitely married." Running her hands up his chest and over the tops of his shoulders, she pushed the garment off of him.

"Enchanted," he said in a tone made husky by the effect of her perfume and attentions.

"What?"

"Enchanted would describe me perfectly." Thrusting his hands through her rich auburn tresses, he tugged her hard against him. "Captivated."

"Do you find any oddness in our sudden fascination with one another?" she asked in a tone that begged for reassurance.

"Is it so sudden? I cannot seem to remember a time when I did not think you were perfect for me."

"I have always thought you were perfection, but never did I think you were perfect *for me*."

"Yes, you did, or you would not have wed me." He nuzzled his mouth against hers. "But you did not think I was perfect for loving, which I am."

"We really must work on building your self-confidence," she whispered.

Gerard twisted her head slightly to better fit their kiss and then licked across her lips. When her tongue flicked out to meet his, he hummed a soft chastising sound. "Allow me to kiss you. Just take it. Take me."

"Give me more then."

His smile curved against hers. A woman after his own heart. "I want to lick away every trace of any other kiss you have ever had." Cupping her nape in a hold that established his dominance, he followed the velvety softness of her upper lip with the tip of his tongue. "I want to give you your first kiss."

"Gerard," she whimpered, trembling.

"Do not be frightened."

"How can I help it? You are destroying me."

He nipped her plump lower lip with his teeth and then suckled it rhythmically, his eyes closing as the wanton taste of her inundated his senses. "I am rebuilding you, rebuilding *us*. I want to be the only man whose kiss you remember."

Sliding one hand down to the curve of her derriere, he urged her against him. With his arms filled with alluring softness, his nostrils filled with exotic flowers and aroused woman, his taste buds soaked in rich flavor, Gerard was left with no doubt that he loved Isabel more than anything. It was like nothing he had ever felt for anyone and it made him happy in a way nothing in his life ever had, or ever could. He tasted her tears and knew what she couldn't yet say.

He was about to say it for her when the scratching at the door parted them. It took far too long to have the bath prepared and the servants dismissed, but the resulting feel of Pel's fingers sifting soap through his hair and over his back was worth the wait. Then he noted the shaking of her hands and knew he had to distract her from her fears until he could take her to bed. There they'd never had any difficulty connecting intimately. With that in mind, he hurried the process.

"Would you like to discuss what lured you and Lady Ansell out to the garden earlier?" he asked, belting his robe before accepting the warmed brandy she offered him.

"Fresh air?" She took a seat in a nearby chair.

Gerard moved to the window. "You can simply tell me to mind my own affairs."

"Mind your own affairs," she retorted with laughter in her voice.

"Now I am intrigued."

"I knew you would be." He heard her sigh. "Apparently, conception is a problem for them, and it is causing a strain."

"Lady Ansell is barren?"

"Yes, her physician says the state is due to her advanced years."

He shook his head in sympathy. "Unfortunate for them that Ansell is an only child, so the burden rests entirely upon their shoulders." Taking a large swallow, he considered his own good fortune in having siblings. "You and I will never face that strain."

"I suppose not."

There was something in her tone that made his stomach clench in apprehension, but he hid the reaction by keeping his back to her and his tone casual. "Are you considering pregnancy?"

"Did you not say that you wished to build something lasting? What is more lasting than lineage?"

"Having two brothers negates that concern somewhat," he said carefully, fighting off the sudden tremor that moved him. The mere thought of Isabel increasing struck terror in him like he had never known. His hand shook so badly, the liquor in his glass sloshed precariously. He was only grateful that she could not see his upset from her vantage behind him. *Emily.*

Her death and the death of their child had very nearly destroyed him, and he had not loved Em like he loved Isabel. If something were to happen to his wife, if he should lose her . . .

He squeezed his eyes shut and forced his grip to relax before he shattered the goblet.

"Does it negate your wish to have issue?" she asked behind him.

He heaved out his breath. *How in hell was he to respond to that?* He would give up everything to have a family with her. But he would not give *her* up. Though the possible result would be bliss, the risk innate in that possibility was agonizing even to contemplate.

"Is there a rush?" he asked finally, turning to meet her gaze to search for the strength of her resolve. She sat nearby, her back ramrod straight, her legs crossed primly, her gown draped loosely about her shoulders and slightly gaping between the breasts. The perfect dichotomy of impeccable breeding and carnal seduction. Perfect for him. Irreplaceable.

She shrugged, which relieved him immeasurably. She was making conversation, nothing more. "I was not implying a need for haste."

Waving his hand in deliberately careless fashion, Gerard affected a complete lack of concern and changed the subject. "I hope you enjoy Waverly Park. It is the closest of my residences to London and one of my favorites. Perhaps, if you agree, we can arrange to spend more time there."

"That would be wonderful," she agreed.

There was a distance fraught with tension between them, such as two fencers would experience while circling one another. He could not bear it.

"I would like to retire now," he murmured, studying her over the rim of his goblet. There was never any distance between them in bed.

A faint hint of a smile teased her mouth. "You suffer no weariness after tramping through hedges?"

"No." He moved toward her with obvious purpose.

Her eyes widened and the ephemeral curve of her lips turned into the come-hither grin of a siren. "How delicious."

"Would you like to nibble on me?" He set the glass on a tabletop as he passed it.

Isabel laughed as he caught her about the waist. "You do realize that I always know when you have an ulterior motive?" She followed the curve of his brows with her fingertips. "You have the devil in your eyes when you are attempting to distract me."

He kissed the tip of her nose. "Do you mind, vixen?"

"No. I would indeed love to nibble on you." Her expert fingertips deftly loosened and then parted his robe. "There is so much to tempt me. I cannot decide where to begin."

"Are you soliciting suggestions?"

Running her fingertips lightly down the center of his chest, she tilted her head to the side as if pondering and said, "That is not necessary." His cock rose up. "I think it's plain which part of you is the most eager for my touch."

Every cell in his body, though tensed in expectation, sighed with satisfaction at her nearness. It always had. Being with Isabel made the world around him a better place, as maudlin as others would find that sentiment.

Her lips, so plump and hot, pressed against his neck, her tongue flicking out to taste his skin. "Ummm . . ." She hummed the pleasure she found with him, her hands sliding beneath his robe to caress his back. "Thank you for the rose. I have never had a rose picked by hand just for me."

"I would pick a hundred for you," he said gruffly, the memories of thorn pricks and muttered curses fading into obscurity. "A thousand."

"My darling. One is more than enough. It's perfection."

Everywhere she touched him heated and grew hard. No one else in his life had loved him like this. He felt it in her fingertips, in the brush of her breath across his flesh, in the way she trembled and grew aroused merely looking at him. Her tiny hands were everywhere, stroking, kneading. She loved the hard ridges of his muscles, despite how unfashionable they were.

She licked down his chest, taking tiny bites with her teeth, arousing him so fully that cum beaded up on the head of his cock and then slid down the upthrust length. As Pel dropped to her knees, she followed the glistening trail with her tongue, making him shudder and groan.

"Your mouth would ruin a saint," he growled, thrusting

his fingers into her fiery tresses. Staring down at her, he watched as she gripped the base of his shaft and angled him down to her waiting mouth.

"What does it do to a man who is far from saintly?"

Before he could catch his breath to reply, she'd engulfed the straining tip in burning, liquid heat. His eyelids grew heavy, his breathing labored as she suckled him between those lush, ripe lips. He swelled in response to the steady, rhythmic pulls, sweat beading along his pores as the flush of pure lust swept across his flesh.

None of the women in his past who had serviced him in this manner could compete with his wife. For Isabel it was not a duty or a prelude to sex. For her it was a joy in and of itself, something she enjoyed as much as he. Something that heated her skin, soaked her sex, beaded her nipples. She moaned along with him, worshipped him with her tongue, fondled the hardened cheeks of his ass.

She loved him.

The skin of his cock was dry and stretched tight where he could not fit. The weight of his balls drew up, ready to spurt the gift of life he would never give her.

It was this last thought that urged him to finish in her eager mouth. Isabel loved it when he came in that fashion, loved to feel him quiver on unsteady legs and cry out her name. But she also loved it when he was hard and thick like this. Loved how deeply he could stroke inside her, and right now that was where he needed to be—connected with her. From now until death parted them, they would have only each other. She was all he needed. He hoped she felt the same about him.

"No more." Pushing her head away, he stepped back from temptation, his cock an angry red and jerking in frustration.

Isabel pouted her protest.

Gerard stepped backward, sinking onto the settee she had

recently risen from, and gesturing impatiently for her to join him. Shrugging out of her dressing gown, she did just that, approaching him in a cloud of flame-touched tresses and seductively swaying hips. Then she climbed over him, straddling him, her hands on his shoulders, her full breasts swaying before his eyes.

Consumed with fever for her, he buried his face in the fragrant valley between her breasts, pulling the scent of her into his blood with deep desperate breaths.

"Gerard," she crooned, her fingers drifting into his damp hair and massaging the roots. "How I adore you."

Incapable of speech, he turned his head and ran his tongue across her nipple before closing his lips and suckling her, taking from her all the sustenance his soul needed. She gasped, a sound tinged with pain, and he cupped the warm undercurve and lifted, to make it more comfortable for her. Then he noted how heavy her breast was, and tender, if her sharp whimper was any indication.

He'd come in her!

The sudden flare of panic he felt nearly unmanned him. If not for Pel choosing that moment to sink her drenched cunt around his cock, he might have lost his erection altogether, which had never happened to him in his twenty-six years.

"Have I hurt you?" he managed, keeping his head lowered to hide his horror. *Surely it was too soon . . . It couldn't be . . .*

Isabel hugged him closer and began to move, mewling softly as she stroked deep inside herself with the hard length of him. "My courses approach," she gasped. "It's nothing."

The relief that flooded him was so powerful, he had to remember to breathe, every muscle drained by the receding tide of terror. He held his wife's straining body to his, biting his lip to keep some semblance of control as she undulated against him in perfect rhythm. Their bodies fit perfectly, as did their personalities, their tastes, their likes and dislikes.

And she loved him. He knew that like he knew nothing else—with bone-deep clarity and assurance. For all that he was, with all of his faults and failings, she adored him anyway. She had given him joy when he had been certain there was no more joy to be had. If he lost her . . .

He would die.

"Isabel." His hands rested on either side of her spine, absorbing the feel of her slender muscles flexing with her exertions. Up and down, she worked their bodies with an understanding of what pleased him as only a woman who loved him would know. It made their joining more than sex, more than carnal gratification.

"Slide a little lower," she instructed, urging him to alter the cant of his hips. "Right there." Pel sank deep onto him, the slick lips of her cunt encircling the very root of his cock. "Ohhhh . . ."

She tightened around him deliciously, and lust singed its way up his spine, making him arch away from the damask embroidered settee back and into her. "Ah, Christ!"

"That's it," she praised, her nails biting into the flesh of his shoulder. "Enjoy the ride."

"Pel," he managed, gasping with fear. "I can't last."

He could not spill in her again . . .

She rose and fell with such grace, her curvy body lithe and filled with quiet feminine strength. She was so tight, so hot and drenched, he knew he was losing his mind just as he had lost his heart.

"Come," he bit out, clutching her hips and thrusting madly into her. A silken fist. A burning glove. "Come, damn you!"

Gerard yanked her down as he ground upward, listening as she gave a thready cry, watching as her head fell back, feeling her clench tight around him and then milk his tortured cock with the same rhythmic suckling as he had felt in her mouth.

The moment she rested limp against his chest he withdrew,

catching his cock in hand and pumping, spurting his seed outside of his wife.

Agonized, he pressed his cheek to her heart, listening to the rapid, passionate beat as he hid his tears in the exotic floral sweat that pooled between her breasts.

Chapter 19

For Isabel, the ride to Waverly was a lovely one, despite the presence of her mother-in-law. The pride with which Gray brought attention to and explained various landmarks was obvious. It deepened their growing bond to share this day and this place, to build these memories. She listened with rapt attentiveness as he spoke in his raspy voice, watching the light in his eyes and the animation of his features.

How different he was from the young, jaded man who had left her side so long ago. That man had died with Emily. The husband she had now was entirely her own and had never given his heart to another. And though he had not yet said it aloud, she suspected he loved her.

The knowledge made her day brighter, her mood lighter, her steps surer. Certainly with love between them, they could conquer any difficulties. True love meant accepting a person with all their faults. Isabel couldn't help but hope that Grayson would love her in spite of hers.

As the carriage rolled to a stop before the Waverly Park manse, Isabel drew herself up and prepared to meet the staff. Today the formality held new significance. In the past, she had not truly felt like Grayson's marchioness, and while she had no trouble assuming the authority of the station she was bred for, it had not previously given her the sense of satisfaction it gave her now.

Over the course of the next few hours, she toured the manse with the efficient housekeeper and took note of the deference paid to Gray's mother, who appeared to have no trouble praising the servants for a job well done, despite her difficulty in doing the same for her sons. Still, the dignified compliments the dowager paid to the staff for remembering certain tasks impeded the passing of the reins to Isabel.

When they were done, she and the dowager sat in the upstairs family parlor for tea. The room, though slightly dated in its décor, was lovely and soothing with shades of deep gold and pale yellow. They managed to hold a civilized conversation regarding the nuances unique to running that particular household. Briefly.

"Isabel," the dowager said, in a tone that made her tense. "Grayson seems determined to establish you in all ways as his marchioness."

Lifting her chin, Isabel replied, "I am equally determined to fulfill that role to the best of my abilities."

"Including discarding your lovers?"

"My private affairs are none of your concern. However, I will say that my marriage is solid."

"I see." The dowager gifted her with a smile that did not reach her eyes. "And Grayson is not disturbed by the prospect of lacking an heir from his own loins?"

Isabel paused with a piece of buttered scone lifted halfway to her mouth. "Beg your pardon?"

Gray's mother narrowed her pale blue eyes and studied her over the rim of her flowered teacup. "Grayson makes no objection to your refusal to bear him children?"

"I am curious as to why you believe I do not want children."

"Your years are advanced."

"I know my age," Isabel said curtly.

"You have never shown any desire to be a mother before."

"How would you know that? You have never expended any effort to ask me."

The dowager took her time returning her saucer and cup to the table before asking, "So you do wish to have children?"

"I believe most women have that desire. I am no exception."

"Well, that is good to hear," came the murmured, distracted reply.

Staring at the woman across from her, Isabel attempted to collect her aim. There was one, if only she could puzzle it out.

"*Isabel.*" The sound of her favorite raspy voice soothed her immensely.

She turned with a bright smile to face Gray as he entered. His hair was windblown and his cheeks flushed, the handsomest man she had ever seen. She had always thought so. Now, looking at him with all the love she possessed, she was rendered breathless by the sight of him. "Yes, my lord?"

"The vicar's wife gave birth to their sixth child today." He held out both hands to her, and then pulled her to her feet. "A small crowd gathered with well-wishes. Instruments were brought out to provide music, others brought food. Now something of a celebration is happening in the village and I would dearly love to take you there."

"Yes, yes." Her excitement was sparked by his, her fingers tightening in response to his affectionate squeeze.

"May I come?" his mother asked, rising.

"I doubt it would be something you would enjoy," Gerard said, tearing his gaze away from Pel's radiant face. Then he shrugged. "But I have no objection."

"A moment to refresh, if you would, please," Isabel asked softly.

"Take all the time you need," he assured her. "I will have the landaulet brought around. It is a short distance, but neither of you are dressed for the walk."

Isabel left the room with her customary graceful glide. He began to follow her when his mother halted his egress.

"How will you know if the children she bears are truly yours?"

Gerard stilled, then turned slowly about. "What the devil are you talking about?"

"You don't honestly believe she will be faithful to you, do you? When she increases, the whole of society will wonder who the father is."

He sighed. *Would his mother ever leave well enough alone?* "Since Isabel will never become pregnant, your distasteful scenario will never come to fruition."

"I beg your pardon?"

"You heard me clearly the first time. After what happened to Emily, how could you think I would ever go through that ordeal again? Michael or Spencer's eldest male issue will inherit. I will not risk Isabel when there is no dire need to."

She blinked, and then broke out in a broad grin. "I see."

"I hope you do." Shaking a finger at her, he narrowed his gaze and said, "Do not think to blame this on my wife as a shortcoming. *I* have made the decision."

His mother nodded with unusual docility. "I understand completely."

"Good." He turned away again and strode to the door. "We shall be departing shortly. If you want to come, be ready."

"Never fear, Grayson," she called after him. "I would not miss this for the world."

"Celebration" was an apt description for the merry crowd that filled the lawn before the vicar's small house and the church next to it. Beneath two large trees gathered a few dozen dancing and loudly conversing villagers, and one beaming vicar.

Isabel could not help but offer a wide smile to everyone who approached their equipage in welcome. Grayson made a grand show of introducing her to the boisterous group, and she was greeted with great excitement.

For the next hour, she watched as Gray mingled. He spoke at length with the gentlemen he had labored alongside while building part of the stone wall, and deepened their regard with his ability to recall the names of their family members and neighbors. He lifted small children into the air, and reduced a group of smitten young girls to fits of giggles by complimenting their pretty hair ribbons.

All the while, Isabel basked in his charm from afar and fell so deeply in love, she ached all over with it. Her chest grew tight, and her heart clenched. The innocent infatuation she had felt for Pelham was nothing, *nothing* compared to the mature joy she found with Grayson.

"His father had the same charisma," the dowager said beside her. "My other sons do not display it in quite the same measure and I am afraid their wives will dilute the trait further. A pity it will not be passed down from Grayson, who has it in such abundance."

Shielded by her enjoyment of the day, Isabel shrugged off the usual irritation she felt with the dowager. "Who can foretell what traits a child will bear when it has yet to be conceived?"

"Since Grayson assured me back at the manse that he has no wish to beget issue off you, I think it's safe to say that he will not be passing along any traits at all."

Isabel glanced aside at her mother-in-law. With her once pretty features shielded by the brim of her hat, the dowager revealed no outward sign to the milling guests of the ugliness hidden beneath the façade. But that underlying rot was all Isabel could see.

"What are you talking about?" she snapped, turning to face her antagonist head-on. She could take poorly veiled barbs, but pure undiluted venom was too much.

"I offered my felicitations to Grayson on his decision to dedicate himself to preserving the title as he should." The dowager's chin lowered, shielding her eyes, but still revealing the smug curve to her thin lips. "He was quick to assure me that Emily is the only woman who would ever carry a child of his. He loved her, and she is irreplaceable."

Isabel's stomach roiled at the sudden remembrance of Gray's happiness over Em's condition. Thinking back, she found she couldn't recall a time since his return when Grayson had ever mentioned wanting to have children with *her*. Even last night, he had avoided the subject rather than address it, stressing that his brothers would see to the task of begetting an heir. "You lie."

"Why would I lie about something so easily disproved?" the dowager asked with mock innocence. "Truly, Isabel, you two are the most mismatched pair. Of course, if you can put aside any desire for children of your own and live with the knowledge that Grayson's heir will be the product of another woman, you may manage to rub along with some semblance of contentment."

Isabel's hands clenched into fists, and she fought the urge to hiss and scratch like a furious cat. Or cry. She couldn't decide which. But she knew either response would only give the dowager an advantage. So she managed a smile and a shrug. "I will take great pleasure in proving you wrong."

Moving a short distance away, she rounded the trunk of a large tree. There, safe from prying eyes, she fell back against the rough bark, heedless of the dirt and possible damage to her gown. Shaking, she laced her fingers together and took deep breaths. She could not appear less than fully composed.

Despite everything inside her that told her to have faith, to believe that she was good enough for Grayson, to trust that he cared for her and wanted her happiness, there was still the voice inside her that reminded her that Pelham had found her lacking.

"Isabel?"

As Grayson stepped beneath the shade of the tree, she met his concerned gaze. "Yes, my lord?"

"Are you well?" he asked, stepping closer. "You look pale."

She waved her hand carelessly. "Your mother is stirring the pot again. It's nothing. A moment and I will regain my composure."

The warning rumble in his throat soothed her, the sound of a man ready to defend his mate. "What did she say to you?"

"Lies, lies, and more lies. What recourse is left to her? You and I are no longer estranged, and we share the same bed, so the only thing she could wound me with was the topic of children."

Gray tensed visibly, something she noted with a flare of unease.

"What about children?" he asked gruffly.

"She claims you do not want any with me."

He stood unmoving for a long while and then winced. Her heart stopped, and then caught in her throat.

"Is it true?" Her hand lifted to her bosom. "Gerard?" she prodded when he did not answer.

Growling, he looked away. "I want to give you things, *all* things. I want to make you happy."

"But no children?"

His jaw tightened.

"Why?" she cried, her heart breaking.

Lifting his gaze to hers, he bit out, "I will not lose you. I *cannot* lose you. Risking you to childbirth is not an option."

Stumbling away, Isabel covered her mouth.

"For God's sake, don't look at me like that, Pel! We can be happy just the two of us."

"Can we? I remember the joy you felt when Emily was pregnant. I remember your exuberance." Shaking her head, she pressed her fingertips hard against her lower lip to still its quivering. "I wanted to give you that."

"Do you also remember my pain?" he asked, on the defensive. "What I feel for you is beyond anything I have ever felt for anyone. To lose you would destroy me."

"You think I am too old for you." Unable to bear the sight of his torment, which reflected her own, she stepped around him.

"This has nothing to do with age."

"Yes, it does."

Gray caught her arm as she walked by. "I promised you I would be enough, and I will be. I can make you happy."

"Release me," she said softly, meeting his gaze. "I need to be alone."

The blue of his eyes swirled with frustration, fear, and a tinge of anger. None of that affected her. She was numb, as she had learned long ago how to be when pierced with a mortal wound.

No children.

Pressing a hand over her aching chest, she tugged the arm that was still trapped in his grip.

"I cannot allow you to go like this, Pel."

"You have no choice," she said simply. "You will not hold me against my will in front of all these people."

"Then I shall go with you."

"I want to be alone," she reiterated.

Gerard stared at his wife's frigid shell and felt a gulf between them so wide he wondered if they could cross it. Panic made his heart race and his breathing shallow. "For Christ's sake, you never said anything about wanting children. You made me promise not to spill my seed in you!"

"That was before you made our temporary bargain into a permanent marriage!"

"How in hell was I to know that your feelings on the matter had changed?"

"Foolish me." Her eyes burned with amber fire. "I should have said, 'By the way, before I fall in love with you and want children, let me ask if you have any objections.'"

Before I fall in love with you . . .

At any other moment those words would have raised him

to the heights. Now they cut him to the quick. "Isabel . . ." he breathed, tugging her closer. "I love you, too."

She shook her head, causing the artless curls at her nape to sway violently. "No." Her hand came up to ward him off. "That is the last thing I want to hear from you. I wanted to be a wife to you in all ways, I was willing to try, but you refuse me. We have nothing left now. *Nothing!*"

"What the devil are you talking about? We have each other."

"No, we do not," she said, with such finality his throat clenched tight as a fist, cutting off his air. "You took us beyond friendship and we cannot go back. And now . . ." She choked on a sob. "I cannot make love to you now, so we have no marriage either."

He froze, the beat of his heart faltering. *"What?"*

"I would resent you every time you sheathed yourself in a French letter or withdrew to spill your seed. To know that you will not allow me to carry your child—"

Catching her about the shoulders, Gerard attempted to shake some sense into his wife. Isabel retaliated with a booted kick to his shin, causing him to swear and release her in surprise. She raced swiftly back to the waiting landaulet, and he hurried after her as fast as decorum would allow. Just as Isabel clambered without assistance into the equipage, his mother stepped into his path.

"Witch!" he growled, grabbing her by the elbow and yanking her roughly aside. "When I depart today, I am leaving you here."

"Grayson!"

"You like this property, so refrain from looking so horrified." He loomed over her, making her cringe. "Save your horror for the day you see me again. I pray you never do, because it will mean that Isabel would not take me back. And if that happens, even God himself will not be able to spare you from my wrath."

He threw her aside and followed the fleeing landaulet on foot, but found his way repeatedly blocked by reveling villagers. When he finally arrived at the manse, Pel had already taken the traveling coach and departed.

Fighting a near crippling fear that he had damaged Isabel's love beyond repair, Gerard saddled a horse and gave chase.

Chapter 20

R hys waited in the hallway of the wing that housed
Abby's rooms. He paced nervously and tugged at his
cravat, but never took his gaze away from her door. His coach
waited out front, and the servants were loading his trunks.
Time was growing short. He would be leaving soon, but refused to do so until he had spoken with Abigail.

He had been trying all morning, to no avail. He had attempted to take the seat next to her at breakfast, but she
moved too quickly, picking a chair bracketed with guests on
either side. A deliberate avoidance.

Blowing out an impatient breath, he heard the lock turn,
then Abigail stepped out. He pounced.

"Abby." Striding toward her quickly, he noted the pleasure
that lit her eyes, before she lowered her lids and shielded
them.

Damned wench was playing at something, and he would
get to the bottom of it, by God! Make him fall in love with
her and then toss him aside, would she? He would see about
that.

"Lord Trenton. How are you this—Oh my!"

Catching her elbow, he dragged her down the hall and into
the servant's stairwell. He paused on the tiny landing and
looked at her, noting the slight parting of her lips. Before she
could protest, he drew her to him and kissed her, taking her

mouth in near desperation, needing her response like he needed to breathe.

When she whimpered and surged into him, Rhys had to bite back the shout of triumph. She tasted like sweet cream and warm honey, a simple flavor that cleansed his jaded senses, and made the world fresh and new. He had to tear himself away, something he barely managed after spending a miserable, sleepless night without her.

"You will marry me," he said gruffly.

Abby sighed and kept her eyes closed. "Now, why did you have to ruin a perfect farewell with that nonsense?"

"It is not nonsense!"

"It is," she insisted, shaking her head as she looked at him. "I will not say yes. So please, cease."

"You want me," he said stubbornly, rubbing his thumb across her swollen bottom lip.

"For sex."

"That is enough." It wasn't, but if he had her beneath him whenever he wanted, perhaps he could reclaim the ability to think. Once he could think, he could plan to win her. Grayson was bumbling along that path. He could simply follow the trail of crushed greenery.

"It isn't," she argued gently.

"Have you any idea how many unions have no passion at all?"

"Yes." She set her hand over his heart. "But I do not believe that passion will be enough to bear the things others will say about you taking an American to wife."

"Curse them all," he grumbled. "We have more than passion, Abby. You and I rub along well. We enjoy each other's companionship even out of bed. And we both like gardens."

She smiled and his heart leapt. Then she dashed it to pieces. "I want love, and I won't settle for less."

Rhys swallowed hard. It was obvious she did not love him, but to hear her say it aloud was painful in the extreme. "Love can grow."

Her lip quivered beneath his thumb. "I do not want to take the chance that it won't grow. I must feel it, Rhys, in order to be happy."

"Abigail," he breathed, pressing his cheek to hers. He could win her heart. If she would only give him the chance.

Unfortunately, before he could press further, a door opened on a lower floor and the sounds of two maids speaking to one another rose up to them.

"Farewell, my lord," Abby whispered, before rising to her toes and gifting him with a bittersweet kiss. "Save that dance for me."

Then she was gone, and the sudden emptiness in his arms was echoed in his heart.

Pulling into the drive before the Hammond estate, Isabel was relieved to see Rhys' black lacquered coach preparing for departure. After spending the last hour soaking her kerchief over the demise of her marriage and her broken dreams, she needed her brother's shoulder to cry on and advice on how to proceed.

"Rhys!" she cried, descending the steps with the help of a footman and running toward him.

He turned with a frown, one hand set at his waist, the other rubbing the back of his neck. He stood tall and proud, his mahogany hair capped with a hat, his long legs sheathed in trim, fitted trousers. To her aching heart, the sight of her brother offered comfort in and of itself.

"Bella? I thought you had left for the day. What has happened? You've been crying."

"I am riding with you back to London," she said hoarsely, her throat raw. "I can be ready within moments."

Looking over her head, he asked, "Where is Grayson?"

She shook her head violently in answer.

"Bella?"

"Please," she murmured, lowering her gaze because his compassion and concern threatened to instigate a torrent of tears. "You will turn me into a watering pot in front of the servants. I shall tell you everything, once I've refreshed myself and collected my abigail."

Rhys muttered an oath under his breath and tugged at his cravat. "Make haste," he growled, shooting an anxious glance at the front entrance. "Please believe that I don't mean to be harsh or uncaring, but truly ten minutes is all I can spare."

Nodding, Isabel hurried into the house. Everything she had with her could not be packed in ten minutes, so she splashed water on her face, took what she needed to be comfortable on the long drive, and left a note for Grayson to see to the rest of her belongings.

At any moment, she expected her husband to appear and the anxiousness of waiting made the cold knot in her belly tighten. She felt rushed, off-kilter, breathless. Her entire world was spinning without the steady core she thought she had discovered in Gray. She should have known she would be lacking in some way. This tightness in her chest that made her dizzy was her own fault. The reality had always been there—she was too old for Gray and he did not trust that her body could give him the children she knew he desired. If she were younger, she doubted he would have such fears about her health.

"Come along," she said to Mary, and they followed the footman, who carried her valise down the stairs to the front driveway.

Rhys waited out front, pacing restlessly. "Damned if you didn't take forever," he muttered, gesturing her abigail to the nearby servants' coach, before catching Isabel's arm and pulling her toward the waiting carriage. He pulled open the door and nearly thrust her inside.

Isabel had to scramble to stay on her feet and as she lifted her head within the confines of the coach, she understood her brother's need for haste. Above a gag, eyes of bright blue with golden flecks met hers.

"Dear heaven," she muttered, backing out quickly. She glanced around in search of a possible audience, then whispered furiously, "What are you doing with Miss Abigail in the coach trussed up like a dinner fowl?"

He heaved out his breath and then set his hands on his hips. "Blasted woman won't listen to reason."

"*What?*" Her arms akimbo pose mimicked his. "*This* is reason? The future Duke of Sandforth kidnapping an unmarried girl?"

"What recourse do I have?" Holding out his hands to her, he asked, "Was I simply to walk away when she refused me?"

"So you will force the girl into marriage by compromising her? What basis is that for a lasting union?"

He winced again. "I love her, Bella. I cannot imagine going on with my life without her. Tell me what to do."

"Oh, Rhys," Isabel breathed, her tears beginning anew. "Do you not think that if I knew how to create love where none existed, I would have done so with Pelham?"

Perhaps it was a familial curse of some terrible sort.

She had wished desperately for Rhys to find a true loving partner. What was left of her heart was broken further to learn that he had fallen in love with a woman who did not return his affections.

Fierce kicking against the interior of the carriage drew their attention. When Rhys moved toward the door, Isabel stepped into his path. "Allow me. You have done quite enough, I think."

Raising her skirts, she used the small step to gain entry into the coach. She sat on the opposite squab, pulled off her gloves, and began to work on removing the gag that allowed only muffled protests to be heard over Rhys' constant muttering about "*impossible women.*"

"Please do not scream when this comes off," she begged softly as she worked at the knot. "I realize you have been treated abominably by Lord Trenton, but he truly does care for you. He is simply misguided. He would not have—"

Abigail writhed frantically as the gag worked free. "My hands, my lady! Free my hands!"

"Yes, of course." Isabel swiped at the tears that wet Abigail's cheeks, then tugged at the soft cloth that wrapped around her wrists. The moment the tie loosened, Abigail worked her arms free and threw herself out the open door of the coach at Rhys. His tall frame absorbed the impact easily, though his hat was knocked away.

"Abby, please!" he begged as she pounded ineffectually at his shoulders. "I *must* have you. Yield to me! I will make you love me, I promise."

"I already love you, you idiot!" she sobbed.

He pulled back with wide eyes. "*What?* You said you only wanted— Damnation, you *lied* to me?"

"I'm sorry." Her feet dangled above the ground as he hugged her.

"What the devil is your objection to marrying me then?"

"You did not tell me you felt the same."

Setting her down, Rhys scrubbed a hand over his face and growled. "Why in the world would a man marry a woman who drives him insane if not for love?"

"I thought you only wished to marry me because we were caught kissing."

"Good God." His eyes closed, even as he reached for her again. "You will be the death of me."

"Say it again," she implored, her lips pressed to the line of his jaw.

"I love you madly."

Isabel looked away from the scene, a fresh kerchief pressed to her face. "Remove his bags," she said to the nearby footman, who hurried to do as she ordered. She settled into the seat, leaned her head back and closed her eyes, which didn't stop the tears from leaking out regardless.

Perhaps it was only she who was cursed.

"Bella."

Opening her eyes, she glanced at Rhys, whose torso filled the doorway.

"Stay," he said softly. "Talk to me."

"But it is so annoying when women start discussing their feelings," she replied with a watery smile.

"Don't make light. You should not be alone now."

"I want to be alone, Rhys. Staying here, pretending to be well when I am not, would be the worst form of torture."

"What in hell happened with you and Grayson? He was sincere in his wish to win your affections. I know he was."

"He succeeded." Leaning forward, she spoke urgently. "You took a risk for love, and it has paid you handsomely. Promise me you will always put your love above everything else, just as you did today. And never underestimate Miss Abigail."

Rhys scowled. "Please do not speak in riddles, Bella. I am a man. I lack comprehension of the female language."

She set her hand over his where it curled around the door frame. "I must go before Grayson arrives. We will talk more when you return to London with your fiancée."

It was that one-word reminder that caused him to nod and step back. He would stay and speak with the Hammonds. She would survive, as she always had.

"I will hold you to that, Bella," he warned.

"Of course." She offered him a wavering smile. "I am so happy for you. I do not approve of your methods," she amended hastily, "but I am glad that you have found the one woman for you. Please make my apologies for me. I did not have the time."

He nodded. "I love you."

"My, you are becoming proficient at saying that, aren't you?" Isabel sniffled and swiped at her eyes. "I love you, as well. Now let me go."

Rhys stepped back and shut the door. The coach lurched

into motion, leaving the setting of fleeting bliss behind, but taking the memories with it.

Isabel curled into the corner and cried.

Gerard rode his mount hard through the Hammond park gate. When he drew to a halt before the front steps, he threw himself down and tossed the reins to the startled groomsman. Disregarding any semblance of decorum, he ran up the stairs to his rooms.

Only to find his wife gone and a tersely worded note requesting that her belongings be sent to her. His response knotted his gut and stole his breath like a physical blow.

He realized then how wounded she was. He sank onto the nearest chair, Pel's missive crushed within his clenched fist. He was stunned, unable to comprehend what had happened to the happiness they'd enjoyed upon waking mere hours ago.

"What transpired?" asked a voice from the open doorway to the main gallery.

Glancing up, Gerard found Trenton leaning against the jamb. "I wish I knew." He sighed. "Were you aware that Isabel wanted children?"

Trenton pursed his lips a moment. "I do not recall ever discussing the topic with her, but it stands to reason that she would. She is romantically inclined. I cannot imagine a woman finding anything more romantic than a family."

"How could I have missed that?"

"I've no notion. Why is having a child a problem? Surely you want the same." Trenton pushed upright and entered, taking the wingback opposite.

"A woman I once cared for died in childbirth," Gerard murmured, staring down at the wedding band on his finger.

"Ah, yes. Lady Sinclair."

Gerard's gaze lifted with a scowl. "How in hell can Isabel ask me to relive the experience? The mere thought of her increasing fills me with such terror I can hardly bear it. The reality would kill me."

"Ah, I see." Settling back into the chair, Trenton crossed one foot over the opposite knee and gave a thoughtful hum. "Forgive me for discussing something delicate, but I am not blind. Over the weeks since your return, I have seen bruises on Isabel. Occasional bite marks. Scratches. I would venture to say you are not a man who practices moderation in his appetites. And somewhere along the way, you found some confidence that she could withstand such depth of ardor."

"Damned if this isn't uncomfortable to discuss," Gerard muttered.

"But I am not wrong?" Trenton prodded. When Gerard gave a jerky nod, he said, "If memory serves me correctly, Lady Sinclair was of delicate stature. In fact, the difference between her and Bella is so extreme one cannot help but wonder how it is that you were so attracted to both."

"Different motivators behind the two attractions." Gerard stood and walked slowly about the room, searching out pockets of exotic floral scent in the air. Em had appealed to his pride. Pel appealed to his soul. "Very different."

"My point exactly."

Taking a deep breath, Gerard leaned against the mantel and closed his eyes. Isabel was a tigress. Em had been a kitten. The sunset to the sunrise. Opposites in every way.

"Women survive childbirth daily, Grayson. Women far less spirited than our Isabel."

This was true, there could be no denying it. But while his mind spoke reason, his heart knew only the unreasonableness of love.

"If I were to lose her," Gerard said, his tone anguished, "I do not know what would become of me."

"Seems to me, you are already well on your way to losing her. Would it not be better to take the risk and chance keeping her, than to do nothing and lose her for certain?"

The logic of that statement was undeniable. Gerard knew

that if he did not bend in this, he would lose Pel. Her distress today had made that abundantly clear.

He heard Trenton rise and turned to face him. "Before you go, Trenton, may I beg the use of your carriage?"

"No need. Bella took mine."

"Why?" The dead weight of apprehension settled in Gerard's stomach. Had his fear caused Isabel to forsake everything that belonged to him?

"It was hitched and ready in the drive. No, don't ask. It is a long story, and you had best be off if you hope to make it back to London before sunrise."

"Lord and Lady Hammond?"

"Are blissfully unaware of any unpleasantness. With minor effort you can keep it that way."

Nodding his agreement, Gerard straightened and mentally began the preparations he needed to excuse himself and his wife from the party without arousing undue suspicions. "Thank you, Trenton," he said gruffly.

"Just fix what has gone awry. I want Bella happy. That is all the thanks I require."

Chapter 21

Gerard judged the distance to the second floor window of his London residence, leaned back, and took aim with a pebble. He waited until he heard the small but satisfying *tink*, before drawing his arm back and throwing another.

The sky was beginning to lighten, turning the dark charcoal gray to a pale pink. He was reminded of another morning, and another window. But the goal he sought was the same.

It took several hits before he achieved the desired result—the sash lifted and Pel thrust her sleep-mussed head out.

"What are you doing, Grayson?" she asked in that low, throaty tone he adored. "I warn you, I am not in the mood to recite Shakespeare."

"Thank God for that," he said with a hesitant laugh.

Apparently, she had vivid remembrances of that morning, too. There was hope in that.

With an audible sigh she settled into the window seat and arched a brow in silent query. No surprise to Isabel to find a man tossing things to win her attention. The whole of her adult life, men had been trying to gain entry to her bedroom.

Now, her body was promised to *his* bed, for the rest of her life. The pleasure the thought gave him spread rapidly through his body and warmed his blood. Then he chilled just as swiftly.

As the rising sun revealed her beloved face, he saw that her sherry-colored eyes were sad, and the tip of her nose was red. She had cried herself to sleep by the look of it, and it was entirely his fault.

"Isabel." His voice was a raw plea. "Let me in. It's cold out here."

Her wary expression turned to one even more guarded. Leaning farther out the window, her unbound tresses drifted over a shoulder bared by her loosely belted dressing gown. From the soft sway of her full breasts he knew she was naked beneath. The effect that knowledge had on him was as predictable as the sunrise. "Is there some reason you cannot enter?" she asked. "Last I queried, this was your home."

"Not the manse, Pel," he clarified. "Your heart."

She stilled.

"Please. Let me explain. Let me make things right between us. I *need* to make things right between us."

"Gerard," she breathed, so softly he barely heard his name drift down upon the chilly morning breeze.

"I love you desperately, Isabel. I cannot live without you."

Her hand came up and covered trembling lips. He stepped closer to the house, every cell in his body reaching out to her.

"I pledge my troth to you, my wife. Not for my needs, as I did before, but for yours. You have given me so much— friendship, laughter, acceptance. You have never judged me or chastised. When I did not know who I was, you cared for me anyway. When I make love to you, I am content and I wish for nothing else."

"Gerard."

His name, spoken in her broken voice, struck deeply. "Will you let me in?" he implored.

"Why?"

"I want to give all that I am to you. Including children, should we be so blessed."

She was silent for so long he grew dizzy from holding his breath. "I agree to talk. Nothing more."

His lungs burned. "If you still love me, we can manage the rest."

Her arm extended out to him. "Come up."

Turning on his heel, Gerard ran to the door and then up the stairs, the desperate need to be with his wife riding him hard. But when he entered their rooms, he drew up short. The sight that greeted him was *home*, despite the tension that crackled between him and Pel.

A fire lay banked in the marble-framed hearth, ivory satin tented the ceiling, and Isabel stood before the window, her lush curves draped in deep red silk. It was an excellent color for his wife, whose lush flamboyance needed a bold setting. And this room, where they had spent so many hours talking and laughing, was an excellent setting for a new beginning. Here, they would conquer the inner demons that strove to drive them apart.

"I've missed you," he said softly. "When you are not beside me, I feel very alone."

"I missed you, too," she admitted, swallowing hard. "But then, I wonder if I ever really had you. I think, perhaps, Emily still holds a part of you captive."

"As Pelham holds you captive?" He shrugged out of his great coat, and then his coat, taking his time because he noted how warily she watched him. Turning his head, his gaze met Pelham's in the portrait. "You and I both made poor choices for ourselves earlier in life, and we are both scarred by them."

"Yes, perhaps we are each ruined in our own way," she said wearily, moving to her favorite chaise.

"I refuse to believe that. There is a reason for everything." Gerard tossed his waistcoat across the back of a gilded chair and crouched before the fire, stoking it and throwing on more coal until heat began to fill the room. "I'm certain that had I not known Emily, I would not be able to appreciate you as I do. I would not have had the comparison required to recognize how perfect you are for me."

She snorted softly. "You only thought I was perfect when you assumed I had forsaken motherhood."

"And you," he continued, ignoring her. "I doubt you would find my uncontrollable passion for you to be so welcome had you not been wooed with calculated seduction by Pelham."

The silence that greeted him was rife with possibilities. He felt the spark of hope he'd tucked close to his heart expand into a blaze to match the one in the hearth before him.

He stood. "However, I think it is time to reduce this marriage of four into a more intimate union of two."

Turning to face her, he found her sitting upright on the chaise, her face pale and beautiful, her eyes welling with tears. Her fingers were laced so tightly together they were white, and he went to her, sat at her feet, and warmed her icy hands with his own.

"Look at me, Pel." When she met his gaze, he offered a smile. "Let's make another bargain, shall we?"

"A bargain?" One finely arched brow rose.

"Yes. I agree to start anew with you. In every way. I will not burden our love with guilt from the past."

"Every way?"

"Yes. Nothing held back, I swear it. In return, you will take down that portrait. You will agree to believe that you are perfection itself. That there is nothing—" His voice broke, forcing him to close his eyes and take a shuddering breath.

Parting the ends of her gown, Gerard nuzzled his cheek against the satin skin of her thigh and breathed in her scent, calming the emotion that overwhelmed him.

Her fingers drifted into his hair, stroking the roots, loving him silently.

"There is nothing I would change about you, Isabel," he whispered, drinking in the sight of the mature beauty and inner strength that made her who she was. Unique and priceless. "Most especially not your age. Only an experienced woman could manage a man as overbearing as I can be."

"Gerard." She slid down beside him, and pulled him to her breast. There, she held him to her heart. "I suppose I should expect that any time you throw stones at my window, it is a herald to how drastically my life is about to change."

"Yes, you should."

"Wicked rogue." Her lips curved against his forehead.

"Ah, but I am *your* wicked rogue."

"Yes." She laughed softly. "That's true. You are far different from the man I married, but your wickedness is one thing that, thankfully, did not change. You are just exactly the way I want you."

He moved, cradling her spine as he lowered her to the floor. "I want you, too."

Isabel gazed up at him, her hair a banner of fire, her skin as pale as ivory where it was revealed by the parted edges of her gown. His dark hand brushed aside the intruding material, revealing the full breasts and ripe curves he worshipped. He shoved his hand into his pocket and withdrew the ruby ring he had purchased for her. With shaking fingers, Gerard slipped it into place, kissing the stone before turning her hand and pressing his lips against her palm.

Heat swept across his skin like a hot breeze, nerve endings tingling to acute awareness, his mouth watering. Bending his head, he licked the softness of one nipple and then the other, parting his lips more fully and drawing her into his mouth. His eyes slid closed, his blood growing sluggish with desire and love, as he drank in her taste with long, deep pulls.

"Yes . . ." she breathed, when he bit gently down on the hardened crest, relishing as always the fierce need he had to devour her whole.

They moved languidly, in no rush. Every touch, caress, and murmur was a promise made. To forsake all others. To love one another, trust one another, and leave the past behind.

Theirs was a union made for all the wrong reasons, but in the end it was one that could not have been more *right*.

Clothing fell away until their skin touched everywhere and he cupped her thigh and opened her, sinking the hard length of his cock into tight hot depths. Joining them more fully than the golden bands they wore ever could.

Gerard lifted his head and watched Isabel's face as he pumped deep into her. Her soft whimper filled the air, made his balls draw up, made his arms shake as he supported his weight. She tossed her head restlessly, her heels in his back, her nails in his forearms. The fiery skeins of her dark hair were spread across the Aubusson rug, releasing the heady scent that intoxicated him.

God, how he loved this. He doubted he would ever have his fill of the sight of her helpless to her desire or the feel of her cunt so tight and slick.

"Sweet Isabel," he crooned, freed for the first time from the desperation that had marked their past encounters.

"*Gerard.*"

He groaned. His name was a tactile caress when spoken in that throaty voice. Lowering over her, he pressed his mouth to hers, drinking in her gasps as he worked her with his cock in exactly the way she liked, stroking her with long, deep, slow drives.

"Oh God!" she gasped, her depths rippling around him, her back arching in the throes of climax.

"I love you," he breathed, his mouth to her ear, his chest pressed to hers. Then he followed her, shuddering, spilling his seed in a rush of longing, giving her the promise of the life they would create together with boundless joy in his heart.

She met him stroke for stroke, his match in every way.

If you loved *The Stranger I Married*, don't miss *Seven Years to Sin*, available now.

Within hours, she would be wed.

As the dark of night lightened into the gray of pre-dawn, Jessica hugged her shawl tighter about her shoulders and walked Temperance deeper into the forest surrounding the Pennington manse. The pug's rapid steps crunched atop the loose gravel trail in a staccato that was soothing in its familiarity.

"Why must you be so picky?" Jess chastised. Her breath puffed visibly in the chill air, making her long for the warmth of the bed she had yet to crawl into. "Any spot should suffice."

Temperance glanced up with an expression Jess swore was akin to exasperation.

"Very well," she said reluctantly, unable to refuse that look. "We'll go a bit farther."

They rounded a corner and Temperance paused, sniffing. Apparently satisfied with the location, the pug presented her back to Jess and squatted in front of a tree.

Smiling at the bid for privacy, Jess turned away and took in her surroundings, deciding to explore the trail more thoroughly in the light of day. Unlike so many estates where the gardens and woodlands were invaded by obelisks, reproductions of Grecian statues and temples, and the occasional pagoda, the Pennington estate displayed a welcome appreciation of the natural landscape. There were places along the pathway where it felt as if civilization and all its inhabitants were miles away. She had not expected to enjoy the feeling so much but found she did, especially after hours of meaningless interactions with people who cared only for the title she was marrying into.

"I shall enjoy walking you through here," she said over her shoulder, "when the sun is up and I am properly attired for the activity."

Temperance finished her business and moved into view. The pug started back toward the house, tugging on the leash with notable impatience after taking so long to find a proper piddle spot. Jess was following when a rustling noise to the left put Temperance on alert. The dog's dark ears and tail perked up, while her tan muscular body tensed with expectation.

Jess's heart beat faster. If it was a wild boar or feral fox, the situation would be disastrous. She would be devastated if something untoward happened to Temperance, who was the only creature on earth who did not judge Jess by standards she struggled greatly to meet.

A squirrel darted across the path. Jess melted with relief and gave a breathless laugh. But Temperance did not stand down. The pug lunged, ripping her leash from Jess's slackened grip.

"Bloody hell. Temperance!"

In a flash of tiny limbs and fur, the two creatures were gone. The sounds of the chase—the rustling of leaves and the pug's low growling—quickly faded.

Tossing up her hands, Jess left the walkway and followed the path of trampled foliage. She was so focused on tracking, she failed to realize she'd come upon a large gazebo until she very nearly ran into it. She veered to the right . . .

A female's throaty laugh broke the quiet. Jess stumbled to a startled halt.

"Hurry, Lucius," the woman urged breathlessly. "Trent will note my absence."

Wilhelmina, Lady Trent. Jess stood unmoving, barely breathing.

There was a slow, drawn-out creaking of wood.

"Patience, darling." A recognizable masculine voice rejoined in a lazy, practiced drawl. "Let me give you what you paid for."

The gazebo creaked again, louder this time. Quicker and harder. Lady Trent gave a thready moan.

Alistair Lucius Caulfield. *Inflagrente delicto* with the Countess of Trent. Dear God. The woman was nearly a score of years his senior. Beautiful, yes, but of an age with his mother.

The use of his middle name was startling. And, perhaps, telling . . . ? Aside from the obvious, perhaps they were intimate in a deeper sense. Was it possible the roguish Caulfield had a *tendre* for the lovely countess, enough that she would have reason to call him by a name not used by others?

"You," the countess purred, "are worth every shilling I pay for you."

Dear God. Perhaps not an intimacy at all, but a . . . transaction. An arrangement. With a man providing the services . . .

Hoping to move on without giving herself away, Jess took a tentative step forward. A slight movement in the gazebo prompted her to still again. Her eyes narrowed, struggling to overcome the insufficient light. It was her misfortune to be bathed in the faint glow of the waning moon while the interior of the gazebo remained deeply shadowed by its roof and overhanging trees.

She saw a hand wrapped around one of the domed roof's supporting poles and another set a short ways above it. A man's hands, gripping for purchase. From their height on the beam, she knew he was standing.

"Lucius . . . For God's sake, don't stop now."

Lady Trent was pinned between Caulfield and the wood. Which meant he was facing Jess.

Twin glimmers in the darkness betrayed a blink.

He saw her. Was in fact staring at her.

Jess wished the ground would open and swallow her whole. What was she to say? How was one supposed to act when caught in such a situation?

"Lucius! Damn you." The weathered wood whined in response to its pressures. "The feel of your big cock in me is delicious, but far more so when it's moving."

Jess's hand went to her throat. Despite the cold, perspiration misted her forehead. The horror she should have felt at finding a man engaged in sexual congress was markedly absent. Because it was Caulfield, and he fascinated her. It was a terrible sort of captivation with which she viewed him—a mixture of envy for his freedom and horror at the ease with which he disregarded public opinion.

She had to get away before she was forced to acknowledge her presence to Lady Trent. She took a careful step forward . . .

"Wait." Caulfield's voice was gruffer than before.

She froze.

"I cannot!" Lady Trent protested breathlessly.

But it was not the countess Caulfield spoke to.

One of his hands was outstretched, extended toward Jess. The request stunned her into immobility.

A long moment passed in which her gaze remained fixed on the twin sparkles of his eyes. His breathing became harsh and audible.

Then, he gripped the pole again and began to move.

His thrusts began slowly at first, then became more fervent with a building tempo. The rhythmic protests of the wood battered Jess from all sides. She could see no detail beyond those two hands and glistening gaze that smoldered with a tangible heat, but the sounds she heard filled her mind with images. Caulfield never took his eyes from her, even as he rutted so furiously she wondered how the countess could take pleasure in such violence of movement. Lady Trent was nearly incoherent, coarse words of praise spilling from her lips between high-pitched squeals.

Jess was riveted by this exposure to a side of sexual congress she'd been mostly ignorant of. She knew the mechanics; her stepmother had been most thorough. *Do not cringe or cry when he enters you. Try to relax; it will decrease the discomfort. Make no sound of any kind. Never voice a complaint.* And yet Jess had seen the knowing looks of other women and heard whispers behind fans that hinted at more. Now she had the proof. Every pleasured sound Lady Trent made echoed through her, tripping over her senses like a stone skipping over water. Her body responded instinctively—her skin became sensitive and her breathing came in quick pants.

She began to quiver under the weight of Caulfield's gaze. Although she longed to run from the purloined intimacy, she was unable to move. It was impossible, but it seemed as if he looked right through her, past the façade forged by her father's hand.

The bonds holding her in place broke only when Caulfield did. His serrated groan at the moment of crisis acted like a spur to her flank. She ran then, clinging to her shawl with both arms crossed over full and aching breasts. When Temperance dashed out of a bush to greet her, Jess sobbed with relief. Scooping up the pug, she rushed toward the trail leading back to the manse.

Coming in December, ASK FOR IT by Sylvia Day.

Marcus found Elizabeth before he even set foot in the Moreland ballroom. In fact, he was trapped on the staircase as impatient peers and dignitaries sought a word with him. He was oblivious to those who vied for his attention, arrested by a brief glimpse of her.

She was even lovelier than before. How that was possible he couldn't say. She had always been exquisite. Perhaps absence had made his heart grow fonder.

A derisive smile curved his lips. Obviously, Elizabeth did not return the sentiment. When their eyes met, he allowed his pleasure at seeing her again to show on his face. In return, she lifted her chin and looked away.

A deliberate snub.

The cut direct, exactly administered but unable to draw blood. She had already inflicted the most grievous laceration years ago, making him impervious to further injury. He brushed off her disregard with ease. Nothing could alter their fate, however she might wish it otherwise.

For years now he'd served as an agent to the crown, and in that time he had led a life that would rival the stories written in any sensational novel. He'd fought numerous sword fights, been shot twice, and dodged more than any man's fair share of cannon fire. In the process, he had lost three of his own ships and sunk a half dozen others before he'd been forced to remain in England by the demands of his title. And yet the sudden fiery lick of awareness along his nerve endings only ever happened when he was in the same room as Elizabeth.

Avery James, his partner, stepped around him when it became obvious he was rooted to the spot. "There is Viscountess Hawthorne, my lord," he pointed out with an almost imperceptible thrust of his chin. "She is standing to the right, on the edge of the dance floor, in the violet silk gown. She is—"

"I know who she is."

Avery looked at him in surprise. "I was unaware that you were acquainted."

Marcus's lips, known widely for their ability to charm women breathless, curved in blatant anticipation. "Lady Hawthorne and I are . . . old friends."

"I see," Avery murmured, with a frown that said he didn't at all.

Marcus rested his hand on the shorter man's shoulder. "Go on ahead, Avery, while I deal with this crush, but leave Lady Hawthorne to me."

Avery hesitated a moment, then nodded reluctantly and continued to the ballroom, his path clear of the crowd that besieged Marcus.

Tempering his irritation with the importunate guests blocking his path, Marcus tersely acknowledged the flurry of greetings and inquiries directed at him. This melee was the reason he disliked these events. Gentlemen who did not have the initiative to seek him out during calling hours felt free to approach him in a more relaxed social setting. He never mixed business with pleasure. At least that had been his rule until tonight.

Elizabeth would be the exception. As she had always been an exception.

Twirling his quizzing glass, Marcus watched as Avery moved through the crowd with ease, his gaze drifting past his partner to the woman he was assigned to protect. He drank in the sight of her like a man dying of thirst.

Elizabeth had never cared for wigs and was not wearing one tonight, as most of the other ladies did. The effect of stark white plumes in her dark hair was breathtaking, drawing every eye inexorably toward her. Nearly black, her hair set off eyes so stunningly colored they brought to mind the luster of amethysts.

Those eyes had locked with his for only a moment, but the sharp shock of her magnetism lingered, the pull of it undeniable. It drew him forward, called to him on the primitive level it always had, like a moth to a flame. Despite the danger of burning, he could not resist.

She had a way of looking at a man with those amazing eyes. Marcus could almost have believed he was the only man in the room, that everyone had disappeared and nothing stood between where he was trapped on the staircase and where she waited on the other side of the dance floor.

He imagined closing the distance between them, pulling her into his arms, and lowering his mouth to hers. He knew already that her lips, so erotic in their shape and plumpness, would melt into his. He wanted to trail his mouth down the slim column of her throat and lick along the ridge of her collarbone. He wanted to sink into her lush body and sate his driving hunger, a hunger that had become so powerful he was very nearly mad with it.

He'd once wanted everything—her smiles, her laughter, the sound of her voice, and the view of the world through her eyes. Now his need was baser. Marcus refused to allow it to be more than that. He wanted his life back, the life free of pain, anger, and sleepless nights. Elizabeth had taken it away and she could damn well give it back.

His jaw clenched. It was time to close the distance between them.

One look had shaken his control. What would it be like when he held her in his arms again?

*   *   *

Elizabeth, Viscountess Hawthorne, stood for a long moment in shock, heat spreading across her cheeks.

Her gaze had locked on the man on the staircase for only a moment and yet during that brief time her heart had increased its rhythm to an alarming pace. She was held motionless, arrested by the masculine beauty of his face, a face which had clearly shown pleasure at seeing her again. Startled and disturbed by her reaction to him after all these years, she had forced herself to cut him, to look away with haughty disregard.

Marcus, now the Earl of Westfield, was still magnificent. He remained the handsomest man she had ever encountered. When his gaze met hers, she felt the spark that passed between them as if it were a tangible force. An intense attraction had always existed between them. She was profoundly disturbed to discover it had not abated in the slightest.

After what he'd done, he should repulse her.

Elizabeth felt a hand at her elbow, jolting her back into the conversation. She turned to find George Stanton at her side, his concerned gaze searching her face. "Are you feeling unwell? You look a bit flushed."

She fluffed the lace at the end of her sleeve to hide her unease. "It is warm in here." Snapping her fan open, she waved it rapidly to cool her hot cheeks.

"I think a beverage is in order," George offered and she rewarded his thoughtfulness with a smile.

Once George had departed, Elizabeth directed her attention toward the group of gentlemen who surrounded her. "What were we discussing?" she asked no one in particular. Truthfully, she hadn't been paying attention to the conversation for most of the past hour.

Thomas Fowler replied, "We were discussing the Earl of Westfield." He gestured discreetly to Marcus. "Surprised to see him in attendance. The earl is notorious for his aversion to social events."

"Indeed." She feigned indifference while her palms grew damp within her gloves. "I had hoped that predilection of the earl's would hold true this evening, but it appears I am not so fortunate."

Thomas shifted, his countenance revealing his discomfort. "My apologies, Lady Hawthorne. I had forgotten your past association with Lord Westfield."

She laughed softly. "No need for apologies. Truly, you have my heartfelt appreciation. I'm certain you are the only person in London who has the sense to forget. Pay him no mind, Mr. Fowler. The earl was of little consequence to me then, and is of even less consequence now."

Elizabeth smiled as George returned with her drink and his eyes sparkled with pleasure at her regard.

As the conversation around her continued, Elizabeth slowly altered her position to better secure furtive glimpses of Marcus navigating the clogged staircase. It was obvious his libidinous reputation had not affected his power and influence. Even in a crowd, his presence was compelling. Several highly esteemed gentlemen hurried to greet him rather than wait for him to descend to the ballroom floor. Women, dressed in a dazzling array of colors and frothy with lace, glided surreptitiously toward the staircase. The influx of admirers moving in his direction shifted the balance of the entire room. To his credit, Marcus looked mostly indifferent to all of the fawning directed toward him.

As he made his way down to the ballroom, he moved with the casual arrogance of a man who always obtained precisely what he desired. The crowd around him attempted to pin him in place, but Marcus cut through it with ease. He attended intently to some, offhandedly to others, and to a few he simply raised an imperious hand. He commanded those around him with the sheer force of his personality and they were content to allow him to do so.

Feeling the intensity of her regard, his gaze met hers again.

The corners of his generous mouth lifted upward as perception passed between them. The glint in his eyes and the warmth of his smile made promises that he as a man could never keep.

There was an air of isolation about Marcus and a restless energy to his movements that had not been there four years ago. They were warning signs, and Elizabeth had every intention of heeding them.

George looked easily over her head to scrutinize the scene. "I say. It appears Lord Westfield is heading this way."

"Are you quite certain, Mr. Stanton?"

"Yes, my lady. Westfield is staring directly at me as we speak."

Tension coiled in the pit of her stomach. Marcus had literally frozen in place when their eyes had first met and the second glance had been even more disturbing. He was coming for her and she had no time to prepare. George looked down at her as she resumed fanning herself furiously.

Damn Marcus for coming tonight! Her first social event after three years of mourning and he unerringly sought her out within hours of her reemergence, as if he'd been impatiently waiting these last years for exactly this moment. She was well aware that that had not been the case at all. While she had been crepe-clad and sequestered in mourning, Marcus had been firmly establishing his scandalous reputation in many a lady's bedroom.

After the callous way he'd broken her heart, Elizabeth would have discounted him regardless of the circumstances but tonight especially. Enjoyment of the festivities was not her aim. She had a man she was waiting for, a man she had arranged covertly to meet. Tonight she would dedicate herself to the memory of her husband. She would find justice for Hawthorne and see it served.

The crowd parted reluctantly before Marcus and then regrouped in his wake, the movements heralding his progress toward her. And then Westfield was there, directly before her.

"You have had a number of willing women who suited you just as well."

"Never, my love. You have always been separate and apart from every other female."

Elizabeth had met her share of scoundrels and rogues but always their slick confidence and overtly intimate manners left her unmoved. Marcus was so skilled at seducing women, he managed the appearance of utter sincerity. She'd once believed every declaration of adoration and devotion that had fallen from his lips. Even now, the way he looked at her with such fierce longing seemed so genuine she almost believed it.

He made her want to forget what kind of man he was—a heartless seducer. But her body would not let her forget. She felt feverish and faintly dizzy.

"Three years of mourning," he said, with a faint note of bitterness. "I am relieved to see grief has not unduly ravaged your beauty. In fact, you are even more exquisite than when we were last together. You do recall that occasion, do you not?"

"Vaguely," she lied. "I have not thought of it in many years."

Wondering if he suspected her deception, she studied him as they changed partners. Marcus radiated an aura of sexual magnetism that was innate to him. The way he moved, the way he talked, the way he smelled—it all boasted of powerful energies and appetites. She sensed the barely leashed power he hid below the polished surface and she recollected how dangerous he was.

His voice poured over her with liquid heat as the steps of the minuet returned her to him. "I am wounded you are not more pleased to see me, especially when I braved this miserable event solely to be with you."

"Ridiculous," she scoffed. "You had no notion I would be here this evening. Whatever your purpose, please go about it and leave me in peace."

His voice was alarmingly soft. "My purpose is you, Elizabeth."

She stared a moment, her stomach churning with heightened unease. "If my brother sees us together he will be furious."

The flare of Marcus's nostrils made her wince. Once he and William had been the best of friends, but the end of her engagement had also brought about the demise of their friendship. Of all the things she regretted, that was paramount.

"What do you want?" she asked when he said nothing more.

"The fulfillment of your promise."

"What promise?"

"Your skin against mine with nothing in between."